Debating Federalism

Debating Federalism

From the Founding to Today

Edited and Introduced by
Aaron N. Coleman and Christopher S. Leskiw

LEXINGTON BOOKS
Lanham • Boulder • New York • London

Published by Lexington Books
An imprint of The Rowman & Littlefield Publishing Group, Inc.
4501 Forbes Boulevard, Suite 200, Lanham, Maryland 20706
www.rowman.com

6 Tinworth Street, London SE11 5AL, United Kingdom

British Library Cataloguing in Publication Information Available

Library of Congress Cataloging-in-Publication Data

ISBN 978-1-4985-4287-6 (cloth : alk. paper)
ISBN 978-1-4985-4289-0 (pbk. : alk. paper)
ISBN 978-1-4985-4288-3 (electronic)

♾️™ The paper used in this publication meets the minimum requirements of American
National Standard for Information Sciences—Permanence of Paper for Printed Library
Materials, ANSI/NISO Z39.48-1992.

Printed in the United States of America

Aaron: To my parents, Jerry and Sue. For instilling in me a love of learning, the value of hard work, the importance and necessity of sacrifice, and for showing me, through example, how to be a loving and devoted parent, I dedicate this work to you.

Chris: To my family, my students, and to the Lord Almighty.

Contents

Acknowledgments

This project developed quickly and soon became one of love. But like most who seek to turn a project into a publication, we needed our fair share of assistance. Those who aided us in completing this edition share in its successes, but are absolved from any potential oversights we might have made. In particular, we must thank our two tireless assistants, Ms. Esmerelda Garcia and Ms. Sara Donahue. Ms. Garcia may be one of the most joyful people we have known. As an undergraduate student, her tireless energy, unflagging happiness, and incredible work ethic made the tracking down, typing, and formatting of a large number of the documents in the collection possible. Simply put, without her, this project would not have seen the light of day. We are honored to know her and be her teachers. We look forward to the bright future that she has. Ms. Donahue, the History and Political Science Department's administrative assistant, not only typed a number of documents, aided us in formatting them, and setting the table of contents, but she did all of this while also juggling the other responsibilities of running a department full of forgetful professors. For that alone, we are amazed. Considering how she did all this while keeping a wonderful sense of humor and her ever-present laugh, makes it all the more impressive. A huge thanks and our deepest gratitude to the both of them. In all seriousness, this project would not have been possible without you!

Also, we would like to thank Brian Hill and Eric Kuntzman, our acquisitions editors at Lexington. From the initial email where we broached the idea of a federalism reader, both Brian and Eric have been supportive—and intensely patient—of this project. Knowing we had their enthusiastic backing made us even more determined to see this work in print. Thank you both!

Finally, we would like to thank the teachers who attended our "Federalism: From the Founding to Today" Professional Development training in late 2015. It was from this event and our excellent discussions that lead us to consider publishing a document collection on federalism. Thank you!

AARON

First, I must thank my coeditor, Chris Leskiw. This project was a team effort, and I could not have had a better teammate. Although the academic life can sometimes lead to jading and cynicism, Chris remains bereft of these traits. I consider myself very blessed to call him my Vice President for Academic Affairs, colleague, coeditor, and, more importantly, friend.

Additional thanks to my great friends David Hollingsworth and Adam Tate who encouraged the development of this work and offered suggestions for documents. Also deserving of thanks is Josh DeBorde. Our Appleby's conversations about history, politics, and the differences and similarities of teaching High School and College courses are always a bright spot for me. Thank you for what you do in the classroom and for your enthusiasm for this project!

Thanks to my parents, Jerry and Sue, who gave the kind of encouragement that only excellent parents can. I love you both dearly and my appreciation for all you've done for me is more profound than you realize.

Finally, to my wife, Emily, and our two kids, Alex and Lorelei, go my deepest thanks and love. Without the three of them, none of this would be worth it. Thank you for your patience, faith in me, and, greatest of all, your love.

CHRIS

I too open with a word of thanks for my coeditor and friend, Aaron Coleman. The idea of this project is really one that developed out of Coleman's notable text, *The American Revolution, State Sovereignty, and the American Constitutional Settlement, 1765–1800*. His text exemplifies the importance of primary source research. As educators, it is our desire to equip our students with the ability to make well-informed arguments and decisions. Primary source materials play a key role in this process.

I am grateful for the students whom I taught over the last decade and a half. It never gets old to see them captivated by the richness and complexity only a primary source document can provide.

A Note on Documents and Editing

The documents included in this collection range from treatises, pamphlets, letters, speeches, presidential actions, and court cases. Many have never been published in any modern collection. The book is divided into four themes: sovereignty/reserved powers, civil rights, commerce clause, and incorporation. We selected these themes partially because of the quantity of sources on these topics, but, more importantly, because they are the key themes debates over federalism have historically revolved. Although thematically organized, the documents are arranged chronologically. Doing so allows readers to trace the historical development of that particular theme. Many of the documents could be put in various categories, of course, but we elected to place them in the most relevant theme. For example, President Johnson's veto of the 1866 Civil Rights Act addressed the fundamental question of sovereignty and reserved powers, but it did so because of the context of civil rights. Thus, we placed it under the Civil Rights section.

A note on the editing method needs mentioning. The quantity and size of some of the sources demanded editing, but we took every effort to preserve as much of the documents as possible. Doing so, we believe, allows the sources to speak for themselves as much as possible. This, in turn, gives readers a greater understanding of author's arguments. In editing the documents, we used ellipses to signify breaks inside of sentences and within paragraphs as well as at the start of a paragraph that was not the original next paragraph in the document. If a paragraph continued but we edited it out, we did not use ellipses to signify that the paragraph continued. We stopped the paragraph with the last relevant word. We felt that too many ellipses would be too confusing to readers (and some documents, court cases especially, already have numerous ellipses). In the court cases, we edited out most of the citations to other cases. Also, we elected to not include any description or background to the individual documents. Doing so would have not only consumed valuable space, thus leading to fewer documents, but since we hope this book will be used in various history and political science courses, we do not want to provide any undue influence to students and other readers. We want readers to develop their own interpretations rather than be influenced by ours. Instead, each document segment has its own broad introduction that ties into the introductory essay. Finally, we did not include the Declaration of Independence nor the Constitution in our collection. The absence of these two foundational documents may appear odd in a collection on federalism but given the ease of access to these documents, we did not believe it necessary to include them.

Aaron N. Coleman and Christopher S. Leskiw,
May 17, 2018

Introductory Essay

Aaron N. Coleman and Christopher Leskiw

"SPLITTING THE ATOM OF SOVEREIGNTY?": FEDERALISM IN AMERICAN HISTORY

Federalism represents one of the most important American contributions to constitutionalism. Most Americans today, however, have very little understanding of what federalism means and its importance throughout American history. While Americans recognize the value of their state governments, the natural assumption today is that the federal government can exercise nearly any power it wants over any issue. This belief manifested itself during the contentious debate over the Affordable Care Act when a constituent questioned California representative, Pete Stark, on the constitutionality of the then-proposed bill. A constituent asked that since the Constitution "specifically enumerates certain powers to the federal government and leaves the other authority to the states . . . or the people. . . . And if they [the federal government] can do this, what can't they do?" Representative Stark's answer was reflexive, blunt, and perhaps more honest than he realized. "The federal government, yes, can do most anything in this country."[1] Although Stark's reply epitomizes modern assumptions on federal power, it nevertheless represents a recent, and radical, departure from American history. For most of American history, the federal government remained relatively confined in its power, with most authority resting with the states. This division of authority between the states and the federal government is known as federalism.

This essay provides an overview of federalism from the time of the American founding to today but leaves the details of those arguments and developments to the documents and the classroom.[2] Quite often, scholars and textbooks describe federalism using the metaphors of either a layered, or marbled, cake. In the layered metaphor, each level of government contains its own separate powers, static and unchanging. A marble cake federalism, by contrast, offers a blending of governmental powers. Rather than being separate and defined, they are mixed so thoroughly as to not know where one element ends and the other begins. These examples are unsatisfactory. The more accurate metaphor is "separate spheres." Not only was the term used at the time of the founding, but it better represents the division between the states and the general government. Even during the founding, however, explaining the nature and comparative sizes of these spheres proved controversial. What this collection reveals, and this essay helps explain, is that defining the size and boundaries of those separate spheres *is* the debate over federalism. This makes a federalism an attempt, often bitter and fiercely contended, to find an equilibrium within constant political, legal, social, and economic, and constitutional change.

The history of American federalism is not one of a process of a gradual evolution. Rather, crises have shaped federalism. A punctuated equilibrium model captures the contentious debate rather well. In this model, the extant system functions almost without notice to most, providing a perception of stability. This perception persists until an event occurs which brings with it the potential for sudden and possibly radical change. These shocks to the system range anywhere from long-simmering issues such as civil liberties or commerce between the states to the rather mundane, or even historically obscure issues. Any number of forces or players, such as federal and state bureaucracies, individual leaders in elected office, judges and justices, or individual citizens or corporations can upset the balance and force a recalibration of the system.

At the same time, and even with these punctuated moments, there can be no doubt that throughout the twentieth and twenty-first centuries American federalism has declined erratically, but persistently. The moments of crisis that often punctuate federalism have almost always resulted in the growth and power of the federal government. As the federal sphere has grown, the states' has atrophied, thus establishing an equilibrium that much more difficult. This decline, however, should not be viewed as a rout, at least not yet. The growth of centralization, while undeniable, has not gone unchallenged. They have been met, stymied, and sometimes defeated by those advancing a greater parity of the spheres. Excavating the history of federalism in America, therefore, uncovers a contentious constitutional concept whose influence has waxed and waned over the course of two centuries.

Sovereignty and Reserved Powers

The most important element of federalism is sovereignty. Since the writings of Jean Bodin and Thomas Hobbes of the sixteenth and seventeenth centuries, sovereignty has been defined as the supreme, unappealable power or authority in a governmental system. This belief in its indivisibility explains why sovereignty underlies practically every moment of punctuation; the core of those conflicts hinge on the question of sovereignty's location in a system of federalism. For the first century of the American experience, most Americans accepted the idea that sovereignty rested with the states, with the federal government's powers being a grant of particular powers voluntarily surrendered to the federal government. Since the Civil War, and especially during the twentieth century, that notion has flipped. Sovereignty now rests with the federal government, with the states exercising only those powers the federal government does not want.

While this dichotomy of state or federal sovereignty provides the axis of American belief on sovereignty, opposition to each side has always existed. This opposition, and their calls for sovereignty residing with the nondominant side, often provide those moments of punctuation and crisis. It is what led to the American Revolution, the writing and adoption of the Constitution, the battles between Federalists and Jeffersonians, and drove the conflict of the Civil War and Reconstruction Amendments. It provided a key source of conflict with the Progressives, the New Deal, the Great Society, and Civil Rights Movement while being a major element of Ronald Regan's political success. In more recent times, questions of sovereignty underpin major issues such as education, homosexual marriage, drug legalization, and even euthanasia.

The American Revolution represents the first of these crises over sovereignty's location. Both sides, interestingly, agreed that sovereignty remained undivided. Where they differed widely and irreconcilably was over whether that sovereignty rested with the Parliament or with the Colonial Assemblies. Parliament argued that it resided exclusively with them. By claiming an indivisible sovereignty over the whole empire, Parliament argued it could govern the colonies "in all cases, whatsoever." The American argument, of course, rejected Parliament's claim. The colonial argument drew upon a traditional imperial arrangement rooted in decentralization. This tradition led colonial Americans to consider sovereignty as being located in the Colonial Assembly, meaning that the actions of the individual colonies, which received monarchial approval, was the supreme power over each colony. Hence, instead of colonies living under a unified sovereignty in Parliament, it was thirteen separate sovereigns united only in their mutual acceptance and loyalty to the British crown.

The colonial argument against Parliamentary sovereignty established four primary ideas behind American federalism. With some modifications, these elements provide the basic refrain which has guided American understanding of federalism's importance ever since. First, they argued that sovereignty resting in the individual assemblies allowed for actual self-government.

Since colonial (and later, state) legislatures come from the same environs, possess the same concerns, wants, and desires as their neighbors, Americans believed these governments responded better to the will of the people and became harder to succumb to tyranny. A neighbor, rather than a Member of Parliament, was far less likely to enact oppressive legislation that applied to him just as much as it did his neighbor. Second, and building directly from the first point, federalism allowed diversity to flourish. It acknowledged and respected the distinct varieties of climates, geographies, economies, cultures, and religious beliefs, yet still allowed the pursuit of the common good of the collective group. Third, embracing federalism reflected the traditional Anglo-American fear of centralized, or consolidated, government. Americans considered consolidated government the opposite of self-governing; it epitomized empire and tyranny. It transformed local self-government into empire and empire brought with it a flattening—not a social leveling, necessarily, but a flattening of liberty. Under empire, the distinctions that federalism respected succumbed to a one-size-fits-all universal legislation, no matter how ungainly, counterproductive, or oppressive it might be to a particular area. In short, empire meant slavery, not chattel slavery, but political slavery, of being subjected to the arbitrary will of far-distant rulers in charge of peoples they knew little about, cared even less, and whose only concern was the glory and power of the empire. Finally, these three lessons culminated into federalism's fourth, and most important, influence on American constitutionalism, namely that federalism protected liberty. By protecting self-government, respecting the diversity of people and places, and preventing the tyranny of consolidated empire, a federalism that divided sovereignty safeguarded liberty. And since liberty required constant vigilance, a federalism allowed for the sentinels of liberty to stand guard and thwart the growth of consolidation and political slavery.

These four elements of federalism, rooted in the sovereignty of the states, became the foundational constitutional points during the American founding. Americans first constitutionalized the idea in the Article II of the Articles of Confederation. That Article, arguably the greatest expression of the American understanding of federalism and sovereignty, confirmed that "Each state retains its sovereignty, freedom, and independence, and every power, jurisdiction, and right, which is not by this Confederation expressly delegated to the United States, in Congress assembled." By noting that the states retained all authority not expressly delegated the Confederation Congress, Article II maintained an indivisible sovereignty located in the states but granted the Confederation only those powers necessary to promote the general welfare of the United States.

Not all Americans believed the states should maintain their sovereignty. A distinct minority believed, like Alexander Hamilton did, that "a want of power in Congress" represented the primary "defect" in the Articles. These nationalist Americans believed that, by 1787, the United States was in a constitutional crisis that threatened the Revolution. Hence, they sought a national government lodged with full sovereign powers. Although the Constitution that emerged from the Philadelphia Convention addressed some of their concerns, the persistent American belief in an indivisible sovereignty residing in their states defeated most of their objectives. Nevertheless, and in an attempt to win acceptance of the Constitution, supporters of the new Constitution argued that the proposed government established a "partly national, partly federal" scheme that divided sovereignty into separate spheres, with overlapping kept to a minimum and confined to issues of taxation and the militia.

Most Americans, however, initially opposed the adoption of the Constitution. They considered the Nationalists' cries of crisis little more than hyperbole with the idea of dividing sovereignty into separate spheres a "solecism." Employing the same arguments used against English during the Revolution, the Constitution's opponents believed the proposed government offered little more than a chimera of protection since no government could "suit so extensive a country, embracing so many climates and containing inhabitants so very different in manners, habits, and customs." With decision making "into the hands of a set of men who live one thousand miles distant," the taxing power; the Federal Judiciary; the Necessary and Proper Clause; the General Welfare Clause; the Times, Place, and Manner Clause of Article I, Section 4, promised to sink federalism the into an abyss of "consolidation."

Not until the Constitution's supporters agreed to amend the Constitution to include a bill of rights, and a provision acknowledging that all powers not granted to the Constitution remained reserved to the states did opponents acquiesce. By securing this amendment—what ultimately became the Tenth Amendment—and different language from Article II of the Articles of Confederation, many of the Constitution's opponents believed they secured the continuation of sovereignty resting indivisibility in the states and the new federal government only receiving the powers voluntarily surrendered by the states. In essence, they considered the amendment an acknowledgment that the Constitution represented a compact of the several states and provide an interpretative guide on the powers of the federal government.

The ratification of the Constitution and the Tenth Amendment did not end the debate. The entire decade of the 1790s was one of crisis as proponents of federal sovereignty made repeated attempts to achieve their goal. The first, and most important, punctuation came from Alexander Hamilton and his "Report on the Constitutionality of the Bank of the United States." In his report, Hamilton advanced the idea of separate spheres of sovereignty, noting how "the powers of sovereignty are in this country divided between the National and State governments." More importantly, he offered for a robust defense of what that sovereignty meant at the national level. To Hamilton, "it is unquestionably incident to sovereign power to erect corporations, and consequently to that of the United States, in relation to the objects intrusted to the management of the government."

Sovereignty, as Hamilton understood it, therefore, rejected the idea that the states still retained an indivisible sovereignty, with the Constitution containing powers surrendered by the states. His understanding of separate spheres meant that, in those areas where the federal government possessed power, the federal government wielded an indisputable sovereignty. This sovereignty, moreover, provided wide latitude in how the federal government chose to carry out its responsibilities. The Tenth Amendment, he argued, in what would become the standard interpretation of the amendment in the twentieth century, acknowledged this separate sphere claiming it "nothing more than a consequence of this republican maxim." The Constitution's enumerated powers provided only the categories of the sovereign power, rather than the actual powers, possessed by the national government. Instead of being confined by those powers, Hamilton insisted that, since the powers were categorical, the federal government, and the federal government only, could decide on how to discharge those powers. Thus, they could execute those powers as widely or narrowly as it so pleased. If those powers happened to breach powers possessed by the states, the states must yield. Since the Constitution was sovereign, it "conceded that implied powers are to be considered as delegated equally with express ones . . . because it is incident to a general sovereign or legislative power to regulate a thing, to employ all the means which relate to its regulation to the best and greatest advantage." Thus, to Hamilton and future advocates of federal power ever since, the Constitution provided the broad means in which to fulfill the sovereign ends of the national government.

Hamilton's argument remains the single most important and influential argument made in defense of national sovereignty and provided intellectual foundations to those defending expansive federal powers. John Marshall and Joseph Story in the early nineteenth century, and Abraham Lincoln and Charles Sumner later that century, and, in the twentieth and twenty-first centuries, Theodore and Franklin Roosevelt, Lyndon Johnson and George W. Bush and Barack Obama have all echoed its primary arguments. At its core, Hamilton's argument allowed the federal government to achieve broad sweeping goals and objectives, often when no clear or obvious Constitutional proscription existed. It provided the justification for the federal intervention in an issue the federal government deemed necessary. While his advocacy of separate spheres acknowledged the sovereignty of the states, his argument made it clear that the federal sphere should be the largest.

Hamilton's argument directly challenged that of his colleague, Secretary of State, Thomas Jefferson. Like Hamilton's opinion, Jefferson's emerged as an authority for those maintaining a sovereignty resting with the states. Defending the traditional American position of sovereignty resting with the states, Jefferson argued for the powers of the federal government as limited, finite, and confined strictly to the Constitution's enumerations. Should the government "take a single step beyond the boundaries thus specially drawn around the powers of Congress," meant it could claim "possession of a boundless field of power, no longer susceptible of any definition." Acquiring this unbridled power completely contradicted the language of the Tenth Amendment, which Jefferson, echoing most American's thoughts, considered the "foundation of the Constitution."

Hamilton's argument punctured state sovereignty-based federalism. While it swam upstream from the majority of American thought, it nevertheless established the groundwork for the future shift in sovereignty location to the federal government. From Hamilton's opinion onward, Americans could no longer assume or take for granted the notion of a state sovereignty-based federalism. It had to compete with repeated attempts to rupture the system and replace it with federal sovereignty.

The second great episode of punctuation in the decade occurred in 1798. In that year, the Federalist Party-controlled Congress, working from Hamilton's argument for a broad sphere of federal sovereignty, enacted the infamous Alien and Sedition Acts. The measures violated the clear language of the First and Tenth Amendments. In response, Thomas Jefferson and James Madison anonymously authored the Kentucky and Virginia Resolutions. Passed by those states respective legislatures, the Resolutions restated the principle that, when adopting the Constitution, "the several states composing the United States of America, are not united on the principle of unlimited submission to their General Government." Rather than being a separate sovereign, both Jefferson and Madison argued that the Constitution represented a compact between the several states. When states, acting through their separate ratification conventions, created the Constitution to aid in the pursuit of the more perfect union, the states retained all the powers not delegated to the federal government. The powers of the Constitution were not categorical, but confined the federal government to only those exact powers. Since the Constitution did not grant the federal government the power to limit the freedom of speech and press as well as limit the immigration of people into a state, it could not exercise that power.

As a compact between the states, Jefferson maintained "that whensoever the General Government assumes undelegated powers, its acts are unauthoritative, void, and of no force; that to this compact each state acceded as a state, and is an integral party; that the Government created by this compact was not made the exclusive or final judge of the extent of the powers delegated to itself; since that would have made its discretion, and not the Constitution, the measure of its powers; but that, as in all other cases of compact among powers having no common judge, each party has an equal right to judge for itself, as well of infractions as of the mode and measure of redress." In other words, the nature of the compact meant that the only states, not the federal government, could determine whether the federal government violated the Constitution. Madison added that whenever the federal government threatened the liberty of the people, "states who are parties thereto, have the right, and are in duty bound, to interpose for arresting the progress of the evil, and for maintaining within their respective limits, the authorities, rights and liberties appertaining to them."

Jefferson and Madison's argument represents perhaps the most aggressive defense in American history of a federal system based upon the sovereignty of the states. Not only were the states clearly sovereign and the federal government limited to only those powers the states decided to give it, but, through the exercise of their sovereignty via interposition, the states checked centralized power. At the same time, however, the idea of interposition did not emerge from Jefferson or Madison. Instead, those ideas drew from previous arguments. Merriweather Smith, for example, in his 1783 pamphlet against provisions in the Treaty of Paris, maintained that states needed to intervene to protect the liberties of their citizens. Madison himself made an argument for interposition in his contributions as "Publius" in the Federalist papers. Perhaps most ironic of all, Hamilton echoed his coauthor's argument in Federalist 26, arguing that "the State legislatures, who will always be not only vigilant but suspicious and jealous guardians of the rights of the citizens against encroachments from the federal government, will constantly have their attention awake to the conduct of the national rulers, and will be ready enough, if any thing improper appears, to sound the alarm to the people, and not only to be the VOICE, but, if necessary, the ARM of their discontent."

The arguments of Hamilton, Jefferson, and Madison became the poles of American constitutionalism. During this time, and with the election of Jefferson in 1800, the idea that the sovereignty rested with the states and the Constitution was a compact of the states dominated constitutional thinking. Moments of intense controversy certainly occurred. Two, in particular, are worth noting. The first came in 1819 with Chief Justice John Marshall's *McCulloch v. Maryland* decision. In this case, Marshall drew upon Hamilton's "Bank Opinion" and the broad definition of sovereignty it contained to defend the Second Bank of the United States. The decision proved a considerable puncturing of state sovereignty federalism. Prior to Marshall's decision, only state sovereignty received constitutional recognition through the Tenth Amendment. Hamilton's argument, while a major punctuation to that idea, remained confined to political debate only; it lacked Constitutional sanctioning. By using Hamilton's opinion and reasoning to defend the Court's opinion, the *McCulloch* decision converted the idea of broad federal sovereignty into a constitutional reality.

The Nullification Crisis of the 1830s represents the greatest moment of constitutional crisis between Jefferson's election and the Civil War. The controversy surrounded whether a state possessed the power to nullify—to make void and unenforceable in their borders—a law passed by the federal government. South Carolina's effort to nullify the Tariff of 1828, which they called the Tariff of Abominations due to its disastrous economic effect to the state, became the first real attempt to put the arguments of the Kentucky and Virginia Resolutions into practice. President Andrew Jackson, despite being an advocate of limited government and state sovereignty, rejected South Carolina's argument. Calling nullification a "strange position," that gave states the "power of resisting all laws," he noted that, "by the theory, there is no appeal, the reasons alleged by the State, good or bad, must prevail." What makes Jackson's proclamation interesting is how it straddled the Hamilton/Jefferson axis. While Jackson acknowledged the traditional Jeffersonian position that, in cases when measures are "too oppressive to be endured," the states could interpose to protect liberty. Yet, taking the more Hamiltonian position, Jackson maintained that the Constitution "forms a government, not a league and whether it be formed by compact between the States, or in any other manner, its character is the same." In those areas where the federal government had clear constitutional authority, its power was supreme. The 1828 Tariff, enacted with clear constitutional authority, meant that the states had to obey.

These two moments of punctuation, the *McCulloch* decision and the Nullification crisis, prepared the ground floor for the fundamental shift away from a federalism of sovereignty states to one of the federal government. That shift began in earnest with the greatest crisis in American history, the Civil War. When the southern states seceded in 1860–1861, they invoked the compact theory of the union as part of their justification. President Lincoln, however, rejected those arguments. He maintained, much like Daniel Webster in his famous debate with Senator Hayne in 1830, the perpetuity and indissolubility of the union. Lincoln even argued, against historical evidence, that the Union predated the states, thereby making the states the creature of the national government. This argument flipped on its head the traditional notion that sovereignty resting with the states. Complete sovereignty, in this line of thinking, rested with the federal government with the states exercising only those power the Constitution did not seek to exercise. This explains why Lincoln, in the Gettysburg Address, made the subtle, but immensely important, rhetorical shift from "union" to "nation." Union signified compact, a gathering of separate peoples into a unit while still maintaining their distinctiveness. Nation, however, meant one whole and indistinguishable body.

In other words, Lincoln's argument refuted the many of the core arguments behind federalism. This belief in a perpetual, indissoluble nation, he maintained, necessitated the need for military force. The Northern victory in the Civil War transformed Lincoln's argument into an American creed.

The theoretical transformation of the federal system emerged more prominently with other members of Lincoln's party, the Republicans. Massachusetts Senator, Charles Sumner, advanced the radical idea that when the southern states attempted to leave the union, they committed suicide and reverted to territorial status. As territories, they lacked the sovereignty possessed by the states and became subjected wholesale to the sovereignty of the federal government. This "state suicide theory" drove some of the more aggressive reconstruction policies and helped secure the idea of complete federal sovereignty. But, the domination of the radical notion of state suicide did not last. In the 1877 case of *Texas v. White*, Chief Justice, Salmon P. Chase, a Lincoln appointee, constitutionalized the slain president's general theme on the perpetuity of American federalism. In the case, Chase maintained that the "Constitution, in all its provisions, looks to an indestructible Union, composed of indestructible States."

The most important constitutional development that emerged from Civil War was the Fourteenth Amendment. Nothing has done more to alter the nature of American federalism. It recalibrated the location of sovereignty within the federal system by dramatically increasing the federal sphere while shrinking that of the states. Whether or not the drafters of the amendment intended for this alteration remains a subject of serious academic debate, but it is indisputable that the 150-year history of the amendment has accomplished this transformation. Through the amendment's provision prohibiting "State's from depriving any person of life, liberty, or property, without due process of law" the federal government, federal courts more specifically, can intervene in state actions over practically any issue, including provisions contained within the states' constitutions. As will be seen in the separate sections of this essay, the Supreme Court's interpretation of the Fourteenth Amendment as incorporating the Bill of Rights against the states sweeps across an array of issues traditionally reserved to the states. With the shift from state to federal sovereignty via the Fourteenth Amendment, the result has been the increasing elimination of the diversity that federalism preserves and the ensconcement of that one-size-fits all mentality that federalism resists. In many ways, the Fourteenth Amendment accomplishes what Virginia Plan at the Constitutional Convention failed to do, give the national government a veto over state laws.

While Civil War and Reconstruction era punctuated the traditional arrangement of federalism by initiating the transformation to federal sovereignty, the revolution was not immediate or total. The full ramifications of the Fourteenth Amendment's effect upon federalism would not occur until the twentieth century. Thus, for the first few decades after the Civil War, the traditional arrangement of federalism remained, although significantly weaker. The pace of the transformation begun by the Civil War accelerated with the two most important moments of the first half of the twentieth-century, the Progressive Movement and the New Deal.

The Progressive Movement emerged in response to the dramatic economic growth of the United States in the last decades of nineteenth century. Deeply influenced by the German political system that removed democratic processes into bureaucratic control, and believing gross inequalities and exploitation existed in America's economic expansion, self-proclaimed Progressive's sought an unelected administrative apparatus to cure these woes. This administrative state, Progressives maintained, would cure the social and economic ills they believe existed by moving the political and democratic process into the hands of unelected experts. Progress toward this utopia, therefore, required a robust, active, and indisputably supreme federal government. Federalism, however, hampered those efforts and thus became a target of progressive reform.

This desire for an expanded sphere of federal power explains why the Progressives attacked the federalism and Constitution and an outdated and obsolete obstacle. They argued instead for a "living constitution." Rather than being confined to the limits of federalism and enumerated powers as constructed by the American founders and even modified by the Civil War, Progressives, such as Albert Beveridge and Woodrow Wilson, argued that the Founders realized "the necessities of the people for all time could not possibly have been foreseen by the men who wrote the Constitution, it follows that they could not have intended to confine the purposes of the Constitution and the powers it confers to the necessities of the people of 1789; that they so wrote it that it might meet the requirements of the people for all time. . . . If that is so, it follows that the Constitution must steadily grow, because the requirements of the people steadily grow." In other words, the Founders drafted a Constitution detached from historical fetters with the flexibility necessary to address Progressive concerns.

Federalism became a casualty of the Progressive argument for a living constitution. As Progressives advanced federal policies of economic regulation, all under the guise that the new industrial age provided constitutional sanctioning of this expansion of federal sovereignty, the authority of the states became increasingly less important. Perhaps the most direct Progressive attack on federalism came from the Seventeenth Amendment. Ratified in 1913, the amendment ended the practice of state legislatures selecting Senators. Instead, Senators became elected directly through popular vote. Although Progressives asserted the Amendment was a response to the corruption of state legislatures, by removing the state legislatures from the selection process, the Amendment detached the states completely from having any role in federal policymaking. As a result, as the power of the federal government expanded, states became less able to halt invasions into their sovereignty and those powers traditionally reserved to them.

The deep puncturing to the separate spheres of federalism during the Progressive era set the stage for what remains as the greatest expansion of federal sovereignty in American history, President Franklin Roosevelt's "New Deal." Containing large elements of the earlier Progressive agenda, the New Deal sought "national planning for and supervision of all forms of transportation and of communications and other utilities which have a definitely public character." The New Deal was a complicated scheme of nationalization of large portions of the economy and a myriad of federal programs such as Social Security. Roosevelt defended the New Deal through the progressive idea of the living constitution, that "Our Constitution is so simple and practical that it is possible always to meet extraordinary needs by changes in emphasis and arrangement without loss of essential form."

Rooted in the living constitution, the Hamiltonian understanding of expansive federal sovereignty, and aided by a Supreme Court that dismissed the Tenth Amendment's stipulation for reserved powers as nothing more than a "truism" that had no interpretive power, the New Deal attacked the foundations of federalism. With its centralized program of economic recovery all rooted in bureaucratic executive agencies administered, distant and unelected rulers made decisions for people and places they knew little about. Federalism's purpose of stopping one-size-fits-all legislation ill-suited for distinct geographies and peoples died as the New Deal came alive. The broad sweeping powers and intervention of the New Deal left little room for the states to act in ways that they believed best for their state. In other words, the federal government, and only the federal government, provided the ways and means economic recovery. Although Roosevelt claimed that his actions would not alter the "essential form" of the Constitution, nevertheless, a fundamental alteration did occur. The New Deal moved sovereignty away from the separate spheres into a single sphere of federal power.

The half-century following the New Deal witnessed the near uninterrupted growth of federal sovereignty. In areas of Housing and Urban Development and Education, to President Lyndon Johnson's Great Society and War on Poverty, the federal government increasingly nationalized areas historically and constitutionally reserved to the states. The result was the final and complete puncturing of federalism as understood at the time of the founding. Sanctioned by nearly six decades of uninterrupted Supreme Court decisions that upheld the expansive use of federal power, sovereignty was now located in the federal government. What was left to the states were only those powers the federal government chose not to exercise. Attempts to explain this new extant system often used the term "corporative federalism." Under this reasoning, the federal government worked with the states to provide grants for the state governments to administer federal programs. Proponents asserted that this "marbled cake" approach, the other name for corporative federalism, allowed for a shared governance and responsibility. Instead of sovereignty flowing from the states, or even the Hamiltonian idea of sovereignty being divided into two separate spheres, corporative federalism turned the states into administrative agencies of the federal government. When corporative federalism was combined with the Fourteenth Amendment and the incorporation doctrine (discussed below), the authority of the states became negligible as they answered to the federal government on practically every area of governance, even in areas, such as criminal law.

Yet, federal dominance did not, and has not, go unchallenged. As with the federal system based upon state sovereignty, punctuations to federal sovereignty emerged. Beginning with the election of Ronald Reagan in 1980, signs that corporative federalism might be weakening appeared. In his inaugural address in 1981 and throughout his presidency, Reagan singled his "intention to curb the size and influence of the Federal establishment and to demand recognition of the distinction between the powers granted to the Federal Government and those reserved to the States or to the people. All of us need to be reminded that the Federal Government did not create the States; the States created the Federal Government." The first major politician in decades to speak of federalism in this traditional sense, Reagan's policies, which he styled "New Federalism," sought to weaken the administrative state and return decision making back to the states. In areas of judicial appointments, Reagan nominated jurists who advocated a return to the "original intent" of the founders.

While not completely successful in living up to its lofty goals, Reagan's New Federalism not only helped somewhat revive a federalism that seeks equilibrium, but it had one major, and often overlooked, consequence. It saved the idea of a federalism of state sovereignty from it mid-twentieth-century association with racism. During the Civil Rights movements of the 1950s and 1960s, opponents of desegregation and other federal civil rights actions used the language of state sovereignty to defend objectively racist and discriminatory practices and legislation. While these arguments ignored the obvious intent and language of the Fourteenth Amendment, a consequence of their rhetoric was to attach federalism to white supremacy. Reagan's administration, however, reassured that federalism and state sovereignty was not inherently racist nor discriminatory. His administration followed the traditional idea that linked federalism to self-government and liberty.

For all its shortcomings, Reagan's administration did begin a resurgence in the understanding of a federalism rooted in state sovereignty. Nowhere was this resurgence more noticeable than in the Supreme Court. Starting with the 1793 case of *Chisholm v. Georgia*, the Supreme Court has served as a bastion of centralization. Under the Chief Justiceship of William Rehnquist, however, the Court reasserted a federalism of divided sovereignty. In cases such as *New York v. United States* and *Printz v. United States, United States v. Lopez*, the Court moved away from its long practice of upholding federal actions against the states. Instead, the Court recognized that a "residual state sovereignty was also implicit, of course, in the Constitution's conferral upon Congress of not all governmental powers, but only discrete, enumerated ones, Art. I, § 8, which implication was rendered express by the Tenth [Amendment]." When compared to the judicial reasoning of the previous half-century, Rehnquist Court of the 1990s returned, at least to some degree, a federalism of separate spheres.

Although much of this early resurgence of federalism seemed confined to the Supreme Court, it remains unclear how vibrant or enduring it may be. Over the past two decades, several moments of particular—and contentious—punctuations reveal that the resurgence might not be lasting. Take for instance the issue of homosexual marriage. For most of American history, this issue never presented itself on any political agenda. What has transpired with this issue over just the last decade is truly remarkable. When homosexual marriage rose to national discussion in the 1980s and 1990s, the overwhelming majority of State and National political leaders staunchly opposed it. In fact, the Defense of Marriage Act (DOMA) which the federal government enacted in 1996 and defined marriage as the union of one man and one woman, received support from a Democratic President and bipartisan supermajorities from the House (342) and the Senate (85). Additionally, in a ten-year period started in 1998, roughly thirty states drafted constitutional amendments to ban same-sex marriage. During the same time, only a handful of states moved in the other direction. All these actions indicated that the issue remained one reserved to the sovereignty of the states with the federal government, beyond establishing its own definition of federal law, having practically no interference.

All of these limitations on same-sex marriage abruptly changed in 2013 with the Supreme Court case of *United States v. Windsor*, which declared key elements of DOMA as unconstitutional. Following just two years later, the *Obergefell v Hodges* case invoked the Fourteenth Amendment to declare that same-sex couples possessed a fundamental right to marry that the states nor federal government could impair. Fueled by interested parties and the echo chambers of a 24-hour news cycle and social media, federal protection of same-sex marriage is arguably one of the fastest and abrupt changes not only in our constitutional history, but for our culture as well. While the full explanation of this sudden change is far beyond the scope of this essay, suffice it to say the case points to the complete sovereignty of the federal government. The Federal government, the Supreme Court more specifically, pushed back against the majority of states in effectively overruling their constitutional prohibitions against homosexual marriage.

Another current example, however, reveals that the return of state sovereignty might have teeth after all. That issue is the legality of certain recreational drugs, primarily marijuana. Like many nations, the United States has an interesting history with the degree to which mind-altering substances were given various levels of legalization and restriction. The federal government declared its sovereignty over the topic by determining which drugs had legitimate medical uses, and which were strictly prohibited for their lack of medical purpose. With the passage of the Controlled Substances Act in 1970, the federal government initiated its modern "war on drugs" campaign. The Reagan administration renewed emphasis on the war in the 1980s, but in a time line that is the mirror image of the same-sex marriage debate, the situation is primed for a radical change. Since the mid-1990s, efforts at the state levels to legalize marijuana for certain uses grew. At the same time as thirty states were banning same-sex marriage, a similar number of were legalizing marijuana in either medical usage or, more recently, as a purely recreational drug. The federal government exerted its sovereignty over the issue in the 2005 case of the *Gonzales v. Raich*. Even with this decision that allows the Federal government to maintain its control and ban of marijuana, states continue to venture forth by passing laws in contradiction to this outcome. With the growth of the state recognized the legal sale of this drug into the billions of dollars in sales, it seems inevitable that another confrontation between the federal and state governments will occur.

At the same time, in the early twenty-first century, states began a more concerted effort at reaffirming their sovereignty. Starting around 2008, a number of states enacted "Tenth Amendment Resolutions." Designed as responses to the War on Terror and legislation such as the Patriot Act, federal intervention into health care, and deepening involvement in education, the Resolutions reminded the federal government that limits to its powers existed. Although it is too early to know what the effect of these resolutions may have in preserving at least some semblance of federalism, what is clear that the notion of federalism has not completely disappeared from the constitutional and political landscape.

Civil Liberties

Freedoms or rights guaranteed to citizens by the government are typically known as civil liberties. That is, those rights that are given or delineated as a condition of entering the social contract. The government acknowledges these rights and often provides a procedure or guiding principles for their interpretation or for their boundaries to be maintained. The right of a trial by an impartial jury in a criminal case is an example of a civil liberty granted to citizens via the Sixth Amendment of the U.S. Constitution. In the selected documents that follow, it will be evident that there is a give and take the type of relationship between the Federal government and the State governments on this issue.

Starting in the mid-1950s, the Supreme Court grew increasingly concerned with civil liberty issues. Most of these cases were in response to the growing demands of the Civil Rights movement which sought to promote equality of opportunity. In *Brown v. Board of Education*, the differences in how equality was perceived by the federal government and those of state governments became readily apparent. This case ushered in several more in which the sovereignty of the federal government eclipsed that of the states. These substantive issues changed over time, from segregation to same-sex marriage and abortion, but the general tone remained. The federal government has its thumb on the scale of federalism. The Supreme Court consistently overruled state laws and governmental actions as violations of civil rights. If the federalism can be seen as separate spheres, clearly the federal sphere is the largest in issues of civil rights.

Commerce Clause

The modern era of Commerce Clause cases is not easily parsed into a winning or losing camp. First, it is important to recognize that the Commerce Clause is indeed an explicit power given to the National government via Article I, Section 8 of the U.S. Constitution. The clause, however, suggests more than just a means of conveying the sovereignty of the federal government. In many ways, the Commerce Clause provides a mindset or even a culture of power. That is, Supreme Court has used the clause to justify federal power and action into areas that seem far removed from commerce or the enumeration of powers in the Constitution. The Court employed the clause during the Civil Rights movement to combat segregation. As the commerce cases herein reveal, the economic dimension of an issue is often not the Court's first consideration, but is the means by which the government is spurred into action. For instance, in the case of *Katzenbach v. McClung*, the Court relied upon commerce powers in establishing the need to seek rest and nourishment as a part of interstate travel. This line of reasoning allowed the federal government to legally force desegregation on individual business owners. In recent times, the Supreme Court has applied the Commerce Clause into novel areas like women's rights, gun laws, and recreational drug use.

Incorporation

When asked in national surveys, the average American consistently demonstrates a cursory knowledge of the exact substance of the Amendments. More worrying, however, is the fact that they also lose sight of the purpose of the Amendments, their intended targets, and the requisite historical events that gave rise to them. Do the Amendments only apply to the National government or are they relevant to the States as well? The notion of incorporation touches upon all these facets of the Amendments.

The procedure of actually amending the Constitution is relatively straightforward as is provided in Article V of the Constitution itself. The procedure is effectively where the easy to understand part of the Amendments end. The philosophical discussions surrounding the notion of amendments, and the Bill of Rights in particular, is far beyond the scope of this current work. What needs to be stated though, is that the first ten Amendments do not create new rights. Not when they were first proposed, nor do we find new rights in them today. Rather, the Bill of Rights sets limits. Far too often, the Amendments are thought of as the enumerated rights given by the government to its citizens. Nothing could be farther from the truth. How can a government that operates on a social contract whereby its citizens enter voluntarily give its people something that is not it's own to give? In other words, the Amendments themselves do not establish rights but set the government on notice of the boundaries of those possessed by the people. Much of the discussion of the Amendments focuses on what those rights actually mean, however, an equally prescient question is determining the target of those boundaries or limitations.

On its face, the Constitution is the very document that creates the National government. Thus, as the preamble to the Bill of Rights asserted, the amendments were "to prevent misconstruction or abuse of its powers." Thus, the Bill of Rights could reasonably be assumed to provide limitations and boundaries that were intended to constrain the National government. A relatively early Supreme Court case, *Barron v. Baltimore* (1833), reinforced this notion. This case, however, settled until the ratification of the Fourteenth Amendment. That amendment covers a lot of ground, but, as the section on sovereignty revealed, it placed prohibitions on State governments. Which prohibitions and their degree of restraint have been the subject of debate over the last 150 years.

The *Gitlow v. New York* (1925) case ushered in the modern area of the incorporation doctrine. Incorporation means that the rights are not just applicable to the National government, but to the states as well. Instead of settling this issue of law, the case added a new wrinkle. The *Gitlow* case introduced the doctrine of selective incorporation. Selective incorporation works just as a simple reading of the phrase leads one to believe. It provides for rights supported in the Bill of Rights to be applied to State governments in a step-wise fashion. That is, the protections of the Bill of Rights are not automatically applied to States. Consequently, the tension between an individual's rights and protections from the Federal government can very much be at odds with those afforded by State governments.

For a selective incorporation to proceed, there first needs to be some sort of perceived rights-based infringement at the state level that provides the ripeness needed for the Supreme Court to act. The Court then narrowly considers whether and how that right constrains a state's actions. As explored in this text, the progression of selective incorporation fits with the punctuated equilibrium model of change. These applications of rights emerge as a response to sudden swings in public opinion or after a particular case of a gross violation of what is believed to be a fundamental right. The most recent incorporation case was *McDonald v. City of Chicago* (2010) and its net effect was to apply an individual's Second Amendment rights and protections against state prohibition of such rights.

NOTES

1. Pete Stark, "The Federal Government, yes, can do almost anything" at https://www.youtube.com/watch?v=W1-eBz8hyoE accessed on July 21, 2018.

2. We intend this essay as an overview of federalism's development in American history. The intricacies and complexities of the debates surrounding federalism throughout American history forced us to simplify and compress many events and issues. Thus, in no way are we claiming this essay as a comprehensive or that it represents the only interpretation available from the documents in this collection. We want this interpretative essay to provide readers with a way to understand arguments contained within these documents. Additionally, we have not included notes to the quotations mentioned throughout. Except for the previous note, all quotations originate from documents within this collection. Citations to those documents are provided throughout the collection.

Part I

Sovereignty and Reserved Powers

Editors' Note: The location of sovereignty is the most critical element of American federalism. The documents in this section cover how Americans have addressed that question throughout their history. They draw attention to those contrasting visions, first explained in the introductory essay, between state versus federal sovereignty. Readers should note the arguments each side employed in defending their respected positions. While examining the differences between both sides, also consider what, if anything, these documents may reveal about possible internal differences within each camp. Did those defending state sovereignty emphasize one element over another over two centuries? Have arguments for federal sovereignty always concentrated on the same points? If different times lead to different emphasis, consider how the role of historical contexts and the importance of crisis, in particular, shaped the historical understanding and arguments behind sovereignty and federalism.

The structure of this section follows the general chronology established in the introductory essay. It opens with the intellectual arguments on nature of sovereignty, the quality of large republics, and the idea of confederations. These ideas represent the received wisdom on the subject by the time of the mid-eighteenth century. The crisis that became the American Revolution required Americans to either accept or challenge this wisdom. The documents reveal how Americans, although certainly not all, accepted the idea of state sovereignty federalism at the time of the founding and early republic. It is in this section that the notion of "separate spheres" first takes hold. The shift from state to federal sovereignty, which began as a result of the Civil War but accelerated in the late nineteenth-century, is characterized by two elements. First, the degree to which the documents attacked the notion of state sovereignty, or "states' rights," as an antiquated limitation

1

to addressing national concerns and achieving national greatness. Secondly, how, in the midst of attacking state sovereignty, they appealed to the idea of undivided federal sovereignty. When the section moves into the 20th century, the concept of state sovereignty all but disappears. Supplanting it was the notion that sovereignty in the federal government can address and cure practically any concern and social ill and serve as a caretaker of the people. State sovereignty federalism declines, even more, when the racial segregationists of the mid-twentieth century appeal to state sovereignty in their attempts to perpetuate the violation of civil rights of African Americans. The section concludes with the recovery of the importance of state sovereignty federalism. The re-emphasis on state sovereignty began with Reagan administration of the 1980s and its somewhat sputtering invocation in the decades since. In particular, readers should notice that much of the return to the idea of state sovereignty emerged, not from the states themselves, but from the United States Supreme Court. Consider what it means to have federal courts, rather than state governments, defend or explain the nature of state sovereignty. How does this affect the efforts of the states in their recent appeals to the Tenth Amendment?

JEAN BODIN *ON SOVEREIGNTY*[1]

Sovereignty is the absolute and perpetual power vested in a commonwealth which in Latin is termed *majestas*.

. . . A perpetual authority therefore must be understood to mean one that lasts for the lifetime of him who exercises it. If a sovereign magistrate is given office for one year, or for any other predetermined period, and continues to exercise the authority bestowed on him after the conclusion of his term, he does so either by consent or by force and violence. If he does so by force, it is manifest tyranny. The tyrant is a true sovereign for all that. The robber's possession by violence is true and natural possession although contrary to the law, for those who were formerly in possession have been disseized. But if the magistrate continues in office by consent, he is not a sovereign prince, seeing that he only exercises power on sufferance. Still less is he a sovereign if the term of his office is not fixed, for in that case he has no more than a precarious commission.

. . . Let us now turn to the other term of our definition and consider the force of the word *absolute*. The people or the magnates of a commonwealth can bestow simply and unconditionally upon someone of their choice a sovereign and perpetual power to dispose of their property and persons, to govern the state as he thinks fit, and to order the succession, in the same way that any proprietor, out of his liberality, can freely and unconditionally make a gift of his property to another. Such a form of gift, not being mad qualified in any way, is the only true gift, being at once unconditional and irrevocable. Gifts burdened with obligations and hedged with conditions are not true gifts. Similarly sovereign power given to a prince charged with conditions is neither properly sovereign, nor absolute, unless the conditions of appointment are only such as are inherent in the laws of God and of nature . . .

. . . On the other hand it is the distinguishing mark of the sovereign that he cannot in any way be subject to the commands of another, for it is he who makes law for the subject, abrogates law already made, and amends obsolete law. No one who is subject either to the law or to some other person can do this. That is why it is laid down in the civil law that the prince is above the law, for the word *law* in Latin implies the command of him who is invested with sovereign power. Therefore we find in all statutes the phrase "notwithstanding all edicts and ordinances to the contrary that we have infringed, or do infringe by these present." This clause applies both to former acts of the prince himself, and to those of his predecessors. For all laws, ordinances, letters patent, privileges, and grants whatsoever issued by the prince, have force only during his own lifetime, and must be expressly, or at least tacitly, confirmed by the reigning prince who was cognizance of them . . . In proof of which, it is the custom of this realm for all corporations and corporate bodies to ask for the confirmation of their privileges, rights, and jurisdictions, on the accession of a new king. Even Parliaments and high courts do this, as well as individual officers of the crown.

. . . It is far otherwise with divine and natural laws. All the princes of the earth are subject to them, and cannot contravene them without treason and rebellion against God. His yoke is upon them, and they must bow their heads in fear and reverence before His divine majesty. The absolute power of princes and sovereign lords does not extend to the laws of God and of nature. He who best understood the meaning of absolute power, and made kings and emperors submit to his will, defined his sovereignty as a power to override positive law; he did not claim power to set aside divine and natural law.

. . . From all this it is clear that the principal mark of sovereign majesty and absolute power is the right to impose laws generally on all subjects regardless of their consent. . . And if it is expedient that if he is to govern his state well, a sovereign prince must be above the law, it is even more expedient that the ruling class in an aristocracy should be so, and inevitable in a popular state. A monarch in a kingdom is set apart from his subjects, and the ruling class from the people in an aristocracy. There are therefore in each case two parties, those that rule on the one hand, and those that are ruled on the other. This is the cause of the disputes about sovereignty that arise in them, but cannot in a popular state . . . There the people, rulers and ruled, form a single body and cannot bind themselves by their own laws.

. . . A distinction must therefore be made between right and the law, for one implies what is equitable and the other what is commanded. Law is nothing else than the command of the sovereign in the exercise of his sovereign power. A sovereign prince is not the subject to the laws of the Greeks, or any other alien power, or even those of the Romans, much less to his own laws, except in so far as they embody the law of nature which, according to Pindar, is the law to which all kings and princes are subject. Neither Pope nor Emperor is exempt from this law, though certain flatters say they can take the goods of their subjects at will. But both civilians and canonists have repudiated this opinion as contrary to the law of God. They err who assert that in virtue of their sovereign power princes can do this. It is rather the law of the jungle, an act of force and violence. For as we have shown above, absolute power implies freedom in relation to positive laws, and not in relation to the law of God. God has declared explicitly in His Law that it is not just to take, or even to cover, the goods of another. Those who defend such opinions are even more dangerous than those who act on them. They show the lion his claws, and arm princes under a cover of just claims. The evil will of a tyrant, drunk with such flatteries, urges him to an abuse of absolute power and excites his violent passions to the pitch where avarice issues in confiscations, desire in adultery, and anger in murder . . .

Since then the prince has no power to exceed the laws of nature which God Himself, whose image he is, has decreed, he cannot take his subject's property without just and reasonable cause, that is to say by purchase, exchange, legitimate confiscation, or to secure peace with the enemy when it cannot be otherwise achieved. Natural reason instructs us that the public good must be preferred to the particular, and that subjects should give up not only their mutual antagonisms and animosities, but also their possessions, for the safety of the commonwealth . . .

. . . If justice is the end of the law, the law the work of the prince, and the prince the image of God, it follows of necessity that the law of the prince should be modelled on the law of God.

THOMAS HOBBES, *LEVIATHAN*[2]

The final Cause, End, or Desire of men, (who naturally love Liberty, and Dominion over others,) in the introduction of that restraint upon themselves, (in which we see them live in Commonwealths) is the foresight of their own preservation, and of a more contended life thereby; that is to say, of getting themselves out from that miserable condition of War, which is necessarily consequent (as has been shown) to the natural Passions of men, when there is no visible Power to keep them in awe, and tie them by fear of punishment to the performance of their Covenants, and observation of those Laws of Nature.

For the Laws of Nature (as *Justice, Equity, Modesty, Mercy,* and (in sum) *doing to others, as we would be done to,*) of themselves, without the terror of some Power to cause them to be observed, are contrary to our natural Passions, that carry us to Partiality, Pride, Revenge, and the like. And Covenants, without the Sword, are but Words, and of no strength to secure a man at all. Therefore notwithstanding the Laws of Nature, (which every one has then kept, when he has the will to keep them, when he can do it safely,) if there be no Power erected, or not great enough for our security; every man will, and may lawfully rely on his own strength and art, for caution against all other men. And in all places, where men have lived by small Families, to rob and spoil one another, has been a Trade, and so far from being reputed against the Law of Nature, that the greater spoils they gained, the greater was their honor; and men observed no other Laws therein, but the Laws of Honor; that is, to abstain from cruelty, leaving to men their lives, and instruments of husbandry. And as small Families did then; so now do Cities and Kingdoms which are but greater Families (for their own security) enlarge their Dominions, upon all pretenses of danger, and fear of Invasion, or assistance that may be given to Invaders, endeavor as much as they can, to subdue, or weaken their neighbors, by open force, and secret arts, for want of other Caution, justly; and are remembered for it in after ages with honor.

Nor is it the joining together of a final number of men, that gives them this security; because in small numbers, small additions on the one side or the other, make the advantage of strength so great, as is sufficient to carry the Victory; and therefore gives encouragement to an Invasion. The Multitude sufficient to confide in for our Security, not determined by any certain number, but by comparison with the Enemy we fear; and is then sufficient, when the odds of the Enemy is not of so visible and conspicuous moment, to determine the event of war, as to move him to attempt.

And be there never so great a Multitude; yet if their actions be directed according to their particular judgements, and particular appetites, they can expect thereby no defense, nor protection, neither against a Common enemy, nor against the injuries of one another. For being distracted in opinions concerning the best use and application of their strength, they do not help, but hinder one another; and reduce their strength by mutual opposition to nothing: whereby they are easily, not only subdued by a very few that agree together; but also when there is no common enemy, they make war upon each other, for their particular interests. For if we could suppose a great Multitude of men to consent in the observation of Justice, and other Laws of Nature, without a common Power to keep them all in awe; we might as well suppose all Man-kind to do the same; and then there neither would be, nor need to be any Civil Government, or Common-wealth at all; because there would be Peace without subjection.

Nor is it enough for the security, which men desire should last all the time of their life, that they be governed, and directed by one judgment, for a limited time; as in one Battle, or one War. For though they obtain a Victory by their unanimous endeavor against a foreign enemy; yet afterwards, when either they have no common enemy, or he that by one part is held for an enemy, is by another part held for a friend, they must needs by the difference of their interests dissolve, and fall again into a War amongst themselves.

It is true, that certain living creatures, as Bees, and Ants, live sociably one with another, (which are therefore by *Aristotle* numbered amongst Political creatures;) and yet have no other direction, than their particular judgements and appetites; nor speech, whereby one of them can signify to another, what he thinks expedient for the common benefit: and therefore some man may perhaps desire to know, why Man-kind cannot do the same. To which I answer,

First, that men are continually in competition for Honor and Dignity, which these creatures are not; and consequently amongst men there arises on that ground, Envy and Hatred, and finally War; but amongst these not so.

Secondly, that amongst these creatures, the Common good differed not from the Private; and being by nature inclined to their private, they procure thereby the common benefit. But man, whose Joy consisted in comparing himself with other men, can relish nothing but what is eminent.

Thirdly, that these creatures, having not (as man) the use of reason, do not see, nor think they see any fault, in the administration of their common business: whereas amongst men, there are very many, that think themselves wiser, and abler to govern the Public, better than the rest; and these strive to reform and innovate, one this way, another that way; and thereby bring it into Distraction and Civil war.

Fourthly, that these creatures, though they have some use of voice, in making known to one another their desires, and other affections; yet they want that art of words, by which some men can represent to others, that which is Good, in the likenesses of Evil; and Evil, in the likenesses of Good; and augment, or diminish the apparent greatness of Good and Evil; discontenting men, and rumbling their Peace at their pleasure.

Fifthly, Irrational creatures cannot distinguish between *Injury*, and *Damage*; and therefore as long as they be at ease, they are not offended with their fellows: whereas Man is then most troublesome, when he is most at ease: for then it is that he loves to show his Wisdom, and control the Actions of them that govern the Common-wealth.

Lastly, the agreement of these creatures is Natural; that of men, is by Covenant only, which is Artificial: and therefore it is no wonder if there be somewhat else required (besides Covenant) to make their Agreement constant and lasting; which is a Common Power, to keep them in awe, and to direct their actions to the Common Benefit.

The only way to erect such a Common Power, as may be able to defend them from the invasion of Foreigners, and the injuries of one another, and thereby to secure them in such sort, as that by their own industry, and by the fruits of the Earth, they may nourish themselves and live contentedly; is, to confrere all their power and strength upon one Man, or upon one Assembly of men, to bear their Person; and every one to own, and acknowledge himself to be Author of whatsoever he that so bear their Person, shall Act, or cause to be Acted, in those things which concern the Common Peace and Safety; and therein to submit their Wills, every one to his Will, and their Judgements, to his Judgment. This is more than Consent, or Concord; it is a real Unity of them all, in one and the same Person, made by Covenant of every man with every man, in such manner, as if every man should say to every man, *I Authorize and give up my Right of Governing myself, to this Man, or to this Assembly of men, on this condition, that thou give up thy Right to him, and Authorize all his Actions in lie manner.* This done, the Multitude so united in one Person, is called a COMMON-WEALTH, in latin CIVITAS. This is the Generation of that great LEVIATHAN, or rather (to speak more reverently) of that *Mortal God*, to which we owe under the *Immortal God*, our peace and defense. For by this Authority, given him by every particular man in the Common-Wealth, he hath the use of so much Power and Strength conferred on him, that by terror thereof, he is enabled to conform the wills of them all, to Peace at home, and mutual aid against their enemies abroad. And in him consisted the Essence of the Commonwealth; which (to define it,) is *One Person, of whose Acts a great Multitude, by mutual covenants one with another, have made themselves every one the Author, to the end he may use the strength and means of them all, as he shall think expedient, for their Peace and Common Defense.*

And he that carried this Person, is called SOVEREIGN, and said to have *Sovereign Power*: and every one besides, his SUBJECT.

The attaining to this Sovereign Power, is by two ways. One, by Natural force; as when a man make his children, to submit themselves, and their children to his government, as being able to destroy them if they refuse; or by War subdue his enemies to his will giving them their lives on that condition. The other, is when men agree amongst themselves, to submit to some Man, or Assembly of men, voluntarily, on confidence to be protected by him against all others. This letter, may be called a Political Commonwealth by *Acquisition*.

MONTESQUIEU, *SPIRIT OF LAWS*[3]

... It is natural for a republic to have only a small territory; otherwise it cannot long subsist. In an extensive republic there are men of large fortunes, and consequently of less moderation; there are trusts too considerable to be placed in any single subject; he has interests of his own; he soon begins to think that he may be happy and glorious, by oppressing his fellow-citizens; and that he may raise himself to grandeur on the ruins of his country.

In an extensive republic the public good is sacrificed to a thousand private views; it is subordinate to exceptions, and depends on accidents. In a small one, the interest of the public is more obvious, better understood, and more within the reach of every citizen; abuses have less extent, and, of course, are less protected.

... A large empire supposes a despotic authority in the person who governs. It is necessary that the quickness of the prince's resolutions should supply the distance of the places they are sent to; that fear should prevent the remissness of the distant governor or magistrate; that the law should be derived from a single person, and should shift continually, according to the accidents which incessantly multiply in a state in proportion to its extent.

VATTEL, *LAW OF NATIONS*[4]

A nation or a state is, as has been said at the beginning of this work, a body politic, or a society of men united together for the purpose of promoting their mutual safety and advantage by their combined strength.

From the very design that induces a number of men to form a society which has its common interests, and which is to act in concert, it is necessary that there should be established a *Public Authority*, to order and direct what is to be done by each in relation to the end of the association. This political authority is the *Sovereignty*; and he or they who are invested with it are the *Sovereign*.

It is evident, that, by the very act of the civil or political association, each citizen subjects himself to the authority of the entire body, in everything that relates to the common welfare. The authority of all over each member, therefore, essentially belongs to the body politic, or state; but the exercise of that authority may be placed in different hands, according as the society may have ordained.

... Every nation that governs itself, under what form so ever, without dependence on any foreign power, is a *Sovereign State*. Its rights are naturally the same as those of any other state. Such are the moral persons who live together in a natural society, subject to the law of the nations. To give a nation a right to make an immediate figure in this grand society, it is sufficient that it be really sovereign and independent, that is, that it govern itself by its own authority and laws.

. . . Finally, several sovereign and independent states may unite themselves together by a perpetual confederacy, without ceasing to be, each individually, a perfect state. They will together constitute a federal republic: their joint deliberations will not impair the sovereignty of each member, though they may, in certain respects, put some restraint on the exercise of it, in virtue of voluntary engagements. A person does not cease to be free and independent, when he is obliged to fulfil engagements which he has voluntarily contracted.

BLACKSTONE'S *COMMENTARIES*[5]

. . . There is and must be . . . a supreme, irresistible, absolute, uncontrolled authority, in which the *jura summi imperii*, or the rights of sovereignty, reside. And this authority is placed in those hands, wherein (according to the opinion of the founders of such respective states, either expressly given, or collected from their tacit approbation) the qualities requisite for supremacy, wisdom, goodness, and power, are not the most likely to be found.

. . . By the sovereign power, as was before observed, is meant the making of laws; for wherever that power resides, all others must conform to, and be directed by it, whatever appearance the outward form and administration of the government may put on. For it is at any time in the option of the legislature to alter that form and administration by a new edict or rule, and to put the execution of the laws into whatever hands it pleases; by constituting one, or a few, or many executive magistrates: and all the other powers of the state must obey the legislature power in the discharge of their several functions, or else the constitution is at an end.

. . . But, happily for us of this island, the British constitution has long remained . . . . For, as with us the executive power of the laws is lodged in a single person, they have all the advantages of strength and dispatch, that are to be found in the most absolute monarchy: and as the legislature of the kingdom is entrusted to three distinct powers, entirely independent of each other; first, the king; secondly, the lords spiritual and temporal, which is an aristocratical assembly of persons selected for their piety, their birth, their wisdom, their valor, or their property; and, thirdly, the house of the commons, freely chosen by the people form among themselves, which makes it a kind of democracy; as this aggregate body, actuated by different springs, and attentive to different interests, composes the British parliament, and has the supreme disposal of everything; there can no inconvenience be attempted by either of the three branches, but will be withstood by one of the other two;

each branch being armed with a negative power, sufficient to repel any innovation which it shall think inexpedient or dangerous.

Here then is lodged the sovereignty of the British constitution; and lodged as beneficially as is possible for society. For in no other shape could we be so certain of finding the three great qualities of government so well and so happily united. If the supreme power were lodged in any one of the three branches separately, we must be exposed to the inconveniences of either absolute monarchy, aristocracy, or democracy; and so want two of the three principal ingredients of good polity, either virtue, wisdom, or power. If it were lodged in any two of the branches; for instance, in the king and house of lords; our laws might be providently made, and well executed, but they might not always have the good of the people in view: if lodged in the king and commons, we should want that circumspection and mediatory caution, which the wisdom of the peers is to afford: if the supreme rights of legislature were lodged in the two houses only, and the king had no negative upon their proceedings, they might be tempted to encroach upon the royal prerogative, or perhaps to abolish the kingly office, and thereby weaken (if not totally destroy) the strength of the executive power. But the constitutional government of this island is so admirably tempered and compounded, that nothing can endanger or hurt it, but destroying the equilibrium of power between one branch of the legislature and the rest. For if ever it should happen that the independence of any one of the three should be lost, or that it should become subservient to the views of either of the other two, there would soon be an end of our constitution. The legislature would be changed from that, which (upon the supposition of an original contract, either actual or implied) is presumed to have been originally set up by the general consent of the bands of government; and the people are thereby reduced to a state of anarchy, with liberty to constitute to themselves a new legislature power.

Having thus curiously considered the three usual species of government, and our own singular constitution, selected and compounded from them all, I proceed to observe, that, as the power of making laws constitutes the supreme authority, so wherever the supreme authority in any state resides, it is the right of that authority to make laws; that is, in the words of our definition, *to prescribe the rule of civil action.* And this may be discovered from the very end and institution of civil states. For a state is a collective body, composed of a multitude of individuals, united for their safety and convenience, and intending to act together as one man. If it therefore is to act as one man, it ought to act by one uniform will. But, inasmuch as political communities are made up of many natural persons, each of whom has his particular will and inclination, these several wills cannot by any *natural* union be joined together, or tempered and disposed into a lasting harmony, so as to constitute and produce that one uniform will of the whole. It can therefore be no otherwise produced than by a *political* union; by the consent of all persons to submit their own private wills to the will of one man, or of one or more assemblies of men, to whom the supreme authority is entrusted: and this will of that one man, or assemblage of men, is in different states, according to their different constitutions, understood to be law.

Thus far as to the *right* of the supreme power to make laws; but farther, it is its *duty* likewise. For since the respective members are bound to conform themselves to the will of the state, it is expedient that they receive directions from the state declaratory of that its will. But, as it is impossible, in so great a multitude, to give injunctions to every particular man, relative to each particular action, it is therefore incumbent on the state to establish general rules, for the perpetual information and direction of all persons in all points, whether of positive or negative duty. And this, in order that every man may know what to look upon as his own, what as another's; what absolute and what relative duties are required at his hands; what is to be esteemed honest, dishonest, or indifferent; what degree every man retains of his natural liberty; what he has given up as the price of the benefits of society; and after what manner each person is to moderate the use and exercise of those rights which the state assigns him, in order to promote and secure the public tranquility.

DECLARATORY ACT[6]

An act for the better securing the dependency of his majesty's dominions in America upon the crown and parliament of Great Britain.

Whereas several of the houses of representatives in his Majesty's colonies and plantations in America, have of late against law, claimed to themselves, or to the general assemblies of the same, the sole and exclusive right of imposing duties and taxes upon his majesty's subjects in the said colonies and plantations; and have in pursuance of such claim, passed certain votes, resolutions, and orders derogatory to the legislative authority of parliament, and inconsistent with the dependency of the said colonies and plantations upon the crown of Great Britain: may it therefore please your most excellent Majesty, that it may be declared; and be it declared by the King's most excellent majesty, by and with the advice and consent of the lords spiritual and temporal, and commons, in this present parliament assembled, and by the authority of the same, That the said colonies and plantations in America have been, are, and of right ought to be, subordinate unto, and dependent upon the imperial crown and parliament of Great Britain; and that the King's majesty, by and with the advice and consent of the lords spiritual and temporal, and commons of Great Britain, in parliament assembled, had hath, and of right ought to have, full power and authority to make laws and statutes of sufficient force and validity to bind the colonies and people of America, subjects of the crown of Great Britain, in all cases whatsoever,

And be it further declared and enacted by the authority aforesaid, That all resolutions, votes, orders, and proceedings, in any of the said colonies or plantations, whereby the power and authority of the parliament of Great Britain, to make laws and statutes as aforesaid, is denied, or drawn into question, arc, and are hereby declared to be, utterly null and void to all in purposes whatsoever.

RICHARD BLAND, *INQUIRY INTO THE RIGHTS OF THE BRITISH COLONIES*[7]

. . . From this Detail of the Charters, and other Acts of the Crown, under which the first Colony in North America was established, it is evident that "the Colonists were not a few unhappy Fugitives who had wandered into a distant Part of the World to enjoy their civil and religious Liberties, which they were deprived of at home," but had a regular Government long before the first Act of Navigation, and were respected as a distinct State, independent, as to their *internal* Government, of the original Kingdom, but united with her, as to their *external* Polity, in the closest and most intimate LEAGUE AND AMITY, under the same Allegiance, and enjoying the Benefits of a reciprocal Intercourse.

STEPHEN HOPKINS, *THE RIGHTS OF THE COLONIES EXAMINED*[8]

We are not insensible that when liberty is in danger, the liberty of complaining is dangerous . . . And we believe no good reason can be given why the colonies should not modestly and soberly inquire what right the Parliament of Great Britain have to tax them . . . . If the British House of Commons are rightfully possessed of a power to tax the colonies in America, this power must be vested in them by the British constitution, as they are one branch of the great legislative body of the nation. As they are the representatives of all the people in Britain, they have beyond doubt all the power such a representation can possibly give; yet great as this power is, surely it cannot exceed that of their constituents. And can it possibly be shown that the people in Britain have a sovereign authority over their fellow subjects in America? Yet such is the authority that must be exercised in taking people's estates from them by taxes, or otherwise without their consent. In all aids granted to the crown by the Parliament, it is said with the greatest propriety, "We freely give unto Your Majesty"; for they give their own money and the money of those who have entrusted them with a proper power for that purpose. But can they with the same propriety give away the money of the Americans, who have never given any such power? Before a thing can be justly given away, the giver must certainly have acquired a property in it; and have the people in Britain justly acquired such a property in the goods and estates of the people in these colonies that they may give them away at pleasure?

In an imperial state, which consists of many separate governments each of which hath peculiar privileges and of which kind it is evident the empire of Great Britain is, no single part, though greater than another part, is by that superiority entitled to make laws for or to tax such lesser part; but all laws and all taxations which bind the whole must be made by the whole. . . . Indeed, it must be absurd to suppose that the common people of Great Britain have a sovereign and absolute authority over their fellow subjects in America, or even any sort of power whatsoever over them; but it will be still more absurd to suppose they can give a power to their representatives which they have not themselves. If the House of Commons do not receive this authority from their constituents it will be difficult to tell by what means they obtained it, except it be vested in them by mere superiority and power.

ALEXANDER HAMILTON, *THE FARMER REFUTED*[9]

There seems to be a necessity for vesting the regulation of our trade there, because in time our commercial interests might otherwise interfere with hers. But with respect to making laws for us, there is not the least necessity, or even propriety, in it. Our Legislatures are confined to ourselves, and cannot interfere with Great Britain. We are best acquainted with our own circumstances, and therefore best qualified to make suitable regulations. It is of no force to object that no particular colony has power to enact general laws for all the colonies. There is no need of such general laws. Let every colony attend to its own internal police, and all will be well. How have we managed heretofore? The Parliament has made no general laws for our good, and yet our affairs have been conducted much to our ease and satisfaction. If any discord has sprung up among us, it is wholly imputable to the incursions of Great Britain. We should be peaceable and happy, if unmolested by her. We are not so destitute of wisdom as to be in want of her assistance to devise proper and salutary laws for us.

ARTICLES OF CONFEDERATION

Article II

Each state retains its sovereignty, freedom, and independence, and every Power, Jurisdiction and right, which is not by this confederation expressly delegated to the United States, in Congress assembled.

Article III

The said states hereby severally enter into a firm league of friendship with each other, for their common defence, the security of their Liberties, and their mutual and general welfare, binding themselves to assist each other, against all force offered to, or attacks made upon them, or any of them, on account of religion, sovereignty, trade, or any other pretense whatever.

Article IX

The united states in congress assembled, shall have the sole and exclusive right and power of determining on peace and war, except in the cases mentioned in the sixth article—of sending and receiving ambassadors—entering into treaties and alliances, provided that no treaty of commerce shall be made whereby the legislative power of the respective states shall be restrained from imposing such imposts and duties on foreigners as their own people are subjected to, or from prohibiting the exportation or importation of any species of goods or commodities, whatsoever—of establishing rules for deciding in all cases, what captures on land or water shall be legal, and in what manner prizes taken by land or naval forces in the service of the united states shall be divided or appropriated—of granting letters of marque and reprisal in times of peace—appointing courts for the trial of piracies and felonies committed on the high seas and establishing courts for receiving and determining finally appeals in all cases of captures, provided that no member of congress shall be appointed a judge of any of the said courts.

ALEXANDER HAMILTON, "THE CONTINENTALIST NO. 1"[10]

It would be the extreme of vanity in us not to be sensible, that we began this revolution with very vague and confined notions of the practical business of government. To the greater part of us it was a novelty: Of those, who under the former constitution had had opportunities of acquiring experience, a large proportion adhered to the opposite side, and the remainder can only be supposed to have possessed ideas adapted to the narrow colonial sphere, in which they had been accustomed to move, not of that enlarged kind suited to the government of an INDEPENDENT NATION.

There were no doubt exceptions to these observations—men in all respects qualified for conducting the public affairs, with skill and advantage; but their number was small; they were not always brought forward in our councils; and when they were, their influence was too commonly borne down by the prevailing torrent of ignorance and prejudice.

On a retrospect however, of our transactions, under the disadvantages with which we commenced, it is perhaps more to be wondered at, that we have done so well, than that we have not done better. There are indeed some traits in our conduct, as conspicuous for sound policy, as others for magnanimity. But, on the other hand, it must also be confessed, there have been many false steps, many chimerical projects and utopian speculations, in the management of our civil as well as of our military affairs. A part of these were the natural effects of the spirit of the times dictated by our situation. An extreme jealousy of power is the attendant on all popular revolutions, and has seldom been without its evils. It is to this source we are to trace many of the fatal mistakes, which have so deeply endangered the common cause; particularly that defect, which will be the object of these remarks, A WANT OF POWER IN CONGRESS.

The present Congress, respectable for abilities and integrity, by experience convinced of the necessity of a change, are preparing several important articles to be submitted to the respective states, for augmenting the powers of the Confederation. But though there is hardly at this time a man of information in America, who will not acknowledge, as a general proposition, that in its present form, it is unequal, either to a vigorous prosecution of the war, or to the preservation of the union in peace; yet when the principle comes to be applied to practice, there seems not to be the same agreement in the modes of remedying the defect; and it is to be feared, from a disposition which appeared in some of the states on a late occasion, that the salutary intentions of Congress may meet with more delay and opposition, than the critical posture of the states will justify.

It will be attempted to show in a course of papers what ought to be done, and the mischiefs of a contrary policy.

In the first stages of the controversy it was excusable to err. Good intentions, rather than great skill, were to have been expected from us. But we have now had sufficient time for reflection and experience, as ample as unfortunate, to rectify our errors. To persist in them, becomes disgraceful and even criminal, and belies that character of good sense and a quick discernment of our interests, which, in spite of our mistakes, we have been hitherto allowed.

It will prove, that our sagacity is limited to interests of inferior moment; and that we are incapable of those enlightened and liberal views, necessary to make us a great and a flourishing people.

History is full of examples, where in contests for liberty, a jealousy of power has either defeated the attempts to recover or preserve it in the first instance, or has afterwards subverted it by clogging government with too great precautions for its felicity, or by leaving too wide a door for sedition and popular licentiousness. In a government framed for durable liberty, not less regard must be paid to giving the magistrate a proper degree of authority, to make and execute the laws with rigor, than to guarding against encroachments upon the rights of the community. As too much power leads to despotism, too little leads to anarchy, and both eventually to the ruin of the people. These are maxims well known, but never sufficiently attended to, in adjusting the frames of governments. Some momentary interest or passion is sure to give a wrong bias, and pervert the most favorable opportunities.

No friend to order or to rational liberty, can read without pain and disgust the history of the commonwealth of Greece. Generally speaking, they were a constant scene of the alternate tyranny of one part of the people over the other, or of a few usurping demagogues over the whole. Most of them had been originally governed by kings, whose despotism (the natural disease of monarchy) had obliged their subjects to murder, expel, depose, or reduce them to a nominal existence, and institute popular governments. In these governments, that of Sparta excepted, the jealousy of power hindered the people from trusting out of their own hands a competent authority, to maintain the repose and stability of the commonwealth; whence originated the frequent revolutions and civil broils with which they were distracted. This, and the want of a solid federal union to restrain the ambition and rivalship of the different cities, after a rapid succession of bloody wars, ended in their total loss of liberty and subjugation to foreign powers.

In comparison of our governments with those of the ancient republics, we must, without hesitation, give the preference to our own; because, every power with us is exercised by representation, not in tumultuary assemblies of the collective body of the people, where the art or impudence of the ORATOR or TRIBUNE, rather than the utility or justice of the measure could seldom fail to govern. Yet whatever may be the advantage on our side, in such a comparison, men who estimate the value of institutions, not from prejudices of the moment, but from experience and reason, must be persuaded, that the same JEALOUSY of POWER has prevented our reaping all the advantages, from the examples of other nations, which we ought to have done, and has rendered our constitutions in many respects feeble and imperfect.

Perhaps the evil is not very great in respect to our constitutions; for notwithstanding their imperfections, they may, for some time, be made to operate in such a manner, as to answer the purposes of the common defense and the maintenance of order; and they seem to have, in themselves, and in the progress of society among us, the seeds of improvement.

But this is not the case with respect to the FEDERAL GOVERNMENT; if it is too weak at first, it will continually grow weaker. The ambition and local interests of the respective members, will be constantly undermining and usurping upon its prerogatives, till it comes to a dissolution; if a partial combination of some of the more powerful ones does not bring it to a more SPEEDY and VIOLENT END.

1783 TREATY OF PEACE

Article 1

His Brittanic Majesty acknowledges the said United States, viz., New Hampshire, Massachusetts Bay, Rhode Island and Providence Plantations, Connecticut, New York, New Jersey, Pennsylvania, Maryland, Virginia, North Carolina, South Carolina and Georgia, to be free sovereign and independent states, that he treats with them as such, and for himself, his heirs, and successors, relinquishes all claims to the government, propriety, and territorial rights of the same and every part thereof.

Article 4

It is agreed that creditors on either side shall meet with no lawful impediment to the recovery of the full value in sterling money of all bona fide debts heretofore contracted.

Article 5

It is agreed that Congress shall earnestly recommend it to the legislatures of the respective states to provide for the restitution of all estates, rights, and properties, which have been confiscated belonging to real British subjects; and also of the estates, rights, and properties of persons resident in districts in the possession on his Majesty's arms and who have not borne arms against the said United States. And that persons of any other description shall have free liberty to go to any part or parts of any of the thirteen United States and therein to remain twelve months unmolested in their endeavors to obtain the restitution of such of their estates, rights, and properties as may have been confiscated; and that Congress shall also earnestly recommend to the several states a reconsideration and revision of all acts or laws regarding the premises, so as to render the said laws or acts perfectly consistent not only with justice and equity but with that spirit of conciliation which on the return of the blessings of peace should universally prevail. And that Congress shall also earnestly recommend to the several states that the estates, rights, and properties, of such last mentioned persons shall be restored to them, they refunding to any persons who may be now in possession the bona fide price (where any has been given) which such persons may have paid on purchasing any of the said lands, rights, or properties since the confiscation.

And it is agreed that all persons who have any interest in confiscated lands, either by debts, marriage settlements, or otherwise, shall meet with no lawful impediment in the prosecution of their just rights.

Article 6

That there shall be no future confiscations made nor any prosecutions commenced against any person or persons for, or by reason of, the part which he or they may have taken in the present war, and that no person shall on that account suffer any future loss or damage, either in his person, liberty, or property; and that those who may be in confinement on such charges at the time of the ratification of the treaty in America shall be immediately set at liberty, and the prosecutions so commenced be discontinued.

MERIWETHER SMITH, "OBSERVATIONS ON THE FOURTH AND FIFTH ARTICLES OF THE PRELIMINARIES"[11]

Sensible that, by the laws of nations upon the principal of revolution, where the people, changing their political capacity, cease to be the *same people*, everything not expressly received in the new social compact, and which was dependent on the old government, was abrogated, dissolved, and become void; it has been judged necessary to renew the claims of individuals by the fourth article. How far this stipulation [i.e., Article 4 of the Treaty of Peace] on the parts of the *ministers* of *congress* is consistent with the *sovereignty* and rights of *legislation* of an individual state is worthy of consideration, and perhaps it will be found, that being *contrary to the laws of the state*, and to the rights of the citizens *derived from the resolution and the positive law of the state, that the ministers of congress* had no right to stipulate in the *manner* they have agreed as to the 4th article, and consequently that there is no authority to carry it into execution but that which arises from the *consent* of the *legislature* of the *state* and of the individuals inscribed herein. The individuals have a positive law of this state in their favor which leaves them not at the unity of British creditors, and the authority of congress extends to no individual in any state. For, the ministers of congress to say then, that there shall be no lawful impeachment to the recovery of the full value of their debts in storing money, is affirming the right of legislation here,—it is subjecting the citizens within the state to their authority, and directing a repeal of such laws as they disapprove—in fine, it is depriving the state of its sovereignty and independence received by the confederation. If congress found it necessary for the sake of peace, it might have stipulated to make good the losses of British creditors of British subjects in any point of view, and the equivalent might have been paid out of the vast conquests of the unites states or such other funds as they had a power over, but congress has no right to contradict the act of the legislature of this state, to compel us to receive British subjects or others whom we disapprove, or to subject the citizens of this state, to the mercy of British subjects, within the same.

2d. When the 4th and 5th articles are compared, it will be difficult to reconcile the principals on which they have been agreed. The 5th article discovers a partially in favor of the *state and of the individuals in possession of confiscated property*;—it does not bind the state to restore the confiscated property even to *risk British subjects* (as they are called) which certainly comprehends all those who did not enter into the new social compact; and it is *recommended* that *traitors* shall be reported *on paying a compensation*. Here is *tenderness* with respect to the *sovereignty* of the individual states and to the *authority of their laws*. Here is at least a tactic acknowledgement of the authority of the *state* to confiscate the property *even of British subjects* without any power in *congress* to compel restitution; and in this case, the *right* and the *interest* of the *state*, that is, of the *majority of the citizens within a state* have been considered; and the *states* may, if it be their interest, retain the benefit arising from confiscated property, and this they will probably do where it is considerable, and where the present possessors are not disposed to give it up.

But the *interest* of some states differ from that of others, inasmuch as some have great of confiscated property, and but few debts; others, were greatly indebted, and have but little confiscated property. In the letter case the individuals, who have risked their lives, their liberty and their property to assist their *fellow citizens* in establishing and securing *their* rights and *property*, are to be given up to the *mercy of British creditors* and sacrificed to the *interest of British subjects* their enemies, and of those who support their cause among us, without any compensation for their various losses, during this unequal war. They are to be left to answer the debts due, *before this revolution*, to the very persons who by various means have been contributing to plunder and ruin them, contrary to every principal of the usage of nations.

Here the right of the state and of the citizens is exactly the same herein the case of confiscation; for the principal of revolution applies equally; and congress have no more authority in the one case than in the other. It is the duty of the individuals to defend themselves, and it is the duty of the state to preserve its authority and the dignity of its laws, and to save its citizens from the ruin which threatens them. *Wisdom* and *firmness* in the *legislature* will be a sure state guard to the people.

. . . Every individual who was indebted to British subjects, and entered into a new community, laid the community under obligation to him, not only for his *personal services* but also for the *use of property which* he was *possessed* of. Every *individual* of the community also was under obligations to him, because he shared the same *common danger* and the same *common expense.* Had he withdrawn himself and his property, he would have risked nothing, and he would have weakened their case: He is therefore entitled to justice and to the protection of his fellow-citizens.

By entering into the new social compact, the *individual* indebted to British subjects, risked his *life*, his *liberty* and not only that where withal he might have discharged the debt, but also the *remaining part of his property*. If he was indebted a *fourth* part, and hath lost *three fourths* of his property, by the 4th article of the preliminaries, he is to lose the *other* part also. Here the *British subject* who is an *enemy*, risks *nothing* the *citizen* of the state, risks *all*; and having risked all, must give up to an enemy that which he hath saved. The terms are unequal and unjust with respect to the citizen;—they are disgraceful to the state.

VIRGINIA PLAN[12]

6. Resolved that each branch ought to possess the right of originating Acts; that the National Legislature ought to be impowered to enjoy the Legislative Rights vested in Congress bar the Confederation & moreover to legislate in all cases to which the separate States are incompetent, or in which the harmony of the United States may be interrupted by the exercise of individual Legislation; to negative all laws passed by the several States, contravening in the opinion of the National Legislature the articles of Union; and to call forth the force of the Union agst any member of the Union failing to fulfill its duty under the articles thereof.

8. Res^d that the Executive and a convenient number of the National Judiciary, ought to compose a Council of revision with authority to examine every act of the National Legislature before it shall operate, & every act of a particular Legislature before a Negative thereon shall be final; and that the

dissent of the said Council shall amount to a rejection, unless the Act of the National Legislature be again passed, or that of a particular Legislature be again negatived by of the members of each branch.

NEW JERSEY PLAN[13]

1. Resd. that the articles of Confederation ought to be so revised, corrected & enlarged, as to render the federal Constitution adequate to the exigencies of Government, & the preservation of the Union.

2. Resd. that in addition to the powers vested in the U. States in Congress, by the present existing articles of Confederation, they be authorized to pass acts for raising a revenue, by levying a duty or duties on all goods or merchandizes of foreign growth or manufacture, imported into any part of the U. States, by Stamps on paper, vellum or parchment, and by a postage on all letters or packages passing through the general post-office, to be applied to such federal purposes as they shall deem proper & expedient; to make rules & regulations for the collection thereof; and the same from time to time, to alter & amend in such manner as they shall think proper: to pass Acts for the regulation of trade & commerce as well with foreign nations as with each other: provided that all punishments, fines, forfeitures & penalties to be incurred for contravening such acts rules and regulations shall be adjudged by the Common law Judiciaries of the State in which any offence contrary to the true intent & meaning of such Acts rules & regulations shall have been committed or perpetrated, with liberty of commencing in the first instance all suits & prosecutions for that purpose in the superior common law Judiciary in such State, subject nevertheless, for the correction of all errors, both in law & fact in rendering Judgment, to an appeal to the Judiciary of the U. States.

6. Resd. that all Acts of the U. States in Congs. made by virtue & in pursuance of the powers hereby & by the articles of Confederation vested in them, and all Treaties made & ratified under the authority of the U. States shall be the supreme law of the respective States so far forth as those Acts or Treaties shall relate to the said States or their Citizens, and that the Judiciary of the several States shall be bound thereby in their decisions, any thing in the respective laws of the Individual States to the contrary notwithstanding; and that if any State, or any body of men in any State shall oppose or prevent yd. carrying into execution such acts or treaties, the federal Executive shall be authorized to call forth ye. power of the Confederated States, or so much thereof as may be necessary to enforce and compel an obedience to such Acts, or an observance of such Treaties.

JAMES WILSON, "STATE HOUSE SPEECH"[14]

When the people established the powers of legislation under their separate governments, they invested their representatives with every right and authority which they did not in explicit terms reserve; and therefore upon every question respecting the jurisdiction of the House of Assembly, if the frame of government is silent, the jurisdiction is efficient and complete. But in delegating federal powers, another criterion was necessarily introduced, and the congressional power is to be collected, not from tacit implication, but from the positive grant expressed in the instrument of the union. Hence, it is evident, that in the former case everything which is not reserved is given; but in the latter the reverse of the proposition prevails, and everything which is not given is reserved.

This distinction being recognized, will furnish an answer to those who think the omission of a bill of rights a defect in the proposed constitution; for it would have been superfluous and absurd to have stipulated with a federal body of our own creation, that we should enjoy those privileges of which we are not divested, either by the intention or the act that has brought the body into existence. For instance, the liberty of the press, which has been a copious source of declamation and opposition—what control can proceed from the Federal government to shackle or destroy that sacred palladium of national freedom? If, indeed, a power similar to that which has been granted for the regulation of commerce had been granted to regulate literary publications, it would have been as necessary to stipulate that the liberty of the press should be preserved inviolate, as that the impost should be general in its operation.

Another objection that has been fabricated against the new constitution, is expressed in this disingenuous form—"The trial by jury is abolished in civil cases." I must be excused, my fellow citizens, if upon this point I take advantage of my professional experience to detect the futility of the assertion. Let it be remembered then, that the business of the Federal Convention was not local, but general—not limited to the views and establishments of a single State, but co-extensive with the continent, and comprehending the views and establishments of thirteen independent sovereignties. When, therefore, this subject was in discussion, we were involved in difficulties which pressed on all sides, and no precedent could be discovered to direct our course. The cases open to a trial by jury differed in the different States. It was therefore impracticable, on that ground, to have made a general rule. The want of uniformity would have rendered any reference to the practice of the States idle and useless; and it could not with any propriety be said that, "The trial by jury shall be as heretofore," since there has never existed any federal system of jurisprudence, to which the declaration could relate. Besides, it is not in all cases that the trial by jury is adopted in civil questions; for cases depending in courts of admiralty, such as relate to maritime captures, and such as are agitated in courts of equity, do not require the intervention of that tribunal. How, then was the line of discrimination to be drawn? The Convention found the task too difficult for them, and they left the business as it stands, in the fullest confidence that no danger could possibly ensue, since the proceedings of the Supreme Court are to be regulated by the Congress, which is a faithful representation of the people; and the oppression of government is effectually barred, by declaring that in all criminal cases the trial by jury shall be preserved.

. . . The next accusation I shall consider is that which represents the federal constitution, as not only calculated, but designedly framed, to reduce the State governments to mere corporations and eventually to annihilate them. Those who have employed the term corporation upon this occasion are not perhaps aware of its extent. In common parlance, indeed, it is generally applied to petty associations for the ease and convenience of a few individuals; but in its enlarged sense, it will comprehend the government of Pennsylvania, the existing union of the States, and even this projected system is nothing more than a formal act of incorporation. But upon what presence can it be alleged that it was designed to annihilate the State governments? For I will undertake to prove that upon their existence depends the existence of the Federal plan. For this purpose, permit me to call your attention to the manner in which the President, Senate and House of Representatives are proposed to be appointed. The President is to be chosen by electors, nominated in such manner as the legislature of each State may direct; so that if there is no legislature there can be no electors, and consequently the office of President cannot be supplied.

The Senate is to be composed of two Senators from each State, chosen by the Legislature; and, therefore, if there is no Legislature, there can be no Senate. The House of Representatives is to be composed of members chosen every second year by the people of the several States, and the electors in each State shall have the qualifications requisite for electors of the most numerous branch of the State Legislature; unless, therefore, there is a State Legislature, that qualification cannot be ascertained, and the popular branch of the federal constitution must be extinct. From this view, then, it is evidently absurd to suppose that the annihilation of the separate governments will result from their union; or, that having that intention, the authors of the new system would have bound their connection with such indissoluble ties. Let me here advert to an arrangement highly advantageous, for you will perceive, without prejudice to the powers of the Legislature in the election of Senators, the people at large will acquire an additional privilege in returning members to the House of Representatives; whereas, by the present confederation, it is the Legislature alone that appoints the delegates to Congress.

FEDERALIST NO. 10[15]

Among the numerous advantages promised by a well-constructed Union, none deserves to be more accurately developed than its tendency to break and control the violence of faction.

By a faction, I understand a number of citizens, whether amounting to a majority or a minority of the whole, who are united and actuated by some common impulse of passion, or of interest, adverse to the rights of other citizens, or to the permanent and aggregate interests of the community.

. . . Liberty is to faction what air is to fire, an aliment without which it instantly expires. But it could not be less folly to abolish liberty, which is essential to political life, because it nourishes faction, than it would be to wish the annihilation of air, which is essential to animal life, because it imparts to fire its destructive agency.

. . . The latent causes of faction are thus sown in the nature of man; and we see them everywhere brought into different degrees of activity, according to the different circumstances of civil society.

. . . The two great points of difference between a democracy and a republic are: first, the delegation of the government, in the latter, to a small number of citizens elected by the rest; secondly, the greater number of citizens, and greater sphere of country, over which the latter may be extended.

The effect of the first difference is, on the one hand, to refine and enlarge the public views, by passing them through the medium of a chosen body of citizens, whose wisdom may best discern the true interest of their country, and whose patriotism and love of justice will be least likely to sacrifice it to temporary or partial considerations. Under such a regulation, it may well happen that the public voice, pronounced by the representatives of the people, will be more consonant to the public good than if pronounced by the people themselves, convened for the purpose. On the other hand, the effect may be inverted. Men of factious tempers, of local prejudices, or of sinister designs, may, by intrigue, by corruption, or by other means, first obtain the suffrages, and then betray the interests, of the people. The question resulting is, whether small or extensive republics are more favorable to the election of proper guardians of the public weal; and it is clearly decided in favor of the latter by two obvious considerations:

In the first place, it is to be remarked that, however small the republic may be, the representatives must be raised to a certain number, in order to guard against the cabals of a few; and that, however large it may be, they must be limited to a certain number, in order to guard against the confusion of a multitude. Hence, the number of representatives in the two cases not being in proportion to that of the two constituents, and being proportionally greater in the small republic, it follows that, if the proportion of fit characters be not less in the large than in the small republic, the former will present a greater option, and consequently a greater probability of a fit choice.

In the next place, as each representative will be chosen by a greater number of citizens in the large than in the small republic, it will be more difficult for unworthy candidates to practice with success the vicious arts by which elections are too often carried; and the suffrages of the people being more free, will be more likely to center in men who possess the most attractive merit and the most diffusive and established characters.

It must be confessed that in this, as in most other cases, there is a mean, on both sides of which inconveniences will be found to lie. By enlarging too much the number of electors, you render the representatives too little acquainted with all their local circumstances and lesser interests; as by reducing it too much, you render him unduly attached to these, and too little fit to comprehend and pursue great and national objects. The federal Constitution forms a happy combination in this respect; the great and aggregate interests being referred to the national, the local and particular to the State legislatures.

The other point of difference is, the greater number of citizens and extent of territory which may be brought within the compass of republican than of democratic government; and it is this circumstance principally which renders factious combinations less to be dreaded in the former than in the latter. The smaller the society, the fewer probably will be the distinct parties and interests composing it; the fewer the distinct parties and interests, the more frequently will a majority be found of the same party; and the smaller the number of individuals composing a majority, and the smaller the compass within which they are placed, the more easily will they concert and execute their plans of oppression. Extend the sphere, and you take in a greater variety of parties and interests; you make it less probable that a majority of the whole will have a common motive to invade the rights of other citizens; or if such a common motive exists, it will be more difficult for all who feel it to discover their own strength, and to act in unison with each other. Besides other impediments, it may be remarked that, where there is a consciousness of unjust or dishonorable purposes, communication is always checked by distrust in proportion to the number whose concurrence is necessary.

Hence, it clearly appears, that the same advantage which a republic has over a democracy, in controlling the effects of faction, is enjoyed by a large over a small republic,—is enjoyed by the Union over the States composing it. Does the advantage consist in the substitution of representatives whose enlightened views and virtuous sentiments render them superior to local prejudices and schemes of injustice? It will not be denied that the representation of the Union will be most likely to possess these requisite endowments. Does it consist in the greater security afforded by a greater variety of parties, against the event of any one party being able to outnumber and oppress the rest? In an equal degree does the increased variety of parties comprised within the Union, increase this security. Does it, in fine, consist in the greater obstacles opposed to the concert and accomplishment of the secret wishes of an unjust and interested majority? Here, again, the extent of the Union gives it the most palpable advantage.

The influence of factious leaders may kindle a flame within their particular States, but will be unable to spread a general conflagration through the other States. A religious sect may degenerate into a political faction in a part of the Confederacy; but the variety of sects dispersed over the entire face of it must secure the national councils against any danger from that source. A rage for paper money, for an abolition of debts, for an equal division of property, or for any other improper or wicked project, will be less apt to pervade the whole body of the Union than a particular member of it; in the same proportion as such a malady is more likely to taint a particular county or district, than an entire State.

In the extent and proper structure of the Union, therefore, we behold a republican remedy for the diseases most incident to republican government. And according to the degree of pleasure and pride we feel in being republicans, ought to be our zeal in cherishing the spirit and supporting the character of Federalists.

FEDERALIST NO. 26[16]

. . . the State legislatures, who will always be not only vigilant but suspicious and jealous guardians of the rights of the citizens against encroachments from the federal government, will constantly have their attention awake to the conduct of the national rulers, and will be ready enough, if any thing improper appears, to sound the alarm to the people, and not only to be the VOICE, but, if necessary, the ARM of their discontent.

FEDERALIST NO. 39[17]

. . . If we resort for a criterion to the different principles on which different forms of government are established, we may define a republic to be, or at least may bestow that name on, a government which derives all its powers directly or indirectly from the great body of the people, and is administered by persons holding their offices during pleasure, for a limited period, or during good behavior. It is ESSENTIAL to such a government that it be derived from the great body of the society, not from an inconsiderable proportion, or a favored class of it; otherwise a handful of tyrannical nobles, exercising their oppressions by a delegation of their powers, might aspire to the rank of republicans, and claim for their government the honorable title of republic. It is SUFFICIENT for such a government that the persons administering it be appointed, either directly or indirectly, by the people; and that they hold their appointments by either of the tenures just specified; otherwise every government in the United States, as well as every other popular government that has been or can be well organized or well executed, would be degraded from the republican character.

. . . "But it was not sufficient," say the adversaries of the proposed Constitution, "for the convention to adhere to the republican form. They ought, with equal care, to have preserved the FEDERAL form, which regards the Union as a CONFEDERACY of sovereign states; instead of which, they have framed a NATIONAL government, which regards the Union as a CONSOLIDATION of the States." And it is asked by what authority this bold and radical innovation was undertaken? The handle which has been made of this objection requires that it should be examined with some precision.

. . . In order to ascertain the real character of the government, it may be considered in relation to the foundation on which it is to be established; to the sources from which its ordinary powers are to be drawn; to the operation of those powers; to the extent of them; and to the authority by which future changes in the government are to be introduced.

On examining the first relation, it appears, on one hand, that the Constitution is to be founded on the assent and ratification of the people of America, given by deputies elected for the special purpose; but, on the other, that this assent and ratification is to be given by the people, not as individuals composing one entire nation, but as composing the distinct and independent States to which they respectively belong. It is to be the assent and ratification of the several States, derived from the supreme authority in each State, the authority of the people themselves. The act, therefore, establishing the Constitution, will not be a NATIONAL, but a FEDERAL act.

That it will be a federal and not a national act, as these terms are understood by the objectors; the act of the people, as forming so many independent States, not as forming one aggregate nation, is obvious from this single consideration, that it is to result neither from the decision of a MAJORITY of the people of the Union, nor from that of a MAJORITY of the States. It must result from the UNANIMOUS assent of the several States that are parties to it, differing no otherwise from their ordinary assent than in its being expressed, not by the legislative authority, but by that of the people themselves. Were the people regarded in this transaction as forming one nation, the will of the majority of the whole people of the United States would bind the minority, in the same manner as the majority in each State must bind the minority; and the will of the majority must be determined either by a comparison of the individual votes, or by considering the will of the majority of the States as evidence of the will of a majority of the people of the United States. Neither of these rules have been adopted. Each State, in ratifying the Constitution, is considered as a sovereign body, independent of all others, and only to be bound by its own voluntary act. In this relation, then, the new Constitution will, if established, be a FEDERAL, and not a NATIONAL constitution.

The next relation is, to the sources from which the ordinary powers of government are to be derived. The House of Representatives will derive its powers from the people of America; and the people will be represented in the same proportion, and on the same principle, as they are in the legislature of a particular State. So far the government is NATIONAL, not FEDERAL. The Senate, on the other hand, will derive its powers from the States, as political and coequal societies; and these will be represented on the principle of equality in the Senate, as they now are in the existing Congress. So far the government is FEDERAL, not NATIONAL. The executive power will be derived from a very compound source. The immediate election of the President is to be made by the States in their political characters. The votes allotted to them are in a compound ratio, which considers them partly as distinct and coequal societies, partly as unequal members of the same society. The eventual election, again, is to be made by that branch of the legislature which consists of the national representatives; but in this particular act they are to be thrown into the form of individual delegations, from so many distinct and coequal bodies politic. From this aspect of the government it appears to be of a mixed character, presenting at least as many FEDERAL as NATIONAL features.

The difference between a federal and national government, as it relates to the OPERATION OF THE GOVERNMENT, is supposed to consist in this, that in the former the powers operate on the political bodies composing the Confederacy, in their political capacities; in the latter, on the individual citizens composing the nation, in their individual capacities. On trying the Constitution by this criterion, it falls under the NATIONAL, not the FEDERAL character; though perhaps not so completely as has been understood. In several cases, and particularly in the trial of controversies to which States may be parties, they must be viewed and proceeded against in their collective and political capacities only. So far the national countenance of the government on this side seems to be disfigured by a few federal features. But this blemish is perhaps unavoidable in any plan; and the operation of the government on the people, in their individual capacities, in its ordinary and most essential proceedings, may, on the whole, designate it, in this relation, a NATIONAL government.

But if the government be national with regard to the OPERATION of its powers, it changes its aspect again when we contemplate it in relation to the

EXTENT of its powers. The idea of a national government involves in it, not only an authority over the individual citizens, but an indefinite supremacy over all persons and things, so far as they are objects of lawful government. Among a people consolidated into one nation, this supremacy is completely vested in the national legislature. Among communities united for particular purposes, it is vested partly in the general and partly in the municipal legislatures. In the former case, all local authorities are subordinate to the supreme; and may be controlled, directed, or abolished by it at pleasure. In the latter, the local or municipal authorities form distinct and independent portions of the supremacy, no more subject, within their respective spheres, to the general authority, than the general authority is subject to them, within its own sphere. In this relation, then, the proposed government cannot be deemed a NATIONAL one; since its jurisdiction extends to certain enumerated objects only, and leaves to the several States a residuary and inviolable sovereignty over all other objects. It is true that in controversies relating to the boundary between the two jurisdictions, the tribunal which is ultimately to decide, is to be established under the general government. But this does not change the principle of the case. The decision is to be impartially made, according to the rules of the Constitution; and all the usual and most effectual precautions are taken to secure this impartiality. Some such tribunal is clearly essential to prevent an appeal to the sword and a dissolution of the compact; and that it ought to be established under the general rather than under the local governments, or, to speak more properly, that it could be safely established under the first alone, is a position not likely to be combated.

If we try the Constitution by its last relation to the authority by which amendments are to be made, we find it neither wholly NATIONAL nor wholly FEDERAL. Were it wholly national, the supreme and ultimate authority would reside in the MAJORITY of the people of the Union; and this authority would be competent at all times, like that of a majority of every national society, to alter or abolish its established government. Were it wholly federal, on the other hand, the concurrence of each State in the Union would be essential to every alteration that would be binding on all. The mode provided by the plan of the convention is not founded on either of these principles. In requiring more than a majority, and principles. In requiring more than a majority, and particularly in computing the proportion by STATES, not by CITIZENS, it departs from the NATIONAL and advances towards the FEDERAL character; in rendering the concurrence of less than the whole number of States sufficient, it loses again the FEDERAL and partakes of the NATIONAL character.

The proposed Constitution, therefore, is, in strictness, neither a national nor a federal Constitution, but a composition of both. In its foundation it is federal, not national; in the sources from which the ordinary powers of the government are drawn, it is partly federal and partly national; in the operation of these powers, it is national, not federal; in the extent of them, again, it is federal, not national; and, finally, in the authoritative mode of introducing amendments, it is neither wholly federal nor wholly national.

FEDERALIST NO. 44[18]

. . . "power to make all laws which shall be necessary and proper for carrying into execution the foregoing powers, and all other powers vested by this Constitution in the government of the United States, or in any department or officer thereof." Few parts of the Constitution have been assailed with more intemperance than this; yet on a fair investigation of it, no part can appear more completely invulnerable. Without the SUBSTANCE of this power, the whole Constitution would be a dead letter. Those who object to the article, therefore, as a part of the Constitution, can only mean that the FORM of the provision is improper. But have they considered whether a better form could have been substituted? There are four other possible methods which the Constitution might have taken on this subject. They might have copied the second article of the existing Confederation, which would have prohibited the exercise of any power not EXPRESSLY delegated; they might have attempted a positive enumeration of the powers comprehended under the general terms "necessary and proper"; they might have attempted a negative enumeration of them, by specifying the powers excepted from the general definition; they might have been altogether silent on the subject, leaving these necessary and proper powers to construction and inference. Had the convention taken the first method of adopting the second article of Confederation, it is evident that the new Congress would be continually exposed, as their predecessors have been, to the alternative of construing the term "EXPRESSLY" with so much rigor, as to disarm the government of all real authority whatever, or with so much latitude as to destroy altogether the force of the restriction.

. . . If it be asked what is to be the consequence, in case the Congress shall misconstrue this part of the Constitution, and exercise powers not warranted by its true meaning, I answer, the same as if they should misconstrue or enlarge any other power vested in them; as if the general power had been reduced to particulars, and any one of these were to be violated; the same, in short, as if the State legislatures should violate the irrespective constitutional authorities. In the first instance, the success of the usurpation will depend on the executive and judiciary departments, which are to expound and give effect to the legislative acts; and in the last resort a remedy must be obtained from the people who can, by the election of more faithful representatives, annul the acts of the usurpers. The truth is, that this ultimate redress may be more confided in against unconstitutional acts of the federal than of the State legislatures, for this plain reason, that as every such act of the former will be an invasion of the rights of the latter, these will be ever ready to mark the innovation, to sound the alarm to the people, and to exert their local influence in effecting a change of federal representatives.

BRUTUS 1[19]

... The first question that presents itself on the subject is, whether a confederated government be the best for the United States or not? Or in other words, whether the thirteen United States should be reduced to one great republic, governed by one legislature, and under the direction of one executive and judicial; or whether they should continue thirteen confederated republics, under the direction and control of a supreme federal head for certain defined national purposes only?

This enquiry is important, because, although the government reported by the convention does not go to a perfect and entire consolidation, yet it approaches so near to it, that it must, if executed, certainly and infallibly terminate in it.

This government is to possess absolute and uncontrollable power, legislative, executive and judicial, with respect to every object to which it extends for by, the last clause of section 8th, article 1st, it is declared "that the Congress shall have power to make all laws which shall be necessary and proper for carrying into execution the foregoing powers, and all other powers vested by this constitution, in the government of the United States; or in any department or office thereof" And by the 6th article, it is declared "that this constitution, and the laws of the United States, which shall be made in pursuance thereof and the treaties made, or which shall be made, under the authority of the United States, shall be the supreme law of the land; and the judges in every state shall be bound thereby, anything in the constitution, or law of any state to the contrary notwithstanding." It appears from these articles that there is no need of any intervention of the state governments, between the Congress and the people, to execute any one power vested in the general government, and that the constitution and laws of every state are nullified and declared void, so far as they are or shall be inconsistent with this constitution, or the laws made in pursuance of it, or with treaties made under the authority of the United States.—The government then, so far as it extends, is a complete one, and not a confederation. It is as much one complete government as that of New-York or Massachusetts, has as absolute and perfect powers to make and execute all laws, to appoint officers, institute courts, declare offences, and annex penalties, with respect to every object to which it extends, as any other in the world. So far therefore as its powers reach, all ideas of confederation are given up and lost. It is true this government is limited to certain objects, or to speak more properly, some small degree of power is still left to the states, but a little attention to the powers vested in the general government, will convince every candid man, that if it is capable of being executed, all that is reserved for the individual states must very soon be annihilated, except so far as they are barely necessary to the organization of the general government. The powers of the general legislature extend to every case that is of the least importance—there is nothing valuable to human nature, nothing dear to freemen, but what is within its power. It has authority to make laws which will affect the lives, the liberty, and property of everyman in the United States; nor can the constitution or laws of any state, in anyway prevent or impede the full and complete execution of every power given.

   . . . Let us now proceed to enquire, as I at first proposed, whether it be best the thirteen United States should be reduced to one great republic, or not? It is here taken for granted, that all agree in this, that whatever government we adopt, it ought to be a free one; that it should be so framed as to secure the liberty of the citizens of America, and such an one as to admit of a full, fair, and equal representation of the people. The question then will be, whether a government thus constituted, and founded on such principles, is practicable, and can be exercised over the whole United States, reduced into one state?

If respect is to be paid to the opinion of the greatest and wisest men who have ever thought or wrote on the science of government, we shall be constrained to conclude, that a free republic cannot succeed over a country of such immense extent, containing such a number of inhabitants, and these increasing in such rapid progression as that of the whole United States. Among the many illustrious authorities which might be produced to this point, I shall content myself with quoting only two. The one is the baron de Montesquieu, spirit of laws, chap. xvi. vol. 1. "It is natural to a republic to have only a small territory, otherwise it cannot long subsist. In a large republic there are men of large fortunes, and consequently less moderation; there are trusts too great to be placed in any single subject; he has interest of his own; he soon begins to think that he may be happy, great and glorious, by oppressing his fellow citizens; and that he may raise himself to grandeur on the ruins of his country. In a large republic, the public good is sacrificed to a thousand views; it is subordinate to exceptions, and depends on accidents. In a small one, the interest of the public is easier perceived, better understood, and more within the reach of every citizen; abuses are of less extent, and of course are less protected."

History furnishes no example of a free republic, any thing like the extent of the United States. The Grecian republics were of small extent; so also was that of the Romans. Both of these, it is true, in process of time, extended their conquests over large territories of country; and the consequence was, that their governments were changed from that of free governments to those of the most tyrannical that ever existed in the world.

Not only the opinion of the greatest men, and the experience of mankind, are against the idea of an extensive republic, but a variety of reasons may be drawn from the reason and nature of things, against it. In every government, the will of the sovereign is the law.

... In a free republic, although all laws are derived from the consent of the people, yet the people do not declare their consent by themselves in person, but representatives, chosen by them, who are supposed to know the minds of their constituents, and to be possessed of integrity to declare this mind.

In every free government, the people must give their assent to the laws by which they are governed. This is the true criterion between a free government and an arbitrary one. The former are ruled by the will of the whole, expressed in any manner they may agree upon; the latter by the will of one, or a few. If the people are to give their assent to the laws, by persons chosen and appointed by them, the manner of the choice and the number chosen, must be such, as to possess, be disposed, and consequently qualified to declare the sentiments of the people; for if they do not know, or are not disposed to speak the sentiments of the people, the people do not govern, but the sovereignty is in a few. Now, in a large extended country, it is impossible to have a repre-sentation, possessing the sentiments, and of integrity, to declare the minds of the people, without having it so numerous and unwieldy, as to be subject in great measure to the inconveniency a democratic government.

The territory of the United States is of vast extent; it now contains near three millions of souls, and is capable of containing much more than ten times that number. Is it practicable for a country, so large and so numerous as they will soon become, to elect a representation, that will speak their sentiments, without their becoming so numerous as to be incapable of transacting public business? It certainly is not.

In a republic, the manners, sentiments, and interests of the people should be similar. If this be not the case, there will be a constant clashing of opinions; and the representatives of one part will be continually striving against those of the other. This will retard the operations of government, and prevent such conclusions as will promote the public good. If we apply this remark to the condition of the United States, we shall be convinced that it forbids that we should be one government. The United States includes a variety of climates. The productions of the different parts of the union are very variant, and their interests, of consequence, diverse. Their manners and habits differ as much as their climates and productions; and their sentiments are by no means coin-cident. The laws and customs of the several states are, in many respects, very diverse, and in some opposite; each would be in favor of its own interests and customs, and, of consequence, a legislature, formed of representatives from the respective parts, would not only be too numerous to act with any care or decision, but would be composed of such heterogenous and discordant principles, as would constantly be contending with each other.

The laws cannot be executed in a republic, of an extent equal to that of the United States, with promptitude.

The magistrates in every government must be supported in the execution of the laws, either by an armed force, maintained the public expense for that purpose; or by the people turning out to aid the magistrate upon his command, in case of resistance.

In despotic governments, as well as in all the monarchies of Europe, standing armies are kept up to execute the commands of the prince or the magistrate, and are employed for this purpose when occasion requires: But they have always proved the destruction of liberty, and is abhorrent to the spirit of a free republic. In England, where they depend upon the parliament for their annual support, they have always been complained of as oppressive and unconstitutional, and are seldom employed in executing of the laws; never except on extraordinary occasions, and then under the direction of a civil magistrate.

A free republic will never keep a standing army to execute its laws. It must depend upon the support of its citizens. But when a government is to receive its support from the aid of the citizens, it must be so constructed as to have the confidence, respect, and affection of the people. Men who, upon the call of the magistrate, offer themselves to execute the laws, are influenced to do it either by affection to the government, or from fear; where a standing army is at hand to punish offenders, every man is actuated by the latter principle, and therefore, when the magistrate calls, will obey: but, where this is not the case, the government must rest for its support upon the confidence and respect which the people have for their government and laws. The body of the people being attached, the government will always be sufficient to support and execute its laws, and to operate upon the fears of any faction which maybe opposed to it, not only to prevent an opposition to the execution of the laws themselves, but also to compel the most of them to aid the magistrate; but the people will not be likely to have such confidence in their rulers, in a republic so extensive as the United States, as necessary for these purposes. The confidence which the people have in their rulers, in a free republic, arises from their knowing them, from their being responsible to them for their conduct, and from the power they have of displacing them when they misbehave: but in a republic of the extent of this continent, the people in general would be acquainted with very few of their rulers: the people at large would know little of their proceedings, and it would be extremely difficult to change them. The people in Georgia and New-Hampshire would not know one another's mind, and therefore could not act in concert to enable them to effect a general change representatives. The different parts of so extensive a country could not possibly be made acquainted with the conduct of their representatives, nor be informed of the reasons upon which measures were founded. The consequence will be, they will have no confidence in their legislature, suspect them of ambitious views, be jealous of every measure they adopt, and will not support the laws they pass. Hence the government will be nerveless and inefficient, and no way will be left to render it otherwise, but by establishing an armed force to execute the laws at the point of the bayonet—a government of all others the most to be dreaded.

In a republic of such vast extent as the United-States, the legislature cannot attend to the various concerns and wants of its different parts. It cannot be sufficiently numerous to be acquainted with the local condition and wants of the different districts, and if it could, it is impossible it should have sufficient time to attend to and provide for all the variety of cases of this nature, that would be continually arising.

In so extensive a republic, the great officers of government would soon become above the control of the people, and abuse their power to the purpose aggrandizing themselves, and oppressing them. The trust committed to the executive offices, in a country of the extent of the United-States, must be various and of magnitude. The command of all the troops and navy of the republic, the appointment of officers, the power of pardoning offences, the collecting of all the public revenues, and the power of expending them, with a number of other powers, must be lodged and exercised in every state, in the hands of a few. When these are attended with great honor and emolument, as they always will be in large states, so as greatly to interest men to pursue them, and to be proper objects for ambitious and designing men, such men will be ever restless in their pursuit after them. They will use the power, when they have acquired it, to the purposes of gratifying their own interest and ambition, and it is scarcely possible, in a very large republic, to call them to account for their misconduct, or to prevent their abuse of power.

These are some of the reasons by which it appears, that a free republic cannot long subsist over a country of the great extent of these states. If then this new constitution is calculated to consolidate the thirteen states into one, as it evidently is, it ought not to be adopted.

BRUTUS 6[20]

. . . The question therefore between us, this being admitted, is, whether or not this system is so formed as either directly to annihilate the state governments, or that in its operation it will certainly effect it. If this is answered in the affirmative, then the system ought not to be adopted, without such amendments as will avoid this consequence. If on the contrary it can be show, that the state governments are secured in their rights to manage the internal police of the respective states, we must confine ourselves in our enquiries to the organization of the government and the guards and provisions it contains to prevent a misuse or abuse of power . . .

The general government is to be vested with authority to levy and collect taxes, duties, and excises; the separate states have also power to impose taxes, duties, and excises, except that they cannot lay duties on exports and imports without the consent of Congress. Here then the two governments have concurrent jurisdiction; both may lay impositions of this kind. But then the general government have supperadded to this power, authority to make all laws which shall be necessary and proper for carrying the foregoing power into execution. Suppose then that both governments should lay taxes, duties, and excises, and it should fall so heavy on the people that they would be unable, or be so burdensome that they would refuse to pay them both—would it not be necessary that the general legislature should suspend the collection of the state tax? It certainly would. For, if the people could not, or would not pay both, they must be discharged from the tax to the state, or the tax to the general government could not be collected.—The conclusion therefore is inevitable, that the respective state governments will not have the power to raise one shilling in any way, but by the permission of the Congress. I presume no one will pretend, that the states can exercise legislative authority, or administer justice among their citizens for any length of time, without being able to raise a sufficiency to pay those who administer their governments.

If this be true, and if the states can raise money only by permission of the general government, it follows that the state governments will be dependent on the will of the general government for their existence.

What will render this power in Congress effectual and sure in its operation is, that the government will have complete judicial and executive authority to carry all their laws into effect, which will be paramount to the judicial and executive authority of the individual states: in vain therefore will be all interference of the legislatures, courts, or magistrates of any of the states on the subject; for they will be subordinate to the general government, and engaged by oath to support it, and will be constitutionally bound to submit to their decisions.

The general legislature will be empowered to lay any tax they chose, to annex any penalties they please to the breach of their revenue laws; and to appoint as many officers as they may think proper to collect the taxes. They will have authority to farm the revenues and to vest the farmer general, with his subalterns, with plenary powers to collect them, in anyway which to them may appear eligible. And the courts of law, which they will be authorized to institute, will have cognizance of every case arising under the revenue laws, the conduct of all the officers employed in collecting them; and the officers of these courts will execute their judgments. There is no way, therefore, of avoiding the destruction of the state governments, whenever the Congress please to do it, unless the people rise up, and, with a strong hand, resist and prevent the execution constitutional laws. The fear of this, will, it is presumed, restrain the general government, for some time, within proper bounds; but it will not be many years before they will have a revenue, and force, at their command, which will place them above any apprehensions on that score.

How far the power to lay and collect duties and excises, may operate to dissolve the state governments, and oppress the people, it is impossible to say. It would assist us much in forming just opinion on this head, to consider the various objects to which this kind of taxes extend, in European nations, and the infinity of laws they have passed respecting them. Perhaps, if leisure will permit, this may be essayed in some future paper.

. . . This power, exercised without limitation, will introduce itself into every corner of the city, and country-It will wait upon the ladies at their toilet, and will not leave them in any of their domestic concerns; it will accompany them to the ball, the play, and the assembly; it will go with them when they visit, and will, on all occasions, sit beside them in their carriages, nor will it desert them even at church; it will enter the house of every gentleman, watch over his cellar, wait upon his cook in the kitchen, follow the servants into the parlor, preside over the table, and note down all he eats or drinks; it will attend him to his bed-chamber, and watch him while he sleeps; it will take cognizance of the professional man in his office, or his study; it will watch the merchant in the counting-house, or in his store; it will follow the mechanic to his shop, and in his work, and will haunt him in his family, and in his bed; it will be a constant companion of the industrious farmer in all his labor, it will be with him in the house, and in the field, observe the toil of his hands, arid the sweat of his brow; it will penetrate into the most obscure cottage; and finally, it will light upon the head of every person in the United States. To all these different classes of people, and in all these circumstances, in which it will attend them, the language in which it will address them, will be GIVE! GIVE!

A power that has such latitude, which reaches every person in the community in every conceivable circumstance, and lays hold of every species of property they possess, and which has no bounds set to it, but the discretion of those who exercise it. I say, such a power must necessarily, from its very nature, swallow up all the power of the state governments.

SAMUEL ADAMS TO RICHARD HENRY
LEE, DECEMBER 3, 1787[21]

I confess, as I enter the Building I stumble at the Threshold. I meet with a National Government, instead of a Federal Union of Sovereign States. I am not able to conceive why the Wisdom of the Convention led them to give the Preference to the former before the latter. If the several States in the Union are to become one entire Nation, under one Legislature, the Powers of which shall extend to every Subject of Legislation, and its Laws be supreme & control the whole, the Idea of Sovereignty in these States must be lost. Indeed I think, upon such a Supposition, those Sovereignties ought to be eradicated from the Mind; for they would be *Imperia in Imperio* justly deemed a Solecism in Politics, & they would be highly dangerous, and destructive of the Peace Union and Safety of the Nation. And can this National Legislature be competent to make Laws for the free internal Government of one People, living in Climates so remote and whose "Habits & particular Interests" are and probably always will be so different. Is it to be expected that General Laws can be adapted to the Feelings of the more Eastern and the more Southern Parts of so extensive a Nation? It appears to me difficult if practicable. Hence then may we not look for Discontent, Mistrust, Disaffection to Government and frequent Insurrections, which will require standing Armies to suppress them in one Place & another where they may happen to arise. Or if Laws could be made, adapted to the local Habits, Feelings, Views & Interests of those distant Parts, would they not cause Jealousies of Partiality in Government which would excite Envy and other malignant Passions productive of Wars and fighting. But should we continue distinct sovereign States, confederated for the Purposes of mutual Safety and Happiness, each contributing to the federal Head such a Part of its Sovereignty as would render the Government fully adequate to those Purposes and no more, the People would govern themselves more easily, the Laws of each State being well adapted to its own Genius & Circumstances, and the Liberties of the United States would be more secure than they can be, as I humbly conceive, under the proposed new Constitution. You are sensible, Sir, that the Seeds of Aristocracy began to spring even before the Conclusion of our Struggle for the natural Rights of Men, Seeds which like a Canker Worm lie at the Root of free Governments. So great is the Wickedness of some Men, & the stupid Servility of others, that one would be almost inclined to conclude that Communities cannot be free. The few haughty Families, think They must govern. The Body of the People tamely consent & submit to be their Slaves. This unravels the Mystery of Millions being enslaved by the few!

AN OLD WHIG II[22]

The first principle which the gentleman [James Wilson] endeavors to establish in his speech is a very important one, if true; and lays a sure foundation to reason upon, in answer to the objection which is made to the new constitution, from the want of a bill of rights. The principle is this: that "in delegating federal powers, the congressional authority is to be collected, not from tacit implication, but from the positive grant expressed in the instrument of union," "that every thing which is not given is reserved." If this be a just representation of the matter, the authority of the several states will be sufficient to protect our liberties from the encroachments of Congress, without any continental bill of rights; unless the powers which are expressly given to Congress are too large.

Without examining particularly present, whether the powers expressly given to Congress are too large or too small, I shall beg leave to consider, whether the author of this speech is sufficiently accurate in his statement of the proposition above referred to- To strip it of unnecessary words, the position may be reduced to this short sentence, "that every thing which is not expressly given to Congress is reserved;" or in other words "that Congress cannot exercise any power or authority that is not in express words delegated to them." This certainly is the case under the first articles confederation which hitherto have been the rule and standard of the powers of Congress; for in the second of those articles "each state retains its sovereignty freedom and independence and every power, jurisdiction and right which is not by this confederation expressly delegated to the United States in Congress assembled." It was the misfortune of these articles of confederation that they did not by express words give to Congress power sufficient for the purposes of the union; for Congress could not go beyond those powers so expressly given. The position of the speech, therefore is strictly true if applied to the first articles confederation; "that everything which is not expressly given is reserved." We are not however to suppose that the speaker meant insidiously to argue from an article in the old confederation in favor of the new constitution, unless the same thing was also in the new constitution. Let us then fairly examine whether in the proposed new constitution there be any thing from which the gentleman can be justified in his opinion, "that every thing which is not expressly given to Congress is reserved."

In the first place then it is most certain that we find no such clause or article in the new constitution. There is nothing in the new constitution which either in form or substance bears the least resemblance to the second article of the confederation. It might nevertheless be a fair argument to insist upon from the nature of delegated powers, that no more power is given in such cases than is expressly given. Whether or not this ground of argument would be such as we might safely rest our liberties upon; or whether it would be more prudent to stipulate expressly as is done in the present confederation for the reservation of all such powers as are not expressly given, it is hardly necessary to determine at present. It strikes me that by the proposed constitution, so far from the reservation of all powers that are not expressly given, the future Congress will be fully authorized to assume all such powers as they in their wisdom or wickedness, according as the one or the other may happen to prevail, shall from time to time think proper to assume.

Let us weigh this matter carefully; for it is certainly of the utmost importance, and, if I am right in my opinion, the new constitution vests Congress with such unlimited powers as ought never to be entrusted to any men or body of men. It is justly observed that the possession of sovereign power is a temptation too great for human nature to resist; and although we have read in history of one or two illustrious characters who have refused to enslave their country when it was in their power;-although have seen one illustrious character in our own times resisting the possession of power when set in competition with his duty to his country, yet these instances are so very rare, that it would be worse than madness to trust to the chance of their being often repeated.

To proceed then with the enquiry, whether the future Congress will be restricted to those powers which are expressly given to them. I would observe that in the opinion of Montesquieu, and of most other writers, ancient as well as modern, the legislature is the sovereign power . . . Let us then see what are the powers expressly given to the legislature of Congress, and what checks are interposed in the way of the continental legislature's assuming what further power they shall think proper to assume.

To this end let us look to the first article of the proposed new constitution, which treats of the legislative powers of Congress; and to the eighth section which pretends to define those powers. We find here that the congress, in its legislative capacity, shall have the power "to lay and collect taxes, duties and excises; to borrow money; to regulate commerce; to fix the rule for naturalization and the laws of bankruptcy; to coin money; to punish counterfeiters; establish post offices and post roads; to secure copyrights to authors; to constitute tribunals; to define and punish piracies; to declare war; to raise and support armies; to provide and support a navy; to make rules for the army and navy; to call forth the militia; to organize, arm and discipline the militia; to exercise absolute power over a district of ten miles square, independent of all the state legislatures, and to be alike absolute over all forts, magazines, arsenals, dockyards and other needful buildings thereunto belonging." This is a short abstract of the powers expressly given to Congress. These powers are very extensive, but I shall not stay at present to inquire whether these express powers were necessary to be given to Congress? whether they are too great or too small? My object is to consider that undefined, unbounded and immense power which is comprised in the following clause; "And, to make all laws which shall be necessary and proper for carrying into execution the foregoing powers and all other powers vested by this constitution in the government of the United States; or in any department or offices thereof." Under such a clause as this can any thing be said to be reserved and kept back from Congress? Can it be said that the Congress have no power but what is expressed? "To make all laws which shall be necessary and proper" is in other words to make all such laws which the Congress shall think necessary and proper, for who shall judge for the legislature what is necessary and proper-Who shall set themselves above the sovereign? What inferior legislature shall set itself above the supreme legislature?—To me it appears that no other power on earth can dictate to them or control them, unless by force; and force either internal or external is one of those calamities which every good man would wish his country at all times to be delivered from. -This generation in America have seen enough of war and its usual concomitants to prevent all of us from wishing to see anymore of it; -all except those who make a trade of war. But to the question; -without force what can restrain the Congress from making such laws as they please? What limits are there to their authority? I fear none at all; for surely it cannot justly be said that they have no power but what is expressly given to them, whereby the very terms of their creation they are vested with the powers of making laws in all cases necessary and proper; when from the nature of their power they must necessarily be the judges, what laws are necessary and proper. The British act of Parliament, declaring the power of Parliament to make laws to bind America in all cases whatsoever, was not more extensive; for it is as true as a maxim, that even the British Parliament neither could nor would pass any law in any case in which they did not either deem it necessary and proper to make such law or pretend to deem it so. And in such cases it is not of a farthing consequence whether they really are of opinion that the law is necessary and proper, or only pretend to think so; for who can overrule their pretensions?-No one, unless we had a bill of rights to which we might appeal, and under which we might contend against any assumption of undue power and appeal to the judicial branch of the government to protect us by their judgements. This reasoning I fear Mr. Printer is but too just; and yet, if any man should doubt the truth of it; let me ask him one other question, what is the meaning of the latter part of the clause which vests the Congress with the authority of making all laws which shall be necessary and proper for carrying into execution ALL OTHER POWERS;—besides the foregoing powers vested, &c. &c. Was it thought that the foregoing powers might perhaps admit of some restraint in their construction as to what was necessary and proper to carry them into execution? Or was it deemed right to add still further that they should not be restrained to the powers already named? -besides the powers already mentioned, other powers may be assumed hereafter as contained by implication in this constitution. The Congress shall judge of what is necessary and proper in all these cases and in all other cases;—in short in all cases whatsoever.

Where then is the restraint? How are Congress bound down to the powers expressly given? what is reserved or can be reserved?

Yet even this is not all—as if it were determined that no doubt should remain, by the sixth article of the constitution it is declared that, "this constitution, and the laws of the United States which shall be made in pursuance thereof; and all treaties made, or which shall be made, under the authority of the United States, shall be the supreme law of the land, and the judges in every state shall be bound thereby, any thing in the constitutions or laws of any state to the contrary notwithstanding." The Congress are therefore vested with the supreme legislative power, without control. In giving such immense, such unlimited powers, was there no necessity of a bill of rights to secure to the people their liberties? Is it not evident that we are left wholly dependent on the wisdom and virtue of the men who shall from time to time be the members of Congress? and who shall be able to say seven years hence, the members of Congress will be wise and good men, or of the contrary character.

PATRICK HENRY, VIRGINIA
RATIFYING CONVENTION[23]

I am not free from suspicion: I am apt to entertain doubts: I rose yesterday to ask a question, which arose in my own mind. When I asked the question, I thought the meaning of my interrogation was obvious: The fate of this question and America may depend on this: Have they said, we the States? Have they made a proposal of a compact between States? If they had, this would be a confederation: It is otherwise most clearly a consolidated government. The question turns, Sir, on that poor little thing—the expression, We, the people, instead of the States of America. I need not take much pains to show, that the principles of this system, are extremely pernicious, impolitic, and dangerous. Is this a Monarchy, like England—a compact between Prince and people; with checks on the former, to secure the liberty of the latter? Is this a Confederacy, like Holland—an association of a number of independent States, each of which retain its individual sovereignty? It is not a democracy, wherein the people retain all their rights securely. Had these principles been adhered to, we should not have been brought to this alarming transition, from a Confederacy to a consolidated Government. We have no detail of those great considerations which, in my opinion, ought to have abounded before we should recur to a government of this kind. Here is a revolution as radical as that which separated us from Great Britain. It is as radical, if in this transition our rights and privileges are endangered, and the sovereignty of the States be relinquished: And cannot we plainly see, that this is actually the case? The rights of conscience, trial by jury, liberty of the press, all your immunities and franchises, all pretensions to human rights and privileges, are rendered insecure, if not lost, by this change so loudly talked of by some, and inconsiderately by others. Is this same relinquishment of rights worthy of freemen? Is it worthy of that manly fortitude that ought to characterize republicans: It is said eight States have adopted this plan. I declare that if twelve States and an half had adopted it, I would with manly firmness, and in spite of an erring world, reject it. You are not to inquire how your trade may be increased, nor how you are to become a great and powerful people, but how your liberties can be secured; for liberty ought to be the direct end of your Government.

. . . The distinction between a National Government and a Confederacy is not sufficiently discerned. Had the delegates who were sent to Philadelphia a power to propose a Consolidated Government instead of a Confederacy? Were they not deputed by States, and not by the people? The assent of the people in their collective capacity is not necessary to the formation of a Federal Government. The people have no right to enter into leagues, alliances, or confederations: They are not the proper agents for this purpose: States and sovereign powers are the only proper agents for this kind of Government: Show me an instance where the people have exercised this business: Has it not always gone through the Legislatures? I refer you to the treaties with France, Holland, and other nations: How were they made? Were they not made by the States? Are the people therefore in their aggregate capacity, the proper persons to form a Confederacy? This, therefore, ought to depend on the consent of the Legislatures; the people having never sent delegates to make any proposition of changing the Government. Yet I must say, at the same time, that it was made on grounds the most pure, and perhaps I might have been brought to consent to it so far as to the change of Government; but there is one thing in it which I never would acquiesce in. I mean the changing it into a Consolidated Government; which is so abhorrent to my mind. The Honorable Gentleman then went on to the figure we make with foreign nations; the contemptible one we make in France and Holland; which, according to the system of my notes, he attributes to the present feeble Government. An opinion has gone forth, we find, that we are a contemptible people: The time has been when we were thought otherwise: Under this same despised Government, we commanded the respect of all Europe: Wherefore are we now reckoned otherwise? The American spirit has fled from hence: It has gone to regions, where it has never been expected: It has gone to the people of France in search of a splendid Government—a strong energetic Government. Shall we imitate the example of those nations who have gone from a simple to a splendid Government. Are those nations more worthy of our imitation? What can make an adequate satisfaction to them for the loss they suffered in attaining such a Government for the loss of their liberty? If we admit this Consolidated Government it will be because we like a great splendid one. Some way or other we must be a great and mighty empire; we must have an army, and a navy, and a number of things: When the American spirit was in its youth, the language of America was different: Liberty, Sir, was then the primary object. We are descended from a people whose Government was founded on liberty: Our glorious forefathers of Great-Britain, made liberty the foundation of every thing. That country is become a great, mighty, and splendid nation; not because their Government is strong and energetic; but, Sir, because liberty is its direct end and foundation: We drew the spirit of liberty from our British ancestors; by that spirit we have triumphed over every difficulty: But now, Sir, the American spirit, assisted by the ropes and chains of consolidation, is about to convert this country to a powerful and mighty empire: If you make the citizens of this country agree to become the subjects of one great consolidated empire of America, your Government will not have sufficient energy to keep them together: Such a Government is incompatible with the genius of republicanism: There will be no checks, no real balances, in this Government: What can avail your specious imaginary balances, your rope-dancing, chain-rattling, ridiculous ideal checks and contrivances? But, Sir, we are not feared by foreigners: we do not make nations tremble: Would this, Sir, constitute happiness, or secure liberty? I trust, Sir, our political hemisphere will ever direct their operations to the security of those objects. Consider our situation, Sir: Go to the poor man, ask him what he does; he will inform you, that he enjoys the fruits of his labor, under his own fig-tree, with his wife and children around him, in peace and security. Go to every other member of the society, you will find the same tranquil ease and content; you will find no alarms or disturbances: Why then tell us of dangers to terrify us into an adoption of this new Government? and yet who knows the dangers that this new system may produce; they are out of the sight of the common people: They cannot foresee latent consequences: I dread the operation of it on the middling and lower class of people: It is for them I fear the adoption of this system.

TENTH AMENDMENT (RATIFIED DECEMBER 15, 1791)

The powers not delegated to the United States by the Constitution, nor prohibited by it to the States, are reserved to the States respectively, or to the people.

THOMAS JEFFERSON OPINION ON THE
CONSTITUTIONALITY OF A NATIONAL BANK[24]

. . . I consider the foundation of the Constitution as laid on this ground: That " all powers not delegated to the United States, by the Constitution, nor prohibited by it to the States, are reserved to the States or to the people." [10th amendment.] To take a single step beyond the boundaries thus specially drawn around the powers of Congress, is to take possession of a boundless field of power, no longer susceptible of any definition.

. . . II. Nor are they within either of the general phrases, which are the two following:

1. To lay taxes to provide for the general welfare of the United States, that is to say, "to lay taxes for *the purpose of* providing for the general welfare." For the laying of taxes is the *power*, and the general welfare the *purpose* for which the power is to be exercised. They are not to lay taxes *ad libitum for any purpose they please*; but only *to pay the debts or provide for the welfare of the Union*. In like manner, they are not *to do anything they please* to provide for the general welfare, but only to *lay taxes* for that purpose. To consider the latter phrase, not as describing the purpose of the first, but as giving a distinct and independent power to do any act they please, which might be for the good of the Union, would render all the preceding and subsequent enumerations of power completely useless.

It would reduce the whole instrument to a single phrase, that of instituting a Congress with power to do whatever would be for the good of the United States; and, as they would be the sole judges of the good or evil, it would be also a power to do whatever evil they please.

. . . 2. The second general phrase is, "to make all laws *necessary* and proper for carrying into execution the enumerated powers." But they can all be carried into execution without a bank. A bank therefore is not *necessary*, and consequently not authorized by this phrase.

If has been urged that a bank will give great facility or convenience in the collection of taxes, Suppose this were true: yet the Constitution allows only the means which are "*necessary*," not those which are merely "convenient" for effecting the enumerated powers. If such a latitude of construction be allowed to this phrase as to give any non-enumerated power, it will go to everyone, for there is not one which ingenuity may not torture into a *convenience* in some instance *or other*, to *some one* of so long a list of enumerated powers. It would swallow up all the delegated powers, and reduce the whole to one power, as before observed. Therefore it was that the Constitution restrained them to the *necessary* means, that is to say, to those means without which the grant of power would be nugatory.

ALEXANDER HAMILTON OPINION ON THE
CONSTITUTIONALITY OF A NATIONAL BANK[25]

Now it appears to the Secretary of the Treasury that this general principle is inherent in the very definition of government, and essential to every step of progress to be made by that of the United States, namely: That every power vested in a government is in its nature sovereign, and includes, by force of the term, a right to employ all the means requisite and fairly applicable to the attainment of the ends of such power, and which are not precluded by restrictions and exceptions specified in the Constitution, or not immoral, or not contrary to the essential ends of political society.

This principle, in its application to government in general, would be admitted as an axiom; and it will be incumbent upon those who may incline to deny it, to prove a distinction, and to show that a rule which, in the general system of things, is essential to the preservation of the social order, is inapplicable to the United States.

The circumstance that the powers of sovereignty are in this country divided between the National and State governments, does not afford the distinction required. It does not follow from this, that each of the portion of powers delegated to the one or to the other, is not sovereign with regard to its proper objects. It will only follow from it, that each has sovereign power as to certain things, and not as to other things. To deny that the government of the United States has sovereign power, as to its declared purposes and trusts, because its power does not extend to all cases would be equally to deny that the State governments have sovereign power in any case, because their power does not extend to every case. The tenth section of the first article of the Constitution exhibits a long list of very important things which they may not do. And thus the United States would furnish the singular spectacle of a political society without sovereignty, or of a people governed, without government.

If it would be necessary to bring proof to a proposition so clear, as that which affirms that the powers of the federal government, as to its objects, were sovereign, there is a clause of its Constitution which would be decisive. It is that which declares that the Constitution, and the laws of the United States made in pursuance of it, and all treaties made, or which shall be made, under their authority, shall be the serene law of the land. The power which can create the supreme law of the land in any case, is doubtless sovereign as to such case.

. . . The first of these arguments is, that the foundation of the Constitution is laid on this ground: "That all powers not delegated to the United States by the Constitution, nor prohibited to it by the States, are reserved for the States, or to the people." Whence it is meant to be inferred, that Congress can in no case exercise any power not Included in those not enumerated in the Constitution.

And it is affirmed, that the power of erecting a corporation is not included in any of the enumerated powers.

The main proposition here laid down, in its true signification is not to be questioned. It is nothing more than a consequence of this republican maxim, that all government is a delegation of power. But how much is delegated in each case, is a question of fact, to be made out by fair reasoning and construction, upon the particular provisions of the Constitution, taking as guides the general principles and general ends of governments.

It is not denied that there are implied well as express powers, and that the former are as effectually delegated as the tatter. And for the sake of accuracy it shall be mentioned, that there is another class of powers, which may be properly denominated resting powers. It will not be doubted, that if the United States should make a conquest of any of the territories of its neighbors, they would possess sovereign jurisdiction over the conquered territory. This would be rather a result, from the whole mass of the powers of the government, and from the nature of political society, than a consequence of either of the powers specially enumerated.

. . . To return: . . . The only question must be in this, as in every other case, whether the mean to be employed or in this instance, the corporation to be erected, has a natural relation to any of the acknowledged objects or lawful ends of the government.

. . . It is certain that neither the grammatical nor popular sense of the term requires that construction. According to both, necessary often means no more than needful, requisite, incidental, useful, or conducive to. It is a common mode of expression to say, that it is necessary for a government or a person to do this or that thing, when nothing more is intended or understood, than that the interests of the government or person require, or will be promoted by, the doing of this or that thing. The imagination can be at no loss for exemplifications of the use of the word in this sense. And it is the true one in which it is to be understood as used in the Constitution. The whole turn of the clause containing it indicates, that it was the intent of the Convention, by that clause, to give a liberal latitude to the exercise of the specified powers. The expressions have peculiar comprehensiveness. They are thought to make all laws necessary and proper for carrying into execution the foregoing powers, and all other powers vested by the Constitution in the government of the United States, or in any department or officer thereof."

. . . It may be truly said of every government, as well as of that of the United States, that it has only a right to pass such laws as are necessary and proper to accomplish the objects intrusted to it. For no government has a right to do merely what it pleases. . . .

The degree in which a measure is necessary, can never be a test of the legal right to adopt it; that must be a matter of opinion, and can only be a test of expediency. The relation between the measure and the end; between the nature of the mean employed toward the execution of a power, and the object of that power must be the criterion of constitutionality, not the more or less of necessity or utility.

. . . The truth is, that difficulties on this point are inherent in the nature of the Federal Constitution; they result inevitably from a division of the legislative power. The consequence of this division is, that there will be cases clearly within the power of the national government; others, clearly without its powers; and a third class, which will leave room for controversy and difference of opinion, and concerning which a reasonable latitude of judgment must be allowed.

But the doctrine which is contended for is not chargeable with the consequences imputed to it. It does not affirm that the national government is sovereign in all respects, but that it is sovereign to a certain extent; that is, to the extent of the objects of its specified powers.

It leaves, therefore, a criterion of what is constitutional, and of what is not so. This criterion is the end, to which the measure relates as a mean. If the end be clearly comprehended within any of the specified powers, and if the measure have an obvious relation to that end, and is not forbidden by any particular provision of the Constitution, it may safely be deemed to come within the compass of the national authority. There is also this further criterion, which may materially assist the decision: Does the proposed measure abridge a pre-existing right of any State or of any individual? If it does not, there is a strong presumption in favor of its constitutionality, and slighter relations to any declared object of the Constitution may be permitted to turn the scale.

CHISHOLM v. GEORGIA[26]

[Justice Wilson:] This is a case of uncommon magnitude. One of the parties to it is a State—certainly respectable, claiming to be sovereign. The question to be determined is whether this State, so respectable, and whose claim soars so high, is amenable to the jurisdiction of the Supreme Court of the United States? This question, important in itself, will depend on others more important still, and, may, perhaps, be ultimately resolved into one no less radical than this: "do the people of the United States form a Nation?"

. . . To the Constitution of the United States, the term SOVEREIGN, is totally unknown. There is but one place where it could have been used with propriety. But even in that place, it would not, perhaps, have comported with the delicacy of those who ordained and established that Constitution. They might have announced themselves "SOVEREIGN" people of the United States. But serenely conscious of the fact, they avoided the ostentatious declaration.

. . . In one sense, the term "sovereign" has for its correlative "subject." In this sense, the term can receive no application, for it has no object in the Constitution of the United states. Under that Constitution, there are citizens, but no subjects. "Citizen of the United states." "Citizens of another state." "Citizens of different states." "A state or citizen thereof." The term, subject, occurs, indeed, once in the instrument; but to mark the contrast strongly, the epithet "foreign" is prefixed. In this sense, I presume the state of Georgia has no claim upon her own citizens. In this sense, I am certain, she can have no claim upon the citizens of another state.

In another sense, according to some writers, state, which governs itself without any dependence on another power is a sovereign state. Whether, with regard to her own citizens, this is the case of the state of Georgia; whether those citizens have done, as the individuals of England are said by their late instructors to have done, surrendered the supreme power to the state or government, and reserved nothing to themselves; or whether, like the people of other states, and of the United states, the citizens of Georgia have reserved the supreme power in their own hands, and on that supreme power have made the state dependent, instead of being sovereign—these are questions to which, as a judge in this cause, I can neither know nor suggest the proper answers, though, as a citizen of the Union, I know, and am interested to know that the most satisfactory answers can be given. As a citizen, I know the government of that state to be republican; and my short definition of such a government is one constructed on this principle—that the supreme power resides in the body of the people. As a judge of this court, I know, and can decide upon the knowledge that the citizens of Georgia, when they acted upon the large scale of the Union, as a part of the "People of the United states," did not surrender the supreme or sovereign power to that state, but, as to the purposes of the Union, retained it to themselves. As to the purposes of the Union, therefore, Georgia is NOT a sovereign state. If the judicial decision of this case forms one of those purposes, the allegation that Georgia is a sovereign state is unsupported by the fact. Whether the judicial decision of this cause is or is not one of those purposes is a question which will be examined particularly in a subsequent part of my argument.

There is a third sense, in which the term "sovereign" is frequently used, and which it is very material to trace and explain, as it furnishes a basis for what I presume to be one of the principal objections against the jurisdiction of this court over the State of Georgia. In this sense, sovereignty is derived from a feudal source, and, like many other parts of that system so degrading to man, still retains its influence over our sentiments and conduct, though the cause by which that influence was produced never extended to the American states.

. . . The principle is that all human law must be prescribed by a superior. This principle I mean not now to examine. Suffice it at present to say that another principle, very different in its nature and operations, forms, in my judgment, the basis of sound and genuine jurisprudence; laws derived from the pure source of equality and justice must be founded on the CONSENT of those whose obedience they require. The sovereign, when traced to his source, must be found in the man.

. . . I find nothing which tends to evince an exemption of the state of Georgia from the jurisdiction of the court. I find everything to have a contrary tendency.

. . . I am, thirdly, and chiefly, to examine the important question now before us by the Constitution of the United states, and the legitimate result of that valuable instrument. Under this view, the question is naturally subdivided into two others. 1. Could the Constitution of the United states vest a jurisdiction over the State of Georgia? 2. Has that Constitution vested such jurisdiction in this Court? I have already remarked that, in the practice, and even in the science, of politics, there has been frequently a strong current against the natural order of things, and an inconsiderate or an interested disposition to sacrifice the end to the means. This remark deserves a more particular illustration. Even in almost every nation which has been denominated free, the state has assumed a supercilious preeminence above the people who have formed it. Hence the haughty notions of state independence, state sovereignty and state supremacy

. . . In the United states, and in the several states, which compose the Union, we go not so far, but still we go one step farther than we ought to go in this unnatural and inverted order of things. The states, rather than the people, for whose sakes the states exist, are frequently the objects which attract and arrest our principal attention. This, I believe, has produced much of the confusion and perplexity which have appeared in several proceedings and several publications on state politics, and on the politics, too, of the United states. Sentiments and expressions of this inaccurate kind prevail in our common, even in our convivial, language. Is a toast asked? "The United states," instead of the "People of the United states," is the toast given. This is not politically correct. The toast is meant to present to view the first great object in the Union: it presents only the second. It presents only the artificial person, instead of the natural persons who spoke it into existence. A state I cheerfully fully admit, is the noblest work of Man. But, Man himself, free and honest, is, I speak as to this world, the noblest work of God.

Concerning . . . the sovereignty of states, much has been said and written; but little has been said and written concerning a subject much more dignified and important, the majesty of the people. The mode of expression, which I would substitute in the place of that generally used, is not only politically, but also (for between true liberty and true taste there is a close alliance) clas-sically more correct. . . . With the strictest propriety, therefore, classical and political, our national scene opens with the most magnificent object which the nation could present. "The PEOPLE of the United states" are the first personages introduced. Who were those people? They were the citizens of thirteen states, each of which had a separate constitution and government, and all of which were connected together by Articles of Confederation. To the purposes of public strength and felicity, that Confederacy was totally inad-equate. A requisition on the several states terminated its legislative authority. Executive or judicial authority it had none. In order therefore to form a more perfect union, to establish justice, to ensure domestic tranquility, to provide for common defense, and to secure the blessings of liberty, those people, among whom were the people of Georgia, ordained and established the pres-ent Constitution. By that Constitution legislative power is vested, executive power is vested, judicial power is vested.

The question now opens fairly to our view, could the people of those states, among whom were those of Georgia, bind those states, and Georgia among the others, by the legislative, executive, and judicial power so vested? If the principles on which I have founded myself are just and true, this question must unavoidably receive an affirmative answer. If those states were the work of those people, those people, and that I may apply the case closely, the people of Georgia, in particular, could alter as they pleased their former work. To any given degree, they could diminish as well as enlarge it. Any or all of the former state powers, they could extinguish or transfer. The inference which necessarily results is that the Constitution ordained and established by those people, and, still closely to apply the case, in particular by the people of Georgia, could vest jurisdiction or judicial power over those states and over the State of Georgia in particular.

The next question under this head, is has the Constitution done so? Did those people mean to exercise this, their undoubted power? These ques-tions may be resolved either by fair and conclusive deductions or by direct and explicit declarations. In order ultimately to discover whether the people of the United states intended to bind those states by the judicial power vested by the national Constitution, a previous enquiry will naturally be: did those people intend to bind those states by the legislative power vested by that Constitution? The Articles of Confederation, it is well known, did not oper-ate upon individual citizens, but operated only upon states. This defect was remedied by the national Constitution, which, as all allow, has an operation on individual citizens. But if an opinion which some seem to entertain be just, the defect remedied on one side was balanced by a defect introduced on the other. For they seem to think that the present Constitution operates only on individual citizens, and not on states. This opinion, however, appears to be altogether unfounded. When certain laws of the states are declared to be "subject to the revision and control of the Congress," it cannot, surely, be contended that the legislative power of the national government was meant to have no operation on the several states. The fact, uncontrovertibly established in one instance, proves the principle in all other instances to which the facts will be found to apply. We may then infer that the people of the United states intended to bind the several states by the legislative power of the national government.

In order to make the discovery at which we ultimately aim, a second previous enquiry will naturally be: did the people of the United states intend to bind the several states by the executive power of the national government? The affirmative answer to the former question directs, unavoidably, an affirmative answer to this. . . . Fair and conclusive deduction, then, evinces that the people of the United states did vest this court with jurisdiction over the State of Georgia. The same truth may be deduced from the declared objects and the general texture of the Constitution of the United states. One of its declared objects is to form an Union more perfect than, before that time, had been formed. Before that time, the Union possessed legislative, but unenforced legislative power over the states. Nothing could be more natural than to intend that this legislative power should be enforced by powers executive and judicial. Another declared object is, "to establish justice." This points, in a particular manner, to the judicial authority. And when we view this object in conjunction with the declaration, "that no state shall pass a law impairing the obligation of contracts," we shall probably think that this object points, in a particular manner, to the jurisdiction of the court over the several states. What good purpose could this constitutional provision secure if a state might pass a law impairing the obligation of its own contracts, and be amenable, for such a violation of right to no controlling judiciary power? We have seen that on the principles of general jurisprudence, a state, for the breach of a contract, may be liable for damages. A third declared object is "to ensure domestic tranquility." This tranquility is most likely to be disturbed by controversies between states. These consequences will be most peaceably and effectually decided by the establishment and by the exercise of a superintending judicial authority. By such exercise and establishment, the law of nations, the rule between contending states, will be enforced among the several states in the same manner as municipal law.

Whoever considers, in a combined and comprehensive view, the general texture of the Constitution will be satisfied that the people of the United states intended to form themselves into a nation for national purposes. They instituted for such purposes a national government, complete in all its parts, with powers legislative, executive and judicial, and in all those powers extending over the whole nation.

ELEVENTH AMENDMENT (RATIFIED FEBRUARY 7, 1798)

The Judicial power of the United States shall not be construed to extend to any suit in law or equity, commenced or prosecuted against one of the United States by Citizens of another State, or by Citizens or Subjects of any Foreign State.

THE KENTUCKY RESOLUTION[27]

Resolved, That the several States composing the United States of America, are not united on the principle of unlimited submission to their General Government; but that, by a compact under the style and title of a Constitution for the United States, and of amendments thereto, they constituted a General Government for special purposes,—delegated to that government certain definite powers, reserving, each State to itself, the residuary mass of right to their own self-government; and that whensoever the General Government assumes undelegated powers, its acts are unauthoritative, void, and of no force; that to this compact each State acceded as a State, and is an integral party, its co-States forming, as to itself, the other party: that the government created by this compact was not made the exclusive or final judge of the extent of the powers delegated to itself; since that would have made its discretion, and not the Constitution, the measure of its powers; but that, as in all other cases of compact among powers having no common judge, each party has an equal right to judge for itself, as well of infractions as of the mode and measure of redress.

Resolved, That the Constitution of the United States, having delegated to Congress a power to punish treason, counterfeiting the securities and current coin of the United States, piracies, and felonies committed on the high seas, and offences against the law of nations, and no other crimes whatsoever; and it being true as a general principle, and one of the amendments to the Constitution having also declared, that "the powers not delegated to the United States by the Constitution, nor prohibited by it to the States, are reserved to the States respectively, or to the people," therefore the act of Congress, passed on the 14th day of July, 1798, and entitled "An Act in addition to the act entitled An Act for the punishment of certain crimes against the United States," as also the act passed by them on the—day of June, 1798, entitled "An Act to punish frauds committed on the bank of the United States," (and all their other acts which assume to create, define, or punish crimes, other than those so enumerated in the Constitution,) are altogether void, and of no force; and that the power to create, define, and punish such other crimes is reserved, and, of right, appertains solely and exclusively to the respective States, each within its own territory.

Resolved That it is true as a general principle, and is also expressly declared by one of the amendments to the Constitution, that "the powers not delegated to the United States by the Constitution, nor prohibited by it to the States, are reserved to the States respectively, or to the people;" and that no power over the freedom of religion, freedom of speech, or freedom of the press being delegated to the United States by the Constitution, nor prohibited by it to the States, all lawful powers respecting the same did of right remain, and were reserved to the States or the people: that thus was manifested their determination to retain to themselves the right of judging how far the licentiousness of speech and of the press may be abridged without lessening their useful freedom, and how far those abuses which cannot be separated from their use should be tolerated, rather than the use be destroyed. And thus also they guarded against all abridgment by the United States of the freedom of religious opinions and exercises, and retained to themselves the right of protecting the same, as this State, by a law passed on the general demand of its citizens, had already protected them from all human restraint or interference. And that in addition to this general principle and express declaration, another and more special provision has been made by one of the amendments to the Constitution, which expressly declares, that "Congress shall make no law respecting an establishment of religion, or prohibiting the free exercise thereof, or abridging the freedom of speech or of the press:" thereby guarding in the same sentence, and under the same words, the freedom of religion, of speech, and of the press: insomuch, that whatever violated either, throws down the sanctuary which covers the others, and that libels, falsehood, and defamation, equally with heresy and false religion, are withheld from the cognizance of federal tribunals. That, therefore, the act of Congress of the United States, passed on the 14th day of July, 1798, entitled "An Act in addition to the act entitled An Act for the punishment of certain crimes against the United States," which does abridge the freedom of the press, is not law, but is altogether void, and of no force.

Resolved, That alien friends are under the jurisdiction and protection of the laws of the State wherein they are: that no power over them has been delegated to the United States, nor prohibited to the individual States, distinct from their power over citizens. And it being true as a general principle, and one of the amendments to the Constitution having also declared, that "the powers not delegated to the United States by the Constitution, nor prohibited by it to the States, are reserved to the States respectively, or to the people," the act of the Congress of the United States, passed on the—day of July, 1798, entitled "An Act concerning aliens," which assumes powers over alien friends, not delegated by the Constitution, is not law, but is altogether void, and of no force.

Resolved, That in addition to the general principle, as well as the express declaration, that powers not delegated are reserved, another and more special provision, inserted in the Constitution from abundant caution, has declared that "the migration or importation of such persons as any of the States now existing shall think proper to admit, shall not be prohibited by the Congress prior to the year 1808;" that this commonwealth does admit the migration of alien friends, described as the subject of the said act concerning aliens: that a provision against prohibiting their migration, is a provision against all acts equivalent thereto, or it would be nugatory: that to remove them when migrated, is equivalent to a prohibition of their migration, and is, therefore, contrary to the said provision of the Constitution, and void.

Resolved, That a committee of conference and correspondence be appointed, who shall have in charge to communicate the preceding resolutions to the legislatures of the several States; to assure them that this commonwealth continues in the same esteem of their friendship and union which it has manifested from that moment at which a common danger first suggested a common union: that it considers union, for specified national purposes, and particularly to those specified in their late federal compact, to be friendly to the peace, happiness and prosperity of all the States: that faithful to that compact, according to the plain intent and meaning in which it was understood and acceded to by the several parties, it is sincerely anxious for its preservation: that it does also believe, that to take from the States all the powers of self-government and transfer them to a general and consolidated government, without regard to the special delegations and reservations solemnly agreed to in that compact, is not for the peace, happiness or prosperity of these States; and that therefore this commonwealth is determined, as it doubts not its co-States are, to submit to undelegated, and consequently unlimited powers in no man, or body of men on earth: that in cases of an abuse of the delegated powers, the members of the General Government, being chosen by the people, a change by the people would be the constitutional remedy; but, where powers are assumed which have not been delegated, a nullification of the act is the rightful remedy: that every State has a natural right in cases not within the compact, (*casus non foederis*,) to nullify of their own authority all assumptions of power by others within their limits: that without this right, they would be under the dominion, absolute and unlimited, of whosoever might exercise this right of judgment for them: that nevertheless, this commonwealth, from motives of regard and respect for its co-States, has wished to communicate with them on the subject: that with them alone it is proper to communicate, they alone being parties to the compact, and solely authorized to judge in the last resort of the powers exercised under it, Congress being not a party, but merely the creature of the compact, and subject as to its assumptions of power to the final judgment of those by whom, and for whose use itself and its powers were all created and modified: that if the acts before specified should stand, these conclusions would flow from them; that the General Government may place any act they think proper on the list of crimes, and punish it themselves whether enumerated or not enumerated by the Constitution as cognizable by them: that they may transfer its cognizance to the President, or any other person, who may himself be the accuser, counsel, judge and jury, whose *suspicions* may be the evidence, his *order* the sentence, his *officer* the executioner, and his breast the sole record of the transaction: that a very numerous and valuable description of the inhabitants of these States being, by this precedent, reduced, as outlaws, to the absolute dominion of one man, and the barrier of the Constitution thus swept away from us all, no rampart now remains against the passions and the powers of a majority in Congress to protect from a like exportation, or other more grievous punishment, the minority of the same body, the legislatures, judges, governors, and counsellors of the States, nor their other peaceable inhabitants, who may venture to reclaim the constitutional rights and liberties of the States and people, or who for other causes, good or bad, may be obnoxious to the views, or marked by the suspicions of the President, or be thought dangerous to his or their election, or other interests, public or personal: that the friendless alien has indeed been selected as the safest subject of a first experiment; but the citizen will soon follow, or rather, has already followed, for already has a sedition act marked him as its prey: that these and successive acts of the same character, unless arrested at the threshold, necessarily drive these States into revolution and blood, and will furnish new calumnies against republican government, and new pretexts for those who wish it to be believed that man cannot be governed but by a rod of iron: that it would be a dangerous delusion were a confidence in the men of our choice to silence our fears for the safety of our rights: that confidence is everywhere the parent of despotism—free government is founded in jealousy, and not in confidence; it is jealousy and not confidence which prescribes limited constitutions, to bind down those whom we are obliged to trust with power: that our Constitution has accordingly fixed the limits to which, and no further, our confidence may go; and let the honest advocate of confidence read the alien and sedition acts, and say if the Constitution has not been wise in fixing limits to the government it created, and whether we should be wise in destroying those limits. Let him say what the government is, if it be not a tyranny, which the men of our choice have conferred on our President, and the President of our choice has assented to, and accepted over the friendly strangers to whom the mild spirit of our country and its laws have pledged hospitality and protection: that the men of our choice have more respected the bare *suspicions* of the President, than the solid right of innocence, the claims of justification, the sacred force of truth, and the forms and substance of law and justice.

In questions of power, then, let no more be heard of confidence in man, but bind him down from mischief by the chains of the Constitution. That this commonwealth does therefore call on its co-States for an expression of their sentiments on the acts concerning aliens, and for the punishment of certain crimes herein before specified, plainly declaring whether these acts are or are not authorized by the federal compact. And it doubts not that their sense will be so announced as to prove their attachment unaltered to limited government, whether general or particular. And that the rights and liberties of their co-States will be exposed to no dangers by remaining embarked in a common bottom with their own. That they will concur with this commonwealth in considering the said acts as so palpably against the Constitution as to amount to an undisguised declaration that that compact is not meant to be the measure of the powers of the General Government, but that it will proceed in the exercise over these States, of all powers whatsoever: that they will view this as seizing the rights of the States, and consolidating them in the hands of the General Government, with a power assumed to bind the States, not merely as the cases made federal, (*casus foederis,*) but in all cases whatsoever, by laws made, not with their consent, but by others against their consent: that this would be to surrender the form of government we have chosen, and live under one deriving its powers from its own will, and not from our authority; and that the co-States, recurring to their natural right in cases not made federal, will concur in declaring these acts void, and of no force, and will each take measures of its own for providing that neither these acts, nor any others of the General Government not plainly and intentionally authorized by the Constitution, shall be exercised within their respective territories.

VIRGINIA RESOLUTION[28]

. . . That this assembly most solemnly declares a warm attachment to the Union of the States, to maintain which it pledges all its powers; and that for this end, it is their duty to watch over and oppose every infraction of those principles which constitute the only basis of that Union, because a faithful observance of them, can alone secure its existence and the public happiness.

That this Assembly does explicitly and peremptorily declare, that it views the powers of the federal government, as resulting from the compact, to which the states are parties; as limited by the plain sense and intention of the instrument constituting the compact; as no further valid that they are authorized by the grants enumerated in that compact; and that in case of a deliberate, palpable, and dangerous exercise of other powers, not granted by the said compact, the states who are parties thereto, have the right, and are in duty bound, to interpose for arresting the progress of the evil, and for maintaining within their respective limits, the authorities, rights and liberties appertaining to them.

That the General Assembly does also express its deep regret, that a spirit has in sundry instances, been manifested by the federal government, to enlarge its powers by forced constructions of the constitutional charter which defines them; and that implications have appeared of a design to expound certain general phrases (which having been copied from the very limited grant of power, in the former articles of confederation were the less liable to be misconstrued) so as to destroy the meaning and effect, of the particular enumeration which necessarily explains and limits the general phrases; and so as to consolidate the states by degrees, into one sovereignty, the obvious tendency and inevitable consequence of which would be, to transform the present republican system of the United States, into an absolute, or at best a mixed monarchy.

That the General Assembly doth particularly protest against the palpable and alarming infractions of the Constitution, in the two late cases of the "Alien and Sedition Acts" passed at the last session of Congress; the first of which exercises a power no where delegated to the federal government, and which by uniting legislative and judicial powers to those of executive, subverts the general principles of free government; as well as the particular organization, and positive provisions of the federal constitution; and the other of which acts, exercises in like manner, a power not delegated by the constitution, but on the contrary, expressly and positively forbidden by one of the amendments thereto; a power, which more than any other, ought to produce universal alarm, because it is levelled against that right of freely examining public characters and measures, and of free communication among the people thereon, which has ever been justly deemed, the only effectual guardian of every other right.

That this state having by its Convention, which ratified the federal Constitution, expressly declared, that among other essential rights, "the Liberty of Conscience and of the Press cannot be cancelled, abridged, restrained, or modified by any authority of the United States," and from its extreme anxiety to guard these rights from every possible attack of sophistry or ambition, having with other states, recommended an amendment for that purpose, which amendment was, in due time, annexed to the Constitution; it would mark a reproachable inconsistency, and criminal degeneracy, if an indifference were now show, to the most palpable violation of one of the Rights, thus declared and secured; and to the establishment of a precedent which may be fatal to the other.

That the good people of this commonwealth, having ever felt, and continuing to feel, the most sincere affection for their brethren of the other states; the truest anxiety for establishing and perpetuating the union of all; and the most scrupulous fidelity to that constitution, which is the pledge of mutual friendship, and the instrument of mutual happiness; the General Assembly doth solemnly appeal to the like dispositions of the other states, in confidence that they will concur with this commonwealth in declaring, as it does hereby declare, that the acts aforesaid, are unconstitutional; and that the necessary and proper measures will be taken by each, for co-operating with this state, in maintaining the Authorities, Rights, and Liberties, referred to the States respectively, or to the people.

JAMES MADISON, REPORT OF 1800[29]

"Resolved, That the General Assembly of Virginia doth unequivocally express a firm resolution to maintain and defend the Constitution of the United States, and the Constitution of this state, against every aggression, either foreign or domestic; and that they will support the government of the United States in all measures warranted by the former."

No unfavorable comment can have been made on the sentiments here expressed. To maintain and defend the Constitution of the United States, and of their own state, against every aggression, both foreign and domestic, and to support the government of the United States in all measures warranted by their Constitution, are duties which the General Assembly ought always to feel, and to which, on such an occasion, it was evidently proper to express their sincere and firm adherence.

In their next resolution—"The General Assembly most solemnly declares a warm attachment to the union of the states, to maintain which it pledges all its powers; and that, for this end, it is their duty to watch over and oppose every infraction of those principles which constitute the only basis of that Union, because a faithful observance of them can alone secure its existence and the public happiness."

The observation just made is equally applicable to this solemn declaration of warm attachment to the Union, and this solemn pledge to maintain it; nor can any question arise among enlightened friends of the Union, as to the duty of watching over and opposing every infraction of those principles which constitute its basis, and a faithful observance of which can alone secure its existence, and the public happiness thereon depending.

The third resolution is in the words following:— "That this Assembly doth explicitly and peremptorily declare, that it views the powers of the federal government, as resulting from the compact to which the states are parties, as limited by the plain sense and intention of the instrument constituting that compact—as no further valid than they are authorized by the grants enumerated in that compact; and that, in case of a deliberate, palpable, and dangerous exercise of other powers, not granted by the said compact, the states who are parties thereto have the right, and are in duty bound, to interpose, for arresting the progress of the evil and for maintaining, within their respective limits, the authorities, rights, and liberties, appertaining to them."

. . . The resolution declares, first, that "it views the powers of the federal government as resulting from the compact to which the states are parties"; in other words, that the federal powers are derived from the Constitution; and that the Constitution is a compact to which the states are parties.

Clear as the position must seem, that the federal powers are derived from the Constitution, and from that alone, the committee are not unapprised of a late doctrine which opens another source of federal powers, not less extensive and important than it is new and unexpected. The examination of this doctrine will be most conveniently connected with a review of a succeeding resolution. The committee satisfy themselves here with briefly remarking that, in all the contemporary discussions and comments which the Constitution underwent, it was constantly justified and recommended on the ground that the powers not given to the government were withheld from it; and that, if any doubt could have existed on this subject, under the original text of the Constitution, it is removed, as far as words could remove it, by the 12th amendment, now a part of the Constitution, which expressly declares, "that the powers not delegated to the United States by the Constitution, nor prohibited by it to the states, are reserved to the states respectively, or to the people."

The other position involved in this branch of the resolution, namely, "that the states are parties to the Constitution," or compact, is, in the judgment of the committee, equally free from objection. It is indeed true that the term "states" is sometimes used in a vague sense, and sometimes in different senses, according to the subject to which it is applied. Thus it sometimes means the separate sections of territory occupied by the political societies within each; sometimes the particular governments established by those societies; sometimes those societies as organized into those particular governments; and lastly, it means the people composing those political societies, in their highest sovereign capacity. Although it might be wished that the perfection of language admitted less diversity in the signification of the same words, yet little inconvenience is produced by it, where the true sense can be collected with certainty from the different applications. In the present instance, whatever different construction of the term "states," in the resolution, may have been entertained, all will at least concur in that last mentioned; because in that sense the Constitution was submitted to the "states;" in that sense the "states" ratified it; and in that sense of the term "states," they are consequently parties to the compact from which the powers of the federal government result.

The next position is, that the General Assembly views the powers of the federal government "as limited by the plain sense and intention of the instrument constituting that compact," and "as no further valid than they are authorized by the grants therein enumerated." It does not seem possible that any just objection can lie against either of these clauses. The first amounts merely to a declaration that the compact ought to have the interpretation plainly intended by the parties to it; the other, to a declaration that it ought to have the execution and effect intended by them. If the powers granted be valid, it is solely because they are granted; and if the granted powers are valid because granted, all other powers not granted must not be valid.

The resolution, having taken this view of the federal compact, proceeds to infer, "That, in case of a deliberate, palpable, and dangerous exercise of other powers, not granted by the said compact, the states, who are parties thereto, have the right, and are in duty bound, to interpose for arresting the progress of the evil, and for maintaining, within their respective limits, the authorities, rights, and liberties, appertaining to them."

It appears to your committee to be a plain principle, founded in common sense, illustrated by common practice, and essential to the nature of compacts, that, where resort can be had to no tribunal superior to the authority of the parties, the parties themselves must be the rightful judges, in the last resort, whether the bargain made has been pursued or violated. The Constitution of the United States was formed by the sanction of the states, given by each in its sovereign capacity. It adds to the stability and dignity, as well as to the authority, of the Constitution, that it rests on this legitimate and solid foundation. The states, then, being the parties to the constitutional compact, and in their sovereign capacity, it follows of necessity that there can be no tribunal, above their authority, to decide, in the last resort, whether the compact made by them be violated; and consequently, that, as the parties to it, they must themselves decide, in the last resort, such questions as may be of sufficient magnitude to require their interposition.

It does not follow, however, because the states, as sovereign parties to their constitutional compact, must ultimately decide whether it has been violated, that such a decision ought to be interposed either in a hasty manner or on doubtful and inferior occasions. Even in the case of ordinary conventions between different nations, where, by the strict rule of interpretation, a breach of a part may be deemed a breach of the whole,—every part being deemed a condition of every other part, and of the whole,—it is always laid down that the breach must be both willful and material, to justify an application of the rule. But in the case of an intimate and constitutional union, like that of the United States, it is evident that the interposition of the parties, in their sovereign capacity, can be called for by occasions only deeply and essentially affecting the vital principles of their political system.

The resolution has, accordingly guarded against any misapprehension of its object, by expressly requiring, for such an interposition, "the case of a deliberate, palpable, and dangerous breach of the Constitution, by the exercise of powers not granted by it." It must be a case not of a light and transient nature, but of a nature dangerous to the great purposes for which the Constitution was established. It must be a case, moreover, not obscure or doubtful in its construction, but plain and palpable. Lastly, it must be a case not resulting from a partial consideration or hasty determination, but a case stamped with a final consideration and deliberate adherence. It is not necessary, because the resolution does not require, that the question should be discussed, how far the exercise of any particular power, ungranted by the Constitution, would justify the interposition of the parties to it. As cases might easily be stated, which none would contend ought to fall within that description,—cases, on the other hand, might, with equal ease, be stated, so flagrant and so fatal as to unite every opinion in placing them within the description.

But the resolution has done more than guard against misconstruction, by expressly referring to cases of a deliberate, palpable, and dangerous nature. It specifies the object of the interposition, which it contemplates to be solely that of arresting the progress of the evil of usurpation, and of maintaining the authorities, rights, and liberties, appertaining to the states as parties to the Constitution.

From this view of the resolution, it would seem inconceivable that it can incur any just disapprobation from those who, laying aside all momentary impressions, and recollecting the genuine source and object of the Federal Constitution, shall candidly and accurately interpret the meaning of the General Assembly. If the deliberate exercise of dangerous powers, palpably withheld by the Constitution, could not justify the parties to it in interposing even so far as to arrest the progress of the evil, and thereby to preserve the Constitution itself, as well as to provide for the safety of the parties to it, there would be an end to all relief from usurped power, and a direct subversion of the rights specified or recognized under all the state constitutions, as well as a plain denial of the fundamental principle on which our independence itself was declared.

But it is objected, that the judicial authority is to be regarded as the sole expositor of the Constitution in the last resort; and it may be asked for what reason the declaration by the General Assembly, supposing it to be theoretically true, could be required at the present day, and in so solemn a manner.

On this objection it might be observed, first, that there may be instances of usurped power, which the forms of the Constitution would never draw within the control of the judicial department; secondly, that, if the decision of the judiciary be raised above the authority of the sovereign parties to the Constitution, the decisions of the other departments, not carried by the forms of the Constitution before the judiciary, must be equally authoritative and final with the decisions of that department. But the proper answer to the objection is, that the resolution of the General Assembly relates to those great and extraordinary cases, in which all the forms of the Constitution may prove ineffectual against infractions dangerous to the essential rights of the parties to it. The resolution supposes that dangerous powers, not delegated, may not only be usurped and executed by the other departments, but that the judicial department, also, may exercise or sanction dangerous powers beyond the grant of the Constitution; and, consequently, that the ultimate right of the parties to the Constitution, to judge whether the compact has been dangerously violated, must extend to violations by one delegated authority as well as by another—by the judiciary as well as by the executive, or the legislature.

However true, therefore, it may be, that the judicial department is, in all questions submitted to it by the forms of the Constitution, to decide in the last resort, this resort must necessarily be deemed the last in relation to the authorities of the other departments of the government; not in relation to the rights of the parties to the constitutional compact, from which the judicial, as well as the other departments, hold their delegated trusts. On any other hypothesis, the delegation of judicial power would annul the authority delegating it; and the concurrence of this department with the others in usurped powers, might subvert forever, and beyond the possible reach of any rightful remedy, the very Constitution which all were instituted to preserve.

The truth declared in the resolution being established, the expediency of making the declaration at the present day may safely be left to the temperate consideration and candid judgment of the American public. It will be remembered, that a frequent recurrence to fundamental principles is solemnly enjoined by most of the state constitutions, and particularly by our own, as a necessary safeguard against the danger of degeneracy, to which republics are liable, as well as other governments, though in a less degree than others. And a fair comparison of the political doctrines not infrequent at the present day, with those which characterized the epoch of our revolution, and which form the basis of our republican constitutions, will best determine whether the declaratory recurrence here made to those principles ought to be viewed as unseasonable and improper, or as a vigilant discharge of an important duty. The authority of constitutions over governments, and of the sovereignty of the people over constitutions, are truths which are at all times necessary to be kept in mind; and at no time, perhaps, more necessary than at present.

. . . These observations appear to form a satisfactory reply to every objection which is not founded on a misconception of the terms employed in the resolutions. There is one other, however, which may be of too much importance not to be added. It cannot be forgotten that, among the arguments addressed to those who apprehended danger to liberty from the establishment of the general government over so great a country, the appeal was emphatically made to the intermediate existence of the state governments between the people and that government, to the vigilance with which they would descry the first symptoms of usurpation, and to the promptitude with which they would sound the alarm to the public. This argument was probably not without its effect; and if it was a proper one then to recommend the establishment of a constitution, it must be a proper one now to assist in its interpretation.

McCULLOCH v. MARYLAND[30]

The first question made in the cause is—has congress power to incorporate a bank? It has been truly said, that this can scarcely be considered as an open question, entirely unprejudiced by the former proceedings of the nation respecting it. The principle now contested was introduces at a very early period of our history, has been recognized by many successive legislatures, and has been acted upon by the judicial department, in cases of peculiar delicacy, as the law undoubted obligation . . .

In discussing this question, the counsel for the state of Maryland have deemed it of some importance, in the construction of the constitution, to consider that instrument, not as emanating from the people, but as the act of sovereign and independent states. The powers of the general government, it has been said, are delegated by the states, who alone are truly sovereign; and must be exercised in subordination to the states, who alone possesses supreme dominion. It would be difficult to sustain this proposition. The convention which framed the constitution was indeed elected by the state legislatures. But the instrument, when it came from their hands, was a mere proposal, without obligation, or pretentions to it. It was reported to the then existing congress of the United States, with a request that it might "be submitted" to a convention of delegates, chosen in each state by the people thereof, under the recommendation of its legislature, for their assent and ratification." This mode of processing was adopted: and by the convention, by congress, and by the state legislatures, the instrument was submitted was submitted to the *people*. They acted upon it in the only manner in which they can act safely, effectively and wisely, on such a subject, by assembling in convention. It is true, they assembled in their several states—and where else should they has assembled? No political dreamer was ever wild enough to think of breaking down the lines which separate the states, and of compounding the American people into one common mass. Of consequence, when they act, they act in their states. But the measures they adopt do not, on that account, cease to be the measures of the people themselves, or become the measures of the state governments.

From these conventions, the constitution derives its whole authority. The government proceeds directly from the people; is "ordained and established," in the name of the people; and is declared to be ordained, "in order to from a more perfect union, establish justice, insure domestic tranquility, and secure the blessings of liberty to themselves and to their posterity." The assent of the states, in their sovereign capacity, is implied, in calling a convention, and thus submitting that instrument to the people. But the people were at perfect liberty to accept or reject it; and their act was final. It required not the affirmance, and could not be negatived, by the state governments. The constitution, when thus adopted, was of complete obligation, and bound the state sovereignties . . .

The government of the Union, then (whatever may be the influence of this fact on the case), is emphatically and truly, a government of the people. In form, and in substance, it emanates from them. Its powers are granted by them, and are to be exercised directly on them, and for their benefit.

This government is acknowledged by all, to be one of enumerated powers. The principle, that it can exercise only the powers granted to it, would seem to be apparent, to have required to be enforced by all those arguments, which its enlightened friends, while it was depending before the people, found it necessary to urge; that principle is now universally admitted. But the question respecting the extent of the powers actually granted, is perpetually arising, and will probably continue to arise, so long as our system shall exist. In discussing these questions, the conflicting powers of the general and state governments must be brought into view, and the supremacy of their respective laws, when they are in opposition, must be settled.

If any one proposition could command the universal assent of mankind, we might expect it would be this—that the government of the Union, though limited in its powers, is supreme within its sphere of action. This would seem to result, necessarily, from its nature. It is the government of all; its powers are delegated by all; it represents all, and acts for all. Though any one state may be willing to control its operations, no state is willing to allow others to control them. The nation, on those subjects on which it can act, must necessarily bind its component parts. But this question is not left to mere reason: the people have, in express terms decided it, by saying, "this constitution, and the laws of the United States, which 'shall be made in pursuance thereof,' shall be the supreme law of the land," and by requiring that the members of the state legislatures, and the officers of the executive and judicial departments of the states, shall take the oath of fidelity to it. The government of the United States, then, though limited in its powers, is supreme; and its laws, when made in pursuance of the constitution, form the supreme law of the land, "anything in the constitution or laws of any state to the contrary notwithstanding."

Among the enumerated powers, we do not find that of establishing a bank or creating a corporation. But there is no phrase in the instrument which, like the articles of confederation, excludes incidental or implied powers; and which requires that everything granted shall be expressly and minutely described. Even the 10th amendment, which was framed for the purpose of quieting the excessive jealousies which had been excited, omits the word "expressly," and declares only, that the powers "not delegated to the United States, nor prohibited to the states, are reserved to the states or to the people"; thus leaving the question, whether the particular power which may become the subject of the contest, has been delegated to the one government, or prohibited to the other, to depend on a fair construction of the whole instrument. The men who drew and adopted this amendment had experienced the embarrassments resulting from the insertion of this world in the articles of confederation, and probably omitted it to avoid those embarrassments. A constitution, to contain an accurate detail of all the subdivisions of which its great powers will admit, and of all the means by which they may be carried into execution, would partake of the prolixity of a legal code, and could scarcely be embraced by the human mind. It would, probably, never be understood by the public. Its nature, therefore, requires, that only its great outlines should be marked, its important objects designated, and the minor ingredients which compose those objects, be deduced from the mature of the objects themselves. That this idea was entertained by the framers of the American constitution is not only to be inferred from the nature of the instrument, but from the language. Why else were some of the limitations, found in the 9th section of the 1st article introduced? It is also, in some degree, warranted, by their having omitted to use any restrictive term which might prevent its receiving a fair and just interpretation. In considering this question, then, we must never forget that it is a *constitution* we are expounding.

. . . The government which has a right to do an act, and has imposed on it, the duty of performing the act, must, according to the dictates of reason, be allowed to select the means; and those who contend that is may not select any appropriate means, that one particular mode of effecting the objects is excepted, take upon themselves the burden of establishing that exception.

The creation of a corporation, it is said, appertains to sovereignty. This is admitted. But to what portion of sovereignty does it appertain? Does it belong to one more than to another? In America, the powers of sovereignty are divided between the government of the Union, and those of the states. They are each sovereign, with respect to the objects committed to it, and neither sovereign, with respect to the objects committed to the other. We cannot comprehend that train of reasoning, which would maintain, that the extent of power granted by the people is to be ascertained, not by the nature and terms of the grant, but by its date. Some state constitutions were formed before, some since that of the United States. We cannot believe, that their relation to each other is in any degree dependent on upon this circumstance. Their respective powers must, we think, be precisely the same, as if they had been formed at the same time. Had they been formed at the same time, and had the people conferred on the general government the power contained in the constitution, and on the states the whole residuum of power, would it have been asserted, that the government of the Union was not sovereign, with respect to those objects which were entrusted to it, in relation to which its laws were declared to be supreme? If this could not have been asserted, we cannot well comprehend the process of reasoning which maintains, that a power appertaining to sovereignty cannot be connected with that vast portion of it which is granted to the general government, so far as it is calculated to subserve the legitimate objects of that government. The power of creating a corporation, though appertaining to sovereignty, is not, like the power of making war, or levying taxes, or of regulating commerce, a great substantive and independent power, which cannot be implied as incidental to other powers, or used as a means of executing them. It is never the end for which other powers are exercised, but a means by which other objects are accomplished. No contributions are made to charity, for the sake of an incorporation, but a corporation is created to administer the charity; no seminary of learning is instituted, in order to be incorporated, but the corporate character is conferred to subserve the purpose of education.

. . . We admit, as all must admit, that the powers of the government are limited, and that its limits are not to be transcended. But we think the sound construction of the constitution must allow to the national legislature that discretion, with respect to the means by which the powers it confers are to be carried into execution, which will enable that body to perform the high duties assigned to it, in the manner most beneficial to the people. Let the end be legitimate, let it be within the scope of the constitution, and all means which are appropriate, which are plainly adapted to that end, which are not prohibited, but consist with the letter and spirit of the constitution, are constitutional.

. . . That the power to tax involves the power to destroy; that the power to destroy may defeat and render useless the power to create; that there is a plain repugnance is conferring on one government a power to control the constitutional measures of another, which other, with respect to those very measures, is declared to be supreme over that which exerts the control, are propositions not to be denied. But all inconsistencies are to be reconciled by the magic of the word confidence.

. . . If we apply the principle for which the state of Maryland contends, to the constitution, generally, we shall find it capable of changing totally the character of measures of the government, and of prostrating it at the foot of the states. The American people have declared their constitution and the laws made in pursuance thereof, to be supreme; but this principle would transfer the supremacy, in fact, to the states. If the states may tax one instrument, employed by the government in the execution of its powers, they may tax any and every other instrument. They may tax the mail; they may tax the mint; they may tax patent—rights; they may tax all the means employed by the government, to an excess which would defeat all the ends of government. This was not intended by the American people. They did not design to make their government dependent on the states . . .

The question is, in truth, a question of supremacy; and if the right of the states to tax the means employed by the general governmental be conceded, the declaration that the constitution, and the laws made in pursuance thereof, shall be the supreme law of the land, is empty and unmeaning declamation . . .

It has also been insisted, that, as the power of taxation in the general and state governments is acknowledged to be concurrent, every argument which would sustain the right of the general government to tax banks chartered by the general government. But the two cases are not on the same reason. The people of all the states have created the general government, and have conferred upon in the general power of taxation. The people of all the states, and the states themselves, are represented in congress, and, by their representatives, exercise this power. When they tax the chartered institutions of the states, they tax their constituents; and these taxes must be uniform.

But when a state taxes the operations of the government of the United States, it acts upon institutions created, not by their own constituents, but by people over whom they claim no control. It acts upon the measures of a government created by others as well as themselves, for the benefit of others in common with themselves. The difference is that which always exists, and always must exist, between the action of the whole on a part, and the action of a part on the whole—between the laws of a government declared to be supreme, and those of a government which, when in opposition to those laws, is not supreme . . .

The court has bestowed on this subject its most deliberate consideration. The result is a conviction that the states have no power, by taxation or otherwise, to retard, impede, burden, or in any manner control, the operations of the constitutional laws enacted by congress to carry into execution the powers vested in the general government. This is, we think, the unavoidable consequence of that supremacy which the constitution has declared. We are unanimously of opinion, that the law passed by the legislature of Maryland, imposing a tax on the Bank of the United States, is unconstitutional and void . . .

JOHN TAYLOR OF CAROLINE, *NEW VIEWS OF THE CONSTITUTION OF THE UNITED STATES*[31]

The reader has perceived that the question concerning state powers, is condensed in the word sovereignty, and therefore any new ideas upon the subject, if to be found, would not be unedifying. A will to enact, and a power to execute, constitute its essence. Take away either, and it expires. The state government and the federal government, are the monuments by which state sovereignty, attended with these attributes, is demonstrated. But as the consolidating school will not see it, I will endeavor further to establish its existence, in order to prevent these beautiful examples of political science from falling into ruin.

The constitution, like the declaration of independence, was framed by deputies from the "states of New-Hampshire," &c. and at the threshold of the transaction, we discern a positive admission of the existence of separate states invested with separate sovereignties. This admission expounds the phrase "We, the people of the United States," which co-operates with the separate powers given to their deputies in the convention, and is distinctly repeated by the words "do ordain and establish this constitution for *the United States of America*." Had the sovereignty of each state been wholly abandoned, and the people of all been considered as constituting one nation, the idea would have been expressed in different language . . . The appellation adopted by the declaration of independence, was, "The United States of America." The first confederation declares, that the style of this confederacy shall be, "The United States of America." And the union of 1787, ordains and establishes the constitution for "The United States of America." The three instruments, by adhering to the same style, coextensively affirmed the separate sovereignties of these states. It was a style proper to describe a confederacy of independent states, and improper for describing a consolidated nation. If neither the declaration of independence nor the confederation of 1777, created an American nation, or a concentrated sovereignty, by this style, the conclusion is inevitable, that the constitution was not intended to produce such consequences by the same style. The word America is used to designate the quarter of the globe in which the recited states were established, and not to designate a nation of Americans . . . If the word state does not intrinsically imply sovereign power, there was no word which we could use better calculated for that purpose.

This construction bestows the same meaning upon the same words in our three constituent or elemental instruments, and exhibits the reason why the whole language of the constitution is affianced to the idea of a league between sovereign states, and hostile to that of a consolidated nation. There are many states in America, but no state of America, nor any people of an American state. A constitution for America or Americans, would therefore have been similar to a constitution for Utopia or Utopians.

Hence the constitution is declared to be made for the "United States of America," that is, for certain states enumerated by their names, established upon that portion of the earth's surface, called America. Though no people or nation of America existed, considering these words as defining a political association, states did exist in America, each constituted by a people. By these political individual entities, called states, the constitution was framed; by these individual entities it was ratified; and by these entities it can only be altered. It was made by them and for them, and not by or for a nation of Americans. The people of each state, or each state as constituted by a people, conveyed to a federal authority, organized by states, a portion of state sovereign powers, and retained another portion. In this division, all the details of the constitution are comprised, one dividend consisting of the special powers conferred upon a federal government, and the other, of the powers reserved by the states which conferred these special powers. The deputation and reservation are both bottomed upon the sovereignty of the states, and must both fall or both stand with that principle. If each state, or the people of each state, did not possess a separate sovereignty, they had no right to convey or retain powers. If they had a right both to convey and to retain powers, it could only be in virtue of state sovereignty. Admitting the utmost which can be asked, and more than ought to be conceded, by supposing that these sovereignties, in conveying limited powers to the federal government, conveyed also a portion of sovereignty, it must also be allowed, that by retaining powers, they retained also a portion of sovereignty. If sovereignty was attached to the ceded powers, it was also attached to the powers not ceded, because all or none of the powers of the states must have proceeded from this principle. In this observation, not use is made of the power reserved to the states to amend the federal form of government, by which a positive sovereignty is retained to the states over that government, subversive of the doctrine, that the constitution bestows a sovereignty upon it over the states. But a delegation of limited powers, being an act of sovereignty, could be a renunciation of the sovereignty attached to the powers not delegated. A power to resume the limited delegation, was the strongest expression of sovereignty, and rejects the idea, that the delegated authority may positively or constructively subject the sovereign power to its own will; that no sovereignty may destroy an actual sovereignty. By this power of amendment, the states may re-establish the confederation of 1777, and thus unquestionably revive their separate sovereignties said to be extinct; because they are positively asserted by that confederation. If it is not absurd, it is yet a new idea, that a dead sovereignty contains an inherent power to revive itself whenever it pleases.

The mode of making amendments to the constitution, expresses its true construction, and rejects the doctrine, that an American people created a federal government. Their ratification is to be the act of states. It is the same with that of the confederation, which asserted the sovereignties of the states, in concomitancy with this mode of ratification, with only two differences. By the first confederation, the ratification was to be the act of state legislatures, and unanimous; by the constitution, the ratification of alterations is to be the act of "state conventions, or legislatures by three-fourths." The last differences extended the power of the states, by removing the obstacle of unanimity, and was not intended to diminish it. State legislatures and conventions are united, as equivalent state organs. Thus the constitution construes the phrase, "We, the people of the United States," and refutes the doctrine of an American people, as the sources of federal powers; because, had these powers been derived from that source, it would have referred to the same source for their modification, and not to state legislatures. It declares that both state legislatures and state conventions, are representations of state sovereignties, equally competent to express their will. The same opinion is expressed by declaring that "ratification of the conventions of nine states, shall be sufficient for its establishment between the ratifying states." Of the two equivalent modes of ratification, it selects one for that special occasion, not because it substantially differed from the other, and was not an expression of state will, but because it was apprehended that a considerable transfer of powers from the state governments to a federal government, might produce an opposition from men in the exercise of these powers, although when experience should have ascertained the benefits of the innovation, and time should have cured the wounds of individual ambition, a further adherence to one equivalent mode in preference to the other, might be unnecessary and inconvenient to the states. The equivalency of the modes is obvious, as state legislatures are empowered to revoke the act of state conventions, by which the residence of state sovereignties in these legislatures is considered as the same as its residence in state conventions, upon no other ground, than that both constituted a representation of the state, and not a representation of an unassociated people.

An adherence to our original principle of state sovereignty is demonstrated both by the confederation and constitution. Unanimity was necessary to put the first, and a concurrence of nine states to put the second, "to the states ratifying only." Both consequences are deduced from state sovereignty, by which one state could defeat a union predicted upon unanimity, and four states might have refused to unite with nine. The latter circumstance displays the peculiar propriety or ordaining and establishing the constitution "for the United States of America." The refusing states, though states of America, did not constitute a portion of an American nation; and their right of refusal resulted from their acknowledged sovereignty and independence.

"The United States of America" would have consisted of nine states only, had four refused to accede to the union; and therefore thirteen states could not have been contemplated by the constitution, as having been consolidated into one people. Hence it adheres to the idea of a league, by a style able to describe "the United States of America," had they consisted but of nine, and avoids a style applicable only to one nation or people consisting of thirteen states. By acknowledging the sovereignty of the refusing, it admits equally an evidence of it. The limitation of federal powers by assent, establishes the principle from which the assent flowed. There could be no sound assent, nor any sound limitation, unless one was given, and the other imposed, by a competent authority; and no authority is competent to the establishment of a government, except it is sovereign. The same authority could only possess the right of rejecting the constitution. Had it been the act of an American nation or people, a state would have possessed no such right. The judicial sages have allowed the federal to be a limited government, but how can it be limited if the state sovereignties by which it was limited, do not exist, and if the state powers reserved, which define the limitation, are subject to its control?

Having proved that state sovereignties were established by the declaration of independence; that their existence was asserted by the confederation of 1777; that they are recognized by the constitution of 1787, in the modes of its formation, ratification, and amendment; that this constitution employs the same words to describe the United States, used by the two preceding instruments; that the word state implies a sovereign community; that each state contained an associated people; that an American people never existed; that the constitution was ordained and established, for such states situated in America, as might accede to a union; that its limited powers was a partial and voluntary endowment of state sovereignties, to be exercised by a Congress of the states which should unite; that the word Congress implies a deputation from sovereignties, and was so expounded by the confederation; and that a reservation of sovereign powers cannot be executed without sovereignty; the reader will consider, whether all these principles, essential for the preservation both of the federal and state governments, were intended to be destroyed by the details of the constitution. The attempt to lose twenty-four states, in order to find a consolidated nation, or a judicial sovereignty, reverses the mode of reasoning hitherto admitted to be correct, by deducing principles from effects, and not effects from principles. But in construing the constitution, we shall never come at truth, if we suffer its details, intended to be subservient to established political principles, to deny their allegiance, and rebel against their sovereigns. A will to act, and a power to execute, constitutes sovereignty. The state governments, says the Federalist, are no more dependent on the federal government is on them, in the exercise of its delegated powers.

The treaty between his Britannick majesty and the *United States of America*, acknowledges "the said United States, viz. New-Hampshire, Massachusetts-Bay, Rhode-Island and Providence Plantations, Connecticut, New-York, New-Jersey, Pennsylvania, Delaware, Maryland, Virginia, North-Carolina, South-Carolina, and Georgia, to be free, *sovereign*, and independent states; as such he treats with them, and relinquishes all claim to their government and territorial rights." This king acknowledges, individually, the sovereignty of the states; he relinquishes to them, individually, his territorial rights; three eminent envoys demanded this acknowledgment and relinquishment, as appertaining, individually, to the states; a Congress of the United States ratified the act and the doctrine; the treaty was then unanimously hailed, and is still generally considered, as a consummation of right, justice, and liberty; but now it is said that the states are corporations, subordinate bodies politick, and not sovereign. By the admirers of royal sovereignty, the treat ought to be considered as valid; by those who confide in authority, it ought to be considered as authentic; by such as respect our revolutionary patriots, it ought to be venerated; and by honest expositors of the constitution, it will be allowed to afford conclusive proof, that the phrase "United States of America," used both in the treaty and the constitution, implied the existence, and not the abrogation, of state sovereignty. Consolidators, suprematists, and conquerors, however, will all equally disregard any instrument, however solemn and explicit, by which ambition and avarice will be restrained, and the happiness of mankind improved.

THE WEBSTER-HAYNE DEBATE[32]

Hayne: . . . Sir, I am one of those who believe that the very life of our system is the independence of the States, and that there is no evil more to be deprecated than the consolidation of this Government. It is only by a strict adherence to the limitations imposed by the constitution on the Federal Government, that this system works well, and can answer the great ends for which it was instituted. I am opposed, therefore, in any shape, to all unnecessary extension of the powers, or the influence of the Legislature or Executive of the Union over the States, or the people of the States, and most of all, I am opposed to those partial distributions of favors, whether by appropriation, which has a direct and powerful tendency to spread corruption through the land; to create an abject spirit of dependence; to sow the seeds of dissolution; to produce jealousy among the different portions of the Union, and finally to sap the very foundations of the Government itself.

Webster: . . . Consolidation!—that perpetual cry, both of terror and delusion—consolidation! Sir, when gentleman speak of the effects of a common fund, belonging to all States, as having a tendency to consolidation, what do they mean? Do they mean, or can they mean, anything more than that the Union of all States will be strengthened, by whatever continues or furnishes inducements to the people of the States to hold together? If they mean merely this, then, no doubt, the public lands as well as every thing else in which we have a common interest, tends to consolidation; and to this species of consolidation every true American ought to be attacked; it is neither more nor less than strengthening the Union itself. This is the sense in which the framers of the constitution use the word consolidation; and in which sense I adopt and cherish it. They tell us, in the letter submitting the constitution to the consideration of the country, that, "in all our deliberations on this subject, we kept steadily in our view that which appears to us the greatest interest of every true American—the consolidation of our Union—in which is involved our prosperity, felicity, safety; perhaps our national existence. This is important consideration, seriously and deeply impressed on our minds, led each State in the Convention to be less rigid, on points of inferior magnitude, than might have been otherwise expected."

Hayne: . . . I am proud of having belonged from the very commencement of my political life to the present day, were the democrats of '98. Anarchists, anti-federalist, revolutionists, I think they were sometimes called. They assumed the name of democratic republicans in 1812, and have retained their name and their principles up to the present hour. True to their political faith, they have always, as a party, been in favor of limitations of power; they have insisted that all powers not delegated to the Federal Government as reserved, and have been constantly struggling, as they are now struggling, to preserve the rights of the States, and prevent them from being drawn into the vortex, and swallowed up by one great consolidated Government.

Who then, Mr. President, are the true friends of the Union? Those who would confine the federal government strictly within the limits prescribed by the constitution—who would preserve to the States and the people all powers not expressly delegated—who would make this a federal and not a national Union—and who, administering the government in a spirit of equal justice, would make it a blessing and not a curse. And who are its enemies? Those who are in favor of consolidation; who are constantly stealing power from the States and adding strength to the federal government; who, assuming an unwarrantable jurisdiction over the States and the people, undertake to regulate the whole industry and capital of the country. But, Sir, of all descriptions of men, I consider those as the worst enemies of the Union, who sacrifice the equal rights which belong to every member of the confederacy, to combinations of interested majorities for personal or political objects. But the gentleman apprehends no evil from the dependence of the States on the federal Government; he can see no danger of corruption from the influence of money or of patronage.

The Senator from Massachusetts, in denouncing what he is pleased to call the *Carolina doctrine*, has attempted to throw ridicule upon the idea that the State had any constitutional remedy by the exercise of its sovereign authority against "a gross, palpable, and deliberate violation of the Constitution." He called it an "an idle" or "a ridiculous notion," or something to that effect; and added, that it would make the Union "a mere rope of sand." Now, Sir, as the gentleman has not condescended to enter into an examination of the question, and has been satisfied with throwing the weight of his authority into the scale, I do not deem it necessary to do more than to throw into the opposite scale, the authority on which South Carolina relies; and there, for the present, I am perfectly willing to leave the controversy. The South Carolina doctrines, that is to say, the doctrine contained in the exposition reported by a committee of the legislature in December, 1828, and published by their authority, is the good old Republican doctrine of '98, the doctrine of the Celebrated "Virginia Resolutions," of that year, and of "Madison's Report" of '00.

Webster: . . . What he contends for, is, that it is constitutional to interrupt the administration of the Constitution itself, in the hands of in the hands of those who are chosen and sworn to administer it, by the direct interference, in from of law, of the States, in virtue of their sovereign capacity. The inherent right in the People to reform their government, I do not deny; and they have another right, and that is, to resist unconstitutional laws, without overturning the Government. It is no doctrine of mine, that unconstitutional laws bind the People. The great question is, whose prerogative is it to decide on the unconstitutionality of the laws? On that, the main debate hinges. The proposition, that, in case of a supposed violation of the Constitution by Congress, the Sates have a constitutional right to interfere, and annul the law of Congress, is the proposition of the gentleman: I do not admit it. If the gentleman had intended no more than to assert the right of revolution, for justifiable cause, he would have said only what all agree to. But I cannot conceive that there can be a middle course, between submission to the laws, when regularly pronounced constitutional, on the one hand, and open resistance, which is revolution, or rebellion, on the other. I say, the right of a Sate to annul a law of Congress, cannot be maintained, but on the ground of the unalienable right of man to resist oppression; that is to say, upon the ground of revolution. I admit that there is an ultimate violent remedy, above the Constitution, and in defiance of the Constitution, which may be resorted to, when a revolution is to be justified. But I do not admit that, under the Constitution, and in conformity with it, there is any mode in which a State Government, as a member of the Union, can interfere and stop the progress of the General Government, by force of her own laws, under any circumstances what so ever. This leads us to inquire into the origin of this Government, and the source of its power. Whose agent is it? Is it the creature of the State Legislature, or the creature of the People?

If the Government of the United States be the agent of the State Government, then they may control it, provided they can agree in the manner of controlling it; if it be the agent of the People, then the People alone can control it, restrain it, modify, or reform it. It is observable enough, that the doctrine for which the honorable gentleman contends, leads him to the necessity of maintaining, not only that this General Government is the creature of the States, but that it is the creature of each of the States severally; so that each may assert the power, for itself, of determining whether its acts within the limits of its authority. It is the servant of four-and-twenty masters, of different wills and different purposes, and yet bound to obey all. This absurdity (for it seems no less) arises form a misconception as to the origin of this Government and its true character. It is, sir, the People's Constitution, the People's Government; made for the People; made by the People; and answerable to the People. The People of the United States have declared that this Constitution shall be the Supreme Law. We must either admit the proposition, or dispute their authority. The States are, unquestionably, sovereign, so far as their sovereignty is not affected by this supreme law. But the State Legislatures, as political bodies, however sovereign, are yet not sovereign over the People. So far as the People have given power to the General Government, so far the grant is unquestionably good, and the Government holds of the People, and not of the State Governments. We are all agents of the same supreme power, the People. The General Government and the State Governments derive their authority form the same source. Neither can, in relation to the other, be called primary, though one is definite and restricted, and the other general and residuary. The National Government possesses those powers which it can be shown the People have conferred on it, and no more. All the rest belongs to the State Governments or to the People themselves.

. . . If there be no power to settle such questions, independent of either of the States, is not the whole Union a rope of sand? Are we not thrown back again, precisely, upon the old Confederation?

. . . I must now beg to ask, sir, whence is this supposed right [Interposition] of the States derived?—where do they find the power to interfere with the laws of the Union? Sir, the opinion which the honorable gentleman maintains, is a notion, founded in a total misapprehension, in my judgement, of the origin of this Government, and of the foundation on which it stands. I hold it to be a popular Government, erected by the People; those who administer it reasonable to the People; and itself being capable of being amended and modified, just as the People may choose it to be. It is popular, just as truly emanating from the People, as the State Governments. It is created for one purpose; the State Governments for one another. It has its own powers; they have theirs. There is no more authority with them to arrest the operation of a law of Congress, than with Congress to arrest the operation of their laws.

We are here to administer a Constitution emanating immediately from the People, and trusted, by them, to our administration. It is not the creature of the State Governments. It is of no moment to the argument, that certain acts of the State Legislatures are necessary to fill our seats in this body. That is not one of their original Sate powers, a part of the sovereignty of the State. It is a duty which the People, by the Constitution itself, have imposed on the State Legislatures; and which they might have left to be performed elsewhere, if they had seen fit. So they have left the choice of President with electors; but all this does not affect the proposition, that this whole Government, President, Senate, and House of Representatives, is popular Government. It leaves it still all its popular character. The governor of a State, (in some of the States) is chosen, not directly by the People, but by those who are chosen by the People, for the purpose of performing, among other duties, that of electing a Governor. Is the Government of the State, on that account, not a popular Government? This Government, sir, is the independent offspring of the popular will. It is not the creature of State Legislatures; nay, more, if the whole truth must be told, the People brought it into existence, established it, and have hitherto supported it, for the very purpose, amongst others, of imposing certain salutary restraints on State sovereignties. The States can not now make war; they cannot contract alliances; they cannot make, each for itself, separate regulations of commerce; they cannot lay imposts; they cannot coin money. If this Constitution, sir, be the creature of the State Legislatures, it must be admitted that it has obtained a strange control over the violations of its creators.

The People, then, sir, erected this Government. They gave it a Constitution, and in that Constitution they have enumerated the powers which they bestow on it. They have made it a limited Government. They have defined its authority. They have restrained it to the exercise of such powers as are granted; and all others, they declare, are reserved to the States or the People. But, sir, they have not stopped here. If they had, they would have accomplished but half their work. No definition can be so clear, as to avoid possibility of doubt; no limitation so precise, as to exclude all uncertainty. Who, then, shall construe this giant of the People? Who shall interpret their will, where it may be supposed they have left it doubtful? With whom do they repose this ultimate right of deciding on the powers of the Government? Sir, they have settled all this in the fullest manner. They have left it, with the Government itself, in its appropriate branches. Sir, the very chief end, the main design, for which the whole Constitution was framed and adopted, was to establish a Government that should not be obliged to act through State agency, or depend on State opinion and State discretion. The People had had quite enough of that kind of Government, under the Confederacy. Under that system, the legal action— the application of law to individuals, belonged exclusively to the States. Congress could only recommend—their acts were not of binding force, till the Stated had adopted and sanctioned them. Are we in that condition still? Are we yet at the mercy of State discretion, and the State construction? Sir, if we are, then vain will be our attempt to maintain the Constitution under which we sit.

But, sir, the People have wisely provided, in the Constitution itself, a proper, suitable mode and tribunal for settling questions of constitutional law. There are, in the Constitution, grants of powers to Congress; and restrictions on these powers. There are, also, prohibitions on the States. Some authority must, therefore, necessarily exist, having the ultimate jurisdiction to fix and ascertain the interpretation of these grants, restrictions, and prohibitions. The Constitution has itself pointed out, ordained, and established that authority. How has it accomplished this great and essential end? By declaring, sir, that "*the Constitution and the laws of the United States, made in pursuance thereof, shall be the supreme law of the land, any thing in the Constitution or the laws of any State to the contrary notwithstanding.*"

. . . Sir, I deny this power of State Legislature altogether. It cannot stand the test of examination. Gentleman may say, that in an extreme case, a State Government might protect the People from intolerable oppression. Sir, in such a case, the People might protect themselves, without the aid of the State Governments. Such a case warrants revolution. It must make, when it comes, a law for itself. A nullifying act of a State Legislature cannot alter the case, nor make resistance any more lawful. In maintaining these sentiments, sir, I am but asserting the rights of the People. I state what they have declared, and insist on their right to declare it. They have chosen to repose this power to the General Government, and I think it my duty to support it, like other constitutional powers.

. . . If, sir, the People, in these respects, had done otherwise than they have done, their Constitution could neither have been preserved, nor would it have been worth preserving. And, if its plain provisions shall now be disregarded, and these new doctrines interpolated in it, it will become as feeble and help-less a being as its enemies, whether early or more recent, could possibly desire. It will exist in every State, but as a poor dependent on State permis-sion. It must borrow leave to be; and will be, no longer than State pleasure, or State discretion, sees fit to grant the indulgence, and to prolong its poor existence.

. . . Mr. President, I have thus stated the reason of my dissent to the doc-trines which have been advanced and maintained. I am conscious of having detained you and the Senate much too long. I was drawn into the debate, with no previous deliberation such as is suited to the discussion of so grave and important a subject. But it is a subject of which my heart is full, and I have not been willing to suppress the utterance of its spontaneous sentiments. I cannot, even now, persuade myself to relinquish it, without expressing, once more, my deep conviction, that, since it respects nothing less than the Union of the States, it is of most vital and essential importance to the public happiness. I profess, sir, in my career, hitherto, to have kept steadily in view the prosperity and honor of the whole country, and the preservation of our Federal Union. It is to that Union we owe our safety at home, and our consideration and dignity abroad. It is to that Union that we are chiefly indebted for whatever makes us most proud of our country. That Union we reached only by the discipline of our virtues in the severe school of adversity. It had its origin in the necessities of disordered finance, prostrate commerce, and ruined credit. Under its benign influences, these great interests immediately awoke, as from the dead, and sprang forth with newness of life. Every year of its duration has teemed with fresh proofs of its utility and its blessings; and, although our territory has stretched out wider and wider, and our population spread farther and farther, they have not outrun its protection or its benefits. It has been to us all a copious fountain of a national, social, and personal happiness. I have not allowed myself, sir, to look beyond the Union, to see what might lie hidden in the dark recess behind. I have not coolly weighed the chances of preserving liberty, when the bonds that unite us together shall be broken asunder. I have not accustomed myself to hang over the principle of disunion, to see whether, with my short sight, I can fathom the depth of the abyss below; nor could I regard him as a safe counsellor in the affairs of this Government, whose thoughts should be mainly bent on considering, not how the Union should be best preserved, but how tolerable might be the condition of the People when it shall be broken up and destroyed. While the Union lasts, we have high, exciting, gratifying prospects spread out before us, for us and our children. Beyond that I seek not to penetrate the veil. God grant that, in my day, at least, that curtain may not rise. God grant that on my vision never may be opened what lies behind. When my eyes shall be turned to behold, for the last time, the sun in Heaven, may I not see him shining on the broken and dishonored fragments of a once glorious Union; on the States dissevered, discordant, belligerent; on the land rent with civil feuds, or drenched, it may be, in fraternal blood! Let their last feeble and lingering glance, rather behold the gorgeous Ensign of the Republic, now known and honored throughout the earth, still full high advanced, its arms and trophies streaming in their original lustre, not a stripe erased or polluted, nor a single star obscured—bearing for its motto, no such miserable interrogatory as, *What is all this worth?* Nor those other words of delusion and folly, *Liberty first, and Union afterwards*—but everywhere, spread all over in characters of living light, blazing on all its ample folds, as they float over the sea and over the land, and in every wind under the whole Heavens, that other sentiment, dear to every true American heart—Liberty *and* Union, now and forever, one and inseparable!

JOHN C. CALHOUN "THE FORT HILL ADDRESS"[33]

The question of the relation which the States and General Government bear to each other is not one of recent origin. From the commencement of our system, it has divided public sentiment. Even in the Convention, while the Constitution was struggling into existence, there were two parties as to what this relation should be, whose different sentiments constituted no small impediment in forming that instrument. After the General Government went into operation, experience soon proved that the question had not terminated with the labors of the Convention. The great struggle that preceded the political revolution of 1801, which brought Mr. Jefferson into power, turned essentially on it; and the doctrines and arguments on both sides were embodied and ably sustained—on the one, in the Virginia and Kentucky Resolutions, and the Report to the Virginia Legislature—and on the other, in the replies of the Legislature of Massachusetts and some of the other States.

The great and leading principle is, that the General Government emanated from the people of the several States, forming distinct political communities, and acting in their separate and sovereign capacity, and not from all of the people forming one aggregate political community; that the Constitution of the United States is, in fact, a compact, to which each State is a party, in the character already described; and that the several States, or parties, have a right to judge of its infractions; and in case of a deliberate, palpable, and dangerous exercise of power not delegated, they have the right, in the last resort, to use the language of the Virginia Resolutions, "to interpose for arresting the progress of the evil, and for maintaining, within their respective limits, the authorities, rights, and liberties appertaining to them." This right of interposition, thus solemnly asserted by the State of Virginia, be it called what it may—State-right, veto, nullification, or by any other name—I conceive to be the fundamental principle of our system, resting on facts historically as certain as our revolution itself, and deductions as simple and demonstrative as that of any political, or moral truth whatever; and I firmly believe that on its recognition depend the stability and safety of our political institutions.

I am not ignorant, that those opposed to the doctrine have always, now and formerly, regarded it in a very different light, as anarchical and revolutionary. Could I believe such, in fact, to be its tendency, to me it would be no recommendation. I yield to none, I trust, in a deep and sincere attachment to our political institutions and the union of these States. I never breathed an opposite sentiment; but, on the contrary, I have ever considered them the great instruments of preserving our liberty, and promoting the happiness of ourselves and our posterity; and next to these I have ever held them most dear.

. . . So numerous and diversified are the interests of our country, that they could not be fairly represented in a single government, organized so as to give to each great and leading interest, a separate and distinct voice, as in governments to which I have referred. A plan was adopted better suited to our situation, but perfectly novel in its character. The powers of government were divided, not, as heretofore, in reference to classes, but geographically. One General Government was formed for the whole, to which were delegated all the powers supposed to be necessary to regulate the interests common to all the States, leaving others subject to the separate control of the States, being, from their local and peculiar character, such, that they could not be subject to the will of a majority of the whole Union, without the certain hazard of injustice and oppression. It was thus that the interests of the whole were subjected, as they ought to be, to the will of the whole, while the peculiar and local interests were left under the control of the States separately, to whose custody only, they could be safely confided. This distribution of power, settled solemnly by a constitutional compact, to which all the States are parties, constitutes the peculiar character and excellence of our political system. It is truly and emphatically *American, without example or parallel.*

To realize its perfection, we must view the General Government and those of the States as a whole, each in its proper sphere, sovereign and independent; each perfectly adapted to its respective objects; the States acting separately, representing and protecting the local and peculiar interests; and acting jointly through one General Government, with the weight respectively assigned to each by the Constitution, representing and protecting the interest of the whole; and thus perfecting, by an admirable but simple arrangement, the great principle of representation and responsibility, without which no government can be free or just. To preserve this sacred distribution, as originally settled, by coercing each to move in its prescribed orbit, is the great and difficult problem, on the solution of which, the duration of our Constitution, of our Union, and, in all probability, our liberty depends. How is this to be effected? . . .

Whenever separate and dissimilar interests have been separately represented in any government; whenever the sovereign power has been divided in its exercise, the experience and wisdom of ages have devised but one mode by which such political organization can be preserved—the mode adopted in England, and by all governments, ancient and modern, blessed with constitutions deserving to be called free—to give to each co-estate the right to judge of its powers, with a negative or veto on the acts of the others, in order to protect against encroachments, the interests it particularly represents: a principle which all of our constitutions recognize in the distribution of power among their respective departments, as essential to maintain the independence of each; but which, to all who will duly reflect on the subject, must appear far more essential, for the same object, in that great and fundamental distribution of powers between the states and General Government. So essential is the principle, that, to withhold the right from either, where the sovereign power is divided, is, in fact, *to annul the division* itself, and to *consolidate*, in the one left in the exclusive possession of the right, *all* powers of government; for it is not possible to distinguish, practically, between a government having all power, and one having the right to take what powers it pleases. Nor does it in the least vary the principle, whether the distribution of power be between co-estates, as in England, or between distinctly organized, but connected governments, as with us. The reason is the same in both cases, while the necessity is greater in our case, as the danger of conflict is greater where the interests of a society are divided geographically than in any other, as has already been shown. . . .

I do not deny that a power of so high a nature may be abused by a State; but when I reflect that the States unanimously called the General Government into existence with all of its powers, which they freely delegated on their part, under the conviction that their common peace, safety, and prosperity required it; that they are bound together by a common origin, and the recollection of common suffering and common triumph in the great and splendid achievement of their independence; and that the strongest feelings of our nature, and among them the love of national power and distinction, are on the side of the Union; it does seem to me that the fear which would strip the States of their sovereignty, and degrade them, in fact, to mere dependent corporations, lest they should abuse a right indispensable to the peaceable protection of those interests which they reserved under their own peculiar guardianship when they created the General Government, is unnatural and unreasonable. If those who voluntarily created the system cannot be trusted to preserve it, what power can?

So, far from extreme danger, I hold that there never was a free State in which this great conservative principle, indispensable to all, was ever so safely lodged. In others, when the co-estates representing the dissimilar and conflicting interests of the community came into contact, the only alternative was compromise, submission, or force. Not so in ours. Should the General Government and a State come into conflict, we have a higher remedy: the power which called the General Government into existence, which gave it all of its authority, and can enlarge, contract, or abolish its powers at its pleasure, may be invoked. The States themselves may be appealed to—three-fourths of which, in fact, form a power, whose decrees are the Constitution itself, and whose voice can silence all discontent. The utmost extent, then, of the power is, that a State, acting in its sovereign capacity, as one of the parties to the constitutional compact, may compel the Government, created by that compact, to submit a question touching its infraction, to the parties who created it; to avoid the supposed dangers of which, it is proposed to resort to the novel, the hazardous, and, I must add, fatal project of giving to the General

Government the sole and final right of interpreting the Constitution—thereby reversing the whole system, making that instrument the creature of its will, instead of a rule of action impressed on it at its creation, and annihilating, in fact, the authority which imposed it, and from which the Government itself derives its existence. . . .

Against these conclusive arguments, as they seem to me, it is objected, that, if one of the parties has the right to judge of infractions of the Constitution, so has the other; and that, consequently, in cases of contested powers between a State and the General Government, each would have a right to maintain its opinion, as is the case when sovereign powers differ in the construction of treaties or compacts; and that, of course, it would come to be a mere question of force. The error is in the assumption that the General Government is a party to the constitutional compact. The States, as has been shown, formed the compact, acting as Sovereign and independent communities. The General Government is but its creature; and though, in reality, a government, with all the rights and authority which belong to any other government, within the orbit of its powers, it is, nevertheless, a government emanating from a compact between sovereigns, and partaking, in its nature and object, of the character of a joint commission, appointed to superintend and administer the interests in which all are jointly concerned; but having, beyond its proper sphere, no more power than if it did not exist. To deny this would be to deny the most incontestable facts, and the clearest conclusions; while to acknowledge its truth is, to destroy utterly the objection that the appeal would be to force, in the case supposed. For if each party has a right to judge, then, under our system of government, the final cognizance of a question of contested power would be in the States, and not in the General Government. It would be the duty of the latter, as in all similar cases of a contest between one or more of the principals and a joint commission or agency, to refer the contest to the principals themselves. Such are the plain dictates of both reason and analogy.

SOUTH CAROLINA, ORDINANCE OF NULLIFICATION[34]

Whereas the Congress of the United States by various acts, purporting to be acts laying duties and imposts on foreign imports, but in reality intended for the protection of domestic manufactures and the giving of bounties to classes and individuals engaged in particular employments, at the expense and to the injury and oppression of other classes and individuals, and by wholly exempting from taxation certain foreign commodities, such as are not produced or manufactured in the United States, to afford a pretext for imposing higher and excessive duties on articles similar to those intended to be protected, bath exceeded its just powers under the constitution, which confers on it no authority to afford such protection, and bath violated the true meaning and intent of the constitution, which provides for equality in imposing the burdens of taxation upon the several States and portions of the confederacy: And whereas the said Congress, exceeding its just power to impose taxes and collect revenue for the purpose of effecting and accomplishing the specific objects and purposes which the constitution of the United States authorizes it to effect and accomplish, hath raised and collected unnecessary revenue for objects unauthorized by the constitution.

We, therefore, the people of the State of South Carolina, in convention assembled, do declare and ordain and it is hereby declared and ordained, that the several acts and parts of acts of the Congress of the United States, purporting to be laws for the imposing of duties and imposts on the importation of foreign commodities, and now having actual operation and effect within the United States, and, more especially, an act entitled "An act in alteration of the several acts imposing duties on imports," approved on the nineteenth day of May, one thousand eight hundred and twenty-eight and also an act entitled "An act to alter and amend the several acts imposing duties on imports," approved on the fourteenth day of July, one thousand eight hundred and thirty-two, are unauthorized by the constitution of the United States, and violate the true meaning and intent thereof and are null, void, and no law, nor binding upon this State, its officers or citizens; and all promises, contracts, and obligations, made or entered into, or to be made or entered into, with purpose to secure the duties imposed by said acts, and all judicial proceedings which shall be hereafter had in affirmance thereof, are and shall be held utterly null and void.

And it is further ordained, that it shall not be lawful for any of the constituted authorities, whether of this State or of the United States, to enforce the payment of duties imposed by the said acts within the limits of this State; but it shall be the duty of the legislature to adopt such measures and pass such acts as may be necessary to give full effect to this ordinance, and to prevent the enforcement and arrest the operation of the said acts and parts of acts of the Congress of the United States within the limits of this State, from and after the first day of February next, and the duties of all other constituted authorities, and of all persons residing or being within the limits of this State, and they are hereby required and enjoined to obey and give effect to this ordinance, and such acts and measures of the legislature as may be passed or adopted in obedience thereto.

And it is further ordained, that in no case of law or equity, decided in the courts of this State, wherein shall be drawn in question the authority of this ordinance, or the validity of such act or acts of the legislature as may be passed for the purpose of giving effect thereto, or the validity of the aforesaid acts of Congress, imposing duties, shall any appeal be taken or allowed to the Supreme Court of the United States, nor shall any copy of the record be permitted or allowed for that purpose; and if any such appeal shall be attempted to be taken, the courts of this State shall proceed to execute and enforce their judgments according to the laws and usages of the State, without reference to such attempted appeal, and the person or persons attempting to take such appeal may be dealt with as for a contempt of the court.

And it is further ordained, that all persons now holding any office of honor, profit, or trust, civil or military, under this State (members of the legislature excepted), shall, within such time, and in such manner as the legislature shall prescribe, take an oath well and truly to obey, execute, and enforce this ordinance, and such act or acts of the legislature as may be passed in pursuance thereof, according to the true intent and meaning of the same, and on the neglect or omission of any such person or persons so to do, his or their office or offices shall be forthwith vacated, and shall be filled up as if such person or persons were dead or had resigned; and no person hereafter elected to any office of honor, profit, or trust, civil or military (members of the legislature excepted), shall, until the legislature shall otherwise provide and direct, enter on the execution of his office, or be he any respect competent to discharge the duties thereof until he shall, in like manner, have taken a similar oath; and no juror shall be impaneled in any of the courts of this State, in any cause in which shall be in question this ordinance, or any act of the legislature passed in pursuance thereof, unless he shall first, in addition to the usual oath, have taken an oath that he will well and truly obey, execute, and enforce this ordinance, and such act or acts of the legislature as may be passed to carry the same into operation and effect, according to the true intent and meaning thereof.

And we, the people of South Carolina, to the end that it may be fully understood by the government of the United States, and the people of the co-States, that we are determined to maintain this our ordinance and declaration, at every hazard, do further declare that we will not submit to the application of force on the part of the federal government, to reduce this State to obedience, but that we will consider the passage, by Congress, of any act authorizing the employment of a military or naval force against the State of South Carolina, her constitutional authorities or citizens; or any act abolishing or closing the ports of this State, or any of them, or otherwise obstructing the free ingress and egress of vessels to and from the said ports, or any other act on the part of the federal government, to coerce the State, shut up her ports, destroy or harass her commerce or to enforce the acts hereby declared to be null and void, otherwise than through the civil tribunals of the country, as inconsistent with the longer continuance of South Carolina in the Union; and that the people of this State will henceforth hold themselves absolved from all further obligation to maintain or preserve their political connection with the people of the other States; and will forthwith proceed to organize a separate government, and do all other acts and things which sovereign and independent States may of right do.

ANDREW JACKSON, "PROCLAMATION REGARDING NULLIFICATION"[35]

. . . The ordinance is founded, not on the indefeasible right of resisting acts which are plainly unconstitutional, and too oppressive to be endured, but on the strange position that any one State may not only declare an act of Congress void, but prohibit its execution—that they may do this consistently with the Constitution—that the true construction of that instrument permits a State to retain its place in the Union, and yet be bound by no other of its laws than those it may choose to consider as constitutional. It is true they add, that to justify this abrogation of a law, it must be palpably contrary to the Constitution, but it is evident, that to give the right of resisting laws of that description, coupled with the uncontrolled right to decide what laws deserve that character, is to give the power of resisting all laws. For, as by the theory, there is no appeal, the reasons alleged by the State, good or bad, must prevail. If it should be said that public opinion is a sufficient check against the abuse of this power, it may be asked why it is not deemed a sufficient guard against the passage of an unconstitutional act by Congress. There is, however, a restraint in this last case, which makes the assumed power of a State more indefensible, and which does not exist in the other. There are two appeals from an unconstitutional act passed by Congress-one to the judiciary, the other to the people and the States. There is no appeal from the State decision in theory; and the practical illustration shows that the courts are closed against an application to review it, both judges and jurors being sworn to decide in its favor. But reasoning on this subject is superfluous, when our social compact in express terms declares, that the laws of the United States, its Constitution, and treaties made under it, are the supreme law of the land; and for greater caution adds, "that the judges in every State shall be bound thereby, anything in the Constitution or laws of any State to the contrary notwithstanding." And it may be asserted, without fear of refutation, that no federative government could exist without a similar provision.

. . . If the doctrine of a State veto upon the laws of the Union carries with it internal evidence of its impracticable absurdity, our constitutional history will also afford abundant proof that it would have been repudiated with indignation had it been proposed to form a feature in our Government.

In our colonial state, although dependent on another power, we very early considered ourselves as connected by common interest with each other. Leagues were formed for common defense, and before the Declaration of Independence, we were known in our aggregate character as the United Colonies of America. That decisive and important step was taken jointly. We declared ourselves a nation by a joint, not by several acts; and when the terms of our confederation were reduced to form, it was in that of a solemn league of several States, by which they agreed that they would, collectively, form one nation, for the purpose of conducting some certain domestic concerns, and all foreign relations. In the instrument forming that Union, is found an article which declares that "every State shall abide by the determinations of Congress on all questions which by that Confederation should be submitted to them."

Under the Confederation, then, no State could legally annul a decision of the Congress, or refuse to submit to its execution, but no provision was made to enforce these decisions. Congress made requisitions, but they were not complied with. The Government could not operate on individuals. They had no judiciary, no means of collecting revenue.

But the defects of the Confederation need not be detailed. Under its operation we could scarcely be called a nation. We had neither prosperity at home nor consideration abroad. This state of things could not be endured, and our present happy Constitution was formed, but formed in vain, if this fatal doctrine prevails. It was formed for important objects that are announced in the preamble made in the name and by the authority of the people of the United States, whose delegates framed, and whose conventions approved it.

The most important among these objects, that which is placed first in rank, on which all the others rest, is *"to form a more perfect Union."* Now, is it possible that, even if there were no express provision giving supremacy to the Constitution and laws of the United States over those of the States, it can be conceived that an Instrument made for the purpose of *"forming; a more perfect Union"* than that of the confederation, could be so constructed by the assembled wisdom of our country as to substitute for that confederation a form of government, dependent for its existence on the local interest, the party spirit of a State, or of a prevailing faction in a State? Every man, of plain, unsophisticated understanding, who hears the question, will give such an answer as will preserve the Union. Metaphysical subtlety, in pursuit of an impracticable theory, could alone have devised one that is calculated to destroy it.

I consider, then, the power to annul a law of the United States, assumed by one State, *incompatible with the existence of the Union, contradicted expressly by the letter of the Constitution, unauthorized by its spirit, inconsistent with every principle on which It was founded, and destructive of the great object for which it was formed.*

After this general view of the leading principle, we must examine the particular application of it which is made in the ordinance.

The preamble rests its justification on these grounds: It assumes as a fact, that the obnoxious laws, although they purport to be laws for raising revenue, were in reality intended for the protection of manufactures, which purpose it asserts to be unconstitutional; that the operation of these laws is unequal, that the amount raised by them is greater than is required by the wants of the Government; and, finally, that the proceeds are to be applied to objects unauthorized by the Constitution. These are the only causes alleged to justify an open opposition to the laws of the country, and a threat of seceding from the Union, if any attempt should be made to enforce them. The first virtually acknowledges that the law in question was passed under a power expressly given by the Constitution, to lay and collect imposts, but its constitutionality is drawn in question from the motives of those who passed it. However apparent this purpose may be in the present case, nothing can be more dangerous than to admit the position that an unconstitutional purpose, entertained by the members who assent to a law enacted under a constitutional power, shall make that law void; for how is that purpose to be ascertained? Who is to make the scrutiny? How often may bad purposes be falsely imputed? In how many cases are they concealed by false professions? In how many is no declaration of motive made? Admit this doctrine and you give to the States an uncontrolled right to decide, and every law may be annulled under this pretext. If, therefore, the absurd and dangerous doctrine should be admitted, that a State may annul an unconstitutional law, or one that it deems such, it will not apply to the present case.

The next objection is, that the laws in question operate unequally. This objection may be made with truth to every law that has been or can be passed. The wisdom of man never yet contrived a system of taxation that would operate with perfect equality. If the unequal operation of a law makes it unconstitutional and if all laws of that description may be abrogated by any State for that cause, then, indeed, is the federal Constitution unworthy of the slightest effort for its preservation. We have hitherto relied on it as the perpetual bond of our Union. We have received it as the work of the assembled wisdom of the nation We have trusted to it as to the sheet-anchor of our safety, in the stormy times of conflict with a foreign or domestic foe. We have looked to it with sacred awe as the palladium of our liberties, and with all the solemnities of religion have pledged to each other our lives and fortunes here, and our hopes of happiness hereafter, in its defense and support. Were we mistaken, my countrymen, in attaching this importance to the Constitution of our country? Was our devotion paid to the wretched, inefficient, clumsy contrivance, which this new doctrine would make it? Did we pledge ourselves to the support of an airy nothing-a bubble that must be blown away by the first breath of disaffection? Was this self-destroying, visionary theory the work of the profound statesmen, the exalted patriots, to whom the task of constitutional reform was intrusted? Did the name of Washington sanction, did the States deliberately ratify, such an anomaly in the history of fundamental legislation? No. We were not mistaken. The letter of this great instrument is free from this radical fault; its language directly contradicts the imputation, its spirit, its evident intent, contradicts it. No, we did not err. Our Constitution does not contain the absurdity of giving power to make laws, and another power to resist them. The sages, whose memory will always be reverenced, have given us a practical, and, as they hoped, a permanent constitutional compact. The Father of his Country did not affix his revered name to so palpable an absurdity. Nor did the States, when they severally ratified it, do so under the impression that a veto on the laws of the United States was reserved to them, or that they could exercise it by application. Search the debates in all their conventions-examine the speeches of the most zealous opposers of federal authority-look at the amendments that were proposed. They are all silent— not a syllable uttered, not a vote given, not a motion made, to correct the explicit supremacy given to the laws of the Union over those of the States, or to show that implication, as is now contended, could defeat it. No, we have not erred! The Constitution is still the object of our reverence, the bond of our Union, our defense in danger, the source of our prosperity in peace. It shall descend, as we have received it, uncorrupted by sophistical construction to our posterity; and the sacrifices of local interest, of State prejudices, of personal animosities, that were made to bring it into existence, will again be patriotically offered for its support.

. . . In vain have these sages declared that Congress shall have power to lay and collect taxes, duties, imposts, and excises-in vain have they provided that they shall have power to pass laws which shall be necessary and proper to carry those powers into execution, that those laws and that Constitution shall be the "supreme law of the land; that the judges in every State shall be bound thereby, anything in the constitution or laws of any State to the contrary not-withstanding." In vain have the people of the several States solemnly sanctioned these provisions, made them their paramount law, and individually sworn to support them whenever they were called on to execute any office.

Vain provisions! Ineffectual restrictions! Vile profanation of oaths! Miserable mockery of legislation! If a bare majority of the voters in any one State may, on a real or supposed knowledge of the intent with which a law has been passed, declare themselves free from its operation—say here it gives too little, there too much, and operates unequally—here it suffers articles to be free that ought to be taxed, there it taxes those that ought to be free-in this case the proceeds are intended to be applied to purposes which we do not approve, in that the amount raised is more than is wanted. Congress, it is true, are invested by the Constitution with the right of deciding these questions according to their sound discretion. Congress is composed of the representatives of all the States, and of all the people of all the states; but WE, part of the people of one State, to whom the Constitution has given no power on the subject from whom it has expressly taken it away-we, who have solemnly agreed that this Constitution shall be our law-we, most of whom have sworn to support it-we now abrogate this law, and swear, and force others to swear, that it shall not be obeyed-and we do this, not because Congress have no right to pass such laws; this we do not allege; but because they have passed them with improper views. They are unconstitutional from the motives of those who passed them, which we can never with certainty know, from their unequal operation; although it is impossible from the nature of things that they should be equal-and from the disposition which we presume may be made of their proceeds, although that disposition has not been declared. This is the plain meaning of the ordinance in relation to laws which it abrogates for alleged unconstitutionality. But it does not stop here. It repeals, in express terms, an important part of the Constitution itself, and of laws passed to give it effect, which have never been alleged to be unconstitutional. The Constitution declares that the judicial powers of the United States extend to cases arising under the laws of the United States, and that such laws, the Constitution and treaties, shall be paramount to the State constitutions and laws. The judiciary act prescribes the mode by which the case may be brought before a court of the United States, by appeal, when a State tribunal shall decide against this provision of the Constitution. The ordinance declares there shall be no appeal; makes the State law paramount to the Constitution and laws of the United States; forces judges and jurors to swear that they will disregard their provisions; and even makes it penal in a suitor to attempt relief by appeal. It further declares that it shall not be lawful for the authorities of the United States, or of that State, to enforce the payment of duties imposed by the revenue laws within its limits.

. . . This right to secede is deduced from the nature of the Constitution, which they say is a compact between sovereign States who have preserved their whole sovereignty, and therefore are subject to no superior; that because they made the compact, they can break it when in their opinion it has been departed from by the other States. Fallacious as this course of reasoning is, it enlists State pride, and finds advocates in the honest prejudices of those who have not studied the nature of our government sufficiently to see the radical error on which it rests.

The people of the United States formed the Constitution, acting through the State legislatures, in making the compact, to meet and discuss its provisions, and acting in separate conventions when they ratified those provisions; but the terms used in its construction show it to be a government in which the people of all the States collectively are represented. We are ONE PEOPLE in the choice of the President and Vice President. Here the States have no other agency than to direct the mode in which the vote shall be given. The candidates having the majority of all the votes are chosen. The electors of a majority of States may have given their votes for one candidate, and yet another may be chosen. The people, then, and not the States, are represented in the executive branch.

. . . The Constitution of the United States, then, forms a government, not a league, and whether it be formed by compact between the States, or in any other manner, its character is the same. It is a government in which all the people are represented, which operates directly on the people individually, not upon the States; they retained all the power they did not grant. But each State having expressly parted with so many powers as to constitute jointly with the other States a single nation, cannot from that period possess any right to secede, because such secession does not break a league, but destroys the unity of a nation, and any injury to that unity is not only a breach which would result from the contravention of a compact, but it is an offense against the whole Union. To say that any State may at pleasure secede from the Union, is to say that the United States are not a nation because it would be a solecism to contend that any part of a nation might dissolve its connection with the other parts, to their injury or ruin, without committing any offense. Secession, like any other revolutionary act, may be morally justified by the extremity of oppression; but to call it a constitutional right, is confounding the meaning of terms, and can only be done through gross error, or to deceive those who are willing to assert a right, but would pause before they made a revolution, or incur the penalties consequent upon a failure.

Because the Union was formed by compact, it is said the parties to that compact may, when they feel themselves aggrieved, depart from it; but it is precisely because it is a compact that they cannot. A compact is an agreement or binding obligation. It may by its terms have a sanction or penalty for its breach, or it may not. If it contains no sanction, it may be broken with no other consequence than moral guilt; if it have a sanction, then the breach incurs the designated or implied penalty. A league between independent nations, generally, has no sanction other than a moral one; or if it should contain a penalty, as there is no common superior, it cannot be enforced. A government, on the contrary, always has a sanction, express or implied; and, in our case, it is both necessarily implied and expressly given. An attempt by force of arms to destroy a government is an offense, by whatever means the constitutional compact may have been formed; and such government has the right, by the law of self-defense, to pass acts for punishing the offender, unless that right is modified, restrained, or resumed by the constitutional act. In our system, although it is modified in the case of treason, yet authority is expressly given to pass all laws necessary to carry its powers into effect, and under this grant provision has been made for punishing acts which obstruct the due administration of the laws.

. . . The States severally have not retained their entire sovereignty. It has been shown that in becoming parts of a nation, not members of a league, they surrendered many of their essential parts of sovereignty. The right to make treaties, declare war, levy taxes, exercise exclusive judicial and legislative powers, were all functions of sovereign power. The States, then, for all these important purposes, were no longer sovereign. The allegiance of their citizens was transferred in the first instance to the government of the United States; they became American citizens, and owed obedience to the Constitution of the United States, and to laws made in conformity with the powers vested in Congress. This last position has not been, and cannot be, denied. How then, can that State be said to be sovereign and independent whose citizens owe obedience to laws not made by it, and whose magistrates are sworn to disregard those laws, when they come in conflict with those passed by another? What shows conclusively that the States cannot be said to have reserved an undivided sovereignty, is that they expressly ceded the right to punish treason-not treason against their separate power, but treason against the United States. Treason is an offense against sovereignty, and sovereignty must reside with the power to punish it. But the reserved rights of the States are not less sacred because they have for their common interest made the general government the depository of these powers. The unity of our political character (as has been shown for another purpose) commenced with its very existence. Under the royal government we had no separate character; our opposition to its oppression began as UNITED COLONIES. We were the UNITED STATES under the Confederation, and the name was perpetuated and the Union rendered more perfect by the federal Constitution. In none of these stages did we consider ourselves in any other light than as forming one nation. Treaties and alliances were made in the name of all. Troops were raised for the joint defense. How, then, with all these proofs, that under all changes of our position we had, for designated purposes and with defined powers, created national governments-how is it that the most perfect of these several modes of union should now be considered as a mere league that may be dissolved at pleasure ? It is from an abuse of terms. Compact is used as synonymous with league, although the true term is not employed, because it would at once show the fallacy of the reasoning. It would not do to say that our Constitution was only a league, but it is labored to prove it a compact (which, in one sense, it is), and then to argue that as a league is a compact, every compact between nations must, of course, be a league, and that from such an engagement every sovereign power has a right to recede. But it has been shown that in this sense the States are not sovereign, and that even if they were, and the national

Constitution had been formed by compact, there would be no right in any one State to exonerate itself from the obligation.

So obvious are the reasons which forbid this secession, that it is necessary only to allude to them. The Union was formed for the benefit of all. It was produced by mutual sacrifice of interest and opinions. Can those sacrifices be recalled? Can the States, who magnanimously surrendered their title to the territories of the West, recall the grant? Will the inhabitants of the inland States agree to pay the duties that may be imposed without their assent by those on the Atlantic or the Gulf, for their own benefit? Shall there be a free port in one State, and enormous duties in another? No one believes that any right exists in a single State to involve all the others in these and countless other evils, contrary to engagements solemnly made. Everyone must see that the other States, in self-defense, must oppose it at all hazards.

These are the alternatives that are presented by the convention: A repeal of all the acts for raising revenue, leaving the government without the means of support; or an acquiescence in the dissolution of our Union by the secession of one of its members. When the first was proposed, it was known that it could not be listened to for a moment. It was known if force was applied to oppose the execution of the laws, that it must be repelled by force-that Congress could not, without involving itself in disgrace and the country in ruin, accede to the proposition; and yet if this is not done in a given day, or if any attempt is made to execute the laws, the State is, by the ordinance, declared to be out of the Union. The majority of a convention assembled for the purpose have dictated these terms, or rather this rejection of all terms, in the name of the people of South Carolina. It is true that the governor of the State speaks of the submission of their grievances to a convention of all the States; which, he says, they "sincerely and anxiously seek and desire." Yet this obvious and constitutional mode of obtaining the sense of the other States on the construction of the federal compact, and amending it, if necessary, has never been attempted by those who have urged the State on to this destructive measure. The State might have proposed a call for a general convention to the other States, and Congress, if a sufficient number of them concurred, must have called it. But the first magistrate of South Carolina, when he expressed a hope that "on a review by Congress and the functionaries of the general government of the merits of the controversy," such a convention will be accorded to them, must have known that neither Congress, nor any functionary in the general government, has authority to call such a convention, unless it be demanded by two-thirds of the States. This suggestion, then, is another instance of the reckless inattention to the provisions of the Constitution with which this crisis has been madly hurried on; or of the attempt to persuade the people that a constitutional remedy has been sought and refused. If the legislature of South Carolina "anxiously desire" a general convention to consider their complaints, why have they not made application for it in the way the Constitution points out? The assertion that they "earnestly seek" is completely negatived by the omission.

This, then, is the position in which we stand. A small majority of the citizens of one State in the Union have elected delegates to a State convention; that convention has ordained that all the revenue laws of the United States must be repealed, or that they are no longer a member of the Union. The governor of that State has recommended to the legislature the raising of an army to carry the secession into effect, and that he may be empowered to give clearances to vessels in the name of the State. No act of violent opposition to the laws has yet been committed, but such a state of things is hourly apprehended, and it is the intent of this instrument to PROCLAIM, not only that the duty imposed on me by the Constitution, "to take care that the laws be faithfully executed," shall be performed to the extent of the powers already vested in me by law or of such others as the wisdom of Congress shall devise and Entrust to me for that purpose; but to warn the citizens of South Carolina, who have been deluded into an opposition to the laws, of the danger they will incur by obedience to the illegal and disorganizing ordinance of the convention—to exhort those who have refused to support it to persevere in their determination to uphold the Constitution and laws of their country, and to point out to all the perilous situation into which the good people of that State have been led, and that the course they are urged to pursue is one of ruin and disgrace to the very State whose rights they affect to support.

. . . Your pride was aroused by the assertions that a submission to these laws was a state of vassalage, and that resistance to them was equal, in patriotic merit, to the opposition our fathers offered to the oppressive laws of Great Britain. You were told that this opposition might be peaceably—might be constitutionally made—that you might enjoy all the advantages of the Union and bear none of its burdens. Eloquent appeals to your passions, to your State pride, to your native courage, to your sense of real injury, were used to prepare you for the period when the mask which concealed the hideous features of DISUNION should be taken off. It fell, and you were made to look with complacency on objects which not long since you would have regarded with horror. Look back to the arts which have brought you to this state-look forward to the consequences to which it must inevitably lead! Look back to what was first told you as an inducement to enter into this dangerous course. The great political truth was repeated to you that you had the revolutionary right of resisting all laws that were palpably unconstitutional and intolerably oppressive-it was added that the right to nullify a law rested on the same principle, but that it was a peaceable remedy! This character which was given to it, made you receive with too much confidence the assertions that were made of the unconstitutionality of the law and its oppressive effects. Mark, my fellow-citizens, that by the admission of your leaders the unconstitutionality must be *palpable*, or it will not justify either resistance or nullification! What is the meaning of the word *palpable* in the sense in which it is here used? that which is apparent to everyone, that which no man of ordinary intellect will fail to perceive. Is the unconstitutionality of these laws of that description? Let those among your leaders who once approved and advocated the principles of protective duties, answer the question; and let them choose whether they will be considered as incapable, then, of perceiving that which must have been apparent to every man of common understanding, or as imposing upon your confidence and endeavoring to mislead you now. In either case, they are unsafe guides in the perilous path they urge you to tread. Ponder well on this circumstance, and you will know how to appreciate the exaggerated language they address to you. They are not champions of liberty emulating the fame of our Revolutionary fathers, nor are you an oppressed people, contending, as they repeat to you, against worse than colonial vassalage. You are free members of a flourishing and happy Union. There is no settled design to oppress you. You have, indeed, felt the unequal operation of laws which may have been unwisely, not unconstitutionally passed; but that inequality must necessarily be removed. At the very moment when you were madly urged on to the unfortunate course you have begun, a change in public opinion has commenced. The nearly approaching payment of the public debt, and the consequent necessity of a diminution of duties, had already caused a considerable reduction, and that, too, on some articles of general consumption in your State. The importance of this change was underrated, and you were authoritatively told that no further alleviation of your burdens was to be expected, at the very time when the condition of the country imperiously demanded such a modification of the duties as should reduce them to a just and equitable scale. But as apprehensive of the effect of this change in allaying your discontents, you were precipitated into the fearful state in which you now find yourselves.

I have urged you to look back to the means that were used to burly you on to the position you have now assumed, and forward to the consequences they will produce. Something more is necessary. Contemplate the condition of that country of which you still form an important part; consider its government uniting in one bond of common interest and general protection so many different States—giving to all their inhabitants the proud title of AMERICAN CITIZEN—protecting their commerce-securing their literature and arts—facilitating their intercommunication—defending their frontiers—and making their name respected in the remotest parts of the earth! Consider the extent of its territory its increasing and happy population, its advance in arts, which render life agreeable, and the sciences which elevate the mind! See education spreading the lights of religion, morality, and general information into every cottage in this wide extent of our Territories and States! Behold it as the asylum where the wretched and the oppressed find a refuge and support! Look on this picture of happiness and honor, and say, WE TOO, ARE CITIZENS OF AMERICA—Carolina is one of these proud States her arms have defended-her best blood has cemented this happy Union! And then add, if you can, without horror and remorse this happy Union we will dissolve—this picture of peace and prosperity we will deface—this free intercourse we will interrupt—these fertile fields we will deluge with blood-the protection of that glorious flag we renounce—the very name of Americans we discard. And for what, mistaken men! For what do you throw away these inestimable blessings-for what would you exchange your share in the advantages and honor of the Union? For the dream of a separate independence-a dream interrupted by bloody conflicts with your neighbors, and a vile dependence on a foreign power. If your leaders could succeed in establishing a separation, what would be your situation? Are you united at home—are you free from the apprehension of civil discord, with all its fearful consequences? Do our neighboring republics, every day suffering some new revolution or contending with some new insurrection—do they excite your envy? But the dictates of a high duty oblige me solemnly to announce that you cannot succeed. The laws of the United States must be executed. I have no discretionary power on the subject-my duty is emphatically pronounced in the Constitution. Those who told you that you might peaceably prevent their execution, deceived you-they could not have been deceived themselves. They know that a forcible opposition could alone prevent the execution of the laws, and they know that such opposition must be repelled. Their object is disunion, hut be not deceived by names; disunion, by armed force, is TREASON. Are you really ready to incur its guilt? If you are, on the head of the instigators of the act be the dreadful consequences-on their heads be the dishonor, but on yours may fall the punishment-on your unhappy State will inevitably fall all the evils of the conflict you force upon the government of your country. It cannot accede to the mad project of disunion, of which you would be the first victims-its first magistrate cannot, if he would, avoid the performance of his duty-the consequence must be fearful for you, distressing to your fellow-citizens here, and to the friends of good government throughout the world. Its enemies have beheld our prosperity with a vexation they could not conceal—it was a standing refutation of their slavish doctrines, and they will point to our discord with the triumph of malignant joy. It is yet in your power to disappoint them. There is yet time to show that the descendants of the Pinckneys, the Sumpters, the Rutledges, and of the thousand other names which adorn the pages of your Revolutionary history, will not abandon that Union to support which so many of them fought and bled and died. I adjure you, as you honor their memory—as you love the cause of freedom, to which they dedicated their lives—as you prize the peace of your country, the lives of its best citizens, and your own fair fame, to retrace your steps. Snatch from the archives of your State the disorganizing edict of its convention—hid its members to re-assemble and promulgate the decided expressions of your will to remain in the path which alone can conduct you to safety, prosperity, and honor—tell them that compared to disunion, all other evils are light, because that brings with it an accumulation of all-declare that you will never take the field unless the star-spangled banner of your country shall float over you—that you will not be stigmatized when dead, and dishonored and scorned while you live, as the authors of the first attack on the Constitution of your country!-its destroy-ers you cannot be. You may disturb its peace-you may interrupt the course of its prosperity-you may cloud its reputation for stability—but its tranquillity will be restored, its prosperity will return, and the stain upon its national char-acter will be transferred and remain an eternal blot on the memory of those who caused the disorder.

Fellow-citizens of the United States! the threat of unhallowed disunion-the names of those, once respected, by whom it is uttered—the array of military force to support it-denote the approach of a crisis in our affairs on which the continuance of our unexampled prosperity, our political existence, and perhaps that of all free governments, may depend. The con-juncture demanded a free, a full, and explicit enunciation, not only of my intentions, but of my principles of action, and as the claim was asserted of a right by a State to annul the laws of the Union, and even to secede from it at pleasure, a frank exposition of my opinions in relation to the origin and form of our government, and the construction I give to the instrument by which it was created, seemed to be proper. Having the fullest confidence in the justness of the legal and constitutional opinion of my duties which has been expressed, I rely with equal confidence on your undivided support in my determination to execute the laws-to preserve the Union by all constitutional means—to arrest, if possible, by moderate but firm measures, the necessity of a recourse to force; and, if it be the will of Heaven that the recurrence of its primeval curse on man for the shedding of a brother's blood should fall upon our land, that it be not called down by any offensive act on the part of the United States.

Fellow-citizens! the momentous case is before you. On your undivided support of your government depends the decision of the great question it involves, whether your sacred Union will be preserved, and the blessing it secures to us as one people shall be perpetuated. No one can doubt that the unanimity with which that decision will be expressed, will he such as to inspire new confidence in republican institutions, and that the prudence, the wisdom, and the courage which it will bring to their defense, will transmit them unimpaired and invigorated to our children.

May the Great Ruler of nations grant that the signal blessings with which he has favored ours may not, by the madness of party or personal ambition, be disregarded and lost, and may His wise providence bring those who have produced this crisis to see the folly, before they feel the misery, of civil strife, and inspire a returning veneration for that Union which, if we may dare to penetrate his designs, he has chosen, as the only means of attaining the high destinies to which we may reasonably aspire.

ANDREW JACKSON, INTERNAL IMPROVEMENTS VETO[36]

The constitutional power of the Federal Government to construct or promote works of internal improvement presents itself in two points of view—the first as bearing upon the sovereignty of the States within whose limits their execution is contemplated, if jurisdiction of the territory which they may occupy be claimed as necessary to their preservation and use; the second as asserting the simple right to appropriate money from the National Treasury in aid of such works when undertaken by State authority, surrendering the claim of jurisdiction. In the first view the question of power is an open one, and can be decided without the embarrassments attending the other, arising from the practice of the Government. Although frequently and strenuously attempted, the power to this extent has never been exercised by the Government in a single instance. It does not, in my opinion, possess it; and no bill, therefore, which admits it can receive my official sanction.

. . . The bill before me does not call for a more definite opinion upon the particular circumstances which will warrant appropriations of money by Congress to aid works of internal improvement, for although the extension of the power to apply money beyond that of carrying into effect the object for which it is appropriated has, as we have seen, been long claimed and exercised by the Federal Government, yet such grants have always been professedly under the control of the general principle that the works which might be thus aided should be "of a general, not local, national, not State," character. A disregard of this distinction would of necessity lead to the subversion of the federal system. That even this is an unsafe one, arbitrary in its nature, and liable, consequently, to great abuses, is too obvious to require the confirmation of experience.

Considering the magnitude and importance of the power, and the embarrassments to which, from the very nature of the thing, its exercise must necessarily be subjected, the real friends of internal improvement ought not to be willing to confide it to accident and chance. What is properly national in its character or otherwise is an inquiry which is often extremely difficult of solution. The appropriations of one year for an object which is considered national may be rendered nugatory by the refusal of a succeeding Congress to continue the work on the ground that it is local. No aid can be derived from the intervention of corporations. The question regards the character of the work, not that of those by whom it is to be accomplished. Notwithstanding the union of the Government with the corporation by whose immediate agency any work of internal improvement is carried on, the inquiry will still remain. Is it national and conducive to the benefit of the whole, or local and operating only to the advantage of a portion of the Union?

. . . Although many of the States, with a laudable zeal and under the influence of an enlightened policy, are successfully applying their separate efforts to works of this character, the desire to enlist the aid of the General Government in the construction of such as from their nature ought to devolve upon it, and to which the means of the individual States are inadequate, is both rational and patriotic, and if that desire is not gratified now it does not follow that it never will be.

ANDREW JACKSON VETO MESSAGE REGARDING THE BANK OF THE UNITED STATES[37]

. . . If the opinion of the Supreme Court covered the whole ground of this act, it ought not to control the coordinate authorities of this Government. The Congress, the Executive, and the Court must each for itself be guided by its own opinion of the Constitution . . . The authority of the Supreme Court must not, therefore, be permitted to control the Congress or the Executive when acting in their legislative capacities, but to have only such influence as the force of their reasoning may deserve.

. . . The several States reserved the power at the formation of the Constitution to regulate and control titles and transfers of real property, and most, if not all, of them have laws disqualifying aliens from acquiring or holding lands within their limits. But this act, in disregard of the undoubted right of the States to prescribe such disqualifications, gives to aliens stockholders in this bank an interest and title, as members of the corporation, to all the real property it may acquire within any of the States of this Union. This privilege granted to aliens is not "necessary" to enable the bank to perform its public duties, nor in any sense "proper," because it is vitally subversive of the rights of the States.

. . . By its silence, considered in connection with the decision of the Supreme Court in the case of McCulloch against the State of Maryland, this act takes from the States the power to tax a portion of the banking business carried on within their limits, in subversion of one of the strongest barriers which secured them against Federal encroachments. Banking, like farming, manufacturing, or any other occupation or profession, is a business, the right to follow which is not originally derived from the laws. Every citizen and every company of citizens in all of our States possessed the right until the State legislatures deemed it good policy to prohibit private banking by law. If the prohibitory State laws were now repealed, every citizen would again possess the right. The State banks are a qualified restoration of the right which has been taken away by the laws against banking, guarded by such provisions and limitations as in the opinion of the State legislatures the public interest requires. These corporations, unless there be an exemption in their charter, are, like private bankers and banking companies, subject to State taxation. The manner in which these taxes shall be laid depends wholly on legislative discretion. It may be upon the bank, upon the stock, upon the profits, or in any other mode which the sovereign power shall will.

Upon the formation of the Constitution the States guarded their taxing power with peculiar jealousy. They surrendered it only as it regards imports and exports. In relation to every other object within their jurisdiction, whether persons, property, business, or professions, it was secured in as ample a manner as it was before possessed. All persons, though United States officers, are liable to a poll tax by the States within which they reside. The lands of the United States are liable to the usual land tax, except in the new States, from whom agreements that they will not tax unsold lands are exacted when they are admitted into the Union. Horses, wagons, any beasts or vehicles, tools, or property belonging to private citizens, though employed in the service of the United States, are subject to State taxation. Every private business, whether carried on by an officer of the General Government or not, whether it be mixed with public concerns or not, even if it be carried on by the Government of the United States itself, separately or in partnership, falls within the scope of the taxing power of the State. Nothing comes more fully within it than banks and the business of banking, by whomsoever instituted and carried on. Over this whole subject-matter it is just as absolute, unlimited, and uncontrollable as if the Constitution had never been adopted, because in the formation of that instrument it was reserved without qualification.

The principle is conceded that the States can not rightfully tax the operations of the General Government. They can not tax the money of the Government deposited in the State banks, nor the agency of those banks in remitting it; but will any man maintain that their mere selection to perform this public service for the General Government would exempt the State banks and their ordinary business from State taxation? Had the United States, instead of establishing a bank at Philadelphia, employed a private banker to keep and transmit their funds, would it have deprived Pennsylvania of the right to tax his bank and his usual banking operations? It will not be pretended. Upon what principal, then, are the banking establishments of the Bank of the United States and their usual banking operations to be exempted from taxation ? It is not their public agency or the deposits of the Government which the States claim a right to tax, but their banks and their banking powers, instituted and exercised within State jurisdiction for their private emolument-those powers and privileges for which they pay a bonus, and which the States tax in their own banks. The exercise of these powers within a State, no matter by whom or under what authority, whether by private citizens in their original right, by corporate bodies created by the States, by foreigners or the agents of foreign governments located within their limits, forms a legitimate object of State taxation. From this and like sources, from the persons, property, and business that are found residing, located, or carried on under their jurisdiction, must the States, since the surrender of their right to raise a revenue from imports and exports, draw all the money necessary for the support of their governments and the maintenance of their independence. There is no more appropriate subject of taxation than banks, banking, and bank stocks, and none to which the States ought more pertinaciously to cling.

It can not be necessary to the character of the bank as a fiscal agent of the Government that its private business should be exempted from that taxation to which all the State banks are liable, nor can I conceive it "proper" that the substantive and most essential powers reserved by the States shall be thus attacked and annihilated as a means of executing the powers delegated to the General Government. It may be safely assumed that none of those sages who had an agency in forming or adopting our Constitution ever imagined that any portion of the taxing power of the States not prohibited to them nor delegated to Congress was to be swept away and annihilated as a means of executing certain powers delegated to Congress.

If our power over means is so absolute that the Supreme Court will not call in question the constitutionality of an act of Congress the subject of which "is not prohibited, and is really calculated to effect any of the objects intrusted to the Government," although, as in the case before me, it takes away powers expressly granted to Congress and rights scrupulously reserved to the States, it becomes us to proceed in our legislation with the utmost caution. Though not directly, our own powers and the rights of the States may be indirectly legislated away in the use of means to execute substantive powers. We may not enact that Congress shall not have the power of exclusive legislation over the District of Columbia, but we may pledge the faith of the United States that as a means of executing other powers it shall not be exercised for twenty years or forever. We may not pass an act prohibiting the States to tax the banking business carried on within their limits, but we may, as a means of executing our powers over other objects, place that business in the hands of our agents and then declare it exempt from State taxation in their hands. Thus may our own powers and the rights of the States, which we can not directly curtail or invade, be frittered away and extinguished in the use of means employed by us to execute other powers. That a bank of the United States, competent to all the duties which may be required by the Government, might be so organized as not to infringe on our own delegated powers or the reserved rights of the States I do not entertain a doubt. Had the Executive been called upon to furnish the project of such an institution, the duty would have been cheerfully performed. In the absence of such a call it was obviously proper that he should confine himself to pointing out those prominent features in the act presented which in his opinion make it incompatible with the Constitution and sound policy. A general discussion will now take place, eliciting new light and settling important principles; and a new Congress, elected in the midst of such discussion, and furnishing an equal representation of the people according to the last census, will bear to the Capitol the verdict of public opinion, and, I doubt not, bring this important question to a satisfactory result.

. . . Nor is our Government to be maintained or our Union preserved by invasions of the rights and powers of the several States. In thus attempting to make our General Government strong we make it weak. Its true strength consists in leaving individuals and States as much as possible to themselves—in making itself felt, not in its power, but in its beneficence; not in its control, but in its protection; not in binding the States more closely to the center, but leaving each to move unobstructed in its proper orbit.

JOHN C. CALHOUN, *A DISCOURSE ON THE CONSTITUTION AND GOVERNMENT OF THE UNITED STATES*[38]

Ours is a system of governments, compounded of the separate governments of the several States composing the Union, and of one common government of all its members, called the Government of the United States. The former preceded the latter, which was created by their agency. Each was framed by written constitutions; those of the several States by the people of each, acting separately, and in their sovereign character; and that of the United States, by the same, acting in the same character—but jointly instead of separately. All were formed on the same model. They all divide the powers of government into legislative, executive, and judicial; and are founded on the great principle of the responsibility of the rulers to the ruled. The entire powers of government are divided between the two; those of a more general character being specifically delegated to the United States; and all others not delegated, being reserved to the several States in their separate character. Each, within its appropriate sphere, possesses all the attributes, and performs all the functions of government. Neither is perfect without the other. The two combined, form one entire and perfect government. With these preliminary remarks, I shall proceed to the consideration of the immediate subject of this discourse.

The Government of the United States was formed by the Constitution of the United States—and ours is a democratic, federal republic.

It is federal, because it is the government of States united in political union, in contradistinction to a government of individuals socially united; that is, by what is usually called, a social compact. To express it more concisely, it is federal and not national, because it is the government of a community of States, and not the government of a single State or nation.

That it is federal and not national, we have the high authority of the convention which framed it. General Washington, as its organ, in his letter submitting the plan to the consideration of the Congress of the then confederacy, calls it, in one place—"the general government of the Union"—and in another—"the federal government of these States." Taken together, the plain meaning is, that the government proposed would be, if adopted, the government of the States adopting it, in their united character as members of a common Union; and, as such, would be a federal government. These expressions were not used without due consideration, and an accurate and full knowledge of their true import. The subject was not a novel one. The convention was familiar with it. It was much agitated in their deliberations. They divided, in reference to it, in the early stages of their proceedings. At first, one party was in favor of a national and the other of a federal government. The former, in the beginning, prevailed; and in the plans which they proposed, the constitution and government are styled "National." But, finally, the latter gained the ascendency, when the term "National" was superseded, and *"United States"* substituted in its place. The constitution was accordingly styled— *"The constitution of the United States of America"*—and the government— *"The government of the United States"* leaving out "America," for the sake of brevity. It cannot admit of a doubt, that the Convention, by the expression "United States," meant the States united in a federal Union; for in no other sense could they, with propriety, call the government, *"the federal government of these States"*—and *"the general government of the Union"*—as they did in the letter referred to. It is thus clear, that the Convention regarded the different expressions—"the federal government of the United States"— "the general government of the Union"—and—"government of the United States"—as meaning the same thing—a federal, in contradistinction to a national government.

The style of the present constitution and government is precisely the style by which the confederacy that existed when it was adopted, and which it superseded, was designated. The instrument that formed the latter was called—"Articles of Confederation and Perpetual Union." Its first article declares that the style of this confederacy shall be, "The United States of America"; and the second, in order to leave no doubt as to the relation in which the States should stand to each other in the confederacy about to be formed, declared—"Each State retains its sovereignty, freedom and independence; and every power, jurisdiction, and right, which is not, by this confederation, expressly delegated to the United States in Congress assembled." If we go one step further back, the style of the confederacy will be found to be the same with that of the revolutionary government, which existed when it was adopted, and which it superseded. It dates its origin with the Declaration of Independence. That act is styled—"The unanimous Declaration of the thirteen United States of America." And here again, that there might be no doubt how these States would stand to each other in the new condition in which they were about to be placed, it concluded by declaring—"that these United Colonies are, and of right ought to be, free and independent States"; "and that, as free and independent States, they have full power to levy war, conclude peace, contract alliances, and to do all other acts and things which independent States may of right do." The "United States" is, then, the baptismal name of these States—received at their birth—by which they have ever since continued to call themselves; by which they have characterized their constitution, government and laws—and by which they are known to the rest of the world.

The retention of the same style, throughout every stage of their existence, affords strong, if not conclusive evidence that the political relation between these States, under their present constitution and government, is substantially the same as under the confederacy and revolutionary government; and what that relation was, we are not left to doubt; as they are declared expressly to be "*free, independent* and *sovereign* States." They, then, are now united, and have been, throughout, simply as confederated States. If it had been intended by the members of the convention which framed the present constitution and government, to make any essential change, either in the relation of the States to each other, or the basis of their union, they would, by retaining the style which designated them under the preceding governments, have practised a deception, utterly unworthy of their character, as sincere and honest men and patriots.

It may, therefore, be fairly inferred, that, retaining the same style, they intended to attach to the expression—"the United States," the same meaning, substantially, which it previously had; and, of course, in calling the present government—"the federal government of these States," they meant by "federal," that they stood in the same relation to each other—that their union rested, without material change, on the same basis—as under the confederacy and the revolutionary government; and that federal, and confederated States, meant substantially the same thing. It follows, also, that the changes made by the present constitution were not in the foundation, but in the superstructure of the system. We accordingly find, in confirmation of this conclusion, that the convention, in their letter to Congress, stating the reasons for the changes that had been made, refer only to the necessity which required a different "*organization*" of the government, without making any allusion whatever to any change in the relations of the States towards each other—or the basis of the system. They state that, "the friends of our country have long seen and desired, that the power of making war, peace, and treaties; that of levying money and regulating commerce, and the correspondent executive and judicial authorities, should be fully and effectually vested in the Government of the Union: but the impropriety of delegating such extensive trusts to one body of men is evident; hence results the necessity of a *different organization.*"

We thus have the authority of the convention itself for asserting that the expression, "United States," has essentially the same meaning, when applied to the present constitution and government, as it had previously; and, of course, that the States have retained their separate existence, as independent and sovereign communities, in all the forms of political existence, through which they have passed. Such, indeed, is the literal import of the expression—"the United States"—and the sense in which it is ever used, when it is applied politically—I say, *politically*—because it is often applied, *geographically*, to designate the portion of this continent occupied by the States composing the Union, including territories belonging to them. This application arose from the fact, that there was no appropriate term for that portion of this continent; and thus, not unnaturally, the name by which these States are politically designated, was employed to designate the region they occupy and possess. The distinction is important, and cannot be overlooked in discussing questions involving the character and nature of the government, without causing great confusion and dangerous misconceptions.

But as conclusive as these reasons are to prove that the government of the United States is federal, in contradistinction to national, it would seem, that they have not been sufficient to prevent the opposite opinion from being entertained. Indeed, this last seems to have become the prevailing one; if we may judge from the general use of the term "national," and the almost entire disuse of that of "federal." National, is now commonly applied to "the general government of the Union"—and "the federal government of these States"— and all that appertains to them or to the Union. It seems to be forgotten that the term was repudiated by the convention, after full consideration; and that it was carefully excluded from the constitution, and the letter laying it before Congress. Even those who know all this—and, of course, how falsely the term is applied—have, for the most part, slided into its use without reflection. But there are not a few who so apply it, because they believe it to be a national government in fact; and among these are men of distinguished talents and standing, who have put forth all their powers of reason and eloquence, in support of the theory. The question involved is one of the first magnitude, and deserves to be investigated thoroughly in all its aspects. With this impression, I deem it proper—clear and conclusive as I regard the reasons already assigned to prove its federal character—to confirm them by historical references; and to repel the arguments adduced to prove it to be a national government. I shall begin with the formation and ratification of the constitution.

That the States, when they formed and ratified the constitution, were distinct, independent, and sovereign communities, has already been established. That the people of the several States, acting in their separate, independent, and sovereign character, adopted their separate State constitutions, is a fact uncontested and incontestable; but it is not more certain than that, acting in the same character, they ratified and adopted the constitution of the United States; with this difference only, that in making and adopting the one, they acted without concert or agreement; but, in the other, with concert in making, and mutual agreement in adopting it. That the delegates who constituted the convention which framed the constitution, were appointed by the several States, each on its own authority; that they voted in the convention by States; and that their votes were counted by States—are recorded and unquestionable facts. So, also, the facts that the constitution, when framed, was submitted to the people of the several States for their respective ratification; that it was ratified by them, each for itself; and that it was binding on each, only in consequence of its being so ratified by it. Until then, it was but the plan of a constitution, without any binding force. It was the act of ratification which established it as a constitution between the States ratifying it; and only between *them*, on the condition that not less than nine of the then thirteen States should concur in the ratification—as is expressly provided by its seventh and last article. It is in the following words: "The ratification of the conventions of nine States shall be sufficient for the establishment of this constitution between the States so ratifying the same." If additional proof be needed to show that it was only binding between the States that ratified it, it may be found in the fact, that two States, North Carolina and Rhode Island, refused, at first, to ratify; and were, in consequence, regarded in the interval as foreign States, without obligation, on their parts, to respect it, or, on the part of their citizens, to obey it. Thus far, there can be no difference of opinion. The facts are too recent and too well established—and the provision of the constitution too explicit, to admit of doubt.

That the States, then, retained, after the ratification of the constitution, the distinct, independent, and sovereign character in which they formed and ratified it, is certain; unless they divested themselves of it by the act of ratification, or by some provision of the constitution. If they have not, the constitution must be federal, and not national; for it would have, in that case, every attribute necessary to constitute it federal, and not one to make it national. On the other hand, if they have divested themselves, then it would necessarily lose its federal character, and become national. Whether, then, the government is federal or national, is reduced to a single question; whether the act of ratification, of itself, or the constitution, by some one, or all of its provisions, did, or did not, divest the several States of their character of separate, independent, and sovereign communities, and merge them all in one great community or nation, called the American people?

. . . Of all the questions which can arise under our system of government, this is by far the most important. It involves many others of great magnitude; and among them, that of the allegiance of the citizen; or, in other words, the question to whom allegiance and obedience are ultimately due. What is the true relation between the two governments—that of the United States and those of the several States? and what is the relation between the individuals respectively composing them? For it is clear, if the States still retain their sovereignty as separate and independent communities, the allegiance and obedience of the citizens of each would be due to their respective States; and that the government of the United States and those of the several States would stand as equals and co-ordinates in their respective spheres; and, instead of being united socially, their citizens would be politically connected through their respective States. On the contrary, if they have, by ratifying the constitution, divested themselves of their individuality and sovereignty, and merged themselves into one great community or nation, it is equally clear, that the sovereignty would reside in the whole—or what is called the American people; and that allegiance and obedience would be due to them. Nor is it less so, that the government of the several States would, in such case, stand to that of the United States, in the relation of inferior and subordinate, to superior and paramount; and that the individuals of the several States, thus fused, as it were, into one general mass, would be united *socially*, and not *politically*. So great a change of condition would have involved a thorough and radical revolution, both socially and politically—a revolution much more radical, indeed, than that which followed the Declaration of Independence.

They who maintain that the ratification of the constitution effected so mighty a change, are bound to establish it by the most demonstrative proof. The presumption is strongly opposed to it. It has already been shown, that the authority of the convention which formed the constitution is clearly against it; and that the history of its ratification, instead of supplying evidence in its favor, furnishes strong testimony in opposition to it. To these, others may be added; and, among them, the presumption drawn from the history of these States, in all the stages of their existence down to the time of the ratification of the constitution. In all, they formed separate, and, as it respects each other, independent communities; and were ever remarkable for the tenacity with which they adhered to their rights as such. It constituted, during the whole period, one of the most striking traits in their character.

. . . another circumstance of no little weight, drawn from the preliminary steps taken for the ratification of the constitution. The plan was laid, by the convention, before the Congress of the confederacy, for its consideration and action, as has been stated. It was the sole organ and representative of these States in their confederated character. By submitting it, the convention recognized and acknowledged its authority over it, as the organ of distinct, independent, and sovereign States. It had the right to dispose of it as it pleased; and, if it had thought proper, it might have defeated the plan by simply omitting to act on it. But it thought proper to act, and to adopt the course recommended by the convention—which was, to submit it—"to a convention of delegates, chosen in each State, by the people thereof, for their assent and adoption." All this was in strict accord with the federal character of the constitution, but wholly repugnant to the idea of its being national. It received the assent of the States in all the possible modes in which it could be obtained: first—in their confederated character, through its only appropriate organ, the Congress; next, in their individual character, as separate States, through their respective State governments, to which the Congress referred it; and finally, in their high character of independent and sovereign communities, through a convention of the people, called in each State, by the authority of its government. The States acting in these various capacities, might, at every stage, have defeated it or not, at their option, by giving or withholding their consent.

Nothing more is necessary, in order to show by whom it was ordained and established, than to ascertain who are meant by—"We, the people of the United States"; for, by their authority, it was done. To this there can be but one answer—it meant the people who ratified the instrument; for it was the act of ratification which ordained and established it. Who they were, admits of no doubt. The process preparatory to ratification, and the acts by which it was done, prove, beyond the possibility of a doubt, that it was ratified by the several States, through conventions of delegates, chosen in each State by the people thereof; and acting, each in the name and by the authority of its State: and, as all the States ratified it—"We, the people of the United States"— mean,—We, the people of the several States of the Union. The inference is irresistible. And when it is considered that the States of the Union were then members of the confederacy—and that, by the express provision of one of its articles, "each State retains its sovereignty, freedom, and independence," the proof is demonstrative, that—"We, the people of the United States of America," mean the people of the several States of the Union, acting as free, independent, and sovereign States. This strikingly confirms what has been already stated; to wit, that the convention which formed the constitution, meant the same thing by the terms—"United States"—and, "federal"—when applied to the constitution or government—and that the former, when used politically, always mean—these States united as independent and sovereign communities.

It remains to be shown, *over whom*, it was ordained and established. That it was not over *the several States*, is settled by the seventh article beyond controversy. It declares, that the ratification by nine States shall be sufficient to establish the constitution between the States so ratifying. "Between," necessarily excludes "over"—as that which is *between* States cannot be *over* them. Reason itself, if the constitution had been silent, would have led, with equal certainty, to the same conclusion. For it was the several States, or, what is the same thing, their people, in their sovereign capacity, who ordained and established the constitution. But the authority which ordains and establishes, is higher than that which is ordained and established; and, of course, the latter must be subordinate to the former—and cannot, therefore, be *over* it. "Between," always means more than "over"—and implies in this case, that the authority which ordained and established the constitution, was the joint and united authority of the States ratifying it; and that, among the effects of their ratification, it became a contract between them; and, *as a compact*, binding on them—but only as such. In that sense the term, "between," is appropriately applied. In no other, can it be. It was, doubtless, used in that sense in this instance; but the question still remains, *over whom*, was it ordained and established? After what has been stated, the answer may be readily given. It was *over the government* which it created, and all its functionaries in their official character—and the individuals composing and inhabiting the several States, as far as they might come within the sphere of the powers delegated to the United States.

JOSEPH STORY, *COMMENTARIES ON THE CONSTITUTION OF THE UNITED STATES*[39]

The next and last amendment is: "The powers not delegated to the United States Constitution, nor prohibited by it to the States, are reserved to the States respectively, or to the people.

This amendment is a mere affirmation of what, upon any just reasoning, is a necessary rule of interpreting the Constitution. Being an instrument of limited and enumerated powers, it follows, irresistibly, that what is not conferred is withheld, and belongs to the State authorities if invested by their constitutions of government respectively in them; and if not so invested, it is retained BY THE PEOPLE, as a part of their residuary sovereignty. When this amendment was before Congress, a proposition was moved to insert the world "expressly" before "delegated," so as to read, "the powers not *expressly* delegated to the United States by the Constitution," &c. On that occasion it was remarked, that it is impossible to confine a government to the exercise of express powers. There must necessarily be admitted powers by implication, unless the Constitution descended to the most minute details. It is a general principal that all corporate bodies possess all powers incident to a corporate capacity, without being absolutely expressed. The motion was accordingly negatived. Indeed, one of the great defects of the confederation was (as we have already seen), that it contained a clause prohibiting the exercise of any power, jurisdiction, or right not *expressly delegated.* The consequence was, that Congress were crippled at every step of their progress, and were often compelled, by the very necessities of the times, to usurp powers which they did not constitutionally possess; and thus, in effect, to break down all the great barriers against tyranny and oppression.

It is pain, therefore, that it could not have been the intention of the framers of this amendment to give it effect, as an abridgment of any of the powers granted under the Constitution, whether they are express or implied, direct or incidental. Is sole design is to exclude any interpretation by which other powers should be assumed beyond those which are granted. All that are granted in the original instrument, whether express or implied, whether direct or incidental, are left in their original state. All powers not delegated (not all powers not *expressly* delegated) and not prohibited, are reserved. The attempts then which have been made from time to time to force upon this language an abridging or restrictive influence are utterly unfounded in any just rules of interpreting the words or the sense of the instrument. Stripped of the ingenious disguises in which they are clothed, they are neither more nor less than attempts to foist into the text the word "expressly; " to qualify what is general, and obscure what is clear and defined. They make the sense of the passage bend to the wishes and prejudices of the interpreter, and employ criticism to support a theory, and not to guide it. One should suppose, if the history of the human mind did not furnish abundant proof to the contrary, that no reasonable man would contend for an interpretation founded neither in the letter nor in the spirit of an instrument. Where is controversy to end if we desert both the letter and the spirit? What is to become of constitutions of government if they are to rest, not upon the plain import of their words, but upon conjectural enlargements and restraints, to suit the temporary passions and interests of the day? Let us never forget that our constitutions of government are solemn instruments, addressed to the common sense of the people, and designed to fix and perpetuate their rights and their liberties. They are not to be fritted away to please the demagogues of the day. They are not to be violated to gratify the ambition of political leaders. They are to speak in the same voice now and forever. They are of no man's private interpretation.

They are ordained by the will of the people; and can be changed only by the sovereign command of the people.

It has been justly remarked that the erection of a new government, whatever care or wisdom may distinguish the work, cannot fail to originate questions of intricacy and nicety; and these may, in a particular manner, be expected to flow from the establishment of a constitution founded upon the total or partial incorporation of a number of distinct sovereignties. Time alone can mature and perfect so compound a system; liquidate the meaning of all parts; and adjust them to each other in a harmonious and consistent whole.

ABEL UPSHUR, *A BRIEF ENQUIRY INTO THE TRUE NATURE AND CHARACTER OF OUR FEDERAL GOVERNMENT*[40]

The tenth article of the amendments of the Constitution provides that "The powers not delegated to the United States by the Constitution, nor prohibited by it to the States, are reserved to the States respectively, or to the people." The powers thus reserved, are not only reserved against the federal government in whole, but against each and every department thereof. The judiciary is no more excepted out of the reservation than is the legislature or the executive. Of what nature, then, are those reserved powers? Not the powers, if any such there be, which are possessed by all the States together, for the reservation is to "the States respectively"; that is, to each State separately and distinctly. Now we can form no idea of any power possessed by a State as such, and independent of every other State, which is not, in its nature, a sovereign power. Every power so reserved, therefore, must be of such a character that each State may exercise it, without the least reference or responsibility to any other State whatever.

We have already seen that the Constitution of the United States was formed by States as such, and the reservation above quoted is an admission that, in performing that work, they acted as independent and sovereign States. It is incident to every sovereignty to be alone the judge of its own compacts and agreements. No other State or assemblage of States has the least right to interfere with it, in this respect, and cannot do so without impairing its sovereignty. The Constitution of the United States is but the agreement which each State has made, with each and all the other States, and is not distinguishable, in the principle we are examining, from any other agreement between sovereign States. Each State, therefore, has a right to interpret that agreement for itself, unless it has clearly waived that right in favor of another power. That the right is not waived in the case under consideration, is apparent from the fact already stated, that if the judiciary be the sole judges of the extent of their own powers, their powers are universal, and the enumeration in the Constitution idle and useless. But it is still farther apparent from the following view.

The Federal Government is the creature of the States. It is not a party to the Constitution, but the result of it—the creation of that agreement which was made by the States as parties. It is a mere agent, entrusted with limited powers for certain specific objects; which powers and objects are enumerated in the Constitution. Shall the agent be permitted to judge of the ex-tent of his own powers, without reference to his constituent? To a certain extent he is compelled to do this, in the very act of exercising them, but this is always in subordination to the authority by whom his powers were conferred. If this were not so, the result would be, that the agent would possess every power which the constituent could confer, notwithstanding the plainest and most express terms of the grant. This would be against all principle and all reason. If such a rule should prevail in regard to government, a written constitution would be the idlest thing imaginable. It would afford no barrier against the usurpations of the government, and no security for the rights and liberties of the people. If then the federal government has no I authority to judge, in the last resort, of the extent of its own powers, with what propriety can it be said that a single department of that government may do so? Nay, it is said that this department may not only judge for itself, but for the other department also. This is an absurdity as pernicious as it is gross and palpable. If the judiciary may determine the powers of the federal government, it may pronounce them either less or more than they really are. That government at least would have no right to complain of the decisions of an umpire which it had chosen for itself, and endeavored to force upon the States and the people. Thus a single department might deny to both the others, salutary powers which they really possessed, and which the public interest or the public safety might require them to exercise; or it might confer on them powers never conceded, inconsistent with private right, and dangerous to public liberty.

In construing the powers of a free and equal government, it is enough to disprove the existence of any rule, to show that such consequences as these will result from it. Nothing short of the plainest and most unequivocal language should reconcile us to the adoption of such a rule. No such language can be found in our Constitution. The only clause, from which the rule can be supposed to be derived, is that which confers juris-diction in "all cases arising under the Constitution, and the laws made in pursuance thereof; but this clause is clearly not susceptible of any such construction. Every right may be said to be a constitutional right, because no right exists which the Constitution disallows; and consequently every remedy to enforce those rights presents "a case arising under the Constitution." But a construction so latitudinous will scarcely be con- tended for by any one. The clause under consideration gives jurisdiction only as to those matters, and between those parties, enumerated in the Constitution itself. Whenever such a case arises, the federal courts have cognizance of it; but the right to decide a case arising under the Constitution does not necessarily imply the right to determine in the last resort what that Constitution is. If the federal courts should, in the very teeth of the eleventh amendment, take jurisdiction of cases "commenced or prosecuted against one of the States by citizens of another State," the decision of those courts, that they had jurisdiction, would certainly not settle the Constitution in that particular. The State would be under no obligation to submit to such a decision, and it would resist it by virtue of its sovereign right to decide for itself, whether it had agreed to the exercise of such a jurisdiction or not.

Considering the nature of our system of government, the States ought to be, and I presume always will be, extremely careful not to interpose their sovereign power against the decisions of the supreme court in any case where that court clearly has jurisdiction. Of this character are the cases already cited at the commencement of this inquiry; such, for example, as those between two States, those affecting foreign ministers, those of admiralty and maritime jurisdiction, &c. As to all these subjects the jurisdiction is clear, and no State can have any interest to dispute it. The decisions of the supreme court, therefore, ought to be considered as final and conclusive, and it would be a breach of the contract on the part of any State to refuse submission to them. There are, how-ever, many cases involving questions of the powers of government. State and federal, which cannot assume a proper form for judicial investigation. Most questions of mere political power, are of this sort; and such are all questions between a State and the United States. As to these, the Constitution confers no jurisdiction on the federal courts, and, of course, it provides no common umpire to whose decision they can be referred. In such cases, therefore, the State must of necessity decide for itself. But there are also cases between citizen and citizen, arising under the laws of the United States, and between the United States and the citizen, arising in the same way. So far as the federal tribunals have cognizance of such cases, their decisions are final. If the constitutionality of the law under which the case arises, should come into question, the court has authority to decide it, and there is no relief for the parties, in any other judicial proceeding. If the decision, in a controversy between the United States and a citizen, should be against the United States, it is, of course, final and conclusive. If the decision should be against the citizen, his only relief is by an appeal to his own State. He is under no obligation to submit to federal decisions at all, except so far only as his own State has commanded him to do so; and he has, therefore, a perfect right to ask his State whether her commands extend to the particular case or not. He does not ask whether the federal court has interpreted the law correctly or not, but whether or not she ever consented that congress should pass the law. If congress had such power, he has no relief, for the decision of the highest federal court is final; if congress had not such power, then he is oppressed by the action of a usurped authority, and has a right to look to his own State for redress. His State may interpose in his favor or not, as she may think proper. If she does not, then there is an end of the matter; if she does, then it is no longer a judicial question. The question is then between new parties, who are not bound by the former decision between a sovereign State and its own agent; between a State and the United States. As between these parties the federal tribunals have no jurisdiction, there is no longer a common umpire to whom the controversy can be referred. The State must of necessity judge for itself, by virtue of that inherent, sovereign power and authority, which, as to this matter, it has never surrendered to any other tribunal. Its decision, whatever it may be, is binding upon itself and upon its own people, and no farther.

LUTHER v. BORDEN[41]

[Roger Taney, Chief Justice] The existence and authority of the government under which the defendants acted was called in question, and the plaintiff insists that, before the acts complained of were committed, that government had been displaced and annulled by the people of Rhode Island, and that the plaintiff was engaged in supporting the lawful authority of the State, and the defendants themselves were in arms against it.

This is a new question in this court, and certainly a very grave one, and, at the time when the trespass is alleged to have been committed, it had produced a general and painful excitement in the State, and threatened to end in bloodshed and civil war.

. . . Moreover, the Constitution of the United States, as far as it has provided for an emergency of this kind and authorized the general government to interfere in the domestic concerns of a State, has treated the subject as political in its nature, and placed the power in the hands of that department.

The fourth section of the fourth article of the Constitution of the United States provides that the United States shall guarantee to every State in the Union a republican form of government, and shall protect each of them against invasion, and on the application of the legislature or of the executive (when the legislature cannot be convened) against domestic violence.

Under this article of the Constitution, it rests with Congress to decide what government is the established one in a State. For as the United States guarantee to each State a republican government, Congress must necessarily decide what government is established in the State before it can determine whether it is republican or not. And when the senators and representatives of a State are admitted into the councils of the Union, the authority of the government under which they are appointed, as well as its republican character, is recognized by the proper constitutional authority. And its decision is binding on every other department of the government, and could not be questioned in a judicial tribunal. It is true that the contest in this case did not last long enough to bring the matter to this issue, and, as no senators or representatives were elected under the authority of the government of which Mr. Dorr was the head, Congress was not called upon to decide the controversy. Yet the right to decide is placed there, and not in the courts.

. . . The remaining question is whether the defendants, acting under military orders issued under the authority of the government, were justified in breaking and entering the plaintiff's house. In relation to the act of the legislature declaring martial law, it is not necessary in the case before us to inquire to what extent, nor under what circumstances, that power may be exercised by a State. Unquestionably a military government, established the permanent government of the State, would not be a republican government, and it would be the duty of Congress to overthrow it. But the law of Rhode Island evidently contemplated no such government. It was intended merely for the crisis, and to meet the peril in which the existing government was placed by the armed resistance to its authority. It was so understood and construed by the State authorities. And unquestionably a State may use its military power to put down an armed insurrection too strong to be controlled by the civil authority. The power is essential to the existence of every government, essential to the preservation of order and free institutions, and is as necessary to the States of this Union as to any other government. The State itself must determine what degree of force the crisis demands. And if the government of Rhode Island deemed the armed opposition so formidable and so ramified throughout the State as to require the use of its military force and the declaration of martial law, we see no ground upon which this court can question its authority. It was a state of war, and the established government resorted to the rights and usages of war to maintain itself, and to overcome the unlawful opposition. And in that state of things, the officers engaged in its military service might lawfully arrest anyone who, from the information before them, they had reasonable grounds to believe was engaged in the insurrection, and might order a house to be forcibly entered and searched when there were reasonable grounds for supposing he might be there concealed. Without the power to do this, martial law and the military array of the government would be mere parade, and rather encourage attack than repel it. No more force, however, can be used than is necessary to accomplish the object. And if the power is exercised for the purposes of oppression, or any injury willfully done to person or property, the party by whom, or by whose order, it is committed would undoubtedly be answerable.

. . . Much of the argument on the part of the plaintiff turned upon political rights and political questions, upon which the court has been urged to express an opinion. We decline doing so. The high power has been conferred on this court of passing judgment upon the acts of the State sovereignties, and of the legislative and executive branches of the federal government, and of determining whether they are beyond the limits of power marked out for them respectively by the Constitution of the United States. This tribunal, therefore, should be the last to overstep the boundaries which limit its own jurisdiction. And while it should always be ready to meet any question confided to it by the Constitution, it is equally its duty not to pass beyond its appropriate sphere of action, and to take care not to involve itself in discussions which properly belong to other forums. No one, we believe, has ever doubted the proposition that, according to the institutions of this country, the sovereignty in every State resides in the people of the State, and that they may alter and change their form of government at their own pleasure. But whether they have changed it or not by abolishing an old government and establishing a new one in its place is a question to be settled by the political power. And when that power has decided, the courts are bound to take notice of its decision, and to follow it.

ORDINANCES OF SECESSION[42]

South Carolina

AN ORDINANCE to dissolve the union between the State of South Carolina and other States united with her under the compact entitled "The Constitution of the United States of America."

We, the people of the State of South Carolina, in convention assembled, do declare and ordain, and it is hereby declared and ordained, That the ordinance adopted by us in convention on the twenty-third day of May, in the year of our Lord one thousand seven hundred and eighty-eight, whereby the Constitution of the United States of America was ratified, and also all acts and parts of acts of the General Assembly of this State ratifying amendments of the said Constitution, are hereby repealed; and that the union now subsisting between South Carolina and other States, under the name of the "United States of America," is hereby dissolved.

Mississippi

AN ORDINANCE to dissolve the union between the State of Mississippi and other States united with her under the compact entitled "The Constitution of the United States of America."

The people of the State of Mississippi, in convention assembled, do ordain and declare, and it is hereby ordained and declared, as follows, to wit:

Section 1. That all the laws and ordinances by which the said State of Mississippi became a member of the Federal Union of the United States of America be, and the same are hereby, repealed, and that all obligations on the part of the said State or the people thereof to observe the same be withdrawn, and that the said State doth hereby resume all the rights, functions, and powers which by any of said laws or ordinances were conveyed to the Government of the said United States, and is absolved from all the obligations, restraints, and duties incurred to the said Federal Union, and shall from henceforth be a free, sovereign, and independent State.

Sec. 2. That so much of the first section of the seventh article of the constitution of this State as requires members of the Legislature and all officers, executive and judicial, to take an oath or affirmation to support the Constitution of the United States be, and the same is hereby, abrogated and annulled.

Sec. 3. That all rights acquired and vested under the Constitution of the United States, or under any act of Congress passed, or treaty made, in pursuance thereof, or under any law of this State, and not incompatible with this ordinance, shall remain in force and have the same effect as if this ordinance had not been passed.

Sec. 4. That the people of the State of Mississippi hereby consent to form a federal union with such of the States as may have seceded or may secede from the Union of the United States of America, upon the basis of the present Constitution of the said United States, except such parts thereof as embrace other portions than such seceding States.

Florida

We, the people of the State of Florida, in convention assembled, do solemnly ordain, publish, and declare, That the State of Florida hereby withdraws herself from the confederacy of States existing under the name of the United States of America and from the existing Government of the said States; and that all political connection between her and the Government of said States ought to be, and the same is hereby, totally annulled, and said Union of States dissolved; and the State of Florida is hereby declared a sovereign and independent nation; and that all ordinances heretofore adopted, in so far as they create or recognize said Union, are rescinded; and all laws or parts of laws in force in this State, in so far as they recognize or assent to said Union, be, and they are hereby, repealed.

Alabama

An Ordinance to dissolve the union between the State of Alabama and the other States united under the compact styled "The Constitution of the United States of America"

Whereas, the election of Abraham Lincoln and Hannibal Hamlin to the offices of president and vice-president of the United States of America, by a sectional party, avowedly hostile to the domestic institutions and to the peace and security of the people of the State of Alabama, preceded by many and dangerous infractions of the constitution of the United States by many of the States and people of the Northern section, is a political wrong of so insulting and menacing a character as to justify the people of the State of Alabama in the adoption of prompt and decided measures for their future peace and security, therefore:

Be it declared and ordained by the people of the State of Alabama, in Convention assembled, That the State of Alabama now withdraws, and is hereby withdrawn from the Union known as "the United States of America," and henceforth ceases to be one of said United States, and is, and of right ought to be a Sovereign and Independent State.

Sec 2. Be it further declared and ordained by the people of the State of Alabama in Convention assembled, That all powers over the Territory of said State, and over the people thereof, heretofore delegated to the Government of the United States of America, be and they are hereby withdrawn from said Government, and are hereby resumed and vested in the people of the State of Alabama.

And as it is the desire and purpose of the people of Alabama to meet the slaveholding States of the South, who may approve such purpose, in order to frame a provisional as well as permanent Government upon the principles of the Constitution of the United States,

Georgia

We the people of the State of Georgia in Convention assembled do declare and ordain and it is hereby declared and ordained that the ordinance adopted by the State of Georgia in convention on the 2nd day of January in the year of our Lord seventeen hundred and eighty-eight, whereby the constitution of the United States of America was assented to, ratified and adopted, and also all acts and parts of acts of the general assembly of this State, ratifying and adopting amendments to said constitution, are hereby repealed, rescinded and abrogated.

We do further declare and ordain that the union now existing between the State of Georgia and other States under the name of the United States of

America is hereby dissolved, and that the State of Georgia is in full possession and exercise of all those rights of sovereignty which belong and appertain to a free and independent State.

Louisiana

AN ORDINANCE to dissolve the union between the State of Louisiana and other States united with her under the compact entitled "The Constitution of the United States of America."

We, the people of the State of Louisiana, in convention assembled, do declare and ordain, and it is hereby declared and ordained, That the ordinance passed by us in convention on the 22nd day of November, in the year eighteen hundred and eleven, whereby the Constitution of the United States of America and the amendments of the said Constitution were adopted, and all laws and ordinances by which the State of Louisiana became a member of the Federal Union, be, and the same are hereby, repealed and abrogated; and that the union now subsisting between Louisiana and other States under the name of "The United States of America" is hereby dissolved.

We do further declare and ordain, That the State of Louisiana hereby resumes all rights and powers heretofore delegated to the Government of the United States of America; that her citizens are absolved from all allegiance to said Government; and that she is in full possession and exercise of all those rights of sovereignty which appertain to a free and independent State.

We do further declare and ordain, That all rights acquired and vested under the Constitution of the United States, or any act of Congress, or treaty, or under any law of this State, and not incompatible with this ordinance, shall remain in force and have the same effect as if this ordinance had not been passed.

Texas

AN ORDINANCE To dissolve the Union between the State of Texas and the other States united under the Compact styled "the Constitution of the United States of America."

WHEREAS, The Federal Government has failed to accomplish the purposes of the compact of union between these States, in giving protection either to the persons of our people upon an exposed frontier, or to the property of our citizens, and

WHEREAS, the action of the Northern States of the Union is violative of the compact between the States and the guarantees of the Constitution; and,

WHEREAS, The recent developments in Federal affairs make it evident that the power of the Federal Government is sought to be made a weapon with which to strike down the interests and property of the people of Texas, and her sister slave-holding States, instead of permitting it to be, as was intended, our shield against outrage and aggression; THEREFORE,

SECTION 1.—We, the people of the State of Texas, by delegates in convention assembled, do declare and ordain that the ordinance adopted by our convention of delegates on the 4th day of July, A.D. 1845, and afterwards ratified by us, under which the Republic of Texas was admitted into the Union with other States, and became a party to the compact styled "The Constitution of the United States of America," be, and is hereby, repealed and annulled; that all the powers which, by the said compact, were delegated by Texas to the Federal Government are revoked and resumed; that Texas is of right absolved from all restraints and obligations incurred by said compact, and is a separate sovereign State, and that her citizens and people are absolved from all allegiance to the United States or the government thereof.

SEC. 2. This ordinance shall be submitted to the people of Texas for their ratification or rejection, by the qualified voters, on the 23rd day of February, 1861, and unless rejected by a majority of the votes cast, shall take effect and be in force on and after the 2d day of March, A.D. 1861. PROVIDED, that in the Representative District of El Paso said election may be held on the 18th day of February, 1861.

Virginia

AN ORDINANCE to repeal the ratification of the Constitution of the United State of America by the State of Virginia, and to resume all the rights and powers granted under said Constitution.

The people of Virginia in their ratification of the Constitution of the United States of America, adopted by them in convention on the twenty-fifth day of June, in the year of our Lord one thousand seven hundred and eighty-eight, having declared that the powers granted under said Constitution were derived from the people of the United States and might be resumed whensoever the same should be perverted to their injury and oppression, and the Federal Government having perverted said powers not only to the injury of the people of Virginia, but to the oppression of the Southern slave-holding States:

Now, therefore, we, the people of Virginia, do declare and ordain, That the ordinance adopted by the people of this State in convention on the twenty-fifth day of June, in the year of our Lord one thousand seven hundred and eighty-eight, whereby the Constitution of the United States of America was ratified, and all acts of the General Assembly of this State ratifying and adopting amendments to said Constitution, are hereby repealed and abrogated; that the union between the State of Virginia and the other States under the Constitution aforesaid is hereby dissolved, and that the State of Virginia is in the full possession and exercise of all the rights of sovereignty which belong and appertain to a free and independent State.

And they do further declare, That said Constitution of the United States of America is no longer binding on any of the citizens of this State.

This ordinance shall take effect and be an act of this day, when ratified by a majority of the voter of the people of this State cast at a poll to be taken thereon on the fourth Thursday in May next, in pursuance of a schedule hereafter to be enacted.

Arkansas

AN ORDINANCE to dissolve the union now existing between the State of Arkansas and the other States united with her under the compact entitled "The Constitution of the United States of America."

Whereas, in addition to the well-founded causes of complaint set forth by this convention, in resolutions adopted on the 11th of March, A.D. 1861, against the sectional party now in power in Washington City, headed by Abraham Lincoln, he has, in the face of resolutions passed by this convention pledging the State of Arkansas to resist to the last extremity any attempt on the part of such power to coerce any State that had seceded from the old Union, proclaimed to the world that war should be waged against such States until they should be compelled to submit to their rule, and large forces to accomplish this have by this same power been called out, and are now being marshaled to carry out this inhuman design; and to longer submit to such rule, or remain in the old Union of the United States, would be disgraceful and ruinous to the State of Arkansas:

Therefore we, the people of the State of Arkansas, in convention assembled, do hereby declare and ordain, and it is hereby declared and ordained, That the "ordinance and acceptance of compact" passed and approved by the General Assembly of the State of Arkansas on the 18th day of October, A.D. 1836, whereby it was by said General Assembly ordained that by virtue of the authority vested in said General Assembly by the provisions of the ordinance adopted by the convention of delegates assembled at Little Rock for the purpose of forming a constitution and system of government for said State, the propositions set forth in "An act supplementary to an act entitled 'An act for the admission of the State of Arkansas into the Union, and to provide for the due execution of the laws of the United States within the same, and for other purposes,'" were freely accepted, ratified, and irrevocably confirmed, articles of compact and union between the State of Arkansas and the United States, and all other laws and every other law and ordinance, whereby the State of Arkansas became a member of the Federal Union, be, and the same are hereby, in all respects and for every purpose herewith consistent, repealed, abrogated, and fully set aside; and the union now subsisting between the State of Arkansas and the other States, under the name of the United States of America, is hereby forever dissolved.

And we do further hereby declare and ordain, That the State of Arkansas hereby resumes to herself all rights and powers heretofore delegated to the Government of the United States of America; that her citizens are absolved from all allegiance to said Government of the United States, and that she is in full possession and exercise of all the rights and sovereignty which appertain to a free and independent State.

We do further ordain and declare, That all rights acquired and vested under the Constitution of the United States of America, or of any act or acts of Congress, or treaty, or under any law of this State, and not incompatible with this ordinance, shall remain in full force and effect, in nowise altered or impaired, and have the same effect as if this ordinance had not been passed.

North Carolina

AN ORDINANCE to dissolve the union between the State of North Carolina and the other States united with her, under the compact of government entitled "The Constitution of the United States."

We, the people of the State of North Carolina in convention assembled, do declare and ordain, and it is hereby declared and ordained, That the ordinance adopted by the State of North Carolina in the convention of 1789, whereby the Constitution of the United States was ratified and adopted, and also all acts and parts of acts of the General Assembly ratifying and adopting amendments to the said Constitution, are hereby repealed, rescinded, and abrogated.

We do further declare and ordain, That the union now subsisting between the State of North Carolina and the other States, under the title of the United States of America, is hereby dissolved, and that the State of North Carolina is in full possession and exercise of all those rights of sovereignty which belong and appertain to a free and independent State.

Tennessee

DECLARATION OF INDEPENDENCE AND ORDINANCE dissolving the federal relations between the State of Tennessee and the United States of America.

First. We, the people of the State of Tennessee, waiving any expression of opinion as to the abstract doctrine of secession, but asserting the right, as a free and independent people, to alter, reform, or abolish our form of government in such manner as we think proper, do ordain and declare that all the laws and ordinances by which the State of Tennessee became a member of the Federal Union of the United States of America are hereby abrogated and annulled, and that all the rights, functions, and powers which by any of said laws and ordinances were conveyed to the Government of the United States, and to absolve ourselves from all the obligations, restraints, and duties incurred thereto; and do hereby henceforth become a free, sovereign, and independent State.

Second. We furthermore declare and ordain that article 10, sections 1 and 2, of the constitution of the State of Tennessee, which requires members of the General Assembly and all officers, civil and military, to take an oath to support the Constitution of the United States be, and the same are hereby, abrogated and annulled, and all parts of the constitution of the State of Tennessee making citizenship of the United States a qualification for office and recognizing the Constitution of the United States as the supreme law of this State are in like manner abrogated and annulled.

Third. We furthermore ordain and declare that all rights acquired and vested under the Constitution of the United States, or under any act of Congress passed in pursuance thereof, or under any laws of this State, and not incompatible with this ordinance, shall remain in force and have the same effect as if this ordinance had not been passed.

ABRAHAM LINCOLN, MESSAGE TO CONGRESS IN SPECIAL SESSION[43]

At the beginning of the present Presidential term, four months ago, the functions of the Federal Government were found to be generally suspended within the several States of South Carolina, Georgia, Alabama, Mississippi, Louisiana, and Florida, excepting only those of the Post Office Department.

. . . And this issue embraces more than the fate of these United States. It presents to the whole family of man, the question, whether a constitutional republic, or a democracy—a government of the people, by the same people—can, or cannot, maintain its territorial integrity, against its own domestic foes. It presents the question, whether discontented individuals, too few in numbers to control administration, according to organic law, in any case, can always, upon the pretenses made in this case, or on any other pretenses, or arbitrarily, without any pretense, break up their Government, and thus practically put an end to free government upon the earth. It forces us to ask: "Is there, in all republics, this inherent, and fatal weakness?" "Must a government, of necessity, be too strong for the liberties of its own people, or too weak to maintain its own existence?"

. . . The course taken in Virginia was the most remarkable—perhaps the most important. A convention, elected by the people of that State, to consider this very question of disrupting the Federal Union, was in session at the capital of Virginia when Fort Sumter fell. To this body the people had chosen a large majority of professed Union men. Almost immediately after the fall of Sumter, many members of that majority went over to the original disunion minority, and, with them, adopted an ordinance for withdrawing the State from the Union. Whether this change was wrought by their great approval of the assault upon Sumter, or their great resentment at the government's resistance to that assault, is not definitely known. Although they submitted the ordinance, for ratification, to vote of the people, to be taken on a day then somewhat more than a month distant, the convention, and the Legislature, (Which was also in session at the same time and place) with leading men of the State, not members of either, immediately commenced acting, as if the State were already out of the Union. They pushed military preparations vigorously forward all over the state. They seized the United States Armory at Harper's Ferry, and the Navy-yard at Gosport, near Norfolk. They received—perhaps invited—into their state, large bodies of troops, with their warlike appointments, from the so-called seceded States. They formally entered into a treaty of temporary alliance, and co-operation with the so-called "Confederate States," and sent members to their Congress at Montgomery. And, finally, they permitted the insurrectionary government to be transferred to their capital at Richmond.

The people of Virginia have thus allowed this giant insurrection to make its nest within her borders; and this government has no choice left but to deal with it, where it finds it. And it has the less regret, as the loyal citizens have, in due form, claimed its protection. Those loyal citizens, this government is bound to recognize, and protect, as being Virginia.

In the border States, so called—in fact, the middle states—there are those who favor a policy which they call "armed neutrality"—that is, an arming of those states to prevent the Union forces passing one way, or the disunion, the other, over their soil. This would be disunion completed. Figuratively speaking, it would be the building of an impassable wall along the line of separation. And yet, not quite an impassable one; for, under the guise of neutrality, it would tie the hands of the Union men, and freely pass supplies from among them, to the insurrectionists, which it could not do as an open enemy. At a stroke, it would take all the trouble off the hands of secession, except only what proceeds from the external blockade. It would do for the disunionists that which, of all things, they most desire—feed them well, and give them disunion without a struggle of their own. It recognizes no fidelity to the Constitution, no obligation to maintain the Union; and while (very many who have favored it) are, doubtless, loyal citizens, it is, nevertheless, treason in effect.

. . . It might seem, at first thought, to be of little difference whether the present movement at the South be called "secession" or "rebellion."

The movers, however, well understand the difference. At the beginning, they knew they could never raise their treason to any respectable magnitude, by any name which implies violation of law. They knew their people possessed as much of moral sense, as much of devotion to law and order, and as much pride in, and reverence for, the history, and government, of their common country, as any other civilized, and patriotic people. They knew they could make no advancement directly in the teeth of these strong and noble sentiments. Accordingly they commenced by an insidious debauching of the public mind. They invented an ingenious sophism, which, if conceded, was followed by perfectly logical steps, through all the incidents, to the complete destruction of the Union. The sophism itself is, that any state of the Union may, consistently with the national Constitution, and therefore lawfully, and peacefully, withdraw from the Union, without the consent of the Union, or of any other state. The little disguise that the supposed right is to be exercised only for just cause, themselves to be the sole judge of its justice, is too thin to merit any notice.

. . . This sophism derives much—perhaps the whole—of its currency, from the assumption, that there is some omnipotent, and sacred supremacy, pertaining to a State—to each State of our Federal Union. Our States have neither more, nor less power, than that reserved to them, in the Union, by the Constitution—no one of them ever having been a State out of the Union. The original ones passed into the Union even before they cast off their British colonial dependence; and the new ones each came into the Union directly from a condition of dependence, excepting Texas. And even Texas, in its temporary independence, was never designated a State. The new ones only took the designation of States, on coming into the Union, while that name was first adopted for the old ones, in, and by, the Declaration of Independence. Therein the "United Colonies" were declared to be "Free and Independent States"; but, even then, the object plainly was not to declare their independence of one another, or of the Union; but directly the contrary, as their mutual pledge, and their mutual action, before, at the time, and afterwards, abundantly show. The express plighting of faith, by each and all of the original thirteen, in the Articles of Confederation, two years later, that the Union shall be perpetual, is most conclusive. Having never been States, either in substance, or in name, outside of the Union, whence this magical omnipotence of "State rights," asserting a claim of power to lawfully destroy the Union itself? Much is said about the "sovereignty" of the States; but the word, even, is not in the national Constitution; nor, as is believed, in any of the State constitutions. What is a "sovereignty," in the political sense of the term? Would it be far wrong to define it "A political community, without a political superior"? Tested by this, no one of our States, except Texas, ever was a sovereignty. And even Texas gave up the character on coming into the Union; by which act, she acknowledged the Constitution of the United States, and the laws and treaties of the United States made in pursuance of the Constitution, to be, for her, the supreme law of the land. The States have their status IN the Union, and they have no other legal status. If they break from this, they can only do so against law, and by revolution. The Union, and not themselves separately, procured their independence, and their liberty. By conquest, or purchase, the Union gave each of them, whatever of independence, and liberty, it has. The Union is older than any of the States; and, in fact, it created them as States. Originally, some dependent colonies made the Union; and, in turn, the Union threw off their old dependence, for them, and made them States, such as they are. Not one of them ever had a State constitution, independent of the Union. Of course, it is not forgotten that all the new States framed their constitutions, before they entered the Union; nevertheless, dependent upon, and preparatory to, coming into the Union.

Unquestionably the States have the powers, and rights, reserved to them in, and by the National Constitution; but among these, surely, are not included all conceivable powers, however mischievous, or destructive; but, at most, such only, as were known in the world, at the time, as governmental powers; and certainly, a power to destroy the government itself, had never been known as a governmental—as a merely administrative power. This relative matter of National power, and State rights, as a principle, is no other than the principle of generality, and locality. Whatever concerns the whole, should be confided to the whole—to the general government; while, whatever concerns only the State, should be left exclusively, to the State. This is all there is of original principle about it. Whether the National Constitution, in defining boundaries between the two, has applied the principle with exact accuracy, is not to be questioned. We are all bound by that defining, without question.

. . . The seceders insist that our Constitution admits of secession. They have assumed to make a National Constitution of their own, in which, of necessity, they have either discarded, or retained, the right of secession, as they insist, it exists in ours. If they have discarded it, they thereby admit that, on principle, it ought not to be in ours. If they have retained it, by their own construction of ours they show that to be consistent they must secede from one another, whenever they shall find it the easiest way of settling their debts, or effecting any other selfish, or unjust object. The principle itself is one of disintegration, and upon which no government can possibly endure.

If all the States, save one, should assert the power to drive that one out of the Union, it is presumed the whole class of seceder politicians would at once deny the power, and denounce the act as the greatest outrage upon State rights. But suppose that precisely the same act, instead of being called "driving the one out," should be called "the seceding of the others from that one," it would be exactly what the seceders claim to do; unless, indeed, they make the point, that the one, because it is a minority, may rightfully do, what the others, because they are a majority, may not rightfully do. These politicians are subtle, and profound, on the rights of minorities. They are not partial to that power which made the Constitution, and speaks from the preamble, calling itself "We, the People."

. . . This is essentially a People's contest. On the side of the Union, it is a struggle for maintaining in the world, that form, and substance of government, whose leading object is, to elevate the condition of men—to lift artificial weights from all shoulders—to clear the paths of laudable pursuit for all—to afford all, an unfettered start, and a fair chance, in the race of life. Yielding to partial, and temporary departures, from necessity, this is the leading object of the government for whose existence we contend.

. . . Our popular government has often been called an experiment. Two points in it, our people have already settled—the successful establishing, and the successful administering of it. One still remains—its successful maintenance against a formidable [internal] attempt to overthrow it. It is now for them to demonstrate to the world, that those who can fairly carry an election, can also suppress a rebellion—that ballots are the rightful, and peaceful, successors of bullets; and that when ballots have fairly, and constitutionally, decided, there can be no successful appeal, back to bullets; that there can be no successful appeal, except to ballots themselves, at succeeding elections. Such will be a great lesson of peace; teaching men that what they cannot take by an election, neither can they take it by a war—teaching all, the folly of being the beginners of a war.

. . . The Constitution provides, and all the States have accepted the provision, that "The United States shall guarantee to every State in this Union a republican form of government." But, if a State may lawfully go out of the Union, having done so, it may also discard the republican form of government; so that to prevent its going out, is an indispensable means, to the end, of maintaining the guaranty mentioned; and when an end is lawful and obligatory, the indispensable means to it, are also lawful, and obligatory.

ABRAHAM LINCOLN, GETTYSBURG ADDRESS[44]

Four score and seven years ago our fathers brought forth on this continent, a new nation, conceived in Liberty, and dedicated to the proposition that all men are created equal.

Now we are engaged in a great civil war, testing whether that nation, or any nation so conceived and so dedicated, can long endure. We are met on a great battle-field of that war. We have come to dedicate a portion of that field, as a final resting place for those who here gave their lives that that nation might live. It is altogether fitting and proper that we should do this. But, in a larger sense, we can not dedicate—we can not consecrate—we can not hallow—this ground. The brave men, living and dead, who struggled here, have consecrated it, far above our poor power to add or detract. The world will little note, nor long remember what we say here, but it can never forget what they did here. It is for us the living, rather, to be dedicated here to the unfinished work which they who fought here have thus far so nobly advanced. It is rather for us to be here dedicated to the great task remaining before us—that from these honored dead we take increased devotion to that cause for which they gave the last full measure of devotion—that we here highly resolve that these dead shall not have died in vain—that this nation, under God, shall have a new birth of freedom—and that government of the people, by the people, for the people, shall not perish from the earth.

CHARLES SUMNER, STATE SUICIDE RESOLUTIONS[45]

Resolutions declaratory of the Relations between the United States and the Territory once occupied by certain states, and now usurped by the pretended Governments without Constitutional or Legal Right.

Whereas certain states, rightfully belonging to the Union of the United States, have, through their respective Governments, wickedly undertaken to abjure all those duties by which their connection with the Union was maintained, to renounce all allegiance to the Constitution, to levy war upon the National Government, and, for the consummation of this treason, have unconstitutionally and unlawfully confederated together with the declared purpose of putting an end, by force, to the supremacy of the Constitution within their respective limits.

And whereas this condition of insurrection, organized by pretended Governments, openly exists in North Carolina, South Carolina, Georgia, Florida, Alabama, Mississippi, Louisiana, Texas, Arkansas, Tennessee, and Virginia,—except in Eastern Tennessee and Western Virginia,—and the President of the United States, in a proclamation duly made in conformity with an Act of Congress, has declared the same to exist throughout this territory, with the exceptions already named;

And whereas the extensive territory thus usurped by these pretended Governments and organized into a hostile confederation *belongs to the United States, as an inseparable part thereof, under the sanctions of the Constitution*, to be held in trust for the inhabitants in the present and future generations, and is so completely interlinked with the Union that is forever dependent thereupon.

And whereas the Constitution, which is the supreme law of the land, cannot be displaced within this territory, but must ever continue the supreme law thereof, notwithstanding the doing of any pretended Governments, acting singly or in confederation, hostile to its supremacy: Therefore, -

1. *Resolved*, That any vote of secession, or other act, by a State hostile to the supremacy of the Constitution within its territory, *is inoperative and void against the Constitution*, and, when sustained by *force*, becomes a practical abdication by the State of all rights under the Constitution, while treason in it involves works instant forfeiture of all functions and powers essential to the continued existence of the State as a body politic; so that from such time forward the territory falls under the exclusive jurisdiction of Congress, as other territory, and the State becomes, according to the language of the law, *felo de sc.*
2. That any combination of men assuming to act in the place of such State, and attempting to ensure or coerce its inhabitants into a confederation hostile to the Union, is rebellious, treasonable, and destitute of all moral authority; and such combination is a usurpation incapable of constitutional existence and utterly lawless, *so that everything dependent upon it is without constitutional or legal support.*
3. That the termination of a State under the Constitution necessarily causes the termination of those peculiar local institutes which, having no origin in the Constitution, or in natural right independent of the Constitution, are upheld by the sole and exclusive authority of the State.
4. That Slavery, being a peculiar local institution, derived from local law, *without any origin in the Constitution or in natural right*, is upheld by the sole and exclusive authority of the State, and must therefore cease, legally and constitutionally, when the State on which it depends has lapsed; for the incident must follow the principal.
5. That, in the exercise of exclusive jurisdiction over the territory once occupied by the States, it is the duty of Congress to see that the supremacy of the Constitution is maintained in its essential principles, so that everywhere in this extensive territory Slavery shall cease to exist in fact, as it has already ceased to exist in law or Constitution.
6. That any recognition of Slavery in such territory, or surrender of slaves under pretended laws of such states, by an officer of the United States, civil of military, is a practical recognition of the pretended Governments, to the exclusion of the jurisdiction of Congress under the Constitution, and is in the nature of aid and comfort to the Rebellion that has been organized.
7. That any such recognition of Slavery, or surrender of pretended slaves besides being a practical recognition of the pretended Governments,

giving them aid and comfort, is a denial of the rights of persons who by the action of the States have become free, so that, under the Constitution, they cannot again be enslaved.

8. That allegiance from the inhabitant and protection from the Government are corresponding obligations, dependent upon each other; so that, while the allegiance of every inhabitant of this territory, without distinction of class or color, is due to the United States, and cannot in any way be defeated by the action of any pretended Government, or by any pretence of property or claim to service, the corresponding obligation of protection is at the same time due from the Unites States to every such inhabitant, without distinction of class or color; and it follows that inhabitants held as slaves, whose paramount allegiance is to the United States, may justly look to the National Government for protection.

9. That the duty cast upon Congress by the action of the States is enforced by the positive requirement of the Constitution, that "no State shall enter into any confederation," or "without the consent of Congress, keep troops or ships of war in time of peace," or "enter into any agreement or compact with another State," or "grant letters of marque and reprisal," or "coin money," or "emit bills of credit," or, "without the consent of the Congress, lay any imposts or duties on imports or exports," all of which have been done by these pretended Governments, and also by the positive injunction of the Constitution, addressed to the Nation, that "the United States shall guaranty to every State in this Union a republican form of Government" ; and that, in pursuance of this duty cast upon Congress, and further enjoined by the Constitution, *Congress will assume complete jurisdiction of such vacated territory, where such unconstitutional and illegal things have been attempted, and will proceed to establish therein republican forms of government under the Constitution*, and, in the execution of this trust, will provide carefully for the protection of all the inhabitants thereof, for the security of families, the organization of labor, the encouragement of industry, and the welfare of society, and will in every way discharge the duties of a just, merciful, and paternal Government.

ANDREW JOHNSON, VETO OF THE
FIRST RECONSTRUCTION ACT[46]

. . . The bill places all the people of the ten States therein named under the absolute domination of military rule; and the preamble undertakes to give the reason upon which the measure is based and the ground upon which it is justified. It declares that there exists in those States no legal governments and no adequate protection for life or property, and asserts the necessity of enforcing peace and good order within their limits. This is not true as a matter of fact.

It is not denied that the States in question have each of them an actual government, with all the powers—executive, judicial, and legislative—which properly belong to a free State. They are organized like the other States of the Union, and, like them, they make, administer, and execute the laws which concern their domestic affairs. An existing de facto government, exercising such functions as these, is itself the law of the State upon all matters within its jurisdiction. To pronounce the supreme law making power of an established State illegal is to say that law itself is unlawful.

The provisions which these governments have made for the preservation of order, the suppression of crime, and the redress of private injuries are in substance and principle the same as those which prevail in the Northern States and in other civilized countries. They certainly have not succeeded in preventing the commission of all crime, nor has this been accomplished any where in the world . . . . But that people are maintaining local governments for themselves which habitually defeat the object of all government and render their own lives and property insecure is in itself utterly improbable, and the averment of the bill to that effect is not supported by any evidence which has come to my knowledge.

The bill, however, would seem to show upon its face that the establishment of peace and good order is not its real object. The fifth section declares that the preceding sections shall cease to operate in any State where certain events shall have happened. These events are, first, the selection of delegates to a State convention by an election at which Negroes shall be allowed to vote; second, the formation of a State constitution by the convention so chosen; third, the insertion into the State constitution of a provision which will secure the right of voting at all elections to Negroes and to such white men as may not be disfranchised for rebellion or felony; fourth, the submission of the constitution for ratification by their vote; fifth, the submission of the State constitution to Congress for examination and approval, and the actual approval of it by that body; sixth, the adoption of a certain amendment to the Federal Constitution by a vote of Legislature elected under the new constitution; seventh, the adoption of said amendment by a sufficient number of other States to make it a part of the Constitution of the United States. All these conditions must be fulfilled before the people of any of these States can be relieved from the bondage of military domination; but when they are fulfilled, then immediately the pains and penalties of the bill are to cease, no matter whether there be peace and order or not, and without any reference to the security of life or property.

The excuse given for the bill in the preamble is one of necessity. The military rule which it establishes is plainly to be used, not for any purpose of order or for the prevention of crime, but solely as a means of coercing the people into the adoption of principles and measures to which it is known that they are opposed, and upon which they have an undeniable right to exercise their own judgment.

I submit to Congress whether this measure is not in its whole character, scope, and object without precedent and without authority, in palpable conflict with the plainest provisions of liberty and humanity for which our ancestors on both sides of the Atlantic have shed so much blood, and expended so much treasure.

. . . If, therefore, the Southern States were in truth out of the Union, we could not treat their people in a way which the fundamental law forbids. Some persons assume that the success of our arms in crushing the opposition which was made in some of the States to the execution of the Federal laws reduced those States and all their people—the innocent as well as the guilty—to the condition of vassalage and gave us a power over them which the Constitution does not bestow or define or limit. No fallacy can be more transparent than this. Our victories subjected the insurgents to legal obedience, not to the yoke of an arbitrary despotism. When an absolute sovereign reduces his rebellious subjects, he may deal with them according to his pleasure, because he had that power before. But when a limited monarch puts down an insurrection, he must still govern according to law.

. . . I have always contended that the Government of the United States was sovereign within its constitutional sphere; that it executed its laws like the States themselves, by applying its coercive power directly to individuals; and that it could put down insurrection with the same effect as a State and no other. The opposite doctrine is the worst heresy of those who advocated secession, and can not be agreed to without admitting that heresy to be right.

. . . That the measure proposed by this bill does violate the Constitution in the particulars mentioned and in many other ways which I forbear to enumerate is too clear to admit the least doubt. It only remains to consider whether the injunctions of that instrument ought to be obeyed or not. I think they ought to be obeyed, for reasons which I will proceed to give as briefly as possible. In the first place, it is the only system of free Government which we can hope to have as a Nation. When it ceases to be the rule of our conduct, we may perhaps take our choice between complete anarchy, a consolidated despotism, and a total dissolution of the Union; but national liberty regulated by law will have passed beyond our reach.

It was to punish the gross crime of defying the Constitution and to vindicate its supreme authority that we carried on a bloody war of four years' duration. Shall we now acknowledge that we sacrificed a million of lives and expended billions of treasure to enforce a Constitution which is not worthy of respect and preservation?

TEXAS v. WHITE[47]

The first inquires to which our attention was directed by counsel, arose upon the allegations . . . that the State, having severed her relations with a majority of the States of the Union, and having by her ordinance of secession attempted to throw off her allegiance to the Constitution and government of the United States, has so far changed her status as to be disabled from prosecuting suits in the National courts . . .

If, therefore, it is true that the state of Texas was not at the time of filing this bill, or is not now, one of the United States, we have no jurisdiction of this suit, and it is our duty to dismiss it

. . . In the Constitution the term state most frequently expresses the combined idea just noticed, of people, territory, and government. A state, in the ordinary sense of the Constitution, is a political community of free citizens, occupying a territory of defined boundaries, and organized under a government sanctioned and limited by a written constitution, and established by the consent of the governed. It is the union of such states, under a common constitution, which forms the distinct and greater political unit, which that Constitution designates as the United States, and makes of the people and states which compose it one people and one country . . .

. . . From the date of admission, until 1861, the State was represented in the Congress of the United States by her senators and representatives, and her relations as a member of the Union remained unimpaired. In that year, acting upon the theory that the rights of a State under the Constitution might be renounced, and her obligations thrown off at pleasure, Texas undertook to sever the bond thus formed, and to break up her constitutional relations with the United States.

The position thus assumed could only be maintained by arms, and Texas accordingly took part, with the other Confederate States, in the war of the rebellion, which these events made inevitable. During the whole of that war there was no governor, or judge, or any other State officer in Texas, who recognized the National authority. Nor was any officer of the United States permitted to exercise any authority whatever under the National government within the limits of the State, except under the immediate protection of the National military forces.

Did Texas, in consequence of these acts, cease to be a State? Or, if not, did the State cease to be a member of the Union?

It is needless to discuss, at length, the question whether the right of a State to withdraw from the Union for any cause, regarded by herself as sufficient, is consistent with the Constitution of the United States.

The Union of the States never was a purely artificial and arbitrary relation. It began among the Colonies, and grew out of common origin, mutual sympathies, kindred principles, similar interests, and geographical relations. It was confirmed and strengthened by the necessities of war, and received definite form, and character, and sanction from the Articles of Confederation. By these the Union was solemnly declared to "be perpetual." And when these Articles were found to be inadequate to the exigencies of the country, the Constitution was ordained "to form a more perfect Union." It is difficult to convey the idea of indissoluble unity more clearly than by these words. What can be indissoluble if a perpetual Union, made more perfect, is not?

But the perpetuity and indissolubility of the Union, by no means implies the loss of distinct and individual existence, or of the right of self-government by the States. Under the Articles of Confederation each State retained its sovereignty, freedom, and independence, and every power, jurisdiction, and right not expressly delegated to the United States. Under the Constitution, thought the powers of the States were much restricted, still, all powers not delegated to the United States, nor prohibited to the States, are reserved to the States respectively, or to the people. And we have already had occasion to remark at this term, that "the people of each State compose a State, having its own government, and endowed with all the functions essential to separate and independent existence," and that "without the States in Union, there could be no loss of separate and independent autonomy to the States, through their union under the Constitution, but it may be not unreasonably said that the preservations of the States, and the maintenance of their governments, are as much within the design and care of the Constitution as the preservation of the Union and the maintenance of the National government. The Constitution, in all its provisions, looks to an indestructible Union, composed of indestructible States.

When, therefore, Texas became one of the United States, she entered into an indissoluble relation. All the obligations of perpetual union, and all of the guaranties of republican government in the Union, attached at once to the State. The act which consummated her admission into the Union was something more than a compact; it was the incorporation of a new member into the political body. And it was final. The union between Texas and the other States was as complete, as perpetual, and as indissoluble as the union between the original States. There was no place for reconsideration, or revocation, except through revolution, or through consent of the States.

Considered therefore as transactions under the Constitution, the ordinance of secession, adopted by the convention and ratified by a majority of the citizens of Texas, and all the acts of her legislature intended to give effect to that ordinance, were absolutely null. They were utterly without operation in law. The obligations of the State, as a member of the Union, and of every citizen of the State, as a citizen of the United States, remained perfect and unimpaired. It certainly follows that the State did not cease to be the State, nor her citizens to be citizens to be citizens of the Union. If this were otherwise, the State must have become foreign, and her citizens foreigners. The war must have ceased to become a war for conquest and subjugation.

Our conclusion therefore is, that Texas continued to be a State, and a State of the Union, notwithstanding the transactions to which we have referred. And this conclusion, in our judgement, is not in conflict with any act or declaration of any department of the National government, but entirely in accordance with the whole series of such acts and declarations since the outbreak of the rebellion.

WOODROW WILSON, "THE STATES AND THE FEDERAL GOVERNMENT"[48]

The question of the relation of the States to the Federal Government is the cardinal question of our constitutional system. At every turn of our national development we have been brought face to face with it, and no definition either of statesmen or of judges has ever quieted or decided it. It cannot, indeed, be settled by the opinion of any one generation, because it is a question of growth, and every successive stage of our political and economic development gives it a new aspect, makes it a new question. The general lines of definition which were to run between the powers granted to Congress and the powers reserved to the States the makers of the Constitution were able to draw with their characteristic foresight and lucidity; but the subject-matter of that definition is constantly changing, for it is the life of the nation itself. Our activities change alike their scope and their character with every generation. The old measures of the Constitution are every day to be filled with new grain as the varying crop of circumstances comes to maturity. It is clear enough that the general commercial, financial, economic interests of the country were meant to be brought under the regulation of the Federal Government, which should act for all; and it is equally clear that what are the general commercial, financial, economic interests of the country is a question of fact, to be determined by circumstances which change under our very eyes, and that, case by case, we are inevitably drawn on to include under the established definitions of the law matters new and unforeseen which seem in their magnitude to give to the powers of Congress a sweep and vigor certainly never conceived possible by earlier generations of statesmen, sometimes almost revolutionary even in our own eyes. The subject-matter of this troublesome definition is the living body of affairs.

The principle of the division of powers between State and Federal governments is a very simple one when stated in its most general terms. It is that the Legislatures of the States shall have control of all the general subject-matter of law, of private rights of every kind, of local interests and of everything that directly concerns their people as communities,—free choice with regard to all matters of local regulation and development, and that Congress shall have control only of such matters as concern the peace and the commerce of the country as a whole.

. . . Which parts of the many-sided processes of the nation's economic development shall be left to the regulation of the States, which parts shall be given over to the regulation of the Federal Government? I do not propound this as a mere question of statesmanship, but also as a question, a very fundamental question, of constitutional law. What, reading our Constitution in its true spirit, neither stinking in its letter nor yet forcing it arbitrarily to mean what we wish it to mean, shall be the answer of our generation to the old question of the distribution of powers between Congress and the States? For us, as for previous generations, it is a deeply critical question. The very stuff of all our political principles, of all our political experience, is involved in it. In this all too indistinctly marked field of right choice our statesmanship shall achieve new triumphs or come to eventual shipwreck.

The old theory of the sovereignty of the States, which used so to engage our passions, has lost its vitality. The war between the States established at least this principle, that the Federal Government is, through its courts, the final judge of its own powers. Since that stern arbitrament it would be idle, in any practical argument, to ask by what law of abstract principle the Federal Government is bound and restrained. Its power is "to regulate commerce between the States," and the attempts now made during every session of Congress to carry the implications of that power beyond the utmost boundaries of reasonable and honest inference show that the only limits likely to be observed by politicians are those set by the good sense and conservative temper of the country.

It is important, therefore, to look at the at facts and to understand the real character of the political and economic materials of our own day with a clear and statesmanlike vision, as the makers of the Constitution understood the conditions they dealt with. If the jealousies of the colonies and of the little States which sprang out of them had not obliged the makers of the Constitution to leave the greater part of legal regulation in the hands of the States, it would have been wise, it would have been necessary, to invent such a division of powers as was actually agreed upon. It is not, at bottom, a question of sovereignty or of any other political abstraction; it is a question of vitality. Uniform regulation of the economic conditions of a vast territory and a various people like the United States would be mischievous, if not impossible. The statesmanship which really attempts it is premature and unwise. Undoubtedly the recent economic development of the country, particularly the development of the last two decades, has obliterated many boundaries,

made many interests national and common which until our own day were separate and distinct; but the lines of these great changes we have not yet clearly
traced or studiously enough considered. To distinguish them and provide for
them is the task which is to test the statesmanship of our generation; and it is
already plain that, great as they are, these new combinations of interest have
not yet gone so far as to make the States mere units of local government.
Not our legal conscience merely, but our practical interests as well, call upon
us to discriminate and be careful, with the care of men who handle the vital
stuff of a great constitutional system.

The United States are not a single, homogeneous community. In spite of a
certain superficial sameness which seems to impart to Americans a common
type and point of view, they still contain communities at almost every stage of
development, illustrating in their social and economic structure almost every
modern variety of interest and prejudice, following occupations of every
kind, in climates of every sort that the temperate zone affords. This variety
of fact and condition, these substantial economic and social contrasts, do not
in all cases follow State lines. They are often contrasts between region and
region rather than between State and State. But they are none the less real,
and are in many instances permanent and ineradicable.

From the first the United States have been socially and economically
divided into regions rather than into States.

We are too apt to think that our American political system is distinguished
by its central structure, by its President and Congress and courts, which the
Constitution of the Union set up. As a matter of fact, it is distinguished by
its local structure, by the extreme vitality of its parts. It would be an impossibility without its division of powers. From the first it has been a nation in
the making. It has come to maturity by the stimulation of no central force or
guidance but by the abounding self-helping, self-sufficing energy of its parts,
which severally brought themselves into existence and added themselves to
the Union, pleasing first of all themselves in the framing of their laws and
constitutions, not asking leave to exist, but existing first and asking leave
afterwards, self-originated, self-constituted, self-confident, self-sustaining,
veritable communities, demanding only recognition. Communities develop,
not by external, but by internal forces. Else they do not live at all. Our commonwealths have not come into existence by invitation, like plants in a tended
garden; they have sprung up on themselves, irrepressible, a sturdy, spontaneous product of the nature of men nurtured in a free air.

The division of powers between the States and the Federal Government
effected by our Federal Constitution was the normal and natural division for
this purpose. Under it the States possess all the ordinary legal choices that
shape a people's life. Theirs is the whole of the ordinary field of law: the regulation of domestic relations and of the ordinary field of law: the regulation

of domestic relations and of the relations between employer and employee, the determination of property rights and of the validity and enforcement of contracts, the definition of crimes and their punishments, the definition of the many and subtle rights and obligations which lie outside the fields of property and contract, the establishment of the laws of incorporation and of the rules governing the conduct of every kind of business. The presumption insisted upon by the Courts in every argument with regard to the Federal Government is that it has no power not explicitly granted it by the Federal Constitution or reasonably to be inferred as the natural or necessary accompaniment of the powers there conveyed to it; but the presumption with regard to the powers of the States they have always held to be exactly the opposite kind. It is that the States of course possess every power that government has ever anywhere exercised, except only those powers which their own constitutions or the Constitution of the United States explicitly or by plain inference withhold. They are the ordinary governments of the country; the Federal Government is its instrument only for particular purposes.

Congress is, indeed, the immediate government of the people. It does not govern the States, but acts directly upon individuals, as directly as the governments of the States themselves. It does not stand at a distance and look on,—to be ready for an occasional interference,—but is the immediate and familiar instrument of the people in everything that it undertakes, as if there were no States. The States do not stand between it and the people. Bu the field of its action is distinct, restricted, and definite.

Added to this doubt and difficulty of analysis which makes it a constant matter of debate what the powers of Congress are is the growing dissatisfaction with the part the States are playing in the economic life of the day. They either let the pressing problems of the time alone and attempt no regulation at all, however loudly opinion and circumstance itself may call for it, or they try every half-considered remedy, embark upon a thousand experiments, and bring utter confusion upon the industry of the country by contradicting and offsetting each other's measures. No two States act alike. Manufacturers and carriers who serve commerce in many States find it impossible to obey the laws of all, and the enforcement of the laws of the States in all their variety threatens the country with a new war of conflicting regulations as serious as that which made the Philadelphia convention of 1787 necessary and gave us a new Federal Constitution. This conflict of laws in matters which vitally interest the whole country and in which no State or region can wisely stand apart to serve any particular interest of its own constitutes the greatest political danger of our day. It is more apt and powerful than any other cause to bring upon us radical and ill-considered changes. It confuses our thinking up on essential matters and makes us hasty reformers out of mere impatience. We are in danger of acting before we clearly know what we want or comprehend the consequences of what we do,—in danger of altering the character of the government in order to escape a temporary inconvenience.

We are an industrial people. The development of the resources of the country, the command of the markets of the world, is for the time being more important in our eyes than any political theory or lawyer's discrimination of functions. We are intensely "practical," moreover, and insist that every obstacle, whether of law or fact, be swept out of the way. It is not the right temper for constitutional understandings. Too "practical" a purpose may give us a government such as we never should have chosen had we made the choice more thoughtfully and deliberately. We cannot afford to belie our reputation for political sagacity and self-possession by any such hasty processes as those into which such a temper of mere impatience seems likely to hurry us.

... There is, however, something else that comes to the surface, and that explains not a little of our present dissatisfaction with State legislation upon matters of vital national importance. Their failure to correct their own processes may prove that there is something radically wrong with the structure and operation of their governments,—that they have ceased to be sensitive and efficient instruments for the creation and realization of opinion,—the real function of constitutional governments.

It is better to learn the true political lesson than merely to improve business. There is something involved which is deeper than the mere question of the distribution of legislative powers within our Federal system. We have come to the test of the intimate and detailed processes of self-government to which it was supposed that our principles and our experience had committed us. There are many evidences that we are losing confidence in our State Legislatures, and yet it is evident that it is through them that we attempt all the more intimate measures of self-government. To lose faith in them is to lose faith in our very system of government, and that is a very serious matter. It is this loss of confidence in our local legislatures that has led our people to give so much heed to the radical suggestions of change made by those who advocate the use of the initiative and the referendum in our processes of legislation, the virtual abandonment of the representative principle and the attempt to put into the hands of the voters themselves the power to initiate and negative laws,— in order to enable them to do for themselves what they have not been able to get satisfactorily done through the representatives they have hitherto chosen to act for them.

The truth is that our State governments are many of them no longer truly representative governments. We are not, in fact, dissatisfied with local representative assemblies and the government which they impose; we are dissatisfied, rather, with regulations imposed by commissions and assemblies which are no longer representative.

. . . The country feels, therefore, that, however selected, they are in some sense more representative, more to be depended on to register its thoughtful judgments, than the members of State Legislatures are.

It is for this reason as much as for any other that the balance of powers between the States and the Federal Government now trembles at an unstable equilibrium and we hesitate into which scale to throw the weight of our purpose and preference with regard to the legislation by which we shall attempt to thread the maze of our present economic needs and perplexities. It may turn out that what our State governments need is not to be sapped of their powers and subordinated to Congress, but to be reorganized along simpler lines which will make them real organs of popular opinion. A government must have organs; it cannot act inorganically, by masses. It must have a law-making body; it can no more make laws through its voters than it can make them through its newspapers.

It would be fatal to our political vitality really to strip the States of their powers and transfer them to the Federal Government. It cannot be too often repeated that it has been the privilege of separate development secured to the several regions of the country by the Constitution, and not the privilege of separate development only, but also that other more fundamental privilege that lies back of it, the privilege of independent local opinion and individual conviction, which has given speed, facility, vigor, and certainty to the processes of our economic and political growth. To buy temporary ease and convenience for the performance of a few great tasks of the hour at the expense of that would be to pay too great a price and to cheat all generations for the sake of one.

Undoubtedly the powers of the Federal Government have grown enormously since the creation of the Government; and they have grown for the most part without amendment of the Constitution. But they have grown in almost every instance by a process which must be regarded as perfectly normal and legitimate. The Constitution cannot be regarded as a mere legal document, to be read as a will or a contract would be. It must of the necessity of the case be a vehicle of life. As the life of the nation changes so much the interpretation of the document which contains it change, by a nice adjustment determined, not by the original intention of those who drew the paper, but by the exigencies and the new aspects of life itself. Changes of fact and alterations of opinion bring in their train actual extensions of community of interest, actual additions to the catalogue of things which must be included under the general terms of the law. The commerce of great systems of railway is of course not the commerce of wagon roads, the only land commerce known in the days when the Constitution was drafted. The common interests of a nation bound together in thought and interest and action by the telegraph and the telephone, as well as by the rushing mails which every express train carries, have a scope and variety, an infinite multiplication and intricate interlacing of which a simpler day can have had no conception. Every general term of the Constitution has come to have a meaning as varied as the actual variety of the things which the country now shares in common.

The character of the process of constitutional adaptation depends first of all upon the wise or unwise choice of statesmen, but ultimately and chiefly upon the opinion and purpose of the courts. The chief instrumentality by which the law of the Constitution has been extended to cover the facts of national development has been judicial interpretation, the decisions of the courts. The process of formal amendment of the Constitution itself that it has seldom been feasible to use it; and the difficulty of formal amendment has undoubtedly made the courts more liberal, not to say more lax, in their interpretation than they would otherwise have been. The whole business of adaptation was theirs, and they have undertaken it with open minds, sometimes even with boldness and a touch of audacity. But, though they have sometimes been lax, though they have sometimes yielded, it may be, to the pressure of popular agitation and of party interest, they have not often overstepped the bounds of legitimate extension. By legitimate extension I mean extension which does not change the character of the Federal power but only its items,—which does not make new kinds, but only new particulars of power.

The members of courts are necessarily men of their own generation: we would not wish to have them men of another. Constitutional law, as well as statesmanship, must look forward, not backward, and, while we should wish the courts to be conservative, we should certainly be deeply uneasy were they to hold affairs back from their natural alteration. Change as well as stability may be conservative. Conservative change is conservative, not of prejudices, but of principles, of established purposes and conceptions, the only things which in government or in any other field of action can abide. Conservative progress is a process, not of revolution, but of modification. In our own case and in the matter now under discussion it consists in a slowly progressive modification and transfer of functions as between the States and the Federal Government along the lines of actual development, along the lines of actual and substantial alterations of interest and of that national consciousness which is the breath of all true amendment,—and not along lines of party or individual purpose, nor by way of desperate search for remedies for existing evils.

No doubt courts must "make" law for their own day, must have the insight which adapts law to its uses rather than its uses to it, must sometimes venture upon decisions which have a certain touch of statesmanlike initiative in them. We shall often find ourselves looking to them for strong and fearless opinions. But there are two kinds of "strong" opinions, as a distinguished English jurist long ago pointed out. There are those which are strong with the strength of insight and intelligence and those which are strong with the mere strength of will. The latter sort all judges who act with conscience, mindful of their oaths of office, should eschew as they would eschew the actual breaking of law. That the Federal courts should have such a conscience is essential to the integrity of our whole national action. Actual alterations of interest in the make-up of our national life, actual, unmistakable changes in our national consciousness, actual modifications in our national activities such as give a new aspect and significance to the well-known purposes of our fundamental law, should of course be taken up into decisions which add to the number of things in which the national Government must take cognizance and regulative control. That is a function of insight and intelligence. The courage it calls for on the part of the courts is the courage of conviction. But they are, on the other hand, called on to display the more noble courage which defends ancient conviction and established principle against the clamor, the class interest and the changeful moods of parties. They should never permit themselves willfully to seek to find in the phrases of the Constitution remedies for evils which the Federal Government was never intended to deal with.

Moral and social questions originally left to the several States for settlement can be drawn into the field of Federal authority only at the expense of the self-dependence and efficiency of the several communities of which our complex body politic is made up. Paternal morals, morals enforced by the judgment and choices of the central authority at Washington, do not and cannot create vital habits or methods of life unless sustained by local opinion and purpose, local prejudice and convenience,—unless supported by local convenience and interest; and only communities capable of taking care of themselves will, taken together, constitute a nation capable of vital action and control. You cannot atrophy the parts without atrophying the whole. Deliberate adding to the powers of the Federal Government by sheer judicial authority, because the Supreme Court can no longer be withstood or contradicted in the States, both saps the legal morality upon which a sound constitutional system must rest and deprives the Federal structure as a whole of the vitality which has given the Supreme Court itself its increase of power. It is the alchemy of decay.

It would certainly mean that we had acquired a new political temper, never hitherto characteristic of us, that we had utterly lost confidence in what we set out to do, were we now to substitute abolition for reform,—were by degrees to do away with our boasted system of self-government out of mere impatience and disgust, like those who got rid of an instrument they no longer knew how to use. There are some hopeful signs that we may be about to return to the better way of a time when we knew how to restrict government and adapt it to our uses in accordance with principles we did not doubt, but adhered to with an ardent fervor which was the best evidence of youth and virility.

We have long been painfully conscious that we have failed in the matter of city government. It is an age of cities, and if we cannot govern our cities we cannot govern at all. For a little while we acted as if in despair. We began to strip our city governments of their powers and to transfer them to State commissions or back to the Legislatures of the States, very much as we are now stripping the States of their powers and putting them in the hands of Federal commissions. The attempt was made to put the police departments of some of our citifies, for example, in the hands of State officers, and to put the granting of city franchises back into the hands of the central Legislature of the State, in the hope, apparently, that a uniform regulation of such things by the opinion of the whole State might take the place of corrupt control by city politicians. But it did not take us long, fortunately, to see that we were moving in the wrong direction. We have now turned to the better way of reconsidering the whole question of the organization of city governments, and are likely within a generation to purify them by simplifying them, to moralize them by placing their government in the hands of a few persons who can really be selected by popular preference instead of by the private processes of nomination by party managers, and who, because few and conspicuous, can really be watched and held to a responsibility which they will honor because they cannot escape.

It is to be hoped that we shall presently have the same light dawn upon us with regard to our State governments, and, instead of upsetting an ancient system, hallowed by long use and deep devotion, revitalize it by reorganization. And that, not only because it is an old system long beloved, but also because we are certified by all political history of the fact that centralization is not vitalization. Moralization is by life, not by statue, by the interior impulse and experience of communities, not by fostering legislation which is merely the abstraction of an experience which may belong to a nation as a whole or to many parts of it without having yet touched the thought of the rest anywhere to the quick. The object of our Federal system is to bring the understandings of constitutional government home to the people of every part of the nation, to make them part of their consciousness as they go about their daily tasks. If we cannot successfully effect its adjustments by the nice local adaptations of our older practice e, we have failed as constitutional statesmen.

ALBERT BEVERIDGE, "VITALITY OF THE AMERICAN CONSTITUTION"[49]

. . . our Constitution proceeded from "progressive history," and therefore is capable of future growth, just as it is the result of past growth. The Constitution was not a contract between thirteen allies called states, and so to be construed as a contract is to be construed; it was and is an ordinance of nationality springing from the necessities of the people and established directly by the people themselves. And as the Constitution gradually grew out of the necessities of the people in the past and was formulated out of the necessities of the people at the time of its adoption, so it embraces the necessities of the people for all time. But as the necessities of the people for all time could not possibly have been foreseen by the men who wrote the Constitution, it follows that they could not have intended to confine the purposes of the Constitution and the powers it confers to the necessities of the people of 1789; that they so wrote it that it might meet the requirements of the people for all time.

If that is so, it follows that the Constitution must steadily grow, because the requirements of the people steadily grow. . . . So, the vitality of the American Constitution and all constitutions must reside in their power to grow as the people grow, and furnish scope for the people's power and the Nation's necessities in exact proportion as the people's power and the Nation's necessities enlarge.

. . . The Golden Rule of constitutional interpretation is this: *The Constitution exists for the people, not the people for the Constitution.* But how can a written Constitution grow? Its words are there not to be changed. But the people change; conditions change; new problems arise; the happiness and welfare of the Nation constantly demand new methods, enlarging powers, activities in directions hitherto unknown. And if the Constitution cannot keep pace with the needs of the people, it ceases to be useful to the people and becomes oppressive to them.

. . . If the Constitution had locked up the people's energies and prevented the recognition of their ever-increasing necessities and paralyzed their ever-enlarging powers, the people would have made short work of the Constitution. They would have over-thrown it by revolution, if necessary, just as the people will overthrow anything which stands in the way of the prosperity of their homes, the happiness of their firesides. The march of nationality is not to be withstood; and so the salvation of the Constitution is in its capacity for growth; and he is the enemy, no matter how much he may think himself the friend, of our fundamental law, who does not recognize its capacity for self-enlargement, determined by the enlarging necessities of the people. He is the enemy of the American Constitution who binds the American people to the letter of that instrument; for if that were done, the people's expanding necessities would overthrow a constitution which retarded and op-pressed them.

. . . So it follows that whatever may be essential to the development of the people's nationality lies latent in the Constitution's general terms, awaiting the necessity of events to call it into action. . . . [We are] a Nation of the people, deriving its powers directly from them and not from the states. If that is so, if nationality is the great purpose of the Constitution, if the people directly are the source of its power and the object of its beneficence, then unexpressed powers and duties in the National Government were called into being, which upon any other theory could not possibly exist.

... This aspiration of the common people toward nationality has expressed itself through every branch of the Government, legislative as well as judicial, executive as well as legislative. Indeed, the Constitution may be said to have been construed, as it was created, by the people's common instinct of nationality. The doctrinaires declared that internal improvements by the National Government were unconstitutional. Three of our Presidents were sure of it. Jefferson so believed. Madison vetoed the first internal-improvement bill on the ground of its unconstitutionality. Monroe made it the subject of a message to Congress.

But the common people knew better than the theorists. No matter what refined logic, spun from mere words and names, might conclude, the farmer and the trader, the feller of forests, the tiller of fields. the builder of homes, the makers, one and all of the Nation, knew that they were fellow-citizens of the American Republic, and not mere members of friendly localities, and so they said: "It is the business of our common Nation to build canals, construct the national highways; clear the rivers, dredge the harbors of our common country; it is absurd to leave to each neighborhood its portion of the work, which if undone impairs and possibly destroys the whole;" and so internal improvements have become an unquestioned practice of the National Government.

... The exercise of the doctrine of implied powers has surrounded the written Constitution with a body of judicial decisions and legislative and executive practices which have grown to be as firm a part of our fundamental law as the written word of the instrument itself; and so it is that the Constitution has grown steadily and will grow steadily just as long and just as fast as the people themselves make progress. If this had not been so, the Constitution would have been a curse instead of a blessing. It would have been an iron band pressed around a young and growing tree, checking its growth and finally strangling it to death, instead of the bark which surrounds the trunk and expands as the great and substantial body within makes progress toward maturity. For the people are the real tree; the Nation is the real trunk; the Constitution is the vital encasement which sur-rounds and protects it, but which keeps progress with the growth of the tree itself.

... These inherent powers exist in the nature of government. They are a part of the thing called sovereignty, without which government could not exist. The government is a real and not a fictitious thing. It lives. It is not an automaton operated through written instruments alone. Whatever is necessary to its continued life and to its beneficent operation exists by virtue of the existence of the government itself. If you name government, you imply powers needful for that government's operation; and therefore when government is established that very act creates those powers which sleep till necessity awakens them.

. . . Whether you agree to this or not, all must concede that, *as a matter of fact*, both Congress and the Executive are almost daily exercising powers not mentioned in the Constitution. And it is certain that the only two theories upon which this exercise of power may be justified are either, first, that these powers are inherent in sovereignty, or else, second, that they are powers reserved to the people and exercised by the people through their agents.

. . . But the future of the American people is heavy with difficulties; so is all opportunity for great and splendid work. Increasing population; the knitting together by railway, telegraph and telephone of places most remote until the Republic is a single and consolidated community; the combination of capital and labor, which this development makes necessary; the shrinking of the very globe itself by these same agencies, until nations are neighbors and alien peoples are at elbow touch: the new problems and novel responsibilities, which all this brings: the still undreamed of emergencies of a yet undreamed of future—all these will demand of the American people all their resourcefulness, purity and power.

And the American people will solve and overcome them all if their hands are not fettered. The hands of the American people were not fettered, but armed with strength, when the Constitution was adopted. That free hand was not paralyzed, but connected with the mind and heart of the Nation . . . So is our Constitution a source of life and power—the spirit and soul of a mighty people's progress. And so God defend and God preserve the American Constitution—a living spirit and not a dead and fading parchment!

THEODORE ROOSEVELT, "NEW NATIONALISM"[50]

I stand for the square deal. But when I say that I am for the square deal, I mean not merely that I stand for fair play under the present rules of the game, but that I stand for having those rules changed so as to work for a more substantial equality of opportunity and of reward for equally good service.

. . . Now, this means that our government, national and state, must be freed from the sinister influence or control of special interests. Exactly as the special interests of cotton and slavery threatened our political integrity before the Civil War, so now the great special business interests too often control and corrupt the men and methods of government for their own profit. We must drive the special interests out of politics. That is one of our tasks to-day. Every special interest is entitled to justice—full, fair, and complete—and, now, mind you, if there were any attempt by mob-violence to plunder and work harm to the special interest, whatever it may be, that I most dislike, and the wealthy man, whomsoever he may be, for whom I have the greatest contempt, I would fight for him, and you would if you were worth your salt. He should have justice. For every special interest is entitled to justice, but not one is entitled to a vote in Congress, to a voice on the bench, or to representation in any public office. The Constitution guarantees protection to property, and we must make that promise good. But it does not give the right of suffrage to any corporation.

The true friend of property, the true conservative, is he who insists that property shall be the servant and not the master of the commonwealth; who insists that the creature of man's making shall be the servant and not the master of the man who made it. The citizens of the United States must effectively control the mighty commercial forces which they have called into being.

There can be no effective control of corporations while their political activity remains. To put an end to it will be neither a short nor an easy task, but it can be done.

We must have complete and effective publicity of corporate affairs, so that the people may know beyond peradventure whether the corporations obey the law and whether their management entitles them to the confidence of the public. It is necessary that laws should be passed to prohibit the use of corporate funds directly or indirectly for political purposes; it is still more necessary that such laws should be thoroughly enforced. Corporate expenditures for political purposes, and especially such expenditures by public service corporations, have supplied one of the principal sources of corruption in our political affairs.

It has become entirely clear that we must have government supervision of the capitalization, not only of public service corporations, including, particularly, railways, but of all corporations doing an interstate business. I do not wish to see the nation forced into the ownership of the railways if it can possibly be avoided, and the only alternative is thoroughgoing and effective legislation, which shall be based on a full knowledge of all the facts, including a physical valuation of property.

. . . The absence of effective State, and, especially, national, restraint upon unfair money-getting has tended to create a small class of enormously wealthy and economically powerful men, whose chief object is to hold and increase their power. The prime need to is to change the conditions which enable these men to accumulate power which it is not for the general welfare that they should hold or exercise. We grudge no man a fortune which represents his own power and sagacity, when exercised with entire regard to the welfare of his fellows.

. . . This, I know, implies a policy of a far more active governmental interference with social and economic conditions in this country than we have yet had, but I think we have got to face the fact that such an increase in governmental control is now necessary.

. . . Nothing is more true than that excess of every kind is followed by reaction; a fact which should be pondered by reformer and reactionary alike. We are face to face with new conceptions of the relations of property to human welfare, chiefly because certain advocates of the rights of property as against the rights of men have been pushing their claims too far. The man who wrongly holds that every human right is secondary to his profit must now give way to the advocate of human welfare, who rightly maintains that every man holds his property subject to the general right of the community to regulate its use to whatever degree the public welfare may require it.

But I think we may go still further. The right to regulate the use of wealth in the public interest is universally admitted. Let us admit also the right to regulate the terms and conditions of labor, which is the chief element of wealth, directly in the interest of the common good. The fundamental thing to do for every man is to give him a chance to reach a place in which he will make the greatest possible contribution to the public welfare. Understand what I say there. Give him a chance, not push him up if he will not be pushed. Help any man who stumbles; if he lies down, it is a poor job to try to carry him; but if he is a worthy man, try your best to see that he gets a chance to show the worth that is in him. No man can be a good citizen unless he has a wage more than sufficient to cover the bare cost of living, and hours of labor short enough so after his day's work is done he will have time and energy to bear his share in the management of the community, to help in carrying the general load. We keep countless men from being good citizens by the conditions of life by which we surround them. We need comprehensive workman's compensation acts, both State and national laws to regulate child labor and work for women, and, especially, we need in our common schools not merely education in book-learning, but also practical training for daily life and work. We need to enforce better sanitary conditions for our workers and to extend the use of safety appliances for workers in industry and commerce, both within and between the States. Also, friends, in the interest of the working man himself, we need to set our faces like flint against mob-violence just as against corporate greed; against violence and injustice and lawlessness by wage-workers just as much as against lawless cunning and greed and selfish arrogance of employers.

National efficiency has many factors. It is a necessary result of the principle of conservation widely applied. In the end, it will determine our failure or success as a nation. National efficiency has to do, not only with natural resources and with men, but it is equally concerned with institutions. The State must be made efficient for the work which concerns only the people of the State; and the nation for that which concerns all the people. There must remain no neutral ground to serve as a refuge for lawbreakers, and especially for lawbreakers of great wealth, who can hire the vulpine legal cunning which will teach them how to avoid both jurisdictions. It is a misfortune when the national legislature fails to do its duty in providing a national remedy, so that the only national activity is the purely negative activity of the judiciary forbidding the State to exercise power in the premises.

I do not ask for the over centralization; but I do ask that we work in a spirit of broad and far-reaching nationalism where we work for what concerns our people as a whole. We are all Americans. Our common interests are as broad as the continent. I speak to you here in Kansas exactly as I would speak in New York or Georgia, for the most vital problems are those which affect us all alike. The National Government belongs to the whole American people, and where the whole American people are interested, that interest can be guarded effectively only by the National Government. The betterment which we seek must be accomplished, I believe, mainly through the National Government.

The American people are right in demanding that New Nationalism, without which we cannot hope to deal with new problems. The New Nationalism puts the national need before sectional or personal advantage. It is impatient of the utter confusion that results from local legislatures attempting to treat national issues as local issues. It is still more impatient of the impotence which springs from over division of governmental powers, the impotence which makes it possible for local selfishness or for legal cunning, hired by wealthy special interests, to bring national activities to a deadlock. This New Nationalism regards the executive power as the steward of the public welfare. It demands of the judiciary that it shall be interested primarily in human welfare rather than in property, just as it demands that the representative body shall represent all the people rather than any one class or section of the people.

I believe in shaping the ends of government to protect property as well as human welfare. Normally, and in the long run, the ends are the same; but whenever the alternative must be faced, I am for men and not for property, as you were in the Civil War. I am far from underestimating the importance of dividends; but I rank dividends below human character. Again, I do not have any sympathy with the reformer who says he does not care for dividends. Of course, economic welfare is necessary, for a man must pull his own weight and be able to support his family. I know well that the reformers must not bring upon the people economic ruin, or the reforms themselves will go down in the ruin. But we must be ready to face temporary disaster, whether or not brought on by those who will war against us to the knife. Those who oppose reform will do well to remember that ruin in its worst form is inevitable if our national life brings us nothing better than swollen fortunes for the few and the triumph in both politics and business of a sordid and selfish materialism.

. . . The object of government is the welfare of the people. The material progress and prosperity of a nation are desirable chiefly so long as they lead to the moral and material welfare of all good citizens. Just in proportion as the average man and woman are honest, capable of sound judgment and high ideals, active in public affairs,—but, first of all, sound in their home, and the father and mother of healthy children whom they bring up well,—just so far, and no farther, we may count our civilization a success. We must have—I believe we have already—a genuine and permanent moral awakening, without which no wisdom of legislation or administration really means anything; and, on the other hand, we must try to secure the social and economic legislation without which any improvement due to purely moral agitation is necessarily evanescent. . . . No matter how honest and decent we are in our private lives, if we do not have the right kind of law and the right kind of administration of the law, we cannot go forward as a nation. That is imperative; but it must be an addition to, and not a substitute for, the qualities that make us good citizens. In the last analysis, the most important elements in any man's career must be the sum of those qualities which, in the aggregate, we speak of as character. If he has not got it, then no law that the wit of man can devise, no administration of the law by the boldest and strongest executive, will avail to help him. We must have the right kind of character—character that makes a man, first of all, a good man in the home, a good father, and a good husband—that makes a man a good neighbor. You must have that, and, then, in addition, you must have the kind of law and the kind of administration of the law which will give to those qualities in the private citizen the best possible chance for development. The prime problem of our nation is to get the right type of good citizenship, and, to get it, we must have progress, and our public men must be genuinely progressive.

DEMOCRATIC PARTY PLATFORM 1912[51]

Rights of the States

We believe in the preservation and maintenance in their full strength and integrity of the three co-ordinate branches of the Federal government—the executive, the legislative, and the judicial—each keeping within its own bounds and not encroaching upon the just powers of either of the others.

Believing that the most efficient results under our system of government are to be attained by the full exercise by the States of their reserved sovereign powers, we denounce as usurpation the efforts of our opponents to deprive the States of any of the rights reserved to them, and to enlarge and magnify by indirection the powers of the Federal government.

We insist upon the full exercise of all the powers of the Government, both State and national, to protect the people from injustice at the hands of those who seek to make the government a private asset in business. There is no twilight zone between the nation and the State in which exploiting interests can take refuge from both. It is as necessary that the Federal government shall exercise the powers delegated to it as it is that the States shall exercise the powers reserved to them, but we insist that Federal remedies for the regulation of interstate commerce and for the prevention of private monopoly, shall be added to, and not substituted for State remedies.

PROGRESSIVE PARTY PLATFORM 1912[52]

The conscience of the people, in a time of grave national problems, has called into being a new party, born of the nation's sense of justice. We of the Progressive party here dedicate ourselves to the fulfillment of the duty laid upon us by our fathers to maintain the government of the people, by the people and for the people whose foundations they laid.

We hold with Thomas Jefferson and Abraham Lincoln that the people are the masters of their Constitution, to fulfill its purposes and to safeguard it from those who, by perversion of its intent, would convert it into an instrument of injustice. In accordance with the needs of each generation the people must use their sovereign powers to establish and maintain equal opportunity and industrial justice, to secure which this Government was founded and without which no republic can endure.

This country belongs to the people who inhabit it. Its resources, its business, its institutions and its laws should be utilized, maintained or altered in whatever manner will best promote the general interest.

It is time to set the public welfare in the first place.

Amendment of Constitution

The Progressive party, believing that a free people should have the power from time to time to amend their fundamental law so as to adapt it progressively to the changing needs of the people, pledges itself to provide a more easy and expeditious method of amending the Federal Constitution.

Nation and State

Up to the limit of the Constitution, and later by amendment of the Constitution, if found necessary, we advocate bringing under effective national jurisdiction those problems which have expanded beyond reach of the individual States.

It is as grotesque as it is intolerable that the several States should by unequal laws in matter of common concern become competing commercial agencies, barter the lives of their children, the health of their women and the safety and well being of their working people for the benefit of their financial interests.

The extreme insistence on States' rights by the Democratic party in the Baltimore platform demonstrates anew its inability to understand the world into which it has survived or to administer the affairs of a union of States which have in all essential respects become one people.

HERBERT CROLY, *THE PROMISE OF AMERICAN LIFE*[53]

[The Constitution's] success has been due to the fact that its makers [i.e. The Framers], with all their apprehensions about democracy, were possessed of a wise and positive political faith. They believed in liberty. They believed that the essential condition of fruitful liberty was an efficient central government. They knew that no government could be efficient unless its powers equaled its responsibilities. They were willing to trust to such a government the security and the welfare of the American people. The Constitution has proved capable of development chiefly as the instrument of these positive political ideas. Thanks to the theory of implied powers, to the liberal construction of the Supreme Court during the first forty years of its existence, and to the results of the Civil War the Federal government has, on the whole, become more rather than less efficient as the national political organ of the American people. Almost from the start American life has grown more and more national in substance, in such wise that a rigid constitution which could not have been developed in a national direction would have been an increasing source of irritation and protest. But this reinforcement of the substance of American national life has, until recently, found an adequate expression in the increasing scope and efficiency of the Federal government. The Federalists had the insight to anticipate the kind of government which their country needed; and this was a great and a rare achievement—all the more so because they were obliged in a measure to impose it on their fellow-countrymen.

. . . There is, however, another face to the shield. The Constitution was the expression not only of a political faith, but also of political fears. It was wrought both as the organ of the national interest and as the bulwark of certain individual and local rights. The Federalists sought to surround private property, freedom of contract, and personal liberty with an impregnable legal fortress; and they were forced by their opponents to amend the original draft of the Constitution in order to include a still more stringent bill of individual and state rights. Now I am far from pretending that these legal restrictions have not had their value in American national history, and were not the expression of an essential element in the composition and the ideal of the American nation. The security of private property and personal liberty, and a proper distribution of activity between the local and the central governments, demanded at that time, and within limits still demand, adequate legal guarantees. It remains none the less true, however, that every popular government should in the end, and after a necessarily prolonged deliberation, possess the power of taking any action, which, in the opinion of a decisive majority of the people, is demanded by the public welfare. Such is not the case with the government organized under the Federal Constitution. In respect to certain fundamental provisions, which necessarily receive the most rigid interpretation on the part of the courts, it is practically unmodifiable. A very small percentage of the American people can in this respect permanently thwart the will of an enormous majority, and there can be no justification for such a condition on any possible theory of popular Sovereignty. This defect has not hitherto had very many practical inconveniences, but it is an absolute violation of the theory and the spirit of American democratic institutions. The time may come when the fulfillment of a justifiable democratic purpose may demand the limitation of certain rights, to which the Constitution affords such absolute guarantees; and in that case the American democracy might be forced to seek by revolutionary means the accomplishment of a result which should be attainable under the law.

. . . The transformation of the old sense of a glorious national destiny into the sense of a serious national purpose will inevitably tend to make the popular realization of the Promise of American life both more explicit and more serious. As long as Americans believed they were able to fulfill a noble national Promise merely by virtue of maintaining intact a set of political institutions and by the vigorous individual pursuit of private ends, their allegiance to their national fulfillment remained more a matter of words than of deeds; but now that they are being aroused from their patriotic slumber, the effect is inevitably to disentangle the national idea and to give it more dignity. The redemption of the national Promise has become a cause for which the good American must fight, and the cause for which a man fights is a cause which he more than ever values. The American idea is no longer to be propagated merely by multiplying the children of the West and by granting ignorant aliens permission to vote. Like all sacred causes, it must be propagated by the Word and by that right arm of the Word, which is the Sword.

The more enlightened reformers are conscious of the additional dignity and value which the popularity of reform has bestowed upon the American idea, but they still fail to realize the deeper implications of their own program.

In abandoning the older conception of an automatic fulfillment of our national destiny, they have abandoned more of the traditional American point of view than they are aware. The traditional American optimistic fatalism was not of accidental origin, and it cannot be abandoned without involving in its fall some other important ingredients in the accepted American tradition. Not only was it dependent on economic conditions which prevailed until comparatively recent times, but it has been associated with certain erroneous but highly cherished political theories. It has been wrought into the fabric of our popular economic and political ideas to such an extent that its overthrow necessitates a partial revision of some of the most important articles in the traditional American creed.

The extent and the character of this revision may be inferred from a brief consideration of the effect upon the substance of our national Promise of an alteration in its proposed method of fulfillment. The substance of our national Promise has consisted, as we have seen, of an improving popular economic condition, guaranteed by democratic political institutions, and resulting in moral and social amelioration. These manifold benefits were to be obtained merely by liberating the enlightened self-interest of the American people. The beneficent result followed inevitably from the action of wholly selfish motives—provided, of course, the democratic political system of equal rights was maintained in its integrity. The fulfillment of the American Promise was considered inevitable because it was based upon a combination of self-interest and the natural goodness of human nature. On the other hand, if the fulfillment of our national Promise can no longer be considered inevitable, if it must be considered as equivalent to a conscious national purpose instead of an inexorable national destiny, the implication necessarily is that the trust reposed in individual self-interest has been in some measure betrayed. No pre-established harmony can then exist between the free and abundant satisfaction of private needs and the accomplishment of a morally and socially desirable result. The Promise of American life is to be fulfilled—not merely by a maximum amount of economic freedom, but by a certain measure of discipline; not merely by the abundant satisfaction of individual desires, but by a large measure of individual subordination and self-denial. And this necessity of subordinating the satisfaction of individual desires to the fulfillment of a national purpose is attached particularly to the absorbing occupation of the American people,—the occupation, viz.: of accumulating wealth. The automatic fulfillment of the American national Promise is to be abandoned, if at all, precisely because the traditional American confidence in individual freedom has resulted in a morally and socially undesirable distribution of wealth.

    . . . The consequences, then, of converting our American national destiny into a national purpose are beginning to be revolutionary. When the Promise of American life is conceived as a national ideal, whose fulfillment is a matter of artful and laborious work, the effect thereof is substantially to identify the national purpose with the social problem. What the American people of the present and the future have really been promised by our patriotic prophecies is an attempt to solve that problem. They have been promised on American soil comfort, prosperity, and the opportunity for self-improvement; and the lesson of the existing crisis is that such a Promise can never be redeemed by an indiscriminate individual scramble for wealth. The individual competition, even when it starts under fair conditions and rules, results, not only, as it should, in the triumph of the strongest, but in the attempt to perpetuate the victory; and it is this attempt which must be recognized and forestalled in the interest of the American national purpose. The way to realize a purpose is, not to leave it to chance, but to keep it loyally in mind, and adopt means proper to the importance and the difficulty of the task. No voluntary association of individuals, resourceful and disinterested though they be, is competent to assume the responsibility. The problem belongs to the American national democracy, and its solution must be attempted chiefly by means of official national action.

MISSOURI v. HOLLAND[54]

. . . The Treaty of August 16, 1916, 39 Stat. 1702, with Great Britain, providing for the protection, by close seasons and in other ways, of migratory birds in the United States and Canada, and . . . as a necessary and proper means of effectuating the treaty, and the treaty and statute, by bringing such birds within the paramount protection and regulation of the Government do not infringe property rights or sovereign powers respecting such birds reserved to the States by the Tenth Amendment.

This is a bill in equity brought by the State of Missouri to prevent a game warden of the United States from attempting to enforce the Migratory Bird Treaty Act of July 3, 1918 . . . The ground of the bill is that the statute is an unconstitutional interference with the rights reserved to the States by the Tenth Amendment, and that the acts of the defendant done and threatened under that authority invade the sovereign right of the State and contravene its will manifested in statutes. The State also alleges a pecuniary interest, as owner of the wild birds within its borders and otherwise, admitted by the Government to be sufficient, but it is enough that the bill is a reasonable and proper means to assert the alleged *quasi* sovereign rights of a State . . .

On December 8, 1916, a treaty between the United States and Great Britain . . . recited that many species of birds in their annual migrations traversed certain parts of the United States and of Canada, that they were of great value . . . [and] provided for specified close seasons and protection in other forms.

[I]t is not enough to refer to the Tenth Amendment, reserving the powers not delegated to the United States, because, by Article II, § 2, the power to make treaties is delegated expressly, and by Article VI treaties . . . are declared the supreme law of the land. . . .

It is said that a treaty cannot be valid if it infringes the Constitution, that there are limits, therefore, to the treaty-making power, and that one such limit is that what an act of Congress could not do unaided, in derogation of the powers reserved to the States, a treaty cannot do . . . What was said in that case with regard to the powers of the States applies with equal force to the powers of the nation in cases where the States individually are incompetent to act. . . .

The State, as we have intimated, founds its claim of exclusive authority upon an assertion of title to migratory birds, an assertion that is embodied in statute. No doubt it is true that, as between a State and its inhabitants, the State may regulate the killing and sale of such birds, but it does not follow that its authority is exclusive of paramount powers. . . . Wild birds are not in the possession of anyone, and possession is the beginning of ownership. . . . we cannot put the case of the State upon higher ground than that the treaty deals with creatures that, for the moment are within the state borders, that it must be carried out by officers of the United States within the same territory, and that, but for the treaty, the State would be free to regulate this subject itself.

. . . Here, a national interest of very nearly the first magnitude is involved. It can be protected only by national action in concert with that of another power. The subject matter is only transitorily within the State, and has no permanent habitat therein. But for the treaty and the statute, there soon might be no birds for any powers to deal with. We see nothing in the Constitution that compels the Government to sit by while a food supply is cut off and the protectors of our forests and our crops are destroyed. It is not sufficient to rely upon the States. The reliance is vain, and were it otherwise, the question is whether the United States is forbidden to act. We are of opinion that the treaty and statute must be upheld.

FRANKLIN ROOSEVELT, FIRST INAUGURAL ADDRESS[55]

I am certain that my fellow Americans expect that on my induction into the Presidency I will address them with a candor and a decision which the present situation of our Nation impels. This is preeminently the time to speak the truth, the whole truth, frankly and boldly. Nor need we shrink from honestly facing conditions in our country today. This great Nation will endure as it has endured, will revive and will prosper. So, first of all, let me assert my firm belief that the only thing we have to fear is fear itself—nameless, unreasoning, unjustified terror which paralyzes needed efforts to convert retreat into advance. In every dark hour of our national life a leadership of frankness and vigor has met with that understanding and support of the people themselves which is essential to victory. I am convinced that you will again give that support to leadership in these critical days.

. . . This Nation asks for action, and action now.

. . . Hand in hand with this we must frankly recognize the overbalance of population in our industrial centers and, by engaging on a national scale in a redistribution, endeavor to provide a better use of the land for those best fitted for the land. The task can be helped by definite efforts to raise the values of agricultural products and with this the power to purchase the output of our cities. It can be helped by preventing realistically the tragedy of the growing loss through foreclosure of our small homes and our farms. It can be helped by insistence that the Federal, State, and local governments act forthwith on the demand that their cost be drastically reduced. It can be helped by the unifying of relief activities which today are often scattered, uneconomical, and unequal. It can be helped by national planning for and supervision of all forms of transportation and of communications and other utilities which have a definitely public character. There are many ways in which it can be helped, but it can never be helped merely by talking about it. We must act and act quickly.

. . . If I read the temper of our people correctly, we now realize as we have never realized before our interdependence on each other; that we can not merely take but we must give as well; that if we are to go forward, we must move as a trained and loyal army willing to sacrifice for the good of a common discipline, because without such discipline no progress is made, no leadership becomes effective. We are, I know, ready and willing to submit our lives and property to such discipline, because it makes possible a leadership which aims at a larger good. This I propose to offer, pledging that the larger purposes will bind upon us all as a sacred obligation with a unity of duty hitherto evoked only in time of armed strife.

With this pledge taken, I assume unhesitatingly the leadership of this great army of our people dedicated to a disciplined attack upon our common problems.

Action in this image and to this end is feasible under the form of government which we have inherited from our ancestors. Our Constitution is so simple and practical that it is possible always to meet extraordinary needs by changes in emphasis and arrangement without loss of essential form. That is why our constitutional system has proved itself the most superbly enduring political mechanism the modern world has produced. It has met every stress of vast expansion of territory, of foreign wars, of bitter internal strife, of world relations.

It is to be hoped that the normal balance of executive and legislative authority may be wholly adequate to meet the unprecedented task before us. But it may be that an unprecedented demand and need for undelayed action may call for temporary departure from that normal balance of public procedure.

I am prepared under my constitutional duty to recommend the measures that a stricken nation in the midst of a stricken world may require. These measures, or such other measures as the Congress may build out of its experience and wisdom, I shall seek, within my constitutional authority, to bring to speedy adoption.

But in the event that the Congress shall fail to take one of these two courses, and in the event that the national emergency is still critical, I shall not evade the clear course of duty that will then confront me. I shall ask the Congress for the one remaining instrument to meet the crisis—broad Executive power to wage a war against the emergency, as great as the power that would be given to me if we were in fact invaded by a foreign foe.

For the trust reposed in me I will return the courage and the devotion that befit the time. I can do no less.

We face the arduous days that lie before us in the warm courage of the national unity; with the clear consciousness of seeking old and precious moral values; with the clean satisfaction that comes from the stem performance of duty by old and young alike. We aim at the assurance of a rounded and permanent national life.

FRANKLIN D. ROOSEVELT, MESSAGE TO THE FIFTH ANNUAL WOMEN'S CONFERENCE[56]

. . . If we limit government to the functions of merely punishing the criminal after crimes have been committed, of gathering up the wreckage of society after the devastation of an economic collapse, or of fighting a war that reason might have prevented, then government fails to satisfy those urgent human purposes, which, in essence, gave it its beginning and provide its present justification.

Modern government has become an instrument through which citizens may apply their reasoned methods of prevention in addition to methods of correction. Government has become one of the most important instruments for the prevention and cure of these evils of society which I have mentioned. Its concern at the moment is unabated. It conceives of itself as an instrument. through which social justice may prevail more greatly among men. In the determination of the standards that make up social justice, the widest discussion is necessary. In the last analysis, government can be no more than the collective wisdom of its citizens. The duty of citizens is to increase this collective wisdom by common counsel, by the discovery and consideration of facts relating to the common life, and by the discouragement of those who for selfish ends or through careless speech distort facts and disseminate untruth.

LYNDON B. JOHNSON, "GREAT SOCIETY SPEECH"[57]

... The purpose of protecting the life of our Nation and preserving the liberty of our citizens is to pursue the happiness of our people. Our success in that pursuit is the test of our success as a Nation.

... The Great Society rests on abundance and liberty for all. It demands an end to poverty and racial injustice, to which we are totally committed in our time. But that is just the beginning. The Great Society is a place where every child can find knowledge to enrich his mind and to enlarge his talents. It is a place where leisure is a welcome chance to build and reflect, not a feared cause of boredom and restlessness. It is a place where the city of man serves not only the needs of the body and the demands of commerce but the desire for beauty and the hunger for community.

It is a place where man can renew contact with nature. It is a place which honors creation for its own sake and for what it adds to the understanding of the race. It is a place where men are more concerned with the quality of their goals than the quantity of their goods.

But most of all, the Great Society is not a safe harbor, a resting place, a final objective, a finished work. It is a challenge constantly renewed, beckoning us toward a destiny where the meaning of our lives matches the marvelous products of our labor.

So I want to talk to you today about three places where we begin to build the Great Society—in our cities, in our countryside, and in our classrooms.

Many of you will live to see the day, perhaps 50 years from now, when there will be 400 million Americans—four-fifths of them in urban areas. In the remainder of this century urban population will double, city land will double, and we will have to build homes, highways, and facilities equal to all those built since this country was first settled. So in the next 40 years we must re-build the entire urban United States.

... A second place where we begin to build the Great Society is in our countryside. We have always prided ourselves on being not only America the strong and America the free, but America the beautiful. Today that beauty is in danger. The water we drink, the food we eat, the very air that we breathe, are threatened with pollution. Our parks are overcrowded, our seashores over-burdened. Green fields and dense forests are disappearing.

. . . For once the battle is lost, once our natural splendor is destroyed, it can never be recaptured. And once man can no longer walk with beauty or wonder at nature his spirit will wither and his sustenance be wasted.

A third place to build the Great Society is in the classrooms of America. There your children's lives will be shaped. Our society will not be great until every young mind is set free to scan the farthest reaches of thought and imagination. We are still far from that goal.

Today, 8 million adult Americans, more than the entire population of Michigan, have not finished 5 years of school. Nearly 20 million have not finished 8 years of school. Nearly 54 million—more than one quarter of all America—have not even finished high school.

Each year more than 100,000 high school graduates, with proved ability, do not enter college because they cannot afford it. And if we cannot educate today's youth, what will we do in 1970 when elementary school enrollment will be 5 million greater than 1960? And high school enrollment will rise by 5 million. College enrollment will increase by more than 3 million.

In many places, classrooms are overcrowded and curricula are outdated. Most of our qualified teachers are underpaid, and many of our paid teachers are unqualified. So we must give every child a place to sit and a teacher to learn from. Poverty must not be a bar to learning, and learning must offer an escape from poverty.

But more classrooms and more teachers are not enough. We must seek an educational system which grows in excellence as it grows in size. This means better training for our teachers. It means preparing youth to enjoy their hours of leisure as well as their hours of labor. It means exploring new techniques of teaching, to find new ways to stimulate the love of learning and the capacity for creation.

These are three of the central issues of the Great Society. While our Government has many programs directed at those issues, I do not pretend that we have the full answer to those problems.

But I do promise this: We are going to assemble the best thought and the broadest knowledge from all over the world to find those answers for America. I intend to establish working groups to prepare a series of White House conferences and meetings—on the cities, on natural beauty, on the quality of education, and on other emerging challenges. And from these meetings and from this inspiration and from these studies we will begin to set our course toward the Great Society.

The solution to these problems does not rest on a massive program in Washington, nor can it rely solely on the strained resources of local authority.

They require us to create new concepts of cooperation, a creative federalism, between the National Capital and the leaders of local communities.

. . . For better or for worse, your generation has been appointed by history to deal with those problems and to lead America toward a new age. You have the chance never before afforded to any people in any age. You can help build a society where the demands of morality, and the needs of the spirit, can be realized in the life of the Nation.

So, will you join in the battle to give every citizen the full equality which God enjoins and the law requires, whatever his belief, or race, or the color of his skin?

Will you join in the battle to give every citizen an escape from the crushing weight of poverty?

Will you join in the battle to make it possible for all nations to live in enduring peace—as neighbors and not as mortal enemies?

Will you join in the battle to build the Great Society, to prove that our material progress is only the foundation on which we will build a richer life of mind and spirit?

There are those timid souls who say this battle cannot be won; that we are condemned to a soulless wealth. I do not agree. We have the power to shape the civilization that we want. But we need your will, your labor, your hearts, if we are to build that kind of society.

RICHARD NIXON, "ADDRESS TO THE NATION ON DOMESTIC PROGRAMS"[58]

Every time I return to the United States after such a trip, I realize how fortunate we are to live in this rich land. We have the world's most advanced industrial economy, the greatest wealth ever known to man, the fullest measure of freedom ever enjoyed by any people, anywhere.

Yet we, too, have an urgent need to modernize our institutions—and our need is no less than theirs.

We face an urban crisis, a social crisis-and at the same time, a crisis of confidence in the capacity of government to do its job.

A third of a century of centralizing power and responsibility in Washington has produced a bureaucratic monstrosity, cumbersome, unresponsive, ineffective.

A third of a century of social experiment has left us a legacy of entrenched programs that have outlived their time or outgrown their purposes.

A third of a century of unprecedented growth and change has strained our institutions, and raised serious questions about whether they are still adequate to the times.

It is no accident, therefore, that we find increasing skepticism—and not only among our young people, but among citizens everywhere—about the continuing capacity of government to master the challenges we face.

Nowhere has the failure of government been more tragically apparent than in its efforts to help the poor and especially in its system of public welfare.

. . . My purpose tonight, however, is not to review the past record, but to present a new set of reforms—a new set of proposals—a new and drastically different approach to the way in which government cares for those in need, and to the way the responsibilities are shared between the State and the Federal Government.

I have chosen to do so in a direct report to the people because these proposals call for public decisions of the first importance; because they represent a fundamental change in the Nation's approach to one of its most pressing social problems; and because, quite deliberately, they also represent the first major reversal of the trend toward ever more centralization of government in Washington, D.C. After a third of a century of power flowing from the people and the States to Washington it is time for a New Federalism in which power, funds, and responsibility will flow from Washington to the States and to the people.

Welfare

Whether measured by the anguish of the poor themselves, or by the drastically mounting burden on the taxpayer, the present welfare system has to be judged a colossal failure.

Our States and cities find themselves sinking in a welfare quagmire, as caseloads increase, as costs escalate, and as the welfare system stagnates enterprise and perpetuates dependency.

What began on a small scale in the depression 30's has become a huge monster in the prosperous 60's. And the tragedy is not only that it is bringing States and cities to the brink of financial disaster, but also that it is failing to meet the elementary human, social, and financial needs of the poor.

It breaks up homes. It often penalizes work. It robs recipients of dignity. And it grows.

. . . What I am proposing is that the Federal Government build a foundation under the income of every American family with dependent children that cannot care for itself—and wherever in America that family may live.

Manpower Training

Therefore, I am also sending a message to Congress calling for a complete overhaul of the Nation's manpower training services.

The Federal Government's job training programs have been a terrible tangle of confusion and waste.

To remedy the confusion, arbitrariness, and rigidity of the present system, the new Manpower Training Act would basically do three things.

- It would pull together the jumble of programs that presently exist, and equalize standards of eligibility.
- It would provide flexible funding-so that Federal money would follow the demands of labor and industry, and flow into those programs that people most want and most need.
- It would decentralize administration, gradually moving it away from the Washington bureaucracy and turning it over to States and localities.

In terms of its symbolic importance, I can hardly overemphasize this last point. For the first time, applying the principles of the New Federalism, administration of a major established Federal program would be turned over to the States and local governments, recognizing that they are in a position to do the job better.

For years, thoughtful Americans have talked of the need to decentralize Government. The time has come to begin.

Revenue Sharing

We come now to a proposal which I consider profoundly important to the future of our Federal system of shared responsibilities. When we speak of poverty or jobs or opportunity or making government more effective or getting it closer to the people, it brings us directly to the financial plight of our States and cities.

We can no longer have effective government at any level unless we have it at all levels. There is too much to be done for the cities to do it alone, for Washington to do it alone, or for the States to do it alone.

For a third of a century, power and responsibility have flowed toward Washington, and Washington has taken for its own the best sources of revenue.

We intend to reverse this tide, and to turn back to the States a greater measure of responsibility—not as a way of avoiding problems, but as a better way of solving problems.

Along with this would go a share of Federal revenues. I shall propose to the Congress next week that a set portion of the revenues from Federal income taxes be remitted directly to the States, with a minimum of Federal restrictions on how those dollars are to be used, and with a requirement that a percentage of them be channeled through for the use of local governments.

The funds provided under this program will not be great in the first year. But the principle will have been established, and the amounts will increase as our budgetary situation improves.

This start on revenue sharing is a step toward what I call the New Federalism. It is a gesture of faith in America's State and local governments and in the principle of democratic self-government.

RONALD REAGAN, FIRST INAUGURAL ADDRESS[59]

The business of our nation goes forward. These United States are confronted with an economic affliction of great proportions. We suffer from the longest and one of the worst sustained inflations in our national history. It distorts our economic decisions, penalizes thrift, and crushes the struggling young and the fixed-income elderly alike. It threatens to shatter the lives of millions of our people.

. . . In this present crisis, government is not the solution to our problem; government is the problem.

From time to time, we have been tempted to believe that society has become too complex to be managed by self-rule, that government by an elite group is superior to government for, by, and of the people. But if no one among us is capable of governing himself, then who among us has the capacity to govern someone else? All of us together, in and out of government, must bear the burden. The solutions we seek must be equitable, with no one group singled out to pay a higher price.

. . . It is my intention to curb the size and influence of the Federal establishment and to demand recognition of the distinction between the powers granted to the Federal Government and those reserved to the States or to the people. All of us need to be reminded that the Federal Government did not create the States; the States created the Federal Government.

Now, so there will be no misunderstanding, it is not my intention to do away with government. It is, rather, to make it work-work with us, not over us; to stand by our side, not ride on our back. Government can and must provide opportunity, not smother it; foster productivity, not stifle it.

If we look to the answer as to why, for so many years, we achieved so much, prospered as no other people on Earth, it was because here, in this land, we unleashed the energy and individual genius of man to a greater extent than has ever been done before. Freedom and the dignity of the individual have been more available and assured here than in any other place on Earth. The price for this freedom at times has been high, but we have never been unwilling to pay that price.

It is no coincidence that our present troubles parallel and are proportionate to the intervention and intrusion in our lives that result from unnecessary and excessive growth of government. It is time for us to realize that we are too great a nation to limit ourselves to small dreams. We are not, as some would have us believe, loomed to an inevitable decline. I do not believe in a fate that will all on us no matter what we do. I do believe in a fate that will fall on us if we do nothing. So, with all the creative energy at our command, let us begin an era of national renewal. Let us renew our determination, our courage, and our strength. And let us renew; our faith and our hope.

RONALD REAGAN, "REMARKS IN ATLANTA, GEORGIA, AT THE ANNUAL CONVENTION OF THE NATIONAL CONFERENCE OF STATE LEGISLATURES"[60]

. . . I believe our campaign to give the government back to the people hit a nerve deeper and quicker than anyone first realized. The government in Washington has finally heard what the people have been saying for years: "We need relief from oppression of big government. We don't want to wait any longer. We want tax relief and we want it now."

The people of this country are saying that we've been on a road that they don't want to stay on. Now we're on a road that leads to growth and opportunity, to increasing productivity and an increasing standard of living for anyone. It was a road once that led to the driveway of a home that could be afforded by all kinds of Americans, not just the affluent.

. . . With the help of these same Americans and with the help of the States, one of our next goals is to renew the concept of federalism. The changes here will be as exciting and even more profound in the long run than the changes produced in the economic package.

This Nation has never fully debated the fact that over the past 40 years, federalism—one of the underlying principles of our Constitution—has nearly disappeared as a guiding force in American politics and government. My administration intends to initiate such a debate, and no more appropriate forum can be found than before the National Conference of State Legislatures.

My administration is committed heart and soul to the broad principles of American federalism which are outlined in the Federalist Papers of Hamilton, Madison, and Jay and, as your President told you, they're in that tenth article of the Bill of Rights.

The designers of our Constitution realized that in federalism there's diversity. The Founding Fathers saw the federal system as constructed something like a masonry wall: The States are the bricks, the National Government is the mortar. For the structure to stand plumb with the Constitution, there must be a proper mix of that brick and mortar. Unfortunately, over the years, many people have come increasingly to believe that Washington is the whole wall—a wall that, incidentally, leans, sags, and bulges under its own weight.

The traumatic experience of the Great Depression provided the impetus and the rationale for a government that was more centralized than America had previously known. You had to have lived then, during those depression years, to understand the drabness of that period.

FDR brought the colors of hope and confidence to the era and I, like millions of others, became an enthusiastic New Dealer. We followed FDR because he offered a mix of ideas and movement. A former Governor himself, I believe that FDR would today be amazed and appalled at the growth of the Federal Government's power. Too many in government in recent years have invoked his name to justify what they were doing, forgetting that it was FDR who said, "In the conduct of public utilities, of banks, of insurance, of agriculture, of education, of social welfare—Washington must be discouraged from interfering."

Well, today the Federal Government takes too much taxes from the people, too much authority from the States, and too much liberty with the Constitution.

Americans have at last begun to realize that the steady flow of power and tax dollars to Washington has something to do with the fact that things don't seem to work anymore. The Federal Government is overloaded, musclebound, if you will, having assumed more responsibilities than it can properly manage. There's been a loss of accountability as the distinction between the duties of the Federal and State governments have blurred, and the Federal Government is so far removed from the people that Members of Congress spend less time legislating than cutting through bureaucratic red tape for their constituents.

Block grants are designed to eliminate burdensome reporting requirements and regulations, unnecessary administrative costs, and program duplication. Block grants are not a mere strategy in our budget as some have suggested; they stand on their own as a federalist tool for transferring power back to the State and to the local level.

In normal times, what we've managed to get through the Congress concerning block grants would be a victory. Yet, we did not provide the States with the degree of freedom in dealing with the budget cuts that we had ardently hoped we could get. We got some categorical grants into block grants, but many of our block grant proposals are still up on the Hill, and that doesn't mean the end of the dream. Together, you and I will be going back and back and back until we obtain the flexibility that you need and deserve.

The ultimate objective, as I have told some of you in meetings in Washington, is to use block grants, however, as only a bridge, leading to the day when you'll have not only the responsibility for the programs that properly belong at the State level, but you will have the tax sources now usurped by

Washington returned to you, ending that round-trip of the peoples' money to Washington, where a carrying charge is deducted, and then back to you.

Now, we also are reviving the cause of federalism by cutting back on unnecessary regulations. The Federal Register is the road atlas of new Federal regulations, and for the past 10 years, all roads have led to Washington . . . Accepting a government grant with its accompanying rules is like marrying a girl and finding out her entire family is moving in with you before the honeymoon.

. . . Now, one of their goals will be recommending allowing States to fulfill the creative role they once played as laboratories of economic and social development. North Dakota enacted one of the country's first child labor laws. Wyoming gave the vote to women decades before it was adopted nationally. And California, during the term of a Governor Reagan—I wonder whatever became of him—[laughter]—we enacted a clear air act that was tougher than the Federal measure that followed years later.

And, incidentally, while it's true that I do not believe in the equal rights amendment as the best way to end discrimination against women, I believe such discrimination must be eliminated. And in California, we found 14 State statutes that did so discriminate. We wiped those statutes off the books. Now, if you won't think me presumptuous, may I suggest that when you go back to your statehouses you might take a look at the statutes and regulations in your respective States.

The constitutional concept of federalism recognizes and protects diversity. Today, federalism is one check that is out of balance as the diversity of the States has given way to the uniformity of Washington. And our task is to restore the constitutional symmetry between the central Government and the States and to reestablish the freedom and variety of federalism. In the process, we'll return the citizen to his rightful place in the scheme of our democracy, and that place is close to his government. We must never forget it. It is not the Federal Government or the States who retain the power—the people retain the power. And I hope that you'll join me in strengthening the fabric of federalism. If the Federal Government is more responsive to the States, the States will be more responsive to the people, and that's the reason that you, as State legislators, and I, as President, are in office—not to retain power but to serve the people.

NEW YORK v. US[61]

[JUSTICE Sandra O'CONNOR] Congress exercises its conferred powers subject to the limitations contained in the Constitution. Thus, for example, under the Commerce Clause Congress may regulate publishers engaged in interstate commerce, but Congress is constrained in the exercise of that power by the First Amendment. The Tenth Amendment likewise restrains the power of Congress, but this limit is not derived from the text of the Tenth Amendment itself, which, as we have discussed is essentially a tautology. Instead, the Tenth Amendment confirms that the power of the Federal Government is subject to limits that may, in a given instance, reserve power to the States. The Tenth Amendment thus directs us to determine, as in this case, whether an incident of state sovereignty is protected by a limitation on an Article I power.

. . . This framework has been sufficiently flexible over the past two centuries to allow for enormous changes in the nature of government. The Federal Government undertakes activities today that would have been unimaginable to the Framers in two senses; first, because the Framers would not have conceived that *any* government would conduct such activities; and second, because the Framers would not have believed that the *Federal* Government, rather than the States, would assume such responsibilities. Yet the powers conferred upon the Federal Government by the Constitution were phrased in language broad enough to allow for the expansion of the Federal Government's role. Among the provisions of the Constitution that have been particularly important in this regard, three concern us here.

. . . In the end, the Convention opted for a Constitution in which Congress would exercise its legislative authority directly over individuals rather than over States; for a variety of reasons, it rejected the New Jersey Plan in favor of the Virginia Plan.

In providing for a stronger central government, therefore, the Framers explicitly chose a Constitution that confers upon Congress the power to regulate individuals, not States. . . .

This is not to say that Congress lacks the ability to encourage a State to regulate in a particular way, or that Congress may not hold out incentives to the States as a method of influencing a State's policy choices.

By contrast, where the Federal Government compels States to regulate, the accountability of both state and federal officials is diminished. If the citizens of New York, for example, do not consider that making provision for the disposal of radioactive waste is in their best interest, they may elect state officials who share their view. That view can always be pre-empted under the Supremacy Clause if it is contrary to the national view, but in such a case it is the Federal Government that makes the decision in full view of the public, and it will be federal officials that suffer the consequences if the decision turns out to be detrimental or unpopular.

. . . But where the Federal Government directs the States to regulate, it may be state officials who will bear the brunt of public disapproval, while the federal officials who devised the regulatory program may remain insulated from the electoral ramifications of their decision. Accountability is thus diminished when, due to federal coercion, elected state officials cannot regulate in accordance with the views of the local electorate in matters not pre-empted by federal regulation.

. . . The Act's first set of incentives, in which Congress has conditioned grants to the States upon the States' attainment of a series of milestones, is thus well within the authority of Congress under the Commerce and Spending Clauses. Because the first set of incentives is supported by affirmative constitutional grants of power to Congress, it is not inconsistent with the Tenth Amendment.

. . . In the second set of incentives, Congress has authorized States and regional compacts with disposal sites gradually to increase the cost of access to the sites, and then to deny access altogether, to radioactive waste generated in States that do not meet federal deadlines.

. . . The Act's second set of incentives thus represents a conditional exercise of Congress' commerce power, along the lines of those we have held to be within Congress' authority. As a result, the second set of incentives does not intrude on the sovereignty reserved to the States by the Tenth Amendment.

. . . The take title provision is of a different character. This third so-called "incentive" offers States, as an alternative to regulating pursuant to Congress' direction, the option of taking title to and possession of the low level radioactive waste generated within their borders and becoming liable for all damages waste generators suffer as a result of the States' failure to do so promptly. In this provision, Congress has crossed the line distinguishing encouragement from coercion.

. . . The take title provision offers state governments a "choice" of either accepting ownership of waste or regulating according to the instructions of Congress. Respondents do not claim that the Constitution would authorize Congress to impose either option as a freestanding requirement. On one hand, the Constitution would not permit Congress simply to transfer radioactive waste from generators to state governments. Such a forced transfer, standing alone, would in principle be no different than a congressionally compelled subsidy from state governments to radioactive waste producers. The same is true of the provision requiring the States to become liable for the generators' damages. Standing alone, this provision would be indistinguishable from an Act of Congress directing the States to assume the liabilities of certain state residents. Either type of federal action would "commandeer" state governments into the service of federal regulatory purposes, and would for this reason be inconsistent with the Constitution's division of authority between federal and state governments. On the other hand, the second alternative held out to state governments-regulating pursuant to Congress' direction—would, standing alone, present a simple command to state governments to implement legislation enacted by Congress. As we have seen, the Constitution does not empower Congress to subject state governments to this type of instruction.

Because an instruction to state governments to take title to waste, standing alone, would be beyond the authority of Congress, and because a direct order to regulate, standing alone, would also be beyond the authority of Congress, it follows that Congress lacks the power to offer the States a choice between the two.

. . . While the Framers no doubt endowed Congress with the power to regulate interstate commerce in order to avoid further instances of the interstate trade disputes that were common under the Articles of Confederation, the Framers did *not* intend that Congress should exercise that power through the mechanism of mandating state regulation. The Constitution established Congress as "a superintending authority over the reciprocal trade" among the States, by empowering Congress to regulate that trade directly, not by authorizing Congress to issue trade-related orders to state governments. As Madison and Hamilton explained, "a sovereignty over sovereigns, a government over governments, a legislation for communities, as contradistinguished from individuals, as it is a solecism in theory, so in practice it is subversive of the order and ends of civil polity."

. . . How can a federal statute be found an unconstitutional infringement of state sovereignty when state officials consented to the statute's enactment?

The answer follows from an understanding of the fundamental purpose served by our Government's federal structure. The Constitution does not protect the sovereignty of States for the benefit of the States or state governments as abstract political entities, or even for the benefit of the public officials governing the States. To the contrary, the Constitution divides authority between federal and state governments for the protection of individuals. State sovereignty is not just an end in itself: "Rather, federalism secures to citizens the liberties that derive from the diffusion of sovereign power."

. . . Where Congress exceeds its authority relative to the States, therefore, the departure from the constitutional plan cannot be ratified by the "consent" of state officials . . . Where state officials purport to submit to the direction of Congress in this manner, federalism is hardly being advanced.

. . . Petitioners also contend that the Act is inconsistent with the Constitution's Guarantee Clause, which directs the United States to "guarantee to every State in this Union a Republican Form of Government." U. S. Const., Art. IV; § 4.

. . . Even if we assume that petitioners' claim is justiciable, neither the monetary incentives provided by the Act nor the possibility that a State's waste producers may find themselves excluded from the disposal sites of another State can reasonably be said to deny any State a republican form of government. As we have seen, these two incentives represent permissible conditional exercises of Congress' authority under the Spending and Commerce Clauses respectively, in forms that have now grown commonplace. Under each, Congress offers the States a legitimate choice rather than issuing an unavoidable command. The States thereby retain the ability to set their legislative agendas; state government officials remain accountable to the local electorate. The twin threats imposed by the first two challenged provisions of the Act hat New York may miss out on a share of federal spending or that those generating radioactive waste within New York may lose out-of-state disposal outlets-do not pose any realistic risk of altering the form or the method of functioning of New York's government. Thus even indulging the assumption that the Guarantee Clause provides a basis upon which a State or its subdivisions may sue to enjoin the enforcement of a federal statute, petitioners have not made out such a claim in these cases.

PRINTZ, SHERIFF/CORONER, RAVALLI COUNTY, MONTANA v. UNITED STATES[62]

[JUSTICE Antonin SCALIA] The question presented in these cases is whether certain interim provisions of the Brady Handgun Violence Prevention Act commanding state and local law enforcement officers to conduct background checks on prospective handgun purchasers and to perform certain related tasks, violate the Constitution.

. . . it is apparent that the Brady Act purports to direct state law enforcement officers to participate, albeit only temporarily, in the administration of a federally enacted regulatory scheme.

. . . Petitioners contend that compelled enlistment of state executive officers for the administration of federal programs is, until very recent years at least, unprecedented. The Government contends, to the contrary, that "the earliest Congresses enacted statutes that required the participation of state officials in the implementation of federal laws," . . . Conversely if, as petitioners contend, earlier Congresses avoided use of this highly attractive power, we would have reason to believe that the power was thought not to exist.

. . . we do not think the early statutes imposing obligations on state courts imply a power of Congress to impress the state executive into its service.

. . . Although the States surrendered many of their powers to the new Federal Government, they retained "a residuary and inviolable sovereignty," This is reflected throughout the Constitution's text, including (to mention only a few examples) the prohibition on any involuntary reduction or combination of a State's territory, Art. IV, § 3; the Judicial Power Clause, Art. III, § 2, and the Privileges and Immunities Clause, Art. IV, § 2, which speak of the "Citizens" of the States; the amendment provision, Article V, which requires the votes of three-fourths of the States to amend the Constitution; and the Guarantee Clause, Art. IV, § 4, which "presupposes the continued existence of the states and . . . those means and instrumentalities which are the creation of their sovereign and reserved rights," Residual state sovereignty was also implicit, of course, in the Constitution's conferral upon Congress of not all governmental powers, but only discrete, enumerated ones, Art. I, § 8, which implication was rendered express by the Tenth Amendment's assertion that "[t]he powers not delegated to the United States by the Constitution, nor prohibited by it to the States, are reserved to the States respectively, or to the people."

. . . the question discussed earlier, whether laws conscripting state officers violate state sovereignty and are thus not in accord with the Constitution. . . . Even assuming, moreover, that the Brady Act leaves no "policymaking" discretion with the States, we fail to see how that improves rather than worsens the intrusion upon state sovereignty. Preservation of the States as independent and autonomous political entities is arguably less undermined by requiring them to make policy in certain fields than by "reduc[ing] [them] to puppets of a ventriloquist Congress." It is an essential attribute of the States' retained sovereignty that they remain independent and autonomous within their proper sphere of authority. It is no more compatible with this independence and autonomy that their officers be "dragooned" into administering federal law, than it would be compatible with the independence and autonomy of the United States that its officers be impressed into service for the execution of state laws.

WILLIAM J. CLINTON, EXECUTIVE ORDER 13132[63]

Federalism

By the authority vested in me as President by the Constitution and the laws of the United States of America, and in order to guarantee the division of governmental responsibilities between the national government and the States that was intended by the Framers of the Constitution, to ensure that the principles of federalism established by the Framers guide the executive departments and agencies in the formulation and implementation of policies, and to further the policies of the Unfunded Mandates Reform Act, it is hereby ordered as follows:

. . . Sec. 2. Fundamental Federalism Principles. In formulating and implementing policies that have federalism implications, agencies shall be guided by the following fundamental federalism principles:

a. Federalism is rooted in the belief that issues that are not national in scope or significance are most appropriately addressed by the level of government closest to the people.

b. The people of the States created the national government and delegated to it enumerated governmental powers. All other sovereign powers, save those expressly prohibited the States by the Constitution, are reserved to the States or to the people.

c. The constitutional relationship among sovereign governments, State and national, is inherent in the very structure of the Constitution and is formalized in and protected by the Tenth Amendment to the Constitution.

d. The people of the States are free, subject only to restrictions in the Constitution itself or in constitutionally authorized Acts of Congress, to define the moral, political, and legal character of their lives.

e. The Framers recognized that the States possess unique authorities, qualities, and abilities to meet the needs of the people and should function as laboratories of democracy.

f. The nature of our constitutional system encourages a healthy diversity in the public policies adopted by the people of the several States according to their own conditions, needs, and desires. In the search for enlightened public policy, individual States and communities are free to experiment with a variety of approaches to public issues. One-size-fits-all approaches to public policy problems can inhibit the creation of effective solutions to those problems.

g. Acts of the national government—whether legislative, executive, or judicial in nature—that exceed the enumerated powers of that government under the Constitution violate the principle of federalism established by the Framers.

h. Policies of the national government should recognize the responsibility of—and should encourage opportunities for—individuals, families, neighborhoods, local governments, and private associations to achieve their personal, social, and economic objectives through cooperative effort.

i. The national government should be deferential to the States when taking action that affects the policymaking discretion of the States and should act only with the greatest caution where State or local governments have identified uncertainties regarding the constitutional or statutory authority of the national government.

Sec. 3. Federalism Policymaking Criteria. In addition to adhering to the fundamental federalism principles set forth in section 2, agencies shall adhere, to the extent permitted by law, to the following criteria when formulating and implementing policies that have federalism implications:

a. There shall be strict adherence to constitutional principles. Agencies shall closely examine the constitutional and statutory authority supporting any action that would limit the policymaking discretion of the States and shall carefully assess the necessity for such action. To the extent practicable, State and local officials shall be consulted before any such action is implemented. Executive Order 12372 of July 14, 1982 ("Intergovernmental Review of Federal Programs") remains in effect for the programs and activities to which it is applicable.

b. National action limiting the policymaking discretion of the States shall be taken only where there is constitutional and statutory authority for the action and the national activity is appropriate in light of the presence of a problem of national significance. Where there are significant uncertainties as to whether national action is authorized or appropriate, agencies shall consult with appropriate State and local officials to determine whether Federal objectives can be attained by other means.

c. With respect to Federal statutes and regulations administered by the States, the national government shall grant the States the maximum administrative discretion possible. Intrusive Federal oversight of State administration is neither necessary nor desirable.

d. When undertaking to formulate and implement policies that have federalism implications, agencies shall:

L (1) encourage States to develop their own policies to achieve program objectives and to work with appropriate officials in other States;

L (2) where poswsible, defer to the States to establish standards;

L (3) in determining whether to establish uniform national standards, consult with appropriate State and local officials as to the need for national standards and any alternatives that would limit the scope of national standards or otherwise preserve State prerogatives and authority; and

L (4) where national standards are required by Federal statutes, consult with appropriate State and local officials in developing those standards.

ARIZONA, ET AL., V. UNITED STATES[64]

[Justice Anthony Kennedy]. To address pressing issues related to the large number of aliens within its borders who do not have a lawful right to be in this country, the State of Arizona in 2010 enacted a statute called the Support Our Law Enforcement and Safe Neighborhoods Act.

. . . The law's provisions establish an official state policy of "attrition through enforcement." The question before the Court is whether federal law preempts and renders invalid four separate provisions of the state law.

The Government of the United States has broad, undoubted power over the subject of immigration and the status of aliens. This authority rests, in part, on the National Government's constitutional power to "establish an uniform Rule of Naturalization," and its inherent power as sovereign to control and conduct relations with foreign nations.

The federal power to determine immigration policy is well settled. Immigration policy can affect trade, investment, tourism, and diplomatic relations for the entire Nation, as well as the perceptions and expectations of aliens in this country who seek the full protection of its laws.

It is fundamental that foreign countries concerned about the status, safety, and security of their nationals in the United States must be able to confer and communicate on this subject with one national sovereign, not the 50 separate States.

Federal governance of immigration and alien status is extensive and complex. Congress has specified categories of aliens who may not be admitted to the United States. Unlawful entry and unlawful reentry into the country are federal offenses. Once here, aliens are required to register with the Federal Government and to carry proof of status on their person. Failure to do so is a federal misdemeanor. Federal law also authorizes States to deny noncitizens a range of public benefits; and it imposes sanctions on employers who hire unauthorized workers.

Congress has specified which aliens may be removed from the United States and the procedures for doing so. Aliens may be removed if they were inadmissible at the time of entry, have been convicted of certain crimes, or meet other criteria set by federal law. Removal is a civil, not criminal, matter. A principal feature of the removal system is the broad discretion exercised by immigration officials. . . . Federal officials, as an initial matter, must decide whether it makes sense to pursue removal at all. If removal proceedings commence, aliens may seek asylum and other discretionary relief allowing them to remain in the country or at least to leave without formal removal.

. . . The pervasiveness of federal regulation does not diminish the importance of immigration policy to the States.

Federalism, central to the constitutional design, adopts the principle that both the National and State Governments have elements of sovereignty the other is bound to respect. From the existence of two sovereigns follows the possibility that laws can be in conflict or at cross-purposes. The Supremacy Clause provides a clear rule that federal law "shall be the supreme Law of the Land; and the Judges in every State shall be bound thereby, any Thing in the Constitution or Laws of any State to the Contrary notwithstanding." There is no doubt that Congress may withdraw specified powers from the States by enacting a statute containing an express preemption provision.

State law must also give way to federal law in at least two other circumstances. First, the States are precluded from regulating conduct in a field that Congress, acting within its proper authority, has determined must be regulated by its exclusive governance.

Second, state laws are preempted when they conflict with federal law. This includes cases where "compliance with both federal and state regulations is a physical impossibility," and those instances where the challenged state law "stands as an obstacle to the accomplishment and execution of the full purposes and objectives of Congress

. . . The framework enacted by Congress leads to the conclusion here, as it did in Hines, that the Federal Government has occupied the field of alien registration. The federal statutory directives provide a full set of standards governing alien registration, including the punishment for noncompliance. It was designed as a "'harmonious whole.'" Where Congress occupies an entire field, as it has in the field of alien registration, even complementary state regulation is impermissible. Field preemption reflects a congressional decision to foreclose any state regulation in the area, even if it is parallel to federal standards.

Federal law makes a single sovereign responsible for maintaining a comprehensive and unified system to keep track of aliens within the Nation's borders.

. . . By authorizing state officers to decide whether an alien should be detained for being removable, [Arizona] violates the principle that the removal process is entrusted to the discretion of the Federal Government.

. . . Congress has put in place a system in which state officers may not make warrantless arrests of aliens based on possible removability except in specific, limited circumstances. By nonetheless authorizing state and local officers to engage in these enforcement activities as a general matter, [Arizona] creates an obstacle to the full purposes and objectives of Congress.

The National Government has significant power to regulate immigration. With power comes responsibility, and the sound exercise of national power over immigration depends on the Nation's meeting its responsibility to base its laws on a political will informed by searching, thoughtful, rational civic discourse. Arizona may have understandable frustrations with the problems caused by illegal immigration while that process continues, but the State may not pursue policies that undermine federal law.

[Justice Antonin Scalia, dissenting] The United States is an indivisible "Union of sovereign States." Today's opinion, approving virtually all of the Ninth Circuit's injunction against enforcement of the four challenged provisions of Arizona's law, deprives States of what most would consider the defining characteristic of sovereignty: the power to exclude from the sovereign's territory people who have no right to be there. Neither the

Constitution itself nor even any law passed by Congress supports this result. I dissent.

As a sovereign, Arizona has the inherent power to exclude persons from its territory, subject only to those limitations expressed in the Constitution or constitution-ally imposed by Congress. That power to exclude has long been recognized as inherent in sovereignty. Emer de Vattel's seminal 1758 treatise on the Law of Nations stated: "The sovereign may forbid the entrance of his territory either to foreigners in general, or in particular cases, or to certain persons, or for certain particular pur-poses, according as he may think it advantageous to the state. There is nothing in all this, that does not flow from the rights of domain and sovereignty: every one is obliged to pay respect to the prohibition; and whoever dares violate it, incurs the penalty decreed to render it effectual."

. . . There is no doubt that "before the adoption of the constitution of the United States" each State had the authority to "prevent [itself] from being burdened by an influx of persons" . . . And the Constitution did not strip the States of that authority. To the contrary, two of the Constitution's provisions were designed to enable the States to prevent "the intrusion of obnoxious aliens through other States." . . . The Articles of Confederation had provided that "the free inhabitants of each of these States, paupers, vagabonds and fugitives from justice excepted, shall be entitled to all privileges and immunities of free citizens in the several States." Articles of Confederation, Art. IV. This meant that an unwelcome alien could obtain all the rights of a citizen of one State simply by first becoming an inhabitant of another. To remedy this, the Constitution's Privileges and Immunities Clause provided that "[t]he Citizens of each State shall be entitled to all Privileges and Immunities of Citizens in the several States." But if one State had particularly lax citizenship standards, it might still serve as a gateway for the entry of "obnoxious aliens" into other States. This problem was solved "by authorizing the general government to establish a uniform rule of naturalization throughout the United States." . . . In other words, the naturalization power was given to Congress not to abrogate States' power to exclude those they did not want, but to vindicate it.

. . . In fact, the controversy surrounding the Alien and Sedition Acts involved a debate over whether, under the Constitution, the States had exclusive authority to enact such immigration laws. Criticism of the Sedition Act has become a prominent feature of our First Amendment jurisprudence but one of the Alien Acts also aroused controversy at the time.

The Kentucky and Virginia Resolutions, written in denunciation of these Acts, insisted that the power to exclude unwanted aliens rested solely in the States. Jefferson's Kentucky Resolutions insisted "that alien friends are under the jurisdiction and protection of the laws of the state wherein they are [and] that no power over them has been delegated to the United States, nor

prohibited to the individual states, distinct from their power over citizens."
Madison's Virginia Resolutions likewise contended that the Alien Act purported to give the President "a power nowhere delegated to the federal government." Notably, moreover, the Federalist proponents of the Act defended
it primarily on the ground that "[t]he removal of aliens is the usual preliminary of hostility" and could therefore be justified in exercise of the Federal
Government's war powers.

One would conclude from the foregoing that after the adoption of the Constitution there was some doubt about the power of the Federal Government
to control immigration, but no doubt about the power of the States to do so.
Since the founding era (though not immediately), doubt about the Federal
Government's power has disappeared. Indeed, primary responsibility for
immigration policy has shifted from the States to the Federal Government.
Congress exercised its power "[t]o establish an uniform Rule of Naturalization." But with the fleeting exception of the Alien Act, Congress did not enact
any legislation regulating immigration for the better part of a century.

I accept that as a valid exercise of federal power—not because of the Naturalization Clause (it has no necessary connection to citizenship) but because
it is an inherent attribute of sovereignty no less for the United States than for
the States . . . That is why there was no need to set forth control of immigration as one of the enumerated powers of Congress, although an acknowledgment of that power (as well as of the States' similar power, subject to federal
abridgment) was contained in Art. I, §9, which provided that "[t]he Migration
or Importation of such Persons as any of the States now existing shall think
proper to admit, shall not be prohibited by the Congress prior to the Year one
thousand eight hundred and eight. . ."

In light of the predominance of federal immigration restrictions in modern
times, it is easy to lose sight of the States' traditional role in regulating immigration—and to overlook their sovereign prerogative to do so. I accept as a
given that State regulation is excluded by the Constitution when (1) it has
been prohibited by a valid federal law, or (2) it conflicts with federal regulation—when, for example, it admits those whom federal regulation would
exclude, or excludes those whom federal regulation would admit.

Possibility (1) need not be considered here: there is no federal law prohibiting the States' sovereign power to exclude (assuming federal authority to
enact such a law). The mere existence of federal action in the immigration
area—and the so-called field preemption arising from that action, upon which
the Court's opinion so heavily relies, ante, at 9–11—cannot be regarded as
such a prohibition. We are not talking here about a federal law prohibiting
the States from regulating bubble-gum advertising, or even the construction
of nuclear plants. We are talking about a federal law going to the core of
state sovereignty: the power to exclude. Like elimination of the States' other

inherent sovereign power, immunity from suit, elimination of the States' sovereign power to exclude requires that "Congress . . . unequivocally expres[s] its intent to abrogate." Implicit "field preemption" will not do.

Nor can federal power over illegal immigration be deemed exclusive because of what the Court's opinion solicitously calls "foreign countries['] concern[s] about the status, safety, and security of their nationals in the United States," ante, at 3. The Constitution gives all those on our shores the protections of the Bill of Rights—but just as those rights are not expanded for foreign nationals because of their countries' views (some countries, for example, have recently discovered the death penalty to be barbaric), neither are the fundamental sovereign powers of the States abridged to accommodate foreign countries' views. Even in its international relations, the Federal Government must live with the inconvenient fact that it is a Union of independent States, who have their own sovereign powers.

What this case comes down to, then, is whether the Arizona law conflicts with federal immigration law—whether it excludes those whom federal law would admit, or admits those whom federal law would exclude. It does not purport to do so. It applies only to aliens who neither possess a privilege to be present under federal law nor have been removed pursuant to the Federal Government's inherent authority.

The Court opinion's looming specter of inutterable horror—"[i]f §3 of the Arizona statute were valid, every State could give itself independent authority to prosecute fed- eral registration violations,"—seems to me not so horrible and even less looming. But there has come to pass, and is with us today, the specter that Arizona and the States that support it predicted: A Federal Government that does not want to enforce the immigration laws as written, and leaves the States' borders unprotected against immigrants whom those laws would exclude. So the issue is a stark one. Are the sovereign States at the mercy of the Federal Executive's refusal to enforce the Nation's immigration laws?

A good way of answering that question is to ask: Would the States conceivably have entered into the Union if the Constitution itself contained the Court's holding? Today's judgment surely fails that test. At the Constitutional Convention of 1787, the delegates contended with "the jealousy of the states with regard to their sovereignty." . . . Through ratification of the fundamental charter that the Convention produced, the States ceded much of their sovereignty to the Federal Government. But much of it remained jealously guarded—as reflected in the innumerable proposals that never left Independence Hall. Now, imagine a provision—perhaps inserted right after Art. I, §8, cl. 4, the Naturalization Clause—which included among the enumerated powers of Congress "To establish Limitations upon Immigration that will be exclusive and that will be enforced only to the extent the President deems appropriate." The delegates to the Grand Convention would have rushed to the exits.

. . . Arizona has moved to protect its sovereignty—not in contradiction of federal law, but in complete compliance with it. The laws under challenge here do not extend or revise federal immigration restrictions, but merely enforce those restrictions more effectively. If securing its territory in this fashion is not within the power of Arizona, we should cease referring to it as a sovereign State. I dissent.

TENTH AMENDMENT RESOLUTIONS[65]

Arkansas

WHEREAS, the Tenth Amendment to the Constitution of the United States provides that "[t]he powers not delegated to the United States by the Constitution, nor prohibited to it by the States, are reserved to the States respectively, or to the people."; and

WHEREAS, the Tenth Amendment defines the total scope of federal power as being that specifically granted by the Constitution of the United States; and

WHEREAS, the scope of power defined by the Tenth Amendment means that the federal government was created by the states specifically to be an agent of the states; and

WHEREAS, today, in 2009, the states are demonstrably treated as agents of the federal government; and

WHEREAS, the United States Supreme Court has ruled in New York v. United States, 505 U.S. 144 (1992), that Congress may not simply commandeer the legislative and regulatory processes of the states; and

WHEREAS, a number of proposals from previous administrations and some now pending from the present administration and from Congress may further violate the Constitution of the United States,

NOW THEREFORE, BE IT RESOLVED BY THE HOUSE OF REPRESENTATIVES OF THE EIGHTY-SEVENTH GENERAL ASSEMBLY OF THE STATE OF ARKANSAS, THE SENATE CONCURRING THEREIN:

THAT the State of Arkansas hereby claims rights under the Tenth Amendment to the Constitution of the United States over all powers not otherwise enumerated and granted to the federal government by the Constitution of the United States.

BE IT FURTHER RESOLVED that this resolution serve as a request to the federal government, as our agent, to refrain from mandates that are beyond the scope of these constitutionally delegated powers.

New Hampshire

A RESOLUTION affirming States' powers based on the Constitution for the United States and the Constitution of New Hampshire.

Whereas, the Constitution of the State of New Hampshire, Part 1, Article 7 declares that the people of this State have the sole and exclusive right of governing themselves as a free, sovereign, and independent State; and do, and forever hereafter shall, exercise and enjoy every power, jurisdiction, and right, pertaining thereto, which is not, or may not hereafter be, by them expressly delegated to the United States of America in congress assembled; and

Whereas, the Constitution of the State of New Hampshire, Part 2, Article 1 declares that the people inhabiting the territory formerly called the province of New Hampshire, do hereby solemnly and mutually agree with each other, to form themselves into a free, sovereign and independent body-politic, or State, by the name of The State of New Hampshire; and

Whereas, each State acceded to the compact titled The Constitution for the United States of America as a State, and is an integral party, its co-States forming, as to itself, the other party: and

Whereas, the State of New Hampshire when ratifying the Constitution for the United States of America recommended as a change, "First That it be Explicitly declared that all Powers not expressly & particularly Delegated by the aforesaid are reserved to the several States to be, by them Exercised"; and

Whereas, the other States that included recommendations, to wit Massachusetts, New York, North Carolina, Rhode Island, and Virginia, included an identical or similar recommended change; and

Whereas, these recommended changes were incorporated as the Ninth Amendment, "The enumeration in the Constitution, of certain rights, shall not be construed to deny or disparage others retained by the people," and the Tenth Amendment, "The powers not delegated to the United States by the Constitution, nor prohibited by it to the States, are reserved to the States respectively, or to the people," to the Constitution for the United States of America. Therefore, the several States composing the United States of America, are not united on the principle of unlimited submission to their General Government; but that, by a compact under the style and title of a Constitution for the United States of America, and of amendments thereto, they constituted a General Government for special purposes, delegated to that government certain definite powers, reserving, each State to itself, all remaining powers for their own self-government; and

Whereas, the construction applied by the General Government (as is evidenced by sundry of their proceedings) to those parts of the Constitution of the United States which delegate to Congress a power "to lay and collect taxes, duties, imports, and excises, to pay the debts, and provide for the common defense and general welfare of the United States," and "to make all laws which shall be necessary and proper for carrying into execution the powers vested by the Constitution in the government of the United States, or in any department or officer thereof," goes to the destruction of all limits prescribed to their power by the Constitution:

I.   Therefore, words meant by the instrument to be subsidiary only to the execution of limited powers, ought not to be so construed as themselves to give unlimited powers, nor a part to be so taken as to destroy the whole residue of that instrument; and

II.   Therefore, whensoever the General Government assumes undelegated powers, its acts are unauthoritative, void, and of no force; and

Whereas, the Constitution of the United States, having delegated to Congress a power to punish treason, counterfeiting the securities and current coin of the United States, piracies, and felonies committed on the high seas, offenses against the law of nations, and slavery, and no other crimes whatsoever:

Therefore, all acts of Congress, the orders of the Executive or orders of the Judiciary of the United States of America which assume to create, define, or punish crimes, other than those so enumerated in the Constitution are altogether void, and of no force; and that the power to create, define, and punish such other crimes is reserved, and, of right, appertains solely and exclusively to the respective States, each within its own territory; and

Whereas, The United States Supreme Court has ruled in New York v. United States, 112 S. Ct. 2408 (1992), that congress may not simply commandeer the legislative and regulatory processes of the States:

Therefore, all compulsory federal legislation that directs States to comply under threat of civil or criminal penalties or sanctions or that requires States to pass legislation or lose federal funding are prohibited; and

Whereas, The Constitution for the United States of America, Article II, Section 2, Clause 2 gives Congress the authority to authorize inferior officers of the government of the United States of America not enumerated in the Constitution by law and for them to be appointed by the manner prescribed by law enacted by the Congress, and that the Constitution gives no such authority to the President:

Therefore, no officer not authorized by the Constitution or by law or exercising a power not authorized by the Constitution, nor their subordinates shall have any authority in, or over the sovereign State of New Hampshire, nor any inhabitant or resident thereof, nor any franchises created under the authority thereof when within the borders of the State of New Hampshire, and

Whereas, the Constitution for the United States of America Article I, Section 1 delegates all legislative power to the Congress, and

Whereas, the Constitution for the United States of America Article II delegates no legislative power to the Executive branch whatsoever. Therefore, any Executive Order that pretends the power to create statutes controlling the States, their inhabitants or their residents is unauthoritive, void and of no force, and

Whereas, the Constitution for the United States of America, Article VI, Section 2 declares "This Constitution, and the Laws of the United States which shall be made in Pursuance thereof; and all Treaties made, or which shall be made, under the Authority of the United States, shall be the supreme Law of the Land; and the Judges in every State shall be bound thereby, any Thing in the Constitution or Laws of any State to the Contrary notwithstanding."; and

Whereas, treaties are ratified by the Senate which being a House of Congress has its jurisdiction limited to the powers enumerated in Article I, Section 8 of the Constitution; and

Whereas, treaties are ratified by the President and the Senate (representing the States) only, but laws are ratified by the House of Representatives (representing the people) and the Senate (representing the States) and the President, no treaty can be lawfully construed to restrict or amend existing law; and

Whereas, treaties are ratified by the President and the Senate (representing the States) only, but the Constitution and its amendments were ratified by the States directly (representing the people), no treaty can be lawfully construed to restrict or amend the Constitution:

Therefore, any treaty which pretends to delegate any powers not delegated to Congress in Article I, Section 8 of the Constitution is altogether void, and of no force; and any order of the Executive or order of the Judiciary which is construed to restrict or amend existing law, or any act of Congress, order of the Executive or order of the Judiciary which is construed to restrict or amend the Constitution for the United States of America based upon compliance with any treaty are altogether void, and of no force; and

Whereas, the government created by this compact was not made the exclusive or final judge of the extent of the powers delegated to itself, since that would have made its discretion, and not the Constitution, the measure of its powers; but that, as in all other cases of compact among powers having no common judge, each party has an equal right to judge for itself, as well of infractions as of the mode and measure of redress:

Therefore, the Legislatures and Legislators of the several States have the right and duty to consider the constitutionality of any legislative act or order promulgated by the government of the United States of America; and to protect their governments, inhabitants, and residents and instruments created under their authority by prohibiting, and if necessary punishing the enforcement any Acts by the Congress of the United States of America, Executive Order of the President of the United States of America or Judicial Order by the Judicatories of the United States of America which assumes a power not delegated to the government of United States of America by the Constitution for the United States of America; and

Whereas, the Constitution for the United States of America guarantees to every State in this Union a Republican Form of Government, and shall protect each of them against Invasion; and on Application of the Legislature (of a State), or of the Executive (when the Legislature cannot be convened) against domestic Violence. Therefore; there exists a class of Acts by the Congress of the United States, Executive Orders of the President of the United States of America or Judicial Orders by the Judicatories of the United States of America that constitutes a direct challenge to the Constitution for the United States of America by the government of the United States including, but not limited to:

I.   Requiring involuntary servitude or governmental service other than pursuant to, or as an alternative to, incarceration after due process of law.
II. Establishing martial law or a state of emergency within one of the States comprising the United States of America without the consent of the legislature of that State or authority derived from that body.
III. Surrendering any power delegated or not delegated to any incorporation or foreign government; now, therefore, be it.

Resolved by the House of Representatives, the Senate concurring:

That the State of New Hampshire urges its co-States to charge to one if its committees with the duty communicating the preceedings of its Legislature in regard to the government of the United States of America to the corresponding committees of Legislatures of the several States; to assure them that this State continues in the same esteem of their friendship and union which it has manifested from that moment at which a common danger first suggested a common union: that it considers union, for specified national purposes, and particularly to those specified in their federal compact, to be friendly to the peace, happiness, and prosperity of all the States: that faithful to that compact, according to the plain intent and meaning in which it was understood and acceded to by the several parties, it is sincerely anxious for its preservation: that it does also believe, that to take from the States all the powers of self-government and transfer them to a general and consolidated government, without regard to the special delegations and reservations solemnly agreed to in that compact, is not for the peace, happiness, or prosperity of these States;

and that therefore this State is determined, as it doubts not its co-States are, to submit to undelegated, and consequently unlimited powers in no man, or body of men on earth: that in cases of an abuse of the delegated powers, the members of the General Government, being chosen by the people, a change by the people would be the constitutional remedy; but, where powers are assumed which have not been delegated, a nullification of the act is the rightful remedy: that every State has a natural right in cases not within the compact, (casus non foederis), to nullify of their own authority all assumptions of power by others within their limits: that without this right, they would be under the dominion, absolute and unlimited, of whosoever might exercise this right of judgment for them; and

Kentucky

A CONCURRENT RESOLUTION claiming sovereignty over powers not granted to the federal government by the United States Constitution; serving notice to the federal government to cease mandates beyond its authority; and stating Kentucky's position that federal legislation that requires states to comply under threat of loss of federal funding should be prohibited or repealed.

WHEREAS, the Tenth Amendment to the Constitution of the United States provides that "The powers not delegated to the United States by the Constitution, nor prohibited to it by the States, are reserved to the States respectively, or to the people."; and

WHEREAS, the Tenth Amendment defines the total scope of federal power as being that specifically granted by the Constitution of the United States and no more; and

WHEREAS, the scope of power defined by the Tenth Amendment means that the federal government was created by the states specifically to be an agent of the state; and

WHEREAS, today, in 2010, the states are demonstrably treated as agents of the federal government; and

WHEREAS, many federal mandates are directly in violation of the Tenth Amendment to the Constitution of the United States; and

WHEREAS, Article IV, Section 4 of the United States Constitution states that "The United States shall guarantee to every State in this Union a Republican Form of Government . . ." and the Ninth Amendment of the United States Constitution states that "The enumeration in the Constitution, of certain rights, shall not be construed to deny or disparage others retained by the people."; and

WHEREAS, the United States Supreme Court has ruled in New York v. United States, 505 U.S. 144 (1992), that Congress may not simply commandeer the legislative and regulatory processes of the states; and

WHEREAS, a number of proposals from previous administrations and some now pending from the present administration and from Congress may further violate the Constitution of the United States;

NOW, THEREFORE,

Be it resolved by the House of Representatives of the General Assembly of the Commonwealth of Kentucky, the Senate concurring therein:

Section 1. The Commonwealth of Kentucky hereby claims sovereignty under the Tenth Amendment to the Constitution of the United States over all powers not otherwise enumerated and granted to the federal government by the Constitution of the United States.

Section 2. This Resolution serves as notice and demand to the federal government, as our agent, to cease and desist, effective immediately, mandates that are beyond the scope of these constitutionally delegated powers.

Section 3. It is the position of the Commonwealth of Kentucky that all compulsory federal legislation that directs states to comply under threat of civil or criminal penalties or sanctions, or requires states to pass legislation or lose federal funding be prohibited or repealed.

Section 4. The Clerk of the House of Representatives shall distribute a copy of this Resolution to the President of the United States, the President of the United States Senate, the Speaker of the United States House of Representatives, the Speaker of the House and President of the Senate of each state's legislature of the United States of America, and to each member of Kentucky's congressional delegation.

Mississippi

A concurrent resolution reinforcing the fundamental principle and authority of state sovereignty under the tenth amendment to the constitution of the United States over certain powers and discouraging the federal government from imposing certain restrictive mandates.

WHEREAS, the Tenth Amendment to the Constitution of the United States reads: "The powers not delegated to the United States by the Constitution, nor prohibited by it to the States, are reserved to the States respectively, or to the people"; and

WHEREAS, the Tenth Amendment defines the total scope of federal power as being that specifically granted by the Constitution of the United States and no more; and

WHEREAS, Federalism is the constitutional division of powers between the national and state governments and is widely regarded as one of America's most valuable contributions to political science; and

WHEREAS, James Madison, "the Father of the Constitution," said, "The powers delegated to the federal government are few and defined. Those which are to remain in the state governments are numerous and indefinite. The former will be exercised principally on external objects, such as war, peace, negotiation, and foreign commerce. The powers reserved to the several states will extend to all the objects which, in the ordinary course of affairs, concern the lives, liberties, and properties of the people"; and

WHEREAS, Thomas Jefferson emphasized that the states are not "subordinate" to the national government, but rather the two are "coordinate departments of one simple and integral whole. The one is the domestic, the other the foreign branch of the same government"; and

WHEREAS, Alexander Hamilton expressed his hope that "the people will always take care to preserve the constitutional equilibrium between the general and the state governments." He believed that "this balance between the national and state governments forms a double security to the people. If one government encroaches on their rights, they will find a powerful protection in the other. Indeed, they will both be prevented from overpassing their constitutional limits by the certain rivalship which will ever subsist between them"; and

WHEREAS, the scope of power defined by the Tenth Amendment means that the federal government was created by the states specifically to be an agent of the states; and

WHEREAS, today, in 2010, the states are demonstrably treated as agents of the federal government; and

WHEREAS, many federal mandates appear to be in violation of the Tenth Amendment to the Constitution of the United States, and the United States Supreme Court's ruling in New York v. United States, 112 S. Ct. 2408 (1992), stated that Congress may not simply "commandeer the legislative and regulatory processes of the States by directly compelling them to enact and enforce a federal regulatory program"; and

WHEREAS, the Supreme Court in that case went on to express that, "No matter how powerful the federal interest involved, the Constitution simply does not give Congress the authority to require the States to regulate. The Constitution instead gives Congress the authority to regulate matters directly and to pre-empt contrary state regulation. Where a federal interest is sufficiently strong to cause Congress to legislate, it must do so directly; it may not conscript state governments as its agents"; and ST: U.S. Congress; urge to be mindful of state sovereignty enumerated in the 10th Amendment to the U.S. Constitution.

WHEREAS, a number of proposals from previous administrations and some now pending from the present administration and from Congress may further violate the Constitution of the United States; and

WHEREAS, it is incumbent upon the Mississippi Legislature, as an agent for the people of the State of Mississippi, to remind the federal government to act only in ways that will ensure the protection and preservation of constitutional rights granted to each state in the framework of the Constitution of the United States as crafted by our nation's founding fathers, so as not to deny each state the enumerated right of self-governance without an over-reaching arm of federal government mandates and implications:

NOW, THEREFORE, BE IT RESOLVED BY THE HOUSE OF REPRESENTATIVES OF THE STATE OF MISSISSIPPI, THE SENATE CONCURRING THEREIN, That the State of Mississippi hereby reinforces the fundamental principles and authority of state sovereignty under the Tenth Amendment to the Constitution of the United States over all powers not otherwise enumerated and granted to the federal government by the Constitution of the United States and discourage the federal government, as our agent, from imposing certain restrictive mandates that are beyond the scope of these constitutionally delegated powers.

Nebraska

WHEREAS, the Ninth Amendment to the United States

Constitution states that "The enumeration in the Constitution, of certain rights, shall not be construed to deny or disparage others retained by the people;" and

WHEREAS, the Tenth Amendment to the United States Constitution declares that "The powers not delegated to the United States by the Constitution, nor prohibited by it to the States, are reserved to the States respectively, or to the people;" and

WHEREAS, the framers of the United States Constitution envisioned a federal government with "few and defined" delegated powers, whereby state governments retained "numerous and indefinite" powers extending "to all the objects which, in the ordinary course of affairs, concern the lives, liberties, and properties of the people, and the internal order, improvement, and prosperity of the State;" and

WHEREAS, the United States Government has historically and continues to expand its enumerated powers in a manner inconsistent with the Ninth Amendment to the United States Constitution; and

WHEREAS, the United States Government has historically and continues to assert powers not enumerated under Article I, section 8, of the United States Constitution in a manner inconsistent with the Tenth Amendment to the United States Constitution; and

WHEREAS, a balanced federalism is necessary to preserve the inherent rights of the people, from whose consent the just powers of both state and federal governments are derived.

NOW, THEREFORE, BE IT RESOLVED BY THE MEMBERS OF THE ONE HUNDRED FIRST LEGISLATURE OF NEBRASKA, SECOND SESSION:

1. That the Legislature encourages the Congress of the United States to adhere to the principles of federalism in accord with the Ninth and Tenth Amendments to the United States Constitution.

South Carolina

TO AFFIRM THE RIGHTS OF ALL STATES INCLUDING SOUTH CAROLINA BASED ON THE PROVISIONS OF THE NINTH AND TENTH AMENDMENTS TO THE UNITED STATES CONSTITUTION.

Whereas, the Tenth Amendment to the United States Constitution provides that "powers not delegated to the United States by the Constitution, nor prohibited by it to the States, are reserved to the States respectively, or to the people"; and

Whereas, the Tenth Amendment defines the limited scope of federal power as being that specifically granted by the United States Constitution; and

Whereas, the limited scope of authority defined by the Tenth Amendment means that the federal government was created by the states specifically to be an agent of the states; and

Whereas, currently the states are treated as agents of the federal government; and

Whereas, many federal mandates are directly in violation of the Tenth Amendment to the United States Constitution; and

Whereas, the United States Supreme Court has ruled that Congress may not simply commandeer the legislative and regulatory processes of the states; and

Whereas, the State recognizes that as an independent sovereign, the State along with the other states of the union took part in an extensive collective bargaining process through the adoption of the Constitution and the various amendments thereto, and like any other party to any other agreement, the State is bound to uphold the terms and conditions of that agreement. Through this agreement, the states have collectively created the federal government, limiting the scope of its power and authority, as well as ensuring that certain fundamental rights are guaranteed. Also, through this process the states have collectively agreed to limit their own governmental authority by providing that the rights and protections afforded to the people as citizens of the United States are also extended to each person as a citizen of an individual state. Pursuant to that agreement, this State is bound to uphold the principals and protections afforded by all of the constitutional amendments, one of the most notable being the protections afforded by the Fourteenth Amendment which guarantees the privileges and immunities of the United States, due process of law, and equal protection under the law; and

Whereas, pursuant to the Tenth Amendment, by limiting the scope of federal power to only those specifically enumerated in the United States Constitution, the states retain plenary power to govern; and

Whereas, included among all states' plenary power to govern is the broad authority of all state legislatures to appropriate funds for the operation of state agencies and to specify and direct the conditions under which appropriated funds shall be spent; and

Whereas, the General Assembly of the State of South Carolina has exercised its broad authority to appropriate and direct the expenditure of funds by appropriating and directing the expenditure of funds in the Fiscal Year 2009–2010 budget. Now, therefore,

Be it resolved by the Senate, the House of Representatives concurring:

That the General Assembly of the State of South Carolina, by this resolution, claims for the State of South Carolina sovereignty under the Tenth Amendment to the Constitution of the United States over all powers not otherwise enumerated and granted to the federal government by the United States Constitution.

Be it further resolved that all federal governmental agencies, quasi governmental agencies, and their agents and employees operating within the geographic boundaries of the State of South Carolina, and all federal governmental agencies and their agents and employees, whose actions have effect on the inhabitants or lands or waters of the State of South Carolina, shall operate within the confines of the original intent of the Constitution of the United States and abide by the provisions of the Constitution of South Carolina, the South Carolina statutes, or the common law as guaranteed by the Constitution of the United States.

Be it further resolved that this resolution serves as notice and demand to the federal government, as South Carolina's agent, to cease and desist immediately all mandates that are beyond the scope of the federal government's constitutionally delegated powers.

Utah

Be it resolved by the Legislature of the state of Utah, the Governor concurring therein:

WHEREAS, the Tenth Amendment to the Constitution of the United States reads: "The powers not delegated to the United States by the Constitution, nor prohibited by it to the States, are reserved to the States respectively, or to the people";

WHEREAS, the Tenth Amendment defines the total scope of federal power as being that specifically granted to the federal government by the Constitution of the United States and no more;

WHEREAS, the states are often treated as agents of the federal government;

WHEREAS, many federal laws directly contravene the Tenth Amendment;

WHEREAS, it is important that all levels of government work together to serve the citizens of the United States by respecting the constitutional provisions that properly delineate the authority of federal, state, and local governments;

WHEREAS, the Tenth Amendment assures that we, the people of the United States, and each sovereign state in the Union of States, now have, and have always had, rights the federal government may not usurp;

WHEREAS, Article IV, Section 4 of the United States Constitution declares in part, "The United States shall guarantee to every State in this Union a Republican Form of Government," and the Ninth Amendment to the United States Constitution further declares that "The enumeration in the Constitution, of certain rights, shall not be construed to deny or disparage others retained by the people";

WHEREAS, the United States Supreme Court ruled in New York v. United States, 505 U.S. 144 (1992), that Congress may not simply commandeer the legislative and regulatory processes of the states by compelling them to enact and enforce regulatory programs;

WHEREAS, the United States Supreme Court, in Printz v. United States/ Mack v. United States, 521 U.S. 898 (1997), reaffirmed that the Constitution of the United States established a system of "dual sovereignty" that retains "a residuary and inviolable sovereignty" by the states;

WHEREAS, this separation of the two spheres is one of the Constitution's structural protections of liberty; and

WHEREAS, a number of proposals by previous administrations, some now pending proposals by the present administration, and some proposals by Congress may further violate the Tenth Amendment restriction on the scope of federal power:

NOW, THEREFORE, BE IT RESOLVED that the Legislature of the state of Utah, the Governor concurring therein, acknowledge and reaffirm residuary and inviolable sovereignty of the state of Utah under the Tenth Amendment to the Constitution of the United States over all powers not otherwise enumerated and granted to the federal government by the Constitution of the United States.

DONALD J. TRUMP, EXECUTIVE ORDER
ENFORCING STATUTORY PROHIBITIONS ON
FEDERAL CONTROL OF EDUCATION[66]

By the authority vested in me as President by the Constitution and the laws of the United States of America, and in order to restore the proper division of power under the Constitution between the Federal Government and the States and to further the goals of, and to ensure strict compliance with, statutes that prohibit Federal interference with State and local control over education, including section 103 of the Department of Education Organization Act (DEOA) (20 U.S.C. 3403), sections 438 and 447 of the General Education Provisions Act (GEPA), as amended (20 U.S.C. 1232a and 1232j), and sections 8526A, 8527, and 8529 of the Elementary and Secondary Education Act of 1965 (ESEA), as amended by the Every Student Succeeds Act (ESSA) (20 U.S.C. 7906a, 7907, and 7909), it is hereby ordered as follows:

Section 1. Policy. It shall be the policy of the executive branch to protect and preserve State and local control over the curriculum, program of instruction, administration, and personnel of educational institutions, schools, and school systems, consistent with applicable law, including ESEA, as amended by ESSA, and ESEA's restrictions related to the Common Core State Standards developed under the Common Core State Standards Initiative.

Sec. 2. Review of Regulations and Guidance Documents. (a) The Secretary of Education (Secretary) shall review all Department of Education (Department) regulations and guidance documents relating to DEOA, GEPA, and ESEA, as amended by ESSA.

(b) The Secretary shall examine whether these regulations and guidance documents comply with Federal laws that prohibit the Department from exercising any direction, supervision, or control over areas subject to State and local control, including:

i.   the curriculum or program of instruction of any elementary and secondary school and school system;
ii. school administration and personnel; and
iii. selection and content of library resources, textbooks, and instructional materials.

(c) The Secretary shall, as appropriate and consistent with applicable law, rescind or revise any regulations that are identified pursuant to subsection (b) of this section as inconsistent with statutory prohibitions. The Secretary shall also rescind or revise any guidance documents that are identified pursuant to subsection (b) of this section as inconsistent with statutory prohibitions. The Secretary shall, to the extent consistent with law, publish any proposed regulations and withdraw or modify any guidance documents pursuant to this subsection no later than 300 days after the date of this order.

NOTES

1. Jean Bodin, *Six Books of the Commonwealth,* M. J. Tooley, ed. and trans (Oxford: Blackwell, 1955), 1–16.

2. Thomas Hobbes, *Leviathan,* A. R. Waller, ed. (originally published 1651; Cambridge: Cambridge University Press, 1904), 115–129.

3. Montesquieu, *The Spirit of Laws,* Thomas Nuget, ed., 2 vols, 2nd edition (London: J. Nourse and P. Vaillant, 1752), 1: 175–179.

4. Vattell, *The Law of Nations* (1758; reprinted, Philadelphia: T and J.W. Johnson Law Booksellers, 1853), 1–3.

5. William Blackstone, *Commentaries on the Laws of England,* 4 vols (Oxford: Clarendon Press, 1765), 1: 49–53.

6. Danby Pickering, ed., *The Statutes at Large,* 42 vols (Cambridge: Printed for Benthem, for C. Bathhurst, 1762–1869), 27: 20.

7. Richard Bland, *Inquiry into the Rights of the British Colonies* (Williamsburg, 1766), 20.

8. Stephen Hopkins, *The Rights of the Colonies Examined* (Providence: William Goddard, 1765), 18–20.

9. Alexander Hamilton, *The Farmer Refuted: or a More Impartial and Comprehensive View of the Dispute between Great-Britain and the Colonies* (New York: James Rivington, 1775), 42–43.

10. Henry Cabot Lodge, ed., *The Works of Alexander Hamilton: Federal Edition,* 12 vols (New York: G.P. Putnam and Sons, 1904), 1: 243–248.

11. Meriweather Smith, *Observations on the Fourth and Fifth Articles of the Preliminaries for a Peace* (Richmond: Dixon and Holt, 1783), 4–7. Used by permission from Readex, a division of Newsbank inc and The American Antiquarian Society.

12. Charles Tansill, ed., *Documents Illustrative of the Formation of the Union of the American States* (Washington, D.C.: Government Printing Office, 1927), 953–963.

13. Charles Tansill, ed., *Documents Illustrative of the Formation of the Union of the American States* (Washington, D.C.: Government Printing Office, 1927), 967–978.

14. James Wilson, "State House Speech," *Pennsylvania Packet,* October 10, 1787.

15. Paul L. Ford, ed., *The Federalist: A Commentary on the Constitution of the United States* (New York: Henry Holt and Company, 1898), 54–64.

16. Paul L. Ford, ed., *The Federalist: A Commentary on the Constitution of the United States* (New York: Henry Holt and Company, 1898), 162–168.

17. Paul L. Ford, ed., *The Federalist: A Commentary on the Constitution of the United States* (New York: Henry Holt and Company, 1898), 245–252.

18. Paul L. Ford, ed., *The Federalist: A Commentary on the Constitution of the United States* (New York: Henry Holt and Company, 1898), 294–303.

19. *New York Journal,* October 18, 1787.

20. *New York Journal,* December 27, 1787.

21. Harry Alonzo Cushing, ed., *The Writings of Samuel Adams,* 4 vols (New York: G. P. Putnan's Sons, 1908), 4: 324–325.

22. *The Independent Gazetteer,* August 18, 1789.

23. Jonathan Elliot, ed., *The Debates in the Several State Conventions on the Adoption of the Federal Constitution,* 4 vols (Washington, D.C.: 1836), 3: 21–23; 43–64.

24. Paul L. Ford, ed., *The Writings of Thomas Jefferson,* 12 vols (New York: G. P. Putnam's Sons, 1904), 6: 197–204.

25. Henry Cabot Lodge, ed., *The Works of Alexander Hamilton in Twelve Volumes: Federal Edition* (New York: G.P. Putnam's Sons, 1904), 3: 445–494.

26. *Chisholm v. Georgia 2 U.S. 419 (1793).*

27. Jonathan Elliot, *The Virginia and Kentucky Resolution of 1798 and '99 with Jefferson's Original Draught Thereof Also, Madison's Report, Calhoun's Address, Resolutions of the Several States in Relation to State Rights with other Documents in Support of The Jeffersonian Doctrines of '98* (Washington, D.C., 1832), 15–19.

28. Jonathan Elliot, *The Virginia and Kentucky Resolution of 1798 and '99 with Jefferson's Original Draught Thereof Also, Madison's Report, Calhoun's Address, Resolutions of the Several States in Relation to State Rights with other Documents in Support of The Jeffersonian Doctrines of '98* (Washington, D.C., 1832), 5–6.

29. Jonathan Elliot, *The Virginia and Kentucky Resolution of 1798 and '99 with Jefferson's Original Draught Thereof Also, Madison's Report, Calhoun's Address, Resolutions of the Several States in Relation to State Rights with other Documents in Support of The Jeffersonian Doctrines of '98* (Washington, D.C., 1832), 21–41.

30. *McCulloch v. Maryland 17 U.S. 316 (1819).*

31. John Taylor of Caroline, *New Views of the Constitution* (Washington, D.C.: Way and Gideon, 1823), 171–177.

32. *Register of Debates* 21st Congress, 1st Session (Washington, D.C.: Gales and Seaton), 31–41; 43–80.

33. Richard K. Cralle, ed., *The Works of John C. Calhoun: Reports and Public Letters of John C. Calhoun,* 6 vols (New York: D. Appleton and Company, 1870), 6: 59–93.

34. Paul L. Ford, ed., *The Federalist: A Commentary on the Constitution of the United States . . . with Notes, Illustrative Documents . . .* (New York: Henry Holt and Company, 1898), 690–692.

35. Paul L. Ford, ed., *The Federalist: A Commentary on the Constitution of the United States . . . with Notes, Illustrative Documents . . .* (New York: Henry Holt and Company, 1898).

36. James D. Richardson, ed., *Compilations of the Messages and Papers of the Presidents,* 11 vols (Washington, D.C.: Government Printing Office, 1897, 1904), 2: 483–493.

37. James D. Richardson, ed., *Compilations of the Messages and Papers of the Presidents,* 11 vols (Washington, D.C.: Government Print Office, 1897, 1904), 2: 576–591.

38. *A Disquisition on Government and a Discourse on the Constitution and Government of the United States*, Richard K. Cralle, ed. (Columbia: A.S. Johnston, 1851), 111–131.

39. Joseph Story, *Commentaries on the Constitution*, 3 vols (Boston: Hillard, Gray, and Company, 1833), 3: 752–755.

40. Abel Upshur, *A Brief Enquiry into the True Nature and Character of Our Federal Government* (originally published 1840; Philadelphia: John Cambell, 1863), 84–87.

41. *Luther v. Borden 48 U.S. 1 (1849)*.

42. Albert Bushnell Hart and Edward Channing, eds., *American History Leaflets: Colonial and Constitutional*, 1–18 vols (New York: A Lovell and Co., 1892), 12: 3–21.

43. James D. Richardson, ed., *Compilations of the Messages and Papers of the Presidents*, 11 vols (Washington, D.C.: Government Print Office, 1897, 1904), 6: 20–31.

44. F.B. Carpenter and John Herbert Clifford, eds., *The Works of Abraham Lincoln*, 6 volumes, Speeches and Presidential Addresses, 1859–1865 (New York: C.S. Hammond, 1908), 5: 183.

45. The Congressional Globe, *37th Congress, 2nd Session* (Washington, D.C.: Congressional Globe Office, 1862), 736–737.

46. James D. Richardson, ed., *Compilations of the Messages and Papers of the Presidents*, 11 vols (Washington, D.C.: Government Printing Office, 1897, 1904), 2498–2511.

47. *Texas v. White 74 U.S. 400 (1873)*.

48. Woodrow Wilson, "The States and the Federal Government," *The North American Review* 187 (May 1908): 684–701.

49. Albert Beveridge, *The Meaning of the Times and Other Speeches* (Indianapolis: The Bobbs-Merrill Company, 1908), 1–20.

50. Theodore Roosevelt, *New Nationalism* (New York: The Outlook Company, 1910), 11–32.

51. *Platforms of the Two Great Parties from 1856–1920* (La Crosse, WI: Arthur Bentley, 1922), 182–196.

52. George Henry Payne, *The Birth of a New Party: Or Progressive Democracy* (New York: J. L. Nichols & Co, 1912), 303–320.

53. Herbert Croly, *The Promise of American Life* (New York: The MacMillan Company, 1911), 21–36.

54. *Missouri v. Holland 252 U.S. 416 (1920)*.

55. Samuel Rosenman, *Public Papers of the Presidents of the United States: Franklin D. Roosevelt*, 13 vols (New York: Random House, 1938–1948), 11–17.

56. Samuel Rosenman, *Public Papers of the Presidents: Franklin D. Roosevelt*, 13 vols (New York: Random House, 1938–1948), 4: 421–423.

57. *Public Papers of the Presidents: Lyndon B. Johnson*, 10 vols (Washington, D.C.: Office of the Federal Register, 1965–1970), 1: 704–707.

58. *Public Papers of the Presidents: Richard M. Nixon*, 6 vols (Washington, D.C.: Government Printing Office, 1971–1975), 1: 639–645.

59. https://www.reaganlibrary.archives.gov/archives/speeches/1981/12081a.htm accessed December 3, 2016.

60. https://www.reaganlibrary.archives.gov/archives/speeches/1981/73081d.htm accessed December 3, 2016.

61. *New York v. U.S. 505 U.S. 144 (1992)*.

62. *Printz v. US 521 U.S. 898 (1997)*.

63. https://www.gpo.gov/fdsys/pkg/FR-1999-08-10/pdf/99-20729.pdf#page=1 accessed March 3, 2017.

64. 567 US___.

65. 10th Amendment Resolutions a collection can be found at http://tenthame ndmentcenter.com/nullification/10th-amendment-resolutions/ accessed November 2, 2016.

66. https://www.whitehouse.gov/the-press-office/2017/04/26/presidential-executi ve-order-enforcing-statutory-prohibitions-federal accessed July 15, 2017.

Part II

Civil Liberties

Editors' Note: Civil liberties are generally known as those protections guaranteed by the government to it citizens. It can range from protections held by individuals or to a more general class of citizens. They are sometimes thought of as a shield that is used against unwanted and unwarranted government action. The artifacts that follow span a time frame starting in 1833 to the present day. It is clear that the majority of these documents are in the modern era. This is not without cause. While the notion of civil liberties has roots in the founding era discussions of our political system, the interplay of these liberties and federalism has more recently accelerated.

The first four documents establish the pre-modern boundaries of the protections afforded to citizens from federal government intrusion. The delineation of specific protections is quite limited as these documents reflect a general attitude of federalism. That is, the protection of civil liberties was seen as more of a responsibility of the state governments than the federal government. These boundaries gave states wide latitude as to how they could treat their respective citizens. The variability in citizen protections between states was the most evident on the distinguishing characteristic of race. Beginning with the Platform of the Dixiecrats (1948) document and stretching to the Katzenbach v. McClung case of 1964, the effort to reverse the pervasive Jim Crow laws and culture captured the center of discussion concerning federalism. In less than 20 years, the previous 100 plus years of the debate of the applicability of federal protections toward citizens was rewritten. Each of the landmark court cases presented in this section demonstrate the continued refinement of Federalism's edge in terms of separating state from their ability to legislate discrimination.

The clarity that was created through the Civil Rights Era struggles continued to sink deeper into issues beyond race. Beginning with the Griswold case, federal protections of civil liberties began to take shape on issues such as marriage, sexual identity, and the rights an individual has over their own body. What will likely come in the near future are clarifications on how federalism relates to all aspects of one's life, whether it involves the upbringing of children to the very decision to end one's own life.

BARRON v. BALTIMORE[1]

. . . The plaintiff in error contends that it comes within that clause in the 5th amendment to the constitution, which inhibits the taking of private property for public use, without just compensation. He insists that this amendment, being in favor of the liberty of the citizen, ought to be so constructed as to restrain the legislative power of the State, as well as that of the United States. If this position be untrue, the court can take no jurisdiction of the cause.

The question thus presented is, we think, of great importance, but not of much difficulty.

The constitution was ordained and established by the people of the United States for themselves, for their own government and not for the government of the individual States. Each State established a constitution for itself, and, in that constitution, provided such limitations and restrictions on the powers of its particular government as its judgment dictated. The people of the United States framed such a government for the United States as they supposed best adapted to their situation, and best calculated to promote their interests. The powers they conferred on this government were to be exercised by itself; and the limitations on power, if expressed in general terms, are naturally, and, we think, necessarily applicable to the government created by the instrument. They are limitations of power granted in the instrument itself; not of distinct governments, framed by different persons and for different purposes.

If these propositions be correct, the 5th amendment must be understood as restraining the power of the general government, not as applicable to the States. In their several constitutions they have imposed such restrictions on their governments as their own wisdom suggested; such as they deemed most proper for themselves. It is a subject on which they judge exclusively, and with which others interfere no further than they are supposed to have a common interest. . .

Had the people of the several States, or any of them, required changes in their constitutions; had they required additional safeguards to liberty from the apprehended encroachments of their particular governments; the remedy was in their own hands, and would have been applied by themselves. A convention would have been assembled by the discontented State, and the required improvements would have been made by itself. The unwieldy and cumbrous machinery of procuring a recommendation from two thirds of congress, and the assent of three fourths of their Sister States, could never have occurred to any human being as a mode of doing that which might be effected by the State itself. Had the framers of these amendments intended them to be limitations on the powers of the state governments, they would have imitated the framers of the original constitution, and have expressed that intention. Had congress engaged in the extraordinary occupation of improving the constitutions of several States by affording the people additional protection from the exercise of power by their own governments in matters which concerned themselves alone, they would have declared this purpose in plain and intelligible language.

But it is universally understood, it is a part of the history of the day, that the great revolution which established the constitution of the United States, was not effected without immense opposition. Serious fears were extensively entertained that those powers which the patriot statesmen, who then watched over the interests of our country, deemed essential to union, and to the attainment of those invaluable objects for which union was sought, might be exercised in a manner dangerous to liberty. In almost every convention by which the constitution was adopted, amendments to guard against the abuse of power were recommended. These amendments demanded security against the apprehended encroachments of the general government, not against those of the local governments.

In compliance with a sentiment thus generally expressed to quiet fears thus extensively entertained, amendments were proposed by the required majority in congress, and adopted by the States. These amendments contain no expression indicating an intention to apply them to the state governments. This court cannot so apply them.

We are of opinion that the provision in the 5th amendment to the constitution, declaring that private property shall not be taken for public use without just compensation, is intended solely as a limitation on the exercise of power by the government of the United States, and is not applicable to the legislation of the States. We are therefore of opinion, that there is no repugnancy between the several acts of the general assembly of Maryland, given in evidence by the defendants at the trial of this case, in the court of the State, and the constitution of the United States. This court, therefore, has no jurisdiction of the cause; and it is dismissed.

CIVIL RIGHTS ACT OF 1866[2]

That all persons born in the United States and not subject to any foreign power, excluding Indians not taxed, are hereby declared to be citizens of the

United States; and such citizens, of every race and color, without regard to any previous condition of slavery or involuntary servitude, except as a punishment for crime whereof the party shall have been duly convicted, shall have the same right, in every State and Territory in the United States, to make and enforce contracts, to sue, be parties, and give evidence, to inherit, purchase, lease, sell, hold, and convey real and personal property, and to full and equal benefit of all laws and proceedings for the security of person and property, as is enjoyed by white citizens, and shall be subject to like punishment, pains, and penalties, and to none other, any law, statute, ordinance, regulation, or custom, to the contrary notwithstanding.

Sec. 2. *And be it further enacted*, That any person who, under color of any law, statute, ordinance, regulation, or custom, shall subject, or cause to be subjected, any inhabitant of any State or Territory to the deprivation of any right secured or protected by this act, or to different punishment, pains, or penalties on account of such person having at any time been held in a condition of slavery or involuntary servitude, except as a punishment for crime whereof the party shall have been duly convicted, or by reason of his color or race, than is prescribed for the punishment of white persons, shall be deemed guilty of a misdemeanor, and, on conviction, shall be punished by fine not exceeding one thousand dollars, or imprisonment not exceeding one year, or both, in the discretion of the court.

Sec. 3. *And be it further enacted*, That the district courts of the United States, within their respective districts, shall have, exclusively of the courts of the several States, cognizance of all crimes and offences committed against the provisions of this act, and also, concurrently with the circuit courts of the United States, of all causes, civil and criminal, affecting persons who are denied or cannot enforce in the courts or judicial tribunals of the State or locality where they may be any of the rights secured to them by the first section of this act; and if any suit or prosecution, civil or criminal, has been or shall be commenced in any State court, against any such person, for any cause whatsoever, or against any officer, civil or military, or other person, for any arrest or imprisonment, trespasses, or wrongs done or committed by virtue or under color of authority derived from this act or the act establishing a Bureau for the relief of Freedmen and Refugees, and all acts amendatory thereof, or for refusing to do any act upon the ground that it would be inconsistent with this act, such defendant shall have the right to remove such cause for trial to the proper district or circuit court in the manner prescribed by the "Act relating to habeas corpus and regulating judicial proceedings in certain cases," approved March three, eighteen hundred and sixty-three, and all acts amendatory thereof. The jurisdiction in civil and criminal matters hereby conferred on the district and circuit courts of the United States shall be exercised and enforced in conformity with the laws of the United States, so far as such laws are suitable to carry the same into effect; but in all cases where such laws are not adapted to the object, or are deficient in the provisions necessary to furnish suitable remedies and punish offences against law, the common law, as modified and changed by the constitution and statutes of the State wherein the court having jurisdiction of the cause, civil or criminal, is held, so far as the same is not inconsistent with the Constitution and laws of the United States, shall be extended to and govern said courts in the trial and disposition of such cause, and, if of a criminal nature, in the infliction of punishment on the party found guilty.

Sec. 5. *And be it further enacted,* That it shall be the duty of all marshals and deputy marshals to obey and execute all warrants and precepts issued under the provisions of this act, when to them directed; and should any marshal or deputy marshal refuse to receive such warrant or other process when tendered, or to use all proper means diligently to execute the same, he shall, on conviction thereof, be fined in the sum of one thousand dollars, to the use of the person upon whom the accused is alleged to have committed the offense. And the better to enable the said commissioners to execute their duties faithfully and efficiently, in conformity with the Constitution of the United States and the requirements of this act, they are hereby authorized and empowered, within their counties respectively, to appoint, in writing, under their hands, any one or more suitable persons, from time to time, to execute all such warrants and other process as may be issued by them in the lawful performance of their respective duties; and the persons so appointed to execute any warrant or process as aforesaid shall have authority to summon and call to their aid the bystanders or posse comitatus of the proper county, or such portion of the land or naval forces of the United States, or of the militia, as may be necessary to the performance of the duty with which they are charged, and to insure a faithful observance of the clause of the Constitution which prohibits slavery, in conformity with the provisions of this act; and said warrants shall run and be executed by said officers anywhere in the State or Territory within which they are issued.

Sec. 8. *And be it further enacted,* That whenever the President of the United States shall have reason to believe that offences have been or are likely to be committed against the provisions of this act within any judicial district, it shall be lawful for him, in his discretion, to direct the judge, marshal, and district attorney of such district to attend at such place within the district, and for such time as he may designate, for the purpose of the more speedy arrest and trial of persons charged with a violation of this act; and it shall be the duty of every judge or other officer, when any such requisition shall be received by him, to attend at the place and for the time therein designated.

Sec. 9. *And be it further enacted,* That it shall be lawful for the President of the United States, or such person as he may empower for that purpose, to employ such part of the land or naval forces of the United States, or of the militia, as shall be necessary to prevent the violation and enforce the due execution of this act.

Sec. 10. *And be it further enacted*, That upon all questions of law arising in any cause under the provisions of this act a final appeal may be taken to the Supreme Court of the United States.

ANDREW JOHNSON, VETO OF
THE CIVIL RIGHTS ACT[3]

. . . By the first section of the bill, all persons born in the United States, and not subject to any foreign power, excluding Indians not taxed, are declared to be citizens of the United States. . . . It does not purport to declare or confer any other right of citizenship than Federal citizenship; it does not propose to give these classes of persons any status as citizens of States, except that which may result from their status as citizens of the United States. The power to confer the right of State citizenship is just as exclusively with the several States, as the power to confer the right of Federal citizenship is with Congress. The right of Federal citizenship, thus to be conferred in the several excepted ratios before mentioned, is now, for the first time, proposed to be given by law. If, as is claimed by many, all persons who are native born, already are, by virtue of the Constitution, citizens of the United States, the passage of the pending bill cannot be necessary to make them such. If, on the other hand, such persons are not citizens, as may be assumed from the proposed legislation to make them such, the grave question presents itself whether, where eleven of the thirty-six States are unrepresented in Congress at the time, it is sound policy to make our entire colored population, and all other excepted classes, citizens of the United States. Four millions of them have just emerged from slavery into freedom. Can it be reasonably supposed that they possess the requisite qualifications to entitle them to all the privileges and immunities of citizenship of the United States? Have the people of the several States expressed such a conviction? It may also be asked, whether it is necessary that they should be declared citizens in order that they may be secured in the enjoyment of the civil rights proposed to be conferred by the bill. Those rights are, by Federals as well as by State laws, secured to all domiciled aliens and foreigners, even before the completion of the process of naturalization; and it may safely be assumed that the same enactments are sufficient to give like protection and benefits to those for whom this bill provides special legislation. Besides the policy of the Government, from its origin to the present time, seems to have been that persons who are strangers to and unfamiliar with our institutions and laws, should pass through a certain probation; at the end of which, before attaining the coveted prize, they must give evidence of their fitness to receive and to exercise the rights of citizens as contemplated by the Constitution of the United States. The bill in effect proposes a discrimination against large numbers of intelligent, worthy and patriotic foreigners, and in favor of the negro, to whom, after long years of bondage, the avenues to freedom and intelligence have just now been suddenly opened. He must of necessity, from his previous unfortunate condition of servitude, be less informed as to the nature and character of our institutions than he who, coming from abroad, has to some extent, at least, familiarized himself with the principles of a Government to which he voluntarily entrusts life, liberty, and the pursuit of happiness. Yet it is now proposed by a single legislative enactment to confer the rights of citizens upon all persons of African descent, born within the excluded limits of the United States, while persons of foreign birth, who make our land their home, must undergo a probation of five years, and can only then become citizens upon proof that they are of good moral character, attached to the principles of the Constitution of the United States, and well disposed to the good order and happiness of the same. The first section of the bill also contains an enumeration of the rights to be enjoyed by those classes so made citizens in every State and Territory of the United States. These rights are, to make and enforce contracts, to sue, be parties and give evidence, to inherit, purchase, lease, sell, hold, or convey real and personal property, and to have full and equal benefit of all laws and proceedings for the security of persons and property as is enjoyed by white citizens. So, too, they are made subject to the same punishments, pains, and penalties common with white citizens, and to none others. Thus a perfect equality of the white and colored races is attempted to be fixed by a Federal law in every State of the Union, over the vast field of State jurisdiction covered by these enumerated rights. In no one of them can any State exercise any power of discrimination between different races. In the exercise of State policy over matters exclusively affecting the people of each State, it has frequently been thought expedient to discriminate between the two races. By the statutes of some of the States, North as well as South, it is enacted, for instance, that no white person shall intermarry with a negro or mulatto. Chancellor Kent says, speaking of the blacks, that marriages between them and the whites are forbidden in some in some of the States where slavery does not exist, and they are prohibited in all the slaveholding States by law; and when not absolutely contrary to law, they are revolting, and regarded as an offence against public decorum. I do not say that this bill repeals State laws, on the subject of marriage between the two races, for as the whites are forbidden to intermarry with the blacks, the blacks can only make such contracts as the whites themselves are allowed to make, and therefore cannot, under this bill, enter into the marriage contract with the whites. I take this discrimination, however, as an instance of the State policy as to discrimination, and to inquire whether, if Congress can abrogate all State laws of discrimination between the two races, in the matter of real estate, of suits, and of contracts generally, Congress may not also repeal the State laws as to the contract of marriage between the races? Hitherto, every subject embraced in the enumeration of rights contained in the bill has been considered as exclusively belonging to the States; they all relate to the internal policy and economy of the respective States. They are matters which, in each State, concern the domestic condition of its people, varying in each according to its peculiar circumstances and the safety and well-being of its own citizens. I do not mean to say that upon all these subjects there are not Federal restraints; as, for instance, in the State power of legislation over contracts, there is a Federal limitation that no State shall pass a law impairing the obligations of contracts; and, as to crimes, that no State shall pass an *ex-post-facto* law; and, as to money, that no State shall make any thing but gold and silver as legal tender. But where can we find a Federal prohibition against the power of any State to discriminate, as do most of them, between aliens and citizens, between artificial persons called corporations, and naturalized persons, in the right to hold real estate? If it be granted that Congress can repeal all State laws discriminating between the two races on the subject of suffrage and office? If Congress shall declare by law who shall hold lands, who shall testify, who shall have capacity to make a contract in a State, that Congress can also declare by law, without regard to race or color, shall have the right to act as a juror or as a judge, to hold any office, and finally to vote, in every State and Territory of the United States. As respects the Territory of the United States, they come within the power of Congress, for as to them the law-making power is the Federal power; but as to the States, no similar provision exists, vesting in Congress the power to make such rules and regulations for them.

The object of the second section of the bill is to afford discriminating protection to colored persons in the full enjoyment of all the rights secured to them by the preceding section. It declares that "any person who, under color of any law, statute, ordinance, regulation, or custom, shall subject or cause to be subjected any inhabitant of any State or Territory to the deprivation of any rights secured or protected by this act, or to different punishment, pains, or penalties on account of such person having at any time been held in a condition of slavery or involuntary servitude, except as a punishment of crime, whereof the party shall have been duly convicted, or by reason of his color or race, than is prescribed for the punishment of white persons, shall be deemed guilty of a misdemeanor, and on conviction shall be punished by fine not exceeding one thousand dollars, or imprisonment not exceeding one year, or both, in the discretion of the court." This section seems to be designed to apply to some existing or future law of a State or Territory, which may conflict with the provisions of the bill now under consideration. It provides for counteracting such forbidden legislation, by imposing fine and imprisonment upon the legislators who may pass such conflicting laws, or upon the officers or agents who shall put or attempt to put them into execution. It means an official offence, not a common crime, committed against law upon the person or property of the black race. Such an act may deprive the black man of his property, but not of his right to hold property. It means a deprivation of the right itself, either by the State Judiciary or the State Legislature. It is, therefore, assumed that, under this section, members of a State Legislature who should vote for laws conflicting with the provisions of the bill, that judges of the State courts who should render judgments in antagonism with its terms, and that marshals and sheriffs who should as ministerial officers execute processes sanctioned by State laws and issued by State judges in execution of their judgments, could be brought before other tribunals and there subjected to fine and imprisonment, for the performance of the duties which such State laws might impose. The legislation thus proposed invades the judicial power of the State. It says to every State court or judge: If you decide that this act is unconstitutional; if you hold that over such a subject-matter the said law is paramount, under color of a State law refuse the exercise of the right to the negro; your error of judgment, however conscientious, shall subject you to fine and imprisonment. I do not apprehend that the conflicting legislation which the bill seems to contemplate is so likely to occur, as to render it necessary at this time to adopt a measure of such constitutionality. In the next place, this provision of the bill seems to be unnecessary, as adequate judicial remedies could be adopted to secure the desired end without invading the immunities of legislators, always important to be preserved in the interest of public liberty, notwithstanding the independence of the judiciary, always essential to the preservation of individual rights, and without impairing the efficiency of ministerial officers, always necessary for the maintenance of public peace and order. The remedy proposed by this section seems to be in this respect not only anomalous but unconstitutional, for the Constitution guarantees nothing with certainty if it does not insure to the several States the right of making index ruling laws in regard to all matters arising within their jurisdiction, subject only to the restriction, in cases of conflict with the Constitution and constitutional laws of the United States—the latter to be held as the supreme law of the land.

The third section gives the district courts of the United States exclusive cognizance of all crimes and offences committed against the provisions of this act, and concurrent jurisdiction with the circuit courts of the United States, of all civil and criminal cases affecting persons that are denied, or cannot enforce in the courts or judicial tribunals of the State or locality where they may be, any of the rights secured to them by the first section. The construction which I have given to the second section is strengthened by this third section, for it makes clear what kind of denial, or deprivation of rights secured by the first section, was in contemplation. It is a denial or deprivation of such rights in the courts or tribunals of the State. It stands, therefore, clear of doubt that the offence and the penalties provided in the second section are intended for the State judge who, in the clear exercise of his functions as a judge, not acting ministerially but judicially, shall decide contrary to this Federal law. In other words, when a State judge, acting upon a question involving a conflict between a State law and a Federal law, and bound, according to his own judgment and responsibility to give an impartial decision between the two, comes to the conclusion that the State law is valid and the Federal law is invalid, he must not follow the dictates of his own judgment, at the peril of fine and imprisonment. The legislative department of the Government of the United States thus takes from the judicial department of the States the sacred and exclusive duty of judicial decision, and converts the State judge into a mere ministerial officer, bound to decide according to the will of Congress. It is clear that in States which deny to persons, whose rights are secured by the first section of the bill, any one of those rights, all criminal and civil cases affecting them will, by the provisions of the third section, come under the executive cognizance of the Federal tribunals. It follows that if in any State, which denies to a colored person any one of all these rights, that person should commit a crime against the laws of a State—murder, arson, rape, or any other crime—all protection and punishment, through the courts of the State, are taken away, and he can only be tried and punished in the Federal courts. How is the criminal to be tried, if the offence is provided for and punished by Federal law? That law, and not the State law, is to govern. It was only when the offence does not happen to be within the province of Federal law that the Federal courts are to try and punish him under any other law. The resort is to be had to the common law, as modified and changed by State legislation, so far as the same is not inconsistent with the Constitution and laws of the United States. So that over this vast domain of criminal jurisprudence, provided by each State for the protection of its citizens and for the punishment of all persons who violate its criminal laws, Federal law, wherever it can be made to apply, displaces State law. The question naturally arises, from what source Congress derives the power to transfer to Federal tribunals certain classes of cases embraced in this section. The Constitution expressly declares that the judicial power of the United States "shall extend to all cases in law and equity, arising under this Constitution, the laws of the

United States, and treaties made, or which shall be made, under their authority; to all cases affecting ambassadors or other public ministers and consuls; to all cases of admiralty and maritime jurisdiction; to controversies to which the United States shall be a party; to controversies between two or more States; between a State and citizens of another State; between citizens of different States; between citizens of the same State claiming land under grants of different States; and between a State, or the citizens thereof, and foreign States, citizens, or subjects."

Here the judicial power of the United States is expressly set forth and defined; and the act of September 24, 1789, establishing the judicial courts of the United States, in conferring upon the Federal courts jurisdiction over cases originating in State tribunals, is careful to confine them to the classes enumerated in the above recited clause of the Constitution. This section of the bill undoubtedly comprehends cases and authorizes the exercise of powers that are not, by the Constitution, within the jurisdiction of the courts of the United States. To transfer them to these courts would be an exercise of authority well calculated to excite distrust and alarm on the part of all the States, for the bill applies alike to all of them, as well as to those who have not been engaged in rebellion. It may be assumed that this authority is incident to the power granted to Congress by the Constitution as recently amended, to enforce, by appropriate legislation, the article declaring that neither slavery nor involuntary servitude, except as a punishment for crime, whereof the party shall have been duly convicted, shall exist within the United States, or any place subject to their jurisdiction. It cannot, however, be justly claimed that, with a view to the enforcement of this article of the Constitution, there is at present any necessity for the exercise of all the powers which this bill confers. Slavery has been abolished, and at present nowhere exists within the jurisdiction of the United States. Nor has there been, nor is it likely there will be any attempts to revive it by the people of the States. If, however, any such attempt shall be made, it will then become the duty of the General Government to exercise any and all incidental powers necessary and proper to maintain inviolate this great law of freedom. The fourth section of the bill provides that officers and agents of the Freedmen's Bureau shall be empowered to make arrests, and also that other officers shall be specially commissioned for that purpose by the President of the United States. It also authorizes the Circuit Courts of the United States and the Superior Courts of the Territories to appoint, without limitation, commissioners, who are to be charged with the performance of quasi judicial duties. The fifth section empowers the commissioners so to be selected by the court, to appoint, in writing, one or more suitable persons from time to time to execute warrants and processes desirable by the bill. These numerous official agents are made to constitute a sort of police in addition to the military, and are authorized to summon a *posse commitatus*, and even to call to their aid such portion of the land and naval forces of the United States, or of the militia, "as may be necessary to the performance of the duty with which they are charged." This extraordinary power is to be conferred upon agents irresponsible to the Government and to the people, to whose number the discretion of the commissioners is the only limit, and in whose hands such authority might be made a terrible engine of wrong, oppression, and fraud. The general statutes regulating the land and naval forces of the United States, the militia, and the execution of the laws are believed to be adequate for any emergency which can occur in time of peace. If it should prove otherwise, Congress can at any time amend those laws in such a manner as, while subserving the public welfare, not to jeopardize the rights, interests, and liberties of the people.

. . . I do not propose to consider the policy of this bill. To me the details of the bill are fraught with evil. The white race and black race of the South have hitherto lived together under the relation of master and slave—capital owning labor. Now that relation is changed; and as to ownership, capital and labor are divorced. They stand now, each master of itself. In this new relation, one being necessary to the other, there will be a new adjustment, which both are deeply interested in making harmonious. Each has equal power in settling the terms; and, if left to the laws that regulate capital and labor, it is confidently believed that they will satisfactorily work out the problem. Capital, it is true, has more intelligence; but labor is never ignorant as not to understand its own interests, not to know its own value, and not to see that capital must pay that value. This bill frustrates this adjustment. It intervenes between capital and labor, and attempts to settle questions of political economy through the agency of numerous officials, whose interest it will be to foment discord between the two races; for as the breach widens, their employment will continue; and when it is closed, their occupation will terminate. In all our history, in all our experience as a people living under Federal and State law, no such system as that contemplated by the details of this bill has ever before been proposed or adopted. They establish for the security of the colored race safeguards which go indefinitely beyond any that the General Government has ever provided for the white race. In fact, the distinction of race and color is by the bill made to operate in favor of the colored against the white race. They interfere with the municipal legislation of the States; with relations existing exclusively between a State and its citizens, or between inhabitants of the same State; an absorption and assumption of power by the General Government which, if acquiesced in, must sap and destroy our federative system of limited power, and break down the barriers which preserve the rights of the States. It is another step, or rather stride, towards centralization and the concentration of all legislative powers in the National Government. The tendency of the bill must be to resuscitate the spirit of rebellion, and to arrest the progress of those influences which are more closely drawing around the States the bonds of union and peace.

14TH AMENDMENT (RATIFIED, 1868)

Section 1. All persons born or naturalized in the United States, and subject to the jurisdiction thereof, are citizens of the United States and of the State wherein they reside. No State shall make or enforce any law which shall abridge the privileges or immunities of citizens of the United States; nor shall any State deprive any person of life, liberty, or property, without due process of law; nor deny to any person within its jurisdiction the equal protection of the laws.

Section 2. Representatives shall be apportioned among the several States according to their respective numbers, counting the whole number of persons in each State, excluding Indians not taxed. But when the right to vote at any election for the choice of electors for President and Vice President of the United States, Representatives in Congress, the Executive and Judicial officers of a State, or the members of the Legislature thereof, is denied to any of the male inhabitants of such State, being twenty-one years of age, and citizens of the United States, or in any way abridged, except for participation in rebellion, or other crime, the basis of representation therein shall be reduced in the proportion which the number of such male citizens shall bear to the whole number of male citizens twenty-one years of age in such State.

Section 3. No person shall be a Senator or Representative in Congress, or elector of President and Vice President, or hold any office, civil or military, under the United States, or under any State, who, having previously taken an oath, as a member of Congress, or as an officer of the United States, or as a member of any State legislature, or as an executive or judicial officer of any State, to support the Constitution of the United States, shall have engaged in insurrection or rebellion against the same, or given aid or comfort to the enemies thereof. But Congress may, by a vote of two-thirds of each House, remove such disability.

Section 4. The validity of the public debt of the United States, authorized by law, including debts incurred for payment of pensions and bounties for services in suppressing insurrection or rebellion, shall not be questioned. But neither the United States nor any State shall assume or pay any debt or obligation incurred in aid of insurrection or rebellion against the United States, or any claim for the loss or emancipation of any slave; but all such debts, obligations and claims shall be held illegal and void.

Section 5. The Congress shall have power to enforce, by appropriate legislation, the provisions of this article.

PLATFORM OF THE STATES RIGHTS
DEMOCRATIC PARTY (DIXIECRATS) 1948

We believe that the Constitution of the United States is the greatest charter of human liberty ever conceived by the mind of man.

We oppose all efforts to invade or destroy the rights guaranteed by it to every citizen of this republic.

We stand for social and economic justice, which, we believe can be guaranteed to all citizens only by a strict adherence to our Constitution and the avoidance of any invasion or destruction of the constitutional rights of the states and individuals. We oppose the totalitarian, centralized bureaucratic government and the police nation called for by the platforms adopted by the Democratic and Republican Conventions.

We stand for the segregation of the races and the racial integrity of each race; the constitutional right to choose one's associates; to accept private employment without governmental interference, and to earn one's living in any lawful way. We oppose the elimination of segregation, the repeal of miscegenation statutes, the control of private employment by Federal bureaucrats called for by the misnamed civil rights program. We favor home-rule, local self-government and a minimum interference with individual rights.

We oppose and condemn the action of the Democratic Convention in sponsoring a civil rights program calling for the elimination of segregation, social equality by Federal fiat, regulations of private employment practices, voting, and local law enforcement.

We affirm that the effective enforcement of such a program would be utterly destructive of the social, economic and political life of the Southern people, and of other localities in which there may be differences in race, creed or national origin in appreciable numbers.

We stand for the check and balances provided by the three departments of our government. We oppose the usurpation of legislative functions by the executive and judicial departments. We unreservedly condemn the effort to establish in the United States a police nation that would destroy the last vestige of liberty enjoyed by a citizen.

We demand that there be returned to the people to whom of right they belong, those powers needed for the preservation of human rights and the discharge of our responsibility as democrats for human welfare. We oppose a denial of those by political parties, a barter or sale of those rights by a political convention, as well as any invasion or violation of those rights by the Federal Government. We call upon all Democrats and upon all other loyal Americans who are opposed to totalitarianism at home and abroad to unite with us in ignominiously defeating Harry S. Truman, Thomas E. Dewey and every other candidate for public office who would establish a Police Nation in the United States of America.

SOUTHERN MANIFESTO[4]

Declaration of Constitutional Principles

The unwarranted decision of the Supreme Court in the public school cases is now bearing the fruit always produced when men substitute naked power for established law.

The Founding Fathers gave us a Constitution of checks and balances because they realized the inescapable lesson of history that no man or group of men can be safely entrusted with unlimited power. They framed this Constitution with its provisions for change by amendment in order to secure the fundamentals of government against the dangers of temporary popular passion or the personal predilections of public officeholders.

We regard the decisions of the Supreme Court in the school cases as a clear abuse of judicial power. It climaxes a trend in the Federal Judiciary undertaking to legislate, in derogation of the authority of Congress, and to encroach upon the reserved rights of the States and the people.

The original Constitution does not mention education. Neither does the 14th Amendment nor any other amendment. The debates preceding the submission of the 14th Amendment clearly show that there was no intent that it should affect the system of education maintained by the States.

The very Congress which proposed the amendment subsequently provided for segregated schools in the District of Columbia.

When the amendment was adopted in 1868, there were 37 States of the Union . . . .

Every one of the 26 States that had any substantial racial differences among its people, either approved the operation of segregated schools already in existence or subsequently established such schools by action of the same law-making body which considered the 14th Amendment.

As admitted by the Supreme Court in the public school case (*Brown v. Board of Education*), the doctrine of separate but equal schools "apparently originated in *Roberts v. City of Boston* (1849), upholding school segregation against attack as being violative of a State constitutional guarantee of equality." This constitutional doctrine began in the North, not in the South, and it was followed not only in Massachusetts, but in Connecticut, New York, Illinois, Indiana, Michigan, Minnesota, New Jersey, Ohio, Pennsylvania and other northern states until they, exercising their rights as states through the constitutional processes of local self-government, changed their school systems.

In the case of *Plessy v. Ferguson* in 1896 the Supreme Court expressly declared that under the 14th Amendment no person was denied any of his rights if the States provided separate but equal facilities. This decision has been followed in many other cases. It is notable that the Supreme Court, speaking through Chief Justice Taft, a former President of the United States, unanimously declared in 1927 in *Lum v. Rice* that the "separate but equal" principle is "within the discretion of the State in regulating its public schools and does not conflict with the 14th Amendment."

This interpretation, restated time and again, became a part of the life of the people of many of the States and confirmed their habits, traditions, and way of life. It is founded on elemental humanity and commonsense, for parents should not be deprived by Government of the right to direct the lives and education of their own children.

Though there has been no constitutional amendment or act of Congress changing this established legal principle almost a century old, the Supreme Court of the United States, with no legal basis for such action, undertook to exercise their naked judicial power and substituted their personal political and social ideas for the established law of the land.

This unwarranted exercise of power by the Court, contrary to the Constitution, is creating chaos and confusion in the States principally affected. It is destroying the amicable relations between the white and Negro races that have been created through 90 years of patient effort by the good people of both races. It has planted hatred and suspicion where there has been heretofore friendship and understanding.

Without regard to the consent of the governed, outside mediators are threatening immediate and revolutionary changes in our public schools systems. If done, this is certain to destroy the system of public education in some of the States.

With the gravest concern for the explosive and dangerous condition created by this decision and inflamed by outside meddlers:

We reaffirm our reliance on the Constitution as the fundamental law of the land.

We decry the Supreme Court's encroachment on the rights reserved to the States and to the people, contrary to established law, and to the Constitution.

We commend the motives of those States which have declared the intention to resist forced integration by any lawful means.

We appeal to the States and people who are not directly affected by these decisions to consider the constitutional principles involved against the time when they too, on issues vital to them may be the victims of judicial encroachment.

Even though we constitute a minority in the present Congress, we have full faith that a majority of the American people believe in the dual system of government which has enabled us to achieve our greatness and will in time demand that the reserved rights of the States and of the people be made secure against judicial usurpation.

We pledge ourselves to use all lawful means to bring about a reversal of this decision which is contrary to the Constitution and to prevent the use of force in its implementation.

In this trying period, as we all seek to right this wrong, we appeal to our people not to be provoked by the agitators and troublemakers invading our States and to scrupulously refrain from disorder and lawless acts.

BROWN v. BOARD OF EDUCATION OF TOPEKA 2[5]

[CHIEF JUSTICE WARREN] These cases were decided on May 17, 1954. The opinions of that date, declaring the fundamental principle that racial discrimination in public education is unconstitutional, are incorporated herein by reference. All provisions of federal, state, or local law requiring or permitting such discrimination must yield to this principle. There remains for consideration the manner in which relief is to be accorded.

Because these cases arose under different local conditions and their disposition will involve a variety of local problems, we requested further argument on the question of relief. In view of the nationwide importance of the decision, we invited the Attorney General of the United States and the Attorneys General of all states requiring or permitting racial discrimination in public education to present their views on that question. The parties, the United States, and the States of Florida, North Carolina, Arkansas, Oklahoma, Maryland, and Texas filed briefs and participated in the oral argument.

These presentations were informative and helpful to the Court in its consideration of the complexities arising from the transition to a system of public education freed of racial discrimination. The presentations also demonstrated that substantial steps to eliminate racial discrimination in public schools have already been taken, not only in some of the communities in which these cases arose, but in some of the states appearing as *amici curiae*, and in other states as well. Substantial progress has been made in the District of Columbia and in the communities in Kansas and Delaware involved in this litigation. The defendants in the cases coming to us from South Carolina and Virginia are awaiting the decision of this Court concerning relief.

Full implementation of these constitutional principles may require solution of varied local school problems. School authorities have the primary responsibility for elucidating, assessing, and solving these problems; courts will have to consider whether the action of school authorities constitutes good faith implementation of the governing constitutional principles. Because of their proximity to local conditions and the possible need for further hearings, the courts which originally heard these cases can best perform this judicial appraisal. Accordingly, we believe it appropriate to remand the cases to those courts.

In fashioning and effectuating the decrees, the courts will be guided by equitable principles. Traditionally, equity has been characterized by a practical flexibility in shaping its remedies and by a facility for adjusting and reconciling public and private needs. These cases call for the exercise of these traditional attributes of equity power. At stake is the personal interest of the plaintiffs in admission to public schools as soon as practicable on a nondiscriminatory basis. To effectuate this interest may call for elimination of a variety of obstacles in making the transition to school systems operated in accordance with the constitutional principles set forth in our May 17, 1954, decision. Courts of equity may properly take into account the public interest in the elimination of such obstacles in a systematic and effective manner. But it should go without saying that the vitality of these constitutional principles cannot be allowed to yield simply because of disagreement with them.

While giving weight to these public and private considerations, the courts will require that the defendants make a prompt and reasonable start toward full compliance with our May 17, 1954, ruling. Once such a start has been made, the courts may find that additional time is necessary to carry out the ruling in an effective manner. The burden rests upon the defendants to establish that such time is necessary in the public interest and is consistent with good faith compliance at the earliest practicable date. To that end, the courts may consider problems related to administration, arising from the physical condition of the school plant, the school transportation system, personnel, revision of school districts and attendance areas into compact units to achieve a system of determining admission to the public schools on a nonracial basis, and revision of local laws and regulations which may be necessary in solving the foregoing problems. They will also consider the adequacy of any plans the defendants may propose to meet these problems and to effectuate a transition to a racially nondiscriminatory school system. During this period of transition, the courts will retain jurisdiction of these cases.

EISENHOWER, "REMARKS ON LITTLE ROCK"[6]

Good Evening, My Fellow Citizens: For a few minutes this evening I want to speak to you about the serious situation that has arisen in Little Rock. To make this talk I have come to the President's office in the White House.

I could have spoken from Rhode Island, where I have been staying recently, but I felt that, in speaking from the house of Lincoln, of Jackson and of Wilson, my words would better convey both the sadness I feel in the action I was compelled today to take and the firmness with which I intend to pursue this course until the orders of the Federal Court at Little Rock can be executed without unlawful interference.

In that city, under the leadership of demagogic extremists, disorderly mobs have deliberately prevented the carrying out of proper orders from a Federal Court. Local authorities have not eliminated that violent opposition and, under the law, I yesterday issued a Proclamation calling upon the mob to disperse.

This morning the mob again gathered in front of the Central High School of Little Rock, obviously for the purpose of again preventing the carrying out of the Court's order relating to the admission of Negro children to that school.

Whenever normal agencies prove inadequate to the task and it becomes necessary for the Executive Branch of the Federal Government to use its powers and authority to uphold Federal Courts, the President's responsibility is inescapable. In accordance with that responsibility, I have today issued an Executive Order directing the use of troops under Federal authority to aid in the execution of Federal law at Little Rock, Arkansas. This became necessary when my Proclamation of yesterday was not observed, and the obstruction of justice still continues.

It is important that the reasons for my action be understood by all our citizens. As you know, the Supreme Court of the United States has decided that separate public educational facilities for the races are inherently unequal and therefore compulsory school segregation laws are unconstitutional.

Our personal opinions about the decision have no bearing on the matter of enforcement; the responsibility and authority of the Supreme Court to interpret the Constitution are very clear. Local Federal Courts were instructed by the Supreme Court to issue such orders and decrees as might be necessary to achieve admission to public schools without regard to race—and with all deliberate speed.

During the past several years, many communities in our Southern States have instituted public school plans for gradual progress in the enrollment and attendance of school children of all races in order to bring themselves into compliance with the law of the land. They thus demonstrated to the world that we are a nation in which laws, not men, are supreme.

I regret to say that this truth—the cornerstone of our liberties—was not observed in this instance.

It was my hope that this localized situation would be brought under control by city and State authorities. If the use of local police powers had been sufficient, our traditional method of leaving the problems in those hands would have been pursued. But when large gatherings of obstructionists made it impossible for the decrees of the Court to be carried out, both the law and the national interest demanded that the President take action.

. . . Proper and sensible observance of the law then demanded the respectful obedience which the nation has a right to expect from all its people. This, unfortunately, has not been the case at Little Rock. Certain misguided persons, many of them imported into Little Rock by agitators, have insisted upon defying the law and have sought to bring it into disrepute. The orders of the court have thus been frustrated.

The very basis of our individual rights and freedoms rests upon the certainty that the President and the Executive Branch of Government will support and insure the carrying out of the decisions of the Federal Courts, even, when necessary with all the means at the President's command.

Unless the President did so, anarchy would result.

There would be no security for any except that which each one of us could provide for himself.

The interest of the nation in the proper fulfillment of the law's requirements cannot yield to opposition and demonstrations by some few persons.

Mob rule cannot be allowed to override the decisions of our courts.

Now, let me make it very clear that Federal troops are not being used to relieve local and state authorities of their primary duty to preserve the peace and order of the community. Nor are the troops there for the purpose of taking over the responsibility of the School Board and the other responsible local officials in running Central High School. The running of our school system and the maintenance of peace and order in each of our States are strictly local affairs and the Federal Government does not interfere except in a very few special cases and when requested by one of the several States. In the present case the troops are there, pursuant to law, solely for the purpose of preventing interference with the orders of the Court.

The proper use of the powers of the Executive Branch to enforce the orders of a Federal Court is limited to extraordinary and compelling circumstances. Manifestly, such an extreme situation has been created in Little Rock. This challenge must be met and with such measures as will preserve to the people as a whole their lawfully-protected rights in a climate permitting their free and fair exercise. The overwhelming majority of our people in every section of the country are united in their respect for observance of the law—even in those cases where they may disagree with that law.

They deplore the call of extremists to violence.

The decision of the Supreme Court concerning school integration, of course, affects the South more seriously than it does other sections of the country. In that region I have many warm friends, some of them in the city of Little Rock. I have deemed it a great personal privilege to spend in our

Southland tours of duty while in the military service and enjoyable recreational periods since that time.

So from intimate personal knowledge, I know that the overwhelming majority of the people in the South—including those of Arkansas and of Little Rock—are of good will, united in their efforts to preserve and respect the law even when they disagree with it.

They do not sympathize with mob rule. They, like the rest of our nation, have proved in two great wars their readiness to sacrifice for America.

A foundation of our American way of life is our national respect for law.

In the South, as elsewhere, citizens are keenly aware of the tremendous disservice that has been done to the people of Arkansas in the eyes of the nation, and that has been done to the nation in the eyes of the world.

At a time when we face grave situations abroad because of the hatred that Communism bears toward a system of government based on human rights, it would be difficult to exaggerate the harm that is being done to the prestige and influence, and indeed to the safety, of our nation and the world.

Our enemies are gloating over this incident and using it everywhere to misrepresent our whole nation. We are portrayed as a violator of those standards of conduct which the peoples of the world united to proclaim in the Charter of the United Nations. There they affirmed "faith in fundamental human rights" and "in the dignity and worth of the human person" and they did so "without distinction as to race, sex, language or religion."

And so, with deep confidence, I call upon the citizens of the State of Arkansas to assist in bringing to an immediate end all interference with the law and its processes. If resistance to the Federal Court orders ceases at once, the further presence of Federal troops will be unnecessary and the City of Little Rock will return to its normal habits of peace and order and a blot upon the fair name and high honor of our nation in the world will be removed.

Thus will be restored the image of America and of all its parts as one nation, indivisible, with liberty and justice for all.

COOPER v. AARON[7]

[Chief Justice] As this case reaches us, it raises questions of the highest importance to the maintenance of our federal system of government. It necessarily involves a claim by the Governor and Legislature of a State that there is no duty on state officials to obey federal court orders resting on this Court's considered interpretation of the United States Constitution. Specifically, it involves actions by the Governor and Legislature of Arkansas upon the premise that they are not bound by our holding in *Brown v. Board of Education*, [t]hat holding was that the Fourteenth Amendment forbids States to use their governmental powers to bar children on racial grounds from attending schools where there is state participation through any arrangement, manage-ment, funds or property. We are urged to uphold a suspension of the Little Rock School Board's plan to do away with segregated public schools in Little Rock until state laws and efforts to upset and nullify our holding in *Brown v. Board of Education* have been further challenged and tested in the courts. We reject these contentions.

. . . the District Courts were directed to require "a prompt and reasonable start toward full compliance," and to take such action as was necessary to bring about the end of racial segregation in the public schools "with all delib-erate speed" . . . State authorities were thus duty bound to devote every effort toward initiating desegregation and bringing about the elimination of racial discrimination in the public school system.

. . . On September 2, 1957, the day before these Negro students were to enter Central High, the school authorities were met with drastic opposing action on the part of the Governor of Arkansas, who dispatched units of the Arkansas National Guard to the Central High School grounds and placed the school "off limits" to colored students. As found by the District Court in subsequent proceedings, the Governor's action had not been requested by the school authorities, and was entirely unheralded.

On the morning of the next day, September 4, 1957, the Negro children attempted to enter the high school, but, as the District Court later found, units of the Arkansas National Guard, "acting pursuant to the Governor's order, stood shoulder to shoulder at the school grounds and thereby forcibly prevented the 9 Negro students . . . from entering," as they continued to do every school day during the following three weeks.

. . . the actions of legislators and executive officials of the State of Arkan-sas, taken in their official capacities, which reflect their own determination to resist this Court's decision in the *Brown* case and which have brought about violent resistance to that decision in Arkansas. In its petition for certiorari filed in this Court, the School Board itself describes the situation in this language: "The legislative, executive, and judicial departments of the state government opposed the desegregation of Little Rock schools by enacting laws, calling out troops, making statements villifying federal law and federal courts, and failing to utilize state law enforcement agencies and judicial pro-cesses to maintain public peace."

. . . The constitutional rights of respondents are not to be sacrificed or yielded to the violence and disorder which have followed upon the actions of the Governor and Legislature.

Thus, law and order are not here to be preserved by depriving the Negro children of their constitutional rights. The record before us clearly establishes that the growth of the Board's difficulties to a magnitude beyond its unaided power to control is the product of state action. Those difficulties, as counsel for the Board forthrightly conceded on the oral argument in this Court, can also be brought under control by state action.

The controlling legal principles are plain. The command of the Fourteenth Amendment is that no "State" shall deny to any person within its jurisdiction the equal protection of the laws.

"A State acts by its legislative, its executive, or its judicial authorities. It can act in no other way. The constitutional provision, therefore, must mean that no agency of the State, or of the officers or agents by whom its powers are exerted, shall deny to any person within its jurisdiction the equal protection of the laws. Whoever, by virtue of public position under a State government, . . . denies or takes away the equal protection of the laws violates the constitutional inhibition; and, as he acts in the name and for the State, and is clothed with the State's power, his act is that of the State. This must be so, or the constitutional prohibition has no meaning."

Thus, the prohibitions of the Fourteenth Amendment extend to all action of the State denying equal protection of the laws; whatever the agency of the State taking the action, or whatever the guise in which it is taken[.] In short, the constitutional rights of children not to be discriminated against in school admission on grounds of race or color declared by this Court in the *Brown* case can neither be nullified openly and directly by state legislators or state executive or judicial officers nor nullified indirectly by them through evasive schemes for segregation whether attempted "ingeniously or ingenuously."

What has been said, in the light of the facts developed, is enough to dispose of the case. However, we should answer the premise of the actions of the Governor and Legislature that they are not bound by our holding in the *Brown* case. It is necessary only to recall some basic constitutional propositions which are settled doctrine.

Article VI of the Constitution makes the Constitution the "supreme Law of the Land." In 1803, Chief Justice Marshall, speaking for a unanimous Court, referring to the Constitution as "the fundamental and paramount law of the nation," declared in the notable case of *Marbury v. Madison*, that "It is emphatically the province and duty of the judicial department to say what the law is." This decision declared the basic principle that the federal judiciary is supreme in the exposition of the law of the Constitution, and that principle has ever since been respected by this Court and the Country as a permanent and indispensable feature of our constitutional system. It follows that the interpretation of the Fourteenth Amendment enunciated by this Court in the *Brown* case is the supreme law of the land, and Art. VI of the Constitution makes it of binding effect on the States "any Thing in the Constitution or Laws of any State to the Contrary notwithstanding." Every state legislator and executive and judicial officer is solemnly committed by oath taken pursuant to Art. VI, cl. 3 "to support this Constitution." Chief Justice Taney, speaking for a unanimous Court in 1859, said that this requirement reflected the framers' "anxiety to preserve it [the Constitution] in full force, in all its powers, and to guard against resistance to or evasion of its authority, on the part of a State. . . ."

No state legislator or executive or judicial officer can war against the Constitution without violating his undertaking to support it. Chief Justice Marshall spoke for a unanimous Court in saying that: "If the legislatures of the several states may at will, annul the judgments of the courts of the United States, and destroy the rights acquired under those judgments, the constitution itself becomes a solemn mockery . . . ."

A Governor who asserts a power to nullify a federal court order is similarly restrained. If he had such power, said Chief Justice Hughes, in 1932, also for a unanimous Court, "it is manifest that the fiat of a state Governor, and not the Constitution of the United States, would be the supreme law of the land; that the restrictions of the Federal Constitution upon the exercise of state power would be but impotent phrases . . . ."

It is, of course, quite true that the responsibility for public education is primarily the concern of the States, but it is equally true that such responsibilities, like all other state activity, must be exercised consistently with federal constitutional requirements as they apply to state action. The Constitution created a government dedicated to equal justice under law. The Fourteenth Amendment embodied and emphasized that ideal. State support of segregated schools through any arrangement, management, funds, or property cannot be squared with the Amendment's command that no State shall deny to any person within its jurisdiction the equal protection of the laws. The right of a student not to be segregated on racial grounds in schools so maintained is indeed so fundamental and pervasive that it is embraced in the concept of due process of law. The basic decision in *Brown* . . . The principles announced in that decision and the obedience of the States to them, according to the command of the Constitution, are indispensable for the protection of the freedoms guaranteed by our fundamental charter for all of us. Our constitutional ideal of equal justice under law is thus made a living truth.

GEORGE WALLACE, "SEGREGATION NOW, SEGREGATION FOREVER"[8]

Today I have stood, where once Jefferson Davis stood, and took an oath to my people. It is very appropriate then that from this Cradle of the Confederacy, this very Heart of the Great Anglo-Saxon Southland, that today we sound the drum for freedom as have our generations of forebears before us done, time and time again through history. Let us rise to the call of freedom-loving blood that is in us and send our answer to the tyranny that clanks its chains upon the South. In the name of the greatest people that have ever trod this earth, I draw the line in the dust and toss the gauntlet before the feet of tyranny . . . and I say . . . segregation today . . . segregation tomorrow . . . segregation forever.

. . . Let us send this message back to Washington by our representatives who are with us today—that from this day we are standing up, and the heel of tyranny does not fit the neck of an upright man . . . that we intend to take the offensive and carry our fight for freedom across the nation, wielding the balance of power we know we possess in the Southland . . . that WE, not the insipid bloc of voters of some sections . . . will determine in the next election who shall sit in the White House of these United States . . . That from this day, from this hour . . . from this minute . . . we give the word of a race of honor that we will tolerate their boot in our face no longer . . . and let those certain judges put that in their opium pipes of power and smoke it for what it is worth.

Hear me, Southerners! You sons and daughters who have moved north and west throughout this nation . . . we call on you from your native soil to join with us in national support and vote . . . and we know . . . wherever you are . . . away from the hearths of the Southland . . . that you will respond, for though you may live in the farthest reaches of this vast country . . . your heart has never left Dixieland.

And you native sons and daughters of old New England's rock-ribbed patriotism . . . and you sturdy natives of the great Mid-West . . . and you descendants of the far West flaming spirit of pioneer freedom . . . we invite you to come and be with us . . . for you are of the Southern spirit . . . and the Southern philosophy . . . you are Southerners too and brothers with us in our fight.

. . . And while the manufacturing industries of free enterprise have been coming to our state in increasing numbers, attracted by our bountiful natural resources, our growing numbers of skilled workers and our favorable conditions, their present rate of settlement here can be increased from the trickle they now represent to a stream of enterprise and endeavor, capital and expansion that can join us in our work of development and enrichment of the educational futures of our children, the opportunities of our citizens and the fulfillment of our talents as God has given them to us. To realize our ambitions and to bring to fruition our dreams, we as Alabamians must take cognizance of the world about us. We must re-define our heritage, re-school our thoughts in the lessons our forefathers knew so well, first hand, in order to function and to grow and to prosper. We can no longer hide our head in the sand and tell ourselves that the ideology of our free fathers is not being attacked and is not being threatened by another idea . . . for it is. We are faced with an idea that if a centralized government assume enough authority, enough power over its people, that it can provide a utopian life . . that if given the power to dictate, to forbid, to require, to demand, to distribute, to edict and to judge what is best and enforce that will produce only "good" . . . and it shall be our father . . . and our God. . . .

We find we have replaced faith with fear . . . and though we may give lip service to the Almighty . . in reality, government has become our god. It is, therefore, a basically ungodly government and its appeal to the pseudo-intellectual and the politician is to change their status from servant of the people to master of the people . . . to play at being God . . . without faith in God . . . and without the wisdom of God. It is a system that is the very opposite of Christ for it feeds and encourages everything degenerate and base in our people as it assumes the responsibilities that we ourselves should assume. Its pseudo-liberal spokesmen and some Harvard advocates have never examined the logic of its substitution of what it calls "human rights" for individual rights, for its propaganda play on words has appeal for the unthinking. Its logic is totally material and irresponsible as it runs the full gamut of human desires . . . including the theory that everyone has voting rights without the spiritual responsibility of preserving freedom. Our founding fathers recognized those rights . . . but only within the framework of those spiritual responsibilities. But the strong, simple faith and sane reasoning of our founding fathers has long since been forgotten as the so-called "progressives" tell us that our Constitution was written for "horse and buggy" days . . . so were the Ten Commandments.

. . . This nation was never meant to be a unit of one . . . but a united of the many . . . that is the exact reason our freedom loving forefathers established the states, so as to divide the rights and powers among the states, insuring that no central power could gain master government control.

In united effort we were meant to live under this government . . . whether Baptist, Methodist, Presbyterian, Church of Christ, or whatever one's denomination or religious belief . . . each respecting the others right to a separate denomination . . . each, by working to develop his own, enriching the total of all our lives through united effort. And so it was meant in our political lives . . . whether Republican, Democrat, Prohibition, or whatever political party . . . each striving from his separate political station . . . respecting the rights of others to be separate and work from within their political framework . . . and each separate political station making its contribution to our lives . . .

And so it was meant in our racial lives . . . each race, within its own framework has the freedom to teach . . . to instruct . . . to develop . . . to ask for and receive deserved help from others of separate racial stations. This is the great freedom of our American founding fathers . . . but if we amalgamate into the one unit as advocated by the communist philosophers . . . then the enrichment of our lives . . . the freedom for our development . . . is gone forever. We become, therefore, a mongrel unit of one under a single all powerful government . . . and we stand for everything . . . and for nothing.

The true brotherhood of America, of respecting the separateness of others . . . and uniting in effort . . . has been so twisted and distorted from its original concept that there is a small wonder that communism is winning the world.

We invite the negro citizens of Alabama to work with us from his separate racial station . . . as we will work with him . . . to develop, to grow in individual freedom and enrichment. We want jobs and a good future for BOTH races . . . the tubercular and the infirm. This is the basic heritage of my religion, if which I make full practice . . . for we are all the handiwork of God.

But we warn those, of any group, who would follow the false doctrine of communistic amalgamation that we will not surrender our system of government . . . our freedom of race and religion . . . that freedom was won at a hard price and if it requires a hard price to retain it . . . we are able . . . and quite willing to pay it.

The liberals' theory that poverty, discrimination and lack of opportunity is the cause of communism is a false theory . . . if it were true the South would have been the biggest single communist bloc in the western hemisphere long ago . . . for after the great War Between the States, our people faced a desolate land of burned universities, destroyed crops and homes, with manpower depleted and crippled, and even the mule, which was required to work the land, was so scarce that whole communities shared one animal to make the spring plowing. There were no government handouts, no Marshall Plan aid, no coddling to make sure that our people would not suffer; instead the South was set upon by the vulturous carpetbagger and federal troops, all loyal Southerners were denied the vote at the point of bayonet, so that the infamous, illegal 14th Amendment might be passed. There was no money, no food and no hope of either. But our grandfathers bent their knee only in church and bowed their head only to God . . . We remind all within hearing of this Southland that a Southerner, Peyton Randolph, presided over the Continental Congress in our nation's beginning . . . that a Southerner, Thomas Jefferson, wrote the Declaration of Independence, that a Southerner, George Washington, is the Father of our country . . . that a Southerner, James Madison, authored our Constitution, that a Southerner, George Mason, authored the Bill of Rights and it was a Southerner who said, "Give me liberty . . . or give me death," Patrick Henry. Southerners played a most magnificent part in erecting this great divinely inspired system of freedom . . . and as God is our witnesses, Southerners will save it.

Let us, as Alabamians, grasp the hand of destiny and walk out of the shadow of fear . . . and fill our divine destination. Let us not simply defend

. . . but let us assume the leadership of the fight and carry our leadership across this nation. God has placed us here in this crisis . . . let is not fail in this . . . our most historical moment.

HEART OF ATLANTA MOTEL, INC. v. UNITED STATES[9]

. . . Title II of the Civil Rights Act of 1964 is a valid exercise of Congress' power under the Commerce Clause as applied to a place of public accommodation serving interstate travelers.

The case comes here on admissions and stipulated facts. Appellant owns and operates the Heart of Atlanta Motel, which has 216 rooms available to transient guests. . . . Appellant solicits patronage from outside the State of Georgia through various national advertising media, including magazines of national circulation; it maintains over 50 billboards and highway signs within the State, soliciting patronage for the motel; it accepts convention trade from outside Georgia and approximately 75% of its registered guests are from out of State. Prior to passage of the Act, the motel had followed a practice of refusing to rent rooms to Negroes, and it alleged that it intended to continue to do so . . .

The appellant contends that Congress, in passing this Act, exceeded its power to regulate commerce under Art. I,§ 8, cl. 3, of the Constitution of the United States; that the Act violates the Fifth Amendment because appellant is deprived of the right to choose its customers . . . resulting in a taking of its liberty and property without due process of law . . . without just compensation . . .

. . . The sole question posed is, therefore, the constitutionality of the Civil Rights Act of 1964 as applied to these facts. The legislative history of the Act indicates that Congress based the Act on § 5 and the Equal Protection Clause of the Fourteenth Amendment, as well as its power to regulate interstate commerce under Art. I, § 8, cl. 3, of the Constitution.

The Senate Commerce Committee made it quite clear that the fundamental object of Title II was to vindicate "the deprivation of personal dignity that surely accompanies denials of equal access to public establishments."

. . . Our study of the legislative record, made in the light of prior cases, has brought us to the conclusion that Congress possessed ample power in this regard, and we have therefore not considered the other grounds relied upon. . . .

While the Act, as adopted, carried no congressional findings, the record of its passage through each house is replete with evidence of the burdens that discrimination by race or color places upon interstate commerce.

. . . In short, the determinative test of the exercise of power by the Congress under the Commerce Clause is simply whether the activity sought to be regulated is "commerce which concerns more States than one" and has a real and substantial relation to the national interest. . . . In framing Title II of this Act, Congress was also dealing with what it considered a moral problem. But that fact does not detract from the overwhelming evidence of the disruptive effect that racial discrimination has had on commercial intercourse. . . .

Nor does the Act deprive appellant of liberty or property under the Fifth Amendment. The commerce power invoked here by the Congress is a specific and plenary one authorized by the Constitution itself. The only questions are: (1) whether Congress had a rational basis for finding that racial discrimination by motels affected commerce, and (2) if it had such a basis, whether the means it selected to eliminate that evil are reasonable and appropriate.

. . . As we have pointed out, 32 States now have such provisions and no case has been cited to us where the attack on a state statute has been successful, either in federal or state courts. . . . As a result, the constitutionality of such state statutes stands unquestioned . . .

We find no merit in the remainder of appellant's contentions, including that of "involuntary servitude." As we have seen, 32 States prohibit racial discrimination in public accommodations. These laws but codify the common law innkeeper rule, which long predated the Thirteenth Amendment. It is difficult to believe that the Amendment was intended to abrogate this principle . . .

We therefore conclude that the action of the Congress in the adoption of the Act as applied here to a motel which concededly serves interstate travelers is within the power granted it by the Commerce Clause of the Constitution, as interpreted by this Court for 140 years. It may be argued that Congress could have pursued other methods to eliminate the obstructions it found in interstate commerce caused by racial discrimination. But this is a matter of policy that rests entirely with the Congress, not with the courts. How obstructions in commerce may be removed—what means are to be employed—is within the sound and exclusive discretion of the Congress. It is subject only to one caveat—that the means chosen by it must be reasonably adapted to the end permitted by the Constitution. We cannot say that its choice here was not so adapted. The Constitution requires no more.

KATZENBACH v. McCLUNG[10]

. . . Ollie's Barbecue is a family owned restaurant in Birmingham, Alabama, specializing in barbecued meats and homemade pies, with a seating capacity of 220 customers. It is located on a state highway 11 blocks from an interstate one and a somewhat greater distance from railroad and bus stations.

The restaurant caters to a family and white-collar trade with a take-out service for Negroes. It employs 36 persons, two-thirds of whom are Negroes.

In the 12 months preceding the passage of the Act, the restaurant purchased locally approximately $150,000 worth of food, $69,683 or 46% of which was meat that it bought from a local supplier who had procured it from outside the State. The District Court expressly found that a substantial portion of the food served in the restaurant had moved in interstate commerce. The restaurant has refused to serve Negroes in its dining accommodations since its original opening in 1927, and, since July 2, 1964, it has been operating in violation of the Act.

. . . On the merits, the District Court held that the Act could not be applied under the Fourteenth Amendment because it was conceded that the State of Alabama was not involved in the refusal of the restaurant to serve Negroes. It was also admitted that the Thirteenth Amendment was authority neither for validating nor for invalidating the Act. . . . There must be, it said, a close and substantial relation between local activities and interstate commerce which requires control of the former in the protection of the latter. The court concluded, however, that the Congress, rather than finding facts sufficient to meet this rule, had legislated a conclusive presumption that a restaurant affects interstate commerce if it serves or offers to serve interstate travelers or if a substantial portion of the food which it serves has moved in commerce. This, the court held, it could not do, because there was no demonstrable connection between food purchased in interstate commerce and sold in a restaurant and the conclusion of Congress that discrimination in the restaurant would affect that commerce.

. . . There, we outlined the overall purpose and operational plan of Title II, and found it a valid exercise of the power to regulate interstate commerce insofar as it requires hotels and motels to serve transients without regard to their race or color. In this case, we consider its application to restaurants which serve food a substantial portion of which has moved in commerce.

. . . Section 201(a) of Title II commands that all persons shall be entitled to the full and equal enjoyment of the goods and services of any place of public accommodation without discrimination or segregation on the ground of race, color, religion, or national origin, and § 201(b) defines establishments as places of public accommodation if their operations affect commerce or segregation by them is supported by state action. Sections 201(b)(2) and (c) place any "restaurant . . . principally engaged in selling food for consumption on the premises" under the Act "if . . . it serves or offers to serve interstate travelers or a substantial portion of the food which it serves . . . has moved in commerce."

. . . As we noted in *Heart of Atlanta Motel*, both Houses of Congress conducted prolonged hearings on the Act. And, as we said there, while no formal findings were made, which, of course, are not necessary, it is well that we make mention of the testimony at these hearings the better to understand the problem before Congress and determine whether the Act is a reasonable and appropriate means toward its solution. The record is replete with testimony of the burdens placed on interstate commerce by racial discrimination in restaurants. . . . This diminutive spending springing from a refusal to serve Negroes and their total loss as customers has, regardless of the absence of direct evidence, a close connection to interstate commerce. The fewer customers a restaurant enjoys, the less food it sells, and consequently the less it buys.

. . . Moreover, there was an impressive array of testimony that discrimination in restaurants had a direct and highly restrictive effect upon interstate travel by Negroes. This resulted, it was said, because discriminatory practices prevent Negroes from buying prepared food served on the premises while on a trip, except in isolated and unkempt restaurants and under most unsatisfactory and often unpleasant conditions. This obviously discourages travel and obstructs interstate commerce, for one can hardly travel without eating.

. . . This Court has held time and again that this power extends to activities of retail establishments, including restaurants, which directly or indirectly burden or obstruct interstate commerce. We have detailed the cases in *Heart of Atlanta Motel*, and will not repeat them here.

Nor are the cases holding that interstate commerce ends when goods come to rest in the State of destination apposite here. That line of cases has been applied with reference to state taxation or regulation, but not in the field of federal regulation.

. . . Here, as there, Congress has determined for itself that refusals of service to Negroes have imposed burdens both upon the interstate flow of food and upon the movement of products generally. Of course, the mere fact that Congress has said when particular activity shall be deemed to affect commerce does not preclude further examination by this Court. But where we find that the legislators, in light of the facts and testimony before them, have a rational basis for finding a chosen regulatory scheme necessary to the protection of commerce, our investigation is at an end. . . .

Insofar as the sections of the Act here relevant are concerned, §§ 201(b) (2) and (c), Congress prohibited discrimination only in those establishments having a close tie to interstate commerce, *i.e.*, those, like the McClungs', serving food that has come from out of the State. We think, in so doing, that Congress acted well within its power to protect and foster commerce in extending the coverage of Title II only to those restaurants offering to serve interstate travelers or serving food, a substantial portion of which has moved in interstate commerce.

. . . The power of Congress in this field is broad and sweeping; where it keeps within its sphere and violates no express constitutional limitation it has been the rule of this Court, going back almost to the founding days of the Republic, not to interfere. The Civil Rights Act of 1964, as here applied, we find to be plainly appropriate in the resolution of what the Congress found to be a national commercial problem of the first magnitude. We find it in no violation of any express limitations of the Constitution and we therefore declare it valid.

GRISWOLD v. CONNECTICUT[11]

[MR. JUSTICE DOUGLAS delivered the opinion of the Court] Appellant Griswold is Executive Director of the Planned Parenthood League of Connecticut. Appellant Buxton is a licensed physician and a professor at the Yale Medical School who served as Medical Director for the League at its Center in New Haven—a center open and operating from November 1 to November 10, 1961, when appellants were arrested.

They gave information, instruction, and medical advice to *married persons* as to the means of preventing conception. They examined the wife and prescribed the best contraceptive device or material for her use. Fees were usually charged, although some couples were serviced free.

. . . we are met with a wide range of questions that implicate the Due Process Clause of the Fourteenth Amendment . . . We do not sit as a super-legislature to determine the wisdom, need, and propriety of laws that touch economic problems, business affairs, or social conditions. This law, however, operates directly on an intimate relation of husband and wife and their physician's role in one aspect of that relation.

The association of people is not mentioned in the Constitution nor in the Bill of Rights. The right to educate a child in a school of the parents' choice—whether public or private or parochial—is also not mentioned. Nor is the right to study any particular subject or any foreign language. Yet the First Amendment has been construed to include certain of those rights. In other words, the State may not, consistently with the spirit of the First Amendment, contract the spectrum of available knowledge. The right of freedom of speech and press includes not only the right to utter or to print, but the right to distribute, the right to receive, the right to read and freedom of inquiry, freedom of thought, and freedom to teach—indeed, the freedom of the entire university community. Without those peripheral rights, the specific rights would be less secure.

[S]pecific guarantees in the Bill of Rights have penumbras, formed by emanations from those guarantees that help give them life and substance. Various guarantees create zones of privacy. The right of association contained in the penumbra of the First Amendment is one, as we have seen.

The Third Amendment, in its prohibition against the quartering of soldiers "in any house" in time of peace without the consent of the owner, is another facet of that privacy. The Fourth Amendment explicitly affirms the "right of the people to be secure in their persons, houses, papers, and effects, against unreasonable searches and seizures." The Fifth Amendment, in its Self-Incrimination Clause, enables the citizen to create a zone of privacy which government may not force him to surrender to his detriment. The Ninth Amendment provides: "The enumeration in the Constitution, of certain rights, shall not be construed to deny or disparage others retained by the people."

. . . The present case, then, concerns a relationship lying within the zone of privacy created by several fundamental constitutional guarantees. And it concerns a law which, in forbidding the use of contraceptives, rather than regulating their manufacture or sale, seeks to achieve its goals by means having a maximum destructive impact upon that relationship. Such a law cannot stand in light of the familiar principle, so often applied by this Court, that a "governmental purpose to control or prevent activities constitutionally subject to state regulation may not be achieved by means which sweep unnecessarily broadly and thereby invade the area of protected freedoms."

Would we allow the police to search the sacred precincts of marital bedrooms for telltale signs of the use of contraceptives? The very idea is repulsive to the notions of privacy surrounding the marriage relationship.

We deal with a right of privacy older than the Bill of Rights—older than our political parties, older than our school system. Marriage is a coming together for better or for worse, hopefully enduring, and intimate to the degree of being sacred. It is an association that promotes a way of life, not causes; a harmony in living, not political faiths; a bilateral loyalty, not commercial or social projects. Yet it is an association for as noble a purpose as any involved in our prior decisions.

LOVING v. VIRGINIA[12]

[MR. CHIEF JUSTICE WARREN delivered the opinion of the Court] This case presents a constitutional question never addressed by this Court: whether a statutory scheme adopted by the State of Virginia to prevent marriages between persons solely on the basis of racial classifications violates the Equal Protection and Due Process Clauses of the Fourteenth Amendment. For reasons which seem to us to reflect the central meaning of those constitutional commands, we conclude that these statutes cannot stand consistently with the Fourteenth Amendment.

. . . The State argues that statements in the Thirty-ninth Congress about the time of the passage of the Fourteenth Amendment indicate that the Framers did not intend the Amendment to make unconstitutional state miscegenation laws. Many of the statements alluded to by the State concern the debates over the Freedmen's Bureau Bill, which President Johnson vetoed, and the Civil Rights Act of 1866, 14 Stat. 27, enacted over his veto. While these statements have some relevance to the intention of Congress in submitting the Fourteenth Amendment, it must be understood that they pertained to the passage of specific statutes, and not to the broader, organic purpose of a constitutional amendment. As for the various statements directly concerning the Fourteenth Amendment, we have said in connection with a related problem that, although these historical sources "cast some light" they are not sufficient to resolve the problem; "[a]t best, they are inconclusive. The most avid proponents of the post-War Amendments undoubtedly intended them to remove all legal distinctions among 'all persons born or naturalized in the United States.' Their opponents, just as certainly, were antagonistic to both the letter and the spirit of the Amendments, and wished them to have the most limited effect."

    . . . There is patently no legitimate overriding purpose independent of invidious racial discrimination which justifies this classification. The fact that Virginia prohibits only interracial marriages involving white persons demonstrates that the racial classifications must stand on their own justification, as measures designed to maintain White Supremacy. We have consistently denied the constitutionality of measures which restrict the rights of citizens on account of race. There can be no doubt that restricting the freedom to marry solely because of racial classifications violates the central meaning of the Equal Protection Clause.

    These statutes also deprive the Lovings of liberty without due process of law in violation of the Due Process Clause of the Fourteenth Amendment. The freedom to marry has long been recognized as one of the vital personal rights essential to the orderly pursuit of happiness by free men.

    Marriage is one of the "basic civil rights of man," fundamental to our very existence and survival . . . To deny this fundamental freedom on so unsupportable a basis as the racial classifications embodied in these statutes, classifications so directly subversive of the principle of equality at the heart of the Fourteenth Amendment, is surely to deprive all the State's citizens of liberty without due process of law. The Fourteenth Amendment requires that the freedom of choice to marry not be restricted by invidious racial discriminations. Under our Constitution, the freedom to marry, or not marry, a person of another race resides with the individual, and cannot be infringed by the State.

ROE v. WADE[13]

    . . . The Texas statutes that concern us here . . . make it a crime to "procure an abortion," as therein defined, or to attempt one, except with respect to "an abortion procured or attempted by medical advice for the purpose of saving the life of the mother." Similar statutes are in existence in a majority of the States.

Roe alleged that . . . that she was unable to get a "legal" abortion in Texas because her life did not appear to be threatened by the continuation of her pregnancy . . .

. . . On the merits, the District Court held that the "fundamental right of single women and married persons to choose whether to have children is protected by the Ninth Amendment, through the Fourteenth Amendment," and that the Texas criminal abortion statutes were void on their face because they were both unconstitutionally vague and constituted an overbroad infringement of the plaintiffs' Ninth Amendment rights. . . .

The principal thrust of appellant's attack on the Texas statutes is that they improperly invade a right, said to be possessed by the pregnant woman, to choose to terminate her pregnancy. Appellant would discover this right in the concept of personal "liberty" embodied in the Fourteenth Amendment's Due Process Clause; or in personal, marital, familial, and sexual privacy said to be protected by the Bill of Rights or its penumbras, *see Griswold v. Connecticut.*

It perhaps is not generally appreciated that the restrictive criminal abortion laws in effect in a majority of States today are of relatively recent vintage. Those laws, generally proscribing abortion or its attempt at any time during pregnancy except when necessary to preserve the pregnant woman's life, are not of ancient or even of common law origin. Instead, they derive from statutory changes effected, for the most part, in the latter half of the 19th century. . . . We are also told, however, that abortion was practiced in Greek times as well as in the Roman Era, . . . that "it was resorted to without scruple." . . . Greek and Roman law afforded little protection to the unborn.

. . . Most Greek thinkers, on the other hand, commended abortion, at least prior to viability. *See* Plato, Republic, V, 461; Aristotle, Politics, VII, 1335b 25 . . . The absence of a common law crime for pre-quickening abortion appears to have developed from a confluence of earlier philosophical, theological, and civil and canon law concepts of when life begins.

. . . In this country, the law in effect in all but a few States until mid-19th century was the preexisting English common law.

The State has a legitimate interest in seeing to it that abortion, like any other medical procedure, is performed under circumstances that insure maximum safety for the patient.

. . . the State retains a definite interest in protecting the woman's own health and safety when an abortion is proposed at a late stage of pregnancy. . . .

The Constitution does not explicitly mention any right of privacy . . . the Court has recognized that a right of personal privacy, or a guarantee of certain areas or zones of privacy, does exist under the Constitution. In varying contexts, the Court or individual Justices have, indeed, found at least the roots of that right in the First Amendment, . . . in the Fourth and Fifth Amendments, . . . in the penumbras of the Bill of Rights, . . . in the Ninth Amendment, . . . or in the concept of liberty guaranteed by the first section of the Fourteenth Amendment . . . These decisions make it clear that only personal rights that can be deemed "fundamental" or "implicit in the concept of ordered liberty," *Palko v. Connecticut,* . . .

This right of privacy, whether it be founded in the Fourteenth Amendment's concept of personal liberty and restrictions upon state action, as we feel it is, or, as the District Court determined, in the Ninth Amendment's reservation of rights to the people, is broad enough to encompass a woman's decision whether or not to terminate her pregnancy. The detriment that the State would impose upon the pregnant woman by denying this choice altogether is apparent. . . . The Court's decisions recognizing a right of privacy also acknowledge that some state regulation in areas protected by that right is appropriate. . . .

As noted above, a State may properly assert important interests in safeguarding health, in maintaining medical standards, and in protecting potential life. At some point in pregnancy, these respective interests become sufficiently compelling to sustain . . .

Although the results are divided, most of these courts have agreed that the right of privacy, however based, is broad enough to cover the abortion decision; that the right, nonetheless, is not absolute, and is subject to some limitations; and that, at some point, the state interests as to protection of health, medical standards, and prenatal life, become dominant. . . .

Where certain "fundamental rights" are involved, the Court has held that regulation limiting these rights may be justified only by a "compelling state interest," . . . and that legislative enactments must be narrowly drawn to express only the legitimate state interests at stake. . . .

. . . The appellee and certain *amici* argue that the fetus is a "person" within the language and meaning of the Fourteenth Amendment . . . . The Constitution does not define "person" in so many words. . . . the use of the word is such that it has application only post-natally. . . .

All this, together with our observation, *supra,* that, throughout the major portion of the 19th century, prevailing legal abortion practices were far freer than they are today, persuades us that the word "person," as used in the Fourteenth Amendment, does not include the unborn. . . .

. . . We need not resolve the difficult question of when life begins. When those trained in the respective disciplines of medicine, philosophy, and theology are unable to arrive at any consensus, the judiciary, at this point in the development of man's knowledge, is not in a position to speculate as to the answer.

. . . As we have noted, the common law found greater significance in quickening. Physician and their scientific colleagues have regarded that event with less interest and have tended to focus either upon conception, upon live birth, or upon the interim point at which the fetus becomes "viable," that is, potentially able to live outside the mother's womb, albeit with artificial aid. Viability is usually placed at about seven months (28 weeks) but may occur earlier, even at 24 weeks.

. . . With respect to the State's important and legitimate interest in the health of the mother, the "compelling" point, in the light of present medical knowledge, is at approximately the end of the first trimester. . . . It follows that, from and after this point, a State may regulate the abortion procedure to the extent that the regulation reasonably relates to the preservation and protection of maternal health. . . . With respect to the State's important and legitimate interest in potential life, the "compelling" point is at viability. . . . A state criminal abortion statute of the current Texas type, that excepts from criminality only a lifesaving procedure on behalf of the mother, without regard to pregnancy stage and without recognition of the other interests involved, is violative of the Due Process Clause of the Fourteenth Amendment.

. . . The decision leaves the State free to place increasing restrictions on abortion as the period of pregnancy lengthens, so long as those restrictions are tailored to the recognized state interests.

[MR. JUSTICE REHNQUIST, dissenting] . . . I would reach a conclusion opposite to that reached by the Court. I have difficulty in concluding, as the Court does, that the right of "privacy" is involved in this case.

. . . The decision here to break pregnancy into three distinct terms and to outline the permissible restrictions the State may impose in each one, for example, partakes more of judicial legislation than it does of a determination of the intent of the drafters of the Fourteenth Amendment.

The fact that a majority of the States reflecting, after all, the majority sentiment in those States, have had restrictions on abortions for at least a century is a strong indication, it seems to me, that the asserted right to an abortion is not "so rooted in the traditions and conscience of our people as to be ranked as fundamental," *Snyder v. Massachusetts.*

PLANNED PARENTHOOD OF SOUTHEASTERN PENNSYLVANIA ET AL. V CASEY[14]

. . . The Act requires that a woman seeking an abortion give her informed consent prior to the abortion procedure, and specifies that she be provided with certain information at least 24 hours before the abortion is performed. . . . For a minor to obtain an abortion, the Act requires the informed consent of one of her parents, but provides for a judicial bypass option if the minor does not wish to or cannot obtain a parent's consent. . . . Another provision of the Act requires that, unless certain exceptions apply, a married woman seeking an abortion must sign a statement indicating that she has notified her husband of her intended abortion . . .

Roe's essential holding, . . . is a recognition of the right of the woman to choose to have an abortion before viability and . . . . [b]efore viability, the State's interests are not strong enough to support a prohibition of abortion or the imposition of a substantial obstacle to the woman's effective right to elect the procedure. . . . a confirmation of the State's power to restrict abortions after fetal viability, if the law contains exceptions for pregnancies which endanger the woman's life or health . . . the State has legitimate interests from the outset of the pregnancy in protecting the health of the woman and the life of the fetus that may become a child. . . .

Neither the Bill of Rights nor the specific practices of States at the time of the adoption of the Fourteenth Amendment marks the outer limits of the substantive sphere of liberty which the Fourteenth Amendment protects. . . . Our precedents "have respected the private realm of family life which the state cannot enter." *Prince v. Massachusetts,* . . . These matters, involving the most intimate and personal choices a person may make in a lifetime, choices central to personal dignity and autonomy, are central to the liberty protected by the Fourteenth Amendment. At the heart of liberty is the right to define one's own concept of existence, of meaning, of the universe, and of the mystery of human life. Beliefs about these matters could not define the attributes of personhood were they formed under compulsion of the State.

Although *Roe* has engendered opposition, it has in no sense proven "unworkable," . . . representing as it does a simple limitation beyond which a state law is unenforceable.

. . . The ability of women to participate equally in the economic and social life of the Nation has been facilitated by their ability to control their reproductive lives. . . .

While the outer limits of this aspect of [protected liberty] have not been marked by the Court, it is clear that among the decisions that an individual may make without unjustified government interference are personal decisions "relating to marriage, procreation, contraception, family relationships, and child rearing and education." . . .

We have seen how time has overtaken some of *Roe*'s factual assumptions: advances in maternal health care allow for abortions safe to the mother later in pregnancy than was true in 1973, . . . and advances in neonatal care have advanced viability to a point somewhat earlier. . . .

We conclude, however, that the urgent claims of the woman to retain the ultimate control over her destiny and her body, claims implicit in the meaning of liberty, require us to perform that function. Liberty must not be extinguished for want of a line that is clear. . . . We conclude the line should be drawn at viability, so that before that time the woman has a right to choose to terminate her pregnancy. We adhere to this principle for two reasons. First, as we have said, is the doctrine of *stare decisis*

The second reason is that the concept of viability . . . is the time at which there is a realistic possibility of maintaining and nourishing a life outside the womb, so that the independent existence of the second life can in reason and all fairness be the object of state protection that now overrides the rights of the woman.

. . . Those cases decided that any regulation touching upon the abortion decision must survive strict scrutiny, to be sustained only if drawn in narrow terms to further a compelling state interest. . . . The trimester framework no doubt was erected to ensure that the woman's right to choose not become so subordinate to the State's interest in promoting fetal life that her choice exists in theory but not in fact. We do not agree, however, that the trimester approach is necessary to accomplish this objective.

Only where state regulation imposes an undue burden on a woman's ability to make this decision does the power of the State reach into the heart of the liberty protected by the Due Process Clause. . . . Not all burdens on the right to decide whether to terminate a pregnancy will be undue. In our view, the undue burden standard is the appropriate means of reconciling the State's interest with the woman's constitutionally protected liberty.

. . . And a statute which, while furthering the interest in potential life or some other valid state interest, has the effect of placing a substantial obstacle in the path of a woman's choice cannot be considered a permissible means of serving its legitimate ends.

[CHIEF JUSTICE REHNQUIST, with whom JUSTICE WHITE, JUSTICE SCALIA, and JUSTICE THOMAS join, concurring in the judgment in part and dissenting in part: . . . We believe that *Roe* was wrongly decided, and that it can and should be overruled consistently with our traditional approach to *stare decisis* in constitutional cases. . . .

. . . Although they reject the trimester framework that formed the underpinning of *Roe*, JUSTICES O'CONNOR, KENNEDY, and SOUTER adopt a revised undue burden standard to analyze the challenged regulations. We conclude, however, that such an outcome is an unjustified constitutional compromise . . . One cannot ignore the fact that a woman is not isolated in her pregnancy, and that the decision to abort necessarily involves the destruction of a fetus . . . Nor do the historical traditions of the American people support the view that the right to terminate one's pregnancy is "fundamental."

. . . the "undue burden" standard, which is created largely out of whole cloth by the authors of the joint opinion. It is a standard which even today does not command the support of a majority of this Court . . . the standard will do nothing to prevent "judges from roaming at large in the constitutional field" guided only by their personal views.

OBERGEFELL v. HODGES[15]

[Justice Anthony Kennedy] The centrality of marriage to the human condition makes it unsurprising that the institution has existed for millennia and across civilizations. Since the dawn of history, marriage has transformed strangers into relatives, binding families and societies together . . . There are untold references to the beauty of marriage in religious and philosophical texts spanning time, cultures, and faiths, as well as in art and literature in all their forms. It is fair and necessary to say these references were based on the understanding that marriage is a union between two persons of the opposite sex.

. . . Indeed, changed understandings of marriage are characteristic of a Nation where new dimensions of freedom become apparent to new generations, often through perspectives that begin in pleas or protests and then are considered in the political sphere and the judicial process.

. . . In the late 20th century, following substantial cultural and political developments, same-sex couples began to lead more open and public lives and to establish families. This development was followed by a quite extensive discussion of the issue in both governmental and private sectors and by a shift in public attitudes toward greater tolerance. As a result, questions about the rights of gays and lesbians soon reached the courts, where the issue could be discussed in the formal discourse of the law.

. . . Under the Due Process Clause of the Fourteenth Amendment, no State shall "deprive any person of life, liberty, or property, without due process of law." The fundamental liberties protected by this Clause include most of the rights enumerated in the Bill of Rights . . . In addition these liberties extend to certain personal choices central to individual dignity and autonomy, including intimate choices that define personal identity and beliefs.

. . . The identification and protection of fundamental rights is an enduring part of the judicial duty to interpret the Constitution. That responsibility, however, "has not been reduced to any formula." Rather, it requires courts to exercise reasoned judgment in identifying interests of the person so fundamental that the State must accord them its respect. That process is guided by many of the same considerations relevant to analysis of other constitutional provisions that set forth broad principles rather than specific requirements. History and tradition guide and discipline this inquiry but do not set its outer boundaries . . . That method respects our history and learns from it without allowing the past alone to rule the present.

The nature of injustice is that we may not always see it in our own times. The generations that wrote and ratified the Bill of Rights and the Fourteenth Amendment did not presume to know the extent of freedom in all of its dimensions, and so they entrusted to future generations a charter protecting the right of all persons to enjoy liberty as we learn its meaning. When new insight reveals discord between the Constitution's central protections and a received legal stricture, a claim to liberty must be addressed.

. . . Applying these established tenets, the Court has long held the right to marry is protected by the Constitution. . . . Over time and in other contexts, the Court has reiterated that the right to marry is fundamental under the Due Process Clause.

. . . Choices about marriage shape an individual's destiny. . . . The nature of marriage is that, through its enduring bond, two persons together can find other freedoms, such as expression, intimacy, and spirituality. This is true for all persons, whatever their sexual orientation . . . There is dignity in the bond between two men or two women who seek to marry and in their autonomy to make such profound choices.

A second principle in this Court's jurisprudence is that the right to marry is fundamental because it supports a two-person union unlike any other in its importance to the committed individuals . . . "Marriage is a coming together for better or for worse, hopefully enduring, and intimate to the degree of being sacred. It is an association that promotes a way of life, not causes; a harmony in living, not political faiths; a bilateral loyalty, not commercial or social projects. Yet it is an association for as noble a purpose as any involved in our prior decisions.

. . . A third basis for protecting the right to marry is that it safeguards children and families and thus draws meaning from related rights of childrearing, procreation, and education . . . Under the laws of the several States, some of marriage's protections for children and families are material. But marriage also confers more profound benefits. By giving recognition and legal structure to their parents' relationship, marriage allows children "to understand the integrity and closeness of their own family and its concord with other families in their community and in their daily lives."

. . . Excluding same-sex couples from marriage thus conflicts with a central premise of the right to marry. Without the recognition, stability, and predictability marriage offers, their children suffer the stigma of knowing their families are somehow lesser. They also suffer the significant material costs of being raised by unmarried parents, relegated through no fault of their own to a more difficult and uncertain family life. The marriage laws at issue here thus harm and humiliate the children of same-sex couples.

That is not to say the right to marry is less meaningful for those who do not or cannot have children. An ability, desire, or promise to procreate is not and has not been a prerequisite for a valid marriage in any State. In light of precedent protecting the right of a married couple not to procreate, it cannot be said the Court or the States have conditioned the right to marry on the capacity or commitment to procreate. The constitutional marriage right has many aspects, of which childbearing is only one.

. . . For that reason, just as a couple vows to support each other, so does society pledge to support the couple, offering symbolic recognition and material benefits to protect and nourish the union. Indeed, while the States are in general free to vary the benefits they confer on all married couples, they have throughout our history made marriage the basis for an expanding list of governmental rights, benefits, and responsibilities. These aspects of marital status include: taxation; inheritance and property rights; rules of intestate succession; spousal privilege in the law of evidence; hospital access; medical decision making authority; adoption rights; the rights and benefits of survivors; birth and death certificates; professional ethics rules; campaign finance restrictions; workers' compensation benefits; health insurance; and child custody, support, and visitation rules.

. . . The right of same-sex couples to marry that is part of the liberty promised by the Fourteenth Amendment is derived, too, from that Amendment's guarantee of the equal protection of the laws. The Due Process Clause and the Equal Protection Clause are connected in a profound way, though they set forth independent principles. Rights implicit in liberty and rights secured by equal protection may rest on different precepts and are not always co-extensive, yet in some instances each may be instructive as to the meaning and reach of the other. In any particular case one Clause may be thought to capture the essence of the right in a more accurate and comprehensive way, even as the two Clauses may converge in the identification and definition of the right.

. . . Indeed, in interpreting the Equal Protection Clause, the Court has recognized that new insights and societal understandings can reveal unjustified inequality within our most fundamental institutions that once passed unnoticed and unchallenged. . . . [P]recedents show the Equal Protection Clause can help to identify and correct inequalities in the institution of marriage, vindicating precepts of liberty and equality under the Constitution.

This dynamic also applies to same-sex marriage. It is now clear that the challenged laws burden the liberty of same-sex couples, and it must be further acknowledged that they abridge central precepts of equality. Here the marriage laws enforced by the respondents are in essence unequal: same-sex couples are denied all the benefits afforded to opposite-sex couples and are barred from exercising a fundamental right. Especially against a long history of disapproval of their relationships, this denial to same-sex couples of the right to marry works a grave and continuing harm. The imposition of this disability on gays and lesbians serves to disrespect and subordinate them. And the Equal Protection Clause, like the Due Process Clause, prohibits this unjustified infringement of the fundamental right to marry.

These considerations lead to the conclusion that the right to marry is a fundamental right inherent in the liberty of the person, and under the Due Process and Equal Protection Clauses of the Fourteenth Amendment couples of the same-sex may not be deprived of that right and that liberty. The Court now holds that same-sex couples may exercise the fundamental right to marry. No longer may this liberty be denied to them . . . the State laws challenged by Petitioners in these cases are now held invalid to the extent they exclude same-sex couples from civil marriage on the same terms and conditions as opposite-sex couples.

[Justice Thomas, with whom Justice Scalia joins, dissent].The Court's decision today is at odds not only with the Constitution, but with the principles upon which our Nation was built. Since well before 1787, liberty has been understood as freedom from government action, not entitlement to government benefits. The Framers created our Constitution to preserve that understanding of liberty. Yet the majority invokes our Constitution in the name of a "liberty" that the Framers would not have recognized, to the detriment of the liberty they sought to protect. Along the way, it rejects the idea—captured in our Declaration of Independence—that human dignity is innate and suggests instead that it comes from the Government. This distortion of our Constitution not only ignores the text, it inverts the relationship between the individual and the state in our Republic. I cannot agree with it.

The majority's decision today will require States to issue marriage licenses to same-sex couples and to recognize same-sex marriages entered in other States largely based on a constitutional provision guaranteeing "due process" before a person is deprived of his "life, liberty, or property" . . . It distorts the constitutional text, which guarantees only whatever "process" is "due" before a person is deprived of life, liberty, and property . . . Worse, it invites judges to do exactly what the majority has done here—"'roa[m] at large in the constitutional field' guided only by their personal views" as to the "'fundamental rights'" protected by that document.

By straying from the text of the Constitution, substantive due process exalts judges at the expense of the People from whom they derive their authority. Petitioners argue that by enshrining the traditional definition of marriage in their State Constitutions through voter-approved amendments, the States have put the issue "beyond the reach of the normal democratic process." But the result petitioners seek is far less democratic. They ask nine judges on this Court to enshrine their definition of marriage in the Federal Constitution and thus put it beyond the reach of the normal democratic process for the entire Nation. That a "bare majority" of this Court is able to grant this wish, wiping out with a stroke of the keyboard the results of the political process in over 30 States, based on a provision that guarantees only "due process" is but further evidence of the danger of substantive due process.

As used in the Due Process Clauses, "liberty" most likely refers to "the power of loco-motion, of changing situation, or removing one's person to whatsoever place one's own inclination may direct; without imprisonment or restraint, unless by due course of law." 1 W. Blackstone, Commentaries on the Laws of England 130 (1769) (Blackstone). That definition is drawn from the historical roots of the Clauses and is consistent with our Constitution's text and structure.

. . . Petitioners cannot claim, under the most plausible definition of "liberty," that they have been imprisoned or physically restrained by the States for participating in same-sex relationships. To the contrary, they have been able to cohabitate and raise their children in peace. They have been able to hold civil marriage ceremonies in States that recognize same-sex marriages and private religious ceremonies in all States. They have been able to travel freely around the country, making their homes where they please. Far from being incarcerated or physically restrained, petitioners have been left alone to order their lives as they see fit.

Nor, under the broader definition, can they claim that the States have restricted their ability to go about their daily lives as they would be able to absent governmental restrictions. Petitioners do not ask this Court to order the States to stop restricting their ability to enter same-sex relationships, to engage in intimate behavior, to make vows to their partners in public ceremonies, to engage in religious wedding ceremonies, to hold themselves out as married, or to raise children. The States have imposed no such restrictions. Nor have the States prevented petitioners from approximating a number of incidents of marriage through private legal means, such as wills, trusts, and powers of attorney.

Instead, the States have refused to grant them governmental entitlements. Petitioners claim that as a matter of "liberty," they are entitled to access privileges and benefits that exist solely *because of* the government. They want, for example, to receive the State's *imprimatur* on their marriages—on state issued marriage licenses, death certificates, or other official forms. And they want to receive various monetary benefits, including reduced inheritance taxes upon the death of a spouse, compensation if a spouse dies as a result of a work-related injury, or loss of consortium damages in tort suits. But receiving governmental recognition and benefits has nothing to do with any understanding of "liberty" that the Framers would have recognized.

NOTES

1. *Barron v. Mayor & City Council of Baltimore, 32 U.S. 7 Pet. 243 243 (1833).*

2. *The Public Statues of the United States,* 18 vols (Boston: Little, Brown, and Co, 1847–1873 and Washington, D.C.: Government Printing Office, 1878–1936), 14: 27–30.

3. James D. Richardson, ed., *Compilations of the Messages and Papers of the Presidents,* 11 vols (Washington, D.C.: Government Printing Office, 1897, 1904), 6: 405–413.

4. Congressional Record, 84th Congress Second Session. *Vol. 102, part 4* (March 12, 1956) (Washington, D.C.: Governmental Printing Office, 1956), 4459–4460.

5. *Brown v. Board of Education of Topeka, 347 U.S. 483 (1957).*

6. *Public Papers of the Presidents: Dwight D. Eisenhowser, 1957* (Washington, D.C.: Government Printing Office, 1958), 689-694

7. *Cooper v. Aaron, 358 U.S. 1 (1958).*

8. http://digital.archives.alabama.gov/cdm/singleitem/collection/voices/id/2952/rec/5 accessed March 23, 2017.

9. *Heart of Atlanta Motel, Inc. v. United States, 379 U.S. 241 (1964).*

10. *Katzenbach v. McClung, 379 U.S. 294 (1964).*

11. *Griswold v. Connecticut, 381 U.S. 479 (1965).*

12. *Loving v. Virginia, 388 U.S. 1 (1967).*

13. *Roe v. Wade, 410 U.S. 113 (1973).*

14. *Planned Parenthood of Southeastern Pa. v. Casey 505 U.S. 833 (1992).*

15. *Obergefell v. Hodges 576 US ___ (2015).*

Part III

Commerce Clause

Editors' Note: The Commerce Clause is easy to identify. It is found in Article 1, Section 8, Clause 3 of the United States Constitution. The operative language states the federal government has the right "to regulate commerce with foreign nations, and among the several states, and with the Indian tribes." While the clause is easy to identify, its exact interpretation demonstrates an evolving nature.

A defining characteristic of the federal regime that was established with the Constitution was its positioning in commerce. Under previous political arrangements, this power never fell on a sole U.S. actor. Under the colonial system, the Crown dictated the larger boundaries and orientation of commerce in the Americas. With the War of Independence came a rejection of this centralization of commerce power. This era of decentralization was short lived as commerce power was gathered together with the ratification of the Constitution and centralized under the purview of Congress. The Commerce Clause developed into one of the strongest powers wielded by the federal government. It, however, was not always this straightforward.

In keeping with a punctuated equilibrium model, the development of the Commerce Clause is rather stable until a critical event or juncture occurs on the political landscape. Many of the developments of this aspect of federalism arise out of growth and complexity of the economy. The first document, the Supreme Court case of Gibbons v. Ogden, *sets the tone for the expanse of the Commerce Clause for well over 100 years. The author of this case, Chief Justice John Marshall, lays out in simple terms the federal preeminence in commerce that occurs outside and between state boundaries. Justice Marshall derives his opinion from his understanding of what the Founding Fathers intended for the field of play in commerce. His understanding placed the federal government in the driver's seat if you will. This overall impression would fluctuate someone over the next 100 years, however the peak of Commerce Clause power is reached with the case of* Wickard v Filburn. *On its face, the authority of an individual property and business owner to grow crops for their own consumption would not seem to create a situation ripe for the application of the Commerce Clause. The situation surrounding the case, however, was not so simple. The case occurs during World War II and in a context of a nation, and its industrial and farming might, fully engulfed in contributing to the arsenals of democracy. With this case, the net effect of wheat production on a handful of acres was not too small or protected from the reach of the federal government.*

If the ebb and flow of federalism is seen as a pendulum, as far as commerce was concerned there was no more swing, no more movement for 50 years. The Commerce Clause became one of the primary tools utilized by the government to legislate. At the turn of the last century, the Congressional use of the Commerce Clause was knocked back on its heels with the Lopez *and* Morrison *cases. The waters were quickly muddied with the* Gonzales v. Raich *case which allowed federal law to overrule state law. The coming years will likely reap a series of cases that more finely delineate the boundaries of federal commerce powers.*

GIBBONS v. OGDEN (1824)[1]

. . . [T]he enlightened patriots who framed our Constitution, and the people who adopted it, must be understood to have employed words in their natural sense, . . . "Congress shall have power to regulate commerce with foreign nations, and among the several States, and with the Indian tribes."

. . . Commerce, undoubtedly, is traffic, but it is something more: it is intercourse. It describes the commercial intercourse between nations, and parts of nations, in all its branches, and is regulated by prescribing rules for carrying on that intercourse. . . .

. . . The power over commerce, including navigation, was one of the primary objects for which the people of America adopted their government, and must have been contemplated in forming it. . . . The subject to which the power is next applied is to commerce "among the several States." The word "among" means intermingled with. . . . Commerce among the States cannot stop at the external boundary line of each State, but may be introduced into the interior. . . .

But, in regulating commerce with foreign nations, the power of Congress does not stop at the jurisdictional lines of the several States. It would be a very useless power if it could not pass those lines. . . .

It is the power to regulate, that is, to prescribe the rule by which commerce is to be governed. This power, like all others vested in Congress, is complete in itself, may be exercised to its utmost extent, and acknowledges no limitations other than are prescribed in the Constitution

. . . It is obvious that the government of the Union, in the exercise of its express powers—that, for example, of regulating commerce with foreign nations and among the States—may use means that may also be employed by a State in the exercise of its acknowledged powers—that, for example, of regulating commerce within the State.

The acknowledged power of a State to regulate its police, its domestic trade, and to govern its own citizens may enable it to legislate on this subject to a considerable extent, and the adoption of its system by Congress, and the application of it to the whole subject of commerce, does not seem to the Court to imply a right in the States so to apply it of their own authority. . . .

In one case and the other, the acts of New York must yield to the law of Congress, . . . [as] the framers of our Constitution foresaw this state of things, and provided for it by declaring the supremacy not only of itself, but of the laws made in pursuance of it. . . .

UNITED STATES v. E. C. KNIGHT CO. (1895)[2]

. . . "The object in purchasing the Philadelphia refineries was to obtain a greater influence or more perfect control over the business of refining and selling sugar in this country."

. . . The bill charged that the contracts under which these purchases were made constituted combinations in restraint of trade, and that in entering into them, the defendants combined and conspired to restrain the trade and commerce in refined sugar among the several states and with foreign nations, contrary to the Act of Congress of July 2, 1890.

. . . Commerce succeeds to manufacture, and is not a part of it. The power to regulate commerce is the power to prescribe the rule by which commerce shall be governed, and is a power independent of the power to suppress monopoly.

. . . The regulation of commerce applies to the subjects of commerce, and not to matters of internal police. Contracts to buy, sell, or exchange goods to be transported among the several states, the transportation and its instrumentalities, and articles bought, sold, or exchanged for the purposes of such transit among the states or put in the way of transit, may be regulated; but this is because they form part of interstate trade or commerce. The fact that an article is manufactured for export to another state does not, of itself, make it an article of interstate commerce, and the intent of the manufacturer does not determine the time when the article or product passes from the control of the state and belongs to commerce.

. . . Manufacture is transformation—the fashioning of raw materials into a change of form for use. The functions of commerce are different. The buying and selling, and the transportation incidental thereto, constitute commerce, and the regulation of commerce in the constitutional sense embraces the regulation at least of such transportation. . .

Contracts, combinations, or conspiracies to control domestic enterprise in manufacture, agriculture, mining, production in all its forms, or to raise or lower prices or wages might unquestionably tend to restrain external as well as domestic trade, but the restraint would be an indirect result, however inevitable, and whatever its extent, and such result would not necessarily determine the object of the contract, combination, or conspiracy.

. . . There was nothing in the proofs to indicate any intention to put a restraint upon trade or commerce, and the fact, as we have seen, that trade or commerce might be indirectly affected was not enough to entitle complainants to a decree. . . . [T]o grant the relief prayed, and dismissed the bill, and we are of opinion that the circuit court of appeals did not err in affirming that decree.

HAMMER v. DAGENHART (1918)[3]

. . . The controlling question for decision is: is it within the authority of Congress in regulating commerce among the States to prohibit the transportation in interstate commerce of manufactured goods, the product of a factory in which . . . children under the age of fourteen have been employed or permitted to work . . .

. . . The thing intended to be accomplished by this statute is the denial of the facilities of interstate commerce to those manufacturers in the States who employ children within the prohibited ages. The act, in its effect, does not regulate transportation among the States, but aims to standardize the ages at which children may be employed in mining and manufacturing within the States. . . . The making of goods and the mining of coal are not commerce, nor does the fact that these things are to be afterwards shipped or used in interstate commerce make their production a part thereof. . . . If it were otherwise, all manufacture intended for interstate shipment would be brought under federal control to the practical exclusion of the authority of the States. . . . In other words, that the unfair competition thus engendered may be controlled by closing the channels of interstate commerce to manufacturers in those States where the local laws do not meet what Congress deems to be the more just standard of other States.

. . . The Commerce Clause was not intended to give to Congress a general authority to equalize such conditions. . . . The grant of authority over a purely federal matter was not intended to destroy the local power always existing and carefully reserved to the States in the Tenth Amendment to the Constitution.

That there should be limitations upon the right to employ children in mines and factories in the interest of their own and the public welfare, all will admit. . . . The power of the States to regulate their purely internal affairs by such laws as seem wise to the local authority is inherent, and has never been surrendered to the general government.

To sustain this statute would not be, in our judgment, a recognition of the lawful exertion of congressional authority over interstate commerce, but would sanction an invasion by the federal power of the control of a matter purely local in its character, and over which no authority has been delegated to Congress in conferring the power to regulate commerce among the States.

. . . In our view, the necessary effect of this act is, by means of a prohibition against the movement in interstate commerce of ordinary commercial commodities, to regulate the hours of labor of children in factories and mines within the States, a purely state authority. Thus, the act in a two-fold sense is repugnant to the Constitution. It not only transcends the authority delegated to Congress over commerce, but also exerts a power as to a purely local matter to which the federal authority does not extend.

A. L. A. SCHECHTER POULTRY CORP. v. UNITED STATES (1935)[4]

. . . The "Live Poultry Code" was promulgated under the National Industrial Recovery Act. . . . [It] authorizes the President to approve "codes of fair competition." . . . Such codes "shall not permit monopolies or monopolistic practices." . . . The Code fixes the number of hours for workdays.

. . . Congress cannot delegate legislative power to the President to exercise an unfettered discretion to make whatever laws he thinks may be needed or advisable for the rehabilitation and expansion of trade or industry. . . . In view of the scope of that broad declaration, . . . the discretion of the President in approving or prescribing codes . . . is virtually unfettered. We think that the code-making authority this conferred is an unconstitutional delegation of legislative power.

. . . The undisputed facts thus afford no warrant for the argument that the poultry handled by defendants at their slaughterhouse markets was in a "*current*" or "*flow*" of interstate commerce, and was thus subject to congressional regulation. The mere fact that there may be a constant flow of commodities into a State does not mean that the flow continues after the property has arrived, and has become commingled with the mass of property within the State, and is there held solely for local disposition and use. So far as the poultry here in question is concerned, the flow in interstate commerce had ceased. . . . Hence, decisions which deal with a stream of interstate commerce—where goods come to rest within a State temporarily and are later to go forward in interstate commerce—and with the regulations of transactions involved in that practical continuity of movement, are not applicable here.

. . . In determining how far the federal government may go in controlling intrastate transactions upon the ground that they "affect" interstate commerce, there is a necessary and well established distinction between direct and indirect effects. The precise line can be drawn only as individual cases arise, but the distinction is clear in principle. . . . But where the effect of intrastate transactions upon interstate commerce is merely indirect, such transactions remain within the domain of state power.

. . . The persons employed in slaughtering and selling in local trade are not employed in interstate commerce. Their hours and wages have no direct relation to interstate commerce.

It is not the province of the Court to consider the economic advantages or disadvantage of such a centralized system. It is sufficient to say that the Federal Constitution does not provide for it.

On both the grounds we have discussed, the attempted delegation of legislative power, and the attempted regulation of intrastate transaction which affect interstate commerce only indirectly, we hold he code provisions here in question to be invalid and that the judgment of conviction must be reversed.

NLRB v. JONES & LAUGHLIN STEEL
CORP., 301 U.S. 1 (1937)[5]

In a proceeding under the National Labor Relations Act of 1935, . . . [t]he unfair labor practices charged were that the corporation was discriminating against members of the union with regard to hire and tenure of employment, and was coercing and intimidating its employees in order to interfere with their self-organization.

. . . The authority of the federal government may not be pushed to such an extreme as to destroy the distinction, which the commerce clause itself establishes, between commerce "among the several States" and the internal concerns of a State. That distinction between what is national and what is local in the activities of commerce is vital to the maintenance of our federal system.

Fully recognizing the legality of collective action on the part of employees in order to safeguard their proper interests, we said that Congress was not required to ignore this right, but could safeguard it.

. . . Undoubtedly the scope of this power must be considered in the light of our dual system of government, and may not be extended so as to embrace effects upon interstate commerce so indirect and remote that to embrace them, in view of our complex society, would effectually obliterate the distinction between what is national and what is local and create a completely centralized government

. . . The close and intimate effect which brings the subject within the reach of federal power may be due to activities in relation to productive industry although the industry, when separately viewed, is local. This has been abundantly illustrated in the application of the federal Anti-Trust Act.

When industries organize themselves on a national scale, making their relation to interstate commerce the dominant factor in their activities, how can it be maintained that their industrial labor relations constitute a forbidden field into which Congress may not enter when it is necessary to protect interstate commerce from the paralyzing consequences of industrial war? . . . Instead of being beyond the pale, we think that it presents in a most striking way the close and intimate relation which a manufacturing industry may have to interstate commerce, and we have no doubt that Congress had constitutional authority to safeguard the right of respondent's employees to self-organization and freedom in the choice of representatives for collective bargaining.

Our conclusion is that the order of the Board was within its competency, and that the Act is valid as here applied. The judgment of the Circuit Court of Appeals is reversed, and the cause is remanded for further proceedings in conformity with this opinion.

UNITED STATES v. DARBY (1941)[6]

. . . [Does] Congress has constitutional power to prohibit the shipment in interstate commerce of lumber manufactured by employees whose wages are less than a prescribed minimum or whose weekly hours of labor at that wage are greater than a prescribed maximum, and, second, whether it has power to prohibit the employment of workmen in the production of goods "for interstate commerce" at other than prescribed wages and hours. . . .

While manufacture is not, of itself, interstate commerce, the shipment of manufactured goods interstate is such commerce, and the prohibition of such shipment by Congress is indubitably a regulation of the commerce.

. . . The motive and purpose of the present regulation are plainly to make effective the Congressional conception of public policy that interstate commerce should not be made the instrument of competition in the distribution of goods produced under substandard labor conditions, which competition is injurious to the commerce and to the states from and to which the commerce flows.

. . . Whatever their motive and purpose, regulations of commerce which do not infringe some constitutional prohibition are within the plenary power conferred on Congress by the Commerce Clause. Subject only to that limitation, presently to be considered, we conclude that the prohibition of the shipment interstate of goods produced under the forbidden substandard labor conditions is within the constitutional authority of Congress.

. . . [I]n *Hammer v. Dagenhart*, . . . [t]he reasoning and conclusion of the Court's opinion there cannot be reconciled with the conclusion which we have reached . . .

. . . There remains the question whether such restriction on the production of goods for commerce is a permissible exercise of the commerce power. The power of Congress over interstate commerce is not confined to the regulation of commerce among the states. It extends to those activities intrastate which so affect interstate commerce or the exercise of the power of Congress over . . .

. . . In the absence of Congressional legislation on the subject, state laws which are not regulations of the commerce itself or its instrumentalities are not forbidden, even though they affect interstate commerce. But it does not follow that Congress may not, by appropriate legislation, regulate intrastate activities where they have a substantial effect on interstate commerce.

. . . A familiar like exercise of power is the regulation of intrastate transactions which are so commingled with or related to interstate commerce that all must be regulated if the interstate commerce is to be effectively controlled.

. . . Our conclusion is unaffected by the Tenth Amendment. The amendment states but a truism that all is retained which has not been surrendered. There is nothing in the history of its adoption to suggest that it was more than declaratory of the relationship between the national and state governments as it had been established by the Constitution before the amendment, or that its purpose was other than to allay fears that the new national government might seek to exercise powers not granted, and that the states might not be able to exercise fully their reserved powers.

WICKARD v. FILBURN (1942)[7]

. . . The appellee filed his complaint against the Secretary of Agriculture of the United States, . . . [and] sought to enjoin enforcement against himself of the marketing penalty imposed by . . . the Agricultural Adjustment Act of 1938, upon that part of his 1941 wheat crop which was available for marketing in excess of the marketing quota established for his farm. He also sought a declaratory judgment that the wheat marketing quota provisions of the Act were unconstitutional because not sustainable under the Commerce Clause or consistent with the Due Process Clause of the Fifth Amendment.

The appellee for many years past has owned and operated a small farm . . . [where it] . . . has been his practice to raise a small acreage of winter wheat . . . to sell a portion of the crop; to feed part to poultry and livestock on the farm, some of which is sold; to use some in making flour for home consumption, and to keep the rest for the following seeding. . . . the Agricultural Adjustment Act of 1938 . . . established for the appellee's 1941 crop a wheat acreage allotment of 11.1 acres . . . [h]e sowed, however, 23 acres . . .

The general scheme of the Agricultural Adjustment Act of 1938 as related to wheat is to control the volume moving in interstate and foreign commerce in order to avoid surpluses and shortages and the consequent abnormally low or high wheat prices and obstructions to commerce.

. . . Appellee says that this is a regulation of production and consumption of wheat. Such activities are, he urges, beyond the reach of . . . the Commerce Clause, since they are local in character. . . . [T]he Government argues that the statute regulates neither production nor consumption, but only marketing, and . . . is sustainable as a "necessary and proper" implementation of the power of Congress over interstate commerce.

. . . But even if appellee's activity be local, and though it may not be regarded as commerce, it may still, whatever its nature, be reached by Congress if it exerts a substantial economic effect on interstate commerce. . . . The effect of consumption of home-grown wheat on interstate commerce is due to the fact that it constitutes the most variable factor in the disappearance of the wheat crop. . . . That appellee's own contribution to the demand for wheat may be trivial by itself is not enough to remove him from the scope of federal regulation where, as here, his contribution, taken together with that of many others similarly situated, is far from trivial.

. . . Home-grown wheat in this sense competes with wheat in commerce. . . . Control of total supply, upon which the whole statutory plan is based, depends upon control of individual supply.

U.S. v. LOPEZ (1995)[8]

. . . We start with first principles. The Constitution creates a Federal Government of enumerated powers. As James Madison wrote: "The powers delegated by the proposed Constitution to the federal government are few and defined. Those which are to remain in the State governments are numerous and indefinite." This constitutionally mandated division of authority "was adopted by the Framers to ensure protection of our fundamental liberties." "Just as the separation and independence of the coordinate branches of the Federal Government serve to prevent the accumulation of excessive power in anyone branch, a healthy balance of power between the States and the Federal Government will reduce the risk of tyranny and abuse from either front."

The commerce power "is the power to regulate; that is, to prescribe the rule by which commerce is to be governed. This power, like all others vested in congress, is complete in itself, may be exercised to its utmost extent, and acknowledges no limitations, other than are prescribed in the constitution."

. . . Under our federal system, the "'States possess primary authority for defining and enforcing the criminal law.'" . . . When Congress criminalizes conduct already denounced as criminal by the States, it effects a "'change in the sensitive relation between federal and state criminal jurisdiction.

. . . In recognizing this fact we preserve one of the few principles that has been consistent since the Clause was adopted. The regulation and punishment of intrastate violence that is not directed at the instrumentalities, channels, or goods involved in interstate commerce has always been the province of the States.

UNITED STATES v. MORRISON (2000)[9]

In these cases we consider the constitutionality of . . . [Violence Against Women Act of 1994] which provides a federal civil remedy for the victims of gender-motivated violence.

. . . this Court has always recognized a limit on the commerce power inherent in "our dual system of government." . . . First, Congress may regulate the use of the channels of interstate commerce. Second, Congress is empowered to regulate and protect the instrumentalities of interstate commerce. . . . Finally, Congress' commerce authority includes the power to regulate those activities having a substantial relation to interstate commerce . . .

. . . But a fair reading of *Lopez* shows that the noneconomic, criminal nature of the conduct at issue was central to our decision in that case.

. . . Gender-motivated crimes of violence are not, in any sense of the phrase, economic activity. While we need not adopt a categorical rule against aggregating the effects of any noneconomic activity in order to decide these cases. . . . the existence of congressional findings is not sufficient, by itself, to sustain the constitutionality of Commerce Clause legislation.

. . . If accepted, petitioners' reasoning would allow Congress to regulate any crime as long as the nationwide, aggregated impact of that crime has substantial effects on employment, production, transit, or consumption. Indeed, if Congress may regulate gender motivated violence, it would be able to regulate murder or any other type of violence since gender-motivated violence, as a subset of all violent crime, is certain to have lesser economic impacts than the larger class of which it is a part.

. . . We accordingly reject the argument that Congress may regulate non-economic, violent criminal conduct based solely on that conduct's aggregate effect on interstate commerce

. . . The regulation and punishment of intrastate violence that is not directed at the instrumentalities, channels, or goods involved in interstate commerce has always been the province of the States. . . . With its careful enumeration of federal powers and explicit statement that all powers not granted to the Federal Government are reserved, the Constitution cannot realistically be interpreted as granting the Federal Government an unlimited license to regulate.

Affirmed.

GONZALES v. RAICH (2005)[10]

. . . The question presented in this case is whether the power vested in Congress . . . includes the power to prohibit the local cultivation and use of marijuana in compliance with California law. . . . Respondents . . . [are] seeking injunctive and declaratory relief prohibiting the enforcement of the federal Controlled Substances Act (CSA).

. . . The question before us, however, is not whether it is wise to enforce the statute in these circumstances; rather, it is whether Congress' power to regulate interstate markets for medicinal substances encompasses the portions of those markets that are supplied with drugs produced and consumed locally.

. . . The main objectives of the CSA were to conquer drug abuse and to control the legitimate and illegitimate traffic in controlled substances. Congress was particularly concerned with the need to prevent the diversion of drugs from legitimate to illicit channels.

. . . Like the farmer in *Wickard*, respondents are cultivating, for home consumption, a fungible commodity for which there is an established, albeit illegal, interstate market. . . . Here too, Congress had a rational basis for concluding that leaving home-consumed marijuana outside federal control would similarly affect price and market conditions.

. . . The parallel concern . . . is the likelihood that the high demand in the interstate market will draw such marijuana into that market. . . . [T]he diversion of homegrown marijuana tends to frustrate the federal interest in eliminating commercial transactions in the interstate market in their entirety.

In both cases, the regulation is squarely within Congress' commerce power because production of the commodity meant for home consumption, be it wheat or marijuana, has a substantial effect on supply and demand in the national market for that commodity.

. . . we have never required Congress to make particularized findings in order to legislate

. . . Given the enforcement difficulties that attend distinguishing between marijuana cultivated locally and marijuana grown elsewhere, . . . we have no difficulty concluding that Congress had a rational basis for believing that failure to regulate the intrastate manufacture and possession of marijuana would leave a gaping hole in the CSA.

. . . The Supremacy Clause unambiguously provides that if there is any conflict between federal and state law, federal law shall prevail.

. . . Under the present state of the law, however, the judgment of the Court of Appeals must be vacated.

NOTES

1. *Gibbons v. Ogden, 22 U.S. 9 Wheat. 1 1 (1824).*
2. *United States v. E. C. Knight Co., 156 U.S. 1 (1895).*
3. *Hammer v. Dagenhart, 247 U.S. 251 (1918).*
4. *A. L. A. Schechter Poultry Corp. v. United States, 295 U.S. 495 (1935).*
5. *NLRB v. Jones & Laughlin Steel Corp., 301 U.S. 1 (1937).*
6. *United States v. Darby, 312 U.S. 100 (1941).*
7. *Wickard v. Filburn, 317 U.S. 111 (1942).*
8. *United States v. Lopez 514 U.S. 549 (1995).*
9. *United States v. Morrison 529 U.S. 598 (2000).*
10. *Gonzales v. Raich 545 U.S. 1 (2005).*

Part IV

Incorporation Cases

Editors' Note: Arguably the most diverse substantive section of artifacts in this collection, falls under the heading of Incorporation. The documents run the gamut from free speech and protections against double jeopardy, to a right to armed self-defense and the protections of private property. While these documents are not strongly united in a particular substantive theme, they are threaded together in terms of their application, and intended target—citizenship. The central question pertains to what, if any, protections are granted to individual citizens via the U.S. Constitution. The extremes of the two schools of thought that govern this topic paint the picture that either none of the elements of the Bill of Rights apply to state governments, or all of these fundamental rights constrain both the federal and state governments.

A cursory view of the documents that follow illustrate the fact that, that like other notions in this volume, there is not a gradual rise having the upper hand in the balance of federalism. Its history is marked by relative calm that is punctuated by crisis which in turn brings change. The word incorporation is not found in the Constitution, nor was it explicitly used by the Founders to describe a process that was to come in the future. Over time, what did develop was more of a debate of whether the Bill of Rights reflected such fundamental elements of citizenship, that they were nonnegotiable regardless if it were state or national governments threatening infringement. This perspective is categorized as total incorporation. On the other hand, the doctrine of selective incorporation more closely reflects the actions of the Supreme Court in the modern era. That is, rights and protections from the Constitution are recognized as held by citizens in more of a step-wise fashion. Take for instance the case of Mcdonald v. Chicago. *Prior to this case, the Second Amendment protections of the "right of the people to keep and bear arms" only applied to the federal government. State governments could, and did, enact legislation that contravened the words and spirit of these protections. This case brought the last of the major Bill of Rights protections to bear against state governments. Notable exceptions that are still not incorporated are some of the various jury rights found in the Fifth, Sixth, and Seventh Amendments, and the no quartering of troops provision found in the Third Amendment. As most amendments are now viewed as inclusive of both state and federal governments, the ongoing debate of incorporation is likely drawing to a close.*

PREAMBLE TO THE BILL OF RIGHTS 1791

The Conventions of a number of the States having at the time of their adopting the Constitution, expressed a desire, in order to prevent misconstruction or abuse of its powers, that further declaratory and restrictive clauses should be added: And as extending the ground of public confidence in the Government, will best insure the beneficent ends of its institution

FIRST AMENDMENT

Gitlow v. People (1925)[1]

. . . The first charged that the defendant had advocated, advised and taught the duty, necessity and propriety of overthrowing and overturning organized government by force, violence and unlawful means, by certain writings therein set forth entitled "The Left Wing Manifesto . . .

There was no evidence of any effect resulting from the publication and circulation of the Manifesto.

. . . the intent, purpose and fair meaning of the Manifesto; that its words must be taken in their ordinary meaning, . . . that a mere statement that unlawful acts might accomplish such a purpose would be insufficient, unless there was a teaching, advising and advocacy of employing such unlawful acts for the purpose of overthrowing government . . .

. . . Manifesto . . . contemplate[d] the overthrow and destruction of the governments of the United States and of all the States, not by the free action of the majority of the people through the ballot box . . . but by immediately organizing the industrial proletariat into militant Socialist unions and at the earliest opportunity through mass strike and force and violence . . .

The Court of Appeals held that the Manifesto "advocated the overthrow of this government by violence, or by unlawful means." . . . it was said: . . . As we read this manifesto, we feel entirely clear that the jury were justified in rejecting the view that it was a mere academic and harmless discussion of the advantages of communism. . . . It is true that there is no advocacy in specific terms of the use of . . . force or violence . . .

. . . The sole contention here is, essentially, that as there was no evidence of any concrete result flowing from the publication of the Manifesto . . ., the statute as construed and applied by the trial court penalizes the mere utterance, as such, of "doctrine" having no quality of incitement, without regard . . . to the likelihood of unlawful sequences . . .

. . . The Manifesto, plainly . . . advocates and urges in fervent language mass action which shall progressively foment industrial disturbances and, through political mass strikes and revolutionary mass action, overthrow and destroy organized parliamentary government.

. . . For present purposes, we may and do assume that freedom of speech and of the press which are protected by the First Amendment from abridgment by Congress are among the fundamental personal rights and "liberties" protected by the due process clause of the Fourteenth Amendment from impairment by the States.

. . . It is a fundamental principle, long established, that the freedom of speech and of the press which is secured by the Constitution does not confer an absolute right to speak or publish, without responsibility, whatever one may choose, or an unrestricted and unbridled license that gives immunity for every possible use of language and prevents the punishment of those who abuse this freedom.

. . . That a State in the exercise of its police power may punish those who abuse this freedom by utterances inimical to the public welfare, tending to corrupt public morals, incite to crime, or disturb the public peace, is not open to question. . . .

. . . That utterances inciting to the overthrow of organized government by unlawful means present a sufficient danger of substantive evil to bring their punishment within the range of legislative discretion is clear. Such utterances, by their very nature, involve danger to the public peace and to the security of the State. . . . A single revolutionary spark may kindle a fire that, smouldering for a time, may burst into a sweeping and destructive conflagration. . . .

We cannot hold that the present statute is an arbitrary or unreasonable exercise of the police power of the State unwarrantably infringing the freedom of speech or press, and we must and do sustain its constitutionality.

. . . And finding, for the reasons stated, that the statute is not, in itself, unconstitutional, and that it has not been applied in the present case in derogation of any constitutional right, the judgment of the Court of Appeals is affirmed.

Near v. Minnesota (1931)[2]

... the County Attorney of Hennepin County brought this action to enjoin the publication of what was described as a "malicious, scandalous and defamatory newspaper, magazine and periodical" ... There is no question but that the articles made serious accusations against the public officers named and others in connection with the prevalence of crimes and the failure to expose and punish them.

... It is no longer open to doubt that the liberty of the press, and of speech, is within the liberty safeguarded by the due process clause of the Fourteenth Amendment from invasion by state action. It was found impossible to conclude that this essential personal liberty of the citizen was left unprotected by the general guaranty of fundamental rights of person and property. ... Liberty of speech, and of the press, is also not an absolute right, and the State may punish its abuse.

... It is apparent that, under the statute, the publication is to be regarded as defamatory if it injures reputation, ... The object of the statute is not punishment, in the ordinary sense, but suppression of the offending newspaper or periodical.

... unless the owner or publisher is able and disposed to bring competent evidence to satisfy the judge that the charges are true and are published with good motives and for justifiable ends, his newspaper or periodical is suppressed and further publication is made punishable as a contempt. This is of the essence of censorship.

... In determining the extent of the constitutional protection, it has been generally, if not universally, considered that it is the chief purpose of the guaranty to prevent previous restraints upon publication.

... The fact that, for approximately one hundred and fifty years, there has been almost an entire absence of attempts to impose previous restraints upon publications relating to the malfeasance of public officers is significant of the deep-seated conviction that such restraints would violate constitutional right. ... The general principle that the constitutional guaranty of the liberty of the press gives immunity from previous restraints has been approved in many decisions under the provisions of state constitutions. ... For these reasons we hold the statute, ... to be an infringement of the liberty of the press guaranteed by the Fourteenth Amendment.

[JUSTICE BUTLER, dissenting]. . . This Court should not reverse the judgment below upon the ground that, in some other case, the statute may be applied in a way that is repugnant to the freedom of the press protected by the Fourteenth Amendment.

The Act was passed in the exertion of the State's power of police, and this court is, by well established rule, required to assume, until the contrary is clearly made to appear, that there exists in Minnesota a state of affairs that justifies this measure for the preservation of the peace and good order of the State.

It is of the greatest importance that the States shall be untrammeled and free to employ all just and appropriate measures to prevent abuses of the liberty of the press.

DeJonge v. Oregon (1937)[3]

. . . The charge is that appellant assisted in the conduct of a meeting which was called under the auspices of the Communist Party, an organization advocating criminal syndicalism. The defense was . . . that, while it was held under the auspices of the Communist Party, neither criminal syndicalism nor any unlawful conduct was taught or advocated at the meeting, either by appellant or by others.

. . . His sole offense as charged, and for which he was convicted and sentenced to imprisonment for seven years, was that he had assisted in the conduct of a public meeting, albeit otherwise lawful, which was held under the auspices of the Communist Party . . . However innocuous the object of the meeting, however lawful the subjects and tenor of the addresses, however reasonable and timely the discussion, all those assisting in the conduct of the meeting would be subject to imprisonment as felons if the meeting were held by the Communist Party. . . .

While the States are entitled to protect themselves from the abuse of the privileges of our institutions through an attempted substitution of force and violence in the place of peaceful political action in order to effect revolutionary changes in government, none of our decisions goes to the length of sustaining such a curtailment of the right of free speech and assembly as the Oregon statute demands in its present application . . . The right of peaceable assembly is a right cognate to those of free speech and free press, and is equally fundamental.

. . . The First Amendment of the Federal Constitution expressly guarantees that right against abridgment by Congress. But explicit mention there does not argue exclusion elsewhere. For the right is one that cannot be denied without violating those fundamental principles of liberty and justice which lie at the base of all civil and political institutions—principles which the Fourteenth Amendment embodies in the general terms of its due process clause. . . .

. . . We hold that the Oregon statute, as applied to the particular charge as defined by the state court, is repugnant to the due process clause of the Fourteenth Amendment.

Everson v. Board of Education (1947)[4]

A New Jersey statute authorizes its local school districts to make rules and contracts for the transportation of children to and from schools . . . this money was for the payment of transportation of some children in the community to Catholic parochial schools. These church schools give their students, in addition to secular education, regular religious instruction conforming to the religious tenets and modes of worship of the Catholic Faith. . . .

. . . It is much too late to argue that legislation intended to facilitate the opportunity of children to get a secular education serves no public purpose.

. . . Prior to the adoption of the Fourteenth Amendment, the First Amendment did not apply as a restraint against the states . . . The "establishment of religion" clause of the First Amendment means at least this: neither a state nor the Federal Government can set up a church. Neither can pass laws which aid one religion, aid all religions, or prefer one religion over another.

. . . New Jersey cannot hamper its citizens in the free exercise of their own religion. Consequently, it cannot exclude individual Catholics, Lutherans, Mohammedans, Baptists, Jews, Methodists, Nonbelievers, Presbyterians, or the members of any other faith, *because of their faith, or lack of it,* from receiving the benefits of public welfare legislation . . . in protecting the citizens of New Jersey against state-established churches, to be sure that we do not inadvertently prohibit New Jersey from extending its general state law benefits to all its citizens without regard to their religious belief.

Measured by these standards, we cannot say that the First Amendment prohibits New Jersey from spending tax-raised funds to pay the bus fares of parochial school pupils as a part of a general program . . . Moreover, state-paid policemen, detailed to protect children going to and from church schools from the very real hazards of traffic, would serve much the same purpose and accomplish much the same result as state provisions intended to guarantee free transportation of a kind which the state deems to be best for the school children's welfare.

. . . the First Amendment . . . requires the state to be a neutral in its relations with groups of religious believers and nonbelievers; it does not require the state to be their adversary. State power is no more to be used so as to handicap religions than it is to favor them.

. . . The First Amendment has erected a wall between church and state. That wall must be kept high and impregnable. We could not approve the slightest breach. New Jersey has not breached it here.

[JUSTICE JACKSON, dissenting] . . . before these school authorities draw a check to reimburse for a student's fare, they must ask just that question, and, if the school is a Catholic one, they may render aid because it is such, while if it is of any other faith or is run for profit, the help must be withheld

. . . it cannot make public business of religious worship or instruction, or of attendance at religious institutions of any character.

Religious teaching cannot be a private affair when the state seeks to impose regulations which infringe on it indirectly, and a public affair when it comes to taxing citizens of one faith to aid another, or those of no faith to aid all.

Edwards v. South Carolina (1963)[5]

. . . The petitioners, 187 in number, were convicted in a magistrate's court in Columbia, South Carolina, of the common law crime of breach of the peace. . . . We granted certiorari, . . . to consider the claim that these convictions cannot be squared with the Fourteenth Amendment of the United States Constitution.

There was no substantial conflict in the trial evidence . . . Late in the morning of March 2, 1961, the petitioners, high school and college students of the Negro race, met at the Zion Baptist Church in Columbia. From there, at about noon, they walked in separate groups of about 15 to the South Carolina State House grounds, an area of two city blocks open to the general public. Their purpose was "to submit a protest to the citizens of South Carolina, along with the Legislative Bodies of South Carolina, our feelings and our dissatisfaction with the present condition of discriminatory actions against Negroes in general, and to let them know that we were dissatisfied, and that we would like for the laws which prohibited Negro privileges in this State to be removed."

. . . and no evidence at all of any threatening remarks, hostile gestures, or offensive language on the part of any member of the crowd . . . There was no obstruction of pedestrian or vehicular traffic within the State House grounds.

In the situation and under the circumstances thus described, the police authorities advised the petitioners that they would be arrested if they did not disperse within 15 minutes . . . Instead of dispersing, the petitioners engaged in . . . loudly singing "The Star Spangled Banner" and other patriotic and religious songs, while stamping their feet and clapping their hands. After 15 minutes had passed, the police arrested the petitioners and marched them off to jail.

. . . the Supreme Court of South Carolina said that . . . "In general terms, a breach of the peace is a violation of public order, a disturbance of the public tranquility, by any act or conduct inciting to violence . . . Nor is actual personal violence an essential element in the offense" . . .

It has long been established that these First Amendment freedoms are protected by the Fourteenth Amendment from invasion by the States . . . The circumstances in this case reflect an exercise of these basic constitutional rights in their most pristine and classic form . . .

These petitioners were convicted of an offense so generalized as to be, in the words of the South Carolina Supreme Court, "not susceptible of exact definition." And they were convicted upon evidence which showed no more than that the opinions which they were peaceably expressing were sufficiently opposed to the views of the majority of the community to attract a crowd and necessitate police protection.

The Fourteenth Amendment does not permit a State to make criminal the peaceful expression of unpopular views.

. . . "The maintenance of the opportunity for free political discussion to the end that government may be responsive to the will of the people and that changes may be obtained by lawful means, an opportunity essential to the security of the Republic, is a fundamental principle of our constitutional system. A statute which, upon its face and as authoritatively construed, is so vague and indefinite as to permit the punishment of the fair use of this opportunity is repugnant to the guaranty of liberty contained in the Fourteenth Amendment."

For these reasons, we conclude that these criminal convictions cannot stand.

[JUSTICE CLARK, dissenting] . . . The priceless character of First Amendment freedoms cannot be gainsaid, but it does not follow that they are absolutes immune from necessary state action reasonably designed for the protection of society . . . For that reason, it is our duty to consider the context in which the arrests here were made. Certainly the city officials would be constitutionally prohibited from refusing petitioners access to the State House grounds merely because they disagreed with their views.

It was only after the large crowd had gathered, among which the City Manager and Chief of Police recognized potential troublemakers, and which, together with the students, had become massed on and around the "horseshoe" so closely that vehicular and pedestrian traffic was materially impeded, . . . that any action against the petitioners was taken . . . The question thus seems to me whether a State is constitutionally prohibited from enforcing laws to prevent breach of the peace in a situation where city officials in good faith believe, and the record shows, that disorder and violence are imminent, merely because the activities constituting that breach contain claimed elements of constitutionally protected speech and assembly. To me, the answer under our cases is clearly in the negative.

SECOND AMENDMENT

Joseph Story, *Commentaries on the Constitution (1833)*[6]

The next amendment is: "A well regulated militia being necessary to the security of a free state, the right of the people to keep and bear arms shall not be infringed."

The importance of this article will scarcely be doubted by any persons, who have duly reflected upon the subject. The militia is the natural defense of a free country against sudden foreign invasions, domestic insurrections, and domestic usurpations of power by rulers. It is against sound policy for a free people to keep up large military establishments and standing armies in time of peace, both from the enormous expenses, with which they are attended, and the facile means, which they afford to ambitious and unprincipled rulers, to subvert the government, or trample upon the rights of the people. The right of the citizens to keep and bear arms has justly been considered, as the palladium of the liberties of a republic; since it offers a strong moral check against the usurpation and arbitrary power of rulers; and will generally, even if these are successful in the first instance, enable the people to resist and triumph over them. And yet, though this truth would seem so clear, and the importance of a well regulated militia would seem so undeniable, it cannot be disguised, that among the American people there is a growing indifference to any system of militia discipline, and a strong disposition, from a sense of its burthens, to be rid of all regulations. How it is practicable to keep the people duly armed without some organization, it is difficult to see. There is certainly no small danger, that indifference may lead to disgust, and disgust to contempt; and thus gradually undermine all the protection intended by this clause of our national bill of rights.

United States v. Cruikshank, (1875)[7]

. . . We have in our political system a government of the United States and a government of each of the several States. Each one of these governments is distinct from the others, and each has citizens of its own who owe it allegiance and whose rights, within its jurisdiction, it must protect. The same person may be at the same time a citizen of the United States and a citizen of a State, but his rights of citizenship under one of these governments will be different from those he has under the other . . .

The people of the United States resident within any State are subject to two governments—one State and the other National—but there need be no conflict between the two. . . . They are established for different purposes, and have separate jurisdictions. . . . True, it may sometimes happen that a person is amenable to both jurisdictions for one and the same act . . . It is the natural consequence of a citizenship which owes allegiance to two sovereignties and claims protection from both.

The Government of the United States is one of delegated powers alone. Its authority is defined and limited by the Constitution. All powers not granted to it by that instrument are reserved to the States or the people . . .

The right of the people peaceably to assemble for lawful purposes existed long before the adoption of the Constitution of the United States. In fact, it is, and always has been, one of the attributes of citizenship under a free government. It "derives its source," to use the language of Chief Justice Marshall in *Gibbons v. Ogden,* . . . "from those laws whose authority is acknowledged by civilized man throughout the world." It is found wherever civilization exists. It was not, therefore, a right granted to the people by the Constitution.

Only such existing rights were committed by the people to the protection of Congress as came within the general scope of the authority granted to the national government.

The first amendment . . . was not intended to limit the powers of the State governments in respect to their own citizens, but to operate upon the National Government alone. . . .

The particular amendment now under consideration assumes the existence of the right of the people to assemble for lawful purposes, and protects it against encroachment by Congress. The right was not created by the amendment; neither was its continuance guaranteed, except as against congressional interference. For their protection in its enjoyment, therefore, the people must look to the States.

The right of the people peaceably to assemble for the purpose of petitioning Congress for a redress of grievances, or for any thing else connected with the powers or the duties of the national government, is an attribute of national citizenship, and, as such, under the protection of, and guaranteed by, the United States. The very idea of a government republican in form implies a right on the part of its citizens to meet peaceably for consultation in respect to public affairs and to petition for a redress of grievances. If it had been alleged in these counts that the object of the defendants was to prevent a meeting for such a purpose, the case would have been within the statute, and within the scope of the sovereignty of the United States. Such, however, is not the case. The offence, as stated in the indictment, will be made out, if it be shown that the object of the conspiracy was to prevent a meeting for any lawful purpose whatever.

The second and tenth counts are equally defective. The right there specified is that of "bearing arms for a lawful purpose." This is not a right granted by the Constitution. Neither is it in any manner dependent upon that instrument for its existence. The second amendment declares that it shall not be infringed, but this, as has been seen, means no more than that it shall not be infringed by Congress. This is one of the amendments that has no other effect than to restrict the powers of the national government, . . .

The very highest duty of the States, when they entered into the Union under the Constitution, was to protect all persons within their boundaries in the enjoyment of these "unalienable rights with which they were endowed by their Creator." Sovereignty, for this purpose, rests alone with the States. . . .

The Fourteenth Amendment prohibits a State from depriving any person of life, liberty, or property without due process of law, but this adds nothing to the rights of one citizen as against another. It simply furnishes an additional guaranty against any encroachment by the States upon the fundamental rights which belong to every citizen as a member of society.

The fourth and twelfth counts charge the intent to have been to prevent and hinder the citizens named, who were of African descent and persons of color, in "the free exercise and enjoyment of their several right and privilege to the full and equal benefit of all laws and proceedings, then and there, before that time, enacted or ordained by the said State of Louisiana and by the United States, and then and there, at that time, being in force in the said State and District of Louisiana aforesaid, for the security of their respective persons and property, then and there, at that time enjoyed at and within said State and District of Louisiana by white persons, being citizens of said State of Louisiana and the United States, for the protection of the persons and property of said white citizens."

There is no allegation that this was done because of the race or color of the persons conspired against. When stripped of its verbiage, the case as presented amounts to nothing more than that the defendants conspired to prevent certain citizens of the United States, being within the State of Louisiana, from enjoying the equal protection of the laws of the State and of the United States.

The Fourteenth Amendment prohibits a State from denying to any person within its jurisdiction the equal protection of the laws; but this provision does not, any more than the one which precedes it, and which we have just considered, add anything to the rights which one citizen has under the Constitution against another. The equality of the rights of citizens is a principle of republicanism. Every republican government is in duty bound to protect all its citizens in the enjoyment of this principle, if within its power. That duty was originally assumed by the States, and it still remains there. The only obligation resting upon the United States is to see that the States do not deny the right. This the amendment guarantees, but no more. The power of the national government is limited to the enforcement of this guaranty.

The sixth and fourteenth counts state the intent of the defendants to have been to hinder and prevent the citizens named, being of African descent, and colored, . . . [the] right and privilege to vote. . . . In *Minor v. Happersett,* . . . we decided that the Constitution of the United States has not conferred the right of suffrage upon anyone, and that the United States have no voters of their own creation in the States. . . . From this, it appears that the right of suffrage is not a necessary attribute of national citizenship, but that exemption from discrimination in the exercise of that right on account of race, &c., is. The right to vote in the States comes from the States, but the right of exemption from the prohibited discrimination comes from the United States. . . .

Inasmuch, therefore, as it does not appear in these counts that the intent of the defendants was to prevent these parties from exercising their right to vote.

Presser v. Illinois (1886)[8]

. . . We think it clear that the sections under consideration, which only forbid bodies of men to associate together as military organizations, or to drill or parade with arms in cities and towns unless authorized by law, do not infringe the right of the people to keep and bear arms. But a conclusive answer to the contention that this amendment prohibits the legislation in question lies in the fact that the amendment is a limitation only upon the power of Congress and the national government, and not upon that of the state. . . .

It is undoubtedly true that all citizens capable of bearing arms constitute the reserved military force or reserve militia of the United States as well as of the states, and, . . . the states cannot, . . . prohibit the people from keeping and bearing arms so as to deprive the United States of their rightful resource for maintaining the public security.

. . . The plaintiff in error next insists that the sections of the Military Code of Illinois under which he was indicted are an invasion of that clause of the first section of the Fourteenth Amendment . . . It is only the privileges and immunities of citizens of the United States that the clause relied on was intended to protect. A state may pass laws to regulate the privileges and immunities of its own citizens, provided that in so doing it does not abridge their privileges and immunities as citizens of the United States . . . The only clause in the Constitution which upon any pretense could be said to have any relation whatever to his right to associate with others as a military company is found in the First Amendment.

. . . This is a right which . . . [is] an attribute of national citizenship, and, as such, under the protection of and guaranteed by the United States. But . . . the right peaceably to assemble was not protected by the clause referred to unless the purpose of the assembly was to petition the government for a redress of grievances.

The right voluntarily to associate together as a military company or organization or to drill or parade with arms without and independent of an act of Congress or law of the state authorizing the same is not an attribute of national citizenship . . . state governments, . . . have the power to regulate or prohibit associations and meetings of the people . . . and have also the power to control and regulate the organization, drilling, and parading of military bodies and associations, . . . The exercise of this power by the states is necessary to the public peace, safety, and good order. To deny the power would be to deny the right of the state to disperse assemblages organized for sedition and treason, and the right to suppress armed mobs bent on riot and rapine.

In respect to these points, we have to say that they present no federal question. It is not, therefore, our province to consider or decide them.

Hamilton v. Regents of University of California (1934)[9]

This is an appeal . . . from a judgment of the highest court of California sustaining a state law that requires students at its University to take a course in military science and tactics, the validity of which was by the appellants challenged as repugnant to the Constitution and laws of the United States.

. . . The primary object of there establishing units of the training corps is to qualify students for appointment in the Officers Reserve Corps. . . . These minors . . . petition the United States government to grant exemption from military service to such citizens who are members of the Methodist Episcopal Church as conscientiously believe that participation in war is a denial of their supreme allegiance to Jesus Christ.

. . . because of their religious and conscientious objections, they declined to take the prescribed course, and . . . [were] suspended . . . from the University.

. . . The state court, [at] a rehearing . . . deny[ed] the application, handed down an opinion in which it held that . . . military tactics is expressly required to be included among the subjects which shall be taught at the University, and that it is the duty of the regents to prescribe the nature and extent of the courses to be given.

. . . By their assignment of errors, appellants call upon this Court to decide whether the challenged provisions of the state Constitution, organic act, and regents' order, insofar as they impose compulsory military training, are repugnant to the privileges and immunities clause of the Fourteenth Amendment, the due process clause of that amendment, or the treaty that is generally called the Briand-Kellogg Peace Pact.

. . . We take judicial notice of the long established voluntary cooperation between federal and state authorities in respect of the military instruction given in the land grant colleges.

. . . Undoubtedly every state has authority to train its able-bodied male citizens . . . to serve in the United States Army or in state militia . . . So long as its action is within retained powers and not inconsistent with any exertion of the authority of the national government and transgresses no right safeguarded to the citizen by the Federal Constitution.

. . . The "privileges and immunities" protected are only those that belong to citizens of the United States, as distinguished from citizens of the states . . . The privilege of the native-born conscientious objector to avoid bearing arms comes not from the Constitution, but from the acts of Congress.

. . . Plainly there is no ground for the contention that the regents' order, requiring able-bodied male students under the age of twenty-four as a condition of their enrollment to take the prescribed instruction in military science and tactics, transgresses any constitutional right asserted by these appellants.

United States v. Miller (1939)[10]

. . . feloniously transport in interstate commerce . . . a certain firearm, to-wit, a double barrel 12-gauge Stevens shotgun having a barrel less than 18 inches in length, . . . transporting said firearm in interstate commerce as aforesaid, not having registered . . . under authority of the said Act of Congress known as the National Firearms Act.

A duly interposed demurrer alleged: the National Firearms Act is not a revenue measure, but an attempt to usurp police power reserved to the States, and is therefore unconstitutional.

Also, it offends the inhibition of the Second Amendment to the Constitution . . .

The District Court held that section eleven of the Act violates the Second Amendment. It accordingly sustained the demurrer and quashed the indictment.

In the absence of any evidence tending to show that possession or use of a "shotgun having a barrel of less than eighteen inches in length" at this time has some reasonable relationship to the preservation or efficiency of a well regulated militia, we cannot say that the Second Amendment guarantees the right to keep and bear such an instrument. Certainly it is not within judicial notice that this weapon is any part of the ordinary military equipment, or that its use could contribute to the common defense.

. . . The Militia which the States were expected to maintain and train is set in contrast with Troops which they were forbidden to keep without the consent of Congress. The sentiment of the time strongly disfavored standing armies; the common view was that adequate defense of country and laws could be secured through the Militia—civilians primarily, soldiers on occasion

. . . the Militia comprised . . . "A body of citizens enrolled for military discipline." And . . . these men were expected to appear bearing arms supplied by themselves and of the kind in common use at the time . . . "In all the colonies, as in England, the militia system was based on the principle of the assize of arms. This implied the general obligation of all adult male inhabitants to possess arms, and, with certain exceptions, to cooperate in the work of defense."

. . . Most if not all of the States have adopted provisions touching the right to keep and bear arms. Differences in the language employed in these have naturally led to somewhat variant conclusions concerning the scope of the right guaranteed. But none of them seems to afford any material support for the challenged ruling of the court below.

We are unable to accept the conclusion of the court below, and the challenged judgment must be reversed.

McDonald v. Chicago (2010)[11]

Two years ago, in *District of Columbia* v. *Heller*, . . . (2008), we held that the Second Amendment protects the right to keep and bear arms for the purpose of self-defense, and we struck down a District of Columbia law that banned the possession of handguns in the home. The city of Chicago (City) . . . argue that their laws are constitutional because the Second Amendment has no application to the States . . . Applying the standard that is well established in our case law, we hold that the Second Amendment right is fully applicable to the States.

. . . Chicago enacted its handgun ban to protect its residents "from the loss of property and injury or death from firearms" . . . The Chicago petitioners and their *amici*, however, argue that the handgun ban has left them vulnerable to criminals.

. . . Petitioners' primary submission is that this right is among the "privileges or immunities of citizens of the United States" and that the narrow interpretation of the Privileges or Immunities Clause adopted in the *Slaughter-House Cases*, *supra*, should now be rejected. As a secondary argument, petitioners contend that the Fourteenth Amendment's Due Process Clause "incorporates" the Second Amendment right.

. . . The *Slaughter-House Cases*, . . . concluded that the Privileges or Immunities Clause protects only those rights "which owe their existence to the Federal government, its National character, its Constitution, or its laws" . . . In drawing a sharp distinction between the rights of federal and state citizenship . . . We therefore decline to disturb the *Slaughter-House* holding.

At the same time, however, this Court's decisions in *Cruikshank*, *Presser*, and *Miller* do not preclude us from considering whether the Due Process Clause of the Fourteenth Amendment makes the Second Amendment right binding on the States.

. . . The Court used different formulations in describing the boundaries of due process . . . In *Snyder* v. *Massachusetts*, (1934), the Court spoke of rights that are "so rooted in the traditions and conscience of our people as to be ranked as fundamental." And in *Palko*, the Court famously said that due process protects those rights that are "the very essence of a scheme of ordered liberty" and essential to "a fair and enlightened system of justice." . . .

With this framework in mind, we now turn directly to the question whether the Second Amendment right to keep and bear arms is incorporated in the concept of due process. In answering that question, as just explained, we must decide whether the right to keep and bear arms is fundamental to *our* scheme of ordered liberty . . . or as we have said in a related context, whether this right is "deeply rooted in this Nation's history and tradition" . . .

Our decision in *Heller* points unmistakably to the answer. Self-defense is a basic right, recognized by many legal systems from ancient times to the present day, and in *Heller,* we held that individual self-defense is "the *central component*" of the Second Amendment right . . . Explaining that "the need for defense of self, family, and property is most acute" in the home, we found that this right applies to handguns because they are "the most preferred firearm in the nation to 'keep' and use for protection of one's home and family," . . . Thus, we concluded, citizens must be permitted "to use [handguns] for the core lawful purpose of self-defense."

. . . *Heller* makes it clear that this right is "deeply rooted in this Nation's history and tradition" . . . *Heller* explored the right's origins, noting that the 1689 English Bill of Rights explicitly protected a right to keep arms for self-defense, . . . and that by 1765, Blackstone was able to assert that the right to keep and bear arms was "one of the fundamental rights of Englishmen[.]"

Blackstone's assessment was shared by the American colonists. As we noted in *Heller*, King George III's attempt to disarm the colonists in the 1760's and 1770's "provoked polemical reactions by Americans invoking their rights as Englishmen to keep arms" . . . The right to keep and bear arms was considered no less fundamental by those who drafted and ratified the Bill of Rights. "During the 1788 ratification debates, the fear that the federal government would disarm the people in order to impose rule through a standing army or select militia was pervasive in Antifederalist rhetoric" . . . Federalists responded, not by arguing that the right was insufficiently important to warrant protection but by contending that the right was adequately protected by the Constitution's assignment of only limited powers to the Federal Government. . . . Thus, Antifederalists and Federalists alike agreed that the right to bear arms was fundamental to the newly formed system of government . . . But those who were fearful that the new Federal Government would infringe traditional rights such as the right to keep and bear arms insisted on the adoption of the Bill of Rights as a condition for ratification of the Constitution . . . In addition to the four States that had adopted Second Amendment analogues before ratification, nine more States adopted state constitutional provisions protecting an individual right to keep and bear arms between 1789 and 1820 . . . Founding-era legal commentators confirmed the importance of the right to early Americans. St. George Tucker, for example, described the right to keep and bear arms as "the true palladium of liberty" and explained that prohibitions on the right would place liberty "on the brink of destruction." . . .

After the Civil War, . . . armed parties, often consisting of ex-Confederate soldiers serving in the state militias, forcibly took firearms from newly freed slaves.

. . . Union Army commanders took steps to secure the right of all citizens to keep and bear arms, . . . but the 39th Congress concluded that legislative action was necessary. Its efforts to safeguard the right to keep and bear arms demonstrate that the right was still recognized to be fundamental.

The most explicit evidence of Congress' aim appears in §14 of the Freedmen's Bureau Act of 1866, which provided that "the right . . . to have full and equal benefit of all laws and proceedings concerning personal liberty, personal security, . . . *including the constitutional right to bear arms*, shall be secured to and enjoyed by all the citizens . . . without respect to race or color, or previous condition of slavery" . . . thus explicitly guaranteed that "all the citizens," black and white, would have "the constitutional right to bear arms."

The Civil Rights Act of 1866 . . . which was considered at the same time as the Freedmen's Bureau Act, similarly sought to protect the right of all citizens to keep and bear arms . . . The unavoidable conclusion is that the Civil Rights Act, like the Freedmen's Bureau Act, aimed to protect "the constitutional right to bear arms" and not simply to prohibit discrimination.

. . . Today, it is generally accepted that the Fourteenth Amendment was understood to provide a constitutional basis for protecting the rights set out in the Civil Rights Act of 1866. . . .

In debating the Fourteenth Amendment, the 39th Congress referred to the right to keep and bear arms as a fundamental right deserving of protection. Senator Samuel Pomeroy described three "indispensable" "safeguards of liberty under our form of Government." . . . Evidence from the period immediately following the ratification of the Fourteenth Amendment only confirms that the right to keep and bear arms was considered fundamental.

. . . The right to keep and bear arms was also widely protected by state constitutions at the time when the Fourteenth Amendment was ratified . . . A clear majority of the States in 1868, therefore, recognized the right to keep and bear arms as being among the foundational rights necessary to our system of Government.

. . . Municipal respondents, in effect, ask us to treat the right recognized in *Heller* as a second-class right, subject to an entirely different body of rules than the other Bill of Rights guarantees that we have held to be incorporated into the Due Process Clause.

. . . There is nothing new in the argument that, in order to respect federalism and allow useful state experimentation, a federal constitutional right should not be fully binding on the States. . . . Under our precedents, if a Bill of Rights guarantee is fundamental from an American perspective, then, . . . that guarantee is fully binding on the States and thus *limits* (but by no means eliminates) their ability to devise solutions to social problems that suit local needs and values . . .

As evidence that the Fourteenth Amendment has not historically been understood to restrict the authority of the States to regulate firearms . . . It is important to keep in mind that *Heller*, while striking down a law that prohibited the possession of handguns in the home, recognized that the right to keep and bear arms is not "a right to keep and carry any weapon whatsoever in any manner whatsoever and for whatever purpose" . . . We made it clear in *Heller* that our holding did not cast doubt on such longstanding regulatory measures as "prohibitions on the possession of firearms by felons and the mentally ill," "laws forbidding the carrying of firearms in sensitive places such as schools and government buildings, or laws imposing conditions and qualifications on the commercial sale of arms."

In *Heller*, we held that the Second Amendment protects the right to possess a handgun in the home for the purpose of self-defense. Unless considerations of *stare decisis* counsel otherwise, a provision of the Bill of Rights that protects a right that is fundamental from an American perspective applies equally to the Federal Government and the States. . . . We therefore hold that the Due Process Clause of the Fourteenth Amendment incorporates the Second Amendment right recognized in *Heller*. The judgment of the Court of Appeals is reversed, and the case is remanded for further proceedings.

[Justice Thomas, concurring in part and concurring in the judgment] I agree with the Court that the Fourteenth Amendment makes the right to keep and bear arms set forth in the Second Amendment "fully applicable to the States" . . . I write separately because I believe there is a more straightforward path to this conclusion through the Fourteenth Amendment's Privileges or Immunities Clause . . . As a consequence of this Court's marginalization of the Clause, litigants seeking federal protection of fundamental rights turned to the remainder of . . . that section's command that every State guarantee "due process" to any person before depriving him of "life, liberty, or property."

. . . The notion that a constitutional provision that guarantees only "process" before a person is deprived of life, liberty, or property could define the substance of those rights strains credulity for even the most casual user of words. Moreover, this fiction is a particularly dangerous one . . . This Court's substantive due process framework fails to account for both the text of the Fourteenth Amendment and the history that led to its adoption, filling that gap with a jurisprudence devoid of a guiding principle. I believe the original meaning of the Fourteenth Amendment offers a superior alternative.

Thus, the objective of this inquiry is to discern what "ordinary citizens" at the time of ratification would have understood the Privileges or Immunities Clause to mean . . . At the time of Reconstruction, the terms "privileges" and "immunities" had an established meaning as synonyms for "rights." The two words, standing alone or paired together, were used interchangeably with the words "rights," "liberties," and "freedoms," and had been since the time of Blackstone . . . A number of antebellum judicial decisions used the terms in this manner. . . .

The fact that a particular interest was designated as a "privilege" or "immunity," rather than a "right," "liberty," or "freedom," revealed little about its substance. Blackstone, for example, used the terms "privileges" and "immunities" to describe both the inalienable rights of individuals and the positive-law rights of corporations.

The group of rights-bearers to whom the Privileges or Immunities Clause applies is, of course, "citizens." By the time of Reconstruction, it had long been established that both the States and the Federal Government existed to preserve their citizens' inalienable rights, and that these rights were considered "privileges" or "immunities" of citizenship.

This tradition begins with our country's English roots . . . As English subjects, the colonists considered themselves to be vested with the same fundamental rights as other Englishmen. They consistently claimed the rights of English citizenship in their founding documents, repeatedly referring to these rights as "privileges" and "immunities."

. . . Even though the Bill of Rights did not apply to the States, other provisions of the Constitution did limit state interference with individual rights. Article IV, §2, cl. 1 provides that "[t]he Citizens of each State shall be entitled to all Privileges and Immunities of Citizens in the several States." The text of this provision resembles the Privileges or Immunities Clause, and it can be assumed that the public's understanding of the latter was informed by its understanding of the former.

Article IV, §2 was derived from a similar clause in the Articles of Confederation, and reflects the dual citizenship the Constitution provided to all Americans after replacing that "league" of separate sovereign States . . . By virtue of a person's citizenship in a particular State, he was guaranteed whatever rights and liberties that State's constitution and laws made available.

. . . When describing those "fundamental" rights, Justice Washington [in the *Corfield v. Coryell* case] thought it "would perhaps be more tedious than difficult to enumerate" them all, but suggested that they could "be all comprehended under" a broad list of "general heads," such as "[p]rotection by the government," "the enjoyment of life and liberty, with the right to acquire and possess property of every kind," "the benefit of the writ of habeas corpus," and the right of access to "the courts of the state," among others. . . .

This evidence plainly shows that the ratifying public understood the Privileges or Immunities Clause to protect constitutionally enumerated rights, including the right to keep and bear arms . . . in light of the States and Federal Government's shared history of recognizing certain inalienable rights in their citizens, is that the privileges and immunities of state and federal citizenship overlap.

. . . I reject *Slaughter-House* insofar as it precludes any overlap between the privileges and immunities of state and federal citizenship . . . In my view, the record makes plain that the Framers of the Privileges or Immunities Clause and the ratifying-era public understood—just as the Framers of the Second Amendment did—that the right to keep and bear arms was essential to the preservation of liberty. The record makes equally plain that they deemed this right necessary to include in the minimum baseline of federal rights that the Privileges or Immunities Clause established in the wake of the War over slavery . . .

[Justice Stevens, dissenting] . . . substantive due process analysis generally requires us to consider the term "liberty" in the Fourteenth Amendment, and that this inquiry may be informed by but does not depend upon the content of the Bill of Rights . . . Liberty claims that are inseparable from the customs that prevail in a certain region, the idiosyncratic expectations of a certain group, or the personal preferences of their champions, may be valid claims in some sense; but they are not of constitutional stature . . .

. . . our law has long recognized that the home provides a kind of special sanctuary in modern life . . . The State generally has a lesser basis for regulating private as compared to public acts, and firearms kept inside the home generally pose a lesser threat to public welfare as compared to firearms taken outside.

The notion that a right of self-defense *implies* an auxiliary right to own a certain type of firearm presupposes not only controversial judgments about the strength and scope of the (posited) self-defense right, but also controversial assumptions about the likely effects of making that type of firearm more broadly available. It is a very long way from the proposition that the Fourteenth Amendment protects a basic individual right of self-defense to the conclusion that a city may not ban handguns . . . The question we must decide is whether the interest in keeping in the home a firearm of one's choosing—a handgun, for petitioners—is one that is "comprised within the term liberty" in the Fourteenth Amendment.

. . . firearms have a fundamentally ambivalent relationship to liberty. Just as they can help homeowners defend their families and property from intruders, they can help thugs and insurrectionists murder innocent victims. The threat that firearms will be misused is far from hypothetical, for gun crime has devastated many of our communities. . . . Hence, in evaluating an asserted right to be free from particular gun-control regulations, liberty is on both sides of the equation . . . *Your* interest in keeping and bearing a certain firearm may diminish *my* interest in being and feeling safe from armed violence . . . It is at least reasonable for a democratically elected legislature to take such concerns into account in considering what sorts of regulations would best serve the public welfare.

. . . If a legislature's response to dangerous weapons ends up impinging upon the liberty of any individuals in pursuit of the greater good, it invariably does so on the basis of more than the majority's " 'own moral code,' " . . . While specific policies may of course be misguided, gun control is an area in which it "is quite wrong . . . to assume that regulation and liberty occupy mutually exclusive zones—that as one expands, the other must contract."

. . . the United States is an international outlier in the permissiveness of its approach to guns does not suggest that our laws are bad laws. It does suggest that this Court may not need to assume responsibility for making our laws still more permissive.

. . . It was the States, not private persons, on whose immediate behalf the Second Amendment was adopted . . . The Second Amendment, in other words, "is a federalism provision" . . . It is directed at preserving the autonomy of the sovereign States, and its logic therefore "resists" incorporation by a federal court *against* the States. . . .

. . . But the reasons that motivated the Framers to protect the ability of militiamen to keep muskets available for military use when our Nation was in its infancy, or that motivated the Reconstruction Congress to extend full citizenship to the freedmen in the wake of the Civil War, have only a limited bearing on the question that confronts the homeowner in a crime-infested metropolis today.

. . . This history of intrusive regulation is not surprising given that the very text of the Second Amendment calls out for regulation, . . . and the ability to respond to the social ills associated with dangerous weapons goes to the very core of the States' police powers . . . So long as the regulatory measures they have chosen are not "arbitrary, capricious, or unreasonable," we should be allowing them to "try novel social and economic" policies . . . It "is more in keeping . . . with our status as a court in a federal system," under these circumstances, "to avoid imposing a single solution . . . from the top down."

FOURTH AMENDMENT

Mapp v. Ohio (1961)[12]

. . . Appellant stands convicted of knowingly having had in her possession and under her control certain lewd and lascivious books, pictures, and photographs. . . . [T]he Supreme Court of Ohio found that her conviction was valid though "based primarily upon the introduction in evidence of lewd and lascivious books and pictures unlawfully seized during an unlawful search of defendant's home."

. . . Cleveland police officers arrived at appellant's residence in that city pursuant to information that "a person [was] hiding out in the home, who was wanted for questioning in connection with a recent bombing, and that there

was a large amount of policy paraphernalia being hidden in the home" . . .
When Miss Mapp did not come to the door immediately, at least one of the
several doors to the house was forcibly opened . . . and the policemen gained
admittance . . . The obscene materials for possession of which she was ultimately convicted were discovered in the course of that widespread search.

At the trial, no search warrant was produced by the prosecution, nor was
the failure to produce one explained or accounted for . . . The State says that,
even if the search were made without authority, or otherwise unreasonably,
it is not prevented from using the unconstitutionally seized evidence at trial,
citing *Wolf v. Colorado*, 338 U. S. 25 (1949), in which this Court did indeed
hold "that, in a prosecution in a State court for a State crime, the Fourteenth
Amendment does not forbid the admission of evidence obtained by an unreasonable search and seizure."

. . . "the Fourth Amendment . . . put the courts of the United States and Federal officials, in the exercise of their power and authority, under limitations
and restraints [and] . . . forever secure[d] the people, their persons, houses,
papers and effects against all unreasonable searches and seizures under the
guise of law . . . and the duty of giving to it force and effect is obligatory upon
all entrusted under our Federal system with the enforcement of the laws."

. . . Nevertheless, after declaring that the "security of one's privacy against
arbitrary intrusion by the police" is "implicit in the concept of ordered liberty" and, as such, enforceable against the States through the Due Process
Clause . . .

Since the Fourth Amendment's right of privacy has been declared enforceable against the States through the Due Process Clause of the Fourteenth, it is
enforceable against them by the same sanction of exclusion as is used against
the Federal Government. Were it otherwise . . . the assurance against unreasonable federal searches and seizures would be "a form of words," valueless
and undeserving of mention in a perpetual charter of inestimable human liberties, so too, without that rule, the freedom from state invasions of privacy
would be so ephemeral and so neatly severed from its conceptual nexus with
the freedom from all brutish means of coercing evidence as not to merit this
Court's high regard as a freedom "implicit in the concept of ordered liberty."

. . . There is no war between the Constitution and common sense. Presently, a federal prosecutor may make no use of evidence illegally seized, but
a State's attorney across the street may, although he supposedly is operating
under the enforceable prohibitions of the same Amendment. Thus, the State,
by admitting evidence unlawfully seized, serves to encourage disobedience
to the Federal Constitution which it is bound to uphold. . . .

[JUSTICE HARLAN, whom MR. JUSTICE FRANKFURTER and MR.
JUSTICE WHITTAKER join, dissenting] . . . This reasoning ultimately rests
on the unsound premise that, because *Wolf* carried into the States, as part of

"the concept of ordered liberty" embodied in the Fourteenth Amendment, the principle of "privacy" underlying the Fourth Amendment . . . it must follow that whatever configurations of the Fourth Amendment have been developed in the particularizing federal precedents are likewise to be deemed a part of "ordered liberty," and as such are enforceable against the States. For me, this does not follow at all.

. . . The preservation of a proper balance between state and federal responsibility in the administration of criminal justice demands patience on the part of those who might like to see things move faster among the States in this respect.

. . . I think this Court can increase respect for the Constitution only if it rigidly respects the limitations which the Constitution places upon it, and respects as well the principles inherent in its own processes. In the present case, I think we exceed both, and that our voice becomes only a voice of power, not of reason.

FIFTH AMENDMENT

Chicago, B. & Q. R. Co. v. Chicago (1897)[13]

. . . certain rulings of the state court, which, it is alleged, were in disregard of that part of the Fourteenth Amendment declaring that no State shall deprive any person of his property without due process of law, or deny the equal protection of the laws to any person within its jurisdiction.

The Constitution of Illinois provides that "no person shall be deprived of life, liberty or property, without due process of law." Article 2, § 2. It also provides: "Private property shall not be taken or damaged for public use without just compensation . . . [and] where no compensation is made to such railroad company, the city shall restore such railroad track, right of way or land to its former state, or in a sufficient manner not to have impaired its usefulness."

. . . Due protection of the rights of property has been regarded as a vital principle of republican institutions. "Next in degree to the right of personal liberty," Mr. Broom, in his work on constitutional Law, says, "is that of enjoying private property without undue interference or molestation." (p. 228.) The requirement that the property shall not be taken for public use without just compensation is but "an affirmance of a great doctrine established by the common law for the protection of private property. It is founded in natural equity, and is laid down as a principle of universal law. Indeed, in a free government, almost all other rights would become worthless if the government possessed an uncontrollable power over the private fortune of every citizen."

. . . The legislature may prescribe a form of procedure to be observed in the taking of private property for public use, but it is not due process of law if provision be not made for compensation. Notice to the owner to appear in some judicial tribunal and show cause why his property shall not be taken for public use without compensation would be a mockery of justice. Due process of law, as applied to judicial proceedings instituted for the taking of private property for public use means, therefore, such process as recognizes the right of the owner to be compensated if his property be wrested from him and transferred to the public. The mere form of the proceeding instituted against the owner, even if he be admitted to defend, cannot convert the process used into due process of law, if the necessary result be to deprive him of his property without compensation.

. . . In *Scott v. Toledo* . . . the late Mr. Justice Jackson, while Circuit Judge, had occasion to consider this question. After full consideration, that able judge said:

"Whatever may have been the power of the States on this subject prior to the adoption of the Fourteenth Amendment to the Constitution, it seems clear that, since that amendment went into effect, such limitations and restraints have been placed upon their power in dealing with individual rights that the States cannot now lawfully appropriate private property for the public benefit or to public uses without compensation to the owner . . . The conclusion of the court on this question is that, since the adoption of the Fourteenth Amendment, compensation for private property taken for public uses constitutes an essential element in 'due process of law,' and that, without such compensation, the appropriation of private property to public uses, no matter under what form of procedure it is taken, would violate the provisions of the federal Constitution."

. . . In our opinion, a judgment of a state court, even if it be authorized by statute, whereby private property is taken for the State or under its direction for public use, without compensation made or secured to the owner, is, upon principle and authority, wanting in the due process of law required by the Fourteenth Amendment of the Constitution of the United States, and the affirmance of such judgment by the highest court of the State is a denial by that State of a right secured to the owner by that instrument.

Malloy v. Hogan (1964)[14]

. . . In this case, we are asked to reconsider prior decisions holding that the privilege against self-incrimination is not safeguarded against state action by the Fourteenth Amendment.

. . . The petitioner was asked a number of questions related to events surrounding his arrest and conviction. He refused to answer any question "on the grounds it may tend to incriminate me" . . . [T]he Connecticut Supreme Court of Errors . . . held that the Fifth Amendment's privilege against self-incrimination was not available to a witness in a state proceeding, that the Fourteenth Amendment extended no privilege to him, and that the petitioner had not properly invoked the privilege available under the Connecticut Constitution.

. . . The Court has not hesitated to reexamine past decisions according the Fourteenth Amendment a less central role in the preservation of basic liberties than that which was contemplated by its Framers when they added the Amendment to our constitutional scheme. . . .

We hold today that the Fifth Amendment's exception from compulsory self-incrimination is also protected by the Fourteenth Amendment against abridgment by the States . . . "[i]n criminal trials in the courts of the United States, wherever a question arises whether a confession is incompetent because not voluntary, the issue is controlled by that portion of the Fifth Amendment to the Constitution of the United States commanding that no person 'shall be compelled in any criminal case to be a witness against himself'" . . . Under this test, the constitutional inquiry is not whether the conduct of state officers in obtaining the confession was shocking, but whether the confession was "free and voluntary: that is, [it] must not be extracted by any sort of threats or violence, nor obtained by any direct or implied promises, however slight, nor by the exertion of any improper influence."

In other words, the person must not have been compelled to incriminate himself. We have held inadmissible even a confession secured by so mild a whip as the refusal, under certain circumstances, to allow a suspect to call his wife until he confessed.

. . . Governments, state and federal, are thus constitutionally compelled to establish guilt by evidence independently and freely secured, and may not, by coercion, prove a charge against an accused out of his own mouth. Since the Fourteenth Amendment prohibits the States from inducing a person to confess through "sympathy falsely aroused" . . . or other like inducement far short of "compulsion by torture" . . . it follows *a fortiori* that it also forbids the States to resort to imprisonment, as here, to compel him to answer questions that might incriminate him. The Fourteenth Amendment secures against state invasion the same privilege that the Fifth Amendment guarantees against federal infringement—the right of a person to remain silent unless he chooses to speak in the unfettered exercise of his own will, and to suffer no penalty.

. . . The philosophy of each Amendment and of each freedom is complementary to, although not dependent upon, that of the other in its sphere of influence—the very least that, together, they assure in either sphere is that no man is to be convicted on unconstitutional evidence."

. . . What is accorded is a privilege of refusing to incriminate one's self, and the feared prosecution may be by either federal or state authorities . . .

It would be incongruous to have different standards determine the validity of a claim of privilege based on the same feared prosecution depending on whether the claim was asserted in a state or federal court. Therefore, the same standards must determine whether an accused's silence in either a federal or state proceeding is justified.

[MR. JUSTICE HARLAN, whom MR. JUSTICE CLARK joins, dissenting] . . . While it is true that the Court deals today with only one aspect of state criminal procedure, and rejects the wholesale "incorporation" of such federal constitutional requirements, the logical gap between the Court's premises and its novel constitutional conclusion can, I submit, be bridged only by the additional premise that the Due Process Clause of the Fourteenth Amendment is a shorthand directive to this Court to pick and choose among the provisions of the first eight Amendments and apply those chosen, freighted with their entire accompanying body of federal doctrine, to law enforcement in the States.

I accept and agree with the proposition that continuing reexamination of the constitutional conception of Fourteenth Amendment "due process" of law is required, and that development of the community's sense of justice may, in time, lead to expansion of the protection which due process affords. In particular, in this case, I agree that principles of justice to which due process gives expression, as reflected in decisions of this Court, prohibit a State, as the Fifth Amendment prohibits the Federal Government, from imprisoning a person *solely* because he refuses to give evidence which may incriminate him under the laws of the State . . . I do not understand, however, how this process of reexamination, which must refer always to the guiding standard of due process of law, including, of course, reference to the particular guarantees of the Bill of Rights, can be short-circuited by the simple device of incorporating into due process, without critical examination, the whole body of law which surrounds a specific prohibition directed against the Federal Government. The consequence of such an approach to due process as it pertains to the States is inevitably disregard of all relevant differences which may exist between state and federal criminal law and its enforcement. The ultimate result is compelled uniformity, which is inconsistent with the purpose of our federal system and which is achieved either by encroachment on the States' sovereign powers or by dilution in federal law enforcement of the specific protections found in the Bill of Rights.

. . . The Court's undiscriminating approach to the Due Process Clause carries serious implications for the sound working of our federal system in the field of criminal law.

The Court concludes, almost without discussion. that "the same standards must determine whether an accused's silence in either a federal or state proceeding is justified" . . . About all that the Court offers in explanation of this conclusion is the observation that it would be "incongruous" if different standards governed the assertion of a privilege to remain silent in state and federal tribunals. Such "incongruity," however, is at the heart of our federal system. The powers and responsibilities of the state and federal governments are not congruent; under our Constitution, they are not intended to be. Why should it be thought, as an *a priori* matter, that limitations on the investigative power of the States are, in all respects, identical with limitations on the investigative power of the Federal Government? This certainly does not follow from the fact that we deal here with constitutional requirements, for the provisions of the Constitution which are construed are different.

As the Court pointed out in *Abbate v. United States* . . . "the States, under our federal system, have the principal responsibility for defining and prosecuting crimes." The Court endangers this allocation of responsibility for the prevention of crime when it applies to the States doctrines developed in the context of federal law enforcement without any attention to the special problems which the States, as a group or particular States, may face. If the power of the States to deal with local crime is unduly restricted, the likely consequence is a shift of responsibility in this area to the Federal Government, with its vastly greater resources. Such a shift, if it occurs, may, in the end, serve to weaken the very liberties which the Fourteenth Amendment safeguards by bringing us closer to the monolithic society which our federalism rejects. Equally dangerous to our liberties is the alternative of watering down protections against the Federal Government embodied in the Bill of Rights so as not unduly to restrict the powers of the States . . . Rather than insisting, almost by rote, that the Connecticut court, in considering the petitioner's claim of privilege, was required to apply the "federal standard," the Court should have fulfilled its responsibility under the Due Process Clause by inquiring whether the proceedings below met the demands of fundamental fairness which due process embodies. Such an approach may not satisfy those who see in the Fourteenth Amendment a set of easily applied "absolutes" which can afford a haven from unsettling doubt. It is, however, truer to the spirit which requires this Court constantly to reexamine fundamental principles and, at the same time, enjoins it from reading its own preferences into the Constitution.

Benton v. Maryland (1969)[15]

. . . because the first jury had found him not guilty of larceny, retrial would violate the constitutional prohibition against subjecting persons to double jeopardy for the same offense.

. . . After consideration of all the questions before us, we find no bar to our decision of the double jeopardy issue. On the merits, we hold that the Double Jeopardy Clause of the Fifth Amendment is applicable to the States through the Fourteenth Amendment, and we reverse petitioner's conviction for larceny.

.. . In 1937, this Court decided the landmark case of *Palko v. Connecticut,* . . . . Palko, although indicted for first-degree murder, had been convicted of murder in the second degree after a jury trial in a Connecticut state court. The State appealed and won a new trial. Palko argued that the Fourteenth Amendment incorporated, as against the States, the Fifth Amendment requirement that no person "be subject for the same offence to be twice put in jeopardy of life or limb." The Court disagreed. Federal double jeopardy standards were not applicable against the States. Only when a kind of jeopardy subjected a defendant to "a hardship so acute and shocking that our polity will not endure it," . . ., did the Fourteenth Amendment apply. The order for a new trial was affirmed. In subsequent appeals from state courts, the Court continued to apply this lesser *Palko* standard . . .

.. . In an increasing number of cases, the Court "has rejected the notion that the Fourteenth Amendment applies to the States only a 'watered-down, subjective version of the individual guarantees of the Bill of Rights . . . "*Malloy v. Hogan* . . . (1964) . . . Only last Term, we found that the right to trial by jury in criminal cases was "fundamental to the American scheme of justice," *Duncan v. Louisiana* . . . (1968), and held that the Sixth Amendment right to a jury trial was applicable to the States through the Fourteenth Amendment . . . For the same reasons, we today find that the double jeopardy prohibition of the Fifth Amendment represents a fundamental ideal in our constitutional heritage, and that it should apply to the States through the Fourteenth Amendment. Insofar as it is inconsistent with this holding, *Palko v. Connecticut* is overruled.

.. . Our recent cases have thoroughly rejected the *Palko* notion that basic constitutional rights can be denied by the States as long as the totality of the circumstances does not disclose a denial of "fundamental fairness." Once it is decided that a particular Bill of Rights guarantee is "fundamental to the American scheme of justice," *Duncan v. Louisiana* . . . the same constitutional standards apply against both the State and Federal Governments . . . The fundamental nature of the guarantee against double jeopardy can hardly be doubted. Its origins can be traced to Greek and Roman times, and it became established in the common law of England long before this Nation's independence . . . As with many other elements of the common law, it was carried into the jurisprudence of this Country through the medium of Blackstone, who codified the doctrine in his Commentaries. "[T]he plea of *autrefois acquit,* or a former acquittal," he wrote, "is grounded on this universal maxim of the common law of England that no man is to be brought into jeopardy of his life more than once for the same offence."

Today, every State incorporates some form of the prohibition in its constitution or common law.

. . . The judgment is vacated, and the case is remanded for further proceedings not inconsistent with this opinion.

[JUSTICE HARLAN, whom MR. JUSTICE STEWART joins, dissenting] . . . I would hold, in accordance with *Palko v. Connecticut* . . . (1937), that the Due Process Clause of the Fourteenth Amendment does not take over the Double Jeopardy Clause of the Fifth, as such. Today *Palko* becomes another casualty in the so-far unchecked march toward "incorporating" much, if not all, of the Federal Bill of Rights into the Due Process Clause. This march began, with a Court majority, in 1961 when *Mapp v. Ohio* . . . was decided and, before the present decision, found its last stopping point in *Duncan v. Louisiana* . . . (1968), decided at the end of last Term. . . . [I]n the *Duncan* case, I undertook to show that the "selective incorporation" doctrine finds no support either in history or in reason.

SIXTH AMENDMENT

In re Oliver (1948)[16]

. . . A Michigan circuit judge summarily sent the petitioner to jail for contempt of court. We must determine whether he was denied the procedural due process guaranteed by the Fourteenth Amendment . . . After petitioner had given certain testimony, the judge-grand jury, still in secret session, told petitioner that neither he nor his advisors believed petitioner's story—that it did not "jell" . . . In carrying out this authority a judge-grand jury is authorized to appoint its own prosecutors, detectives and aides at public expense, all or any of whom may, at the discretion of the justice of the peace or judge, be admitted to the inquiry.

. . . This nation's accepted practice of guaranteeing a public trial to an accused has its roots in our English common law heritage. The exact date of its origin is obscure, but it likely evolved long before the settlement of our land as an accompaniment of the ancient institution of jury trial . . . Today, almost without exception, every state, by constitution, statute, or judicial decision, requires that all criminal trials be open to the public.

The traditional Anglo-American distrust for secret trials has been variously ascribed to the notorious use of this practice by the Spanish Inquisition, to the excesses of the English Court of Star Chamber, and to the French monarchy's abuse of the *lettre de cachet.* All of these institutions obviously symbolized a menace to liberty. In the hands of despotic groups, each of them had become an instrument for the suppression of political and religious heresies in ruthless disregard of the right of an accused to a fair trial. Whatever other benefits the guarantee to an accused that his trial be conducted in public may confer upon our society, the guarantee has always been recognized as a safeguard against any attempt to employ our courts as instruments of persecution . . .

In giving content to the constitutional and statutory commands that an accused be given a public trial, the state and federal courts have differed over what groups of spectators, if any, could properly be excluded from a criminal trial. But, unless in Michigan and in one-man grand jury contempt cases, no court in this country has ever before held, so far as we can find, that an accused can be tried, convicted, and sent to jail when everybody else is denied entrance to the court except the judge and his attaches.

. . . We further hold that failure to afford the petitioner a reasonable opportunity to defend himself against the charge of false and evasive swearing was a denial of due process of law. A person's right to reasonable notice of a charge against him, and an opportunity to be heard in his defense—a right to his day in court—are basic in our system of jurisprudence, and these rights include, as a minimum, a right to examine the witnesses against him, to offer testimony, and to be represented by counsel.

. . . It is "the law of the land" that no man's life, liberty or property be forfeited as a punishment until there has been a charge fairly made and fairly tried in a public tribunal. . . . The petitioner was convicted without that kind of trial.

Gideon v. Wainwright (1963)[17]

. . . Appearing in court without funds and without a lawyer, petitioner asked the court to appoint counsel for him, whereupon the following colloquy took place:

"The COURT: Mr. Gideon, I am sorry, but I cannot appoint Counsel to represent you in this case. . . . the only time the Court can appoint Counsel to represent a Defendant is when that person is charged with a capital offense.

Put to trial before a jury, Gideon conducted his defense about as well as could be expected from a layman . . . The jury returned a verdict of guilty, and . . . petitioner filed in the Florida Supreme Court this habeas corpus petition attacking his conviction and sentence on the ground that the trial court's refusal to appoint counsel for him denied him rights . . . Since 1942, when *Betts v. Brady* . . . was decided by a divided Court, the problem of a defendant's federal constitutional right to counsel in a state court has been a continuing source of controversy and litigation in both state and federal courts.

. . . It was held that a refusal to appoint counsel for an indigent defendant charged with a felony did not necessarily violate the Due Process Clause of the Fourteenth Amendment, which . . . the Court deemed to be the only applicable federal constitutional provision. The Court said: "Asserted denial [of due process] is to be tested by an appraisal of the totality of facts in a given case. That which may, in one setting, constitute a denial of fundamental fairness, shocking to the universal sense of justice, may, in other circumstances, and in the light of other considerations, fall short of such denial."

. . . Upon full reconsideration, we conclude that *Betts v. Brady* should be overruled.

The Sixth Amendment provides, "In all criminal prosecutions, the accused shall enjoy the right . . . to have the Assistance of Counsel for his defense." We have construed this to mean that, in federal courts, counsel must be provided for defendants unable to employ counsel unless the right is competently and intelligently waived. Betts argued that this right is extended to indigent defendants in state courts by the Fourteenth Amendment. In response, the Court stated that, while the Sixth Amendment laid down "no rule for the conduct of the States, the question recurs whether the constraint laid by the Amendment upon the national courts expresses a rule so fundamental and essential to a fair trial, and so, to due process of law, that it is made obligatory upon the States by the Fourteenth Amendment."

. . . We think the Court in *Betts* had ample precedent for acknowledging that those guarantees of the Bill of Rights which are fundamental safeguards of liberty immune from federal abridgment are equally protected against state invasion by the Due Process Clause of the Fourteenth Amendment. This same principle was recognized, explained, and applied in *Powell v. Alabama*, (1932), a case upholding the right of counsel, where the Court held that, despite sweeping language to the contrary in *Hurtado v. California*, (1884), the Fourteenth Amendment "embraced" those "fundamental principles of liberty and justice which lie at the base of all our civil and political institutions,'" even though they had been "specifically dealt with in another part of the federal Constitution.

. . . "We concluded that certain fundamental rights, safeguarded by the first eight amendments against federal action, were also safeguarded against state action by the due process of law clause of the Fourteenth Amendment, and among them the fundamental right of the accused to the aid of counsel in a criminal prosecution." *Grosjean v. American Press Co.,* (1936).

. . . In light of these and many other prior decisions of this Court, it is not surprising that the *Betts* Court, when faced with the contention that "one charged with crime, who is unable to obtain counsel, must be furnished counsel by the State," conceded that "[e]xpressions in the opinions of this court lend color to the argument" . . . The fact is that, in deciding as it did—that "appointment of counsel is not a fundamental right, essential to a fair trial"—the Court in *Betts v. Brady* made an abrupt break with its own well considered precedents. In returning to these old precedents, sounder, we believe, than the new, we but restore constitutional principles established to achieve a fair system of justice. Not only these precedents, but also reason and reflection, require us to recognize that, in our adversary system of criminal justice, any person hauled into court, who is too poor to hire a lawyer, cannot be assured a fair trial unless counsel is provided for him. This seems to us to be an obvious truth. Governments, both state and federal, quite properly spend vast sums of money to establish machinery to try defendants accused of crime . . . The right of one charged with crime to counsel may not be deemed fundamental and essential to fair trials in some countries, but it is in ours. From the very beginning, our state and national constitutions and laws have laid great emphasis on procedural and substantive safeguards designed to assure fair trials before impartial tribunals in which every defendant stands equal before the law. This noble ideal cannot be realized if the poor man charged with crime has to face his accusers without a lawyer to assist him.

Pointer v. Texas (1965)[18]

. . . The question we find necessary to decide in this case is whether the Amendment's guarantee of a defendant's right "to be confronted with the witnesses against him," which has been held to include the right to cross-examine those witnesses, is also made applicable to the States by the Fourteenth Amendment.

. . . It cannot seriously be doubted at this late date that the right of cross-examination is included in the right of an accused in a criminal case to confront the witnesses against him. And probably no one, certainly no one experienced in the trial of lawsuits, would deny the value of cross-examination in exposing falsehood and bringing out the truth in the trial of a criminal case

. . . The fact that this right appears in the Sixth Amendment of our Bill of Rights reflects the belief of the Framers of those liberties and safeguards that confrontation was a fundamental right essential to a fair trial in a criminal prosecution. Moreover, the decisions of this Court and other courts throughout the years have constantly emphasized the necessity for cross-examination as a protection for defendants in criminal cases. This Court, in *Kirby v. United States* . . . referred to the right of confrontation as "[o]ne of the fundamental guarantees of life and liberty," and "a right long deemed so essential for the due protection of life and liberty that it is guarded against legislative and judicial action by provisions in the Constitution of the United States and in the constitutions of most if not of all the States composing the Union."

. . . There are few subjects, perhaps, upon which this Court and other courts have been more nearly unanimous than in their expressions of belief that the right of confrontation and cross-examination is an essential and fundamental requirement for the kind of fair trial which is this country's constitutional goal. Indeed, we have expressly declared that to deprive an accused of the right to cross-examine the witnesses against him is a denial of the Fourteenth Amendment's guarantee of due process of law.

. . . "In the constitutional sense, trial by jury in a criminal case necessarily implies at the very least that the 'evidence developed' against a defendant shall come from the witness stand in a public courtroom where there is full judicial protection of the defendant's right of confrontation, of cross-examination, and of counsel."

. . . We hold that petitioner was entitled to be tried in accordance with the protection of the confrontation guarantee of the Sixth Amendment, and that that guarantee, like the right against compelled self-incrimination, is "to be enforced against the States under the Fourteenth Amendment according to the same standards that protect those personal rights against federal encroachment."

Under this Court's prior decisions, the Sixth Amendment's guarantee of confrontation and cross-examination was unquestionably denied petitioner in this case. As has been pointed out, a major reason underlying the constitutional confrontation rule is to give a defendant charged with crime an opportunity to cross-examine the witnesses against him. . . . Since we hold that the right of an accused to be confronted with the witnesses against him must be determined by the same standards whether the right is denied in a federal or state proceeding, it follows that use of the transcript to convict petitioner denied him a constitutional right, and that his conviction must be reversed.

Parker v. Gladden (1966)[19]

. . . At a hearing on the petition, the trial court found that a court bailiff assigned to shepherd the sequestered jury . . . stated to one of the jurors . . . "Oh that wicked fellow [petitioner], he is guilty."

. . . We believe that the statements of the bailiff to the jurors are controlled by the command of the Sixth Amendment, made applicable to the States through the Due Process Clause of the Fourteenth Amendment. It guarantees that "the accused shall enjoy the right to a . . . trial, by an impartial jury . . . [and] be confronted with the witnesses against him" . . . "the 'evidence developed' against a defendant shall come from the witness stand in a public courtroom where there is full judicial protection of the defendant's right of confrontation, of cross-examination, and of counsel."

Klopfer v. North Carolina (1967)[20]

. . . The question involved in this case is whether a State may indefinitely postpone prosecution on an indictment without stated justification over the objection of an accused who has been discharged from custody.

. . . The consequence of this extraordinary criminal procedure is made apparent by the case before the Court. A defendant indicted for a misdemeanor may be denied an opportunity to exonerate himself in the discretion of the solicitor and held subject to trial, over his objection, throughout the unlimited period in which the solicitor may restore the case to the calendar. During that period, there is no means by which he can obtain a dismissal or have the case restored to the calendar for trial.

. . . Noting that some 18 months had elapsed since the indictment, petitioner, a professor of zoology at Duke University, contended that the pendency of the indictment greatly interfered with his professional activities and with his travel here and abroad . . . deprived him of his right to a speedy trial as required by the Fourteenth Amendment to the United States Constitution . . .

The petitioner is not relieved of the limitations placed upon his liberty by this prosecution merely because its suspension permits him to go "whithersoever he will." The pendency of the indictment may subject him to public scorn and deprive him of employment, and almost certainly will force curtailment of his speech, associations and participation in unpopular causes. By indefinitely prolonging this oppression, as well as the "anxiety and concern accompanying public accusation," the criminal procedure condoned in this case by the Supreme Court of North Carolina clearly denies the petitioner the right to a speedy trial which we hold is guaranteed to him by the Sixth Amendment of the Constitution of the United States.

While there has been a difference of opinion as to what provisions of this Amendment to the Constitution apply to the States through the Fourteenth Amendment, that question has been settled . . . We hold that petitioner was entitled to be tried in accordance with the protection of the confrontation guarantee of the Sixth Amendment, and that that guarantee, like the right against compelled self-incrimination, is "to be enforced against the States under the Fourteenth Amendment according to the same standards that protect those personal rights against federal encroachment" . . . We hold here that the right to a speedy trial is as fundamental as any of the rights secured by the Sixth Amendment. That right has its roots at the very foundation of our English law heritage. Its first articulation in modern jurisprudence appears to have been made in Magna Carta (1215), wherein it was written, "We will sell to no man, we will not deny or defer to any man either justice or right"; but evidence of recognition of the right to speedy justice in even earlier times is found in the Assize of Clarendon (1166). By the late thirteenth century, justices, armed with commissions of gaol delivery and/or oyer and terminer were visiting the countryside three times a year. These justices, Sir Edward Coke wrote in Part II of his Institutes, "have not suffered the prisoner to be long detained, but, at their next coming, have given the prisoner full and speedy justice, . . . without detaining him long in prison."

To Coke, prolonged detention without trial would have been contrary to the law and custom of England; but he also believed that the delay in trial, by itself, would be an improper denial of justice. . . . Coke's Institutes were read in the American Colonies by virtually every student of the law. Indeed, Thomas Jefferson wrote that, at the time he studied law (1762–1767), "*Coke Lyttleton* was the universal elementary book of law students." And . . . when George Mason drafted the first of the colonial bills of rights, he set forth a principle of Magna Carta, using phraseology similar to that of Coke's explication: "[I]n all capital or criminal prosecutions," the Virginia Declaration of Rights of 1776 provided, "a man hath a right . . . to a speedy trial." That this right was considered fundamental at this early period in our history is evidenced by its guarantee in the constitutions of several of the States of the new nation, as well as by its prominent position in the Sixth Amendment. Today, each of the 50 States guarantees the right to a speedy trial to its citizens. The history of the right to a speedy trial and its reception in this country clearly establish that it is one of the most basic rights preserved by our Constitution.

For the reasons stated above, the judgment must be reversed and remanded for proceedings not inconsistent with the opinion of the Court.

Washington v. Texas (1967)[21]

. . . We granted certiorari in this case to determine whether the right of a defendant in a criminal case under the Sixth Amendment to have compulsory process for obtaining witnesses in his favor is applicable to the States through the Fourteenth Amendment, and whether that right was violated by a state procedural statute providing that persons charged as principals, accomplices, or accessories in the same crime cannot be introduced as witnesses for each other.

. . . Two Texas statutes provided at the time of the trial in this case that persons charged or convicted as co-participants in the same crime could not testify for one another, although there was no bar to their testifying for the State.

We have not previously been called upon to decide whether the right of an accused to have compulsory process for obtaining witnesses in his favor, guaranteed in federal trials by the Sixth Amendment, is so fundamental and essential to a fair trial that it is incorporated in the Due Process Clause of the Fourteenth Amendment . . . We have held that due process requires that the accused have the assistance of counsel for his defense, that he be confronted with the witnesses against him, and that he have the right to a speedy and public trial.

The right of an accused to have compulsory process for obtaining witnesses in his favor stands on no lesser footing than the other Sixth Amendment rights that we have previously held applicable to the States. This Court had occasion in *In re Oliver,* (1948), to describe what it regarded as the most basic ingredients of due process of law. It observed that:

"A person's right to reasonable notice of a charge against him, and an opportunity to be heard in his defense—a right to his day in court—are basic in our system of jurisprudence, and these rights include, as a minimum, a right to examine the witnesses against him, to offer testimony, and to be represented by counsel."

The right to offer the testimony of witnesses, and to compel their attendance, if necessary, is in plain terms the right to present a defense, the right to present the defendant's version of the facts as well as the prosecution's to the jury, so it may decide where the truth lies. Just as an accused has the right to confront the prosecution's witnesses for the purpose of challenging their testimony, he has the right to present his own witnesses to establish a defense. This right is a fundamental element of due process of law.

. . . Joseph Story, in his famous Commentaries on the Constitution of the United States, observed that the right to compulsory process was included in the Bill of Rights in reaction to the notorious common law rule that, in cases of treason or felony, the accused was not allowed to introduce witnesses in his defense at all. Although the absolute prohibition of witnesses for the defense had been abolished in England by statute before 1787, the Framers of the Constitution felt it necessary specifically to provide that defendants in criminal cases should be provided the means of obtaining witnesses so that their own evidence, as well as the prosecution's, might be evaluated by the jury.

. . . The federal courts followed the common law restrictions for a time, despite the Sixth Amendment . . . The holding in *United States v. Reid* was not satisfactory to later generations, however, and, in 1918, this Court expressly overruled it, refusing to be bound by "the dead hand of the common law rule of 1789,"

. . . The rule disqualifying an alleged accomplice from testifying on behalf of the defendant cannot even be defended on the ground that it rationally sets apart a group of persons who are particularly likely to commit perjury. . . .

. . . We hold that the petitioner in this case was denied his right to have compulsory process for obtaining witnesses in his favor because the State arbitrarily denied him the right to put on the stand a witness who was physically and mentally capable of testifying to events that he had personally observed, and whose testimony would have been relevant and material to the defense. The Framers of the Constitution did not intend to commit the futile act of giving to a defendant the right to secure the attendance of witnesses whose testimony he had no right to use.

SEVENTH AMENDMENT

Minneapolis & St. Louis R. Co. v. Bombolis (1916)[22]

. . . By the Constitution and laws of Minnesota in civil causes, after a case has been under submission to a jury for a period of twelve hours without a unanimous verdict, five sixths of the jury are authorized to reach a verdict, which is entitled to the legal effect of a unanimous verdict at common law.

It has been so long and so conclusively settled that the Seventh Amendment exacts a trial by jury according to the course of the common law—that is, by a unanimous verdict . . . that it is not now open in the slightest to question that, if the requirements of that Amendment applied to the action of the State of Minnesota in adopting the statute concerning a less than unanimous verdict, or controlled the state court in enforcing that statute in the trial which is under review, both the statute and the action of the court were void because of repugnancy to the Constitution of the United States.

. . . Two propositions as to the operation and effect of the Seventh Amendment are as conclusively determined as is that concerning the nature and character of the jury required by that Amendment, where applicable. (a) That the first ten Amendments, including, of course, the Seventh, are not concerned with state action, and deal only with federal action . . . And, as a necessary corollary, (b) that the Seventh Amendment applies only to proceedings in courts of the United States, and does not in any manner whatever govern or regulate trials by jury in state courts, or the standards which must be applied concerning the same . . . So completely and conclusively have both of these principles been settled, so expressly have they been recognized without dissent or question almost from the beginning in the accepted interpretation of the Constitution, in the enactment of laws by Congress and proceedings in the federal courts, and by state constitutions and state enactments and proceedings in the state courts, that it is true to say that to concede that they are open to contention would be to grant that nothing whatever had been settled as to the power of state and federal governments or the authority of state and federal courts and their mode of procedure from the beginning.

. . . that the right to jury trial which the Seventh Amendment secures is a substantial one in that it exacts a substantial compliance with the common law standard as to what constitutes a jury.

. . . Moreover, the proposition is in conflict with an essential principle upon which our dual constitutional system of government rests—that is, that lawful rights of the citizen, whether arising from a legitimate exercise of state or national power, unless excepted by express constitutional limitation or by valid legislation to that effect, are concurrently subject to be enforced in the courts of the state or nation when such rights come within in the general scope of the jurisdiction conferred upon such courts by the authority, state or nation, creating them. . . . the unity of the governments, national and state, and the common fealty of all courts, both state and national, to both state and national Constitutions, and the duty resting upon them, when it was within the scope of their authority, to protect and enforce rights lawfully created, without reference to the particular government from whose exercise of lawful power the right arose.

EIGHTH AMENDMENT

Robinson v. California (1962)[23]

. . . A California statute makes it a criminal offense for a person to "be addicted to the use of narcotics." This appeal draws into question the constitutionality of that provision of the state law, as construed by the California courts in the present case.

. . . "There can be no question of the authority of the state in the exercise of its police power to regulate the administration, sale, prescription and use of dangerous and habit forming drugs . . . The right to exercise this power is so manifest in the interest of the public health and welfare that it is unnecessary to enter upon a discussion of it beyond saying that it is too firmly established to be successfully called in question."

Such regulation, it can be assumed, could take a variety of valid forms . . . This statute . . . is not one which punishes a person for the use of narcotics, for their purchase, sale or possession, or for antisocial or disorderly behavior resulting from their administration. It is not a law which even purports to provide or require medical treatment. Rather, we deal with a statute which makes the "status" of narcotic addiction a criminal offense, for which the offender may be prosecuted "at any time before he reforms." California has said that a person can be continuously guilty of this offense, whether or not he has ever used or possessed any narcotics within the State, and whether or not he has been guilty of any antisocial behavior there.

It is unlikely that any State at this moment in history would attempt to make it a criminal offense for a person to be mentally ill, or a leper, or to be afflicted with a venereal disease . . . But, in the light of contemporary human knowledge, a law which made a criminal offense of such a disease would doubtless be universally thought to be an infliction of cruel and unusual punishment in violation of the Eighth and Fourteenth Amendments. . . .

We cannot but consider the statute before us as of the same category. In this Court, counsel for the State recognized that narcotic addiction is an illness. Indeed, it is apparently an illness which may be contracted innocently or involuntarily. We hold that a state law which imprisons a person thus afflicted as a criminal, even though he has never touched any narcotic drug within the State or been guilty of any irregular behavior there, inflicts a cruel and unusual punishment in violation of the Fourteenth Amendment. To be sure, imprisonment for ninety days is not, in the abstract, a punishment which is either cruel or unusual. But the question cannot be considered in the abstract. Even one day in prison would be a cruel and unusual punishment for the "crime" of having a common cold.

We are not unmindful that the vicious evils of the narcotics traffic have occasioned the grave concern of government. There are, as we have said, countless fronts on which those evils may be legitimately attacked. We deal in this case only with an individual provision of a particularized local law as it has so far been interpreted by the California courts.

[JUSTICE WHITE, dissenting] . . . I am not at all ready to place the use of narcotics beyond the reach of the States' criminal laws. I do not consider appellant's conviction to be a punishment for having an illness or for simply being in some status or condition, but rather a conviction for the regular, repeated or habitual use of narcotics immediately prior to his arrest and in violation of the California law.

. . . In my opinion, on this record, it was within the power of the State of California to confine him by criminal proceedings for the use of narcotics or for regular use amounting to habitual use.

. . . The Fourteenth Amendment is today held to bar any prosecution for addiction regardless of the degree or frequency of use, and the Court's opinion bristles with indications of further consequences. If it is "cruel and unusual punishment" to convict appellant for addiction, it is difficult to understand why it would be any less offensive to the Fourteenth Amendment to convict him for use on the same evidence of use which proved he was an addict . . . At the very least, it has effectively removed California's power to deal effectively with the recurring case under the statute where there is ample evidence of use but no evidence of the precise location of use. Beyond this, it has cast serious doubt upon the power of any State to forbid the use of narcotics under threat of criminal punishment.

. . . Finally, I deem this application of "cruel and unusual punishment" so novel that I suspect the Court was hard put to find a way to ascribe to the Framers of the Constitution the result reached today rather than to its own notions of ordered liberty. If this case involved economic regulation, the present Court's allergy to substantive due process would surely save the statute and prevent the Court from imposing its own philosophical predilections upon state legislatures or Congress. I fail to see why the Court deems it more appropriate to write into the Constitution its own abstract notions of how best to handle the narcotics problem, for it obviously cannot match either the States or Congress in expert understanding.

Schilb v. Kuebel (1971)[24]

. . . In order to gain his liberty pending trial . . . Schilb deposited $75 in cash with the clerk of the court . . . At his ensuing trial . . . was convicted of traffic obstruction. When he paid his fine, the amount Schilb had deposited was returned to him decreased, however, by $7.50 retained as "bail bond costs" by the court clerk pursuant to the statute. The amount so retained was 1% of the specified bail and 10% of the amount actually deposited.

Schilb, by this purported state class action against the court clerk, the county, and the county treasurer, attacks the statutory 1% charge on Fourteenth Amendment due process and equal protection ground . . . Bail, of course, is basic to our system of law . . . and the Eighth Amendment's proscription of excessive bail has been assumed to have application to the States through the Fourteenth Amendment . . . But we are not at all concerned here with any fundamental right to bail or with any Eighth Amendment-Fourteenth Amendment question of bail excessiveness. Our concern, instead, is with the 1% cost retention provision. This smacks of administrative detail and of procedure, and is hardly to be classified as a "fundamental" right or as based upon any suspect criterion. The applicable measure, therefore, must be the traditional one: is the distinction drawn by the statutes invidious and without rational basis? . . .

With this background, we turn to the appellants' primary argument. It is threefold: (1) that the 1% retention charge . . . is imposed on only one segment of the class gaining pretrial release; (2) that it is imposed on the poor and nonaffluent, and not on the rich and affluent; (3) that its imposition with respect to an accused found innocent amounts to a court cost assessed against the not-guilty person.

We are compelled to note preliminarily that the attack on the Illinois bail statutes, in a very distinct sense, is paradoxical. The benefits of the new system, as compared with the old, are conceded. And the appellants recognize that, under the pre-1964 system, Schilb's particular bail bond cost would have been 10% of his bail, or $75; that this premium price for his pretrial freedom, once paid, was irretrievable; and that, if he could not have raised the $75, he would have been consigned to jail until his trial. Thus, under the old system, the cost of Schilb's pretrial freedom was $75, but under the new it was only $7.50. While acknowledging this obvious benefit of the statutory reform, Schilb and his co-appellants decry the classification the statutes make and present the usual argument that the legislation must be struck down because it does not reform enough.

. . . "The Equal Protection Clause requires more of a state law than non-discriminatory application within the class it establishes. It also imposes a requirement of some rationality in the nature of the class singled out. To be sure, the constitutional demand is not a demand that a statute necessarily apply equally to all persons. 'The Constitution does not require things which are different in fact . . . to be treated in law as though they were the same.' Hence, legislation may impose special burdens upon defined classes in order to achieve permissible ends. But the Equal Protection Clause does require that, in defining a class subject to legislation, the distinctions that are drawn have 'some relevance to the purpose for which the classification is made.'"

. . . The poor man-affluent man argument centers, of course, in *Griffin v. Illinois,* . . . (1956), and in the many later cases that "reaffirm allegiance to the basic command that justice be applied equally to all persons."

In no way do we withdraw today from the *Griffin* principle . . . The situation, therefore, wholly apart from the fact that appellant Schilb himself has not pleaded indigency, is not one where we may assume that the Illinois plan works to deny relief to the poor man merely because of his poverty.

. . . We refrain from nullifying this Illinois statute that, with its companion sections, has brought reform and needed relief to the State's bail system.

[MR. JUSTICE BRENNAN delivered the opinion of the Court] In this case, we are asked to reconsider prior decisions holding that the privilege against self-incrimination is not safeguarded against state action by the Fourteenth Amendment.[25]

. . . The petitioner was arrested during a gambling raid in 1959 by Hartford, Connecticut, police. He pleaded guilty to the crime of pool selling, a misdemeanor, and was sentenced to one year in jail and fined $500. The sentence was ordered to be suspended after 90 days, at which time he was to be placed on probation for two years. About 16 months after his guilty plea, petitioner was ordered to testify before a referee appointed by the Superior Court of Hartford County to conduct an inquiry into alleged gambling and other criminal activities in the county. The petitioner was asked a number of questions related to events surrounding his arrest and conviction. He refused to answer any question "on the grounds it may tend to incriminate me." The Superior Court adjudged him in contempt, and committed him to prison until he was willing to answer the questions. Petitioner's application for a writ of habeas corpus was denied by the Superior Court, and the Connecticut Supreme Court of Errors affirmed . . . The latter court held that the Fifth Amendment's privilege against self-incrimination was not available to a witness in a state proceeding, that the Fourteenth Amendment extended no privilege to him, and that the petitioner had not properly invoked the privilege available under the Connecticut Constitution. We granted certiorari . . . We reverse. We hold that the Fourteenth Amendment guaranteed the petitioner the protection of the Fifth Amendment's privilege against self-incrimination and that, under the applicable federal standard, the Connecticut Supreme Court of Errors erred in holding that the privilege was not properly invoked.

. . . The extent to which the Fourteenth Amendment prevents state invasion of rights enumerated in the first eight Amendments has been considered in numerous cases in this Court since the Amendment's adoption in 1868. Although many Justices have deemed the Amendment to incorporate all eight of the Amendments . . . the view which has thus far prevailed dates from the decision in 1897 in *Chicago, B. & Q. R. Co. v. Chicago*, . . . which held that the Due Process Clause requires the States to pay just compensation for private property taken for public use. . . . It was on the authority of that decision that the Court said in 1908, in *Twining v. New Jersey, supra*, that "it is possible that some of the personal rights safeguarded by the first eight Amendments against National action may also be safeguarded against state action because a denial of them would be a denial of due process of law."

. . . The Court has not hesitated to reexamine past decisions according the Fourteenth Amendment a less central role in the preservation of basic liberties than that which was contemplated by its Framers when they added the Amendment to our constitutional scheme. . . .

Court held that, in the light of later decisions . . . it was taken as settled that ". . . the Fourth Amendment's right of privacy has been declared enforceable against the States through the Due Process Clause of the Fourteenth."

We hold today that the Fifth Amendment's exception from compulsory self-incrimination is also protected by the Fourteenth Amendment against abridgment by the States . . . We discuss first the decisions which forbid the use of coerced confessions in state criminal prosecutions . . . "[i]n criminal trials in the courts of the United States, wherever a question arises whether a confession is incompetent because not voluntary, the issue is controlled by that portion of the Fifth Amendment to the Constitution of the United States commanding that no person 'shall be compelled in any criminal case to be a witness against himself.'"

. . . Under this test, the constitutional inquiry is not whether the conduct of state officers in obtaining the confession was shocking, but whether the confession was "free and voluntary: that is, [it] must not be extracted by any sort of threats or violence, nor obtained by any direct or implied promises, however slight, nor by the exertion of any improper influence."

In other words, the person must not have been compelled to incriminate himself. We have held inadmissible even a confession secured by so mild a whip as the refusal, under certain circumstances, to allow a suspect to call his wife until he confessed . . . The marked shift to the federal standard in state cases began with *Lisenba v. California* . . . where the Court spoke of the accused's "free choice to admit, to deny or to refuse to answer" . . . The shift reflects recognition that the American system of criminal prosecution is accusatorial, not inquisitorial, and that the Fifth Amendment privilege is its essential mainstay.

Governments, state and federal, are thus constitutionally compelled to establish guilt by evidence independently and freely secured, and may not, by coercion, prove a charge against an accused out of his own mouth. Since the Fourteenth Amendment prohibits the States from inducing a person to confess through "sympathy falsely aroused" . . . or other like inducement far short of "compulsion by torture," . . . it follows *a fortiori* that it also forbids the States to resort to imprisonment, as here, to compel him to answer questions that might incriminate him. The Fourteenth Amendment secures against state invasion the same privilege that the Fifth Amendment guarantees against federal infringement—the right of a person to remain silent unless he chooses to speak in the unfettered exercise of his own will, and to suffer no penalty, as held in *Twining,* for such silence.

This conclusion is fortified by our recent decision in *Mapp v. Ohio,* . . . which had held "that, . . . as to the Federal Government, the Fourth and Fifth Amendments, and, as to the States, the freedom from unconscionable invasions of privacy and the freedom from convictions based upon coerced confessions, do enjoy an 'intimate relation' in their perpetuation of 'principles of humanity and civil liberty [secured] . . . only after years of struggle[.]'

The philosophy of each Amendment and of each freedom is complementary to, although not dependent upon, that of the other in its sphere of influence—the very least that, together, they assure in either sphere is that no man is to be convicted on unconstitutional evidence." . . .

The respondent Sheriff concedes in his brief that, under our decisions, particularly those involving coerced confessions, "the accusatorial system has become a fundamental part of the fabric of our society and, hence, is enforceable against the States." . . . The State urges, however, that the availability of the federal privilege to a witness in a state inquiry is to be determined according to a less stringent standard than is applicable in a federal proceeding. We disagree. . . . In the coerced confession cases, involving the policies of the privilege itself, there has been no suggestion that a confession might be considered coerced if used in a federal, but not a state, tribunal. The Court thus has rejected the notion that the Fourteenth Amendment applies to the States only a "watered-down, subjective version of the individual guarantees of the Bill of Rights" . . . What is accorded is a privilege of refusing to incriminate one's self, and the feared prosecution may be by either federal or state authorities . . . It would be incongruous to have different standards

determine the validity of a claim of privilege based on the same feared prosecution depending on whether the claim was asserted in a state or federal
court. Therefore, the same standards must determine whether an accused's
silence in either a federal or state proceeding is justified.

. . . The conclusions of the Court of Errors, tested by the federal standard,
fail to take sufficient account of the setting in which the questions were asked.
The interrogation was part of a wide-ranging inquiry into crime, including
gambling, in Hartford. It was admitted on behalf of the State at oral argument—and indeed it is obvious from the questions themselves—that the
State desired to elicit from the petitioner the identity of the person who ran
the pool-selling operation in connection with which he had been arrested in
1959. It was apparent that petitioner might apprehend that, if this person were
still engaged in unlawful activity, disclosure of his name might furnish a link
in a chain of evidence sufficient to connect the petitioner with a more recent
crime for which he might still be prosecuted. . . .

[MR. JUSTICE HARLAN, whom MR. JUSTICE CLARK joins, dis-
senting] Connecticut has adjudged this petitioner in contempt for refusing
to answer questions in a state inquiry. The courts of the State, whose laws
embody a privilege against self-incrimination, refused to recognize the petitioner's claim of privilege, finding that the questions asked him were not
incriminatory. This Court now holds the contempt adjudication unconstitutional because, it is decided: (1) the Fourteenth Amendment makes the Fifth
Amendment privilege against self-incrimination applicable to the States; (2)
the federal standard justifying a claim of this privilege likewise applies to
the States, and (3) judged by that standard the petitioner's claim of privilege
should have been upheld.

. . . While it is true that the Court deals today with only one aspect of state
criminal procedure, and rejects the wholesale "incorporation" of such federal
constitutional requirements, the logical gap between the Court's premises and
its novel constitutional conclusion can, I submit, be bridged only by the additional premise that the Due Process Clause of the Fourteenth Amendment is a
shorthand directive to this Court to pick and choose among the provisions of
the first eight Amendments and apply those chosen, freighted with their entire
accompanying body of federal doctrine, to law enforcement in the States.

I accept and agree with the proposition that continuing reexamination of
the constitutional conception of Fourteenth Amendment "due process" of
law is required, and that development of the community's sense of justice
may, in time, lead to expansion of the protection which due process affords.
In particular, in this case, I agree that principles of justice to which due process gives expression, as reflected in decisions of this Court, prohibit a State,
as the Fifth Amendment prohibits the Federal Government, from imprisoning
a person *solely* because he refuses to give evidence which may incriminate

him under the laws of the State . . . I do not understand, however, how this process of reexamination, which must refer always to the guiding standard of due process of law, including, of course, reference to the particular guarantees of the Bill of Rights, can be short-circuited by the simple device of incorporating into due process, without critical examination, the whole body of law which surrounds a specific prohibition directed against the Federal Government. The consequence of such an approach to due process as it pertains to the States is inevitably disregard of all relevant differences which may exist between state and federal criminal law and its enforcement. The ultimate result is compelled uniformity, which is inconsistent with the purpose of our federal system and which is achieved either by encroachment on the States' sovereign powers or by dilution in federal law enforcement of the specific protections found in the Bill of Rights.

. . . The Court's undiscriminating approach to the Due Process Clause carries serious implications for the sound working of our federal system in the field of criminal law.

The Court concludes, almost without discussion that "the same standards must determine whether an accused's silence in either a federal or state proceeding is justified." About all that the Court offers in explanation of this conclusion is the observation that it would be "incongruous" if different standards governed the assertion of a privilege to remain silent in state and federal tribunals. Such "incongruity," however, is at the heart of our federal system. The powers and responsibilities of the state and federal governments are not congruent; under our Constitution, they are not intended to be. Why should it be thought, as an *a priori* matter, that limitations on the investigative power of the States are, in all respects, identical with limitations on the investigative power of the Federal Government? This certainly does not follow from the fact that we deal here with constitutional requirements, for the provisions of the Constitution which are construed are different.

As the Court pointed out in *Abbate v. United States* . . . "the States, under our federal system, have the principal responsibility for defining and prosecuting crimes." The Court endangers this allocation of responsibility for the prevention of crime when it applies to the States doctrines developed in the context of federal law enforcement without any attention to the special problems which the States, as a group or particular States, may face. If the power of the States to deal with local crime is unduly restricted, the likely consequence is a shift of responsibility in this area to the Federal Government, with its vastly greater resources. Such a shift, if it occurs, may, in the end, serve to weaken the very liberties which the Fourteenth Amendment safeguards by bringing us closer to the monolithic society which our federalism rejects. Equally dangerous to our liberties is the alternative of watering down protections against the Federal Government embodied in the Bill of Rights so as not unduly to restrict the powers of the States . . . Rather than insisting, almost by rote, that the Connecticut court, in considering the petitioner's claim of privilege, was required to apply the "federal standard," the Court should have fulfilled its responsibility under the Due Process Clause by inquiring whether the proceedings below met the demands of fundamental fairness which due process embodies. Such an approach may not satisfy those who see in the Fourteenth Amendment a set of easily applied "absolutes" which can afford a haven from unsettling doubt. It is, however, truer to the spirit which requires this Court constantly to reexamine fundamental principles and, at the same time, enjoins it from reading its own preferences into the Constitution.

NOTES

1. *Gitlow v. People of New York, 268 U.S. 652 (1925).*

2. *Near v. Minnesota, 283 U.S. 697 (1931).*

3. *DeJonge v. Oregon, 299 U.S. 353 (1937).*

4. *Everson v. Board of Education, 330 U.S. 1 (1947).*

5. *Edwards v. South Carolina, 372 U.S. 229 (1963).*

6. Joseph Story, *Commentaries on the Constitution,* 3 vols (Boston: Hillard, Gray, and Company, 1833), 3: 746–748.

7. *United States v. Cruikshank, 92 U.S. 542 (1875).*

8. *Presser v. Illinois, 116 U.S. 252 (1886).*

9. *Hamilton v. Regents of University of California, 293 U.S. 245 (1934).*

10. *United States v. Miller, 307 U.S. 174 (1939).*

11. *McDonald v. Chicago 561 U.S. 742 (2010).*

12. *Mapp v. Ohio, 367 U.S. 643 (1961).*

13. *Chicago, B. & Q. R. Co. v. Chicago, 166 U.S. 226 (1897).*

14. *Malloy v. Hogan, 378 U.S. 1 (1964).*

15. *Benton v. Maryland, 395 U.S. 784 (1969).*

16. *In re Oliver, 333 U.S. 257 (1948).*

17. *Gideon v. Wainwright, 372 U.S. 335 (1963).*

18. *Pointer v. Texas, 380 U.S. 400 (1965).*

19. *Parker v. Gladden, 385 U.S. 363 (1966).*

20. *Klopfer v. North Carolina, 386 U.S. 213 (1967).*

21. *Washington v. Texas, 388 U.S. 14 (1967).*

22. *Minneapolis & St. Louis R. Co. v. Bombolis, 241 U.S. 211 (1916).*

23. *Robinson v. California, 370 U.S. 660 (1962).*

24. *Schilb v. Kuebel, 404 U.S. 357 (1971).*

25. *Malloy v. Hogan, 378 U.S. 1 (1964).*

Index

About the Editors

Aaron N. Coleman is Associate Professor of History and Chair of the History and Political Science Department at the University of the Cumberlands. Aaron received his PhD in early American history from the University of Kentucky. He is the author of *The American Revolution, State Sovereignty, and the American Constitutional Settlement, 1765–1800* (Lexington Books, 2016). Aaron lives in Williamsburg, KY, with his wife, Dr. Emily Coleman, and their two children.

Christopher S. Leskiw is Professor of Political Science and Vice President for Academic Affairs at the University of the Cumberlands. He received his PhD in International Politics from Vanderbilt University. He resides in Williamsburg, KY, with his wife and two boys.

DAO DOMINION

BRUCE SENTAR

D1528125

CONTENTS

CHAPTER 1

The sun beat down over the stone cliffs, highlighting every nook and cranny in the stone with deep shadows. Dar wiped gritty sweat away from his brow with the back of his forearm, squinting in the bright light to take in their latest progress.

Two days had passed since they had broken ground on their fledgling village, which was situated between the granite cliffs and the Bell River. They had worked together to plan out the basics.

Housing had been their most immediate need. Cherry had taken the lead in building the first homes, much like the hut she'd made for Dar and Sasha on their journey to the city of Bellhaven. Cherry had grown small huts for everyone in a wide arch around the largest cave they had found in the cliffs.

Between the huts and the cave was a wide area where people had set up a large hearth for communal meals. All around the central hearth, the village came to life with work. Tables and stumps were scattered between the hearth and the huts for people to congregate, work or eat.

Dar had been surprised when he had watched Cherry wear herself out building so many huts. All along the way, Cherry had been cautious not to show her real strength and to always hold something in reserve. Of his two women, Cherry was the cautious one and avoided drawing attention to herself.

Chuckling to himself, Dar considered just how much had changed since he had died on Earth and entered this new world. The fact that his body now housed a space where he could increase his power and the fact that it felt almost second nature at this point was insane.

Breathing in the crisp air, Dar smiled. He definitely didn't miss the stale air of his previous life. While there were challenges with being in a less developed world, he loved that it hadn't been tainted by high yield industries. The wide-open land around them held possibilities.

He could wring a living out of the land in a way that was satisfying.

Townspeople bustled around him, working to set up the village. They wore smiles despite the exhaustion that was creeping in from all of the work. But they were doing more than manual labor; they were working to build their future, and he could see the fire it was igniting.

There were about a hundred villagers in all that had taken a chance with Dar, fled Bellhaven, and ventured out to create their own life. They had traveled inland and along the Bell River to a spot where a long line of granite cliffs protected them, and the Bell River helped provide what they'd need. It was the perfect spot for a new life, and it held potential for trade.

They were now positioned directly between Kindrake—the capital named after the small nation they were in—and Bellhaven, which was the center of trade. Dar hoped that they'd be able to play a part in the trade operations, allowing those that had traveled with him to also sell their wares and generate income for the village. He had every intention of making sure their lives were for the better.

Many that had fled had done so because of the way they had been treated in Bellhaven. The city wasn't welcoming to those who walked the dao path, the ancient races, despite the power that they held. They were treated as inferiors and put under oaths that limited their freedom.

Dar sighed. Those in power always feared losing it, and that's what the ancient races represented to wizards and nobles.

Like that had done them any good though. The city, under pressure from a devil horde, had its nobles collapse in on themselves, all the while directing people's anger towards the ancient races. It hadn't been that difficult to accomplish considering the city had been attacked several times by masses of devils.

Dar shook his head. The city had never felt right to him. Out here, though? It was grand. He got what he worked for, and people were honest, unlike the duplicity of the nobles in the city.

Mark and his wife Margret had played him like a fiddle. He had never gotten the chance to pay them back. Helping all these people survive was his first priority; he'd deal with those two if they ever poked their heads out of Bellhaven.

He had a feeling that time would come sooner or later. For now, he focused back on the task at hand. Picking up another cut tree for the palisade, he slung it over his shoulder. Sometimes the physical things he could do so casually boggled his mind.

His body had been enchanted by one of this world's oldest and most powerful demons. It was she who had brought him to this world. Apparently, his soul had been here before and he had a destiny to finish.

Though, right now, he just enjoyed the feeling of working.

"Right here, boss." Glump moved away from another shallow hole he had made with his dao of mud.

Dar lined up the lumber, sank it into the hole and held it straight up.

Glump was a demon. Whatever magic translated things for Dar when people described him, it came across as frogman—an accurate description.

"It's in—seal it up." Dar held the pole as still as he could and left only a small gap between it and its neighbor.

The frogman dumped a bucket of mud into the hole, and his green lips pursed in concentration as he bent down and stuck his finger in the mud. Mud moved on its own, sinking into the ground and solidifying around the pole.

"This is the last one for today. Want to go cool off at the river when we finish?" Dar kept holding the pole as Glump used his dao to pack in mud around the base. It would hold for now, but Dar would have Cherry come to help with this section later.

"Yes, but we need to be back for dinner. My companions were upset at us being late yesterday."

Dar grinned. He had watched the whole thing play out. They had left Dar alone, but Glump hadn't been so lucky. He'd been nearly hen-pecked back into line by his eight dao companions. Glump was a demon, and harems were common in the ancient race societies.

They had small, wild families that tended to focus around a single male and a number of women. It was because spirits were largely female and male demons didn't often get along.

"Sure. We'll make it quick. But it feels so good to stick your feet in the cool water after a hard day." Dar liked the moment of rest, and Glump was becoming a close friend after working so closely to get the initial structure of the city created.

"I'll go get your woman to fix the pole so you don't have to wait for the mud to dry." Glump's monotone could be misleading. He put enthusiasm into his work; he just didn't emote much.

Dar smiled as Glump went to get Cherry and busied himself getting the mud off his hands with a large leaf.

"Is this all of them?" Cherry's youthful voice called as she approached with Glump. The petite dryad surveyed their day's work.

Dar let his eyes roam appreciatively over Cherry's curves. She looked like she'd fit in as a college cheerleader, her toned body curvy in all the right places and a bounce in her hair that barely looked natural. But she was old, ancient even, and while she sometimes played stupid to protect herself, Dar had gotten to love a deeper and wiser Cherry.

"For today. How'd the planting go?"

"Good enough. I'm about to just go rest for a while. Speeding up the growth of so many plants is tough work." Cherry stepped forward. Because she possessed a grand dao, she didn't even have to

touch the poles before limbs sprouted from the two dozen they'd set, intertwining and solidifying their palisade wall.

Dar let out a soft whistle. It was always impressive to see Cherry's grand dao at work.

"There you go. Now, I'm going to go get a quick nap before dinner." Cherry stretched her arms over her head and let out a cute yawn.

"You do that, babe. Maybe we won't stay up all night tonight." Dar had to admit his body was also tired from all the manual labor and evenings with his dao companions, but it wasn't a bad way to live.

Cherry didn't have a lick of shame in her, grinning widely at his statement. "That's why I'm getting a little sleep now, so I don't have to later."

Feeling his cheeks warm at that, Dar waved goodbye and pulled Glump along for their brief respite at the river.

"A happy dao companion makes for a good life, boss," Glump added as they headed to the river.

"Oh, you don't have to worry about that. They are both quite happy. But, at some point, I need to get some sleep."

Dar knew connecting with dao companions was important for their relationship in and of itself, but it was also a way for them to help share and grow on their dao paths. For a little while after sex with his dao companions, he was a touch closer to understanding the dao they had mastered and them his.

"Have you managed to get closer to your greater dao?" Glump asked.

The river starting to come into sight as they walked. The Bell River was massive, providing the main trade route across the small nation. But Dar knew a few tide pools near their area where they could be more comfortable.

"No. I haven't been able to form it yet." Dar tried to keep the frustration from his voice, but he was getting tired of waiting. It felt so close now.

He had managed to quickly get three lesser dao with the help of his body and its ability to absorb dao from trolls he had killed, and he

had hoped they would solidify into a greater dao, but nothing had happened despite his efforts.

Lesser dao allowed him to manipulate the attributes within his body or in something he was touching. From his kills, he'd gotten the lesser dao of heat, heavy, hard, and strength. He had hoped heavy, hard, and strength would form some sort of rock greater dao.

As he looked over the granite cliffs that sheltered their small community, he knew exactly what type of rock he was focusing on.

"Don't push yourself too hard. These things take time, and the community looks to you." Glump padded up to the edge of the tide pool and wiggled his webbed feet into the mud.

Dar did his best not to sigh as he took off his boots. Ancient races were immortal, and he was too now, but it didn't feel like he had forever. Maybe that was the part of him that was still human, his desire to grow and progress ever faster.

"I know, but if I could form the dao of granite, think how much easier this would all be."

"And if you bled out from forcing it, the community would be in shambles." Glump shrugged, wiggling his webbed feet deeper into the mud.

Dar rolled up his pants and found a nice rock to sit on. Using his dao of heat, he warmed it to make a nice seat while he dipped his feet in the cool wading pool of the river. Leaning back on his palms, he let out a sigh of contentment.

"This really does relax you," Glump added, forcing Dar to crack an eye open to look at him.

Unlike Sasha, would could pass for human. Glump was obviously not human. He had an almost olive skin tone but with just a little more green than he should have. His hands and feet had overly long digits and were webbed. Finally, and he did his best to hide it, but Dar had seen his throat expand like a frog when his companions doted on him.

"Well, sticking them in the mud seems odd to me."

Glump croaked, looking away quickly, his face starting to turn red.

Dar was fairly certain that had meant to have been a more human huff. "You don't have to hide what you are."

"You are young and don't understand. Many of us demons have spent a long time trying to blend with human society."

Dar knew he was right. He'd seen bits and pieces of the lifetime of discrimination many in their new town had endured, but he hadn't known it firsthand. "Still, doesn't The White technically rule all that she can see from Frost's Fang?"

Frost's Fang was a lone mountain at the trailing edge of the mountain range that marked the northern borders of Kindrake.

"She is not concerned with the noisy going-ons of mortals, or even us demons and spirits. She is meditating on the dao, trying to form another celestial dao. And it's not always best when she gets involved. She—" Glump stopped himself.

"What?"

"It's nothing, just an old tale some of the older demons say."

"No, go on. I want to hear it."

"I must warn you I have not experienced it myself; it was some five hundred years ago." Glump looked to make sure Dar took note of that.

Dar nodded, noting he should ask Cherry for more information. "That's fine."

"Well, they say there was a fourth major city in Kindrake, called Toldove. However, it is said Toldove started indiscriminately enslaving the ancient races. The White left Frost's Fang, and then there was no more Toldove."

Blinking, Dar stared at him. "You are terrible at telling stories. What did she do to the city?"

Glump shook his head. "That is the most terrifying part. No one knows. One day, she caught wind of what was happening, and the next day, the city was destroyed with no survivors."

Working through that disturbing picture, Dar tried to wrap his head around it. Even if an army attacked a city, there were large traces

of what happened and always some survivors. For The White to destroy an entire city in less than a day and leave no survivors…

A chill went up his spine that had nothing to do with the weather.

Dar had seen Cherry's strength when the nobles had lit her dao tree on fire, but extending that to the power to demolish an entire city was hard to imagine.

"I can see you struggle with the concept. That is why most think it is just an old tale. Truthfully, I've never met a celestial demon and would be happy to never meet one." Glump squished his feet in the mud.

"She sounds downright terrifying. Still, all of you are much stronger than the humans. I was surprised to see you in such trouble in the city."

"It has been the way of things in Bellhaven lately. Things used to be much better, and I had heard Kindrake was better. I'd thought about traveling there."

Suddenly worried he was about to lose his new friend, Dar tried to sound casual as he asked, "Are you going to head to Kindrake?"

"No, not yet at least. This budding village is nice. It's wild, yet we'll see some luxuries of a human city. I'll stay for now."

Dar let out a sigh of relief. Glump, as a male demon and one of only a handful of ancients in the village with a greater dao, was another pillar of the community. "You'd be sorely missed. Your temperance in the community as a demon has set the tone for the younger ones."

"I know." Glump grinned. "Russ would be challenging you every day if he didn't see me between him and yourself in the pecking order."

Russ was one of the other male demons in the village, a gnoll. He and his companions were among the youngest in the community. Russ had been eager to prove himself.

"Good thing we send him hunting every day to use up some of that energy," Dar teased.

But Glump responded seriously. "Oh yes, or he'd be challenging me rather than trotting around camp showing off the head of his latest kill."

Dar could practically see Russ dancing around the fire with a large deer's head. He wasn't very human looking, but it made sense. Russ didn't see humans as strong, and his first step on his dao path had used his limited imagination to reform himself. Most would become more human as they progressed.

It was only the really old demons that became more monstrous with each step of their dao, their sense of strength more bestial than human.

The bushes behind Dar rustled, and he turned enough so that he could watch for any attack out of the corner of his eye.

"Milord, Sasha sent me to fetch you for dinner." Marcie stepped out of the foliage with a few twigs stuck in her mousy brown hair.

She was one of two girls Sasha had picked up to become maids, though Marcie had a habit of fading into the background. Shy was an understatement for her.

But he had to give her credit; she'd been trying harder lately. And he'd been working to make her feel more secure. Apparently in their society, allowing maids to pleasure the man of the house was considered a part of the role in the household, and being shunned from the bedroom would give cause to believe their job may be tenuous.

Dar hadn't felt comfortable with the idea, but he'd eventually given in when he'd seen how happy it had made Amber. Now Marcie was the odd one out, and he was being sensitive to it around her.

He tried to keep his thoughts off his face and give her a wide smile. "Thanks, Marcie, we'll head back right now."

Dar pulled his feet out of the water, and with a little focus, used his dao of heat to steam the water right off and slip back into his boots.

Glump just carried his shoes as his muddy feet slapped on the ground.

"One of your women is going to complain if you track that much mud back."

"It's fine." Glump waved Dar's concern away. "Besides, if I don't have to worry about trying to blend in, I'd rather not wear shoes at all. I like the feel of the dirt on my feet."

"Then no shoes for you." Dar turned to Marcie. "Any idea what is cooking tonight?"

"Right now, it is still just vegetables. We are still waiting for the hunting party to come back." Marcie stepped up to his side, away from Glump as they walked back.

Marcie was human, like about half of their village, though she was still wary of many of the ancient races. Glump was a friend to Dar, but he knew his friend was dangerous given his power, and so did the rest of the villagers.

"Maybe Russ will come back without spoils. It would do him some good. Temper his confidence," Glump mused.

Dar snorted. "Yeah right. If he fails to find a kill today, I'll bet he doesn't come back until tomorrow."

Glump let out a sigh of agreement. "Yes, I think that's likely. Then let us hope he gets something, because those huts Cherry made are comfortable."

"I'm pretty sure you got the biggest one," Dar jabbed.

Glump only gave him a thin smile. "As it should be. I have many women to please."

CHAPTER 2

They stepped off the wild trail and onto a path that had been worn down in the few days they'd travelled it.

Up ahead, the village sprawled out, a collection of small huts nestled up against the stone cliffs and following the new palisade wall out from the cliffs. A few caves in the cliffs were enclosed by the partially complete palisade wall, but no one had taken up residence in them.

Dar and Bart had been having men dig out stone so they could build some more fortified structures. The huts were nice for now, but summer was over, and the leaves had turned into a colorful warning of the winter to come.

Dar wasn't convinced the huts would stand up against the brunt of a winter storm, and there wasn't enough space in the caves as they were at the moment. Dar had also seen first-hand how quickly devils could burn down a town. He liked the idea of having something that would be harder for them to destroy.

So the cave mining was a two-part solution: to both improve their dwellings outside the cave, and to expand the caves should they need them for shelter this winter.

As they continued into the center of the village, they came up to the large communal space. The open area was split in half by a massive fire pit. One side had tables on the outskirts and was dotted with rocks and log stumps for seating closer to the fire pit. The other side

was wide open for larger projects, such as the trees that were being dragged in now.

The area had naturally become a gathering point. The entire village came together to eat meals and work on projects. It had helped build their community and ease some of the tension between the different groups of demons, spirits, and humans.

Dar gave Glump a nod and broke off, spotting Sasha busying herself around one of the tables. She was so focused on her task that she didn't see him approach, so he stopped just a bit away from her and smiled as he watched her work.

Her long, raven black hair was not as tidy as it had been when he'd first met her. She preferred to pull it back with a ribbon now, and she'd abandoned her large witchy hat. He'd found her attractive before, but there was something more natural about the way she styled herself now, although she still wore dresses despite the heat and working up a sweat.

Tailoring clothes seemed to be an integral part of her as a demon. She also had strong ideas about his wardrobe. Given that he was the leader of this new village, she made sure he looked the part.

Sasha was a demon—of what exactly she had purposefully kept to herself—and even naked in bed, he hadn't found a sign of anything hinting at what animal she'd been before she had touched upon her first dao.

Sasha had formed the greater dao of silk and had used it to become a seamstress for the wealthy of Kindrake, creating fanciful dresses and enchanting them to be better than anything a human could make.

Sliding up behind her, Dar wrapped his arms around her midsection and pulled her close.

"Dar!" She let out a surprised squeak. "I was working." Her objection was weakened by the way her body molded into him as she pressed her hips back into his own. "Is someone excited to see me?"

"Always, dear. What are you working on?" He leaned down and gave her a kiss on the cheek while he studied what she'd been doing.

There was a large cloth laying on the table. It looked like she'd been working to enchant it.

"Trying to fix the bed problem," Sasha muttered, clearly frustrated with her progress.

Dar ran his lips along her cheek and up to her ear, nibbling a bit as he went and enjoying the contented sigh he got in return. Placing his hand on her waist, he slowly started sliding his hand up her body until he reached her bountiful chest, eliciting a slight moan.

"You really are an animal sometimes." Her voice was breathy.

Sasha's dao of silk was made up of three lesser dao: soft, fibrous, and elasticity. Mostly the first and last applied to her body, making it the softest body Dar had ever encountered. He loved the feel of her and took the opportunities he had to touch her.

At first, he had avoided doing anything where others could see, but the culture in Granterra was far more open than what he'd known on Earth. It was one of the things he'd been forced to get used to after arriving in this world.

"How does this fix the bed problem?"

She gave him a playful slap on the wrist as his hands got a little too friendly. "If you'd settle down and study enchanting a little more, you'd see and not have to ask." She gave him a stern face before continuing. "I'm trying to make the cloth not only be soft but make anything below it soft and elastic as well."

"So then we could drape it over a rock and have a bed?" Dar asked, taking a closer look at the enchantment.

The characters were blurry, evading his ability to actually read them. That happened whenever he tried to look at a dao he hadn't yet understood. He wanted to push through it, but the previous times he'd done that had ended in nose bleeds.

"Exactly. Now, how's your dao going?" Sasha flipped her focus back to him.

"Nothing yet." He tried and failed to hold back a heavy sigh.

Sasha reached down into her dress and pulled out a book. He knew it actually came from the enchanted pouch tied to her thigh, but it

was always interesting to watch her pull odds and ends out of her dress.

"Study the combustion dao character. Sometimes working on something else is what you need to clear your mind and make progress."

Dar took one last squeeze of her hips before he freed Sasha and took the book. "Love you." He kissed the side of her head and flipped it open.

She had labeled the pages since he had last looked at it. He smiled to himself. He'd been asking her all the time which was which. It looked like she'd wanted to streamline it a bit. Sasha, like many demons and spirits, recorded what dao they knew so they could share with their dao companions, the closest thing they had to marriage.

Besides the three dao he hoped would form the greater dao of granite, he had heat. Sasha's combustion dao would be a perfect pair for him to build closer to fire. The dao of granite he wanted would best help the village build, but fire would be great in combat and defending the village.

With Lilith, a powerful demon, gone, seals were breaking, and more devils were entering the world. According to her words before she had passed on, he had a destiny to stop them.

For now, he sat on a stump close to the fire and tried to trace the character for the dao of combustion. His finger moved as his eyes tracked the lines of the character, hoping to use his muscle memory to imprint the dao character into his mind.

But the character grew fuzzy, and his eyes slipped from the character, losing focus. He tried not to get too frustrated. Demons all spoke of the years it typically took them to reach their next dao.

He was a marvel for reaching four lesser dao in such a short time period, but he'd set the bar high for himself. He needed to grow more powerful to protect the village he was trying to create. Devils were already becoming more bullish in their attacks; it was only a matter of time before he'd need all the firepower he could get.

Frustrated, Dar felt his mana swirling around with his tumultuous feelings. He wondered if he should go for a run or something to work off the extra energy, but as he sat feeling it move through his body, Dar realized that it actually felt like it was trying to build to something.

Closing his eyes, he looked at his inner body and all the channels that he'd created to move mana around his body. They were a network of near infinite possibilities.

The mana continued to swirl, certain areas flickering with a bit of extra mana. The arcs and lines almost formed characters. Dar watched the mana swirl, a thought forming. He knew that mana and dao were closely linked, so it made sense that the two might somehow be connected. And there was something in the shapes he was seeing that felt... right.

Pushing out any other thoughts, Dar focused again on the character he'd been studying for combustion. Instead of tracing it with his finger, he began to flow his mana through his channels, working to find the ones that would line up to create the shape.

Dar had part of it formed when he lost his focus and the mana bled out back into the broader channels, losing the shape. Taking a deep breath, he went back to work, making sure to keep his breathing steady and focus on where he needed the mana.

After a few more failed attempts, he managed to pull mana into the shape he needed and hold it through an entire cycle of his mana. His body resonated with the dao character in a more intimate way than he had ever had studying by tracing the characters.

In his excitement, Dar loosened his focus slightly, and the mana started to drain into its normal pattern and pain began to wrack him, his chest squeezing with the extra pressure.

Slamming all the distractions in his mind to the side, Dar breathed deeply, concentrating only on the dao character and reforming it before it could completely dissolve. His body continued to resonate with the dao of combustion with each pass, growing greater and

greater. He kept his focus, refusing to let his overexcitement mess it up.

"Dar. Get up! We need you," someone shouted, shattering his concentration.

The dao character crumbled, and Dar came to, leaning over and puking up blood. It felt like his entire core was being shredded.

"What did you do?" He could hear Sasha run up behind him. A slight ripple on the wind told him her ribbons were out, and she was ready to fight.

The other voice backed away as Dar continued spitting out blood, but Dar heard the person in the background talking to another villager. "But we need his help to carry Russ back."

Sasha's voice broke through then, turning on whoever had spoken. "As you can see, he's in no—"

"What happened to Russ?" Dar growled through the pain. It was a sudden event; though he was feeling weak from it, it wouldn't stop him.

"Dar, please." Sasha came up behind him and rubbed a hand in slow circles on his back.

He raised a hand, waving her concern away. "Not as bad as it looks. What's wrong with Russ?" He managed to lift his head and see who he was talking to.

The voice had been one of the younger spirits in the village and one of Russ' women, Claire, who went hunting with him most days. Dar couldn't remember what her dao was.

"We were attacked by a demon. She was too fast." The woman looked like she was on the edge of breaking down.

Dar spit out the last of the blood in his mouth and sat up, wiping his chin. He knew he probably looked like a mess, but now wasn't the time to be concerned with how he looked. Russ needed his help.

"Show me." He leaned over, pushing himself up to stand. He was a little lightheaded, but he'd be fine.

"Dar." Sasha pulled at his sleeve.

"I'm fine. We'll talk when I'm back. Despite what it looks like, I think I made progress with something new." He gave Sasha a kiss on the forehead, ignoring the scowl on her face that said she thought he should rest.

Turning to Russ' woman, he nodded. "Lead the way."

Claire darted out to the woods, clearly not wanting to waste a second with more words. Dar increased his pace to keep up with her as she wound around the granite cliffs to the break in between them. He'd been in this area before. The break seemed to have been caused by an inlet to the Bell River once upon a time, but it was now a nice path into the northern forest on the other side of the cliffs.

He had to work to keep an eye on the woman in the woods; she blended in well. Her pale green hair was like the underside of an oak leaf. And, right now, it was braided up and swishing back and forth as she picked her way through the quiet forest.

Dar knew the quiet of the forest was a sign—there was still danger near.

"How much farther?"

"Not much more." Her head snapped to something that Dar didn't make out and then cut a ninety-degree angle, still rushing through the forest. "Almost there."

She didn't have to say anything because Dar could hear people up ahead.

When they came into view, Dar was stunned. Russ was bleeding badly on the forest floor. Three of his other girls were angled around him, holding spears and watching the trees. They looked at Dar as he approached before taking a few steps away from Russ, making room for Dar to check on him.

Russ was a demon, a big burly demon that had kept his coyote face and neck. He only blended to more of a humanoid shape at the shoulders, but he kept his patchy fur all the way down to his feet. From what others had said, many of the male demons tended to stick with many of their previous animal traits because they associated them with strength.

Dar leaned down, feeling for a pulse. It was still there, but weak. He was in bad shape, covered in cuts. "Okay, we need to move him."

"That's what you are here for. We couldn't move him and defend against it," a demon girl with a pair of rams horns curling out of her head said, hissing a bit as she said 'it'.

Dar nodded. He would get the full story out of them later. If there was danger around, they needed to move. He wasn't sure how much longer Russ had in him.

Hefting the demon over his shoulder, he nodded to them, and they started to move as a group, keeping their circle around Dar and watching into the trees.

"What are we looking for?" Dar asked, starting to loop mana through his channels so he would be ready to use any of his dao if he needed to.

"Demon. Cat-like. Very fast." Ram girl spoke in clipped, clearly agitated words.

Dar nodded, keeping his head up as he hauled Russ. The demon was bulky, almost as big as Dar. Luckily for them both, Dar's body was covered in enchantments. Carrying him back to camp wasn't a problem, but if they got in a fight, that would get trickier. He wasn't sure how to balance Russ without hurting him further if he was forced to fight.

"Maybe if it attacks, you should run with Russ," Claire spoke.

"No, if this is a big cat, that's exactly what it probably wants. If we scatter, it can try to pick one of us off." Dar wanted to ask for all of their names, but now wasn't the best time.

A branch cracked and Dar's hand shot up, prepared to blast heat at their enemy. He and a doe stared at each other for a moment before the doe shot off deeper into the woods.

Dar and the girls let out a collective breath, and he lowered his hand. But, just as his arm was halfway down, something flew into him from the other side. Pain laced up his arm as he tumbled to the side. Dar drew on his hard dao for his skin and to protect Russ.

Whatever it was kicked off Dar, right in his stomach.

He righted himself, earning a wheezed grunt from Russ. Crouched on the ground before him was a cat girl. She was slim with curves in the right places, and mostly human with fluffy cat ears and a tail. She had a jaguar pattern to her ears and tail, the black circles with darker red-ish coloring on the inside.

Dar knew a few guys back on Earth that would be in heaven right now. And he had to admit, there was a cuteness to her, even when she was in her fighting stance.

But she would have been cuter if her hands weren't dripping his blood on the forest floor. She licked her plump pink lips, looking at Dar, but it wasn't sexy at all. It looked more like she was ready to eat him as she crouched low, readying to spring again.

"Ha!" The ram demon jumped forward with her spear, but the jaguar girl did a small hop and twisted her body around the spear, lashing out with her hands like they were claws.

Dar could sense the mana in her hands as they tore right through the girl's clothes. The ram girl was barely able to get out of the way.

She and the others settled back into a ring around Dar, trying to guard Russ, but it didn't slip his notice that her clothes were rapidly being dyed red.

"Keep moving. We don't have to kill her." He needed to get them out of the forest and back to the village. He could come back later and deal with the jaguar girl.

"But she hurt Russ. We need to fight back," Ram girl tried to argue, but she was slapped upside the head by one of the others.

"We leave now. Thank you, boss, for helping with Russ. I know the two of you don't always get along."

Dar's eyes never left their attacker, who at the moment was stalking in a slow circle around them, waiting for an opening. Luckily, she didn't have one. The girls held the ring steady.

"We keep going. Come on." Dar stood and touched his own wound. It wasn't deep enough to prevent him from moving, but he was sure Sasha would throw a fit when he got back.

He didn't need to remind the girls again as they moved as one, keeping the feral cat girl in their sights. She didn't take another swipe at them. Instead, she simply perched, watching and waiting for them to slip up.

Eventually, she slipped back into the trees, but given her last attempt to attack them, Dar wasn't going to slacken his attention.

The girls led him back a ways before they pointed out a split tree that looked like it had been struck by lightning. "Turn due east here and we can find our way back to the village."

Ah, that's what Claire had sighted earlier. They were using the tree as a landmark to find their way back. They probably had a few they'd developed in the short time they'd been hunting this forest.

"If I wanted to come back out here by myself, how would I get back to the area we were at before?" Dar asked.

"Up the paths from the cliff, stay straight till you hit the split tree, turn due north and keep going. There's a ravine with a bunch of rotting wood. If you hit that, you went too far."

Dar nodded. He had partly asked to keep their minds sharp. They were starting to relax.

"The path down to the bottom is up ahead," the ram girl called.

Dar cast one last look back at the forest, but he couldn't see anything. With a small shrug, he followed the girls down out of the forest. As soon as there wasn't an overhead canopy for the jaguar demon to hide in, they all relaxed and focused on picking up speed and getting Russ back to the village.

CHAPTER 3

As Dar carried Russ into the center of the village, people scrambled to make way for their injured townsperson.

"Dar, we have this table ready for you." Sasha guided him over to a low table.

Setting Russ down, Dar was nearly pushed aside as Russ' women circled the table defensively and wouldn't let Sasha approach.

"Cut it out," Dar growled. "Now isn't the time for this. Let her get to him."

All but the ram girl wilted in front of Dar, but as he locked eyes with her, she looked ready to pick a fight. He knew her emotions were riding high, so he let the challenge pass, but he kept eye contact with her.

"You need to get a new shirt and get that wound stitched up."

She looked down at the torn shirt plastered to her side, soaked in blood. "I'll be fine. I'm made of tough stuff."

"Mindy," one of her sister wives pleaded.

Dar let out a sigh of relief. Finally, he had her name. "Mindy. Let someone look at your wound and let them tend to Russ. You are currently getting in the way of his recovery."

She glared at Dar and started to move, only to wince and clutch her side.

Dar knew she'd come to the right conclusion soon, but he was tired of waiting. "Lay down. Don't make that cut any worse than it is. We'll have someone look at you after Russ."

Mindy grumbled but eventually used her spear to lower herself down to the ground, refusing to even take her other dao companions' help.

One problem solved, Dar nodded to Sasha and two human women that came to the table. Tabby, Bart's wife, apparently had a knack for healing. She liked to joke she was self-taught from having to bandage Bart so much during his early days in the forge.

Sasha pulled out a spool of thread and got to work. Using her dao, she didn't even need a needle to stitch the wounds closed. Her precision was impeccable. Tabby worked with her, sealing each wound with a paste, while a third woman finished with wraps.

Together, the three women should be able to stop Russ from getting worse, at least long enough that his natural fortitude as a demon would do the rest.

Dar felt somebody come up behind him, but he knew that floral smell. As Cherry reached him, she rubbed his back, standing on her tiptoes to put her chin against his shoulder.

"Let's get you some food, and we can talk about what happened with the leaders."

Nodding, Dar left the healers to do what they did best. His own minor injuries could wait.

They approached the other side of the fire pit where they ate communally. The central fire pit sported three large cauldrons and masses stood around them, waiting their turn to get a serving of food. Dar recognized one of Glump's dao companions managing one of the cauldrons, so he headed over with Cherry to get a bowl of stew.

Dar hoped they'd be able to get things set up for a larger variety, but they could all live on stew for now. It was by far one of the easier meals to cook en masse to feed over a hundred people.

"What are we having today, Darande?" Dar asked the woman ladling food into everybody's bowls.

"We have another lovely assortment of wild herbs with dryad grown corn and potatoes. We even managed to get some rabbit in here." She scooped stew into two rough bowls for Dar and Cherry.

"Thank you." Dar nodded to her in thanks.

"Here." Cherry held her bowl out, offering to swap. It had a slightly larger portion.

Dar took it and gave her a peck on the cheek, but looking up, he noticed a few of the heads of the village looking at him as they formed a rough circle among the seating.

Sighing internally, Dar was reminded that building a town didn't keep to working hours. There was always work to be done. Dar found Cherry and him a seat in the circle, making a mental list of who was in attendance.

Closest to him was Bart, the first human to agree to come with Dar to start the town, and the reason so many other craftsmen had joined. He was also the father of their maid, Amber. He'd naturally become the leader for the humans in the village. He was well-spoken, well-liked, and a bear of a man from his days at the forge. He had helped lead the craftsmen as they built up the town.

Next to him was Glump, a demon from the eldest family unit, and Dar's working companion. Glump's dao companions flitted around him but never sat down at the group. Dar had been told it was something to do with the demon culture; the men would usually take the lead and speak for their group.

Samantha, a human woman, sat next to Glump. She had taken it upon herself to be the voice of the women and children in the village. She'd even set up a schooling program for the little ones. Dar obliged her as much as he could; children were the future, and he wouldn't hamper them unless he had to.

Rex was the last one in the circle. He was a bird demon and led the charge around the village's defenses. His ability to scout and keep an eye on everything around them had already proven valuable. He and his guards had managed to spot and prevent two wolf packs from getting to their budding village in the short time they'd been at this.

A few of the leaders were missing, but the important ones were there. Dar knew Rex would be interested in hearing his report of the attack.

"Evening." Bart waved Dar and Cherry into the conversation.

Dar smiled as he settled into his seat. "A little livelier than I was expecting this late in the day, but all's well that ends well. Russ will get patched up and be back to his boisterous self in no time."

"Maybe he'll be tempered a tad." Glump smiled and a few of the others tried to keep a smile off their own lips. "Still, he should be strong enough to take care of himself. Many in the village are not as strong as he is, so if there is a threat to him, there's a threat to many. Tell us what you found."

Dar told them the story of his flight through the forest, and how he'd found Russ. They paid special attention to his description of the jaguar demon.

Rex was the first to speak. "Sounds like a young demon. We'll double up anyone on night watch. Can't have her prowling down from the cliffs and causing trouble. She'll need to be dealt with though."

Wincing, Dar hazarded a question. "Dealt with how?"

Glump croaked a laugh. "Captured, not killed. This situation isn't that uncommon among demons. Most of us start like that. It isn't as if we go from animals to demons and become magically civilized."

Dar paused. He hadn't really given it much thought, but it made sense. Even though forming a dao and rebuilding their bodies led to higher intelligence, most of them would still not be more than a wild animal. Just far smarter. After all, their life so far had been as wild animals.

"So, we send out a team to wrangle her down. Then what?"

Glump smiled and Rex filled in. "We bring her back and try to socialize her. The women have done this before; they can hen peck the new girl for a while. It'll get them off my back."

Dar looked warily over Rex's shoulder. Sure enough, one of his dao companions walked over and smacked the back of his head, walking away muttering something about ungrateful men.

Rex winced, a sparkle of mirth in his eye as he rubbed the back of his head. "I guess I deserved that one."

"Probably did. Most of us were thinking it, but I have enough sense not to say it aloud," Bart laughed, and the others joined in, the tension lightening.

Dar took another bite of the stew, waiting for the group to settle before getting back to the topic at hand. "So we send a group to go get her. Who's it going to be?"

But Glump surprised Dar when he said, "No, only one can go. A demon like her won't make a move on a large group. She still has the instincts of a predator. She will know when she's outmatched, and it will be almost impossible to flush her out."

Dar nodded, looking around the circle and noticing all the expectant faces watching him.

Sure enough, Glump finished his statement by saying, "I think it should be you, boss."

Dar had thought that was coming. He looked over to Cherry to get her thoughts; she nodded her agreement. "Alright. I'll go see if I can't wrangle us a feral demon and a new member of the village. What other excitement did I miss today?"

Bart leaned forward. "I got those picks made. If you think your dao isn't going to come soon, I'll start some men working the caves into something larger. We can at least dig out some limestone we can crush and start trying to make that concrete you described."

Dar had given him the basic recipe for some simple concrete. He'd recommended crushed and cooked limestone as a great base, with sand and gravel mixed in. It wouldn't be like industrial concrete, but it would do the job just fine.

"Go ahead and get that started. If you can get the guys to dig out a pit and lay a foundation, I'll see about enchanting it."

"Will one of the kilns we were already working on do it? We have the three pits for you almost dug out. Just need to line them so you can enchant them."

Dar thought about it. He knew cooking the limestone would give off some pretty dangerous fumes, so really it just needed to be somewhat kept separate. "Pick one, but let's make sure it is marked. There are some nasty fumes that come off the limestone; I don't want to mix our new pottery dishes and those fumes."

Bart nodded and scratched a note into a piece of wood he had at his side with a knife. "I'll get them marked with stakes. Two for the women's pottery and one for the concrete." He looked up. "You know, Rick is begging to try building with this stuff given how you talked it up. He's excited about the idea of something like mortar but used en masse to make a structure's base."

"Hah, I hope it lives up to his expectations. Just be careful what you put in it. It's meant to be pretty hard to modify once it is set," Dar commented, still a little unsure how the substance would work in Granterra. So far, chemical properties had seemed similar enough to what he was used to. Mana just made everything a bit different.

"Sam, how are the kids?" Dar changed to lighter topics.

There were about two dozen little ones that ran around the village. They were mostly human, but there were a few young demons and spirits in the group. It was fun to watch them all play together, and it seemed to also help the adults get used to intermingling more than they had in Bellhaven.

After all, the kids didn't seem to care if they were human or ancient. They were all just kids.

"Energetic. It would be easier to manage them if we had a proper building to help hold them and reinforce some structure. They like to wander too much." There was a pointed look at Glump, who had a little one in the group that was a bit of a troublemaker.

Dar had seen similar incidents where the kids had all been running in different directions, Sam chasing after them. At her age, Sam struggled a bit to keep up with them.

"Our children are very active; it is okay to let them learn through error," Glump defended himself.

Sensing potential conflict, Dar worked to try to move on without getting in the middle. It wasn't wise to tell somebody how to raise their kids. "Either way, thank you Sam for working with the children."

"My pleasure, Lord Yigg."

Despite his protests, she continued to stick to a formal title. After realizing he wasn't a wizard, the people of Bellhaven had dropped that title and picked up lord. Sam took it even further, using his last name as well.

"How much longer on the palisade?" Rex took the opportunity to change the topic.

Dar shared a glance with Glump and spoke for the both of them. "The biggest delay is the lumber, and I'm worried that, with the recent attack on Russ, we might not have many people willing to go out to collect logs the next few days."

Cherry turned to him, a bit of sadness in her eyes. Her dao, unfortunately, wouldn't help them with this task. They'd thought to use her dao to grow a tree, but it had limitations. She could create new growth or even speed up the growth of a harvest, but creating a several decade old oak that they could cut down for lumber took too much to be worth it.

Her dao worked more so to speed up growth than to magically create a tree.

"Cherry, how's food production going?"

She shifted back to the group to report. "We are still gathering plenty of food. We'll need more storage space soon. Dar, your solution to rotate beans into the field has helped significantly; it is much easier to encourage their growth now."

"Good. How much more storage do you need?" Bart asked, before turning to Dar. "Do you think that would be a suitable job for our first project with the concrete?"

"Yeah, that would work pretty well. It just needs to be a simple cellar. We could dig down maybe six feet and line it with concrete to keep the bugs out."

"Couldn't we just use the caves?" Rex asked. "The houses should be a priority."

The group paused with that question, and Dar put it to a vote.

"Hands up if you think the priority should be housing." The hands went up from Glump, Bart, Sam and Rex. A swift majority put the issue to bed. "Focus on the first foundation then, Bart. We can use the caves for now."

"Any other issues with the crops?" Dar asked.

Last time, he'd had to prod Cherry to tell him that it was getting harder and harder to grow the crops. She'd been exhausting herself and struggling through it. After a look at the little field they were using, it became apparent to Dar that they weren't rotating the crops. They were just growing as much corn as they could because they thought it had the best yield.

Cherry might have been using her dao to speed it up, but the soil wasn't being given time to recover. He'd then suggested growing a few cycles of beans and rotating the crops.

It confirmed that, while her dao could make plants grow faster, it was less taxing if there were better conditions; the mana and her dao only helped supply what was missing for her to speed up the crop growths.

"None, besides the coming winter. I'm not sure if I'll be able to coax crops up through the snow." Cherry bit her lip. She put a lot of pressure on herself, especially as they tracked their current yields. They were doing impressively for a new settlement, but they still would have to work hard to stock enough before winter came.

"How long do we have before our first snow?" Dar shifted the question to address the entire group.

"A moon, maybe a little more if it comes later." Cherry looked to the others for confirmation.

Everyone nodded at her assessment.

"If we could build an enclosure around the field and give it some heat, do you think we could extend it?" Bart asked.

Dar considered it but realized there was more that they needed. "It's the sun that's the problem. In the winter, sunlight is weaker and doesn't provide enough energy to sustain crops."

A few of them looked at Dar like he had a new head growing out of his neck. They generally accepted his odd knowledge based on the story he'd told them that he was from a faraway area, but they got more curious the more that he said.

"Is that why it gets colder in the winter?" Glump asked, sounding genuinely curious.

"Sort of. It's complicated." Dar wasn't about to get into planetary science, especially knowing he'd butcher it anyway. He would have paid more attention in science classes if he'd known he'd have to represent it for an entire world.

"So, how do we make up for the weakened sunlight?" Sam asked, before adding, "Also, you should teach the kids. You have a wealth of knowledge."

Dar had to keep himself from laughing. Back on Earth, his general education and trade skills hadn't made him stand out at all, but they seemed to put him into an elite category here. But he couldn't think of how he'd fit it into his schedule.

"Maybe sometime once we are more set up. For now, I'm focused on getting everything built."

"Bring the kids to the field. We'll give them a lesson and they can pitch in. It should get some of their energy out," Cherry offered, and Sam nodded agreement.

Dar couldn't think of a strong reason not to. They could at least try it, and if it got too much in the way of their production, they'd just change their approach. "Sure. Priority stays on the crops. The kids would be a big help if we can get them to focus, but, Sam, if they are more trouble than they are worth, we need to have enough food for the winter."

Sam nodded, but Dar knew he'd have to keep an eye out. She often put the kids above everything else, so he threw Cherry a knowing

look, making sure she knew he wanted to know the moment there were issues.

Cherry nodded back. "I will not let you all go hungry. If that means shooing out some children from the field, then I'll do it."

"Good, we'll have to think of some other ideas come winter. For now, we'll keep on as we are."

A loud belch resounded in the circle from Glump, breaking the moment and leading to a few of the nearby men from other groups challenging him with belches of their own. They'd all finished their food at that point, so the group started to clear out.

Sasha came over to Dar, who had stayed seated. She wiped grime off her hands and settled down to finally enjoy her own bowl of stew.

"He'll live, but he'll have a few new scars for it. And don't think I didn't notice that you didn't let me look at you for all the grief you gave Mindy." Sasha poked at his side where he'd been cut.

"It's not bad at all." There was a small patch of caked blood, but it looks like it was enough to clot itself.

"Mmm, we'll look at it later," Sasha promised before focusing on her stew.

Cherry handed off her and Dar's empty bowls to Marcie, who'd been hovering nearby, to clean.

"Would you like another bowl, milord?" Amber asked before Marcie could get too far away.

"No, thank you. And please sit down with us when you are finished," Dar added.

Both of them did a small curtsy before moving off. They'd been helpful and had been supporting Cherry in the field during the day. He felt a little guilty that they had signed up for something different, thinking he'd be some big shot wizard in Bellhaven.

They'd done well so far as the plans adjusted, and they seemed to be enjoying their time, but he still worried they wouldn't say anything if they were unhappy.

Once the group had cleared out and just Sasha and Cherry remained with him, Dar broached a topic he'd been thinking about.

"Cherry, do you think if I planted some trees in my inner world, you'd be able to help them get a head start?"

"Why not just gather some wild trees from the forest?"

Pausing, Dar didn't have a good answer. He just hadn't thought of doing that. "That... is a really good idea. I'll see if I can't spot any."

"You should also invite Mika over here," Cherry added, looking over at another group. It was filled with mostly unaffiliated spirits and demons; they had formed their own small group of five women.

"She can decide on her own," Dar grumped. Since they'd started the village, Mika had avoided him for the most part. He didn't want to deal with whatever her problem was; he had enough going on.

"He really needs us to spell it out for him, doesn't he?" Cherry asked Sasha, a smile teasing at the edge of her lips.

"Right? It took brute force for him to win us over, saving me twice and binding you to him with oaths. And yet he seems to think that, if Mika wanted him, she'd just curl up like a little kitten waiting for attention."

Dar stayed silent through their mock discussion, enjoying the light banter despite taking the brunt of their joking. He got their point. Granterra was different. Strong men had multiple women; it was expected of them. And, in the communities of the ancient races, men sought strong dao companions.

But the concept of having multiple dao companions was still an odd concept to him. His brain still was stuck in how he'd been raised. At this point, he had Sasha and Cherry as dao companions and even used Amber for pleasure. That felt like more than enough. Going after another woman seemed selfish, but the girls had a different opinion. They wanted a stronger family unit that measured up to what they felt his prominence should be.

This wasn't the first time Cherry and Sasha had brought up Mika, but they were definitely becoming more direct. He gave them a look, letting them know he heard them and would figure it out in his own time. They just smiled to themselves.

It was growing dark, and groups were starting to break off to their huts, so Dar stood up. Whatever he did, it would have to wait for another night.

"Come on, you two. Time to go get some sleep so we are ready for tomorrow."

"Sleep?" Cherry chuckled. "Is that what we are supposed to do in the hut?"

CHAPTER 4

Dar blinked awake, his arms still wrapped around Sasha's soft, curvy form. He let his fingers sink into her, savoring her body pressing against his for a moment longer.

"Dar?" Sasha asked, her voice giving away that she was still half-asleep.

Kissing her neck, he teased, "I do hope you weren't expecting someone else in bed."

He got his hand slapped away from her chest in response. "Careful, Lug."

Dar could hear the smile in her voice as she used his nickname, and she knew full well he didn't like it.

He pivoted back a bit, looking around, but then he remembered that Cherry wasn't in the hut. The night before, they had all coupled and grown closer as a family, but they'd also shared with each other as dao companions and worked to bring their dao paths closer.

When they were too exhausted to do more than sleep, Cherry had insisted on entering his inner world. When he had joined her, she'd used the time while his body rested to pick up where they'd left off. The ancient dryad might have not lived up to her namesake originally, but she was making up time for it.

Dar took one last look at Sasha's sleeping form. He couldn't see anything that stood out as non-human, and he still wondered what

she had been before she became a demon. Yet she was hesitant to tell him.

"Okay, enough lounging around. Time to get up, Sash." Dar gave her a peck on the cheek and opened his inner world for Cherry to exit.

Cherry stretched out with a yawn as she appeared in front of them. "That was nice."

She moved towards Dar, now sitting on the edge of the cloth-draped mound, and leaned down for a good morning kiss. For once, Cherry towered over him as she kissed him. He smiled. Normally she had to stand on her tiptoes to reach him.

Her breath was fresh and sweet, with a faint trace of cherries to her. Her name did come from the tree she'd been tied to most of her life, a cherry tree. When Dar had met her, she'd protected that tree with her life. But, when it had been destroyed, she'd bound herself to the tree in his inner world.

A smile lingered on Dar's lips as Cherry pulled back. "Morning, my little dryad. Is your tree in good health?"

"The best, for the best tree ever." Her grin grew wide as she looked at him with that slightly obsessive gaze she'd previously had for her cherry tree. Since she'd bound herself to his tree, the gaze was now for him.

"Then let's keep it that way. We have some work to do." He hauled himself up and looked back at Sasha, who was curling back up for another round of sleep. He could prod her out of bed, but she'd been working hard, and he wasn't going to disrupt her if she needed a little longer.

Clothes on, Dar ducked out of their hut that Cherry had made using living saplings. Cherry could easily manipulate the saplings, but she had more trouble with trees large enough for lumber. The more she tried to accelerate past the normal bounds of what the tree would do naturally, the more effort it took.

But his ponderings evaporated as the smell of oatmeal hit his nose.

"Come on. Let's get some food in you before you drool on that new shirt," Cherry laughed, pulling Dar by the hand towards the center of the village to the fire pit. A set of women were stirring pots of oatmeal mixed with some crushed berries.

"That smells great, Tabby." Dar recognized Bart's wife in the morning dawn.

"Morning, lord. I hope you got some sleep." She arched a brow, giving him a somewhat motherly look.

Dar grinned sheepishly. There wasn't much in the way of sound insulation on those huts. But he'd heard other huts grunting into the night, so he didn't feel bad about making noise with his girls.

Cherry spoke up for him though. "He is a great lover. We can't get enough of him."

Dar nearly choked. He still hadn't gotten used to how open everybody was about sex in Granterra.

"Well, maybe I should convince Bart to take on one of the lovely spirits."

Cherry jumped on that. "You should! Bart is the de facto leader of the craftsmen; he deserves all the love he can get."

Tabby only gave Cherry a polite smile and didn't draw out the conversation. "Here, I better not keep you too long." She handed them both bowls.

Cherry took them and shooed Dar to a seat. He had learned not to try to fight it. His attempts so far had been useless. Cherry's culture oriented around women doing smaller tasks for the man in their dao companionships as a way to show affection. It would be like interrupting someone who showed love through small acts of service.

Instead, he just enjoyed how she chose to show her affection.

Dar spotted Marcie and flagged her over. "Can you make sure to get Sasha up if she's not up shortly?"

"Yes, milord. Do you need anything else?"

"No, thank you, Marcie. I think we are set for the day." Dar checked with Cherry as she handed him his bowl.

page

"I am fine as well, Marcie. If you have time, come help with the crops today."

Marcie bowed and stepped away to give them some privacy.

"I feel bad that I don't have more work for her."

"Don't be. I keep her plenty busy in the field; though, you should bed her soon or she might leave on her own."

Dar didn't answer that and just dug into his oatmeal. It wasn't anything fancy, but the berries added a nice swirl of color and sweetness that made it pleasant enough. Which was good, because he had a feeling he'd be eating it for the foreseeable future.

"So, you are going after this demon today?" Cherry asked.

"Seems like the smart thing to do. Glump had no interest in the job, and I'm probably the best to handle her in a one-on-one situation. Unless you want to come with? I bet you could hide in my inner world and give her a big surprise."

Cherry shook her head, but what confused Dar was her almost hungry eyes. "No. This is something you need to do alone. If I went and subdued her, she wouldn't accept it. Not to mention, a day away from the field is a lot of lost food."

Dar nodded. He'd need to bring his axe and be ready for whatever this demon had to throw at him. "Any tips?"

"Bring rope. Pin her and bind her up, then haul her back here. I'm sure Sasha will love the project of civilizing some young demon." Cherry chuckled as she ate.

"You make it sound so casual."

She shrugged. "It is. This is how demons have been doing it for over a thousand years. They take the new demon, teach them language, civilize them to a degree, and then let them decide what they want to do."

Dar still didn't quite understand why it had to be him alone. It made sense that the jaguar demon might not come out if she felt outnumbered, but she had when he'd been with a few of the weaker females. He had a nagging feeling there was some part of the demon

culture he wasn't understanding in the situation. He eyed Cherry skeptically.

"Don't worry. I have no doubt that, if you are prepared, you can deal with her on your own," Cherry added, avoiding his eyes.

"Thanks for the vote of confidence, but she was pretty dangerous yesterday." Whatever Cherry was hiding, Dar didn't dig after it. He trusted her.

"That's because you had several people to guard, and you weren't ready. This time, you will be."

Dar sighed and ate the rest of his oatmeal. Bart was already redirecting the woodcutters to another task for the day.

Dar needed those woodcutters out in the forest, but it was too dangerous with the rogue demon. He couldn't let them get any further behind. They'd been lucky so far at not having any devil attacks, but he knew it was only a matter of time. They needed stronger defenses.

"Alright, I'm heading out. Let's see if I can't bag us a new member of the village," he said halfheartedly, but Cherry nodded with more excitement in response.

"You should really name it, you know? Think about it, Dar. She needs a name as a first step towards being socialized. It's not something she would have done herself."

Dar just nodded as he started heading towards the forest. Picking up his axe on the way, he figured he could see if he could help with any other problems while he spent the day in the woods.

Following the trail up to the top of the cliffs, Dar moved by the morning light until he spotted the split tree and made a right, following the guidance of the hunters. He wondered if finding some game would help lure the cat girl out.

Dar had only hunted a few times before this new life, and it had always been with friends. Now it felt like he was crashing through the woods, sending animals scattering in every direction. He also had to be on the lookout for an attack at any moment. It was far different from setting up at a blind.

Deciding he didn't have the patience for stealth in the moment to hunt small game, he changed his approach and started looking for fruit trees. It took less of the attention he needed to keep on the chance of being attacked.

It wasn't long till he found a tree growing plump orange fruits a dozen feet up hidden in its thick green leaves.

"You look tasty," Dar said, jumping and grabbing hold of one of the ripe oranges.

Peeling the fruit, he took a bite. The orange slice exploded with more flavor than he'd ever had before, fruit juice quickly dripping down his chin. There was even a little trace of mana in the fruit that flowed through his body as he ate.

Putting his hand against the tree, wondering what he could do with it, he tried to pull it into his inner world. He stood for a bit, continuing to try different techniques or visualizations, but it strained against the unyielding ground, not budging.

"Guess that's one limitation. Do I need to dig it up?"

It seemed like as good a project as any while he waited to get attacked.

Holding his axe, he used the hard dao and reinforced the poor weapon before using it like a trowel to loosen the dirt, making it easier to dig out the tree. It was hard work, but he brought out the shovel from his inner world to move the loose dirt. Slowly, he started to unearth the roots of the orange tree.

Dar wiped the sweat from his brow and looked around for any sign of the jaguar. He should be making enough noise in the forest that she knew he was here, but he didn't get any sign of her, so he went back to experimenting with the orange tree.

It wasn't completely uprooted. There were still some roots going far deeper, but it seemed like it might be close enough to shift it back and forth and wiggle it loose. Normally, it would be too much damage to a tree, but he had a feeling Cherry could fix any of that.

Grabbing the tree by the trunk, Dar bent at the knees and tried to push the tree out of the ground.

"Yes!" It was coming loose.

A small rustle of leaves was the only warning Dar had before the attack came. Dar immediately saturated his body in the hard dao before claws raked across his back. They weren't able to find purchase in his hardened skin, but Dar was sure he was going to have nice pink welts from it.

The demon looked at her hands in confusion as she landed in a crouch.

"Do you speak?" Dar asked, squaring up against the demon. This time, he wasn't trying to protect a wounded friend, so she had his sole focus.

She growled back at him. He took that as a 'no'.

Leaping forward, Dar tried to get a hold of the demon, but she sprang back, swiping at his arms as she moved. It was like her legs were made of springs as she cleared several yards with just that small hop. Crouching on the forest floor, she watched Dar carefully with the eyes of a predator.

"Well, since you can't speak, you probably won't understand this. But I'm not trying to hurt you. But I also can't have you attacking our hunters, so I need to bring you back to our camp. I can't promise you won't get a little hurt in the process of tying you up, but I'll do my best."

She tilted her head to the side as he spoke, clearly confused at the noises he was making.

"Yeah, I didn't think you'd understand. And you'll probably take what I'm about to do the wrong way as a result, but know that I am sorry it has to be like this." Dar grabbed a rock he'd dug up and hurled it at the demon. It might seem extreme for a capture, but she was a demon, and her body was far stronger than a human's.

While she was quick on her feet, she wasn't fast enough to move out of the way of the rock. It clipped her hip with a wet crack that made Dar wince. Howling in pain, she turned to run, angling for another tree.

"Sorry, but I don't want to have to do this again." Dar rushed forward before she could get up in a tree. He knew she could easily outmaneuver him in the foliage. Barely catching her in time, Dar ripped her off the side of a tree, and the two of them tumbled down to the forest floor.

She yowled and scratched at Dar. He kept his hard dao in place, avoiding the scratches from doing too much damage. She was still managing to break skin, but it wasn't nearly as deep as it would have been.

Keeping his arms wrapped tightly around her, he used his size to roll her over, putting himself sitting on top of her hips while he held her wrists. Her eyes showed the first moments of fear before they turned desperate as she pawed at him.

"Look, I'm sorry. This isn't how I'd like to do it either."

She hissed at him and tried to use her feet to get him off of her, forcing him to shift his weight a little further down her hips.

"Don't do that. It hurts."

But he knew she didn't understand. All she knew was that she was being pinned down by somebody who had injured her. Heck, if he walked up on the same scene, he'd probably take out the guy in his position. Sighing, he tried to figure out how to get her tied up so he could get her back.

While he was thinking, he felt a sharp sting on his wrists. She'd pivoted her head to bite at his hands.

"I get it. I do. Just bear with me a bit more." He pulled out a rope from his inner world and set it to the side as he shifted both her wrists to one of his big mitts to hold them tight, using his other hand to bind her tight.

Once she was bound, she seemed to calm down and stare at him with a calculating look. He had no doubt she was planning her escape.

Dar looked over at the orange tree and then back at her. He had almost finished with it. After all that work, he really wanted to try

again before he left the area, but he also knew she'd make a break for it if given a chance.

So he'd have to be sure he had a good hold on her for this last attempt.

Grabbing the calmer cat girl by the back of the neck, he got up and hauled her over to the tree. He held her while he tried to bring it into his inner world. This time, it took much less effort. Thankfully, the tree disappeared into his navel.

The cat girl froze, further confusion on her face at what had happened to the tree as she looked between where it had been and Dar as he retrieved the shovel in a similar manner.

"Okay, now let's get you back."

Talking to her seemed to calm her some, and he didn't want to have to chase her if she got loose. He hung his axe on his belt loop as he shifted into position. Keeping one hand on the rope tying her and the other on the back of her neck, he started walking her along the path back towards their village.

They made it about halfway before she jumped. Dar tightened his grip on the back of her neck, but her next move was to tuck her legs in and then launch them out, catching Dar in the chest.

The full force of her leg strength was too much for Dar's grip. She slipped out, landing and biting through her wrist bindings in one swift motion.

There was a cocky grin on her face as she backed away from Dar cautiously.

"Oh, come on now. You were being so good."

She only growled back at him before turning and trying to bound away.

He really didn't want to do it, but he ripped a branch from a tree and chucked it at her with his full strength.

It bounced off her head, and she went down, sliding into the dirt. Dar winced. He hadn't meant to be that rough.

"Dar, go catch the cat girl. It'll be easy," he muttered to himself as he walked up to her cautiously and prodded her with a foot. When

she didn't move, Dar leaned closer. She was either a great actor or unconscious.

He bent down and lifted her hair to see where he hit her, and there was already a bump starting to swell and an abrasion. He cringed, hating that he'd had to use brute force, but glad it hadn't done further damage.

Not bothering to bind her this time since it really had done limited good with her sharp teeth and he was fairly certain she was unconscious, he hauled her over his shoulder and started making his way back to the village again.

She started to stir halfway back, but Dar had both her wrists and ankles tightly in his hands.

CHAPTER 5

Dar stepped within sight of the village and the demons and spirits exploded in applause, hooting and hollering as he came back with the demon.

"Put her down." Sasha came forward and Dar did, though he was ready to take her out if she attacked Sasha.

He noticed Sasha was ready too, her ribbons peeking out of her dress in case she needed to defend and protect herself. Though Sasha wasn't a natural fighter, she'd proven she could step up when needed, but softness didn't lend well to being a warrior. So Dar still kept an eye on the cat girl, protective of Sasha.

But the cat girl just sat there, completely stunned by everyone's reaction. She looked around, taking in all the surrounding villagers. Through the confusion, Dar saw a spark of something like hope in her eyes.

Sasha reached out and grabbed her, leading her into the village amid all the cheering and clapping. She seemed so stunned by the village that she didn't put up a fight.

Dar hadn't expected the village to be together or be so excited. Turning to Cherry, he waited for her to explain.

Beaming, Cherry nearly jumped up and down as she spoke. "It's like the birth of a new demon or spirit for us. They appear in the

untamed areas of the world, and when one wanders close to a community that has other ancient races, we celebrate their arrival."

Cherry watched the cat girl make her way to the group, the smile not shifting on her face. "There are so few of us compared to humans. It is only fair that we celebrate their births so much."

She looked away guiltily. "You sort of deserved something like this too when you became an immortal. But we were hiding it then, so I wanted you to experience it even if they all are doing it for her today."

Dar realized it then. "That's what you were hiding."

She bobbed her head. "Sorry for that. But it wouldn't be the same if you knew it was coming."

"Thank you." Dar pecked her on the cheek and focused back on the village.

Not only was it a celebration for the village, but Dar could tell that, despite the cat girl's confusion, there was something about all the excitement and other ancient races around her that seemed to enrapture her. Dar had a feeling it would make it easier for her to feel comfortable and settle into the new place with a first experience like this.

To properly celebrate, everybody seemed to have taken the day off of their typical tasks to congregate around the central hearth. While they needed to keep moving to build up their village, he looked around at the kids running, young adults laughing, parents half-heartedly scolding their children while cooking up a feast, and even a few starting up some dancing.

He realized just how much everybody needed this moment.

They'd been working since the moment they'd reached the area to establish themselves, and as Dar felt himself settle into the moment, it was clear to him that it was the right thing for their small town.

Community would be important, and life was always uncertain. It was time to party, to celebrate what they'd done.

"This is fantastic, Cherry. Only thing missing is some wine."

She looked away from him for a moment, clearly thinking. "There is wine. Someone must have brought it in the carts from Bellhaven. I don't think it is going to be very good though."

"Boss." Glump came up with a knowing smile. "I see you wrangled a new demon."

"I see there's a tradition you left out."

Glump shrugged. "You are always so focused on what people need to survive. That's not an awful thing. You just were missing some wants."

"I don't know, Glump. It seems like they might have needed this. I just didn't see it."

Women fussed about with smiles, cooking at the common hearth at the center of the village. This place was becoming a community and the hearth here had become the center of it all.

"Well, I'm going to go introduce myself to our new little demon. Does she have a name yet?" Glump asked.

Dar blinked. "Was I supposed to name her?"

"No obligation. But she's like a child. You seem to have a reluctance to name things though." Glump turned to the cat girl and took her hand, leading her over to a bench.

Dar knew Glump was talking about a name for the village. He had called it Dao City when they first broke ground. But that name was quickly squashed. No one felt comfortable calling a gathering of huts a city. He was pushed to come up with another name.

Everything he thought of ended up sounding silly to him, so he'd just kept his thoughts to himself. He figured that, once it was settled and used more, it would fit just like any city. But still he struggled.

Dar's thoughts were interrupted as Glump stepped up onto a bench, pulling the stunned cat girl up alongside him.

"Everyone, can I get your attention? For those of you who don't know, today is an exciting day," he said.

Cheers erupted from the crowd standing around in the open space.

The cat girl scanned quickly over the crowd before her eyes found Dar. As soon as they locked, she stopped looking around, staring dead at him while Glump continued.

"Today, we have the birth of a new demon. Unlike a normal child who is found and cared for at birth, so many demons are left in the wild after awakening their first dao. As a result, they keep to the things that were comfortable as beasts." He paused, letting it settle in across the group.

"She may still be a little rough around the edges, but as a community, we should accept her for who she is. Allow for some rough patches as she acclimates. Most importantly, we should celebrate her birth!" Glump raised his arms up high in celebration. There were cheers from the village, most of all from the demons, who were excited for another to join them.

"Now, our village has its first newborn, yet it doesn't even have a name." Glump turned to Dar with a slightly wicked smile. As Glump kept staring at Dar, the rest of the crowd turned, following the gaze and clearly waiting on Dar to say something.

Dar hated public speaking, but he knew this was a moment he needed to get over. So he stood tall on top of a stump, like a lightning rod for the rest of the village. "Today is our fourth day as a new village, a new community. I'm amazed by all the work we've done so far. Everyone, look around."

He paused and looked around himself. He saw a few hundred yards of palisade wrapping around fifty huts, a field blooming just beyond them, and the communal hearth in the center where they stood.

"We've made so much progress in just this short amount of time. We should be proud of how fast we've set up the start of an incredible village. If I didn't know better, I'd think there was some dao of hearth flowing through each and every one of you."

The people, rightly so, stood a little straighter, proud of what they'd accomplished.

Taking a breath, he continued. "For those of you who walk the dao path, or just live your lives, many of us know that it is about

the journey rather than the destination. With those two concepts in mind, we celebrate not only a new arrival, but a new beginning for our budding village of Hearthway."

Everyone cheered and whistled. Despite trying to calm the crowd, Dar wasn't able to get another word out for almost a solid minute.

"Okay, now, if someone could get me a cup of wine. I think I made a mistake, and we need to get someone started on brewing a batch of wine and beer."

There were more cheers, and Sasha approached him out of the crowd, pulling him down for a kiss.

"You're a good man, Dar, and you'll be a great leader here." She grabbed a cup from someone behind him and handed him the cup of wine he asked for.

He took a sip and had to work not to stutter. It went down harsher than bottom shelf vodka. "Whew." He blew out an astringent breath. "That's strong stuff."

Sasha took a sip from his cup and coughed as she swallowed. "Yes, it is."

Out of the corner of his eye, the cat girl was watching the two of them, her tail flicking back and forth.

"Is it alright to abandon your charge?"

Sasha shrugged. "I'm keeping an eye on her. Can't hold her too close though, or I don't get to enjoy my own dao companion. It is a celebration after all."

Dar pecked her on the lips. "Yes, it is."

A beat rose from the area, and Dar spotted a group of spirits using boxes and a hollow log as a drum set. They quickly fell into a rhythm, building off of each other. It was a pumpy sort of tribal beat that repeated often.

Content, Dar downed the drink and pulled Sasha to an open space near the fire to dance. He wasn't very coordinated on his feet, but he enjoyed himself as the wine started to settle into his body.

Sasha twirled around him, her dress flaring as she danced far more gracefully than he could. She was keeping eye contact with him, a natural smile on her face.

As Dar watched, he realized Sasha must have had some training. She moved with a flourish and practice that felt like it belonged at some noble's ball, not in a clearing of a just beginning village. Watching her was mesmerizing as she swayed her curves to the beats.

Another dancer bumped into Dar's shoulder, breaking his gaze from Sasha's graceful movements. He realized they had kicked off a dance party. More and more townspeople were filling the space and dancing with them.

Cherry moved through the crowd, stopping near them and joining in the dance. Soon after, Sasha flowed away to return to the cat girl, leaving him alone with Cherry.

Cherry's dancing was far different from Sasha's, although still far better than Dar's. Where Sasha moved with a natural grace, Cherry's moves had a wild flow as they wound around each other.

She pulled his head down for a long kiss. "I think you have other takers. I can't hog you all night."

Amber replaced her and might have been Dar's match for dancing as they slowed down to a more stationary dance. The maid seemed content to sway slightly, spending most of her time rubbing her body up against his.

As he started to grow harder against her, he realized he needed a break before he poked a hole in his pants. He also caught Marcie at the edge of the dancing, watching the two of them.

"Marcie, would you care to dance?" Dar offered his hand.

She blushingly took it, and he pulled her in to dance with him.

"Thank you, milord." She ducked her head.

Dar had to lift her chin to talk to her properly. "I enjoyed it as well. You are wonderful, Marcie. You have every reason to keep your chin up and let the world see your beauty."

Marcie had a lovely face, but she hid it too often. He could feel her try to hide her face again as her cheeks went scarlet. Holding her gaze steady for a moment, he let it sink into her before he let go.

She needed some coaxing, but he didn't want to push her too hard, too quickly. He knew it would take a while before she became comfortable with their family, but he hated that she was so insecure about herself.

Not too surprisingly, she only stayed long enough to not immediately flee.

"You did good, Dar," Sasha whispered from behind him.

"I'm trying. I don't see Mika." His eyes went through the crowd.

"She took a liking to the new girl and gave me a break."

He could feel a ribbon tease its way into his pants and search for his member. "Sasha, not here."

"Of course not. I thought we'd take a break from the celebration and celebrate alone for a moment?"

Dar caught sight of a few other whispered conversations between partners that had the same mood.

"Okay, my little vixen. But we can't waste the whole party."

Sasha nearly dragged him back to their hut. On their way, he got a few whistles from Glump's women.

"There's no rush," Dar teased, only to be pulled even harder. As they got back to the hut, Sasha turned around and jumped into his arms. "I still can be in a hurry because I want to be."

He didn't get a chance to talk as she silenced him with a kiss.

Shifting his hands to cup her ass, he lifted her up so she was level with him. He savored her lips. With her dao of silk, Sasha's body was always so soft and flexible.

She pressed herself into him, and her soft mounds mashed against his chest. He couldn't help but pull her closer, chasing that feeling of her body pressed against his.

Sasha came up for air and grinned at him with a wicked smirk. "That never gets old, and I don't think it will. I love you, Dar." Her eyes searched his as she waited for his response.

"And I love you too, Sasha. All of you, even if you won't tell me what you once were. I want you to know it doesn't matter at all."

Vulnerability spread across her face as she watched him and listened to what he said. He could tell she was struggling between whatever held her back and the truth she could see in what he said.

"You really mean it, don't you?" Her voice was quiet as she spoke more to herself than to him, but he answered her anyway.

"Of course."

"Even if I was a worm? A silkworm, to be clear." She looked away slightly, not wanting to meet his eyes.

Dar kept a smile on his face, pulling her to face him again. Her eyes darted back and forth across his face as she searched for the slightest hint that it bothered him.

He hoped he was conveying it clearly, but he wanted to speak the words as well, just in case. "Sasha, it doesn't bother me one bit. I love you all the same. But I have to admit I am curious, what parts of your old form did you keep?"

His fingers trailed along her shoulder, nudging the edge of her dress off as he dipped down to kiss the exposed skin.

Blushing, Sasha pushed back from him, planting her feet back on the ground. "Let me show you." She ran a finger down his chest and used her dao of silk to split his clothing off him. The fabric fell away, leaving him entirely exposed to her.

Putting on a show for him, she let her hand linger and coax his growing erection before turning that finger on herself and slowly splitting her dress, freeing her cleavage, followed by her waist, and moving even slower as she began to reach her sex and the dress fell down to the floor. She stood in front of him in her full, naked glory.

"Sit, Dar."

He sat down with his back laid against the wall of the hut. She sat in his lap with her back to him and looked over her shoulder.

"Feel here." She brought his hand to the dimples in her lower back just before the curve of her butt.

"You have two moles back here? Ah." Dar traced what he now suspected were spinnerets.

Sasha tensed in his lap and used her hands to pull from them, confirming his suspicion as she dragged out two thin threads of silk.

Dar stopped her and wrapped his arms around her. "Amazing. You're amazing in every way, Sasha. But I just have one question."

She tensed in his embrace.

"Am I wearing clothes made of your silk?"

"No, that's different, stronger silk."

He kissed her neck and let his hand roam down to her sex as he started to let his fingers dance around her lower lips. "I want to wear your silk."

She shivered against his chest and relaxed against him. "I can do that, but I'll need some time to make enough thread and to make—"

He flicked her clit and she gasped. "Shh. Later."

Sasha only nodded as his fingers probed deeper, and she melted against his chest. He'd explored her body enough to know what drove her crazy, and he was going to use it. His fingers drew languid shapes as she continued to melt for him.

He enjoyed teasing her, knowing she was hitting her breaking point. Sure enough, she quickly spun around on his lap, facing him with lust filled eyes, and sank herself down on his length.

They didn't need words to coordinate as Dar put his hands on her hips, guiding her to rise and sink upon his length as she took his erection into her silky, warm depths.

Her sex squeezed around the head of his cock as he locked eyes with her bright blue eyes.

"Mmm. Dar. You fill me up so well," she moaned as she closed her eyes, showing the full satisfaction across her face of having him inside of her.

Dar commanded the pace, savoring every inch of her. They rocked like that for a while, slowly building their pleasure and enjoying every shared moment of their union. Sasha's slick sex devoured Dar's cock

with each pump of her hips, his own starting to rise with her craving to stay snug in her.

Dar's body began to crave more, and he gave into it, wanting to feel more friction. He started to speed her up by thrusting his hips up into her downward swing, meeting in the middle with a soft smack.

Sasha groaned at the first time and sped up her own tempo, wanting the same release he was pushing towards. She began to ride him harder, throwing her hair back and staring into his eyes as she brought him to the height of his release.

Feeling himself reach the top of the peak, Dar squeezed her hips and slammed her down, impaling her as deep as he could before he painted her insides with his seed.

Coming down from his release, Dar pulled her close and kissed her. "Now let's work on you."

Sasha kissed him back and rocked her hips on his still hard member. "I just want to make you feel good today." She leaned in to whisper in his ear, "Make the man who wants to wear my silk pop off all night long."

Her warm lips nibbled on his ear and started kissing down his neck as her hips flexed and gently started up a rhythm again.

Growling playfully, Dar pushed his hips up into her, trying to hit a fast tempo for her. But Sasha pushed his hips back down, holding them low as she took him deeply into her. Then she began to rock herself in circles on top of him.

She gasped, sheer pleasure spreading across her face as she moved herself on top of him, making him even harder all over again watching her. Her eyes lit up as she felt him throb inside of her, and a wicked grin spread on her face as they started all over again.

CHAPTER 6

Dar had spent more time with Sasha than he had planned on, but every moment had been incredible. By the time Sasha had rolled over, curling up next to him with a soft smile on her face, the daytime celebration had wound down and people were enjoying dinner by the communal hearth.

As he walked over, Dar saw the group of leaders sitting together, waiting for him.

"Hello. I'm assuming we didn't get much done today?" Dar sat down to get the update first. He could go grab food after.

Bart guffawed. "We got the kilns marked. We just need a hand from you tomorrow to enchant them. A few men piddled around this morning, and we have a handcart full of limestone to try baking tomorrow. The children had a wonderful education today in the birth of a new demon. I think many of us adults learned quite a bit too. She'll be joining the kids in lessons."

Dar did a double take. "The new demon is learning with the kids? Do we think that's such a great idea?"

Someone tapped Dar on the shoulder, and he turned to Marcie, who had a steaming bowl of food she was holding out to him. Inside was a mixture of grilled meat and vegetables, all with some sort of beany puree. It looked a little like hummus, but it must be made with soy since they hadn't harvested any chickpeas.

"Thank you, Marcie." Dar gave her a nod before turning back to the group. "She could be dangerous."

Rex spoke next. "Doubt it. Since you brought her out of the forest, she's been shell-shocked, but she hasn't tried to leave yet."

Dar looked to Glump for confirmation, and Glump nodded his agreement.

Considering it, Dar decided to try to balance the risk. "Maybe we should have someone from the guard nearby. I don't think anything will happen, but it will make everyone less tense."

Everyone nodded, and Rex said he'd put someone on duty.

Russ joined them then, two of his girls steadying him as he sat down.

"Welcome back." Glump smacked Russ on the back, eliciting a groan from the gnoll and gaining glares from Russ' two women.

Russ turned his big dog-like head to Dar. "I hear you brought the new demon back to the village?"

"Yep." Dar could feel the tension mounting in the demon. He knew he had succeeded where Russ had failed, and the young male demon might not take losing well.

"Good. She deserved that much." He grunted in acceptance as one of his women brought him his meal. "What else did I miss?"

The group filled him in quickly on the various happenings since he'd gone off to hunt. While they were talking, Cherry slipped up to Dar's side and joined the conversation.

"Food and shelter are still the priority. I don't think that'll change anytime soon," Dar simplified. "But at least we don't have any issues with water since the river is only a short walk away."

"Maybe you should think about getting something set up to boil water, or melt snow in large quantities," Russ said between mouthfuls.

That... actually wasn't a bad idea. "Bart, that might be a great thing for you guys to try once you feel like you have the hang of concrete. We could just make a heated catch basin, with the option to turn up the heat and boil the water."

"I'll add it to the list. The women are asking for clay to start making dishes, and we'll get men back to woodcutting tomorrow. We'll have our hands full in the short term." Bart took his scrap wood and carved out a list.

"It'll be worth it. Hearthway is growing fast," Dar agreed.

"What about winter?" Samantha asked, one of the few times she'd brought anything up in the leadership group that didn't have to do with the children. "People are starting to get a little worried that we won't be ready in time."

"Cold is obviously going to be a problem. I can enchant heat into a lot of our items to make it less of a problem. And I know we are saving the pelts from Russ' kills—that'll help. The biggest issue, and what we cannot solve once winter comes, is food." He looked at Cherry. They'd be able to hunt, but crops were needed to make the bulk of the village's diet.

"We need to let the soil rest, anyway. We might have to move to a new field if we've depleted the current one too much." Dar explained.

Because they'd been forcing the plants into a growth season every day, there was no way the soil was recouping nutrients it needed. "Try and push through another few days. Let's get a small crew to till a field out on the other side of Hearthway, and you can start there if the current one runs out of nutrients."

"More foreign knowledge?" Samantha asked, arching a brow.

"Your farmers probably already do this, but the husks from the last harvest, the leaves, and rain, all of those bring nutrients back into the soil. With how quickly we are speed harvesting using our dao, they won't have time to recover."

"Will it ever recover?" Samantha prompted.

"Yes, it just needs a rainy season to wash minerals from the cliffs back into the soil and for the debris to decompose. If we can move where we are harvesting every week, we should be able to sustain the growth we are forcing on the soil."

Bart spoke up. "I think we are wrong. The largest concern is housing." He looked across at the village. "No offense, Cherry, but those

huts don't make great insulators. Even if we have Darius' help with heat, it won't stay inside. We have a month to get housing for over a hundred people."

"Agreed. We'll need housing as well. We'll tackle all of this one thing at a time. We'll get some of the concrete made up, and we can lay a single foundation. Until then, we'll focus on lumber and food." Dar looked around the group for any dissenting opinions, but nobody spoke up.

Glump raised his hand. "If you can get water on the ground, I can move the mud to make room for your foundations."

Dar and Bart nodded at that, the old blacksmith using the scrap of wood to etch it into his chores.

Needing a break from all the village planning, Dar turned to Cherry. "Can you make me a new hut? I need a place to practice in solitude." Dar hadn't had a chance to experiment since he'd sat by the stream working on learning his dao. And he didn't want to do that out in the open.

"I can't guarantee you won't be disturbed here in the village. What if I block off a cave entrance?" Cherry offered.

Liking the sound of that, Dar gave her a smile. It would be perfect. "Let's do that. I need to grab Sasha's book of dao first."

"And what would you be trying to do?" Cherry followed along.

"I tried something the other day—" he started to explain, but Cherry cut him off.

"You mean when you vomited blood?" Her tone was clear in her disapproval.

Dar rolled his eyes. "It was going well until someone interrupted me. So, we're fixing the problem by making it private. Good to go."

Cherry squinted her eyes at him, not quite buying it. But Dar had a feeling she'd end up giving in, so he just kept moving.

Dar paused and ducked inside their hut to snatch the book of dao characters. He glanced over at Sasha, who was still passed out with a smile on her face. She didn't even stir as he moved around, so he

darted over, giving her a kiss on the cheek before he left the hut. He and Cherry headed toward the nearby cave.

"So tell me more about this stupid plan you have that leaves you vomiting blood," Cherry prompted.

Dar laughed, pulling her into him as they walked. "It's not like that. I just need to be able to focus. I used the channels I made in my body for moving mana, tracing out the dao character within them. I can't even describe it very well, but it felt so much closer than it ever had before, Cherry. I think that, if I kept going, I would grasp the dao."

Cherry stopped and turned slowly to him. "And which dao character were you... experimenting with?"

Dar started to answer her, but then as he took in her expression, he realized she knew he'd been focusing on combustion recently. He paused, pretty certain that, if he answered, it would not go over well.

But it didn't matter, because Cherry saw right through him, throwing her arms in the air. "Drasils above! You were experimenting with combustion. What if you essentially enchanted your body with it and blew yourself to kingdom come? What if you took out the whole village with you? Dar, this is not something you can do so casually."

Dar went to quickly reassure her, but he realized she was right. He wasn't really sure what would happen when the dao finally clicked. Accepting she had a point, he reached up to pull her to him. "Okay. Fair enough. Maybe this time I try something a little less harmful, like Sasha's dao of softness?"

Cherry harrumphed. "Promise me you won't experiment with the combustion dao. I'll block off one of the caves and even send Amber and Marcie up there to stand guard. But, Dar, I don't want to lose you."

"Have you heard of anything like this before?" He'd been meaning to ask, but too much had been happening.

"No, but you are the first immortal. Demons have their crystalized mana, and spirits have mana-infused souls. Neither of us made chan-

nels in our bodies for mana like you have. I'm not even sure how I'd start to implement such an idea."

She trailed off before meeting his eyes again. "This is dangerous. Please don't push yourself too far."

"Cherry, I'll be careful, but I also need to grow faster than the rest of the ancient races. We might have a peaceful break here, but what happens when Bellhaven or a large pack of devils find us? Heck, we aren't even ready to deal with winter."

He realized he was starting to shout and lowered his voice. "Cherry, I need to try this if it can speed up my dao."

"Fine." Cherry stomped forward towards the cave and checked inside, coming back outside after a moment. "If I end up helping you kill yourself, know I'll never forgive myself. Don't you dare leave me with that, Dar." She shook her finger at him, a stern face warring with clear worry for him.

He gave her his best smile. "I'm not going to push myself that far. Plus, I'd be an idiot to miss out on all your love." He squeezed her hips playfully and managed to bring a small smile to her lips.

"On second thought, you owe me one now. I'll collect later." Cherry shooed him inside.

Dar could tell she was apprehensive, but he also felt confident that he'd been on the right path. He'd made far more progress than when he'd studied, and like Cherry had said, he was something new.

He needed to follow his instincts when his body was telling him something. There was danger in experimentation, but something about this felt far more like an opportunity.

As Dar walked into the cave, darkness surrounded him. His eyes adjusted a bit, but he could barely make out much more than a few feet ahead. Stepping back to grab a nearby branch, Dar held his hands around the end, heating it until it lit on fire.

"Stay safe." Cherry waved from the entrance as he went further inside the cave.

Looking back, he watched as thick vines closed around the entrance, giving him his isolation. He had to admit that it was a little

eerie. He'd been travelling with somebody or out in nature for so long that being isolated in a cave felt odd.

The space within the cave wasn't large, maybe ten square feet. It was one that they had marked off as a potential winter home or storage if they could get housing up. At the moment, there wasn't anything but a few boxes of dried beans. They were using the cool cave to keep them fresher.

Not bothering with any of the boxes, Dar sat down in the center of the cave.

As his bottom settled on the cold, damp ground, he let loose a blast of heat that warmed and dried off the stone. He smiled. He'd gotten so used to the dao that things like that came second nature. It was easy to forget all the extra benefits he was getting from his new body.

Settling in, Dar pulled out and flipped open Sasha's book, searching through the pages until he found the soft dao that made up her dao of silk.

The character was harder to focus on than combustion, but he accepted that it was the right first step. If it did something to his body, he always had his hard dao to rely on to set himself back into some sort of balance. Combustion seemed harder to counter. He was more likely to end up in a lethal mess.

Focusing on the soft character, Dar started. He once again looped mana through the channels he had made when he had become an immortal, working to identify the ones that would line up into the character he wanted.

He traced the pattern while he stared at Sasha's book. Unlike attempts to copy a dao character with writing, his channels were built to handle mana, and the mana channels and dao were inextricably linked. Mana fueled his dao when he put them to use.

Tracing the pattern in his body once, Dar felt something settle within him. He kept his focus this time, cycling two more times, each faster than the previous. Soon, the cycles bled into each other, and he didn't have to study the character in the book. Instead, he focused on

continuing to direct the dao character in his channels, feeding mana into the channels and keeping the cycle going.

Dar's eyelids grew heavy, and he settled down into a meditation, imprinting the shape on his body and mind with each passing.

After a while, the constant cycling made his channels, something he thought were more metaphysical than anything else, start to ache. The aching built, but Dar could feel that the dao was just on the peak of settling into something more, so he continued pushing his body through the ache.

There was something helping him. He could feel his intersection with Sasha's dao path as they had intertwined themselves together as dao companions. Dar continued cycling the mana, even as he ached to stop, reaching further and further just to touch a hint of the dao.

All of a sudden, mana surged up from him in a push to solidify the character. It was a rush, and Dar did his best to manage the increase properly, filling it into one solid character, all lit up at the same moment.

As it settled into the character, something clicked in Dar's brain and soul. The soft dao settled into place beside the other four within him.

Breathing out a heavy breath, Dar fell over sideways, completely exhausted.

"Ha. I did it!" He yelled to no one, ignoring the hard ground in his complete happiness.

Learning that dao had taken everything out of him, and that was just with one lesser dao that his dao companion had already brought him closer to. But it had worked. Dar couldn't wait to keep experimenting. It was a small step, but it held tons of opportunity.

Dar tried to lift himself off the cave floor, but his muscles gave out and he smacked back down on the stone floor.

Okay, maybe I need a minute. Still can't believe that worked.

After lying there for a few minutes huffing the cool cave air, Dar tried to get up again. This time he almost made it, but then he fell

back down, his body not able to keep himself upright. He'd really done a number on himself.

There was noise from the entrance of the cave, and the vine covering split apart. Cherry stood on the other side, her eyes wide as she took in Dar's collapsed form on the ground.

"Morning, Cherry." Dar tried to play it casual, pretending he meant to be on the ground and was examining some nearby dirt, but based on Cherry's face, he wasn't fooling anybody.

"Morning?! It's already past noon, you idiot. And you look like you are about to die."

"Not dying. I promise. But hey, guess what? It worked." He knew he was grinning like an idiot.

Cherry sighed and shook her head. "Oh. Good. So now you're satisfied and will keep trying to kill yourself. I'm so glad. What am I going to do with you?" As she took in his state, a look of further concern spread on her face. "Can you walk?"

"Nope."

With a huff, she raised her arms and vines snaked in, lifting Dar off the cold cave floor and carrying him out. "We need to talk about this later with Sasha. I'm sure she will also have an opinion."

"Of course." Dar had more sense than to argue when Cherry was riled up. "I think I can walk if you can get me on my feet."

Cherry narrowed her eyes but shifted him upright and held him with a few vines as he tottered his first few steps. "We need to get some food into you. Come on."

She stayed close as he started towards the communal hearth. There always seemed to be something there to eat.

Marcie was hanging around outside the cave, and Dar realized she must have gotten Cherry. "Thanks, Marcie. I'll be okay."

She rushed forward and wrapped Dar in a hug before fleeing.

Damn, he really had made them worry, hadn't he?

"I think heavy labor like trying to go set the palisade or help with woodcutting is out for me today," Dar voiced aloud. "But I think I can go enchant the kilns."

His minder glowered at him. "If you can't stand up on your own after lunch, I'm having Sasha tie you up in ribbons and put you to bed."

"Yes, dear." Dar smiled, taking that bet. He was feeling stronger as they went. It seemed like it was just an initial bout of weakness after forming the new character.

Given how sturdy his body was both as an immortal and as an enchanted body, he was fairly sure what he'd just done wasn't repeatable for others. He just had too many advantages for what he had just attempted, yet he had wound up as weak as a kitten.

Still, it was a potent tool to be able to progress his dao path like this. He was already wondering if there was a way to refine this process and enable someone else to do it, but that would mean another person would need to become an immortal.

His mind immediately went to the dao fruit in his inner world. He could bring things in and out; could he bring a dao fruit out for another human to eat?

All his thoughts disappeared as Cherry put a bowl of food in front of him. Dar didn't even know what it was before he was devouring the whole bowl of semi-liquid food without it touching his tongue.

"There's more. Please don't choke." Cherry stayed standing, ready to take the bowl back from him.

"Thanks." Dar wiped the inside of the bowl for more and tasted it this time. It was a simple boiled and crushed corn, sort of like grits. "Did I miss anything?"

"A few people were wondering where you were. I'm also positive that, if I hadn't hidden you in that cave, you would have been interrupted." She stepped away briefly to get more of the grits.

"That's exactly why I wanted my own space. The cave was a great idea." Dar ate a little more slowly, but it felt like his stomach was a bottomless pit.

"More?" Cherry started to take the bowl.

"No. I'll let this settle first and see if I still need more." He stretched his body, which was already starting to rouse after the food. He stood of his own accord. "Let's see about these kilns, shall we?"

Cherry pursed her lips at him. "You know where they are. I need to get back to the field. Don't make me have to come back here to carry you again." Concern showed in her eyes over any sort of anger.

Catching her before she could leave, Dar gave her a kiss. "Thanks, really, Cherry. Sorry to worry you, but it worked, and I might do it again."

She let out a small huff and kissed him on the cheek. "We'll talk about it with Sasha later."

Dar made his way over to where Bart had marked the kilns. Even if he had lost half the day, he needed to do his share.

"Well, I was wondering if you'd pop up today." Bart waved Dar down.

"I was working on some things related to my dao path this morning, but what do we have here?" He looked down at the three pits dug into the ground, topped with large stone lids.

"Here." Bart grunted as he lifted one of the lids and revealed what lay underneath.

There were three layers of material, sand on the outside, loose stones and then a final layer of clay. All of it led to a hole about five feet deep and two feet wide.

Dar reached down and touched the clay; it was dried but not hardened. Of course, they didn't have a kiln yet to harden them. "You want these to turn off and on, right?"

Bart chuckled. "Yeah, that'd be nice."

Dar hung the top half of his body down into the unfinished kiln. "I'll get to work then."

Sasha had taught him the basics. He could simply carve the dao character into the clay and be done. Depending on how deep and how large the character was would lead to how much heat it produced.

He wasn't quite sure how big to do it, but Dar followed his intuition. It had looked like fancy scrollwork the first time Sasha had showed the conditional rules to enchanting, but he had learned the simple parts and he carved those into the clay.

Using his new dao of softness to make it malleable even though it had already dried, Dar was able to dip his finger into the clay and cleanly build the enchantment.

Connecting the dao character to the scrollwork, Dar then connected it all to the large stake markers that Bart had used for each of the kilns. The way he had tried to design it, the further the marker was pulled out of the ground, the hotter the kiln would get. Pushing it all the way in would stop all heat.

It might not be perfect, but it would have to do for the moment. When he explained it to Bart, Bart was nearly giddy, moving the marker up and down to his delight.

Laughing, Dar moved on to the others. He spent hours perfecting the enchantment, realizing an error when he was working on the third and going back to redo the first two. It was tiring, but in the end, he was satisfied with a job well done.

CHAPTER 7

"So, you just push this lever down." Dar demonstrated the motion, and the runes inside the kiln wavered as heat distorted the air. "I thought variability would do better here than trying to fine tune just the right amount of heat."

Bart scratched his chin, nodding. "Trial and error will then be on my guys. It'll take us a bit to get the right heat to fire the pottery and limestone, but at least we won't have to call you over to make adjustments. I think the men will love it. Are you going to do something like this when you make heaters for the homes?"

Dar nodded. "That'll be trickier. I don't want anyone to be able to set their house on fire."

The light labor of enchanting had given Dar's body more time to recover, and he was feeling far better.

"Yeah, I could see that." Bart nodded, giving the kilns another look.

"So, homes. I was thinking lumber will be the big bottleneck. We need to speed that up. What's taking the biggest amount of time?"

Bart hummed to himself in thought. "We might need to get out there and see it for ourselves to really make that call. I just send the men out. Frank leads the woodcutters and knows more than I do."

Nodding, Dar agreed with that thought. "Tomorrow I'll go out and see how we can best speed up the lumber process."

"Boss!" One of Rex's women ran up to Dar panting. "Riverboat. Coming."

"Thanks, take a breather." Dar patted her on the back and nodded to Bart. "Looks like someone heard I had finished up here."

"Go. We'll take the kilns from here. Hopefully, you'll be eating off a clay plate tomorrow." Bart ignored Dar and started playing with the kilns.

Setting himself into a steady jog, Dar hurried over to the river.

The riverboat was different from the one they had seen on their way to Bellhaven. It was far less boxy, but the general structure seemed similar. The shallow boat was covered with various trade goods strapped down to the deck.

As Dar approached, he saw Rex watching the boat approach, but he was clearly keeping himself hidden within the foliage of the nearby trees.

Stopping on his way to the boat, Dar turned to Rex. "Do you want to remain hidden?"

Rex nodded, a look of uncertainty on his face. "They are coming from Bellhaven, I am... cautious to let them know we are here."

That made sense. A little caution would be good. Especially for the ancients.

"I doubt they'd recognize me. I'll go say hello and see if we can't get any news about Bellhaven while I'm at it."

While the nobles of Bellhaven would likely recognize him, he doubted his short time and escape from the city would have merchants hunting for him.

Dar stepped out of the tree line and waved at the boat. It was plodding along at a snail's pace as it tried to trudge up the river. Dar was able to keep pace with it at a brisk walk.

"Hello there," Dar called to the boat.

Someone stuck their head over the side and waved. "We didn't know there was anyone in these parts."

"We keep to ourselves, but we wanted to know what was happening at Bellhaven. We heard recently there were devil troubles."

The man winced. "You must be hidden pretty well. Most of the villages we used to stop at are gone; all of them went to Bellhaven for refuge."

Dar tried to act surprised. "Bellhaven must be packed! Holy cow."

The sailor nodded in agreement. "Yup, bursting at the seams. They kicked out all the non-humans actually. It went pretty poorly, as you can imagine. The city walls are holding, but food is the real problem. The captain would buy any spare food you had."

The last bit was punctuated with a hopeful glimmer in the sailor's eyes. Dar had to wonder if they hadn't sold every ounce of their own food to Bellhaven.

"Sorry, we are tight for this winter, too. What happened to Bellhaven's food?"

"Too many refugees, and the latest devil attack tore apart their farmland. There was this giant troll. The thing had to be thirty feet tall, and it nearly cracked the city open."

"What! I hope everyone is okay." Dar faked some of the extra enthusiasm to try to gain the guy's trust, but the thirty-foot troll had definitely caught his attention. He'd have to ask Cherry what that meant later.

"Yeah, they lost a lot, but the city held on. We have some correspondences from Bellhaven to Kindrake we're carrying; we all think they are requests for aid."

The man paused to look Dar over again. "They are scared of the devils, but I'd be more worried about what all the ancient races they kicked out are going to do." He looked wide-eyed into the woods. "Terrible thing they did, and that sort of thing often brings calamity."

Dar schooled his face, trying not to smirk. "Well, it's a good thing we are out here away from all that trouble."

The sailor looked over his shoulder, listening to something before he turned back to Dar. "Can't laze about too much. Have a good day."

With that, the man turned back to the boat and his tasks. They seemed to be more interested in getting back to Kindrake than any trading Dar could offer.

Dar stopped walking alongside the boat, having learned enough. It sounded like Bellhaven was in trouble, but he had little to no sympathy for them. He had Hearthway to worry about.

Spotting Rex still hiding in the woods as he headed back, Dar headed over to catch him back up. "Nothing we didn't already guess. Bellhaven is struggling with food. They survived the last attack, but there was a huge troll apparently."

Rex's slit pupils narrowed sharply. "How big?"

Dar sighed. "According to that man, thirty feet. I'm hoping it got embellished as the tale was told."

A furrow formed in Rex's brow. "Haven't seen a troll that big before, but I've heard of such things in the past. Back before, a bunch of powerful ancients went on a warpath against the devils and got rid of the really big threats like a grand devil."

Dar nodded, knowing that the devils were going to be a problem at some point. Whether they were able to make it through or not depended more on time than anything else. "Either way, it seems that Bellhaven might have their hands too full to bother us for a while. Better for us to not need to fight and defend ourselves against devils and our old city."

"Yes, that would be good."

"Have we had any devil sightings?"

"A few gremlins have been killed, but they often wander the woods following deer trails looking for food. We kill them and bury the bodies."

A soft rustle was the only warning before a form jumped out of the bushes at Dar. Shifting quickly into a battle stance with his hands up and ready for a fight, Dar tried to process what was happening.

The jaguar girl's body hit his, hands first, but before he fought back, he noticed that her claws weren't out. Confused, he let her

body smack into his as she finished her pounce. She was dripping water as she clung to him, rubbing her face on his shoulder.

Rex loosened up after a moment and laughed. "She likes you."

Dar rolled his eyes and tried to pry her off.

"No," she said, the word carrying more meaning behind it.

"Where did she get off to now?" Sasha's voice came through the woods.

"Over here," he called to Sasha before turning back to the cat girl. "You are going to be in trouble."

"No. Cat. No." She shook her head rapidly.

Dar was amazed she had learned that much of their language so quickly, but it didn't help it make any more sense to him.

"Dar, is that you?" Sasha stepped around a large tree, smirking as she took in the situation.

Dar was still trying to pry the jaguar off, but she was using her claws now to hold tight, and he didn't want to ruin his clothes.

"Yes. Over here. I think I have what you are looking for."

"Don't you always," Sasha purred, then saw Rex and blushed. "Didn't see you there."

"You two are dao companions. There is nothing to apologize for, but I'll be getting back to my duties. Good luck, boss."

Hey, don't leave me here.

"Come here, you. We need to get you to take a bath in the river." Sasha helped Dar pry the cat girl off.

"No. Cat. No." She wriggled free and hid behind Dar.

"I think that means she doesn't want a bath," he chuckled.

As he took his focus off the cat girl and got a good look at Sasha, he did his best to not start laughing. Sasha was splattered with water, and she was not wearing the clothes she normally did for times like that. Based on her exasperated expression, this was not the first tantrum she had dealt with.

"You don't say. The little cat made me chase her all the way over here. If she'd just get a bath, she'd be so much prettier."

Dar took a moment to get a good look at the girl hiding behind him. Sasha was right; she was caked in dirt. But, even through it, he could see that she was like many other demons. She had an attractive body and face, although her hair color was a mystery under all the dirt. Something gave him the impression it might be strawberry blonde once the grime came out.

"Why don't we take a bath?" Dar asked. "Wait, Sasha, is she calling herself 'Cat'?"

His lovely demon sighed. "Yes."

Okay, there were a few problems to fix then. He scooped her up and poked at his chest. "Darius."

She nodded and said his name back, but she sort of growled the end of his name.

"Close enough."

He pointed at her chest, trying to think up a name quickly that would suit her. He'd been thinking of her as 'the cat girl', so maybe he should use that for inspiration? A number of sites he'd seen called cat girls 'neko' something or other.

"Neko." It would work. He tapped her chest.

She looked down at his finger, confused before shifting her head and body, trying to nip at the pointed finger. He moved his hand away, giving her a scowl and a low growl that seemed to do the trick as they continued walking. Sasha followed along with a smirk, watching the two of them.

"No. Cat." She tapped her chest.

"No. Neko." Dar insisted for maybe the fourth time.

"Do all demons name themselves?" he asked Sasha.

"How do you think Glump got a name like that?" Sasha asked, clearly working to control her laughter but failing.

Her laugh was infectious, and Dar burst into laughter, imagining that Glump, like Neko, was right now insisting his name was some sort of frog noise.

Neko looked back and forth between them, not understanding what was happening. She started a barking, fake laughter as she tried to join in, and that only made them laugh louder.

"You are pretty fun, Neko." Dar tried to keep his words simple, not sure what she might be able to pick up. Based on her progress, he was hopeful she'd settle into the town faster than he had expected.

"Neko." She tested out the word, her head tilting as she listened to it. Looking up at Dar, she pointed to herself with a smile. "Neko!"

Dar couldn't help but smile back, enjoying her enthusiasm as he nodded his agreement.

Neko turned back to their walk, the smile quickly vanishing from her face as she spotted the nearby water and realized where Dar had been taking her.

Many of the villagers had found the small pool that came off the Bell River. It was where most people had taken to doing their laundry and bathing. As they approached, there were a few women watching as they washed clothes.

"No. Neko. No." She pointed at the water angrily.

"Yes. Neko. You are going to have to get wet."

She started to turn to go another direction, but Dar held her still as they approached the water. She wasn't using her claws or her dao, luckily, so Dar just had to put up with her thrashing before Sasha stepped in.

"Neko, bath time." Sasha had a wicked grin as she used her dao of silk to bind Neko in ribbons and undress her.

Dar stayed by the side of the small pool and encouraged her, but nothing he said seemed to actually appease the angry Neko. Giving up on verbal encouragement, Dar decided to try joining in and showing that it was normal. He was gross after his meditation in the cave anyway.

As he started taking off his clothes to bathe, he was immediately aware of all the added eyes on him. It seemed he had gotten Neko and the rest of the women's attention.

"Yeah! Take it off!" one of the unaffiliated spirit women whistled at him.

Dar looked over at the white-haired spirit watching him. She was in Mika's group of random spirits and demons that had grouped up together. And she wasn't even attempting to hide her gawking as she stared at him. Realizing that he had started a show, he continued.

Neko had stopped struggling and was staring at Dar with wide eyes.

He waded deeper into the pool and opened his arms for her to come to him. Neko scrambled to him, clinging to him like a drowning cat as she wrapped her legs around his waist.

"Dar, you are going to spoil her," Sasha chided from the shallower water. But he didn't miss the smirk as she threw him a bar of soap that floated in the water.

"She clearly hates the water; I thought I'd make it easier." Dar held onto her and grabbed the bar of soap, rubbing it against her until he made enough suds to start working the dirt off her.

Neko leaned forward, sniffing her shoulder where he had recently lathered. Her nose wrinkled a bit, but she let him continue. She watched with curiosity as he cleaned her and freed her flesh of the forest dirt.

Dar continued to work over her body with his firm hands, trying to make sure not to wear down her skin too much and hurt her. He had a feeling that, if the experience turned painful, they'd have an even harder time the next time she needed a bath.

But, at one point, a small vibration started up in her chest as he cleaned her. He smiled, glad she had finally relaxed, and he enjoyed her purring against his chest.

Neko floated against him, and he stretched out her legs, moving to remove the dirt from them next. The whole process was fairly peaceful except for a few catcalls from the one white-haired spirit.

Dar had waited at first to see if Sasha would go shut the spirit up, but Sasha didn't seem to care at all. If anything, she seemed amused at all of it. Ignoring the continued calls, Dar finished most of Neko's body. It was time for her hair, which was still fairly dry.

"Neko, I'm going to have to dunk your head in the water." He looked at her, trying to gauge how much she understood.

Based on her calm, pleased look she gave him, Dar had a feeling that she didn't understand. Pulling her back slightly from himself so she could float on her own, Dar demonstrated plugging his nose, taking a deep breath, and going underwater.

When he came back up, making sure to smile, he was met with a completely panicked Neko.

"No. Neko. No."

"Neko, we need to work that mud out of your hair," Dar tried to reason with her, pointing at her hair.

"No. Neko. No." Her face turned into a scowl as she tried to move away from him back towards shore.

Dar reached forward, grabbing hold of her and pulling her to him. He took an exaggerated breath and lowered them both in the water slowly. Neko tried to hold her head above the water, but soon she gave up. She took a deep breath, and he pulled them both fully under the water.

When they came back up, she was sputtering with a look of complete and utter betrayal. "No," she stated with a firmness that wouldn't be denied.

Dar grinned. She was getting a lot of mileage out of that single word. Neko continued to pout as Dar worked the mud out of her hair and did his best to comb it with his fingers.

He'd been right. As the sun began to dry some of the strands, they were a nice light strawberry blonde. What was most interesting to him was that her jaguar pattern continued on her scalp. With her hair down, it was largely a mix of reddish blonde, with most of the black blending in with the rest, but framing her face were two extra black locks.

"Neko is beautiful," Dar encouraged as he swished her through the water to get the last of the suds off.

"Dar. No." Neko continued to pout, a calculating look on her face as she watched him.

"No more. Let's go to shore," Dar confirmed.

Walking them back through the water, Dar brought her back out onto the shoreline. He used his own dao of heat to blast himself dry, although it failed a bit as Neko stood near him, shaking herself wildly, trying to get rid of the water.

Looking up, she took in his largely dry state and tilted her head; her gaze shifting down to his manhood before a heated look filled her eyes.

Dar ignored the look, once again working to rid himself of the excess water. As she watched it all disappear, a giant smile lit Neko's face.

"Neko?" She pointed to herself, and Dar understood. He let out a stream of heat at her, sort of like a blow dryer, and she let out a gleeful squeal as she spun around, enjoying the warmth.

As she spun laughing, Dar couldn't help but appreciate her naked body. She may have been learning the language, but she was still a fully mature woman, which showed in her curves. Dar tried to think about other things, but he could feel his manhood rising right there for all to see.

Sasha cleared her throat. "If I had known you'd love this so much, I'd have let you bathe me ages ago."

Dar felt a bit guilty, hoping Sasha wouldn't be offended or upset. "Sorry. She is lovely."

"Oh, yes, she is." Sasha circled Neko and pulled out a bolt of silk. "She needs clothes to match it."

Wanting to let Sasha work, Dar headed over and started putting his own clothes on. He heard some murmurs of amazement from Neko as Sasha crafted the clothes around her body.

Dar remembered the first time Sasha had sculpted clothing right around his body from a bolt of fabric. It had been a sort of magical fairytale experience. There was a reason she'd made so much of her living off her seamstress abilities before they'd met.

When he turned back, he tried not to laugh. Sasha had at least not put the wild woman into a dress, but Sasha was still Sasha. She'd done her best to make Neko more presentable.

A tight-fitted blue top with heavy seams supporting her chest wound around Neko's waist before disappearing and showing her flat stomach. Neko's waist was exposed, with a skirt starting just under her navel. It was short with a high slit, so Neko could still move freely.

Neko was pinching at the fabric, trying to determine what she thought of it as she looked up and caught Dar staring. She tilted her head, waiting to hear what he thought.

"You look wonderful, Neko." He added a smile and an encouraging nod to try to make sure she understood his meaning.

It seemed to work. Neko beamed and spun around for him, though it didn't quite have the same effect as when she had been naked. Just the thought of her spinning naked got his blood pumping again. He quickly shut down the thoughts and worked to change the subject.

"Come on, Neko. I think it is about supper time." He offered one arm to Sasha and the other to Neko, who took his arm after watching Sasha.

Sasha leaned in to whisper in his ear, "She's going to be smitten with you if you keep her this close."

Dar expected himself to baulk at the idea, but somehow it didn't seem so bad. Maybe the culture of the ancient races was starting to wear off on him. Being in a village where multiple women with one man wasn't rare, it seemed more normal to him. And Neko was tough as nails; he'd be honored to have such a fierce dao companion.

Pausing in his steps, Dar looked down at Sasha, still trying to figure out where he stood on all of it. "Are you okay with that?"

Sasha's brows shot up. "Of course. I just didn't expect you to be."

"Me neither, but... I'm feeling perfectly fine pulling her closer into our family, if you are okay with it. Cherry too."

"Yes, I'll talk to her. Though I already know she'll be okay with it. Hun, Cherry really wanted you to grow our little family. She just didn't want to push you."

Dar chewed on that for a moment. He was a bit annoyed that Cherry hadn't said something directly, but to be fair, she had been dropping more than a few casual hints. "Okay."

Talking about starting a relationship with Neko was a little odd when she was standing right there, and she hadn't really indicated that she wanted him sexually. But she did seem to cling to him as they made their way to the central fire.

Spotting the leaders once again circled up for an update, Dar let the girls go off while he headed to join the leaders. The group wasn't fully formed yet, Dar having arrived earlier than usual, so he made small talk with Samantha as more villagers filtered into the area.

Feeling a tap on his shoulder, Dar turned to find Neko holding a bowl of food and a hopeful face.

"Thank you, darling." Dar took the offered bowl and lifted it in thanks with a smile.

Neko did a little skip and hurried away to Sasha, who seemed far too content to not have been the one who had arranged and coached the entire thing.

"I'm not sure how you handle so many women," Samantha commented with just a pinch of judgement.

"I just care for them and love them just like you would any single woman. And we stay a tight family. It's not only me and them; it's all of us together."

Dar waited to see if she rebutted, but he was distracted as he felt a heavy gaze resting on his back.

Turning to see what had set off his senses, he found the source. The white-haired spirit from earlier was whispering in Mika's ear as she glared at Dar.

Oh boy. He could feel a storm brewing over there, but before he could decide what to do about it, Bart and Glump sat down at the circle and their meeting began.

CHAPTER 8

B art held up a clay bowl as he sat down with a particular grin. "The kilns are up and running. Got a crew of gals keeping them furnished with pottery."

"Always good to hear about progress." Dar smiled back, looking down at his own rough wooden bowl.

"The boys are tripping over themselves to play with an enchanted kiln. Calling themselves wizards."

The group chuckled at that. But Dar had been thinking about it during the day. They weren't utilizing enchantments enough yet. There were plenty of people with dao, but enchantments gave dao to the humans as well. It should make their little village more productive.

"What else could we do to make things easier?" Dar's mind was starting to buzz with ideas. He was already thinking about how to get Neko to make some enchantments with her sharp dao.

Before they had replied, Dar already had an idea what they were going to list. Lumber and food continued to be top priorities. Dar listened and nodded. "Bart and I are going to join the lumber crew tomorrow. We will see what we can improve on."

As they sat chatting, Rex launched into the story of the river boat for all of those that hadn't been there to experience it. Dar worked

to fill in additional details where Rex had stopped being able to hear. The news left the group somber.

"Sounds like Bellhaven is going to have some trouble." Samantha spat. "Good riddance."

But Bart was a little more sympathetic. "If we are able to continue growing food during the winter, can we sell them some? Their leadership isn't my favorite, but there are a lot of good villagers still within the city."

Dar nodded, knowing Bart likely had a lot of friends that hadn't joined them that he was thinking about. "Maybe. I'm sure we'll need to start trading, eventually. But I've been thinking it might be best if we traded with a river boat rather than the city directly. I wouldn't want our past interactions to cloud their decision to take the trade. Plus, they may have more unique goods to sell than Bellhaven."

Bart nodded happily, but many of the others grumbled their agreement. The ancients hadn't forgiven the way they had been treated, but they respected that commerce was part of what kept towns alive. There were only so many resources they'd have access to. They needed a broader network to really build up and out.

Russ, who had seemed extra chipper all evening, jumped in, changing the topic as he gave his update. "We were up north along the river today. We spotted a large herd of bison on the other side, several hundred head."

Dar and the rest of the group whistled. If they could open up hunting on that herd, it would be a significant amount of meat. They could even make some jerky to help get them through the winter.

But seeing the meat and capturing and hauling it back were two different things.

"How do you expect to get across the river, not to mention bringing a kill that size back?" Dar asked.

Russ scratched the back of his head. "Uh, I was hoping one of you could figure out that part. We could probably take down a few if we do it right. But, even if we field dressed them, we'd still have over a thousand pounds of bison to bring back."

Dar rubbed his face. The meat was tempting as hell. The Bell River wasn't that fast at the moment. It was likely some of the stronger swimmers could get across on their own, but there was no way they were going to be able to carry a kill back.

Russ looked around nervously. "Maybe a raft? I think we could pull at least a single kill across on one."

"With what lumber?" Bart glared. "I don't have enough as it is for the housing projects. We'd need to build a smoker to make the meat last any length too."

"Just have Blair pack it in salt." Russ shrugged off the last comment, clearly annoyed that they were all questioning his big find.

Dar raised a brow at Russ. "Blair?"

Russ pointed with his bowl back over to Mika and the white-haired spirit. "Salt spirit. She used to make a lot of money back in Bellhaven pulling salt out of the ground and selling it."

Dar paused, realizing that salt was likely worth its weight in gold in Grandterra, at least if the history on Earth was anything to judge its value by.

"Has she started making some here?" Dar asked.

Russ shrugged. "Don't know."

Dar looked over again, which was enough to grab both Mika and the salt spirit's attention. Mika looked excited at the attention, but the salt spirit was still looking a little surly.

But, as his eyes locked with Mika, another thought formed in his mind. She might be able to help them cross the river. They'd just need to create some sort of vehicle that could cross the river.

Dar partially stood up and motioned for Mika and Blair to come join their circle.

Mika nearly tripped over herself, getting up and discarding her bowl. Blair laughed at her and far more casually got up and came towards him.

"What's up?" Mika asked, eyes were wide and hopeful.

"We were discussing plans and news. Russ here saw a large herd of bison today, which would be a huge win for us. But there are a

few issues we have in capturing them." Dar paused, making sure they were following.

When he saw they were, he continued. "We don't have a great way to pack that much meat away for the winter." Dar's eyes slid to Blair before shifting over to Mika. "And they are on the other side of the river. We need to think of a good way to cross. I'm hoping you could advise us on that one."

Mika stood up straighter as he asked for her help, clear pride on her face.

Blair jumped in first. "I can pull salt from the cliffs. I'm pretty sure I've felt some. But it isn't as easy as pulling it from the sea. If you can get me down to the bottom of the river, I could likely fill whatever you needed in a day."

Dar nodded. The sea made sense. She could likely pull salt powder straight from the ocean.

"That would be another reason to get a boat. For now, I think we need you to pull what you can from the cliffs. What would we owe you for that?" Dar asked.

Blair did a small bow, a smile resting on her lips. "It would be my pleasure to help Hearthway get through the winter."

"Thank you. I know you could make a lot more money if you sold the salt in one of the cities; we'll find a way to make this up to you. Until then, you have my thanks. Let me know if my dao companions or I can enchant anything to make your winter more comfortable."

Blair gave him a smile that said she already had something in mind, but she didn't speak whatever she was thinking. "Thank you. I'll keep that in mind."

Several of the others in the group gave her a sincere thank you as well. She seemed to genuinely be glad to help, and Dar was satisfied with that. A strong supply of salt would help them even if they didn't get the bison.

Dar turned his attention back to Mika, who looked a little impatient.

"I could cross the river no problem. Probably even pull a boat across it with a dozen people. But we don't have a boat. I don't think you want me swimming with the carcass; that would do horrible things to the meat." Her foot tapped in frustration, and Dar could tell she was unhappy that she couldn't do more to help.

"You can't carry something on waves over?" Bart asked, hope in his voice.

"No, that wouldn't be feasible. It would need to be able to float."

Bart snapped his fingers. "Darn. I don't suppose you know anyone else here that would be able to get us across the river."

Mika paused, turning and looking at Glump.

"Don't look at me that way. I could swim like you, but I don't know if I could carry a bison or a boat across," the old demon croaked.

"That's fine. I think we'll want a boat eventually anyway. It'll be something to think about. For now, Russ, I think the bison are unfortunately off the table," Dar said.

Russ nodded, clearly frustrated but he seemed to understand that they weren't in a place where they could do anything with the bison.

Mika stood to the side awkwardly, looking pained by a perceived failure. "Thank you. I'll think about it and let you know if I think of another solution."

She hurried away, and Blair threw an apologetic glance over her shoulder at Dar before chasing after her friend.

Cherry grumbled something, clearly annoyed as Blair and Mika hurried away, and Dar remembered what Sasha had said about Cherry wanting him to push for more girls. She must not consider him making Mika feel like she let the town down as good for building a stronger bond.

But that was a problem for another time. Preparing the village for winter had to stay everybody's top goal.

"I'll keep hunting on this side of the river in the meantime. Hunting is about patience more than anything. Something will come." Russ went back to his dinner.

Dar looked around the group. "Samantha, how is Neko doing with her first lessons?"

"Neko?" Sam asked, and the rest of the group looked confused.

"Right, Cat. She was with me this afternoon, and I named her Neko. Cat was a little too on the nose."

"Well, there's your answer. She disappeared after lunch, and I couldn't take too much time from the rest of the kids to find her. But, in the bit of lessons we were able to do, she is learning quickly."

"Yes, she seems quite articulate with her small vocabulary."

Samantha shared a wry grin with Dar. "That's a nice way to put it. You'll also be happy to hear that the kids did very well in the fields today, don't you think, Cherry?" She looked to Cherry for confirmation, knowing Dar had instructed Cherry to shoo the kids away if they got in the way of the progress.

"They did well. We gave them a corner of the field and put two workers with them. The kids behaved enough that I wouldn't mind them back tomorrow. I also sent a few men and a team of horses to try and plow out a new field. This field isn't getting better."

Dar decided to let Sam and the kids stay if they wanted to keep helping in the field.

"That's about how I figured it would go. Sticking with the same size?"

Cherry nodded. "That's about all I can force to grow in a day."

The prior field had been about half the size of a football field, and Cherry had been forcing it to grow a full yield of crops every day.

"Maybe we should double the size and only use half at a time. The day of rest might help it last a little longer." Dar wasn't an expert, but he knew the problem was that they were depleting the soil too quickly. He figured any rest would help.

"We'll get it done." Cherry noted the change in plans.

"Boss, before we get too far, it might be worth thinking about what we could make to trade with the river boats. A rowboat might be something they'd be willing to part with and save us a ton of time and loss of lumber. Some enchantments like you've been meaning to

make for the winter or salt would do. Both would be welcome to the river boat merchants," Glump added.

Dar scratched his chin in thought. "I could make a few of those house heaters I've been thinking about. See how they do. How much do you think I should make?"

"How effective will they be?" Glump croaked.

Dar hadn't made any yet, but the goal was one per home. "They should heat a small home."

Glump nodded along. "Five should be a fair trade, if they have a boat to spare."

Nodding to himself, Dar added it to his mental checklist. "With all of that settled, I say we stop brooding over what to do and enjoy our families."

Bart grumbled in agreement and stood to his own family.

Dar walked with Cherry to sit with Sasha and Neko, but as they sat, Dar couldn't help but feel odd about how the recent days conversation had gone with Mika and Blair.

"Dammit. Marcie, can you go find Mika and Blair and bring them over here, if they are willing?"

"Yes, milord." The mousy maid ducked away.

"Amber, could you get four seats for the circle?"

"Four?"

"Yes. You and Marcie will join us tonight."

She paused for a moment before she started moving the logs scattered around the hearth until their little area had the necessary number of seats.

Sasha claimed the seat to Dar's right without issue. Neko, however, prowled to the seat on Dar's left and gave a challenging glare to the other girls.

Cherry met her challenge with an exasperated sigh. "When you can speak, I'll make sure to whip your ass and let you know this moment is why."

Blair giggled at that as she walked up. "Poor kitty doesn't know what she just brought on herself. But she's pretty cute."

"I don't know. Think I could take the kitty for that seat?" Mika stared down Neko, who was ignoring the girls and looking to Dar.

"Like I'm going to get involved in this. You guys figure it out."

Sasha grinned from her unchallenged perch. "Don't worry, love. I'll make sure this doesn't happen again."

Mika gave Sasha a look and backed down. "We should talk then."

"We'll work something out. Welcome, both of you," Sasha said.

"Ah, so…" Dar wasn't quite sure what the proper protocol was, but he felt like he needed to make sure they knew they were welcome. "You two are welcome at our meals. It seems to have split into a family unit thing, but I wanted to make sure you both knew that you had a standing invitation."

Mika smiled so wide that it threatened to split her face. "I'm honored to join you for meals."

"Me as well. What about sleeping arrangements?" Blair bounced her eyebrows.

Dar coughed into his hand, not expecting the blunt question. "The hut is very cramped at present, even with the three of us. When we start to get homes built for the winter, we'll have something big enough to expand into."

Amber and Marcie squealed, giving a shared look that had a touch of heat. Dar wondered if the two of them… no that was none of his business.

"Shame," Blair pouted, but Dar could see right through it. She was going to be a handful.

"Dar, you promised to explain a few things from this morning," Cherry prompted, reminding him that he did owe her and the others an explanation of what he'd done.

"So, last night into this morning, I tried and succeeded in learning a new dao, but I did it differently from what seems normal."

Sasha sighed. "Of course you did. Which dao?"

"He was going to try it with your dao of combustion." Cherry joined her dao companion in an eye roll. "Idiot. Could have blown himself up."

Now both of them were giving Dar dirty looks, while the others were holding their reservations until they understood more. Well, except for Neko, who just looked excitedly from one person to another, not understanding what they were talking about.

"It worked, so no need to be too judgmental. After listening to Cherry's advice, I instead tested it with the dao of softness." He looked over at the two newcomers and then at the two humans and decided to start a little earlier in the process.

"When I formed my first dao, I made channels in my body for the mana to flow through."

"Like water ways?" Mika asked.

"Sort of. They crisscross all over my body. Anyway, instead of trying to write or memorize a dao character, I started to use all these crisscrossing channels in my body to write the character as I saw it. Then I rapidly continue to draw the character and sort of internalize it."

"Is that what gave you all those wicked tattoos?" Blair leaned forward, looking at his arm.

"No... these are from Lilith, the first witch." He added the last bit as an afterthought.

"Wait, Lilith? THE Lilith? She did those?!" Blair jumped off her stump and grabbed his arm to look at them.

"Yes, and you can study his enchantment another time. We're in the middle of a discussion," Sasha admonished Blair. "His entire body is enchanted by Lilith. He's the Black Knight, or was. It's complicated."

Dar didn't see any reason to try and hide his background. He needed to trust the people he was building relationships with. "I died. She used my body as a sort of living weapon afterwards and only recently pulled my soul back into it. But, before she did that, I was living another life in another world."

Despite the shocked faces, nobody questioned him. Dar had expected a bit more hesitation, but they all just nodded along.

"Anyway, so I used these new channels to learn the soft dao in a little over half a day. But that was with my dao path heavily entwined with Sasha, and all these enchantments on me."

"More importantly, he was weak as a kitten afterwards," Cherry told the group. "I had to drag him out because he couldn't even stand."

"That's not entirely fair."

Cherry crossed her arms under her chest. "You were too weak, Dar. I don't know if I'm comfortable with you trying that again."

"Would it be possible to not do it all in one go?" Blair tried to be helpful.

"I like that idea. Dar, I think you need to be careful. Dao is not meant to be forcibly mastered like this." Sasha put her hand on his arm and stared into his eyes. "Please, Dar. The last thing any of us want is for you to wind up injured."

"I understand, but we also have a ticking bomb. Between Bellhaven and the devils, I need to grow my strength. I have a feeling the worst is yet to come." Dar thought back to the river boat sailor's reflection on a thirty-foot troll. "We've been comfortable here the last few days, but the danger isn't gone."

Sasha nodded. "I understand, but what about..." She looked at the others before turning back to Dar. "The little tree?"

"If there's the opportunity to grow it, I will. But I haven't seen any here yet, unless you are suggesting I lose all my morals for a little bit of strength."

She recoiled. "No, not at all."

"Sasha is right. We need to get you in the action again. That little tree is your secret weapon," Cherry said.

The others were looking confused, but he didn't fill in the blanks. While he had explained much to them already, the little dao tree was a dangerous secret. It was a large advantage if he found a way to fully use it.

"Okay. But it's already evening, so let's enjoy each other's company. Tomorrow I will go help with lumber."

Dar knew they were right. He'd need to balance helping Hearthway prepare for winter while working to prepare to protect them from attacks. While the devils were a danger, nature could also be deadly.

CHAPTER 9

D ar blinked and realized he was once again inside his inner world. Overall, it stayed the same with every visit. This time, there was one new addition. The orange tree sat in the center of the clearing.

Cherry was walking excitedly around it, inspecting the new arrival. "Are we going to plant this in here?" she asked.

"That was the plan," Dar admitted.

He paused for a moment, trying to decide if he wanted to broach the subject with Cherry then or later, and finally decided on then. "Cherry, Sasha told me that the rate at which I was accepting new girls was bothering you."

She studied the orange bush a little longer before looking up and meeting his eyes. "Dar, I want you to be comfortable with what you decide. You didn't seem like you'd react very well to being pushed." Cherry tore herself away from the tree.

"I think ignoring the problem doesn't solve anything."

She blew her tongue out. "There's a difference between waiting and letting a problem solve itself. Mika wasn't going to ignore you, so I figured it just needed a little more time. And then tonight, you more or less gave her and Blair permission to pursue you, too. What changed?"

"Neko. I realized that, if I started including her without giving Mika a fair shot, there would be trouble."

Cherry started laughing. "Yeah. I think that's true. Mika was close to putting her in her place when you first came back with Neko. She knew right there and then that the cat girl was going to stick with you."

"Why is that?"

"She's a jaguar, or was, right? It just goes back to their animal nature. Neko is going to steer towards a man that can beat her."

Dar nodded, but he didn't necessarily like that his main attractive point for Neko at present was that he could beat her to a pulp and hold her down. He'd have to work on getting to know her more and making sure it was a good fit for both of them.

Dar returned to the initial target. "Beyond the other women, I want to make sure you tell me if something is bothering you next time, Cherry."

"Alright." Cherry bobbed her head. "Now, can we talk about this tree?" Her eyes lit up.

"That's what I wanted to ask you. We have two options: we could either plant it here and see what becomes of it, or we start an orchard in town."

"How would you explain suddenly pulling trees out of your gut and planting them in the village?" Cherry grinned. "We can take some seeds in the spring, and I can give them a nice little boost, but they'll have to mature on their own."

Dar nodded. Cherry was right. He could try to lie and say he had carried it in from the forest, but the lie could easily break down.

Moving over, Dar started positioning the orange tree to be near a few seedlings that had sprouted from Cherry's original cherry tree. Despite the tree being withered and dried out, she had managed to coax a few trimmings to start sprouting. They had to have been nearly dead, and Dar had been amazed her dao could still bring them back to life.

Dar picked up the shovel he had brought into his inner world before to bury corpses for the little dao tree and started to dig a new hole for the orange tree.

Cherry helped manipulate the tree's roots into the soil, working to grow back a few spots that Dar's less than delicate removal had damaged. She grumbled a few times about butchery as she tended to the plant, and Dar couldn't help but smile.

As they finished, Cherry stepped back to inspect their work and gave it a nod. Task complete, Dar began strolling around to check on everything in his inner world.

The large dark keep still dominated the inner world, its walls making up the boundaries. Dar looked through the black iron portcullis that blocked him from entering. He had wondered if the gate would eventually open, but so far he'd had no luck. He had tried to break it open or find some sort of latch a number of times with no success. Eyeing it once more, Dar continued past to his dao tree.

While the little dao tree had grown slightly since he'd last visited, the fruits remained frozen in the same state. A number of half-ripe fruits pulsing with various dao hung from the branches. A few of them were duplicates of dao he had already mastered, but some were new. He'd have to find other devils or wild beasts with that dao and bury them in the ground beneath the tree before the fruits would grow further.

"There's been no change, Dar. I think that, if you really want to grow stronger, we need to find something for you to kill and feed the dao tree." Cherry interrupted him as he was sifting through the leaves, looking for anything new.

"Greedy little tree."

"Dar! This tree is a miracle. The way it produces those fruits is amazing." She held one of the half-grown fruits. "Even with your newfound meditation skill, these fruits could birth new demons with ease."

"Or other immortals," Dar added.

Cherry paused, looking up at him in surprise. "Is that what you are planning to do with them?"

"I'm not entirely sure. I think it would be easier than a demon. They would be conscious and able to make the decision, and I'd be able to judge their worth prior to giving them a fruit. But... yeah it has been a thought," Dar admitted.

"They are yours to do with," Cherry stated, nodding and stepping away from the tree, her lips turning up into a smile. "And so am I."

***

Dar woke from the dream in his inner world with a smile. He found himself in bed with his arms wrapped comfortably around Sasha.

For once, she was already awake. "You were grunting quite a bit in your sleep."

"Sorry, blame Cherry later."

She gave a soft snort. "No, it's fine. Just makes me a little jealous that she gets you alone every night."

"Then take my morning. She's still sleeping." Dar got up, moving over to Sasha's side of the bed, and Sasha used her dao to clothe him in perfectly fitting clothes.

"I'm not sure that's going to get old." Dar smirked and headed out to snag breakfast.

Only Neko was lurking nearby the hut. The second he emerged, she pounced on him. "Neko. Dar. Yes."

He stumbled but caught her and picked her up, carrying her to breakfast.

"So much for alone." Sasha gave a playful sigh. "Morning, Neko."

"Sasha."

"Sorry, milord, she's been lurking near your hut since sunrise." Amber appeared with a bowl of steaming oats.

"Thank you." Dar put Neko down and took the bowl with a smile.

Neko glared at the bowl angrily, like it had stolen her moment. She huffed and prowled towards the center, seeming like she was on the hunt.

Dar laughed and sat down. "Did you sleep well, Amber?"

"Yes, though we'll be happy when you have a larger place."

It didn't miss Dar's eyes that she looked scared for a moment. He wondered if the people of Hearthway weren't feeling quite as safe as he thought.

Working through his oats, Dar noticed a group of men carrying axes moving out into the woods with the light of dawn. Ejecting a sleepy Cherry and handing her off to Sasha, he hurried to catch up to the woodsmen.

"Morning. Where are we heading?" he asked the man leading the group as he caught up.

"Not too far. The woods thicken up pretty quickly. I'm Frank." He gave a short salute to Dar and kept going.

Getting the message loud and clear, Dar kept quiet and walked with the woodcutters into the woods. There were about twenty of them in all, making up about a fifth of the village's work force.

With the limited size of their workforce, they had to be strategic about how they divided up their priorities. For this task, they had leaned largely human. There were only a handful of demons, and only one of them was male. His name was Terick, and he generally kept to himself. Dar instantly liked him more for it.

Terick was part of a family that was led by a female spirit, which made them unusual, but Terick seemed plenty content.

As they walked through the woods, Dar could see the stumps of prior timber scattered among smaller trees, thinning out the woods but not clear cutting them.

They passed by a massive tree, the trunk almost big enough for three to four men to wrap their arms around, and Dar stopped and asked Terick, "Why is this one still standing?"

"Huh? Oh, it's too big. It would be too hard for us to cut that big boy down safely." Terick looked up and down the tree with a faint

whistle. "And can you imagine how much trouble that would be to fit with other timber? Not very uniform."

Dar looked again and acknowledged the man was right. It wouldn't work for their current uses given that it was so large. But he realized it could be used for something else where its size was beneficial. A boat, for example. Dar's face spread with a smile as he thought about the solid wood boat they could make if they could bring the tree down.

Making a mental note, Dar realized most of the woodworkers had passed him and were continuing down the trail. His axe bounced on his shoulder as he strode quickly to catch up and found them fanned out around a tree.

"This is the one we are going to take down next." Frank looked around. "Simon, Mark, take your groups in for the next tree."

The group split into three, though Frank's was much larger. Each of the groups was working far apart, chopping away. Dar guessed the added distance was to prevent an accident with a falling tree.

"So, do you want to try and cut the first tree?" Frank asked.

Dar knew how to do it with a chainsaw, but this would be his first time working to cut down a tree with an axe. "Sure. I'm no woodcutter, but I'm happy to help. Show me the ropes?"

Frank nodded, looking pleased with the honesty, and Dar had a feeling that he'd just won a small dose of the man's respect.

"You cut the wedge first," Frank explained, stepping back and swinging his axe over his head, bringing it down hard into the side of the tree. As it hit, he cut a steep angle that went with the grain of the wood. After several more chops, he pried out a doorstop-shaped wedge.

"We want it to fall in that direction." Frank nodded towards the side he had just cut into. "So now we move to the other side and finish the job." Frank picked up the wedge and walked around the tree. "This part is harder. We have to cut against the grain at a sharp angle. We'll take turns."

Frank swung with his full strength for maybe a dozen strokes before stepping back. Another man then stepped in, continuing to hit

in the same spot. Together, they hacked a sharp, narrow cut into the other side of the tree. It took a few minutes, but overall, Dar had a feeling they made it look easier than it would be.

"Now the fun part." Frank took the wedge he had made on the other side of the tree and trimmed the tip off with his axe, then jammed it into the sharp cut they'd been working on. "We hammer this in while two guys take turns hacking into the first cut."

One of the demons and another man stepped up to where the wedge had been taken out. At Frank's nod, they started hacking into the base of the missing wedge.

Meanwhile, Frank started hammering his wedge into the narrow cut. "Want to take a turn?" he asked, stepping back.

Dar shrugged. It seemed simple enough. "Can I put my full strength into this? Or is the goal to go slow?"

"Go ahead and give it your all. You are trying to move several hundred pounds of tree."

The two workers on the other side of the tree watched him as he wound back, preparing to use the back of his axe like a hammer.

He tapped into his dao of hardness and strength to reinforce his axe and his body as he swung for the fences. He hadn't cut down a tree this way before, but he had plenty of experience swinging a hammer in his past life. Not knowing more than to just hit the wedge, Dar wound up his hit like he was going to swing straight through the tree.

A low roar emerged from his throat as he slammed the axe into the wedge. As the axe made contact, the wood shattered, and the axe continued sliding through the tree.

CRACK

The tree started to tip.

"Timber," Frank said before yelling louder. "Timber!" He and everyone else dropped what they were holding and ran.

Dar dropped his own axe and ran clear of the tree with Frank.

It tottered, seeming unsure which way to fall before tilting towards the wedge side. Several more cracks echoed through the woods as the

tree broke free from the stump and fell onto the forest floor with a boom.

Frank gave Dar a completely unamused glare. "That was dangerous. Next time, go slower. Not controlling the fall of a tree is the most dangerous thing you can do out here."

Dar nodded, feeling a bit guilty as he scratched the back of his head. "Yeah, sorry about that. I hadn't realized it would be quite so effective. I'll be more careful."

Frank only grunted as he waved the men back to the tree. "Now the really fun part," he said, his voice flat. "Trimming the tree."

Several of the others grunted and moved over to the felled tree, immediately hacking away limbs. Dar joined them and took the lowest and largest branches, squaring where they joined between his feet and started hacking them off with heavy overhanded swings.

"Good but be careful not to split the trunk. You see here where the grain changes from vertical on the trunk to horizontal with the branch? You want to stay on the horizontal grain and cut against it, or you risk splintering the trunk," Terick pointed out.

"Thank you." Dar meant it. Doing everything manually like this was a bit of a shock to the system. It was definitely making him appreciate the technology he'd once had around him. But, despite the exhaustion, there was something satisfying in what they were doing.

"No problem." Terick went back to his own work, hacking at the limbs.

All of them worked together until about halfway through trimming the limbs. The large ones were all clear and just the upper branches needed to be scraped off. At that point, Frank reconvened the group and started on the next tree while a few continued to trim branches.

"This time, I'll let you give it a try." Frank gave Dar the floor.

Making sure to remember all he had watched, Dar stepped forward. He angled the first cut to remove the wedge well enough, then started on the back. He dialed back his strength as he started to hack the thin cut in the tree.

Given his strength, he was moderating himself not to slam the tree so hard that he might topple it unexpectedly. His axe bit far deeper than Frank's had, but no matter how much strength he used, it wasn't quite sharp enough.

Or maybe, the tree was too hard.

Trying again, Dar focused on his dao of softness and kept one hand on the tree while he brought back the axe for another swing, though with far less power without his torso to pivot with.

"What are you doing?"

"Trying something." Dar swung and his axe bit far deeper than last time, and this time it sank all the way to the shaft. He couldn't help but grin.

Two more swings like the first, and he already had a space big enough for the wedge, which Frank had already trimmed for him.

"Maybe we should all stand back while you try this next one," Frank teased, but Dar didn't miss the couple steps back Frank and the others still seemed to take.

Setting the wedge, Dar tapped it in about halfway. "Okay, next one will be a big swing. Are you all ready?" He checked to make sure everybody still trimming the last tree was clear before he swung for all he was worth, once again using his dao.

This time, Dar knew that first crack was a sign it was going to come down and jogged away to stand with the rest.

"Well, this is certainly going faster," Frank stated, staring at the downed tree with the others. Everybody stood for a moment in silence, seeming shocked. "Well? What are you all waiting for? Get to trimming."

Dar wiped the grin off his face with the second comment and joined the rest in trimming. He was excited about his discovery. If he could get a few charms from Sasha to soften the trees, they could speed up felling by quite a bit for everybody.

But he wasn't sure how to solve the issue of trimming. The majority of the branches came off with one or two swings. It wasn't an issue

of effort to break through; it was the limitation of how many smaller branches there were on the tree.

The modern idea of a delimber wasn't going to work here. It would require moving entire tree trunks through a hoop, and even he wasn't sure he could do that very well with his strength.

Dar considered something like a hand planer. A sharp-bladed hand tool might be able to scrape along the side of the tree and get all the smaller branches in a long scrape, rather than cutting them each free. But it would take a bit of effort to move it through them.

Trying it out with his axe, it was only mildly successful. He'd need to figure out some sort of enchantment to enhance the process to really work.

"Ready for another one, boss?" Frank interrupted his musings with the trimming process.

"Of course." Dar got up, and Frank pointed him to the next tree worthy enough to become building material.

Dar was partway through the new tree when shouting arose deeper in the woods. Wanting to check it out, Dar looked to Frank. "Is it safe for me to leave this part way?"

Frank eyed the tree from top to bottom and shrugged. "It isn't great, but I don't think it is going to fall just yet."

The rest of their work crew was looking up from their work deeper into the forest and grabbed their axes.

"Do you often get trouble?" Dar asked.

"No, not so much as a peep since we've started. But, after logging back in Bellhaven, you always had to be careful. The forest doesn't like it when you take her trees."

Dar grabbed his axe just under the head and hoofed it deeper into the forest, towards the sound of the shouting.

The voices seemed to be coming from an outcropping nearby. Dar leapt up on top of the rocks, finding himself just over the work crew. They had been backed into a corner.

Splayed out in front of them was a hideous manspider. It looked like someone had tried to graft the traits of a spider onto a human.

Eight eyes shifted from the work crew upwards, taking in Dar. It clicked its mandibles as it watched him, carefully crouched on a branch with his humanoid body.

But the manspider wasn't alone; it had a small pack of large spiders with it that were each as big as a dog.

"What is that?" Dar was going to be sick from the sight of them.

"Ettercaps," Frank said as he caught up. "Nasty devils."

CHAPTER 10

"Like actual devils? Not a demon?" Dar wanted to confirm. "Does that look like a demon?" Frank waved his axe at the ettercap.

Dar didn't want to admit that he still was learning all the differences, so he just took Frank's word and focused on the issue at hand. Regardless of what it was, it was a danger to his village and did seem far more monstrous than any demon Dar had encountered.

The purple-skinned creature stood on two legs, with thin arms that ended in two claw-like fingers and the head of a spider on an otherwise humanoid body.

Wanting to insert himself before one of the crewmen was injured, Dar jumped from the rocks and landed on one of the smaller spiders, crushing it underfoot. Whirling, he cleaved the head of another spider.

The rest of the men flowed over the rocks and joined him. They weren't well armed; many had managed to bring a branch to use like a spear. So Dar left the smaller spiders to them and focused on the ettercap.

The purple devil crouched low in preparation for a fight. Its mandibles worked over its maw, which was dripping with a sticky-looking liquid. Dar waited for it to move, but instead, it gave

no other warning before spitting a stringy, sticky webbing out of its mouth.

"Eew." Dar had the stuff plastered to his shoulder. "You're going to make Sasha sew me a new outfit, aren't you?"

It just chittered back at Dar as it attacked with its two large claws.

Dar blocked the attack and spun to the side, dodging out of the way as the ettercap stumbled through where Dar had just been. As it fumbled to right itself, Dar's axe was already whistling through the air, cleaving off one of its arms at the shoulder.

The ettercap let out a wretched screech as its arm was separated. Dar felt a moment of victory before something wrapped around his neck and hauled him into the air.

Confused, Dar worked to reorient himself. The sticky thread around his neck was connected to another ettercap up above in the trees he hadn't spotted before. It was pulling the sticky thread back like a garrote wire.

But, before it could get very far, Dar blasted it and its thread with the dao of heat, cooking through the web and blasting the ettercap with enough heat to pop its bug eyes.

It joined the other in screaming, but it went quiet as Dar swung his axe back over his shoulder and slashed through its face. Ripping the blade free, Dar noticed that, instead of blood, it was covered in the gooey guts of an insect.

He nearly gagged at the smell of the oozing matter, but he didn't have time to focus much on it as the other ettercap regrouped and moved towards Dar with its large mandibles open.

The others were fighting defensively in small groups. So far they had managed to keep anyone from dying. After the ettercaps had lost their advantage of surprise, they were far easier to manage.

The ettercap didn't let him observe for long, leaping into the air. Dar met it head on with a swing of his axe, but the ettercap moved strangely and ducked under it, pushing itself up and into another lunge. Dar's axe and right arm were still overextended, so he gathered

his hard dao around his left arm and punched the monster straight in the face.

The devil tried to sink its fangs into Dar's arm, but it was only able to scratch him through his hardened skin. Dar connected with its face and through it, his fist sinking into the same gooey substance he'd dealt with on his axe.

Stepping back, Dar ripped his hand from its head and quickly looked around for any of the crewmen who needed help. But the rest of the group had fared well enough. Two men had been wounded and were being tended to, but nothing looked mortal. The final spiders were being dispatched by those that remained.

With the immediate concerns taken care of, Dar began immediately scanning the surroundings. That other ettercap had caught him off guard, and he couldn't help the heebie jeebies from dealing with the spiders.

"We need to take these two back to the village. If they were bit, they need to rest and work off the venom's paralytic effect," Frank said.

"Sounds like you are familiar with these ettercaps. Care to give me the rundown?" Dar asked, kneeling on the ground and picking up someone's dropped axe.

"Unfortunately, there's never just one or two. Ettercaps breed like spiders. They have big egg sacks with hundreds of eggs. They work in colonies. Usually, you see the webs before you see them. I hadn't spotted any as we worked, but we must be close to come across these two."

Terick butted into the conversation. "They also absolutely hate fire. If you want to work in the woods, just lighting a fire and keeping it nearby is enough to keep them away."

"Really?" Dar turned to Terick.

"Yep. I've been through woods where they lived and were plentiful. Didn't come within twenty feet of a flame."

Dar picked up a branch and used his dao of heat to char and eventually burn one end, ultimately creating a poor torch. "Then we

should finish this up with a fire burning by each group. No one goes away from the group alone."

Everyone nodded their agreement as Dar made two more torches for the groups to start their own small fires.

Dar looked at the corpses on the ground. "I'll go ahead and drag these away. There's not enough meat to them to warrant trying to cut them up." The beasts seemed to mostly be chitin and guts. There were a few disgusted faces at even the thought of eating them.

"You should have company. No one goes away alone, right?" Frank frowned at Dar.

Dar felt guilty for breaking his own rule so quickly, but he needed privacy to do what he needed to do. "Hah, yeah. That's fair. But I can just blast anything with my dao of heat. Don't worry about me." Dar grabbed the two spiders by their legs and started hauling them into the woods.

Once he was far enough out of sight, Dar pulled them into his inner world. He was curious what dao they possessed, but he'd have to wait until evening to bury them and watch what fruits grew on his dao tree.

While it wasn't good for the village that there was a massive nest nearby, Dar was excited at the chance to get a lot of creatures that likely had the same dao. He'd need to go search for the colony and take it out, but he'd wait until he had a few reinforcements. Enough of these devils could be trouble to take on.

When Dar returned to the group, all the woodcutters had fires burning nearby, but he saw their eyes venturing up to the canopy above them as they worked. Everybody was a bit spooked.

"What are the fires for?" Bart asked, showing up midway through the morning.

"Ettercaps," Frank spat.

"Shit. You're kidding me." Bart seemed to have at least some knowledge of the devils.

"Unfortunately not. Fought two of them, and half a dozen dog-sized spiders." Dar swung his axe over his shoulder. "I'm told the

fires will keep them away, but that means we have a new problem to deal with, Bart."

"Me? Naw. I'm pretty sure you and Rex have a new problem to deal with. I still have my old problem of a shortage of lumber. Quite frankly, I like my problem better."

"They're going to be all our problems if we don't deal with them, Bart." Dar gave him a level stare.

"Right, right. I was just sayin' that it looks like you have things taken care of for now, so we should focus on the lumber piece," Bart corrected.

Dar let the silence linger a bit before letting Bart off the hook. "I do have a couple ideas around the lumber issue. Let me catch you up." Dar walked Bart through the process and explained the two biggest points he saw for improvements.

Bart didn't have anything to offer for the first challenge of cutting through the back end of the tree more quickly, but he did when it came to cutting off all the smaller branches.

"Yeah." Bart took Dar's axe and tried to run the blade under a small branch. Trying to cut it that way for him wasn't working. "I think we need something you could use like this."

Bart put the head of the blade flat against the tree and grabbed the small nub sticking out of the top of the axe and the shaft scraping towards himself. "See? So you can get your full back into it. Two handles, one on each side and a blade in the middle."

"You should probably make the blade shaped a little like a scoop, so you can use the rounded blade either around the curve of the tree or to get a more focused cut," Dar added to the design.

"I like that." Bart nodded. "I think I could work with the boys on the forge and mock one up today. Think you could help with the necessary enchantments?"

There was an excited look on the old blacksmith's face. Enchantments weren't getting old for him.

"Sure, I can put some on to make it tougher, but..." Dar trailed off, thinking of the sharpness he experienced from Neko. He was pretty

sure she had the dao of sharpness, or at least something very close to it. "I'll see if I can't get something to make the blade sharper, too. No promises on that end though."

"Your new friend?" Bart smiled.

Dar rolled his eyes. "I seem to have a lot of new friends lately."

"But only one you bathed recently. Created a lot of rumors with that stunt." Bart chuckled. "I hope you aren't leaving Amber out to dry."

Dar nearly choked when Bart mentioned his daughter. "No. Amber is fine."

"Mhmm." Bart gave him a judgmental fatherly hum. "That's why she isn't even sleeping in the same hut."

Dar recovered from the blunt statement, turning it back on the man. "Yeah, it would be great if we had more stable housing. So when are you going to finish the first house for us?" Dar smiled as Bart harumphed.

"Well, I need some damn more lumber!" Bart threw up his hands, but then let out a chuckle and slapped Dar on the back. "Alright. I'm going to head back and see what we can get hammered out for this scooped blade today."

"Grab a torch and bring someone with you. We can't have you walking these woods alone after the ettercaps. Pass word around the village as well. I don't want others venturing out here to us alone."

"Shit. Right. I'll grab someone. Are you staying here?"

"I'd like to stay close for now. Tell Rex the situation when you get back and have him and a few others come this way to add some reinforcements. Ideally, I'd like to see if we can find this colony and get a sense of what we're dealing with before it becomes a bigger problem. This is the first time we're seeing them, so I'm wondering what started sending them this way."

"Right, can do." Bart nodded and grabbed a torch and a man to head back with, not wasting any time. Dar appreciated that about Bart. He was a man of action and took his work seriously.

Dar continued to work with the woodcutters as each group stacked up a newly trimmed tree every hour or so. Dar's group had sped up with his help, but the limb trimming was still the longest part.

"Boss." Rex approached with two of his wives, both carrying proper cloth-wrapped torches and armed with bows, as well as blades belted to their hips.

"Good to see you. We have an ettercap problem."

Rex's eyes narrowed. "So Bart told me. Which way did they come from?"

"We don't really know. They snuck up on one of our groups. Come with me."

Dar dusted off his hands and picked up a branch from the fire, looping his axe in his belt. He figured his dao of heat was probably the better weapon in this situation. Leading them up to the area of the ambush, Dar walked through the situation as he'd seen it.

Rex surveyed the scene, his eyes scanning the tops of the trees, before heading off to the southeast. "This way."

They only traveled for about twenty minutes before it became apparent that they were on the right path.

At first, the only signs were a few small, lingering spider webs in the lower branches of a tree, or a big funnel web spread between the tree's roots. But then the area seemed to get gloomier as the trees became almost spooky with the number of webs spreading across them and their leaves becoming scarce. Fall had started, but leaves were still on most of the trees, not these though.

The worst was the silence. It took Dar a few minutes to notice the silence in the forest. It was unnaturally quiet, like nothing lived in them.

"Do we continue?" Dar asked.

"Yes. They won't come near us with the torches," Rex explained.

Terick had said the same thing, but it still gave Dar the creeps to walk, knowing they were likely being watched by spidery devils.

"It's like nothing lives past this point," Dar murmured.

"Like most devils, they do not live in harmony with nature. They destroy everything around them," Rex growled.

"You mean they over hunted the area?"

"Like a plague of locusts," one of Rex's wives agreed. "Even the trees are starting to die."

Dar looked more carefully. Sure enough, he could see that many trees showed a number of dead, decaying limbs, smothered by a canopy of webs.

Lifting his torch, Dar thought he saw something in one of them.

But the light caught on something deeper into the forest, and Dar saw a massive wall of white spider web that stretched across the forest. Round tunnels were built into it, like it was a massive fortress. His fears were only confirmed as he saw ettercaps and spiders both crawling through the structure.

"Shit."

"Yes, indeed. That's big enough that we have more than ettercaps to deal with. They are hierarchical, like all devils. If you have a group this size, that means there's something stronger holding the whole group together." Rex backed away and looked over his head and around them. "We should head back. We need to discuss what to do about this as a group."

Dar wanted to deal with the problem, but he also recognized Rex had the right amount of caution. This wasn't a handful or a dozen ettercaps to clear out; this was hundreds of them, and they weren't far from their home.

"Let's hurry back. This place gives me the creeps," Shelia said, before jumping backwards and slashing at the air above her.

Her blade cut through a giant spider that had been descending on her. It split in two and fell to the ground.

Chittering filled the canopy above them, and Dar realized it was already too late. "Go. Now."

Their group ran through the ettercap woods as large spiders crawled around the trees, descending on their group despite the fire they had brought with them.

Dar used his dao of heat to blast the air above them to drive off any descending spiders as they moved, but they only made it a few minutes before they were forced to stop.

"Did we get turned around? There wasn't a web here before." Dar looked at the funnel web big enough to catch an elephant.

"No. This is the way we came. They constructed this behind our backs."

Dar nodded. So they'd been led into a trap. Dar stepped forward, immediately blasting the web with his heat dao and smiling as the threads melted away. But there was still a good bit more.

"Good thinking. We'll hold them off while you clear a path," Rex stated, his blade already moving to cut through a nearby spider.

Dar pushed mana through his body and cooked the web off a section at a time, but it was a slow process.

The twang of bowstrings and the occasional screech of a spider sounded off behind Dar. But he stayed focused on getting rid of the web. The web never caught on fire; instead, it just dried up and shriveled off.

Eventually, the maker of the web poked itself out of the center of the funnel and watched Dar angrily. At least, that was how Dar interpreted the big spider thrashing about in its web like it was throwing a fit. The man-sized spider was black with orange bands running along its legs and bulbous mid-section.

Gross.

Dar fingered his axe, ready for it to make its move. But, as Dar continued to cook away its web, it disappeared back into its funnel. Shifting back to hacking away at the web while waiting for the spider to reemerge, Dar began to see a tunnel further into the funnel. It looked like it led underground into some sort of hole.

"Steer clear of the hole in the ground, we have a big friend in there," Dar called over his shoulder, hoping that the tunnel didn't go further out where more reinforcements could come at them. Feeling confident that he had at least a moment before he'd be attacked, Dar glanced at the situation behind him.

The torches were doing their job, keeping the spiders at least wary. Rex held both torches now and waved them at any spider that got a little too confident. Meanwhile, his girls had their bows out and were putting arrows in any spider that tried to rappel down above them.

Feeling reassured that they were safe, Dar focused back on the last of the funnel web, using his heat to cook away the wisps.

"Come on, we have a path."

Dar stepped through first, giving the hole a wide berth and keeping his head on a swivel for another surprise attack. He stayed by the hole, wanting to give the others better cover.

Rex and his girls didn't miss a beat, following directly behind Dar in the same path he had taken. Rex was still carrying the torches high and waving them about as a warning to any spider spotting a chance to attack.

Rex and the girls had just moved past the hole when the spider finally made its move. It emerged faster than Dar had expected, expanding out of the two-foot-wide hole in seconds, its body seeming far too large to have fit within the space.

It flew across the ground and reared up to cover one of Rex's women. But Dar had been prepared. He'd already been swirling his mana and was able to release a jet of heat straight at the spider.

The spider recoiled instinctively, buying the group an extra moment of time. Rex took the moment to strike.

He was a fury of a demon as he bit where the spider's head met its midsection. The bite was met with a hard crunch as he tore through the exoskeleton. Rex ripped his head back until he tore away the spider's own head. Dar had to admit it was a pretty fast and efficient kill.

The spider twitched, and its legs curled inward as Rex stepped away, his faintly avian features a mask of outrage. Everyone had said that male demons were territorial and prone to fighting amongst themselves, but this was the first time Dar had witnessed just how deadly Rex could be.

Their whole group stood still for just a moment, but all snapped back into battle mode quickly. Based on the growing chittering of the spiders, something was coming.

"Hurry up. Let's get out of here." Dar grabbed one of the torches that Rex had dropped when he had attacked.

"I'm sorry, boss," Rex said, grabbing his own torch and keeping up.

They weren't being cautious at all about their path through the woods this time. They were in full escape mode.

"It doesn't matter. You can be as violent and angry as you want towards a spider attacking your dao companion."

"But we are supposed to blend in with the humans."

Dar scoffed. But they could talk more about it later. "The reality is that you aren't human. I'm not going to ask you to be something you're not. But right now, we need to get the woodcutters out of the woods. I think we just kicked the hornet's nest."

Rex frowned. "Those are very clearly spiders, not hornets."

"It's a saying, Rex," Dar muttered as he saw the first of the wood-cutter groups looking up at them. They had all paused in what they were doing, looking alarmed at Dar, Rex, and the girls charging at them.

Dar worked to snap them out of it. "Quick, grab your stuff. We are getting out of these woods for the day."

A few of them nodded but started to wrap up the task they were on.

Growling, Dar yelled, "You have a group of ettercaps coming. Get your stuff. We need to go now."

That woke the last few up, who scrambled for their belongings and booked it out of the forest.

Dar was hot on their heels, breaking off to get the other two groups' attention and hustle them out of the forest. They needed wood, but it had just gotten too dangerous to be in the woods.

CHAPTER 11

"Thank you for protecting Shelia," Rex said once they had gotten clear of the woods. The chittering of the spiders within hadn't stopped, though. It sounded like there were many just past the tree line.

"No problem at all. We are all in this together." Dar leaned against a tree and looked back at the forest to see if they would follow out of the forest.

"They won't chase clear of the trees," Rex offered.

"Well, earlier I was told they were too afraid of fire to come close. That turned out to be not quite true. I'd rather verify for myself than be caught off guard," Dar grumbled, a little upset and embarrassed about the risk they had taken.

He'd felt confident taking Rex and the others to go investigate, thinking that they'd be home free with the fire. Turned out it just meant the spiders had to get a bit more crafty, not to mention that some of them outright ignored the fire.

"For what it is worth, I've seen ettercaps and spiders retreat from a single torch and not bother a demon. What happened in there was unusual behavior."

"It's fine, Rex." Dar could see his doubt. Rex thought he had failed him. "We all made it out fine. Next time, we'll be ready. That's the

main point of going to scout. Although, I do wish we'd been able to wipe those creepy buggers out."

"Yes, boss." Rex bowed out and went to see his women; Shelia was pretty shaken up.

While Rex cared for the women, Dar stood watching the edge of the forest. So far, they hadn't spilled out, but the chittering was far too close to the village for his comfort. Part of him had expected something to come; it had been too quiet recently.

Now that they'd investigated, he had a feeling that the massive ettercap fortress had blocked anything else coming from the south and had likely decimated the nearby area, venturing further out to find more food.

They were lucky it was deep enough in the woods that they weren't bothered when they'd originally travelled to the spot. Who knows how long it had been there, with so many devils present?

But they needed access to the woods. They couldn't afford to lose their connection to lumber. Dar thought about the number of warriors they had. He couldn't take everybody away from the village in case there was another attack, and he wasn't sure if they'd have enough for whatever was within those walls.

Frustrated, Dar ran his hand through his hair, trying to figure out how they'd even try to attack the fortress. No doubt there were traps and alcoves woven into it, ready to snatch up any prey bold enough to enter. Their best bet was actually tearing it down. But, given how long his heat dao had taken to burn through the quickly constructed web, Dar wasn't very confident in that approach.

His only thought was upping the firepower. Gunpowder didn't exist, but there were other means of creating explosions. The dao of combustion he'd been working on, and Cherry had steered him away from, seemed like his best bet. And who knew, maybe the lesser dao could lead to a greater dao. This devil sighting seemed like a first sign of more to come. Dar wanted a greater dao with more firepower than the granite he was already close to.

The chittering started to quiet, making Dar scan the forest again. As he did, his eyes locked with an ettercap that had stepped up to the edge. The ettercap just stood there, studying him, before it turned back into the forest and the chittering faded away completely.

Dar let out a breath he'd been holding. They seemed to be keeping to the forest, at least for the time being. He watched for another few minutes before turning back himself and heading into Hearthway.

Bart was the first leader he came across, working with all the men who'd been cutting lumber, reassigning them to help at the farm or work on the few projects that were going on in the village.

The blacksmith spotted Dar and stopped what he was doing, asking the question on everyone's mind. "Are they coming?"

"No. Not right now. They retreated after they saw we left the forest, but after our encounter, I'd expect them to become more territorial. But this isn't a small nest. There is a massive colony of them, maybe eight or ten miles southeast from the village. We're going to have to clear it before we can do much in the forest."

That caused a few sharp inhales from the men. The woodcutters shivered, not realizing how close to that danger they'd been.

"How big? Can we muster up our men and drive them out?" Bart switched from fact finding into solutioning. That was one thing Dar appreciated about him; he saw every problem as a nail to hammer.

But this wasn't a matter of just hammering the ettercaps away. "Rex, how many do you think there were?"

"Hundreds, maybe up to a thousand?" But Rex looked hesitant. "If I'm honest, I've heard of a colony before, but even that was only around twenty. This was massive."

"Yeah, it was like a spiderweb fortress, or a small city," Dar agreed, putting it in perspective for everyone.

"Do we move? If we can't deal with it..." Bart was already looking for the next solution.

Dar shook his head. "It would be dangerous to try and head back to Bellhaven. We could head north to Kindrake, but winter is coming on fast."

"We wouldn't make it to Kindrake before the first snowfall," Rex supplied. "It might be better to prepare to bunker down here for the winter." He hesitated.

"Does winter slow down the ettercaps?" Dar asked, thinking if they followed the normal pattern for spiders, they might not be an issue.

"Yes, at least supposedly. They typically wrap themselves up in big cocoons and find tight spaces to retain heat and sort of hibernate," Rex answered, but he still looked uncomfortable.

He doubted himself. Dar knew his prior assessment had rattled the demon's confidence in his knowledge about the devils. And it was hard to trust a fact enough to risk everybody's lives on it.

"Okay, so we continue to prepare to bunker down," Dar announced, making the decision. "Bart, we can try logging the northern forest, at least for the short term. I know it isn't quite as old…" he trailed off in thought and had another idea. "Or we can try across the river. Timber floats."

"Still don't have a boat," Bart said.

"I know, but I have an idea for one." Dar was already hatching a new plan. "But we can get to that later. Today let's focus on what we have immediate resources for. Send the guys into the northern forest to see what they can bring back for today."

Bart looked over his shoulder at Frank, who had been listening to the entire thing and was nodding.

"I got it. We'll see what more we can get done today." Frank gave a lazy salute and gathered his people to do the newly assigned task.

Dar patted Bart on the shoulder. "Let's see about this branch scraper we thought up."

The blacksmith grinned. "Already started. We picked out a rough blank that we should be able to finesse into the tool." He made his way back over to the enchanted forge that Dar had helped set up.

As they walked up, Dar watched several men who were working around the forge repairing various tools. The men barely looked up from their work, clearly focused on getting the tools the town needed

ready. Not wanting to distract them, Dar made a mental note to try to remember to thank the men personally at the next dinner.

Bart had moved ahead and was pulling out a rough form of the tool they'd been designing and laid it down on his anvil with a pair of tongs. "So, we need a curved bill, two protrusions for handles, and then to blade the bill."

He started hammering with that in mind. It was interesting for Dar to watch as Bart paired off two sections, bending them outwards for the handles, and then started on rounding and stretching the bill.

Bart reheated the metal often and continued hammering it into shape several minutes at a time.

"What do you think?" Bart pulled away after his last bit of hammering.

"Let's see." Dar picked up the red-hot piece of metal and Bart nearly lost it.

"You can't touch th—" The blacksmith stared at Dar as he didn't react to the heat.

"Dao of heat, remember?" Dar smirked and looked at the piece, turning it around even as it was starting to cool off. "I think this looks about right. Definitely good enough to give it a try and go from there."

The tool was the shape they had discussed, but it was all a bit theoretical. There probably was something they'd missed that they would find as they put it into practice, especially at scale.

"You scared the crap out of me," Bart admonished, grabbing a rag and wiping his forehead.

Dar shrugged. He hadn't really thought about it very much. It was part of who he was now. "This goes in the water bucket?"

"Yes, please." Bart stepped away from the forge and held his arms out, cooling them off in the fall wind.

The bucket of water hissed for a moment before it settled down and Dar pulled out the tool. If this worked, they'd put a wooden handle on it so it would be easier to use.

"Can you run this out and see if a woodcutter can give it a try for a few hours?" Dar asked.

"Not going to go try it yourself?"

Dar shook his head; he didn't feel comfortable leaving Hearthway so soon after the threats in the nearby forest. "I'm going to stay in case we have a problem with the ettercaps."

"Ah, makes sense. In that case, I'll be happy to bring it out to them and get further away from those creepy things." Bart smiled to himself as he took the tool from Dar and headed out.

Dar turned, starting to walk back out into town, scanning for places he could be useful. A small growl was all the warning he got before Neko pounced on his shoulders and clung to him.

"Oh, come on." Amber came up panting. "Sorry, milord."

"It's fine." He lifted the demon off his shoulders. "Were you causing trouble?"

Neko at least knew enough to shake her head. "Neko. Good," she said with a smile.

"Well, aren't you learning words quickly?" Dar put her down where she molded herself up against his side like a house cat wanting attention.

Amber huffed. "She is learning quickly, milord. But she was kicked out of the field by Cherry this morning. I guess she got bored with picking crops and started tackling and scaring people through the cornstalks."

He tried not to laugh as Neko looked up at him with wide, innocent eyes of someone who knew they did wrong. "Neko. Good. Amber. Bad. Scare people. Scare Neko."

"Really now? That's what we are going with?" Amber huffed and looked ready to dunk the poor cat girl in the lake.

Dar stared at her for a few moments, thinking of what to do with her. "Well, I'm done early for the day. Why don't the three of us go for a walk and see if we can't teach Neko a few new words?"

"That would be wonderful." Amber smiled.

"Maybe we can even lure her over for a bath," Dar said conspiratorially.

His maid gave him a wicked smile. "Oh, yes. I hear she loves baths." Her tone dripped with sarcasm.

Dar felt like things were slipping through after watching the woodcutters; he didn't have enough eyes on what was going on. There had to be more places they could enchant and improve the processes.

Their first stop were the kilns where workers were shoveling cooked limestone out into a simple wheelbarrow. Others then used hardwood bats to crush and break the limestone down further until it was powder. Dar knew that powder would get mixed with sand from the river and crushed granite from the cliffs.

Dar snagged a particular stone that called to him and stuck it in his pocket.

"Boss, is everything okay?"

"Yes, you are all doing great. I'm just watching."

He nudged his fellow worker with an 'I told you so' look.

"Actually, hold up a second. Don't mix that in the wheelbarrow. Let's crush it all up and cart it over to the site." Dar didn't see the value in mixing before they carted it all across. It would create way more trips and be a pain to get out of the wheelbarrow.

Dar helped them move the materials over to where the foundation was being laid, and he tried not to sigh. There were mounds of cement already starting to dry, but they had yet to make a large dent in the total foundation.

"Okay, let's dump all of this in that corner and mix it in the hole." Dar pointed to a corner of the hole and the men got to work mixing it all in the space for the foundation. It was probably not the best with mixing the soil into the mixture, but they needed to speed up the process.

Together, they mixed the whole kiln worth of limestone into the foundation with gravel and sand.

Neko and Amber pitched in, though Neko wasn't quite as helpful as Dar would have liked. In the end, they made short work of mixing

the foundation, leaving a nice ten by ten foundation with a few sunken logs to build on. A solid base that something sturdier than Cherry's huts could be built upon.

Dar still had time to kill before dinner, so he moved through the center of the village, where women and children were doing more idle tasks like weaving or pottery. They were chatting away, working and watching the children who had long abandoned the field.

Continuing on, Dar could see the cliffs proper, where men were coming out of a main cave with carts of crushed stone and smiles on their faces.

Dar gave them a friendly wave and ducked inside.

"Dar." Neko held close to him as her eyes adjusted to the darkness.

"It's okay, Neko. We are expanding the cave, getting stone for foundations, and possibly creating a storage and shelter."

The temperature dropped several degrees as they stepped into the cave. Soaking up the chill, Dar contemplated that there might be options for a cellar or a place to keep cool the next summer.

Still, they had winter to get through. His plans for summer would need to wait. "What do you think, Amber? Is it cool enough for food storage?"

"For the winter? It'll make terrible meat for later and heating it up can be a pain." Amber gave her opinion, blinking her eyes as they adjusted to the darkness too.

"Frozen meat won't kill you. It just doesn't taste quite as good. We might even want to pack the meat in snow if we have any game after the first snowfall."

Amber wrinkled her nose. "Whatever you say, milord."

He wanted to keep the village as happy as he could. No one wanted to be miserable for the winter.

"We'll see what else we can do, Amber. Contentment is a very real concern, especially in the winter where people don't have the ability to do much. Bored and upset people can be as dangerous as a storm at times." Dar scratched his chin. "Still, I think we just need to accept it is going to be a harsh winter."

"We are all tough people." Amber nodded, but the nod continued on as a pondering look crossed her face. She seemed to be talking herself into what was to come.

"What did you do during the winters in the past?"

"Lots of celebrations, and mostly just trying to keep warm. If you make heater stones for everyone, it will be a very different winter for most."

Dar hadn't realized the stones would change their lives so much; it seemed so basic. "So you gathered firewood and stayed indoors in the past?"

"Kids played in the snow, sled down hills, and celebrated. But, for the adults, there was a bit more stress. They had to work to try to keep the younger children from seeing their fear as they worked to keep a fire going and food in everybody's bellies when everything is much scarcer."

Dar nodded along. It would take a lot of extra shelter and resources to be able to comfortably ride out a winter. This world was still in survival mode for most. "Well, let's hope we can get those solved so we can make this winter a little more comfortable."

"En." Amber nodded excitedly. "I think winter here will be far better than it has been in the past."

Dar smiled at her optimism. Maybe he was being too harsh on himself for the winter preparations. If they spent the whole winter trying to survive, that would mean they would continue to forage and hunt through the winter.

They reached the men that were working away in the cave. Men were using bronze pickaxes to chip away at the cavern wall. Dar wanted to jump in and help, but he'd proven that his strength didn't always help when they were cutting trees. Here, a misstep could mean collapse.

"How are you doing, hunky chunk of man meat?" Blair smiled up from where she'd been sitting, working to pull salt out of the ground using her dao. So far, it looked successful. White crystals rose around her in a circle.

"Really, that's what you are going with?" Dar snorted.

"Oh, darn. I guess I'll have to keep trying. Come here to take me for a spin?" She wiggled her eyebrows at him.

Dar just shook his head. She wouldn't stop even if he asked. "No. We had some trouble out by the woodcutters, so I'm just doing rounds around the village to see how everything is going."

Bending down, Dar snapped off a salt crystal protruding from the ground, bringing it to his lips to give it a small lick. Yep, it tasted just like the salt he was used to. And Blair had maybe twenty pounds of it in the circle around her.

"That was fast," Dar commented.

"I'm good at what I do. And you can lick anything of mine you like, Stud." Blair's amethyst eyes twinkled playfully in the dark cave.

"Not Stud," Dar and Amber said together.

"Okay. Not Stud. Sheesh, give a girl a break. It's not my fault you're knickers-dropping hot."

Dar rolled his eyes. Amber was blushing, while Neko just stared back and forth between the two of them.

"Hey, kitty cat, can you speak yet?" Blair changed her target.

"Neko good."

Blair barked in laughter. "Yes, I bet you are going to be really good. You know you're hot as hell, right? If the big guy takes too long with me, we can pair up and have a real good time."

Neko tilted her head at that.

"She didn't understand that," Dar defended her.

"Oh, you'd be surprised. We have almost perfect recall. It's why she's learning so fast. Though she's still a little feral, so doesn't quite understand the quality behind saying more than a few clipped words."

"Really?" Dar paused to try to figure out if it applied to him as well. Now that he thought about it, he was way better with names and faces in the village than he would have been in his previous life.

"I wondered if your memory would be as good too. How about it?"

It wasn't a secret in Hearthway that Dar was an immortal, but Blair was the first to question just what that meant.

"Yeah. It's all surprisingly clear. I'd been taking it for granted." Dar realized he didn't fully understand his transformation as much as he thought he did.

"So, just come to lick my salt, or did you need anything else?"

"I'd love to hear what you were doing before I interrupted. Looked like meditation."

She smiled. "What do I get in return?"

"I didn't realize this was a transaction. Here I thought I was the leader in this town." Dar arched a brow, waiting to see if she would continue to challenge him. She backed down, giving him a small pout before launching into explanation.

"It was a bit like meditation. There's no large vein of raw salt here, but if I focus, I can tap small quantities among the naturally forming minerals. But they are often too small to really push their way out, so I have to try and wiggle them into larger and larger clumps and bring them through the surface." She waved at the surrounding circle.

Dar found her use of her dao interesting, but he was most interested in her meditation. "Ever used that meditation to try to progress on your dao path?"

"Not without a bit of inspiration. Same thing as trying to force the dao characters." It sounded a lot like what Sasha and Cherry had described, but he was curious if working meditation more into his routine could change anything.

Having what he needed, Dar turned to go, but Blair stopped him.

"Wait, are you going to take that salt without paying?" she gasped.

Dar looked down at the crystal. It was pretty big, and he knew salt had quite a bit of value in this society. "How much do I owe you?" He was thinking about grinding it up and giving it to the cooks for seasoning.

"Bend down here and let me have a look to see how big it is," she said with a straight face.

Dar bent over her with the crystal in his palm, but she grabbed his head and kissed him. Her lips were salty, giving off a bit of a saltwater taste as he pulled away. He was more surprised than anything and backed up. It certainly was skipping a few steps—steps Dar thought were important.

"Damn," Blair said with a smirk as she touched her lips and a flash of remorse crossed her face.

"Neko, yes." Neko pointed to her own lips.

"Of course, sexy." Blair practically tackled the demon with a kiss.

Dar watched as the white-haired spirit and the jaguar demon started making out against the wall. Neko even started purring and rubbing herself up against Blair before the spirit had to come up for air.

"Oh, you are going to be a fun little kitty, aren't you?"

Dar cleared his throat. "If you two are done, I think supper is probably starting."

All three girls' eyes slid down to his pants. He didn't have to look to know there was a serious tenting issue down there right now.

"Milord, would you like me to fix that for you?" Amber asked with all the seriousness of a maid just going about her duties.

Dar ground his palms into his face, not sure what he was going to do with all the women in his life.

CHAPTER 12

Dar ended up stopping by his hut and letting Amber do just what she offered, which she seemed immensely pleased by tucking it away with an affectionate kiss.

He didn't really want to show up for dinner sporting that hard on, and he wasn't sure if he was going to be able to get it to go away with his dinner companions. Especially not with Blair egging him on as she had been.

Amber slid her dress back up over her shoulders. "I see you enjoyed them."

"I've never had anybody do that," Dar admitted as he pulled his pants back on. Amber had used her chest to work him most of the way. He'd seen it done in videos and animations, but never felt it personally.

"I'm glad you liked it. Now just imagine it with Marcie's giant ones." Amber cupped her own chest to make it seem larger.

Dar gave an awkward chuckle. He still wasn't entirely used to the girls talking about each other. It was great, but still took some adjustment. "Well, she needs to make the first move. I'm scared to spook her."

Amber hummed in thought. "I think you need to make the first move with her, milord."

"Think you could get her permission for me? I'd like for her to at least voice it to someone. I don't want her feeling like she has to."

She nodded. "Yes, it would make her think about it too."

"Exactly." Dar sat down to put on his boots. "I need her to think about it and accept it beforehand, so she doesn't have to make a choice at the moment. Otherwise, I fear she'd question it during and after, and that would end poorly."

"Yes. I can see how that could end poorly. A normal lord would just force her and continue to, even if she didn't like it. But you aren't a normal lord. You're Darius Yigg, the Black Knight, and the first human to become an Immortal." Amber smirked as she finished all his titles. "It is an honor to serve you."

Amber did a well-practiced bow with a flourish of her dress.

"Cut it out. You know I don't care for that sort of formality."

She swooned. "And ten times more kind than a lord would be with even one of those titles. Makes a girl wish she wasn't a commoner."

Dar needed to get out there to dinner with the whole family. He swatted her on the rear. "Get your shoes on. We are going to dinner."

"Ah, there's the whip," Amber lamented, but a smile cracked her facade.

Dar got up and left, but her antics had put a smile on his face.

As he stepped out of the hut, he saw the village was already gathering for supper. People were splitting into family units as a few women minded the pots on the central hearth. Marcie was over at the pots now, stirring one of the three that would feed people today.

But Dar noticed one thing out of the ordinary. There were fish leaning over the fire on sticks, grilling. Dar felt his mouth water.

"Who got all the fish?" Dar asked, sitting down with his family. The leader meeting could wait until after. He wanted to spend some time with his girls.

Mika blushed. "I did. After everything the other day, I realized I was just doing as I was told when I knew I could do something better."

"This is amazing. Do you want to fish every day?" Dar wondered who else had been underutilized so far.

"I could probably catch quite a few fish. If you got me a solid spear and net, I'd be able to catch more than I did today." Blushing, Mika seemed to have trouble looking him in the eyes. She seemed far different from the girl he'd originally met. That girl had been overly confident, but also happy as a loner. He wondered if the change was as she was trying to join their family.

Then again, they had met under strenuous circumstances. Mika had been more concerned about staying alive.

"Of course. Please. Let me see if Bart can get someone to make you a spear. Actually, let's have you work with a blacksmith tomorrow morning, and we'll get it hammered out." He put his hand on her arm and gave her a smile. If she needed a spear, then she'd get one.

Blair gave her friend an encouraging jab of the elbow. "Wow, I'm jealous. He doesn't offer to make me anything."

Dar rolled his eyes and changed the subject. "What's wrong with Neko?"

The girl in question was angrily batting her tail while hiding it in her lap. A small growl escaped her lips at whatever was wrong.

Cherry reached over and grabbed the cat girl's tail away from her and held it up for all to see. The end of her tail was encrusted with cement. Dar tried to not laugh, knowing it would likely only make Neko upset.

"Poor kitty. We are going to have to cut it off." Shaking her head, Blair took on a sad tone.

Neko shot several feet in the air, like her feet were made of springs, and hurried to hide behind Dar.

The whole group broke out in laughter, and Neko growled quietly behind Dar, bringing him back to the situation. "Blair, you shouldn't tease her like that."

"But she clearly understood everything I said. Proves my point." Blair gave Dar a devilish smile.

Realizing she was right, and that Neko was really learning far faster than he was giving her credit for, he turned his head to look at the jaguar girl. "Let me see it."

Neko held her tail in her hand and gave Dar a wary look, glancing down to his axe.

"Fine. Here, take my axe. I promise I won't cut it." Dar knocked the axe down so it wasn't leaning against his stump where it would be easily reachable. It seemed to satisfy Neko, who carefully gave him her tail with an almost reverent gesture.

It was far softer than Dar had expected. He'd seen her grooming it more than once, but he was surprised at just how velvety it was. At the tip, it looked like the cement had been pressed in, but luckily it seemed to have only gotten caught in the hairs, and not on her skin.

"We could shave some of the hair off and remove it now, or we could just let it grow out. Normally, you use vinegar to get it off your skin, but I'm not sure if we have any." Dar looked over at the rest of the girls.

"It's unlikely. That's not exactly someone's priority when they are running for their lives," Mika answered for him.

"Okay, so no vinegar, Neko. Do you want to let it grow out or do you want me to trim the hairs and get it out?"

Neko pulled away and clutched at her tail, then looked back at Dar before she held up a finger. Sadness filled her face as her finger hummed with dao as she cut it out herself, leaving a little bald patch at the end of her tail. She pouted and sat down next to Dar.

"Or you can do it. Your tail still looks very pretty."

That statement seemed to cheer her up a bit, but she still stared at the bald patch now at the end of the tail sadly.

"Milk it for all it is worth, kitty. You're mine tonight." Blair grinned from across the circle.

"What does that mean?" Dar asked.

"We three are poor souls all alone in our hut. And kitty needs some lessons before she's ready for you." The salt spirit grinned.

Mika hid her face in her hands. "Blair, you can't come on that strong."

"Look at him. He's interested in the idea. You should have seen him earlier," she said, the last part conspiratorially as she trailed off to whisper in Mika's ear.

Neko blushed after a few moments and shot Dar a look that he couldn't quite decipher. Thankfully, Dar was aided by Marcie and Amber, who came around with a dinner of a vegetable stew and a whole roasted fish on top.

Dar tapped his new ceramic bowl. Turning it around to look at it more carefully, he noticed that it wasn't quite round, but it was far superior to the wooden bowls. While a bit more oblong than round, it would be far easier to clean. He could even make an enchantment to steam them. A little box with heat runes and some water should do the trick.

"What new thing did you just invent in your mind?" Cherry asked.

"Oh, nothing." Dar waved it away.

"No, we want to know," Sasha encouraged him, getting her own food.

"Uh, back in my old world, we cleaned our dishes with steam. At least, we did in the restaurants. You'd hose them down to get the big stuff off and then do a steam rinse to kill off any lingering bacteria." Dar picked up his grilled fish and bit into it. It was simple, but fantastic, and a very welcome change from stew.

Dar let out a groan of approval and his idea vanished as everyone tried the grilled fish.

"This is great," Sasha agreed with her first bite. "Is there even a little salt on it?"

Mika nodded. "Yes. Just a little from Blair's work today." Her eyes tracked back to Dar, enjoying the fish, and she smiled warmly at his enjoyment.

"I think you won out on me today. Just a simple fish, yet I gave him pounds of salt and he isn't over here pounding me," Blair teased.

"I thought you already took your reward?" Dar threw it right back.

"Oh? What reward was that?" Sasha could sense there was something there.

Blair, however, looked at Cherry and Sasha with a bit of fear. "Nothing."

"It wasn't nothing," Amber spoke up. "She made out with Dar and then Neko."

"With Neko?" Cherry perked up, completely ignoring that Blair had kissed him. Then again, she was still encouraging him to take more women, so maybe that wasn't a problem for her.

Sasha nudged him and whispered, "Moving fast, well done."

"Dar, are you okay with her being physical with Neko?" Cherry turned to Dar.

"Of course, I have no issue with you girls seeking pleasure in each other. Otherwise, that would be hypocritical of me. But I'd ask you to keep it to our family or those that are going to join."

Cherry traded a look with Sasha before continuing. "That's unusual for male demons."

"It's better than that," Blair continued, clearly feeling emboldened now that his two dao companions weren't going to fry her for it. "He liked it. A lot."

"Enough." Dar stopped it before it went any further. "If it is a question, then yes, I have no issue with girls in our family sharing each other's bodies. In fact, where I came from, that was a common fantasy among men."

Sasha stepped around Dar and kissed Cherry. The two of them leaned into it and really went at it, making out in the public hearth. Their hands tangled in each other's hair as they seemed to go off to their own world.

Dar picked his jaw up off the floor and cleared his throat. "It might be best not to do that in public."

Both of them turned to him with big grins. "That was pleasant. Not quite as enjoyable as my rugged big lug, but you are a skilled kisser, Cherry."

"And our man does seem to really like it."

"That was hot as hell. When's my turn?" Blair leaned forward, about to fall out of her chair.

"When the big lug you love to tease gives you the green light. Not a moment before then." Sasha sat back down on Dar's left and gave the salt spirit a look that warned caution.

Ah, Sasha would be the one to keep her in line. Dar would let the women handle each other, though he realized he was close to overstepping when she kissed him.

The conversation died down as they focused on their food, and they settled into familial silence.

Finishing up, people were looking tired from a hard day's work, and Dar was feeling it as well. But he still needed to discuss plans with the other leaders of the village.

Getting up, Dar kissed Sasha's head just as she started a yawn. "Feel free to get some sleep. I'll come join you later."

The witch wrinkled her nose and sighed, giving up an argument before she even started. "Today was particularly trying. I'll take you up on that."

"Night, love." Dar gave her another kiss before he pulled Cherry along with him to the leader's group. Over his shoulder, he noticed the rest of them tightened into a smaller circle and Sasha started talking.

"What's that about?"

"Women things. Let us sort out things, and you just sit back and enjoy?" Cherry asked.

Dar didn't like that they were keeping him out of it and grunted neither in agreement nor disagreement.

"She's organizing your women for you. Let's leave it at that, okay?" Cherry tried again.

"You know that is still a foreign concept to me... but I'll leave it in yours and Sasha's hands. Not like I'm complaining." In some ways, he felt like he was just the binding agent for these powerful women, but if Cherry and Sasha were going to manage them, then any complaints would be downright silly.

Cherry bumped his hip as they got to the other group's circle. "Didn't think you'd throw much of a fit."

Pushing that aside, Dar spoke to the group as he joined the leaders' circle. "Evening. How was everyone today? I hope we didn't get any more surprises out of the day."

Russ growled. "I've heard about the fun in the woods, but I'd like to hear it again from you. Also, the woodcutters are scaring away game in the northern forest. If you want me to keep bringing back as much as I have been, we can't keep them in those woods."

Dar scratched at his chin. He hadn't considered that. "Then I'm afraid we need to do something about it. While we were felling trees today, one of the groups was attacked by two ettercaps and their pet spiders."

Russ looked confused, but one of his women whispered into his ear and he nodded along with Dar's story.

"We settled that one situation, but then I went with Rex to scout deeper in the forest than we'd been before. We found..." Dar paused, looking over to see if Rex wanted to fill in from there. It was technically his role, and Dar didn't want to take it away.

Rex cleared his throat and stepped back a few steps in the story. "We brought along torches to keep them away as we scouted. Deep in the forest, maybe ten miles southwest, was the largest ettercap colony I've ever heard of. We didn't get too close, but we were able to see it from over a mile away. It was a giant wall of white, tightly woven web, like a fortress made from the stuff."

"That's not good," Russ added unhelpfully.

Dar looked to Glump as the oldest in the group besides Cherry. "Any thoughts on what to make of that?"

"Normally, I'd get the hell out of their way, but we don't have that option now, do we? Winter is coming, and we can't afford to try to pack up and go to either of the cities. They are too far, and there are other risks to this group regardless." Glump was clearly agitated based on the way his throat bloated when he closed his mouth.

"Then we need to fight," Russ growled and knocked over his bowl.

Dar gave the young demon a level look. "How many do you suppose are in there? Our guess is hundreds, Russ. We might have some

powerful fighters, but that's a lot of ettercaps who have the element of knowing the territory and having pet spiders to throw at us to wear us down. We'd be exhausted before we even got to the main battle."

"But you're supposed to be the Black Knight, hunter of devils extraordinaire. The stories all sing of your ability to cut through armies of devils. Or is all that a lie?" Russ' hackles were up as he growled in challenge.

"Careful," Glump warned Russ. "We aren't fighting here."

Dar leveled the young demon with a glare. "I was the Black Knight, but not anymore. But that doesn't mean you have a chance against me."

It sounded aggressive to Dar, but Cherry and Sasha had coached him that, if he was to be challenged, he needed to stand tall and puff out his chest. This was something from a demon's animal heritage, not a human conversation.

Dar stood and rose to Russ' level. "Do we have a problem that needs to be settled?"

Russ growled and stamped his foot. If Dar hadn't fought much worse since coming to Granterra, he might have been intimidated like that first day with the Minotaur. But he'd become accustomed to this world enough to know that this was something he had to do to keep order in the village.

"You two. Why don't we settle down?" Samantha started, but one of Rex's wives held her back and whispered in her ear.

"We will take care of the ettercaps, Russ. It will be on our terms, and we will have a better plan than just charging in and seeing how many we can kill. I agree we can't just let them grow. Do you have any better ideas on how to take care of them?" Dar tried to appeal to his rational brain, to make Russ think about what else could be done.

Russ huffed and backed down. Two of his girls eased him down to his seat and did their best to comfort him. "No. I certainly couldn't walk in there like you said and kill them all."

Maybe his youthful rashness had been more curbed than Dar expected from his encounter with Neko.

"We know they hate fire, but it seemed they were aggressive enough to ignore that," Dar informed everyone. "But they did stop at the edge of the forest for now."

"We could just burn it all down," Russ offered.

Dar tried not to shoot it down immediately and poke his idea full of holes, since Russ already seemed a bit on edge. Instead, Dar just pivoted the conversation. "Let's leave that as a last resort. We'd lose a lot of resources, and it would potentially spread back to the village. It could also create something large enough to draw a bunch more devils to us."

"They will slow down as the weather chills, but fire will also be less of a deterrent in winter," Glump added. "We could try a few probing attacks."

"I was already thinking along those lines. I'll admit I'm terrified that they might come out of the forest en masse and overrun the village, but inaction through fear is no action at all." Dar shook his head.

"But there's something else I wanted to talk to this group about." Dar paused, confirming their attention. "There's a huge tree not far into the forest. I want to send a small team that deep to try and fell it to be carved into a solid wood boat." Dar gave them his plan. "At the same time, we can understand what the situation in the woods is after yesterday."

"A boat? How big?" Russ perked up, knowing that might lead him to the bison that he had been wanting to hunt.

"Big enough to bring at least a few bison back if we pack it correctly," Dar encouraged him.

"Good. With the woodcutters in the northern forest, we won't get much done, anyway. I will go with you tomorrow to get this wood for a boat." Russ nodded to himself.

Dar looked over his shoulder at Cherry. "Can I borrow you for the morning too?"

"Of course. We got ahead with the crops today. I'll wake up early and start a new crop for them to pick today before we go. Sasha will

come too." The last bit was said such that there was no room for argument.

"Sounds good." Dar looked back at Russ.

"Hold up. Is this the big tree that Frank said was too big to safely take down?" Bart interjected.

Dar nodded. "The very same. But I think that, with a skilled crew of heavy hitters like this, we can take it down. We'll have to be careful."

Bart looked around the group and heard no other complaint, so he raised his hands in surrender. "Alright, how about you take Frank too, just to be safe?"

Relenting, Dar nodded. Frank did have great expertise. "Send him our way in the morning. Would love to have him."

Bart grunted at having to tell the woodcutter but nodded. "I'll do that."

Dar waited to see if anybody else had pressing topics to discuss, but it seemed like everyone was tired and the big problem was all they had energy to work out that night.

"I wish I had a few to send your way," Rex said before standing up. "But we've doubled the watch, so I'm not sure we'll be able to spare anyone."

"Good thinking on the watch. Let's keep that up until we have better news." Dar couldn't hold back a yawn. "Sorry."

"No. It's been a long day. Let's hope tomorrow is a better one," Glump said.

Chapter 13

Dar groaned back to consciousness. "That feels good." Sasha was working him to completion, and he groaned in release.

Sasha pulled off and licked her lips. "Morning. You slept in this morning, and I thought you deserved a nice wake up call."

"Not sending Amber this time?" he teased, remembering the last time.

She playfully swatted him. "No, I need to get as much of you as I can get before there's more competition."

"Jealous already?" he probed as he sat up and fished for his clothes. Dar frowned, unable to find them. They were right there last night.

"Not jealous, really, but your time is a limited commodity. I just want to get it while I can." Sasha held up a new set of clothes and beckoned for him to stand.

He eyed the clothes; there was something different about them. "Are those made from your silk?"

She ducked her head as she blushed. "Yes. Now hurry up."

Holding his arms out wide, he let her control the clothes. The seams split and reformed around him to a perfect fit. The silk was soft and flexible when he lifted his arms, trying to see if there would be any mobility issues in his new clothes.

"It fits wonderfully, as always." Dar pulled her close for a lingering kiss. "Thank you."

"Mmm," Sasha hummed happily as she pulled away and went to work on his pants, walking around him, making small adjustments. "They aren't going to be quite as durable as your other set, but at least I'll be able to repair and replace them far easier."

Dar would be able to harden and strengthen the fibers with his dao. It didn't matter too much to him how durable his clothes were naturally.

"How do they feel?"

"Great, like I'm wearing a cloud." He grinned back. "Thank you very much, Sasha. I know this was a step for you."

She went on her tiptoes and kissed him on the cheek. "You accepted me for what I truly am. Nothing could make me happier. There's also just something about you wearing my silk that does send a little thrill through me."

"I know another way to send a thrill through you." Dar smiled, grabbing her hips.

But she swatted his hands away. "As much as I would love to, we can't take that much time. While you slept in, Russ did not, and he's been pacing the center of the village. I'd rather he not get so worked up that he challenges you."

Dar remembered how close they'd been to that the night before. "You saw last night?"

"Yes. I have no doubt you could beat him. However, for the stability of the village, I'd prefer you don't have to put him in his place." Sasha removed his hands and dusted off his shoulders. "Now get."

Ducking out of his hut, Dar saw his group for the day lingering by the central hearth. It wasn't far past dawn, but so many of the villagers started at the crack of dawn, putting in a full day's work to make Hearthway ready for the winter. By comparison, he felt late.

"Morning, Russ," Dar said, sitting down and accepting a bowl of breakfast from Marcie, who went right back to stirring her pot over the fire.

Russ grunted, and Dar noticed Russ only had his goat demon wife, Mindy, with him. Russ must have noticed his look because he

explained. "Others are hunting today. We thought we should bring a smaller, elite team on this trip."

"Fair. We certainly don't want to create a lot of noise on this trip. Though, taking down that tree and transporting it is going to be loud," Dar explained.

Frank sat down and joined them. "That's an understatement. Taking down that tree is risky for all of us involved." Frank gave Dar a look that told him he wasn't entirely on board but that he'd help nonetheless.

"Great, even more reason for us to go with a smaller team. You don't seem to think there will be a problem with taking it down, just that it'll be dangerous?" Dar wasn't about to let Frank seed any doubt for this trip.

"Something that big… it is hard to get it to fall the way you want. And something that big doesn't give you much option to run if it falls your way."

Neko walked up to get her own food and Dar waved her over. Before they got started, he wanted to see if she couldn't help him with an enchantment.

"Dar," Neko said simply, sitting down with her porridge.

"Neko, I was wondering if I couldn't get you to scratch your dao into my axe." He put the weapon on his lap for her to see it.

She stared at it for a moment and shrugged.

"Sasha, could you give her a crash course in enchanting? I'd like to see if we can't get her character on it and speed up our cutting time so we aren't in the woods longer than need be."

"Yes, I think I can. Come here, Neko." Sasha pulled the demon aside for a quick lesson.

"Woods?" Neko asked, as Sasha pulled her away.

Dar knew Sasha would end up doing more of the work, but if they could get Neko to at least enchant the blade, it would go a long way.

"Still amazing how casually you allow everybody to use enchantments. Think once you get your axe done that we could get some for ours?" Frank asked, licking his lips.

"No safety concerns?" Dar shot right back.

The old woodcutter gave a noncommittal grunt. Dar smiled, shifting back to his food so they could get going on the trip and get it done. The whole affair promised to be its own set of troubles.

"Dar!" Mika bounced over to his side, already wide awake and with some black smudges on her hands.

"What are you up to?"

"Just finished talking through the design of the spear with the blacksmiths. Now I just need to work on getting a hearty net made." She seemed excited about her new tools.

Dar was happy for her and excited for the prospect of a steady supply of fish. "I'd love to see it later. We are going to head out here shortly. But definitely show it to me later. I look forward to how much fish you bring in tonight."

"Do you need me to come with?" she asked, but Dar shook his head.

"Not this time. We got our crew all set up. Hopefully, we won't need everyone."

Mika nodded, bouncing away excitedly over to a group of nearby women.

"Sasha, do you have enough to make her a net?" Dar asked.

"Not right now, but that's a great idea." Sasha understood what he wanted.

Russ looked like he was about to bounce out of his seat, so Dar figured it was time to get going.

"Alright, finish up. We are heading out." Dar looked over his shoulder, and Sasha had already taken the axe back from Neko and was adding the conditional scroll work to focus the enchantment on the blade of the axe.

After a few more moments, Sasha looked up and nodded, putting away her wand and holding up the axe for him. "It's at least done. We'll have to test it on this favorite tree of yours."

Dar hefted the axe and looked over the head, careful not to focus on the enchantment. "Great. Thank you."

Standing up, they all grouped together, throwing their bags over their shoulders. The team consisted of Dar, Russ, Mindy, Frank, Sasha, and Cherry. They all had weapons, along with Dar and Frank having axes for the tree.

The edge of the forest was quieter than before, and it was immediately obvious why. Large spider webs hung overhead with ensnared birds and small game wrapped up.

"They just decimated our squirrel and bird population, didn't they?" Dar looked up to see so many of the poor critters trapped and dead.

"Devils," Russ spat. "When they form big groups, it is always like this. They drive the life out of the land."

"There don't seem to be any lurking, though?" Cherry said, although she spun as she walked, clearly still antsy.

Dar's head was on a swivel, and he had yet to spot any, but that didn't mean they weren't there. His experience the day before had taught him that they were masters of ambushing prey. "I don't see any, but we cannot afford to lower our guard. Keep your eyes peeled."

The group nodded and stayed quiet as they walked through the eerie forest. It had only been a day since the same walk had been filled with vibrant, lush greens and the sounds of nature. Now any rustling of leaves caused everybody to startle and spin around. The walk was far less therapeutic.

Breathing a sigh of relief as they reached the tree, the group circled up around it. The tree was large enough that it had beaten out any smaller plants below, leaving an open area around it. It would at least give them some warning before any ambush.

Cherry whistled as she saw the tree. "That's big. I see what you mean by making a boat out of it." Her neck craned back as she tried to look for the top. "There's no way in hell I can control that much plant."

"Good thing you don't have to. The plan is to cut this guy down the old-fashioned way." Dar slung his axe over his shoulder and looked over to Frank. "How do you want to do this one?"

The old woodcutter circled the base of the tree, looking up and down; he picked up some grass and let it flutter in the breeze. "West towards the village is downhill. Wind isn't strong, but it's blowing east. You'd be surprised how much wind the top of a tree like this can catch. It is a bit of a tossup on whether the land or the wind will have the most power to direct the way it falls, but I'd bet on the wind. We'll have to try and use it to help us direct its fall."

Stepping around to the east side of the tree, Dar got to work cutting out the wedge. He activated the new enchantment on his axe and cut into the tree. It wasn't quite like cutting through butter, maybe closer to cutting through a steak, but definitely easier than it would have been before.

Even with the ease that his axe slid through the wood, Dar still had to work to carve out the wedge rather than the few simple cuts it would have been for a smaller tree. Everybody else in the crew kept an eye around Dar, letting him do the brunt of the work given his extra strength.

"That's it. We probably need to go a little deeper right here though." Frank observed the wedge Dar had been making.

"Here?" Dar notched a spot with his axe.

"Yeah. A little deeper. I'm just trying to be extra careful that it goes the way we want."

Grunting, Dar took another few swings, deepening the wedge and taking a break to lean on his axe. "That's good?"

"It'll have to do. Want me to start on the other side?" Frank asked, eyeing Dar's axe.

"You just want to play with my new toy. Not fooling anybody." Dar smiled, holding out the oversized axe. "Go for it."

Frank sank when he grabbed it. "Drasil above! How do you swing this?"

"With my arms." Dar let out a satisfied chuckle.

The woodcutter was unamused. "I'll take a few swings, but I think that's all I'm worth."

Russ grumbled. "As long as you hurry up. I feel like we are being stalked."

Dar knew better than to distrust a demon's instincts. "Danger?"

"Just being watched. Maybe a scout for their colony. Can't see the bugger though." Russ shaded his eyes and looked up into the canopy.

Dar nodded, trusting Russ and the rest of the crew to keep an eye on whatever was stalking them while he focused his efforts on the tree.

Frank pushed through about a dozen swings before he dropped Dar's axe with a thump. "That's all I got in me. New respect for you, lord."

Brow rising up, Dar gave him a slow nod. It seemed he was earning the old man's respect, oddly enough, for his ability to swing an axe of all things.

Taking over the axe, Dar went to work on hacking a narrow channel through the base of the tree. Then Frank and Russ worked to lift the largest piece from cutting the wedge into the thin tract that was made.

"Okay, line her up and drive her home. Try to be a little more careful than last time." Frank backed up away from the tree.

Dar pressed on the wedge and squared up his axe. This was the moment of truth. "Everyone, be ready to move when this starts to fall." Dar swung, hitting it with the shaft of the axe. Once, twice, three times.

It wasn't tipping, at least not yet.

"Give me another piece of the wedge." Dar held his hand out.

Frank gave him another piece, and Dar wedged it in, winding up and slamming it home.

Crack.

It felt almost like the wind and leaves paused in respect for the mighty tree about to fall, everything holding for a moment after the loud noise.

Holding his breath and looking up to see which way the tree would fall, Dar froze as it tottered for a moment. He backed up to get the full view as it swayed and finally tipped.

"Timber," Dar said, just loud enough for everyone to hear. "This way."

He stepped around to the west side as the tree tipped east. It was slow going for just a moment. It felt like it would take minutes to fall. Then it accelerated and crashed down to the forest floor in seconds, tearing apart other trees in its wake and slamming against the dirt with a deafening boom.

Dirt and debris blew up into the air, and Dar had to shield his face to prevent it from getting in his eyes. Blinking away the dirt, the mammoth tree was laid out before him. Now on its side, Dar got a real idea for how thick it was; he couldn't see over the top. He guessed it was about eight feet wide.

"Now how the fuck do you plan on moving that?" Frank asked.

"Cut a section for the boat, and then roll it out of here." Dar answered, not wasting any time. They already felt like they had a watcher, but no doubt more would come from that loud noise.

Dar walked long paces down the length, aiming to count out about thirty feet and starting to hack a section off.

"Could we build more than one boat?" Russ asked, seeing the length of the tree.

"One is already going to be a massive task, so let's start with one. It'll still be here if we want more later."

Digging into the tree with his axe, Dar didn't have to worry about the same finesse that he did when felling the tree. Speed was most important to him at that moment. Frank moved around the other side and worked with Dar to separate the massive log.

"How's that feeling, Russ? Should we be worried?" Dar checked in with the hunter.

"Still feel like we are being watched, but I don't know. If these ettercaps are so aggressive, there's no way they'd not come investigate. But whatever is watching us isn't making a move."

Dar hoped it was some other predator of the forest that had managed to escape the aggressive clearing of the forest wildlife the ettercaps had clearly done.

Focusing back on the task at hand, Dar threw himself into hacking at the tree, sending large chips of wood flying. It wasn't long into the task that a yowl of a large cat sounded in the trees above, and the sounds of chittering spiders reached Dar's ears.

"Where?" Dar said, looking up from his task, his axe buried in the tree at present.

Russ must have spotted it, because he pulled back his bow, lining up a shot in a tree a hundred paces behind them, towards the village. But Dar spotted Neko up in the tree, surrounded by ettercaps and spiders. They had snuck around them and had been trying to block them from returning.

"No, hold your fire," Dar called, not wanting Russ to hit Neko before calling out to her. "Neko, jump down."

He was already running to get underneath the tree and catch her. She looked over the edge of the tree at him, and that was the moment an ettercap attacked. It jumped on Neko's back, pinning her to the tree.

Webs sprang from the surrounded ettercaps, trapping her up in the tree and cutting her off from Dar. In that moment, all Dar could think about were the dozens of dead critters they'd seen in the forest, wrapped up in webs just like Neko was now. She was not going to be one of them.

Dar's concern for her outweighed anything else in the moment. "Frank, spear. Now."

The old woodcutter didn't hesitate for a moment, tossing Dar his spear and pulling out his axe.

Putting his full strength behind it, Dar launched the spear like a missile. As soon as it left his hand, he knew he hit. The branch Neko was pinned to shattered where it connected to the trunk, and the whole lot fell to the forest floor.

Dar was already running, his axe pulled back and swinging for the first ettercap in his path. His newly enchanted blade cut right through the devil—this time closer to butter—and he swung back in a chopping motion. In the backswing, he cut the ettercap on top of Neko.

Reaching the center of the fray, Dar grabbed Neko and slid her out from under the ettercaps, shifting her behind him and pushing her towards his companions. Sasha rushed forward to grab her.

But the ettercaps weren't idle. They jumped on him, trying to tie Dar down with their webs. Sticky threads rapidly coated him from above and around.

But Dar had a new advantage—Neko was out of any blast radius. Dar pumped his dao of heat out of his every pore and cooked the web surrounding him. He even managed to get the nearby ettercaps and their spiders.

But they didn't stop coming, no matter how many he cooked alive. Dar had shifted into single-minded battle focus. He continued blasting his heat, pausing to unleash one of his largest waves yet to get a moment of reprieve to strategize.

But the spiders didn't flinch, continuing to throw themselves at Dar. They poured out of the canopy like a swarm. He could start to feel his heat puttering out. Reaching for more mana for another blast, Dar found that it was like a dry engine sputtering on only fumes.

"DAR!" Sasha screamed behind him.

She was crouched over Neko with her ribbons out, but the spiders were leaving them alone, for the most part. Instead, they all seemed to be focusing on him.

More spiders jumped down, using the opportunity and landing on his back.

Dar reached up and flipped one off of him, finishing it with a swing of his axe, but more threads spat out at his extended arm, tangling it up. Dar was strong, but the sticky webbing had a flex to it that made it hard to break with brute strength. As he worked to break it, more and more webbing piled up on top of him.

Dar continued to swing and cleave his way through the spiders, refusing to give up, but with each added web, his movements grew less effective, until he was barely able to move.

CHAPTER 14

T rapped in the webs, Dar worked to keep himself from panicking. He needed to work his way out of the situation. The town and the world needed him, and if he was going to take down the devils, he needed to be able to handle this group of low-level devils. This wasn't where it all ended.

Relaxing his body, Dar worked to focus his mind. One thought floated to the top: he needed to reach his greater dao.

With adrenaline coursing through his veins, Dar forced himself to focus. He worked to intertwine the lesser dao of hard, strength and heavy. Dar was having trouble breathing through the webs, but he used that as pressure, keeping his mind singularly focused on his task. He ignored the brief yells and noises of battles beyond, continuing to work the lesser dao together.

Like the flicker of a candle wick just catching a spark, Dar sensed the beginning of something more. Dar wasn't sure if it was going to survive and blaze into a true fire or be blown out by a stray wind, but it was all he had to hold onto.

Keeping his concentration on the character, Dar started to cycle what little fumes of mana he had left into the shape of the complex character that was beginning to flicker to life. Over and over again, he cycled his mana.

This time, there was no need to meditate. The sheer determination within him kept him singularly focused on this task. He had to form this dao. Everything depended on it.

But, as he cycled, Dar quickly began to acknowledge that the fumes of mana in his channels weren't enough to complete the character no matter how quickly he sped up his cycling.

Desperate for success, Dar called out mentally to the world around him, the ground beneath him, calling for his body to pull whatever mana it could find. In response, he felt the barest trickle of mana reach him.

Renewed hope sparked in Dar, and he began to pull harder. He breathed deeply both through his mouth and with his body as he drew in more mana, filling his channels with a faint trickle. It wasn't much, but it was enough to complete a full cycle.

Focusing again, Dar continued the cycling of the mana, one after another. Sasha's scream reached him through the webs, but Dar had to work to block it out. He'd be no use to her unless he could finish this.

Dar let the strength of the very earth beneath his feet flow into him. And soon, the cycles became one, the scales tipping in his favor. Granite. It was everything Dar knew it to be and so much more.

Knowledge and power flowed into Dar as the greater dao of granite flowed into him.

Like his first lesser dao, with the new dao came vast amounts of mana. He could even feel trace amounts of the complete dao circling him, as if in this moment of comprehension, he drew the attention of the world itself. It brought with it power, allowing him to change himself.

It was like the complete dao was for a moment surrounding him, and he grasped all that he could change so he could grow into the next stage of his journey as an immortal.

Dar widened his channels, filling himself to the brim with everything this moment offered and expanding his inner world. He could feel it grow and swell to hold as much mana as he could bear.

At the same time, he was thickening all of these containers for mana. Dar recognized he needed to be able to pressurize mana to greater extents; he needed to be able to bear the meditation method he'd started upon. Elation spread through Dar; there was so much potential and power in his current path.

As he shifted his body to accommodate the new changes, Dar realized how flexible his inner world seemed at that moment. Smiling, Dar reached deeper, imagining that dark iron gate that had been immobile for so long. He pictured the bars ripping apart, giving him full access to the space.

At first, the image of the bars only seemed to ripple, but soon he was able to bend and mold them, pulling them apart and creating a path for him to enter.

Dar continued to draw upon this moment of enlightenment to further improve his ability to grow along his dao path. Drawing on imagery of gardening, Dar laid down the necessary foundation for the next stage of its growth, establishing his body as a place to nourish the little dao tree further.

The moment of pure elation faded as quickly as it had begun, and Dar came back to himself, still wrapped up in webs. There he was, tied down while his friends and dao companions struggled for their lives.

But this moment was different. Dar was bursting to the brim with mana, and he had a new tool that he didn't have before.

He could feel granite just a few feet below the hard packed soil beneath him. He had a feeling it was likely connecting all the way back to the cliffs, but he could only feel it in a small field around him.

Calling upon that very stone, Dar roared to the heavens in a new call to war against the ettercaps. The stone rose up against his feet, and he could feel it bending to his will.

Pillars rose up around Dar in a protective cage as he released his dao of heat once more, using his new mana reserves. It took a moment of burning, but soon all the webbing that had encased him was gone once again.

As he was able to see again, Dar spotted spiders and ettercaps trying to break through his pillars to once again dog pile him. But they were having trouble getting between the pillars, and Dar was about to make it far harder. The granite pillars bent and spun, transforming the area around Dar into a grinder that would catch and chew up any who entered.

Unfortunately, that left Dar covered with the foul goo as the ettercaps and spiders ground up in the granite pillars.

The tide didn't stop, as it hadn't before. The spiders continued their reckless pursuit to reach him. He knew his team needed his help, and not wanting to run down his mana again, Dar prepared to break free.

Holding tightly to his axe, Dar crossed his arms over his chest before falling back. The ground split open for him, welcoming him with a coffin of granite. He fell into the ground and shuttled through it for twenty feet before bursting out of the ground with a gasp.

Dar let out a deep breath, glad it had worked. There was a moment of panic from being buried in the ground that he hadn't been expecting. Being entombed alive in the ground by his own hand was not the type of death he envisioned for himself.

"Dar!" Sasha squealed, and wrapped her arms around him. Her clothing was ragged from fighting, but not as if she'd been directly attacked.

Something else had the ettercaps' attention.

Dar's eyes immediately scanned for threats, the first one being the largest spider he had ever seen, just beyond Sasha. But the scene didn't make sense to him... the ettercaps were attacking it?

Dar's brain and eyes fought over what they were seeing for a moment. It wasn't piecing together. But then Dar spotted Cherry behind Sasha, hunched over the ground in concentration, sweat dripping down her face.

Following her line of sight, Dar realized it was woody roots that were swinging down on the crowd of ettercaps, crushing dozens of them. The large creature wasn't a spider at all. Cherry was controlling

the stump of the tree they had cut down, using it to stomp the ettercaps into the forest grounds.

She had kept the devils busy and protected Dar during his epiphany.

"Dar, I'm so glad you're alive." Sasha squeezed him for all he was worth.

"I love you too, but we need to go," Dar declared, prying her off of him.

She snapped back to herself. "Of course. I was just so overwhelmed."

Dar gave her a quick peck and took in the rest of the situation. Frank was unarmed, and Dar cringed. He'd made Frank give up his spear and now the old woodcutter was hanging back by the log with his axe, protected by Russ and his girl, who were firing arrows into the never-ending sea of ettercaps.

Cherry's work seemed to be the most effective at keeping them from being overrun, but Dar knew there was only so long that she could keep up with that kind of power.

"Frank, move," Dar called, pulling on the stone beneath their feet.

The old woodcutter looked at Dar in shock and backed into the felled tree.

"Move," Dar repeated more forcefully, snapping the man out of his shock as he quickly moved out of the way.

They needed to retreat, but the ettercaps now knew what they were after. Dar had no doubt there would be more traps and a larger battle to get access to the large tree. He had to at least try to salvage the mission if he could, although the lives of his crew were more important in the end.

A plan forming in his mind, Dar pulled the granite out of the ground and formed it like clay with his mind into a ridiculously oversized axe. Dar let the idea of a sharp blade take form, and between his control over granite and his strength, he lifted it high over his head.

Lining it up with the section they'd already cut away, Dar let it drop, simultaneously using his dao of heavy to make it fall like a meteor strike.

The granite axe blew right through the remaining section of the tree in a messy cut, blowing splinters of wood as big as his forearm everywhere.

Frank and Russ stared, slack jawed, at the destruction he'd just caused. Even the ettercaps had paused in battle, startled by the massive display of force. Or maybe it was the vibration along the ground that had startled them.

"Come on, push it," Dar said, before slamming his shoulder into the log.

"You're kidding." Frank stared at the massive log. "We can't budge that. We need to get out of here."

It wasn't moving with all Dar's effort, so he changed tactics. Finding purchase in the rough bark, Dar squatted and strained, trying to get it rolling.

"It's downhill to the village; we just need to get it started," Dar grunted between clenched teeth as he pushed.

Russ and his girl joined him, followed by Sasha and Frank. There was a tense moment while it didn't shift, but then, ever so slowly, the log rocked away from them.

"That's it. PUSH." Dar gave it all he had; it felt like the veins in his neck were going to burst, but the log finally moved.

Once it had momentum, it was ten times easier to move, and Dar walked his hands down the log, pulling their side up and rolling the log.

Sasha ducked back and grabbed Neko, who was motionless and still tangled in webbing. Russ grabbed Cherry and carried her, even as she still focused on her monstrous stump, and continued to wreck the ettercap population.

Continuing to pick up speed, the log started on its own path, becoming harder to control, but moving in the direction they needed. Dar took Cherry from Russ and kept pace with the log as it

continued, heading straight for the ettercaps and spiders who hadn't realized what was coming yet.

The log rolled right over the smaller trees that had been left by the woodcutters after the previous day's attack, snapping like twigs as the log continued to roll forward. Soon Dar had to jog to keep up with it.

It moved like a bull in a china shop, plowing over everything in its way, which included ettercaps that had been working to ambush them further down field. The tree crushed their bodies, and Dar did his best to avoid losing his boots in the goo left in its wake.

Cherry had brought along her massive stump, continuing to use it to block any that were able to dodge the tree and attack from the side. Soon, they'd made their way through the thick of enemies, and Cherry relaxed in Dar's grip, the giant stump crashing to the ground with an earthshaking thud.

"I got you, Cherry. We are getting out of here," Dar managed to squeeze out between panted breaths.

"Dar?" Cherry looked up, clearly confused.

He gave her the best smile he could as he ran. "Later."

The log was still picking up speed, and Dar realized he had a new issue. Even if they got out of the forest, that log had the potential to steam roll over Hearthway and everyone still there.

A chuckle of self-deprecation slipped through his lips at the idea that, after all this, he might wreck the village himself. They survived angry nobles, an army of ettercaps, but a big log would be their doom. But that moment was short-lived as Dar pulled himself together.

He needed to change its trajectory. Watching how it moved, Dar decided to try to redirect it a bit.

Pumping his legs for all he was worth, Dar caught up to the log and passed it, drawing upon his new dao and creating small ledges of granite on one side of the log, pushing it into the cliffs and higher ground.

The log bounced off the granite ramps and slowly shifted its direction away from dooming the village and towards the slope of the

cliffs that Dar hoped would starve it of its momentum. He could see it slow down and rock back towards them using the rise of the cliffs as a shallow bowl to halt it.

Dar let out a sigh of relief, brought back to the next crisis as the chittering behind him reminded him of their other problem. Their entire group managed to make it past the edge of the forest, all looking exhausted and worse for wear.

Once again, the spiders and ettercaps stopped at the edge, angrily pacing and chittering for a minute before skulking back deeper into the tree line.

"Think that's it, boss?" Russ' chest heaved as he bent over, placing his hands on his knees. The rest of the group, including Dar, sat down in the grass to catch their breath.

The term 'boss' was a new one for Russ, but Dar didn't comment on it. Maybe he had earned a bit of respect from the battle.

"We can hope," Dar replied, looking over the group once more to assess damage.

"Dar!" Cherry jumped into his arms and smothered him with kisses before he could say anything else. When she finally came up for air, she grabbed his head. "What happened? I thought we lost you."

He noticed everyone else was watching him closely, wanting to hear the story as well. "I broke through on my greater dao. I am now a greater immortal with the dao of granite." He couldn't help but grin as he said it. "I fucking did it!"

"Good for you." Cherry was all smiles and planted one last kiss on his lips before jumping back.

As Cherry moved away, Dar spotted Neko in Sasha's arms, unmoving in the webs.

Dar hurried over and pulled some of the webbing free to feel for a pulse at her neck. A sigh of relief escaped him. It was weak, but she had a steady pulse. Pulling the webbing apart further, he used his dao of heat to burn anywhere his hands touched, working to separate her from the webs.

The first thing Dar saw were two big cuts on her shoulder, and they had an oily sheen on them.

"Poison," Russ answered, looking over Dar's shoulder.

"Anything we can do?" Dar asked.

"She'll need lots of water and time to work it out of her system. That's the best way. We'll see if anyone in the village can make a general-purpose compress for the wound too."

Cherry shook her head. "Stupid girl. She should have stayed back in the village."

"I disagree. If it wasn't for her, think how much closer they would have gotten before we noticed them," Dar explained. "She was the one that started fighting them. If not for that noise, it could have been a much worse ambush."

Russ grunted. "I think she was the one watching us earlier. It would make sense. And for what it is worth, I agree. She saved all of us today. I didn't sense them until they were already on us. She knows the forest well."

Dar nodded and scooped up Neko. "Let's go check on this log and see if this was all worth it."

Everyone got up and Frank hurried ahead to look at the log. The woodcutter was quickly doing circles around it, his hands making motions as he likely strategized the best way to make it into a boat. Dar smiled; the man was back in his element, clearly looking to focus on something other than the near-death experience they'd just had.

Others from the village were now coming out, wanting to see what had created all the commotion.

"What happened?" Shelia asked, holding onto her weapon and looking towards the forest.

"We'll explain later. For now, everything is okay. Or at least, no worse," Dar answered for everyone before turning back to Frank. "What's the damage?"

"Hmmm." Frank walked along the log's length again, stroking his chin. "It seems to be in remarkable condition all things considered. You have a few spots that are going to need to be cut out, and I need

it rolled to see the top and bottom, but I'd say it is still fit to make a boat."

With his words, a small cheer came from the village, and Dar turned to see all the children getting excited over what they likely didn't fully understand. But the laughter and glee brought a weary smile to everyone's faces.

"Okay, Shelia. Get as many people as we can spare. We need to try to bring this into the village carefully." Dar looked at the log with a shake of his head. It had been so much trouble, but he had a feeling it may just save them with all it could unlock as they got access to the other side of the river.

"Uh, boss. Do you really think we can move that?" Shelia stared at the massive log.

Sasha nudged him. "I'm taking Neko back to our hut; I'll have her wounds cleaned and dressed."

"Take good care of our little savior," Dar added and gave Neko's ears a small ruffle before he leaned down and whispered in them. "Stay strong, Neko."

Sasha gave a determined nod before carrying her away.

When he looked back up, Dar found everybody staring at him. "Well come on. We have this massive log to move, and then we need to get started on trimming it. Anyone have a dao that can help?"

CHAPTER 15

D ar wiped the sweat from his brow and looked at the giant tree section sitting to the side of the central hearth. It had taken most of the village and half the afternoon to move it, and he was still amazed they'd managed to do it.

"What now?" Shelia asked.

"Now we start carving a boat out of it," Dar stated simply, knowing it wouldn't be an easy task. With only hand saws, axes and chisels, it was going to be a massive labor effort.

While the men went to begin gathering their tools, Dar took the moment to go check in on Neko.

She wasn't hard to find; Sasha always stood out like a beacon with her choice in clothing. Dar only had to look for the rich, vibrant colors of her dresses. Quickly spotting her, he headed her way.

"Hey, love. How's she doing?" Dar came up behind Sasha and wrapped his arms around her, giving her a kiss on the cheek.

"Stable but see for yourself." Sasha moved over to where Neko was lying in a hut. Neko's face was twisted up in pain, sweat beading down her body as she fought whatever venom the spiders had left in her wounds.

Sasha had Neko's arm banded up tightly with a lump of a compress over her shoulder.

"Stitches to close it up?" Dar asked.

"We washed it out as best we could, but the venom had plenty of time to get in her system." Sasha wrung out a fresh cloth and put it on Neko's forehead, replacing an old one.

Dar reached down and stroked Neko's hair and ruffled her ears. "Get better soon, Neko. But fair warning: I'll have to bathe all this sweat off you when you feel better."

Neko scrunched her eyes in pain before she opened them. She had trouble focusing, but her eyes finally settled on Dar's face, and she gave him a bright smile. "Dar."

"Yes, I'm right here." He sat down with her and just let his presence be there for her.

She nuzzled into his lap for a moment before she was struck with a coughing fit.

"I'll get you some water." Sasha left with a smile.

Dar sat there, rubbing Neko's back as her body revolted against the venom. "Shhh, it'll be okay."

"Dar, Neko bad."

"If it wasn't for you, I'm not sure we would have seen them in time. Neko, you helped us. Now rest."

She really had caught the ettercaps before any of them had sensed their presence. While reckless, he couldn't be upset with her. She had wanted to protect them, and she did know the forest better than any of them.

Sasha brought back a bowl of water. "You'll look after her? I have a few things to take care of."

"Of course. I'll stay with her until she falls asleep again." Dar took the bowl of water and held it for Neko to sip.

Neko drank her fill, resting her head against his lap with a content groan and a lazy swish of her tail.

"Shh, rest. Your body needs it." Dar ran his fingers through her hair, teasing out the black locks mixed in with the strawberry-blonde.

It only took a few minutes, but Neko fell back asleep. Dar sat a bit longer, running his fingers through her hair and studying her. Somehow, the cat girl had wormed her way into his life and heart.

There was something pure about her that called to him. And he'd almost lost her today.

It had shocked him how possessive he'd felt when he'd seen her in trouble. It was more than what he felt for his villagers; he was really starting to care for her and want her in his life.

Dar wasn't sure what that would look like yet, but he knew he wasn't going to give her up easily.

Sighing and giving Neko's soft ears one last stroke, he gingerly slid her head off his lap and stuffed a blanket under it. As he walked out, Dar called over to Marcie to come watch Neko and make sure she was taken care of until Sasha was able to return.

Feeling it was safe to leave, Dar headed out and saw Frank and Bart had the initial boat work well in hand. He then pivoted and instead went to the cave, wanting to test out his new greater dao now that there was a bit of time.

Granite was a relatively common stone, but Dar figured that actually gave his dao more strength. It wasn't some rare mineral that he'd have to gather. No, granite was common enough that he'd be able to find it when he needed it. After seeing Blair's struggle with limited salt around, he recognized the benefit of having a common resource.

As Dar stepped into the cave, a thrum immediately connected to him, the granite around him calling out to his body.

Using his hand, Dar scooped off a chunk of granite and molded it into the same shape as the tool they'd designed to help remove tree limbs. Smiling, he looked around, deciding to head further into the cave where he could get a greater amount of granite; the entrance was largely softer stone.

Miners waved as he walked deeper, coming up to a spot that had a good amount of granite around and fewer workers. Reaching forward, Dar touched the wall and imagined pulling out a huge chunk of stone the size of a small car.

He could feel the rest of the stone and left enough behind that it wouldn't collapse.

The stone flowed and shifted for Dar, until the wall of stone had molded into a lump with a handle that Dar was easily able to pull out from the wall. It was a few thousand pounds of stone, but with his dao helping move the stone, it wasn't a great feat to drag it. When he was touching the granite, he found his power was much stronger.

"Hunky man meat, what on earth do you have there?" Blair looked up from the same spot she'd been sitting in the day before. The larger crystals were gone, the start of smaller crystals all forming around her.

"I'll tell you and everybody else about it at dinner. I want to keep focusing on this." Dar waved to her and continued on out of the cave, receiving gawking looks from all the miners he passed with his giant chunk of granite.

A few people trailed behind him as he moved out of the cave with it and stopped at a patch of dirt, driving it into ground and forming the start of a stone foundation. Stepping back, Dar smiled, appreciating his work. But it was still smaller than he had intended, so he headed back in to grab another piece.

Checking his reserves, his mana was already feeling sluggish from hauling that large piece for that far. Disappointed, Dar paused to try to think of a better way to do it without using so much of his dao.

This time, when he pulled it out, he formed a large cylindrical wheel at the bottom, like a large rolling pin embedded in the bottom. Stone wasn't going to make a good axle and wheel, but he didn't need it to last long. He thought of it as a stone cart.

Using his strength instead of his granite dao, Dar pulled it out and set it next to the original piece he had used to start the foundation. Then he formed it once more, sinking it into the ground.

When he was done, the foundation formed a short, knee-high wall. Dusting himself off, Dar smiled as he looked over the foundation. It seemed like it would work. He could create foundations with half-height walls, which would also help with their lumber issue. Heck, he may even be able to carve out homes within the caves themselves.

Dar went back inside and made one more stone cart, bringing it out to the foundation and adding to the existing half-walls, making them even higher and thickening them to something closer to the cinder block walls he was used to. But as he added, he could sense the granite wasn't the best material for tall walls or the ceiling. It just didn't have any tensile strength, and you needed that for a roof.

He'd have to live with just making the foundations and part of the walls, adding some stability, strength, and warmth to the home. They'd need lumber or another material for the rest of the wall and ceilings.

Bart hovered over his work when he was done. "That was quick; maybe faster than the concrete."

Dar wiped at his forehead. "Yeah, but I'm not sure how many of those I can do before getting worn out." Dar could tell he needed to rest and restore his reserves of mana before he could do more.

"These walls, are they partially hollow?" Bart asked, rapping on one to listen to the sound.

"Sort of," Dar explained what a cinder block looked like, and how they could be stacked in a staggered order to create a solid wall with less material.

"And we can do that with concrete too?" Bart asked.

"Typically, they are made with slightly different mixtures; you use cinders from a fire instead of gravel with the binding agent so they are lighter." A few summers in construction had taught him quite a bit.

"Got plenty of that from the central hearth. Haven't had much to do with it until now besides soap. But if we shoot for a few foundations a day between now and winter, we might just have a shot at getting everyone in a winter home."

"That would take a heavy burden off all our backs," Dar agreed.

Behind Bart, people were crawling all over the massive log, still working to shave and chisel the bark off it.

"Speaking of large projects, how's that going?" Dar pointed to the log.

"People are eager to help with that one. As soon as Russ said that it would be used to hunt and bring back bison, people have started pitching in after they wrapped up with their tasks for the day." Bart shook his head. "Still have a few things to work out, but with that many hands, we'll get it done."

"It's going to be a big boat. You may want to save some of the larger pieces of wood; we'll need paddles."

"Aye, it is almost big enough to need a paddle wheel, but none of us have experience with making one."

Dar remembered the large paddle wheel on the riverboat, but his mind drifted to an enchantment. Mika's dao of waves might just work well enough to make something like a rear-mounted boat motor.

"I have some ideas, but we have time. That's going to take days to carve out."

"Dar," Mika called, coming up from the river.

Dar glanced over, his eyes catching on the wet clothing that was sticking to her body. He found himself gulping as he took in her curves, struggling to keep his focus on her face. It took him a moment to notice the net full of fish hanging over her shoulder, full down to her hips.

"I'll catch you at dinner." Bart clapped Dar's shoulder, a smirk on his face as he went back to the massive log.

"Wow, Mika. That's a lot of fish. Are you hoping to feed the whole village?" Dar teased.

She hefted the bag and eyed it critically. "There isn't that much, but I'm glad you approve." Mika stabbed the butt of her new spear into the ground and struck a pose. What she had gotten created was less like a spear and more like a trident. It had three prongs, with the middle one sticking out slightly above the other two.

"Seems to have worked well for you today." He gave her an appreciative smile. "Want me to carry the fish the rest of the way?"

Mika squinted at Dar, distracted from his offer. "Uh huh. Something about you is different."

Dar grinned, pleased that she could tell. "Yes. We'll talk about it later. Let's get your fish over to the women at the fire, and we can talk about the days we've had. I had some questions about your dao as well." He took the heavy net of fish from her.

"Sure!" Mika hurried over to the group of women working at a table as Dar laid down her net. There were exclamations among the women as they quickly cast aside their current work and started sorting and prepping the fish.

With how much Mika was gathering, Dar was hopeful that they'd soon have more than they needed for the night's dinner and could start packing them away for the winter. Although, there may also be fishing as an option in the winter, depending on how Mika could do in the cold.

Heading over to the massive log, Dar saw Frank using his axe to shave some shape into it. "Which side is the front and which is the back?"

Frank jumped at Dar's question. "Hi, uh... here's your axe back." He held it out for Dar.

"Thanks, but if it's useful for you, feel free to keep using it. For now, I'd just like to make sure we're on the same page around the plan for this boat." Grabbing a lump of burnt-out coal from the fire, Dar then snagged a nearby piece of extra wood. "Bart, come over here. Let's sketch out how this is going to be cut."

"It's a boat, isn't it? Seems straight forward." Bart gave Dar a skeptical look.

"Right, I get that. But we went to a lot of work for this. We can't afford over cutting it. Here." Dar used the coal to mark the smoother of the two cuts with a nice flat-bottomed U for the profile of the boat. "The top is here. We can mark the top out and the curve we want as we go, but we'll make this side the back and the side that's not quite as clean as the front."

Bart whistled. "That's a lot of wood we'll need to shave off."

"It's not a day project for sure. If we can get the top flat, we can use coals to burn down into it. Being able to cross the Bell and maybe even go up or down it for trade will be worth it."

"Can we get some more enchantments like what you have on your axe? Might speed it up," Frank suggested.

Dar winced. "Neko did the enchantment with Sasha's help; we won't be able to make another till she's back on her feet."

"Sorry." The old woodcutter ducked his head. "I didn't know."

"It's fine." Dar waved it off. "She'll pull through and we can get some made. Can we use the mining picks at least for the rough stuff?"

"We could. You risk splitting the wood if you do it that way, but we can use the bills to pulp and scrape out the rough shape. But any of the final inches, we should do more carefully."

"Get the top flat so we can start with the coals; it'll take time, but a lot less effort. Let's focus on that first while we have a thicker exterior. We can trim up the side when we are done with that."

Both men nodded, redirecting the workers to clearing away the top of the log.

The central hearth was bustling now. Everybody had finished up their tasks for the day and were coming back for dinner. But the log still drew a lot of excitement, different folks jumping in to help and taking over for those who had been going at it for a while. Dar smiled, once again enjoying the community that they'd built, something he hadn't really felt before.

After grabbing his dinner in a newly formed clay bowl, Dar once again joined the leaders for an update. Samantha, Rex, Glump, and Cherry were already there chatting.

"Evening, folks. How's the village today?"

Cherry looked a little worn down, but she gave a small smile. "Good. We managed to get two harvests planted today. We've run out of containers to store food though. I'm not sure if that's a good thing or a bad thing."

"That's great news. It means we've made really good progress thanks to all your work, Cherry." Dar leaned over, giving her a kiss

on the shoulder and enjoying the small, delighted blush that spread across her face.

"Let's see if we can't get a solid count of what we have and make sure we're using it up now," he continued. "We can replace it with what we make in the next few weeks. As for containers, I can make some stone boxes or barrels in one of the caves."

"We still need meat," Russ said, sitting down and examining his food.

"Yes. The good news is we have the fish as a meat source that we can get during the winter, thanks to Mika. And with the boat, I'm hopeful we can get you across the river to that bison herd. That might be in..." Dar paused as Bart joined them and shifted what he was going to say into a question. "A week for the boat, Bart?"

"A week?" Bart snorted. "I'd have said it would be a whole winter project, but the way everyone is working it, I'm not sure."

"Then we'll just have to keep an eye on it and adjust. Until then, we have a plan to speed up winter housing and maybe lumber reduction." Dar went into detail about how he and Bart were going to start setting foundations.

"Housing would make many of us feel more comfortable," Rex agreed, "However, it seems like you are ignoring the issue of the ettercaps."

Dar winced. "It's still on my mind; I just don't have an answer to that yet. We don't have the firepower to take them on, and we can't move the village. So for now, I don't have an answer beyond keeping on alert and hoping they don't leave the woods. But I'll keep trying to figure out a better plan."

"I don't know how long we can sustain a high alert and double shifts. The men will start to lose their vigilance," Rex muttered.

Leaning back, Dar looked up into the stars for an answer, but they didn't have one. "We almost died out there today. If we had a full team of woodcutters out there with us, I'm not even sure we would have been able to get them all out alive. How do we fight that?"

"Maybe we could ask the capital for help?" Samantha spoke up. "This is a large enough issue that they should send an army to deal with it."

Dar nodded. But he wasn't sure a human army could do all that much. It would take something much more powerful. Dar looked over to their older member for ideas. "Glump, could we petition The White to act?"

"She would be unlikely to even hear your petition. However, there are many other powerful ancients that reside on her mountain. We could seek their help, but we would have to wait for spring for such a journey. Trying to climb Frost's Fang in the winter is suicide."

"Based on what we heard from the riverboat, Bellhaven already requested aid from Kindrake with their devil problem. If we see the aid, maybe we can ask them for assistance with the ettercap infestation as well." Dar still didn't like relying on that as the answer. For now, they were safe, but he knew it may only last until the ettercaps grew bolder, or hungrier.

"We may be able to slowly chip away at them, but I don't want to risk causing enough trouble that we become a force the ettercaps feel they need to remove. As a first step, I think we should scout the area we fought in today and see if there's anything new we can learn." Dar tried to pitch it as a learning expedition, but he really wanted to gather the corpses he had to leave behind.

"Do we have anyone who used to be a soldier in the village? I'd feel better if we had more villagers with a basic understanding of how to organize and fight."

"My husband was a soldier. He might be too old to fight now—and don't you dare tell him I said that—but he knows how to train men and mold soldiers," Samantha offered.

"That would be perfect." Dar looked to Rex. "I'll let you organize how, but I'd like the guard to start training for now. I think it would also be a great activity for the winter."

Dar's comment sparked a heated debate among the group about fighting and training. It seemed that it was a contentious topic, with

many different views on the best way to train and the best styles of fighting.

Samantha cleared her throat, clearly tired of the bickering. "I can report that everything in the village is going well. The children and the parents are excited about this boat and eager to learn and work on it. The families see it as a sign of hope."

"Good. That's part of what it is. Let's just make sure we don't push people too hard on it. Finishing the boat is going to be a marathon, not a sprint."

Several of them tilted their heads.

"What's a 'marathon'?" Glump asked.

"A race where you run twenty-six miles." Dar realized it likely wasn't something that would exist in Granterra.

Rex looked at him blankly. "Are they training to be runners between cities? Even then, they should learn to ride. Far easier."

The avian demon's blunt assessment brought a slight smile to Dar's face. A marathon did seem pretty silly in a world where survival was still uncertain.

"I... never mind. We need to keep people excited about the boat. Don't push too hard too fast, or we'll tire them out. It's a long job."

Everyone nodded, and Dar clapped his hands to punctuate the end of the meeting. Rising, he and Cherry went to go sit with the rest of their family and enjoy the evening.

CHAPTER 16

B lair was grinning ear to ear as Dar sat down. "Hunk, you really didn't tell Mika yet?"

The spirit in question rolled her eyes. "He said he would at dinner; can you stop pushing him so much?" But Mika did turn to him with her most charming smile immediately afterwards saying, "But I'd love to know."

"Hah, I thought it would be a surprise for everybody, but it makes sense Blair figured it out from what she saw earlier. So, I've formed my first greater dao," Dar laid out without preamble.

"What!" Mika jumped to her feet, knocking over her bowl and giving him a big hug. "That's huge! But you don't seem all that excited?"

He was, but maybe it was just everything that had happened today that made it seem smaller.

"I am. I'm just not sure I want to nearly die to be able to reach the next one. I wish it had been something a bit more sustainable or practiced."

Sasha got up and came over, sitting in his lap. As she snuggled deeply into him, Dar realized he'd neglected her a bit after his near-death, leaving her to tend to Neko. He pulled her into him, rubbing her back as he described the day and the battle to the others.

"The pussy cat is going to be alright?" Blair's first concern was for her new friend.

Dar waited, seeing if Sasha would explain.

She sat back from him a little, looking over to Blair. "She's working through the venom. It's rough on her, but I don't think she's in danger."

"Poor pussy cat. I'll go check on her after dinner."

"We're not sure what we're going to do about the full ettercap problem, but we'll go do some more scouting tomorrow in the forest. See if we can learn any more." As Dar said it, he felt Sasha tense under him.

She sat up, a glare on her face as she positioned herself straight in front of him. "Darius Yigg. You will not."

Dar tucked a loose hair behind her ear and rubbed her arm, wishing he didn't have to make her mad.

"It could help in ways we don't even know, Sasha. All the remains of those spiders..." He trailed off, knowing that Sasha and Cherry would realize what he meant. "I'll go in with the intent not to fight unless forced to."

Sasha turned away, but she didn't manage to hide the tear leaking out. "Fuck you. I'm going with you again. I can't let you go alone. Not after today."

Dar held her more tightly against him. "I know. It scared me today too."

She hit him in the chest, but there was no force behind it. The movement was followed by sobs as she cried into his chest, and it was like a small crack that broke Dar's heart.

"It's alright," Dar tried to soothe her, not quite sure what to do.

The rest of the girls were looking at Sasha with a mix of their own emotions. He could see questions lingering in Mika and Blair's eyes, but they didn't ask why he needed the bodies.

Cherry, by far, was the strangest reaction. He expected her to be angry, but instead she looked thoughtful. After a moment, she spoke.

"I'm going too but for a different reason. I'd like to retrieve that stump and keep it close to the village."

"You were a natural disaster with that stump," Dar encouraged. "I'd love to have it close by should there be more trouble."

"My thoughts exactly. Even if the ettercaps leave us alone, something else will eventually cause trouble."

"Perfect. Cherry and Sasha will come with me tomorrow, and we'll do a quick in and out of the forest."

Mika looked like she wanted to jump forward, but Blair held her back. "You better come back in one piece, hunk. I'm not dealing with a heartbroken Mika."

"Blair!" Mika scowled at her friend.

"What? I'm just telling it how it is. Can't you see the big hunk is just about as straightforward as you can get?"

Dar cleared his throat. He didn't like being discussed, like he wasn't even there. "Well, I'm glad you've figured that out, Blair. How's your salt gathering going?"

"Slow. I'll need a new spot tomorrow. I've pulled up as much as I can there. But you have quite a bit of salt now. It would be enough to live on for a few years if we were still in the city."

"Why weren't you rich if you could pull all this out of the ground, or even the ocean, when you were in Bellhaven?" Salt was almost as valuable as gold.

Blair rolled her eyes. "Some of the merchants called it demon salt or monster salt. They wanted verification of where it all came from. Nobles enforced it, making my salt worth far less than what humans brought out. It was the same stuff! And I'm fairly certain they sold it all the same in the end." Her statement ended in a grumble.

"So, they ripped you off," Dar grunted in agreement.

"Yeah, although it still was lucrative enough. I worked a couple days a moon and lived comfortably. They just never wanted to buy any more than that from me, so I was somewhat limited in my means."

"So what did you do with your time?" Dar asked.

"Oh, you know, lots of time to drink and be merry." She winked.

On second thought, maybe she wasn't working her dao path. "Do you have any other greater dao?"

"Maybe, maybe not. That's not something I'd share until after we get to know each other better," she said demurely as she leaned forward, pretending to tie her shoe, which had no laces that needed tied. Her chest spilling out of the top in the process. She looked up, giving him a beaming smile.

Dar looked away, not wanting to encourage her. But his attention shifted back as a root appeared over Blair's shoulder and smacked her on the top of the head.

"Cut it out." Cherry wasn't amused. "You are making him uncomfortable. He's not used to women being so forward. You need to wait for him to reciprocate some."

"Ouch. Maybe if I throw him off his game, I can sneak in under his guard." Blair's purple eyes looked like they were starting to water.

"Cherry, maybe that was a bit harsh."

"If you give him one crocodile tear, I swear I'll beat you black and blue." Cherry narrowed her eyes at Blair, daring her.

Dar wasn't entirely sure what was going on, but Sasha pulled his arm for his attention. "Let them sort it out. Please, Dar."

"What's she doing wrong?"

"Cherry and I set the pace, not her. While I admire her pursuit, she needs to respect Cherry if she's to work out long term."

"I—okay." Dar wasn't about to get in the middle of that. He respected that Sasha and Cherry needed to feel some control over the women brought into their lives. "Just don't take it so far that I need to intervene. She's mostly harmless."

"Nothing like that, just some simple establishing of the pecking order." Sasha kissed him on the cheek. "Thank you, love. This will go a long way to a stable family."

Dar looked at the two women squaring off and decided that he was best to just remove himself from the situation. "Mika, why don't we go for a walk?"

Blair looked away from Cherry. "Where are you going?"

"Away from you two. Settle it before I get back. I don't want this in our family dinner again."

The salt spirit looked from me to Cherry several times before wilting and bowing her head to Cherry. "Okay."

Sasha gave him a pat on the rear. "Good luck. I'm going to go check on Neko."

Dar paused, considering if he should join.

"You can go with her if you want; I know you are worried about Neko," Mika offered, noticing his hesitation.

Giving Mika a reassuring smile, he started moving, grabbing her hand and pulling her along. "No, she's in great hands. I'll go check on her a little later."

"I'm glad you are okay though." Mika hesitated before continuing. "Do you want me there tomorrow?"

There really wasn't a great answer for that one. "You might have caught a few things I didn't exactly make clear. I have a secret that both of them know, and I'm not comfortable sharing it just yet."

Mika waved her hands in front of her. "No, no. It's totally fine. I just wasn't sure if you—" She snapped her mouth closed. "Sorry, rambling. I seem to be doing that a lot around you lately."

Dar bumped her with his hip. "It's cute. I would have never guessed you were like this when you were a stone-cold badass back in Bellhaven."

She blushed and covered her face. "I'm not normally like this."

"Well then, what do we need to do to get you over it?"

"Talk?" She said it more like a question than an answer.

"Well, I had an idea I wanted to run past you. I'm not sure if you've done much enchanting in the past?" Dar started off.

Mika shrugged. "I've done a few simple ones, but waves aren't exactly in high demand. Though... Henry used to make me do a few simple ones." She cringed, remembering her previous master who abused her.

Dar tried to quickly move on, not wanting to make her relive it. "I had an idea. Maybe we could work your wave dao into something

on the back of the boat, like this." Dar picked up a stick and started drawing in the dirt.

The more Dar talked about her dao and asked questions, the more Mika opened up to him. If there was one thing a spirit could talk all day about, it was their dao. Mika lit up as she talked about waves.

***

Dar had fallen asleep and found himself standing in his inner world.

"Wow. It's so much bigger." Cherry spun around before him. "You at least tripled the size."

"More like five times," Dar said, astounded at the difference in the amount of land around him. The dark stone walls that once made the border of his inner world now stretched far away.

Dar wondered what he was going to do with all this space. What happened if it kept expanding? Would he practically have another world inside of him? He'd need to figure out something to do with it. Maybe bring in more trees and animals? What would he do with them?

Dar paused, not for the first time wishing there was somebody who had gone through what he was before, somebody who could at least give him some guidance as he figured it all out.

Walking towards the lake, he saw the plants on the edge were all doing well. If he could get fish in here, he might have fish to eat one day. Moving over to where Cherry was checking out the little dao tree and her connection to him, he checked in with what she was sensing.

"It is all okay?"

"Yes, no change, despite everything else in here changing."

Dar looked towards the dark stone keep, his eyes lighting up as he instantly started moving towards it. "That's right!" He'd managed to break open the iron gate and could finally see what was on the other side!

"What is it?" Cherry said, hurrying to keep up with him as she hurried over to the keep.

Sure enough, the iron gate was smashed in, like a giant troll had decided to break through.

"What happened? How'd that get smashed?" Cherry's eyes were wide.

"I did it. At least, I think I did. When I expanded my inner world, I also thought to smash that gate. Looks like I didn't just imagine it." He grinned, so eager to explore.

Dar didn't break his stride as he stepped over the remains of the gate and into the keep's yard. Passing by some of the vegetation near the gate, Dar finally was able to see more of what was within. The closest thing that stood out to him was a raised platform with a rack of practice weapons.

"A training area?" he asked.

Cherry shrugged. "That seems like the obvious answer, but this is inside of you. You tell me what it is."

Dar walked the edge of what seemed to be a training yard, looking over the gear. Almost every weapon he could think of sat on the neat racks, and all of them were made with a dark black metal that didn't reflect any light. The weapon racks were spaced by dummies, wearing various armor types.

There was even another dummy wearing the armor with the same twilight black metal in the form of a full set of plate armor.

"Dar..." Cherry was staring at that black set of armor, a faraway look in her eye. "That's the Black Knight's armor."

Dar looked at it with a new sense of respect. "Then these weapons? They are all his? Mine?"

"He used a huge sword..." She spun around, looking at all the racks before going to one and pointing it out. "This one, I'm pretty sure. But it has been a while."

The sword she pointed to was massive, like a sword an anime character would use to crush boulders. Dar stepped over to it and lifted it off the rack, or at least, he tried to. Instead, he simply knocked

it off the rack, and it crashed to the ground with a deep thud, the blade burying into the soil.

"That's heavier than I expected," Dar muttered, a touch embarrassed.

Dar drew upon his enhanced body, working to increase his strength. Feeling his mana pumping, Dar lifted the sword out of the floor, but his shoulders were already aching just picking it up. The sword had to be several thousand pounds.

"I used to swing this around?" Dar asked skeptically.

"And walk around with it over your shoulder." Cherry offered oh so helpfully.

"Maybe another time. Let's try something lighter." Dar hefted the sword back on the rack and looked through the weapons. The one that spoke to him the most was his axe. It didn't quite have the skill that a longsword might have, but it suited his strength, which was overwhelming brute force.

Mentally shrugging, Dar knew enough to admit that he wasn't a trained sword fighter, and brute force had served him well so far.

Dar found something similar to his axe on the racks. It was about as long as his arm from the base to the business end of the axe. It had a large blade with a wicked-looking curve. The curve, along with the pitch-black coloring, gave it evil vibes to Dar.

It was still heavy, but it was far more manageable than the oversized sword.

"You will need to learn how to swing a sword," Cherry teased.

"What's with how dark these are?" Dar tried to inspect the blade, but it was so dark it seemed to absorb all light. He couldn't make out any of the details on the blade.

"They were enchanted by Lilith. There are hundreds, maybe thousands of enchantments, including a dozen to obscure and hide the enchantments themselves so that someone would have to know all of them to even see the enchantments on them."

Dar let out an appreciative whistle. "That's intense. Do you know what they are made of?"

"Not a clue, but it doesn't matter at this point. It might as well be an entirely new material with how many enchantments are on it."

Holding it, Dar tried to will the enchantments to shift or change, but nothing happened. "They are all permanently active enchantments."

"Yup. The armor is the same way."

"I'd be a walking fortress," he said, amazed.

"A walking fortress with a person inside. But you aren't invulnerable with the armor on, nor are the weapons going to magically cut everything in half," Cherry said with narrowed eyes.

Dar scratched the back of his head. "Caught me. So, you don't think this can let me go waltz through the ettercap army?"

Cherry gave him a scolding look. "You'd still get tied down in webs like last time. And you're toast once they strip the armor off you. Don't be stupid."

Sighing, Dar took the axe and walked around the training yard.

Nearby, there was a door that seemed to lead into the furthest edges of the keep. Approaching it, Dar tested the handle, not surprised to find that it was locked. After all the work he had gone through to get through the gate, he should have known the keep wouldn't be wide open. He turned, walking back to Cherry.

"Well, this was a pretty big boon. I have a full armory and different types of armor. Guess I can't expect this to solve all my problems."

"Yeah, just perhaps the strongest armor in the world." Cherry rolled her eyes. "I hope you weren't holding out for a weapon that you just pointed at people and instantly killed them."

"A gun?"

"Wait, that was a thing in your old world?"

Dar explained what a gun was to her as they walked back out of the armory.

"For a world without mana, that is a pretty powerful enchantment. Everyone in your world uses these?" Cherry asked with disbelief.

"No, but everyone could." They exited the keep, and Dar once again appreciated how large his inner world had become. "Cherry,

what do you think about trying to expand the pond and bringing some fish in here. Maybe form a big orchard too?"

"Sounds like it would be a place to live, but I hope you don't expect to keep me here."

Dar waved his hands. "No, that wasn't the idea. I was thinking more of a getaway or an emergency shelter. We've brought in plants and fish. Maybe we could bring in other people if something were to go wrong?"

Cherry's face softened. "You are still worried about the ettercaps."

"Who wouldn't be? Thousands, Cherry. It's hard to imagine just how many that is and the death toll we'd have if they did decide to attack."

"They are staying to the forest for now," Cherry tried to reassure him, but they both knew it may only be a matter of time. They had no idea how long the forest would hold them.

CHAPTER 17

"Did you see Russ this morning?" Cherry chuckled as she, Dar, and Sasha walked away from the village just a little after dawn, headed for the forest.

"Yeah, I think he woke up most of the village as he went to town, trying to carve it out. We might have to ask him to chill out." Dar shook his head.

The gnoll had started on the log far before the sun rose, seeming to not hear any of the groans that were sent his way as a result. Dar had a feeling Russ intended for it to be a regular occurrence, and the village may not completely tolerate it more than the one morning.

Sasha shrugged with a smirk. "I didn't mind it. Gave us some quality morning time."

"You're insatiable." He shot back.

"Says the man who never seems to get flaccid," Cherry chimed in, teaming up with Sasha. He knew better than to take them both on, holding up his hands.

"Got me. But can you blame me surrounded by such lovely ladies?" He slapped Sasha's rear. "Besides, you love it."

"We both do. And we know that you're going to add more here soon; can't blame us for taking all we can get for now."

Dar gave her a kiss on the cheek before holding his fingers to his lips as they approached the forest. "Quiet from here on out."

Both girls nodded, and they crept through the forest.

Déjà vu struck Dar as he walked through the forest, once again keeping an eye and ear out for the spider. It was even creepier this time, after being nearly ambushed the previous time. Part of Dar wished Neko could have joined them, but she was still recovering.

The unnatural quiet and spiderwebs covering branches and trees made the place feel more like a haunted house than a whimsical forest. The calm felt unnatural; Dar found himself bracing for something to jump out from behind every tree or bush.

As they moved towards the main battle area, they first came across the corpses of spiders. Dar was pleased to see that the spiders hadn't eaten each other.

They followed the intense trail that had been created from their flight, and Dar pulled the corpses into his inner world one by one as they walked. Every few steps they'd have to stop for another.

"That's a lot. If those spiders have a trace of dao..." Cherry let her thoughts trail off.

Dar found himself smiling despite the creepy surroundings. He was hopeful Cherry was right. It would mean his little dao tree would soon produce more fruit, likely more than he or they needed.

"I know. We'll cross that bridge when we come to it."

When they got to the site of the big fight, Dar knew without a doubt that they'd get plenty of dao fruits, even if the spiders didn't have a touch of dao. Though, his little dao tree would have to get used to partial bodies.

The whole site was a mess of spider-Armageddon.

Cherry pulled roots from surrounding trees up and started to pick through the mess, placing bodies before him so all he had to do was focus and draw them into his inner world, one by one.

"That's still very odd looking," Sasha said over her shoulder as she continued to scan the surroundings.

"You should see inside," Cherry commented, keeping the conversation a hush, but it still sounded deafening to Dar amid the silent forest.

Sasha was quiet for a moment. "You wouldn't mind? Either of you? Feels a bit like it's your private space."

"No, you're always welcome." Dar felt stupid for not thinking about it earlier. "I have been talking to Cherry about making it a potential safe haven for others should something happen to the village. Can't hurt to have an escape plan."

"Then, yes, I'd like to see this inner world of yours." Sasha peeked at him over her shoulder.

Cherry let out a small laugh. "We could use the extra help tonight, anyway; this is going to be so much work. Dar, do you think you can bring in my stump? Much easier than moving it with us."

Looking at the massive stump that was still covering a large amount of the corpses. Dar tried to gauge how heavy it would be. "I don't think so. Remember when we tried that boulder? Too heavy."

"Right. Then we'll just do this the hard way." Cherry continued at her task, and the three of them fell into a companionable silence as they found their rhythm.

Sasha started pacing away from them, keeping her eyes in the canopy. So far, there hadn't been any trouble. "Are you almost done?"

"Not much more," Cherry said, before looking over to the massive stump. "But I'm going to have to make some noise when I bring that out."

"If you have to focus as much as last time, do you want me to carry you?" Dar paused in his task to try to read her reaction.

"And leave me as the only one ready to fight?" Sasha teased. "I see how it is."

"Hush. I can fight while carrying Cherry." Dar took the last corpse into his inner world and looked at Cherry.

"We're done." Cherry smiled at him.

Dar stretched his back and realized the sun was about halfway up to the middle of the day. They'd spent a solid three hours harvesting the bodies, but the walk back wouldn't be long.

"Then let me scoop you up and get out of here." Dar lifted Cherry into a princess carry, and she closed her eyes in concentration.

The giant stump came to life, rising off the ground. Its roots thundered as it followed them like a massive puppy.

"Well, at least we don't have to worry about being quiet anymore." Sasha breathed a sigh of relief. "That thing is really terrifying."

Dar thought so too, but he didn't like how it took all of Cherry's concentration to move it, leaving her vulnerable like she was at that moment.

With each step of the stump, the spider webs in the trees quivered. It was almost like they were sending out some sort of signal, and a bad feeling started crawling across Dar's skin.

Dar barely recognized what he was sensing before a massive spider sprang out of a funnel web. Dar moved backward quickly, shielding Cherry. Sasha whipped around, throwing her ribbons at the spider and touching the web itself. It shrank and cocooned the spider with its own web.

"Much better. I'd been wanting to do that to one of the buggers." Sasha spit on the squirming spider and touched the web again, completely encasing it in a tight ball. "I don't think it's going to be able to get out without help, but just in case, we better move along."

"Do you want to go just rip down their fortress in the woods?" Dar chuckled while he picked up the pace.

"If only I could control that much, I would. Although, I'd also have to get close enough to it to touch it, and I doubt I could get that close by myself. It's likely heavily protected."

Dar smiled at how literally she was taking his question. "I was teasing. Now, let's keep moving and get my lovely grump back to the village."

"And away from spiders for at least a few days?" Sasha asked hopefully.

Dar had to admit he was tired of the creepy things as well. Even having them in his inner world felt grimy. "I'd like that, but I can't promise anything."

Their group made it clear of the forest just as a wave of chittering spiders reached their ears. "See? In and out. No problem." Dar nudged Sasha.

A loud chorus sounded from the village as the guard rushed out, likely seeing the big stump before they saw the group.

"Cherry, can you get that thing to stab its roots back in the ground? Might let it keep better."

She didn't respond to his comment, but the stump drove its roots in one at a time and began working itself into the soil as he'd asked. When the stump finally settled in, she opened her eyes and yawned. "I need to go sprout the fields today."

"Boss." One of the guards came up and saluted. "Is everything okay?"

"Everything is fine—sorry for the concern. This is Cherry's new toy. She plans to keep that by the village in the event we have trouble."

"To use as a weapon?" the guard asked, his eyes wide as he looked back at the stump with a sort of reverence.

Dar knew then that he'd be fine. "Yep. So don't touch it. She'll have your hide if you do."

"Yes, boss." He snapped another salute and turned around to talk with his partner.

"You are turning out to be quite the leader." Sasha grabbed onto his arm as they walked into the village.

Dar felt himself swell a little at the comment. He'd felt like he'd been doing well, but if he was honest, he'd always been the doer, not the thinker in most projects. He just knew how to get shit done.

"Thanks." Dar kissed the top of her head. "I'm going to go check on Neko."

"Tell her I said 'hi'. I need to go work on some clothes for the kids; they outgrow or destroy clothes faster than I can make them."

Dar gave her a squeeze goodbye and found the hut with Neko in it, wanting to check on her. The jaguar girl looked up drowsily, as if she had been on the verge of going back to sleep.

"Shh, I didn't mean to disturb you." He turned back.

But Neko's eyes shot up on hearing his voice. "Dar. Stay."

"New words?" Dar came back over to her side.

"New words," she confirmed. "Talking important."

"Well, I'm glad to see that you are at least learning quickly. How are you? Do you need water? A new rag?"

"Need Dar." She stared right back into his eyes. The gold of her iris captured his attention, and maybe a small piece of his heart.

He sat down where she lay and scooted her head into his lap. "There you go. Just wait, soon you'll be back on your feet. You already look miles better than yesterday."

Neko hummed and rubbed her head into his lap. "Dar best."

"Yeah? What makes me the best?" he teased.

She grabbed his hand and put it on her head, worming her way deeper into his lap. He just smiled down at her and played with her hair, occasionally stroking one of her soft ears.

Neko's human hum turned into a feline purr as she melted into his lap. "Dar. Best."

"I know, kitten, I know," Dar soothed her back to sleep. He was pleased to see that she was livelier and didn't seem to be in as much pain, but she was still so weak. The curled-up woman in his lap was so far from the strong, ferocious demon he'd fought in the woods only a few days ago.

Still, the woman could bring a smile to his face.

He stayed with her a while after she fell back asleep to see if she'd wake again, but when she didn't, Dar slipped out and went back to work. He'd laughed when she'd given a half-asleep growl as he shifted her off his lap, but she didn't wake.

Ready to take on his next task, Dar headed back to the large cave, passing the men working with a smile. "Afternoon, gents."

"We heard you went back into the woods today. Any trouble?" a nearby worker asked, the others pausing in their tasks to listen in.

"The ettercaps seem to have retreated back deep into the woods. All we encountered was a spider. And Cherry brought back the massive

stump she used to take them down before. She'll have it at the ready to use as a weapon to defend the village if needed."

There were more than a few sighs of relief, but one man spoke up. "That means you are getting ready to fight?" He paused and looked ashamed. "Sorry, lord. It isn't my place to ask those sorts of questions."

Dar waved it off. Some formality helped with his authority, but he didn't mind setting their minds at ease. "I don't mind one bit. Hearthway's safety is everyone's concern. Right now, trying to take them head on is suicide, but we are trying to improve our position, regardless. We don't know if they'll change tactics and come at us."

"With all these demons, we can take them! Charge right in and kill them all." One man pumped his pick like he was ready to join the fight.

"Like I said, it's too dangerous for us to take them head on. Just because our focus is on improving the village for winter right now doesn't mean we're cowards. It means that, unlike the devils, we can use our heads in this fight."

The man who had spoken up to go fight looked away as his two friends elbowed him.

Dar waited a moment to let that sink in before adding some more encouraging words, not wanting to discourage the man's spirit. "But who knows? If they come out of the woods, we won't have an option. If that happens, we'll need each and every one of you to pick up a weapon."

"Thank you, lord. I just wish we could do something now," the first spoke.

"Waiting is sometimes the hardest part. But trust me, it's our best option. I've fought them three times now; there are just too many of them. But we will work towards being more battle-ready. You'll see some changes I'm making to prepare for when we can take the fight to them."

The men nodded eagerly. Dar could see they were ready to fight for Hearthway, eager even. He just hoped that, when the time came, they'd be smart about it.

"Anyway, back to work! I can't dally too long."

"Of course." They smiled and went back to chipping away at a section of limestone and shoveling the broken stone into a wheelbarrow.

Picking his way to the back of the cave, Dar approached the area where he had been collecting stone previously, but the area was blocked off by Blair. She seemed to have shifted her meditation area right to that spot, her bright amethyst eyes popping open as he approached.

"Fancy meeting you here. This was the best spot I could find for drawing more salt out of the stone." A grin split her pink lips, and Dar had no doubt there was some strategy behind her spot choice as well.

Rolling his eyes, he stepped around her.

"Hey."

"Look, I get it. I've welcomed you into our meals, but you need to pump the brakes." Dar was going to let Cherry handle her.

She tilted her head. "Pump the brakes?"

"Pull back on the reins and slow your cart down," Dar tried again. "I have houses to start and a village to organize. Don't get me wrong, you're hot. And I have no doubt you have amazing things to offer, but right now isn't going to be the time. What you do from here is up to you, but all I can offer is continuing to join our dinners and getting to know each other." As her eyes sparkled, he added, "Platonically for now. We'll see where it goes."

Blair opened her mouth, then closed it several times. "You're a tough nut to crack, hunk."

"What do you mean?" Her tone had turned more serious than usual.

"I can't figure out what you want. You seem wholesome, down to earth, but you certainly enjoy your women. From the noises coming

out of your hut at night, you enjoy them wildly. But you don't seem to want me?"

Dar crouched down, so he was eye level with her. "I happen to think physical love is so much sweeter when there's an emotional connection for it to grow off of."

Blair let out a heavy sigh. "Fine. But a little physical won't hurt ya, you know."

Dar chuckled. "Like you said, you've heard evidence that I enjoy the physical as well. And I know Sasha and Cherry want our family to grow. But I'm not going to put this village at risk because I'm getting too distracted. So, for now, we just get to know each other more. Understand?"

Blair sighed, nodding.

"Good. Now, is this really the best spot for you to find salt?"

"Actually, it is really good. You sort of churned the stone around here and loosened things up for me to work," she answered, and he didn't see a lick of dishonesty in her eyes.

"Okay, then I'm going to carve a path around you so I don't disturb you."

She nodded, biting her bottom lip as she studied him.

Turning to focus on the rock, Dar started to pull granite from the surrounding rock and make more stone carts that he could haul out. Deciding to focus on the tasks a bit more, he kept producing cart after cart.

Once he had a number of them, he began wheeling them out one at a time, scattering them around the village into spaces where he'd turn them into foundations later.

Back and forth he went into the mines, hauling out enough for three foundations before Bart stopped him.

"What can I help with?" Dar asked.

Bart looked at his work and whistled. "Maybe we should just leave the foundation work to you. We are only making enough cement for one a day, and we still have to dig out the ground."

"Yeah, I'm starting to get a bit wiped, too. It's still quite a bit of work using the granite to push out the soil." Dar looked at the carts he'd brought out, knowing that each of them would take a toll on his mana reserves for him to push into the ground.

He looked around. It might make sense to try to see if there were parts of the process others could help with to limit the reserves he had to use up.

"Maybe we could use Glump to help move out the soil for the foundations," Dar thought aloud.

Bart nodded, scratching that into a piece of wood. "Great idea, I'll remind you to tell him at dinner."

"Anyway, what did you need?" Dar focused back on Bart.

"Molds. I was hoping you could make some stone molds, so we could start making and laying out roof tiles before it gets too cold."

"I can do that, no problem." Dar reached for one of the nearby carts and pulled off a chunk of granite, starting to mold it in front of Bart. "Like this?"

"Damn, that's still impressive no matter how many times I see it." Bart shook his head.

Dar smiled to himself, hopeful that he may one day be able to help Bart accomplish it himself. Bart was near the top of Dar's list for getting any extra fruits.

"How many do you need?" Dar asked.

"Three should do the trick."

Dar quickly made the other two and looked back at the first few foundations he'd made. "Bart, if we have some lumber, you should bring it over to one of the houses I already started. If I sank a strong piece into the four corners, do you think your men could use that to build up the rest?"

Bart looked at the foundations for a second, eyeing them up. "I think we could work with that. If you sink them into the granite as deep as I'm thinking, then they should be rock solid."

"Great. Can we get your men working on that?"

"Still tight on lumber," Bart reminded him.

Dar nodded. He'd already considered that. "For now, we stop the palisade construction. Maybe even strip it if we need to. I'm not entirely sure it would do us much good in the event we have trouble with the ettercaps anyway. Climbing is their specialty."

Bart stroked his chin. "I see your point, although I still like the idea of a wall. Can we talk about this when we meet at dinner with the others? Even if the palisade isn't much help with them, it would make people feel a whole lot more comfortable."

"So would a home, Bart," Dar countered. Dar understood the concern, but houses still seemed more important. And he could always shift the material for the walls to granite now that he had his new greater dao. His only barrier was his limitations with mana.

CHAPTER 18

Dar worked at the granite foundations all afternoon, only pausing to meditate to restore his mana. He'd sat with Blair a few times, working with her to meditate together. She had been able to pass on some of the techniques she used to get even closer to her dao. He'd also found that being closer to his dao had made meditating and restoring his mana easier.

But what had really surprised him was Blair. Focused on helping him with his technique, she'd put aside some of the constant come-ons, and he'd seen a clearer picture of who she was under all the flirting.

There'd been a few moments when he couldn't help the smile on his face as she'd eagerly talked about her meditation practice, often babbling on about some breathing technique or visualization. He finally felt like they were connecting on a more real level. Maybe the talk had helped.

As the sun started to set, they called it a day, moving to join the community in the center of the village. Neko was well enough that she left the hut and joined them, although she was still weak.

"I got her." Dar scooped Neko up and plopped her on his lap. "Marcie, can you get another bowl of food?"

The quiet maid nodded and hurried to move.

Taking his own bowl, he spooned out a portion and held it up for Neko. "Say, Ah."

"Ah." Neko opened her mouth wide and rested against Dar.

"You spoiled brat." Mika shook her head. "You know she's milking this?"

Neko blew her tongue at Mika before her ears flattened to her head, and she looked back up at Dar innocently. "Neko good. But Neko tired."

The whole circle laughed at her antics.

"What do you say, Sasha? Is she good enough to eat on her own?" Dar asked.

"She still needs the help. But be good, Neko, don't antagonize Mika." Sasha wagged her finger at Neko.

She went quiet and cuddled into Dar. "Neko be good," she said before opening her mouth again, asking for food.

Dar didn't mind helping her eat. In fact, he enjoyed taking care of her like he would any of his girls, but in this moment, she truly needed it and doing so only brought a warmth to his chest.

They finished up dinner and moved onto the leaders' meeting.

After meeting with the other leaders and not hearing anything out of the ordinary, Dar worked to cut the evening short, anxious to get back to their hut. Sasha and Cherry were right on his heels.

As they stepped inside, Dar pulled Sasha to him to give her a kiss, but all he got was a quick peck. Surprised she wasn't moving to rip his clothes off like usual, he was met with a serious face.

"Inner world first!" Her excitement shone in her eyes, and Dar just laughed.

Nodding, he stepped back.

"Now, when you feel it tug you, try to go with it. Don't resist at all or it'll hurt him," Cherry explained.

Sasha leaned back, wariness entering her face. "Maybe I shouldn't? What if I do it wrong? I don't want to hurt you, Dar."

Dar sighed, pulling her into his lap on the bed. "It'll be alright. Deep breath."

She breathed in deep, and he tugged, working to bring her into his inner world. He'd only really done it with Cherry, but it felt about the same as Sasha sank into his navel.

"I'll go make sure she's alright." Cherry dove in herself, a natural now at going into his inner world.

As silence surrounded him, Dar realized it was one of the first times since they'd come to Hearthway that he was alone in his hut for the night. It felt unnatural now that he'd gotten used to it.

Climbing into bed, he tried to fall asleep, but he'd gotten so used to having somebody else in bed with him, he just couldn't seem to nod off. Rolling out of his hut, Dar went to see if Mika might be willing to come join him. As he was walking around looking for Mika, he ran into Marcie. He paused before beckoning her over.

"Milord, do you need something? I was about to turn in."

Dar was afraid to push her too fast with this request, but it might also be a good, easy first step for her. He hoped that by now Amber had at least put some thoughts into Marcie's head. "This is embarrassing, but Sasha and Cherry aren't in my hut tonight, and I'm having trouble falling asleep on my own."

"Oh. OH." Her eyes went wide.

Dar waved his hands, trying to stop her mind from going out of control. "Nothing like what you are thinking."

She suddenly deflated.

He ran his hands through his hair, annoyed he was messing it up at every turn. "Marcie, you are lovely. But I'm not sure what you want or are comfortable with, and I certainly don't want to push you or have you feel like I'm using my position to pressure you. So, if you'd like to sleep, just sleep, in my hut tonight—it would be helpful. But it's not required. Do you understand?"

Marcie looked up at him and swallowed. "Yes, milord." She paused, looking back and forth between him and the nearby hut before meeting his eyes and nodding. "I'd like to join you."

Dar held out his hand, and she tentatively took it, seeming to relax as they started walking.

As they entered the hut, Marcie stared at the pile of blankets before looking up at him. "Do you want my clothes off?"

"However you sleep best. I'll be taking mine off. I find them uncomfortable in the sheets."

"Yes, milord." Marcie slipped off her dress. She was about as buxom as they came, which had been hard to hide. But, when she took off the dress, Dar realized she'd even wrapped her chest tightly to keep them down.

"You have a lovely body, Marcie," Dar said, trying to keep his tone comfortable and relaxed. Shifting over to the bed, he laid down and held the covers out for her.

Marcie blushed, laying down in front of him. "Your body is quite the sight too, milord." Her voice was tentative, but there was a bit of excitement behind it. She shifted in the sheets, burrowing in a bit.

They stayed like that for a few moments before Marcie shifted herself backward, gently pressing her butt against his groin. She didn't move, but he felt her body go from tense to relaxed as she grew more comfortable with the position.

He put a hand on the side of her hip, otherwise holding his body as still as he could, although he wasn't sure how long he could keep his member from responding to the softness of her body.

Dar closed his eyes, working to start to shift himself back to sleep, but soon he felt Marcie's hand on his, guiding it up to wrap around her, pushing her breasts into his palm.

Dar didn't say anything, but he squeezed and teased her breasts gently.

"Milord, if you keep that up, you won't sleep." The shyness in her voice had softened, and a slight gravel had been added.

Dar smiled, pleased at the small step they'd taken. Grunting, he pulled her closer, already feeling the warmth of her body helping lull him to sleep.

***

Dar found himself back in his inner world. Sasha was walking around with Cherry, exclaiming at nearly everything.

"Dar, what took you so long?" Cherry asked.

"Turns out I got so used to having someone with me that I had trouble sleeping, so I invited Marcie in to sleep with me."

Both of them looked at each other. "Truly?"

"Yes. I know, I know. Took me long enough. It was a little awkward, but she relaxed with me after a bit of time. I think it was good for us."

"Did you do anything else?"

Dar shook his head. "No, honestly, we went further than I'd intended. We're snuggled naked right now with my hand on her breast, which she did. So I'd say progress?"

Sasha nodded. "Good, I'm glad she's opening up. It will certainly help her reinforce her position in her mind if nothing else."

Dar shrugged. "Strange how you get used to some things so quickly. Not sure I'm going to be able to fall asleep on my own."

"We'll make sure one of the family is with you every night," Sasha answered quickly, looking worried. "It's our fault for not realizing that need sooner."

"How could you know if I didn't?" he teased, but both women seemed to feel like it was in part their fault. He wasn't sure how he'd gotten so lucky to have women who wanted to please him so much.

"Anyway," he changed the subject. "How do you like my inner world?"

"This is amazing! I wasn't quite sure what to expect. But 'world' is correct; it really feels like a small world here." Sasha stepped around the little dao tree. "So this is where the magic happens?"

There was a massive mound of the spider and ettercap bodies not far away.

"Yes. That's the tree that extracts the dao from our enemies and creates fruits."

Sasha brushed aside the leaves and looked at each fruit. "These are incomplete."

It wasn't a question, but Dar answered it all the same. "Yes, they are. But hopefully not forever. Here's the leftover from the hellhounds." Dar pointed to a dark red fruit.

Sasha's eyes became misty as she touched the fruit. "You almost died for this one. Died saving me, too."

Kissing the side of her head, he whispered, "You were worth it. Now, how about you help Cherry and I bury all of these?"

"Wait..." She narrowed her eyes playfully. "I was tricked!"

Both Dar and Cherry laughed. "Yes, dear, I tricked you. But I think this work will bear unique fruits of your labor. I'm sure you'll enjoy them."

"I can eat them too?" she asked in surprise.

Dar looked to Cherry for her opinion. Cherry shrugged. "I think we can; I think anyone can. Which only makes this secret more dangerous."

Dar knew where she was going. "I still intend to make this place somewhere people could live. I know it might take time, but this could be a haven."

"I don't doubt that, love, but I agree with Cherry. It is dangerous to let others know."

Dar nodded, but he also knew that there would come a time that the secret would be revealed. If his fruits could make their village stronger, he didn't want to hold it back. He just had to be careful in how he did it and whom he trusted.

"We'll cross that bridge when we come to it. For now, let's see how many fruits we can make." Dar took the dirty job of bringing the bodies over to the dark soil, and Sasha and Cherry took turns using the shovel to bury them under the thinnest layer of dirt.

"This is simply amazing! It is like the soil is digesting them." Sasha tipped more soil on a shriveled-up spider, watching closely and marveling at the process.

"Look at the dao tree." Dar pointed to the little tree, which had been steadily growing as they fed it.

Sasha just shook her head. "You cheat. This is so unfair! Do you realize how much work we put in to grow along our dao path?"

"I know, although I can't say I'm sorry. Even the meditation I did to pick up the soft dao felt like cheating, but I'm not going to hold back when there is as much danger as we've been in."

"Nor should you," Cherry agreed. "We need strong dao companions if we are to make the sort of change you want."

Dar threw more bodies into the soil, and they worked quickly together. Sasha made shallow wells for Dar to throw the bodies into, and Cherry sprinkled dirt over the top.

As they worked, flowers bloomed on the little dao tree, slowly building into buds and then fruits covered in dao characters.

"Let's stop here. I think we have plenty for now."

The little dao tree looked weighed down by the dozen or so fruits that had blossomed completely, but Dar partially wanted to pause because he couldn't hold back his curiosity any longer at what type of dao had been produced.

Picking one of them up, Dar bit into the fruit, the juice dribbling down his neck. He immediately picked up on the dao of quiet. It made so much sense! That's how they'd been able to sneak up on them in the forest.

"They had the dao of quiet. Almost all of them." He looked at the remaining fruits, confirming almost all were the same dao element he was holding. There were only two others of the remaining eleven that weren't quiet.

"That would make sense. My turn?" Sasha placed her hands on one of the fruits and gave him a questioning look.

Dar nodded. "That's another quiet fruit."

Sasha took the fruit and took a tentative bite before her eyes lit up. "Mmm! And here I thought things good for you were supposed to be bitter." She eagerly devoured the rest of the fruit.

"They are pretty tasty, aren't they?"

Cherry snatched one off the tree and bit into it the same as Sasha and groaned into it. "These are freaking delicious." She eyed the others.

"And worth far more than their taste," Dar reminded her.

"I know. I won't eat another." She quickly finished off her fruit and licked her fingers clean.

Sasha had also finished and was playing around with the new dao. It looked like she was screaming at him, but not a whisper made it to his ears. She breathed in deep.

"Amazing. So we have seven of those left, along with the other two mystery dao?"

Dar looked at the other two fruits, both felt like the same dao, but he wasn't sure. "Do you both want to do the honors and try the next one?"

"Mine." Cherry snatched another and devoured it quickly. "Eww."

Sasha, about to take a bite out of hers paused, holding it out at arm's length and eyeing it warily. Turning to Cherry, she waited to hear what dao it possessed.

"Sticky. I don't want to be sticky." Cherry blew out her tongue. Dar held back a laugh. He could already think of ways to use it in village construction or even traps outside the village.

"There could be uses for that." Sasha smirked. "Imagine if he couldn't escape your sex."

"Ooh." Cherry's eyes went wide with a grin.

Dar rolled his eyes. "Does it always have to be about sex?"

"Yes," they answered in unison.

Ignoring them, Dar stared at the remaining fruits. He knew they would have plenty more where these came from, considering they still had quite the number of ettercaps and spiders to toss into the soil. They had only planted about half of them so far.

"I'd like to give Neko, Amber, and Marcie fruits tomorrow. Maybe Mika and Blair too."

"That leaves two fruits."

Dar thought on it. "Bart and his wife?"

Cherry gave him a worried stare. "That's a lot of faith you are putting in them."

But Dar disagreed. "I have to trust some people, Cherry. I know you are slow to trust, but if I can't trust them, I'd go crazy."

"Then do it, but you won't be the only immortal. One day, someone is going to realize not only you, but other humans, have stepped onto the dao path. When that time comes, there will be trouble. Bringing other humans onto the dao path will only make that day come sooner."

Dar nodded. He'd already considered it, but he also didn't want to hold back out of fear. "The more good people I elevate, the more help I will have when that day comes. I hope that I can give these fruits out to those who I can trust to do the right thing with their newfound strength."

Cherry closed her mouth, clearly still not pleased. Dar knew she was more cautious than he was, and she had her reasons. She'd lived a long time and spent a lot of her life having to act like an airhead to avoid conflict from those who would consider her power a threat.

But Dar didn't want to live a life hiding who he was or holding back from helping his allies.

"While I have you two here, I'd like to discuss the other women," Dar changed topics, wanting to get their opinions, and having a feeling it would cheer Cherry up.

Cherry smiled and leaned in. "Yes, this is a much better point of conversation. Too bad you didn't see one of the other girls before Marcie. I can only imagine that we'd still be waiting for you if you had brought Blair back to the hut."

Sasha jumped in. "Not so sure on that one. But she's calmed down quite a bit today. I suspect you did something, Dar?"

He sighed and explained his conversation he had with her earlier, that he was interested in the physical, but not without an emotional connection to go with it.

"That she stayed means she'll try for that as well," Sasha explained.

"Right, but I'm not in any rush. I'm not really sure what I'm supposed to do with Mika, either. She was the first we were all interested in, but it's progressed more slowly. We probably need some more one-on-one time."

Dar watched as Sasha tried and failed to hold back an 'I told you so' look. And she was right. Cherry and Sasha had wanted him to approach Mika earlier. Now he had some work to do to make sure she knew he was interested.

"And then there's Neko, who has been worming her way quickly into your life." Cherry smiled. "And she's hot as hell, not to mention that whole mix between both wild yet innocent. If you don't pull Neko into this hut soon, I might just drag her in first."

Dar sighed. "Really? You want more people in the family that much?"

"Sure. It's a way to build bonds, and not just physical. Plus, it will entwine our dao paths, allowing you to try and meditate on their dao as well."

Dar was surprised she'd brought it up. "I thought both of you wanted me to stop doing that now?"

They shared a look, seeming to debate who would tell him. It appeared Sasha lost.

"After the other day, when you almost…" her voice cracked, and she pivoted where she was going. "It's less dangerous for you to pursue more power in the cave than go face a thousand devils without the power. We realize that. But we don't like that both choices are so dangerous."

Dar pulled Sasha close and kissed her. "I love you both, and I'll fight to be here for you every night. But I agree. If I'm to defeat the devils or even fight for Hearthway to become a place in this world, then I'm going to need to be stronger faster."

"We know." Cherry grinned and sank down onto her knees, pulling at his pants. "Which is why we should use this time to further entangle our dao paths, so you can have a fresh boost if you meditate on them soon."

There was no argument from him. He'd take time with his girls whenever he could. Tangling his hands in Cherry's green hair, he felt Sasha press her soft body up behind him. Smiling, Dar turned his head and kissed her.

Cherry had his stiff member out in the cool air, but she paused.

He pulled himself away from Sasha to her biting her lip and a question in her eyes. "Do you really like it when two of your girls enjoy each other?"

"Tremendously," Dar answered and pulled Cherry to her feet. "Would you like to try? Both of you?"

"Wouldn't be the first time with another girl," Sasha purred into his ear.

Dar swallowed loudly as Sasha came around to his front, trailing a finger across his arm only to collect Cherry in her arms and the two of them kissed. There was something about the contrast between Sasha's pink lips and Cherry's red ones tangling together that made Dar's breathing heavier.

Cherry pushed back, coming up to breathe, and gave Dar a half-lidded look. "Oh, he does like that quite a bit."

Still in each other's arms, they both gave him hungry looks.

"You are both gorgeous." He sat down to watch the two of them.

Sasha whirled Cherry around so she was behind the smaller woman, with them both facing Dar. But then Sasha's hands disappeared into Cherry's clothing, caressing the dryad's stomach and working their way up while her pink lips kissed along Cherry's neck.

Cherry looped her arms back over Sasha's neck and extended her own neck for Sasha to continue kissing. "So soft."

"Here I thought you liked hard things," Sasha teased, one hand twisting on Cherry's chest and eliciting a moan.

"Soft can be good sometimes, too. Variety is the spice of life." Cherry pulled on Sasha's head, and they kissed again.

They broke their kiss again and watched him. His throat was dry and his breathing short. Just watching those two was an experience in and of itself.

Sasha's other hand wandered down between Cherry's legs, moving in slow circles while the other kept her chest captive and occupied. "Look at him."

Cherry's eyes were looking hazy with pleasure as Sasha continued to play her like a fiddle. "I like the way he's looking at me."

"I do too. He looks so... hungry for us right now." Sasha licked her lips, but there was a second wet sound down between Cherry's legs just before the dryad let out a long, satisfied moan.

"So hungry." Sasha kept eye contact with him while her finger squished into Cherry's sex.

The dryad rolled her head back, moaning as she wiggled her hips, pushing Sasha's fingers deeper into her sex. "More."

Wet noises accelerated as Sasha's hand continued to work under Cherry's dress and the dryad's moaning pitched up into soft, breathy screams. "Fuck. I love you both. Yes."

Sasha smiled, still locked in a strange staring contest with Dar. "Think I should finish her?"

"Yes." He found himself saying without thinking and watched as the bulge under Cherry's dress vibrated, bringing the dryad to full on screams till she let out one final yell of pleasure and started to come down.

"She's soaking wet for you now, Dar." Sasha spread Cherry's legs. "Join us."

CHAPTER 19

Dar woke up pleasurably and looked down between his legs. Marcie lay between his legs, sucking him off with her eyes closed. The last thing he wanted to do was startle her, so he just propped his head up and watched.

She was clumsy, but any oral sex was a treat as far as he was concerned. It wasn't just the physical pleasure, but a smidge of his own male ego loved the dominance that came from it.

He let out a grunt as she circled the head with her tongue, causing her to look up and see that he was awake.

For a moment, she stopped and stared like a deer in headlights.

"Don't stop. I'm close and you look lovely." Dar took the moment to run his fingers through her brown hair.

"Mmfph." She talked around his cock and went back at it with a gusto, bobbing fast on his cock while her tongue dragged along the sensitive underside till he was forced to tap her head in warning for release.

But she didn't slow down for a second all the way till he blew his load as she coughed, sputtering with seed dripping down her chin.

"Sorry, milord." She struggled with the words between the cough.

"I should have warned you better. Here, use the sheet."

But before she could, Cherry and Sasha both barged out of his inner world.

Cherry took one look at Marcie and pulled her up for a kiss, licking his seed off her chin. "Delicious. Thank you for the breakfast treat, Marcie."

"Ye—eah," Marcie stumbled, looking shocked as she stared between Cherry and Sasha.

Great, Dar had some explaining to do. It wasn't exactly normal for two people to just appear around him.

Though Marcie's hesitation was probably more to do with how bold Cherry had been. Both of the girls seemed to still be wound up from their activities in his inner world. They had been eager to explore the three of them together.

"You missed some on her chest," Sasha pointed out, smiling.

Cherry wiped it up with a finger, giving Marcie's large chest a playful squeeze as she licked it off her fingers. Marcie still stood there, looking a little shell-shocked at what was happening.

"Marcie, I'm sure you have some questions about where they just came from. If you stay a minute, I will help it make more sense."

Cherry kissed him on the cheek. "See you in a few minutes, love."

Both his women ducked out of the hut, leaving him to explain everything.

"Milord, w-where did they come from?"

Dar sighed, giving Marcie the full story of how he came to Granterra and a basic understanding of his inner world. But he ended his description by pulling out the dao fruit of quiet and explaining what he was offering her. Her eyes went wide.

"So, after all I just told you, do you want to become an immortal like me?" He held the fruit out, but Marcie didn't take it.

Instead, she bowed her head, shaking it back and forth. "Milord, I cannot. This is far too precious."

"I will be able to get more, and you have served our family well. The question is if you think you will stay with our family. Being an immortal will come with risks of its own. I want you to go in with your eyes wide open. We will do best if we stick together and protect

each other and this secret for as long as we can. But you will be more powerful. You can be so much more than just our maid, Marcie."

Reaching his hand under her chin, he tilted her face up to look at him, making sure she saw the sincerity in his eyes.

Taking a deep swallow, she started to reach for the fruit, pausing for a brief moment before picking it up. "Thank you."

She took the fruit and ate it. A surprised look flashed across her face at the first bite, and she lost any hesitation. Dar tried to suppress the chuckle. The fruit was addictively sweet.

Once she devoured the fruit, she looked at Dar curiously. "I don't feel that different."

Dar stood, waiting, but nothing happened. He started wondering if he'd been wrong about how it would work. Maybe the enchantments on his body made the difference.

Deciding to try something else, he gave her his most confident smile and nodded like it was entirely expected. "Grab Amber and bring her here, and then we can do the next part together."

Marcie nodded sharply and hurried out of the hut. Dar smirked, feeling just how unnaturally quiet she'd just been. He hoped he could make it work.

Marcie returned with a confused-looking Amber.

Dar had managed to get dressed in that time and smiled at her as he sat cross-legged, pulling out a fruit. Amber snatched it out of his hand and bit into it. Letting out a delighted moan, she devoured the entire thing, not pausing for a moment.

"You didn't even know what that was for," Dar said, surprised at how quickly she'd downed it.

"Marcie said you were going to feed me a special fruit. Didn't matter. I trust you. Tasty, but doesn't feel special."

Dar had them both sit down. "Okay, I'm going to describe something that might feel odd, but trust me. Sit down and cross your legs like me."

Both of them complied, watching him closely.

"Now you both have a new dao, the dao of quiet. It isn't anything grand, but it will start you both on the path of being an immortal like me."

Still, they just nodded and listened to him. There wasn't an ounce of doubt or hesitation in them as he spoke.

"I'm going to try to help you understand it, but I haven't guided anybody through this before, so hang in there with me. Feel for the mana in the air; it is like a sixth sense, like hearing or smell. You'll be able to sense it. Tell me when you can."

He waited for a minute as they both closed their eyes. Marcie was first; he could feel the subtle pull of mana into her, and she gasped. Amber furrowed her brows. But it was only another minute later when she took a deep breath and the draw of mana started for her as well.

"Now, I need both of you to draw as much in as you can and simultaneously push as much as you can into your dao."

Both of them started using their dao of quiet, and the world around them took on an unnatural stillness. Dar meant to explain more, but now realized that they'd be unable to hear him.

Focusing on his own dao of quiet, he cut through theirs and created a small channel for his voice to reach their ears. "Now I need you to draw in all the mana you can and push out. Use all this mana, not just to fuel your dao, but to change who you are. Picture yourself forming a reservoir behind your navel for mana and form channels that crisscross your body. As you do, you may find yourself able to alter your body, make yourself stronger, faster. Feel free to strengthen yourself."

Amber's mouth moved with a question that he couldn't hear. Instead, Dar started tracing the patterns for his channels on their backs as they both closed their eyes. Supernatural silence blanketed the hut.

He could feel the mana and the touch of the complete dao upon them as they blossomed into immortals. Though he felt that, if he

tried to touch it, to use that dao for himself, that there would be disastrous consequences.

Waiting, until finally, he could feel the dao pass them all by, and Dar cut through their dao of quiet. It was difficult, but he overpowered their dao and was able to speak.

"You can open your eyes. It's done."

Marcie breathed deep. "I feel it now. It's so beautiful."

Amber cupped her breasts and looked at them for a moment before looking up at Dar with a smile. "Yes, I didn't know this is what it felt like. I feel like I could go fight a boar!"

"You might even be able to. But first, you'll need to learn how to fight. I know Samantha's husband was going to work on training some of the guards into a real regiment; you two could go by and try to practice with them. I'd suggest at least learning how to use a sword."

"Yes, milord." Amber nodded, excitement clear on her face.

Marcie bowed low. "Milord, can we now swear oaths like the ancient races?"

"Yes. In most ways, you are now an ancient. I can swear oaths, too. But please don't feel any pressure."

Ignoring the last part of his statement, Marcie started talking more firmly than he'd ever heard her speak. "I, Marcie, swear upon my dao to serve you for the rest of my life." She touched her head to the ground.

Amber jumped forward and followed Marcie's lead. "I swear upon my dao to serve you."

"Really, I don't require any of that from either of you," Dar sighed. It was too much, but he was also flattered. He just hoped that the fact that the fruits were so valuable hadn't been why they had done it; he wanted them to genuinely want to be a part of their growing family.

Amber paused. "Milord, will you be giving anyone else these fruits?"

"The number is limited for now. But your father is one of my most trusted people here. I'll give him a fruit later."

Amber's face lit up at his statement. "Thank you, milord!" Licking her lips, she eyed him up and down. "Is there any way I could serve you right now?"

Dar laughed. "Sorry, Marcie beat you to it this morning."

Amber spun around, grabbing Marcie by the shoulders and pulling her into a hug with a kiss on her cheek. "Finally! I'm so proud of you! How was it?" Amber pulled back, looking between Marcie and Dar.

Marcie only blushed and bowed her head, murmuring, "It was nice."

Dar moved towards the door. "We should get going. We have a lot to do today."

"Yes, milord!" They both snapped to attention and headed out of the hut.

As they were about to step back, Dar realized he hadn't clarified the need to keep quiet. "Wait! You are to tell no one about what happened this morning, or any of my secrets."

Amber's brow furrowed, and she looked a bit wounded. "You needn't have commanded that." Marcie nodded with her.

Dar instantly felt guilty. He should have known they'd be loyal and Cherry's worries were unfounded, but he also knew that there was truth to what Cherry said. Word would get out, and they would become targets.

Following them out, he saw a group already crowding around eating breakfast. The sunrise had crested the horizon, and workers were already chipping away at the massive log. It was almost starting to look vaguely boat-shaped. But Dar knew hollowing the inside might be the longest task.

"Morning, hunk," Blair called, waving her fingers as he sat down.

"You look positively lovely today." Dar meant it. She had her white hair braided over her shoulder with a few crystals of salt decoratively woven into it, catching the warm light of the sunrise.

Blair smiled through her blushing cheeks. "Thank you."

"You look lovely as well, Mika."

The nereid had braided shells into her hair, although they were not quite as intricately woven in as Blair's salt; Mika couldn't manipulate shells like Blair could salt.

Dar took another look around the morning breakfast group and realized Neko was missing. "Amber, could you grab Neko and me something for breakfast? I'm going to go make sure she's okay."

At Amber's nod, Dar headed off to find Neko. He spotted her in a tangle of her own clothes and shook his head. "What am I going to do with you?"

"Dar?" Neko looked up and smiled, happy to see him. Then she looked back at her situation with a frown.

Dar picked her up and helped her remove all the misplaced arm and leg holes from her before setting it back on her properly. "I know, Sasha makes clothes a little complicated. I'm just surprised you didn't tear them yet."

"You like them," she said simply.

"That I do." Dar helped her into the tight-fitted trousers. They weren't that different from a pair of skin-tight jeans. Around her chest was a silk top that also provided support.

Neko looked stunning, and Dar couldn't help himself. Scooping her up, he carried her out of the hut. At first, Neko responded with a small growl of surprise, but soon she was cuddling into him and enjoying the ride.

"That pussy cat is so lucky," Blair said as they passed by. "Maybe I should go fight and get injured."

"If you go fight and don't get injured on purpose, I'll treat you the same for a day," he offered.

Blair's eyes shone as she smiled wide. "Deal. Remember that deal, hunk."

Marcie brought over a stump, and Amber set down two bowls within Dar's reach as he settled Neko down on his lap and used one hand to put the bowl to her lips.

"You know, she's milking this for all the attention she can," Cherry offered. The cat girl in his arms at least looked a little guilty.

"Is that true, Neko?" he asked.

She looked away but spoke, "Yes."

"Thank you for being honest." He kissed the side of her head and offered the bowl of grits again. "I don't hate doing this, but tonight you're going to feed yourself."

"Yes." She bobbed her head rapidly and drank the offered breakfast.

"He isn't even mad," Blair huffed. "Is there anything you won't just shrug off?"

"Is it worth getting mad over simple things? Like I said, I don't mind doting on Neko one bit. In fact, I kind of like it."

Sasha cleared her throat. "When the ettercaps attacked Neko, Dar lost it."

Blair made a big O with her mouth. "Got it."

Dar gave Cherry a questioning look. Something was happening here that was going over his head. She shook her head, which meant either she didn't know or wasn't going to tell him now.

"So, what's everyone up to today?" Dar tried to keep the conversation going.

"Salt and more salt." Blair shrugged, trying to hide a smirk. "But I get to see this lovely man enter and exit my cave all day, so it's worth it."

"More fishing for me," Mika said. "They aren't thinning out any, so the Bell River could give us fish for a long time."

"Good. It's probably one of the best places to get meat in the winter. Which reminds me, I've been meaning to ask. How are you in the cold water?" Dar paused, wondering if it bothered her.

"Uh, cold?" Mika asked, confused. "I'm not swimming once there's ice at the edge of the river."

Dar nodded. It made sense, but he was hoping she might have been able to tolerate the cold water more easily. "Cherry, you're back to the field today?"

"Yep. What about you?"

Dar scratched his chin, trying to figure out what needed his attention the most. The village probably needed him to drop a few more

foundations into place, but Bart also needed to speed up his men into building the tops of the homes. Did it make sense for him to keep dropping the foundations if Bart couldn't keep up, or could he start on another project?

"I think I might try to make some more containers for food storage, or a few other enchantments I've been thinking of. Actually, it's about time I tried to make a few heaters to sell in case another river boat comes by."

Before Dar could ask, Sasha answered his next question. "Neko will be with me. We are going to work on enchanting tools for the woodcutters."

Looking around, Dar asked the group, "Mika, Blair, and Neko, would you be willing to swear an oath to keep my secrets?"

Mika and Blair swore it in a heartbeat, while Neko required some coaching.

He pulled out three fruits from behind his back and gave one to each. "Eat them."

Neko did in a heartbeat. The other two watched her for a second before eating the fruits themselves.

"How?" Mika asked, her eyes wide.

"For now, I'll keep that quiet, but hopefully, I'll have more later."

Blair licked her fingers slowly, watching Dar. "You get more mysterious by the day, hunk. Are you sure I can't entice you just yet?"

"We already discussed that. The rest of us have also eaten that particular fruit, and so have Amber and Marcie."

That caused Blair's brows to shoot up. "They are like you then? An immortal?"

"Yes," Dar answered. "I hope that we might have more than a few immortals in this village before the end of the winter."

Blair and Mika seemed to have so many questions, while Neko began using her quiet dao immediately, crouching low and pretending to pounce on prey silently.

Dar held up his hand to pause Blair and Mika. "For now, we need to get to work. Hearthway won't build itself."

Dar went into the cave and hauled out several stone carts, making an alcove for himself to work. Then he got started pulling several large chunks of granite from the cave wall, shaping them in his hands to a square with a flared base. That way, it didn't tip over. Once he finished, he carved the rising part of them with a large dao character for heat.

The character would serve as the heating element, but he still needed to adjust it so that the dao didn't get expressed on the base. He didn't want to burn anybody's home down as he attempted to keep them warm.

Working to morph them slightly more, Dar added a flared shelf that would hopefully draw off and disperse heat coming down from the heating element. Once he finished that, he made a dial-like feature that connected to more conditionals, leading to the rune. It wasn't exactly like a dial; he didn't have a spring that he could use. But the piece could lift and be shifted between slots. Which slot it was in determined the strength of the heating element.

Dar sat, testing it a few times to make sure it was working. Once he was satisfied, Dar studied it, working to solidify the image in his mind.

Setting it down, he moved over to the wall, keeping the image in his mind. He pulled another ball of granite from the wall and more quickly formed it into a heater, like the first.

It went much faster than he'd expected to craft after completing the first. In no time, he had crafted multiple heaters. Dar finally paused in what he was doing to study the surrounding area.

Blair had settled into her spot again, salt circling her body. Past her, the light of day was still strong enough that Dar estimated that it was likely close to noon.

Looking back, Dar looked at the space he'd cleared out and suddenly had an idea. Taking that space and filling it with granite, he shifted the stone to create a pocket behind him and started molding a home into the back of the cave.

Wanting it to not just be a stone box, Dar first made an archway with two columns decorated with a braided pattern. Satisfied, he started scooping out the floor to an even plane and crisscrossing it to look like tile, until there was a reasonably large entryway in front of him.

Wiping his brow, Dar could feel that his mana was running low. He started to meditate, but it wasn't long before he was interrupted.

"Boss, there's been a river boat spotted coming from the north. Wood cutter just came in to report it."

Dar quickly got up from his meditation. "Alright. I'll be out by the river shortly."

Dar had only made three of the heaters, but he wanted to save one to keep copying from. Picking the two up, he found a wheelbarrow and started to cart them out towards the river.

CHAPTER 20

"Milord." Amber caught up to him. "I hear there's a boat."

"There is. You're welcome to come with me, but do hold the 'milord' while we talk to them. I would like to stay relaxed."

"Yes, mi—Dar," she stopped herself.

"Better, but try not to have to correct yourself," Dar teased.

Amber nodded. "I'll try not to have to correct myself again."

"Have you had a chance to get used to the changes?" he asked, curious how it would change for everyone else.

She cupped her chest. "I like the changes."

Dar stared at the swell of her chest. "Are they larger?"

"Yes." She beamed. "Though not overly so, I mostly evened them out. I also didn't get tired at all today helping the men in the field move barrels!"

"Good. Now, let's see what we are dealing with?" Dar stepped through the last of the trees and spotted the river. "I was told they are coming from the north."

Dar eyed the river. It was running faster than he'd seen before. He hoped the boat wasn't making such good time that he'd miss them. Pulling on his dao of heavy, he stepped out into the river far enough to see around the trees and upstream.

"Careful, you'll get swept away," Amber cautioned.

"No need." Dar smiled at her concern, but he was like a rock in the middle of rapids. The river wasn't going to move him.

Looking down the river, he spotted the boat still coming their way. But it looked different from the merchant boats he'd seen previously.

As the boat moved closer, it became clear it was not a merchant vessel. Men in bronze helmets and chain mail walked the bow. There were enough of them that Dar assumed it was largely a vessel to carry men, not goods.

"Amber, it might be best that you step back into the forest. The boat is full of armed men."

Her eyes were wide. "Do they look like trouble?"

"No. If I had to guess, they are coming down from Kindrake to support Bellhaven. But we won't know until I can talk to them. So I'd feel better if they don't know there is a village with girls as lovely as you in it."

She gave him a wry grin. "Thank you. I'll go hide so I don't tempt these men like a siren."

Dar shook his head with a wry smile. "Exactly what I'm worried about; they'll be jealous I have such a beautiful maid."

As she moved away, Dar took an extra moment to look for the subtle changes she'd made to her body as part of becoming an immortal. Her hourglass frame definitely seemed more accentuated. She'd been beautiful before, but Dar couldn't blame her for enhancing her beauty further. She had definitely become exceptionally enticing to any man.

But she also walked with a little more grace that spoke of changes that went further than skin deep. He didn't doubt that she had spent a large portion of her effort on becoming stronger.

As she crossed into the treeline, Dar looked back towards the boat. Standing there in the river, anchored down by his heavy dao, all Dar could do was wait. But it didn't take long for someone at the bow to spot him, and the boat slowed as it approached. A heavy splash indicated someone might have dropped an anchor off the back.

"Hello, is there a village here? It isn't on the maps."

"A small one; we mostly keep to ourselves," Dar said, looking the man over. His armor seemed a notch above the others on the boat. "I'm Dar. I can speak for the village. Our hunters saw you further up the river, and we wanted to know what a group such as yours was doing."

He snorted. "Commander Carlson. Heading down to support Bellhaven. I don't suppose you have the latest news on what we can expect to find?"

"Probably not anything more recent than you have. Another merchant vessel came from Bellhaven four days or so ago. They told us the city survived the latest attack, but there was a big ass troll that was part of it."

The commanded nodded. "Yes, we met them two days ago and got their full story. It was much of the same warning we've been getting the whole way down. We also learned that Bellhaven has quite the food shortage."

At that, two other occupants came up to the commander's sides. One was a younger man in armor with gold trim, the other a demon with a rack of antlers.

The younger man looked down the boat at Dar. "We should requisition your villages food stores for our trip. For the soldiers and to bolster Bellhaven."

Dar scowled. "I'm afraid we are quite the small village. It wouldn't be worth your time."

The commander cleared his throat. "This is Prince Gregor and my second, Rack."

Rack was staring straight at Dar, his eyes wide and puzzled.

Dar realized belatedly that the demon had sensed his use of mana. He hoped the demon would assume, like many others when they met Dar for the first time, that he was just a demon with a less obvious animal aspect. Dar hoped this was just a passing conversation and that he'd never see these people again.

"I would suggest you don't antagonize the man," Rack spoke up to Gregor. "Winter is almost here, and they might not have time to get more food before it comes."

Gregor snorted. "Bring your food here."

"I'm sorry, sir. I wish we could. But our village is quite small, and many of our townspeople are spread out working to prepare for winter. You'd have to wait half the day for us to get enough men to bring the food here." Dar was already regretting conversing with the boat.

The commander spoke back up, once again being a voice of reason. "We can't waste that amount of time. Bellhaven needs you to step up since the death of the duke, sir."

Dar tried to school his reaction. The duke was dead? No wonder the prince was coming down the river. He must be taking over the city for the time being.

"The duke is dead? That's a shame. He was a fair leader." Dar shook his head.

"You knew him?" the prince asked, sounding surprised.

Dar backpedaled, realizing his mistake. "No, just of him. It is a loss for the area."

The prince nodded. "Given that there is so much danger in the area, we should hold here and bring these people to Bellhaven. Why have you not already left your small village like the others? There are reports of large groups of devils wandering the area."

Dar smiled. "Ettercaps in the woods. They stick to the woods south of here and for now we believe they are blocking any other devils from getting through there."

The commander was interested in that fact. "There must be a lot of them if they are that much of a barrier."

"Thousands in the woods," Dar clarified. "I've seen their webbed fortress. But they keep to the woods, so for now, they aren't much more than a mountain that we or others can't pass."

"Even more reason for you to come aboard, and we'll sail down to safety," the prince still pushed. "And bring your food."

There it was.

"No thank you. Bellhaven isn't a very welcoming place lately." Dar started to back out of the river.

"Interesting. I thought you were blocked off from Bellhaven by the ettercaps," the prince stated, narrowed his eyes.

Rack spoke up again. "Sirs, I think it best we go, before you upset this man."

The prince dismissed the comment, but the commander turned wide-eyed to his second. "Truly?"

"Yes, sir."

The commander looked over at Dar once more with more interest as he said, "Then we should get going. I apologize for any insult we might have incurred." The commander went so far as to bow his head slightly.

"What's going on here?" The prince glared at the commander.

The older man glowered back at the prince. "Are you going to demand we stay?"

Dar ignored them, fixing Rack with a stare. "I thank you for moving along. Though, if there is a chance to help with the ettercaps in the near future, we'd appreciate it."

The prince had settled down by that point and was staring intently at Dar, his eye raking over him. "Are you among the ancients that fled Bellhaven recently?"

"If you know about that incident, then you'd understand why there are some in our village that would be against heading to Bellhaven."

"You all should be there fighting for Bellhaven. It is because of your cowardice that the city is in dire straits!" the prince spat.

Dar was done. The commander seemed reasonable enough to deal with, but the prince didn't seem worth talking to. Stepping back out of the river, Dar started walking away, making his stance clear.

"Men, bring him here," the prince shouted.

At his order, several men looked like they were about to jump out of the boat.

Dar let out a heavy sigh. Either way, they were going to see what he was capable of. He might as well make an impression and hope it might spare him showing all of his secrets.

Turning back, Dar took several running steps. The water offered barely any resistance to him as he launched himself upwards onto the bow of the boat, activating his dao of hard and strength as he landed to crack the planks beneath him.

"No need to get out—here I am. Now what did you need?" Dar stood staring the prince down.

The soldiers blinked in shock at Dar's jump. The commander and Rack backed up, pulling the prince with them.

"What the—" the prince stuttered, seeing Dar up close.

Dar dwarfed the prince as he stood tall and beckoned the soldiers forward. "I don't have all day."

They charged, but they didn't draw their swords. They clearly didn't want to fight him to the death, and he couldn't blame them. Their bodies and fists crashed into his but bounced off like waves against a cliff.

Dar didn't budge an inch, using his dao of heavy to root himself on the creaking planks. He grabbed two of the men, tossing them back into the others. They tumbled over each other, and the sudden shift caused the river boat to rock dangerously to the side.

"Are we done yet?" Dar knew he was walking a thin line. He needed to not make complete enemies of these soldiers, but he also needed them to be wary of messing with his village.

"Stop. Go back to your duties," the commander barked.

Dar stepped up to the young prince. "I recommend when you get to Bellhaven that you work to get the real story about what's been happening there. You might want to make some adjustments before The White hears of it and it ends up like Toldove."

All three men winced.

"That was not what we heard." The commander bowed his head in apology.

Meanwhile, the prince stepped back, physically distancing himself from the conflict he'd started. Dar met his eyes and held them.

"We will investigate the matter," the prince promised.

Nodding, Dar looked between them as he continued. "You should also know that, prior to our departure from the city, several noble houses were making attempts at the duke's life. At that point in time, the duke was all that stood between the ancient races and an unfortunate ending. I'm not sure what you will find but know that it will not be good."

They both grimaced, but neither seemed surprised. They clearly knew more about how the duke had died than their previous conversation had implied.

"We... understand. Thank you for sparing our men. We will endeavor to check out this ettercap issue as well." Rack stepped forward, bowing to Dar.

"Thank you. They are just south of here, about four miles from the river deep in the forest. You can't miss it. And I had no interest in your men's blood. I'll be leaving now." He stepped back, giving them a chance for a final question.

When nothing came, he jumped off the boat and let his dao of heavy sink him to the bottom of the river, where he waited for the boat to pass. In response, their anchor came up swiftly, and the boat moved on in a hurry that made Dar smirk.

He wasn't a particularly vindictive man, but he did hope that Mark and his wife would suffer for what they had started back in Bellhaven. Though, he couldn't help a worry tickling the back of his mind. If Mark had taken over, would the prince be able to restore order? Dar had his doubts that Mark would be quite so willing to part with the power he had fought so hard to obtain. Maybe Dar needed to head down to Bellhaven after the boat was finished, if nothing else than to check on the situation.

When he surfaced, Amber rushed out of the woods. "Milord, I was worried."

Dar ruffled her hair, getting it wet in the process. "No worries. But just think, one day soon, you might be able to accomplish something like that."

Her eyes went wide. "I'd never go confront the prince and his commander like that."

Shrugging, Dar decided she could do what she wanted with the strength that came with being an immortal when she had it. However, he knew that this level of strength was changing him.

He was finding it a lot harder to tolerate anybody abusing their power when he had the power to do something about it. He'd felt that way before, but it was always a guess if he'd win the battle. Now that he was more confident, he couldn't help but push back.

That came with the power and responsibility to protect those he held dear. Bellhaven was something he could solve if he needed to.

"Then you just keep being you. We'll see where it goes." Dar picked at his wet clothes before taking a step back and letting his dao of heat blossom and steam himself dry.

Amber nodded. "I'll keep being here to support you, milord."

"Thank you for that." Dar nodded, starting his way back towards the village.

As he got back, he noticed that the top of the log had been cleared and it was a flat surface that would become the top of the boat, but they were still chipping slowly through the tree.

"Excuse me. Do you all plan to chip through the whole boat?" he asked, trying not to startle them. It appeared that Bart and Frank hadn't communicated the use of coals to the men.

One of the men looked up from his work, his eyes widening when he saw it was Dar. "Is there an easier way to get this done?"

"An easier way to clear the rough stuff, sure. Hold on a moment." Dar went over to the central hearth and picked out an armful of hot coals before coming back. "Make way."

The men hurried out of Dar's way before he pitched his load over the edge of the future boat and hauled himself up to spread them

out. Hot coals noticeably started burning through the wood beneath them.

"Now you just need a few guys to fan them to keep them going and to put some kindling over them to keep them cooking."

"I hadn't thought about doing it this way, but I guess it works?" the man said, still watching the coals burn.

Dar shrugged; their options had been limited. "This'll be far easier than chipping it all out."

"Dar!" Neko shouted, walking up with Sasha and thrusting an axe into his hands.

"Thank you, Neko." Dar used the axe to shave off just a bit of wood. The tool was sharp as hell. "Here. Split the crew between men working the top and men shaping the sides." They still needed to rough out the hull and smooth the bottom.

The man took the axe with a look of reverence as he tested it on a small bit of the tree, a smile blossoming on his face as it slid like butter through the wood. "Yes, lord. I'd just like to say thank you for providing us with enchantments. It makes a world of difference."

"Enjoy those as much as you can today. I'm afraid the woodcutters will be after them in the morning for their own use tomorrow."

The man held the axe close, already a little defensive of it. "Yes, sir."

The men rearranged themselves, and Dar got off the boat as Sasha and Neko handed out the rest of their enchanted axes.

"Neko, are you getting the hang of enchanting objects?" Dar prodded the woman.

Sasha snorted. "She just gives me the characters and helps me point out where to start the conditional work."

Dar nodded, a little disappointed but not surprised. He was hoping Neko could soon do her own enchantments without help. Pausing, Dar realized he didn't know exactly what Neko's dao was for sure.

Turning, he asked her. "Neko, what dao is it you have?"

Neko tilted her head slightly making her ears flop. "Sharp." She raised her hand, and Dar could feel mana ripple around her hand like little blades.

He blinked and looked at Sasha, who just shrugged. "Dao paths are infinite and full of potential. This one is definitely very useful. Unlike sticky." Sasha made a face at the mention of the dao.

Dar had to agree. It was also already proving versatile. "Impressive, Neko."

She smiled so wide that her eyes squeezed closed. "Neko best."

Dar gave in and rubbed between her ears, eliciting a purr from the cat girl.

"You better make sure the men know to be careful with these axes. They could do a lot of damage to themselves with the wrong swing." Sasha finished handing out the remaining axes.

Neko had pulled her mana back in and was snuggling up against Dar's arm, rubbing her face into his shoulder as she purred. Dar laughed, scooping her up as he walked off. She kicked her feet up as she let him carry her like a princess and smiled at anyone they passed.

Chapter 21

The next two days went by quickly as the village banded together to get ready for winter. The villagers had adopted Dar's approach to use coal to hollow out the boat, which had sped it up considerably. Food storages had also been filled to the point that more was available for everybody in their day-to-day meals. Morale across the village was increasing; they actually stood a chance at making it through the winter.

Dar had focused on helping with the houses and heaters. They had stopped using lumber for the palisade and had started piling them up for use in the houses. When there was downtime, Dar would work on forming more heaters while simultaneously carving further into the back of the cave.

He had tried to add homey elements into the cave over the last two days, ones he thought the girls might like. Dar hoped to surprise them with the space once he got closer to finishing.

Smiling at the thought, Dar worked to focus back on his task at hand.

The boat was nearly finished. He was in the process of running his hands across the finished exterior of the boat, burning the top layer of the wood with his heat dao and sealing it for use in the river.

They had spent quite a bit of time adding enchantments to the boat and he worked with Mika and Cherry to design a mounted motor on the boat.

"Are you sure we can't use it today?" Russ asked, clear excitement showing on his face.

"Positive. Mika and I need to test it before we put others into it. Either of us can haul it back if there's a problem," Dar answered the gnoll as Russ slung his bow over his shoulder and went off to hunt.

The boat had already been moved closer to the river for the final preparations, so they didn't have far to go. Mika walked up next to him, looking it over.

"This is an amazing boat." Mika's eyes lit up as she spotted the motor at the back that she had worked with Dar to build. Pride shone in her eyes, although Dar also caught a bit of unease. They hadn't tested it out yet.

"With your help, that should get us around nicely. I just wanted to test it with someone who could handle themselves in the river if something went wrong."

Mika beamed with extra pride, standing a bit taller.

Dar smiled, studying the motor once more before they put it in the water. The way they had designed it, the motor used her dao of waves to propel the boat forward. He was pretty proud of it, if he was honest. He wasn't exactly an engineer, but he had enough of an understanding with basic mechanics to get it set up.

Cherry had built the gear system, under his guidance, that connected to the big wheel at the helm that turned the motor. The more he worked to figure out enchantments, the more endless the possibilities felt.

He walked up, feeling the smooth exterior. Cherry had helped with the final touches. She had helped add a deck of branches separating the main area from a small storage area below. Dar couldn't fit comfortably in the lower area, but some of the smaller villagers could if they crouched.

"Alright, let's get it in the water and test this thing out!" Dar cheered, lifting the back of the boat while Mika guided the front into the water.

As the front glided in, she jumped up, getting her front up on the rail. "I'm up," Mika called as she threw her spear on deck and slung herself over the edge.

The boat as a whole floated high in the water with only their weight in it. As Dar jumped onto the back of the boat, the watching villagers cheered them on. He realized how important that moment was for the village. There was so much hope and potential that came with now having a boat.

Pulling back on the lever, the enchanted motor kicked on and the boat lurched forward.

"Whoa!" Mika grabbed onto the railing as it shot forward.

Grinning, Dar spun the wheel, turning it downstream as the boat shot forward.

"It's so fast!" Mika cried, holding onto the railing and putting her face into the wind, a giant smile spreading across her face.

"We aren't even at top speed," Dar teased, grinning as he pulled the lever fully, kicking the boat into high gear. It was enough to pull the front of the boat out of the water as the motor pulled the back end lower, and they raced down the river far faster than any river boat they'd seen previously.

Mika stepped up to the front of the boat, taking in the full view of the water around them. Spreading her arms wide, she looked up at the sky, the wind whisking her hair and clothes back. Dar had never seen her so free.

After a few moments, she looked back at him. "Dar, we could get to the ocean in a day trip. Blair could pull all the salt we need."

Dar gave her a smile, but he had other thoughts. They could easily check on Bellhaven using the boat and its speed, but he didn't want to voice that yet. "This is pretty incredible. How long do you think it would take to get up to Kindrake?"

She shook her head in amazement. "At least half the time of usual, maybe a quarter. So, two to four days by boat."

"That would open a lot of options for trade with a more reasonable city."

Mika looked back at him seriously. "But, with any luck, Bellhaven will be more reasonable here shortly. The prince will fix things, I'm sure."

"I hope so, Mika." He did his best to hide his doubt in his tone, but Dar had a bad feeling in his gut.

They continued downriver for a clip in silence before Dar pulled Mika over. "Do you want to take the wheel?"

"I'm not sure. I don't want to wreck this." She didn't fight it though, as Dar slowed down the motor and shifted her in front of the wheel.

Wrapping his arms around her, he supported her as she turned the wheel. "Give it a turn and get a feel for what it's like. The turning is a bit delayed, so just turn and hold for a second to see it."

Mika focused on steering the ship while Dar was a little more distracted, with her wet rear pressing into him.

"You're doing great. Now, how about we speed up?" Dar shifted the lever, and the front of the boat picked up.

"Wahoo!" Mika let out a shout as the wind picked up and sent her hair into Dar's chest. "This is crazy," she shouted over the wind, holding the wheel steady. "Is this what it feels like to fly?"

Dar chuckled, shouting into the wind. "It's probably as close as we'll get anytime soon."

Mika turned the boat, followed a curve in the river. It forced Dar to hold on to the railing while catching Mika with his body and holding her to the wheel. He made a mental note that they probably needed to get a chair for future trips.

Keeping an eye on the west bank for any ettercaps as they approached the area, Dar saw no signs of them or their spider friends. The forest seemed quiet.

Mika must have seen where he was looking. "Even if they were out there, it would be hard to catch us."

"Not what I'm worried about. I'm just looking to see if our friends the other day would have seen them."

"Ah." Mika made a noise of understanding and focused back on driving the boat.

"Why don't we slow down a little?" Dar suggested.

Mika pulled back the lever most of the way, and the boat settled back down on the water, no longer plowing through the current.

"What do you need?" she asked, clearly eager to keep driving quickly.

Dar felt a little guilty for denying her the thrill, but it was hard to talk with the wind whipping in their ears. "I wanted to just talk. With you hunting fish every day, I haven't had as much of a chance to talk to you as the other girls."

She blushed a darker blue than the rest of her skin. "Ah."

"How are you doing with everything? The village, being part of our little group?"

"The village is nice. There's something satisfying in bringing back the big net of fish and seeing everyone's smiles as it goes towards the dinner pots."

Dar nodded. "Like you earned those smiles. They are all in a small way celebrating your catch."

"Yes, and it helps that you praise me too." She tilted her head back to look into his eyes. "That's my favorite part, if I'm honest."

"Then I'll have to do it more." Dar kissed her forehead.

"Dar..." Mika paused for a moment before she seemed to summon up the courage for what she was going to say. Straightening herself for a moment, she made eye contact and asked, "Do you like me?" She managed to hold his attention a moment further before she looked down, focusing on the steering wheel.

Dar worked to keep his surprise off his face. He knew they hadn't progressed that far, but he thought she knew that he was attracted to her.

"Mika, you are lovely. After our flight from Bellhaven, I was still adjusting to the idea of a family that included Sasha and Cherry, but I've been attracted to you from the beginning."

Mika nodded, looking away, clearly thinking she was about to get turned down.

Wrapping his arms around her, Dar squeezed her in reassurance. "Hey now. None of that. I do like you; we just haven't had time together. So, why don't we make time today? Let's cruise the river, stop and you can catch some fish, and then we'll do a grilled fish lunch on the riverbank."

"Really?" Her eyes lit up as she finally looked back up at him.

Even if he hadn't meant it, he wouldn't want to wipe that look off her face. Putting his hands on either side of her face, Dar leaned down to be nearly forehead to forehead. "Really. I'd like to give this a shot. And, as a bonus, we can see just how far we can get down the river in this boat."

Mika gave him a wicked grin before her arm shot out, pushing the lever to its fastest setting and letting out a gleeful laugh as the nose of the boat rose up out of the water.

"You said before you grew up in a seaside town. Where was that?" Dar asked.

Mika tilted her head in thought. "It wasn't Kindrake. Off the coast, southeast from Bellhaven, there is a collection of islands. Mahaklan is what they call their islands." Dar noticed she didn't refer to it as her islands, but he didn't comment on it.

"Nice islands?"

"Warmer than here; you barely notice the seasons change besides when the rainstorms come."

"And that was where you first found yourself with humans?"

She nodded. "They treated me like a god, or well, they did. Then that tribe was murdered by another. And then that tribe was murdered."

"Sounds bloody." Dar couldn't imagine what it would be like to have all of Hearthway killed.

"Still is, I bet. That's why I left, uhh..." She paused to think. "...maybe a hundred years ago or so. I just jumped into the ocean and swam until I wound up on the shore east of Bellhaven."

"That bad?"

Mika nodded. "It was a very tribal area, much less developed than Kindrake. Most of the tribes were peaceful, but there was always a large war between two tribes every few years. The winner would absorb much of the other tribe, but most would scatter."

The wind shifted slightly, blowing hair into her face. She shifted it away, tucking it behind her ear before continuing. "No real progress was ever made. The most powerful tribe would keep acquiring more until they spread themselves too thin, and then another tribe would break them and start taking their land."

Dar let out a soft whistle. "The ancients participated?"

"Oh yes. They were often the main actors. That violent society and then you throw in something like a male demon that came from a predator? Aggressive is an understatement. I remember this one that used to be a shark—he did terrible things." She shuddered.

"There had to have been good moments." He tried to push her into happier thoughts.

A sad smile spread across her face. "There were. Lovers, tribes I particularly got along with."

"Kids?" Dar probed.

"Never. Not yet at least." She looked over her shoulder as she hurriedly corrected herself. "Not that I'm against it! But, after seeing that cycle a few times, I didn't want to subject a kid to that."

Dar nodded his head. "I understand. You need stability before you want a kid." Changing the subject, Dar prodded a bit further, wanting to understand more about where Mika came from. "What about Bellhaven? You've been in the area for a hundred years?"

She nodded, pushing the boat a little faster. "Yep. It's been getting harsher and harsher towards ancients."

"And Blair? How long have you two known each other?" Based on how they interacted, Dar had a feeling there was a longer history than just the journey to Hearthway.

Mika gave him a curious look, but she answered him. "Blair and I were both drawn to the ocean. I liked to immerse myself in the waves, and she would often go out there to pull salt for sale. That's how we met, at the water."

"That's all? You two seem awfully close."

Mika blushed. "I helped her sell the salt and offered some protection. Blair has a habit of getting herself into trouble."

Dar laughed. He was not surprised at all by that. "With men or other things?"

"Merchants have taken advantage of her salt more than once. I mean, when she can just make something as valuable as salt by the pound out of the ocean, she hadn't really had to worry about money before."

"Ah. She told me about some of them calling it 'monster salt'." Dar remembered the story.

"That's just the tip of the iceberg. She practically gave it away more times than I can count. But she could just go make another basket full with a quick trip to the ocean." Mika rolled her eyes. "Girl has zero business sense."

"So you helped her with that?"

"Sort of. I was the muscle mostly. More recently, we worked with Henry for his help selling the salt, and I eventually swore an oath to help him in a greater capacity. I didn't know that he'd abuse the oath to the extent that he did. That he'd do... what he did..." Her voice cracked slightly before she hardened her face.

It broke Dar's heart to watch. Wrapping his arms around her tighter, he whispered into her ear, "That's all over though."

She dipped her head slightly in a nod. "I still can't thank you enough for that. Neither of us saw the trap Henry was laying until it was too late. He started with small oaths and built them up over time. I..."

"Shh," Dar shushed her and just held her close, reminding her that the threat was gone and that she was safe.

"Thanks." Mika's voice came out soft as a breeze, and she stopped supporting herself, letting Dar bear her weight.

Dar smiled at the trust that showed. "So, how about we see just how fast this thing can go and then take a break for lunch? I'd like to see if we can't get down to check out Bellhaven."

Mika jumped back to attention and slammed the throttle forward with a shout of excitement.

***

Mika came out of the water with two large fish wiggling on the end of her spear. "See? Easy."

"I don't think many people, or even ancients, could chase down fish in water like that. I'm happy to be on your good side. I don't need you coming at me with that spear," Dar said with a wink.

He took a moment to appreciate her. Mika had a toned, athletic frame and often wore what wasn't much more than a bikini showing it off. Her hair was a little wavy and cut just below her chin. The girl would have fit right in with a surfer crowd.

She struck a pose, thrusting the spear point into the shoreline, the fish slung over her shoulder. "I am pretty badass. Nice you finally noticed it." But her bravado quickly melted away into a shy smile as she walked towards him.

They had stopped on the east bank, and Dar had gathered some dry wood that he had blasted with heat until a fire had sprung to life while Mika had gone fishing.

"That's a pretty useful lesser dao," Mika said, wrapping a thin cloth over her hips before sitting down on the sand.

Dar had tried, but there wasn't any granite beneath them that he could pull on to make better seating. "Yes, it is. I hope to push it into something closer to a flame. Sasha has mastered the combustion

dao, which is what I want next. I'm hoping that and one more that's similar might push me towards a greater dao related to fire."

"Nice! But I won't be much help there. Sorry." Mika gutted the two fish and stabbed them through a sharp stick.

Dar sighed. "Please don't be sorry. It's just a goal, anyway. Who knows if I'll find what I need to get there for a long time."

"Is there anything else I can help with?" Mika asked.

Dar gave the question some honest thought. "I could use some live fish? Oh! Or fish eggs, if you find some."

She blinked. "That's not a problem at all. Fish this time of year are coming upstream to lay eggs, anyway. But what do you need eggs for?"

"I want to create a fish farm," Dar stated. In full truth, he wanted to make two fish farms: one in his inner world and one near the village. But he hadn't shared that with Mika yet.

"There's an easier way to do that..." Mika tapped her lips, thinking. "Back in Mahaklan, they did this thing where they'd create a lake next to the river where it bends and then make a channel between the two. Fish swimming upstream to lay eggs would mistakenly go into the lake and lay their eggs. And then the channel could always be closed back off."

Dar nodded. He hadn't considered that, and it didn't seem too difficult. It might be something that Glump could work on, given all the mud surrounding the river. It could be big for them the next spring if they could manage it. "How big does it need to be?"

Mika shrugged. "Not that big. But the bigger you make it, the more it'll provide. But you could also make really small ones and just catch the fish on their own."

"Think when we get back that you could help Glump and I design this?"

"Of course!" She smiled.

"You are just filled with all sorts of knowledge. You should speak up more! This could really help us get sustainable meat next spring."

Mika scratched the back of her head. "I just know a few things from living with people that Kindrake would call savages."

"It's a different way of living, but it doesn't mean it doesn't have its own benefits." Dar grunted as he reached into the fire to poke the fish and see how warm they'd gotten. They still needed a little time. "It sounds like the Mahaklan people knew more about how to live off the land than Kindrake."

Prompting her a bit further, Dar asked. "Anything else they did we should consider?"

But Mika shook her head. "Not that I can think of right now..." she said, trailing off in thought. She shook her head one last time. "Nope. At least, for now that's all."

Mika paused again before she asked. "Where did that fruit you gave us come from? I don't mean to pry, but it seemed to come after you went into the forest? Did you find it there? I've never heard of or seen such a thing."

Dar raised his eyebrow. "You could somewhat say I found it there. It involved the death of the spiders and ettercaps, which were in the forest."

Pausing, Dar considered how much he should tell her. But, after their day together, he wanted to get closer to her, and they wouldn't be able to do that without trust. He got the feeling that she'd close herself off if she sensed he didn't trust her. Decision made, Dar continued.

"It's all part of why I wanted the fish eggs, actually," Dar started, watching as Mika's face twisted in confusion as she tried to guess what he was about to say.

Smiling, Dar launched into explaining his inner world and the dao tree. With each revelation, Mika's eyes grew wider.

"So what happens if you... put me in that soil."

Dar cringed, hating that it was her first question. But it had been Cherry's too and he understood the concern. "I get a partially finished fruit of your dao, but I would need more with the same dao to be able to get to a full fruit. While the devils seem to all be similar and

there are large quantities of the same species, demons and spirits are more unique. So it's difficult to progress using demons and spirits."

Dar paused, realizing by the look on Mika's face that he was not doing a great job at soothing her worry.

Quickly pivoting, Dar added, "But more importantly, I would never do that to you, Mika. You mean much more to me than an opportunity to progress my dao."

Mika nodded, a bit of her unease leaving her face. "That makes sense."

"But, if you were to become my dao companion, I have another method to try to learn your dao that is much more fun." Dar nudged her, wiggling his eyebrows until he saw her face light up in recognition.

She leaned forward as she whispered, "That does sound like a much better way for you to pick up a new dao."

They stayed that way, faces close to each other for a moment before Dar closed the distance. His lips met her eager ones, her tongue snaking out aggressively to explore him. Enjoying her soft mouth, Dar wrapped his hand in her hair and pulled her more tightly against him.

She shifted forward, moving herself into his lap to close any remaining distance. Dar nearly moaned. He'd been attracted to Mika but kissing her had completely revved up his feelings. There was a chemistry he couldn't explain.

Dar went to reposition her on her back as the smell of burning hit his nostrils. Pausing, Dar looked over at the same time as Mika.

Mika jumped out of his lap. "The fish!" She ran over, working to remove them from the flames, and Dar worked to soothe the ache in his lap at her sudden departure.

"You could come back over here, and we could catch more after?" But even as he said it, Dar could see she was not going to be swayed.

"We shouldn't be wasteful of the life they gave, Dar." Mika pulled out a knife and started peeling back the burnt skin, removing any of

the less edible areas. As her face focused on her task, Dar watched her, taking in the woman who had quickly worked deeper into his heart.

CHAPTER 22

Dar and Mika devoured the fish. As they finished, Mika stood up, walking towards the water. Curious, Dar watched as she waded into the water, pausing before diving and submerging below the surface for only a few seconds.

When she came back up, she held a handful of fish eggs.

Standing up, water dripped down her blue hair and toned body as she looked at him with eyes that smoldered as she took in his perusal of her body.

Knowingly, she swung her hips slightly as she walked out of the water, holding out the eggs to him. "Here, these should help your idea for your inner world."

Dar smiled, opening up his inner world and pulling them out of her hands, enjoying the expression on her face as she exclaimed, "That's so cool! It's like a spatial pouch."

"Really?" Dar hadn't asked much about how Sasha's pouch worked.

"Yep. Do you think that, with all those enchantments on you, one could be turning your navel into a spatial artifact?"

Dar paused. He had never thought of it that way, but now that he considered it, it could be possible. But, as he considered it more, he realized one flaw. "There's still the fact that I can enter it when I sleep."

Mika tilted her head as she thought about it, nodding, but clearly not dismissing it entirely. "How many enchantments are on you? Maybe another one is doing that? But I have to admit, I've never heard of a spatial ring that living things can reside within."

Her face puzzled, and Dar could tell that she really wanted to figure out the mystery. He'd grown used to not being able to understand all the intricacies of what Lilith had done to his body.

Knowing they wouldn't be able to get any real answers without their maker, Dar changed the subject. "Thanks for the eggs. We'll see if we can't grow a nice stock of fish inside my inner world, but I also want to create a fish farm for the village too. We can use the method you described."

As Mika nodded, Dar looked at where the sun was in the sky. They should keep moving if they were going to make it to Bellhaven. Walking over, Dar made sure to smother any of the remaining embers before turning to Mika and holding out his hand. "Ready to keep going?"

She put her hand in his in a heartbeat. "Of course."

They walked through the water, back to the boat. Mika pulled herself up on the boat and stood to the side of the wheel, leaving the spot open for him as he got up on the boat.

He looked at it questioningly. "Don't want to drive?"

Mika just smiled wider and shook her head. "Go ahead."

Dar took the wheel and throttled it out into the river while Mika hung off his arm.

It wasn't more than a minute into the trip before Mika leaned closer, first starting with a single kiss on his arm before they turned into slow trailing kisses moving up his arm. Soon, she was at his shoulders, kissing along to the back of his neck. Dar worked to stay focused on the water ahead of them, but it was proving difficult.

"Careful, you're going to make me crash."

But she only seemed further encouraged by his statement as she crept onto his back, positioning her mouth by his ear as she nibbled on his earlobe. Pausing, she whispered into his ear, "Then you better

work on your focus, because I'm not going to stop. And there's no way little ol' me weighs enough to throw you off."

Dar had to admit there wasn't any physical problem, but the desire to close his eyes and let his head fall back to enjoy the moment was pulling at him. He growled playfully in response.

"Oh, so scary," she whispered into his ear before nipping it harder.

Dar cranked back the throttle in response and pulled her off, positioning her facing him, stuck between him and the wheel with his arms braced on either side of her as he drove.

"Careful or the boat might crash." She wiggled, trying to break free from him, causing the boat to veer a bit in the process.

As she squealed, he corrected it, keeping her pinned beneath him. When he got it settled and looked back down, she was grinning like a little nymph. Shaking his head, he leaned down to give her a quick peck before watching the water again.

Pretending to ignore her, he stepped a bit closer, pressing his body against her as he looked over her head. When she gave a small gasp, he knew that she could feel how hard she had made him in the process of her teasing. Smiling, he continued to look ahead at the water as he reached back and let the anchor drop while turning off the motor, slamming the boat to a stop.

Mika lurched against him, but he held her upright. A gleam in his eye as he finally looked back down at her. Her eyes filled with challenge as she ducked under his arm in one fluid motion and ran away, but he grabbed her, carefully pulling her down to the floor of the boat.

"What if somebody comes and sees us?" she asked, her voice breathy.

"Then they see us. My attention is all on you." Dar couldn't hide the hunger in his eyes as he looked at her.

Leaning down over her, Dar went to kiss her again. She tilted her face up, eagerly accepting his kiss. Lowering his body slightly, Dar got free use of his hand and let it roam her body, cupping her ass and pulling her up into him. She wrapped her arms around his neck, and

she arched herself into him, her nipples hardening as they pressed into his chest.

"Someone's excited," Dar commented as he came up for air. Putting his body directly over her, he lowered them completely against the floor of the boat. She wrapped her legs around him in response.

As Mika kissed at his jawline, moving to his neck, she whispered. "Maybe, I am."

Moaning, Dar started slowly rocking himself against her, feeling his member slide along her crevices, with just a few layers of wet clothing separating them.

Letting out a breathy noise herself, Mika reached down, slowly exposing one of her breasts and looking up at him. Taking the hint, Dar leaned down, nipping and sucking on it while Mika pressed her head back against the floor, making more small moans as he worked on her bud.

Mika reached down, trying to pull her clothes off but failing with Dar's weight against her. Grumbling angrily, she continued trying and Dar couldn't help but enjoy her moment of clear sexual frustration. Lifting himself off her slightly, he watched as she quickly peeled her wet top off her body, exposing herself to him.

Cupping her chest, he tweaked her nipples, playing with her handful of soft cushions. They weren't overly large like Sasha's, but they fit Mika's toned, athletic frame.

"What are you thinking about?" She bit her lip, looking hungrily back at him.

"How sexy you are, and the logistical challenge of getting my pants off."

"Oh, we can fix that problem." Shifting her legs around him, she hooked her feet into his pants and pushed them down. "See? Fixed."

Dar couldn't even respond as his cock finally sprang free. The feel of it in the open air was quickly replaced as Mika used her legs to pull her body tight against him again.

As it pressed against her, Mika bit her lip harder. "I had hoped, but..." She let out a soft whistle in place of any words.

"Glad you like it, but we still have one barrier." Dar was close to destroying the simple layers of fabric that separated him from her. Trying to keep his control, Dar waited to see what she wanted.

But, instead of doing anything to remove the fabric, Mika just smiled. "If you move the skirt out of your way, you won't find any resistance."

Brow raised, Dar held himself with one arm as he slowly worked her skirt up her thighs, exposing her full sex. His hunger surged at the sight. He wasn't sure when she'd taken them off, but in that moment, it didn't matter one bit.

Looking up and meeting her eyes, he saw everything he needed. He lowered himself back down, lining himself up at her sex, teasing the entrance slightly. The wet heat coming off of it told him Mika didn't need any help getting ready. Looking into her eyes, Dar slipped just the tip in.

"Oh. Yes," Mika cried out, her fingers digging into his shoulders as she lifted her hips to get the angle just right. As she pulled on his shoulders, Dar followed the motion, pushing himself more deeply into her.

Her sheath was tight, but thankfully, it was soaking wet enough for him to slide in to the hilt.

Dar took the moment to enjoy the feel of her body wrapped around him, her wetness coating him and even covering his balls. Enjoying the moment, Dar's focus was broken as he felt nails rake down his back and her body shift into him. Looking down, he was met with a hungry scowl.

"I finally have you. Get moving." She playfully slapped his bare ass, and Dar chuckled, happy to oblige. Pinning her hips against the floor, he thrust up harder into her, eliciting gasps.

"Yes! Fuck me."

Continuing to pump deeply into her, Mika held her hips up against him, holding onto his shoulders like she was clinging on for her life.

Mika didn't hold back, screaming out her pleasure as he moved, undulating her body to his motions and adding to the friction.

As they moved, a new sensation flooded Dar. He realized that she was controlling her body, undulating against him as he slid inside of her. As he thrust in and out, her body stroked him internally, adding an additional friction element to the moment.

"I don't know how you're doing that, but it feels fantastic," Dar grunted as she squeezed him and coaxed him towards his peak.

"Harder." She bucked against his hips, and Dar started slamming her hips into him as she screamed in release, her sex working him further and bringing him to the edge of his own orgasm.

Wanting to drag her orgasm out, Dar kept pumping hard, chasing his own release. Unable to hold back any longer, Dar painted her insides with his seed before they both collapsed against the ground.

"Whew," Mika let out a rush of breath. "That was fantastic."

Still coming down from his own release, Dar just grunted against her shoulder.

She wiggled to the side, shifting him off her. Looking over, her face turned to surprise. "How is it still hard?" She reached over, taking him in her hand as she stroked him further.

"The girls didn't tell you?"

"No..." She kept stroking. "Is it going to stay hard?"

"Yeah. So, all the enchantments on me... one of them apparently gives me quite a bit of... stamina."

Mika gave him a wicked grin. "Fuck, really?"

"Yes. But I do think we should continue our trip, don't you?" Dar paused at her pout, not wanting to ruin the progress they'd made. "Tonight, maybe you sleep in our hut?"

The smile she gave him nearly blinded him. "I'd be delighted to.... Does this make us dao companions?"

"I'd like that if you would," Dar answered honestly. "Sasha and Cherry have already accepted you."

Mika smiled, grabbing Dar's face and pulling him to her for another kiss. "Yes! Now let's finish this trip."

Mika grabbed her clothes, slipping her top and bikini bottoms back on and hurrying back up to the wheel to get them moving.

Dar just shook his head, unable to hide the giant smile on his face. He'd had no intention of getting that far with her on their trip, but it just felt right. Putting his pants back on, he wandered over to help Mika raise the anchor.

"What do you want to do at Bellhaven, my companion?" Mika asked, her lips curling up as she said the last part.

Dar took the wheel after finishing with the anchor, enjoying as she wrapped her arms around his waist. "I just want to see if the group from before made it down there and get a feeling for the city."

"And maybe see if they are going to be able to come look for us?" Mika asked, clearly having a sense of where his thinking was going.

"Something like that. They are a danger to us, especially if the duke is dead now. If Mark successfully took over, I'm worried that the prince and his guard might be killed or absorbed into the city's defenses."

Mika bobbed her head, squeezing him tighter. "Then to Bellhaven we go." She leaned up, giving him a kiss on the cheek before looking forward with him as they started moving.

***

"Here?" Mika asked, holding the anchor again.

"Perfect," Dar said, his statement punctuated by the plop of the anchor and the rope running into the water. "We'll get out here and cut through these woods to reach the northern side of Bellhaven. I don't want to expose ourselves by going all the way down to the delta and the open ocean."

Mika nodded. "Should one of us stay with the boat?"

Dar paused. He hadn't built any sort of key into the enchantments, but he also doubted someone would be able to get them started without instructions.

"Let me just make it so no one can steal this." He went down to the motor, and with his dao of granite, he shifted some of the conditionals in the enchantment so it wouldn't function. Someone could try to row the boat, but they'd have to bring their own oars, and they'd need a lot of people to power the massive thing.

Dar laughed as he realized that, even if they did that, he was pretty sure Mika would hunt down anybody who tried to steal it.

"Good to go!" Dar jumped off the boat with a splash and held his arms out for Mika, who jumped into them gleefully. Stepping out of the water and using heat to dry their clothes, Dar and Mika trudged through the forest towards Bellhaven.

It was far livelier than their southern forest, reminding him once more of the plague the ettercaps were to their area. He couldn't wait to deal with them as soon as he had enough firepower to take them on.

"Mika, you wouldn't happen to have other lesser dao, perhaps one related to fire?" Dar figured it couldn't hurt to ask.

She cocked her head to the side. "No, I have the wave dao, and I'm close to forming a dao of rain."

"Oh." Dar was surprised that she was so close to another greater dao. "Do you have the lesser dao you need?"

She nodded, keeping her eyes on the ground as she picked her way through the forest. "Three lesser now. I just need to build them into what I believe will be the dao of rain."

"That's incredible!" Dar couldn't help but be impressed. He knew how long it took for most ancients to build up that much power.

"Nowhere near as incredible as you and your fruits. It's taken almost two hundred years to get here, and you're going to catch up to me in a few months." She shook her head. "If more demons knew about the speed you are growing along your dao path, they might act

to prevent you from getting a grand or a celestial dao in the next few years."

"It's not that bad," Dar tried to downplay it.

"Dar, I'm not sure you understand. It is terrifying. You might be physically a great fighter, a great leader, but what makes you overly strong is that your ability to grow is far beyond anyone else. And, at the speed you do it, others will see a need to act quickly before you grow too strong."

"I'm overpowered," Dar suggested.

"Yes. That," Mika agreed. "Your ability for growth is overpowered."

Nodding, Dar was going to continue the discussion as they stepped out of the forest, but the shock of what they saw cleared his mind.

"What! How's the wall almost done?" Mika nearly shouted.

The wall outside the farmland had been nearly a quarter finished when they had fled, but now it wrapped around almost the entire city in a second tier.

"They must have conscripted the entire city to get it done this fast," Dar stated, amazed at the progress. He couldn't think of another way they would have been able to build it so quickly. It didn't look like it was made of anything different from blocks of stone carved from the quarry.

Although, they had likely had great incentive from all the devil attacks.

Dar couldn't quite see the west wall in its entirety, but he could see the top of the gaping hole in the wall. "What the merchant boat said was true." He pointed to the hole.

"I'd hate to see what could take out a chunk of the wall like that." Mika shook her head. "A devil with a grand dao. I haven't heard of one of those in a long while."

"Lilith kept them at bay, but she's gone now," Dar stated, remembering what she had told him. "Now it's up to us to deal with them as her work fades."

Mika nodded slowly. "I see. I guess it is good you are so overpowered then." She smiled up at him.

"Yeah, let's hope it's enough to take on their numbers when the time comes." Seeing the damage done by what they guessed was a grand devil, Dar couldn't help but feel the weight of responsibility settle on him.

He'd been focusing on getting the village ready for winter with the promise that he could then focus on his personal power. He still thought it was the right order, but part of him was excited for winter to come so that he could pivot to focusing more on his dao.

"The city seems fine," Mika broke him from his thoughts.

"No mass fires or charred buildings that I can see," Dar agreed.

The city, besides the hastily built wall and massive hole, seemed the same as when they had left it. Further south, Dar could see the docks and the prince's river boat he'd seen before rocking in the bay.

"Do you want to get closer?" Mika asked.

Dar paused, trying to decide. He had no doubt the city guard would question them if they approached, and some might even recognize him. He had a feeling his exit wouldn't get him welcomed with open arms.

Looking at Mika, he realized she'd quickly be a target as well. "Let's circle around to the east side and see if we can't find anyone near the quarry to ask a few questions." He had a feeling they might be more talkative, and it would keep them away from the city, where they might have more issues.

"Sounds like a plan," Mika stated.

They circled around Bellhaven for the quarry on the north-east side.

Chapter 23

The continuous clang of picks hitting stone sounded before Dar could even see Bellhaven's quarry up ahead. The place was packed, several thousand workers sweating side by side working the quarry for all the stone it was worth.

Mika whistled softly. "They are throwing all the manpower at this that they can. Must be how they got that wall built so quickly."

Dar reached out, sensing what they were chipping away. Feeling a sense of familiarity, Dar instinctively knew the stone was largely granite.

Staying back towards the shadows, Dar didn't want to call any extra attention to himself. He already stood out enough. Looking around for somebody he may be able to talk to, he spotted a minotaur in shackles. The brute wasn't the one he'd met before; this one had a much larger woolen head. Knowing what he did now about demons, Dar suspected he had evolved from a bison.

Dar watched as the minotaur trudged back into the quarry, taking a path that all the humans weren't using. Nobody seemed to keep a firm eye on him, forming Dar's plan. "I'm going to slip down there to talk to that bull and see if I can't free him."

Mika looked worried. "He's not going to be in a great mood. Looks like he's not here by choice."

"He won't trust me at first, but I'm hoping we can come to an arrangement easily. If something goes wrong, there's a lot of granite here. I can do enough to escape."

Dar stepped forward, creating a small alcove in the granite before stepping into it. Focusing on the surrounding stone, Dar shifted the pocket of space through the rock, refilling behind him as he went. It took a lot of concentration and was a tight fit, but Dar could move himself in the direction the minotaur's path had taken.

Soon, his little alcove opened up as it passed up to a passageway. Dar hoped it was the same one the minotaur had gone down. Taking a deep breath, he worked to adjust his eyes to the limited light, sensing for any threats.

There were torches about every twenty feet in the square-cut tunnel, but even under the flickering light, it was hard to make out much further down the tunnel.

Following the clop of the minotaur he could hear up ahead, Dar used his quiet dao to muffle any noise he'd make walking through the tunnel. As he went deeper, he began to hear the pings of a bull's pickaxe and stopped just short of the demon, waiting to be noticed rather than startle the already upset and armed demon.

The demon took a few more swings, and Dar realized he may need to help the demon spot him. Shifting slightly back and forth, it worked. The minotaur looked up slowly, a wary expression on his face as he pulled his tool back for an attack.

"Hey now, I just didn't want to startle you." Dar raised his hands. "I'm not from Bellhaven. I'm from a community up the Bell River and came down here to check on the city after the rumors we heard."

But the bull looked around. "How did you get down here? And why are you down in a cave tunnel talking to me if you just need information?" Distrust covered his face.

"I'm not exactly expecting to be well loved by the humans in the city. For one, I'm not one of them." Dar demonstrated, pulling a chunk of granite off the wall and molding it. The distrust on the

minotaur's face turned to awe as he looked back at Dar with new interest.

"And the last time I was in Bellhaven I sort of took a bunch of the tradesmen, demons, and spirits that were interested and headed out to carve our own way through the world. So, lying low is a better plan for me. I saw you off on your own and was hoping you might be willing to catch me up on what's going on here."

The minotaur snorted and scraped its feet against the ground, the clang of chains echoing off the square walls. "Heard a bit about all of you, although they don't like to talk much about the group that left. Came here a week ago with the rest of my village. As soon as we arrived, the women and men were split up. Women were let into the city and put to work in the farms. All men were given work duty. Most of them are breaking their backs hauling stone for the wall, I'm here digging stone."

"Probably just based on your size and strength, this is tough work." Dar rolled his eyes. "What's your dao?"

The man paused for a moment, seeming to size up if he could trust Dar, but he seemed to decide there wasn't much to lose. "Tough."

Dar gave him a once over. "Fits well enough. So, what's your name?"

"Lou. What else did you want to know? I need to make sure I hit my quota or they're going to know something was up."

"I heard the prince was coming here. I wanted to come check in on how that worked out for him and the city."

Lou snorted a chuckle. "Clearly I didn't get out of my shackles, if that's what you are asking," he grumbled as he looked down at the chains around his ankles. "Last I heard, the prince was confined to the keep. Haven't seen him around, but I also don't get out a lot."

Dar winced, but he wasn't surprised. He had a feeling the prince would struggle against the entrenched nobles of the city. While he wasn't a huge fan of the prince, he did get the sense that the man would do more right by the ancients. "Thanks, I was hoping for some better news."

"You didn't ask for good news. You asked for the news," the minotaur said, his tone even.

"Well, got any good news?"

"The wall's almost finished? Not sure what happens to me when it is, though."

Given the shackles around his ankles, Dar figured it wouldn't be anything good. "Do you want out of here?"

Lou scoffed. "Of course. But fat chance I have at that. It isn't like I can sneak out." He clopped his hooves on the ground. "Not exactly built for stealth."

Dar paused, listening for anybody approaching. The tunnel still seemed quiet. "I may be able to help you, but we should get moving. Up for it? You can bring your pick if you want."

Lou paused, seeming more torn than Dar expected of somebody clearly forced into indentured servitude. "I can't. At least... not until I know for sure..." The minotaur went silent, staring off to the side.

Dar was antsy to get moving, so he tried to coax more out of the demon. "What is it you need to know?"

The minotaur looked back at Dar, pulled out of his thoughts. "I have a friend. A girl that I've known since we were kids. We joked about getting married when we were older. We got separated when we came to the city..." A sad chuckle escaped him. "She's always been a stubborn one. My guess is she stood up to somebody she shouldn't have. I don't know all the details, but I've heard that she's been sentenced to hang in the morning. I know there's nothing I can do to save her, so I should just leave, but it feels wrong. I know her. She doesn't deserve this."

Dar nodded, understanding the demon's hesitation more clearly. "And if we could save her too?" Dar knew Mika was going to kill him for this, but it went against his core beliefs to let an innocent person hang if there was something he could do to help.

The minotaur scoffed, looking Dar over again. "You and what army? Don't get me wrong, you seem powerful and all demonstrat-

ing that greater dao, but I really don't see how you're going to be able to get in and get her out."

Dar nodded. In all honesty, he hadn't pieced that together yet, but he'd work on it as they got out of the cave. "Come with me, and I promise we will do what we can to help her." Seeing the demon still hesitating, Dar added, "What do you really have to lose?"

Lou finally nodded, breaking his pickaxe over his knee while he muttered, "Happy to never see another one of those my whole life." Nodding to Dar, they headed out of the cave.

Dar led the way as they moved back up through the tunnels. When he spotted the alcove he had entered, Dar realized that, while he was large, the opening was clearly not large enough for the minotaur. Opening it up slightly further, Dar motioned to the demon. "This way. It'll be tight, but bear with me."

Lou grunted and stepped in behind Dar. Dar then used the air pocket around them and started slowly shifting it, displacing stone as they moved. The minotaur fidgeted next to him, clearly not loving the confined space, but he didn't say a word as Dar guided them out.

"Dar," Mika whispered, seeing him come out of the ground again. Her clear relief at seeing him quickly turned into a frown as she crossed her arms. "Next time, no vanishing until we've both agreed on a plan."

Dar gave her a sheepish look. "Sorry. I wanted to catch this big guy before he got too far ahead of me. Lou, meet one of my dao companions, Mika."

Lou bowed slightly to Mika. "Hello."

"Mika, I need you to take Lou back to the boat and hunker down for a bit. I have something I need to do in town, but I'll come join you in the next hour or so. If you don't see me by then, fix the enchantment and go back upstream. We can't pilot the boat in the dark, and sunset isn't too far away. I don't want Bellhaven finding the boat and taking control of it. Can you do that?"

Mika's eyebrow arched, clearly not onboard with that plan. "And what exactly are you doing in town?"

Dar paused, knowing she wasn't going to like what he was about to say. "Lou has a friend in town that needs our help and doesn't have long. I'm going to go grab her, and maybe help the prince establish a bit more control while I'm at it." Dar gave Mika his most confident smile, but the skepticism on her face remained.

"Dar, I know you want to help everybody, and the nobles here are definitely corrupt. But how exactly do you plan on getting in and doing all of that without the world crashing down on you? These nobles saw you use dao without any talisman. That's unheard of! I'll bet there's some sort of bounty already on your head. And you're not invincible!"

Taking a deep breath, Mika worked to calm herself down before she stared into his eyes. "I don't want to lose you."

Dar nodded, wanting to console her but also not sure how to answer her concerns. Seeing him pause, Mika softened the moment by saying, "And if I go back without you, Cherry and Sasha are going to kill me."

Chuckling, Dar knew that she had nothing to worry about compared to the fury he'd meet when they did get him back. But his mind was still spinning on what she'd said at the end. He wasn't invincible, but he could make his body much more fortified and manage to hide his identity. All he needed to do was stop being Dar and become The Black Knight.

A smile crossed his face as the pieces of the puzzle started to come together, which only deepened Mika's frown. "I'm not going to like this, am I?" she asked.

"Probably not, but I think it's a good plan, and you helped me get there. Thank you." He stepped forward, pulling her into a hug. She stayed stiff for a moment before giving in and relaxing into his hug.

"Dar, this better be a damn good plan." Mika looked up at him and he kissed her forehead.

"It's the best we've got, but I think it'll work. And I need you to protect the boat and bring it back to Hearthway should anything happen. It's the best chance the village has at getting the resources it

needs, and I won't do something that would risk our village. I know it's a lot to ask, but can you do that, Mika?"

He saw the hesitant acceptance cross her face before she agreed. "One hour. I better see you in one hour." Punctuating her words, she leaned up, wrapping her arms around his neck while she gave him a deep kiss.

"Who wouldn't want to get themselves back when they have a beautiful woman who can kiss like that?" Dar asked, earning himself a smile before sadness entered Mika's eyes again.

"One hour," she reiterated again before turning and motioning for Lou to follow her. Dar watched as they headed off towards the boat, waiting until they were out of sight to kick off his plan.

Looking around to make sure he was alone, Dar brought out the suit of pitch-black armor and quickly donned it before summoning the midnight black axe.

The enchantments on the armor and weapon blazed to life against his skin. There were layers to the enchantments hiding them, further obscured, but Dar could feel the massive draw of mana from the suit of armor as he stepped towards Bellhaven. He couldn't help but enjoy the satisfaction the extra firepower gave him.

Heading from the quarry towards the town, Dar had only made it about halfway toward the gates before guards began swarming in front of them, clearly preparing for a fight.

"Who goes there?" one man shouted from the top of the wall.

Dar considered talking but ended up deciding that an air of mystery might work to his advantage the best. So instead, he swung his axe off his shoulder and planted it firmly in the ground, crossing his wrists over the top and waiting, doing his best to give off an air of boredom.

The guards didn't seem to know what to do in response. There was a long pause as they waited and watched him before trying again.

"Knight. Declare yourself!" the man on the wall shouted again. He had tried to sound authoritative, but Dar could hear the hesitancy in his voice.

Deciding to speed things along since he was on a clock, Dar lifted his axe out of the soil and slung it over his shoulder, strolling towards the city like he didn't have a care in the world. Soldiers raised their weapons as he reached them, but Dar pushed forward, using his dao of heavy to root each of his steps and prevent them from pushing him back.

As a result, their bodies just shifted around him as he plowed forward, unable to move him from each step that he took. They doubled down, trying to all push against him, but Dar just strode forward like he was walking through a strong counter wind.

"I said stop. Stop dammit!" the man atop the wall shouted as Dar finished striding through the men, reaching the gate and looking up.

The men behind him were standing haphazardly, clearly trying to rationalize what they had just experienced. A few of the men started raising their weapons, their arms hesitating in the air as they looked up the wall, clearly waiting for an order.

"Hold, men," an older voice shouted, coming to the wall on horseback.

Dar recognized Commander Carlson that had been on the prince's boat. The man had seemed reasonable enough. He had a feeling he wouldn't sacrifice the lives of his men for no reason, and Dar was happy to not have to hurt anybody that was just following orders.

Focusing on the open gate, Dar strolled right through, hearing the commander shout behind him, "Do not engage that knight. Fuck. If that abomination is here, that means there's a celestial demon in the city."

The soldiers around went so still at his statement that they could have been statues.

"But, commander..."

"Shut up. He could kill the lot of you, and you would die for nothing. If he doesn't attack, don't draw your weapons on him. Just get out of his way. Send word to the rest of the guard."

So far, the armor was doing its job. He was pleased there were still those around who knew of Lilith and the Black Knight well enough to recognize him.

The clop of hooves on cobblestones came up to Dar's right. "I apologize, sir Black Knight. Where... uh might you be going?"

Dar plodded his way down the busy Bellhaven street. The commander's presence atop his horse added extra help to part the crowd ahead of them. Together, the masses parted, the townspeople gaping to the side as they moved past.

"It would seem you are heading to the duke's manor?" the commander tried again, and Dar thought it might be best to work with the man. He'd at least seemed sensible before.

Nodding his large black helmet, Dar agreed that that was his destination. He planned to make one extra stop in addition to saving Lou's friend, and it would be easier to do it without her in tow.

The commander cleared his throat and waved to two men, who hurried over to him. The commander said something in a hushed urgency that Dar couldn't quite hear before the two men sprinted ahead.

Feeling something was wrong, Dar increased his stride, not wanting them to be able to prepare more for him than they already were.

"Ho, Black Knight. No need to hurry." The commander kicked his horse to speed up into a slow trot.

But Dar didn't slow, moving quickly through the familiar streets and heading straight for what had been the duke's manor previously.

As they moved closer, Dar spotted the two men pulling something down from the entryway. Curious about what they were working so hard to hide, Dar moved faster to intercept them. That was when he spotted the limp form of a spirit with a noose around its neck being carted away like some sack of flour.

Dar's blood began boiling. The men were treating the body with no respect, dragging it away along the ground. Stepping forward, Dar swung his axe from his shoulder, cutting through both of the guards' legs like butter. As they fell to the ground screaming, Dar

couldn't help but feel justified. They didn't deserve to walk on the same ground as the spirit they had treated in that way.

"Hold up!" the commander yelled, clearly torn between defending his men and fear over taking Dar on directly.

Dar turned his attention to the commander. "Where is your second in command? The demon with antlers." His voice came out rougher than normal.

The commander swallowed around a lump in his throat, staring at Dar. "Dead, but I didn't have a say in that. The prince is being held hostage, and if I return to Kindrake without him, the king won't forgive me or my family."

"So instead, you allow these atrocities to occur?" Dar growled, his axe only a moment away from killing the coward.

The commander gave a self-deprecating chuckle as he stated, "You think being sent to babysit the third prince was because the king trusted me? No, it is punishment. I'm already on thin ice. I have a family to think about." The man crossed his arms, like that justified anything.

Dar had half a mind to kill him right then and there, but he also sensed that the commander was a fine enough leader if given the right circumstances. The prince might need him to shore things up if Dar could help improve the current circumstances.

"Fine." Dar loosened his grip on the axe and trudged into the manor.

Two guards stood, more alert as he walked up. He recognized them as some of the soldiers the nobles had used previously. Giving them a moment to step aside, they held their ground in front of the manor door. With one wide sweep of his axe, Dar cut through both of them, his axe moving so swiftly that it scored the door between them.

Stepping forward, Dar nudged the door, but it didn't move. It had to be barred from the inside.

"Are you just going to kill everyone?" the commander asked.

Dar turned and glared at the man through his dark helmet. "I'm going to remove the cancerous problem in this city."

"Please, spare the prince. I swear he argued against the new duke's actions. He just didn't have the force to take them on before they kept him isolated here in the manor." The commander looked away, his cheeks flushing in shame.

"I'm disappointed you let this happen. This blood is on your hands." Dar used his axe and cut through the door and the bar behind it.

"I know," the commander whispered, stopping short of the door.

Dar continued into the duke's manor. Men came charging forward, but Dar cut through them, focused on his target. His axe passed through the air, men dying in a shower of blood, their armor clattering to the floor.

If Mark and Margaret were allowed to continue to grow, Hearthway would eventually come into conflict with them. And Dar would feel at least partially responsible for any of the deaths that occurred when he could have helped turn the tide in the prince's favor. With his Black Knight's armor, he had a chance of tipping the scales.

Dar pushed further into the manor, leaving a trail of blood behind him. As he entered what was a dining hall, the room looked like it had been hastily abandoned. A lavish spread was placed around the table, with half-eaten plates of food at each place setting.

The soldiers rallied in the dining hall, but their weapons did nothing to penetrate Dar's armor. Meanwhile, Dar's axe split through them like they were nothing. Dar couldn't wait to see what other goodies his inner world might hold; the armor was proving invaluable.

"Where are Mark and Marget?" Dar grabbed the last soldier by his throat.

The young man panicked and pointed towards a pair of large barred double doors. "They took the prince and the wizards through there."

Dar paused, considering if he should kill the young man. "Do you think killing the demons was the right thing to do?"

The man spit on Dar's helm. "The monsters should be pur—"

Dar's hand tightened around the young man's neck. With a single snap, the man's eyes glazed over as he died.

Dropping him in disgust, Dar continued forward. He knew what he was doing would take a toll on his soul, but he didn't have time to spare. Rehabilitation would have to wait until another day.

Chopping through the center of the double doors, Dar cleaved the bar in two and pushed his way into the duke's living wing.

With his first step up to the doors, ice shards began to rain down. Pausing to see what they did, he watched as the armor took the attack, although the chill still seeped through and crept along his skin. It almost felt like the armor was meant to stop this sort of attack.

"Die, you vermin! This enchantment was granted by The White. You cannot dare come here and defy her." A wizard Dar didn't recognize stood with a crystalline white staff that looked like it was made from ice.

To fight the chill and the ice spreading across his armor, Dar let out a faint dao of heat, which seemed to multiply several times as it passed through the armor, melting away any of the chill. Dar straightened, turning his head to the man with the staff.

"No. Can't be," the wizard stammered, slamming the staff back down and once again pelting Dar with shards of ice.

Dar simply flooded his dao of heat again and pushed through it, continuing to step forward through the spray of ice to grab the wizard by the throat. He felt pure satisfaction in the crunch beneath his palm.

Several other wizards stood ready, sizing him up. Dar recognized Golum and shook his head as they all hesitated to take action. He knew none of them had something more powerful than what The White had given, but they would be formidable if they came together. Luckily for him, their selfishness seemed to make each of them hesitate to be the first to make a move, hoping somebody else would be the fodder.

A part of Dar also knew he needed to leave enough of them that they could defend the city. It wouldn't do any good to free it of

corruption, only to weaken it to the point that the devils would be able to come and sweep through.

Spotting the staff in the dead wizard's hands, Dar smiled as he opened up his inner world and drew it in. Gasps filled the room as the wizards watched, but Dar didn't mind the Black Knight having even more power in their minds.

Moving towards the door they had seemed to be guarding, they all moved aside, allowing him through.

"Knock knock," Dar said, not even bothering to try the door before he smashed it inwards.

CHAPTER 24

S tanding in the room were Mark and Margret. She was holding a knife to the prince's throat while Mark stood boldly in front.

Both of them were deeply imprinted in his mind from his time in Bellhaven. Margret, the flirty woman with a crippled husband, and Mark drooling in his wheelchair. Dar had felt so stupid when he'd trusted Margret enough to the point that she'd managed to drug him. Her husband then revealed to not be crippled at all.

Mark still had the haughty look Dar remembered when the man had stood out of his wheelchair those weeks ago in the jail cell, confident that he would rule and take down the duke.

He'd been right about taking down the duke, but Dar planned to stop whatever he thought he was going to do next. Although, the smirk made Dar wonder what made Mark so confident. He should be cowering.

"Hello, Black Knight. I think we can talk this out, don't you? Or you can bring your master here, and we can talk it out with her."

Tilting his head, Dar debated what to do next. If he stayed quiet, he might be able to use Lilith's prestige. But he wasn't sure he truly needed it. He could kill both of them easily, but at the moment he couldn't do that without risking the prince's death.

Thinking quickly, Dar came up with a plan. He'd use their own desperate need for self-preservation against them.

Dar stepped forward, raising his axe over his head, and intoned, "Death to the prince."

Margret grinned like an idiot, moving out of the way immediately as Dar brought his axe down. But Dar's swing moved to the side, avoiding the prince entirely and catching Margret. It cleaved her arm from her body in a spray of blood.

She slumped to the floor, the blood loss sparing her cognition as she wheezed on the floor.

"Wha—What?!" Mark screamed and jumped on Dar's back, biting at the base of Dar's helmet.

Peeling the idiot off him, Dar threw Mark across the room as Margret's eyes turned glassy with her death.

"What are you doing? You said death to the prince!" Mark sputtered, backing up away from Dar. His eyes were darting around the room, searching for something, anything, he could use.

"I lied." Dar stepped forward, the squish of blood catching his attention. His legs were coated in it. Flicking some of it off, Dar strode towards Mark.

Mark backed into a corner, grabbing a nearby candlestick, like that was going to be able to take on the Black Knight. His face turned panicked; he knew he was about to join his wife.

Keeping his back to the growing but silent crowd behind them, Dar lifted his helmet for just a moment to meet the man's eyes before he killed him. He wanted Mark to know that he was the one that was winning in the end.

"No! No Way!" Mark screamed and tried to scramble away, but Dar dropped his helmet back into place and lunged forward, grabbing Mark by the arms and twisting his shoulder back.

"Unhand him. He deserves the king's justice!" the prince shouted, having come to his senses.

"Yes! Unhand me! This is an issue for the king. Prince, this man, his name is D—"

Dar twisted Mark's arm, ending his communication in a guttural scream as he bent over.

Dar knew there was no way he could let Mark live. The man was corrupt, but he was smart. He'd find a way to shift himself back into a position of power, and Dar couldn't allow that.

Lifting his head, Dar looked at the prince through his helmet. "I apologize, but for what this man has done, he and the Tints will be removed from this world."

Dar was secretly grateful that Mark and Margret had no kids. He needed to remove the problem, but he wasn't sure if he could go quite that far.

"Prince — Agh," Mark started again, but was cut off as Dar twisted his arm again, this time with a snap that sent the pitiful noble into agonizing screams.

Lifting Mark up to look eye to eye with him, Dar spoke slowly for him to understand. "Who else was involved in killing all the ancient races in the city. I saw the spirit you had hung outside the manor."

The prince gasped in what seemed like genuine shock. "What?"

"It's embarrassing that a prince wouldn't even know that his home had a corpse of a spirit hanging from its doors like decoration. I'm going to assume you would not have placed it there were it your choice?" Dar spoke harsher than he meant to. His anger was rising, and he didn't feel like holding it back at that moment. He needed his anger for what was to come.

His axe hovered like a guillotine for the prince.

"I— No. I had nothing to do with that," the young prince stammered and backed away.

"The commander's second is also dead. Any ancients you brought with you to Bellhaven are dead." Dar could see the dread in the prince's face. "And now those who caused this will be too."

Mark tried to get another word out, but Dar broke his other arm. "Who. Else?"

But the man's mind must have snapped as he cackled through the pain, red foam at the corner of his lips. Deciding he wouldn't get anything more of value, Dar ended him and dropped Mark's corpse to the ground.

There was no satisfaction in the kill. Dar was starting to feel the weight of the lives he had taken. The only thing that kept it all from crashing down on Dar was the anger, the anger and what they'd done.

"You killed him," the prince said, his eyes wide.

"Of course. He deserved far worse. Now, I have some other lesions to remove from the city," Dar spoke as he started to take his first strides, but the prince jumped in his way.

Dar had to give the man credit. He stood tall, considering what he'd witnessed from the Black Knight. "You cannot. This is for the country's justice system to handle; they will pay for their crimes. If every citizen were to take justice into their own hands, it would be chaos. It wouldn't be justice unless the Kingdom sees it as such."

The young man had an ideal, and Dar could respect that. But Dar also knew those in powerful positions with strong political ties often slipped by, only to slither back out and become a danger to more.

Snorting, Dar pushed past the prince. "Yes, your system has done an impressive job so far. Really. An incredible job."

"This is savagery! There is a civilized way to handle this!" The prince was red in the face as he tried to argue, but Dar was done.

Continuing to walk, he called over his shoulder, "Make sure this doesn't happen again. And fix this damn city."

"You'll be marked for this. If anyone sees that armor again, you'll be hunted," the prince spat.

Dar didn't really care, since he didn't plan to use the armor too regularly.

"I would recommend reconsidering going to war with me. I can be a powerful ally or a fearsome opponent. I could hunt you down, and all of Kindrake couldn't stop me," Dar lied.

The prince swallowed and stayed quiet.

"Good. Now, I don't care what you do when I'm gone. But pick this mess of a city up and squash whatever anti-ancient rhetoric has been going around. If it remains, I will be back and clean it up myself."

Dar turned around more fully, finding himself in a room full of stunned wizards, looking over his shoulder at Mark's corpse. Stepping forward once more, the wizards kept their distance, their hands holding enchanted charms ready to fight. Dar felt a smug satisfaction in their fear.

Once he passed them, they collapsed back between Dar and the prince, several of them going to whisper to the young man and look back up at Dar.

Already found a new master? Dar snorted. Fight burned in their eyes, but he could tell they were holding back. And he needed to reserve his strength and keep moving.

Leaving the manor quickly, Dar saw the commander sitting outside with a line of men, ready for a fight.

"Is the prince alive?" the commander asked.

Dar nodded his head, and the commander waved at the men, who moved in formation past Dar and rushed into the manor.

"I couldn't give two shits about these petty nobles. I'll have the prince secured in a few minutes, but my guess is he may have to give some orders to do with you. It would be best for you to get out of Bellhaven." The commander eyed Dar. "That's the best I can do. If you go around slaughtering nobles and we don't fight, the city will think we failed them."

Dar nodded. "Fine with me. This is your mess to clean up from here. But I have a couple more things I need to take care of. Where are prisoners to be executed being kept?"

The commander paused, clearly curious, before he seemed to decide it was better if he didn't know. "They're kept in a prison near the hanging racks. Down that way." He pointed.

Nodding, Dar headed off for his last stop before grabbing Lou's friend. Luckily, Mayor Tint's home was located near the duke's residence. As he approached, Dar recognized the men wearing Mayor Tint's colors in formation along the front.

The Tint family had been in league with Mark, operating where he couldn't. After all, a drooling idiot in a wheelchair couldn't whip up

the city to a frothing hate towards the ancients. No, the Tints had been responsible for that. They were the ones that executed Mark's orders, such as setting Cherry up and burning her tree.

Dar's steps turned into strides as he charged the gates, cutting through the bar and wrestling his way in. The men all took a step back, jostling against each other as the ones in back shoved the ones in front, back into their spots.

Seeming to get it together, swords were pulled and pointed at him as he came through the gate. Ignoring them as they bounced off his dark armor, Dar went to move forward. But the combined mass was enough to make it a challenge in the smaller gate.

Not wasting more time, Dar swung his axe, taking out all those near him enough that he could start to make progress forward. He left others behind him, focusing on any in his path as he made his way to the door. He noticed a few that he hadn't touched seem to pretend to be hit and go down with their peers. Cowards.

Dar stepped up to the manor and hacked the door down. He'd expected more soldiers inside, but all he found were servants armed with what looked like the largest kitchen implements they could find. Dar paused. Fighting soldiers was one thing but cutting down regular servants felt different.

A pan struck his armor, and Dar turned, taking in an older woman who froze there, like a deer in headlights, like she couldn't believe what she'd done. Reaching out, Dar plucked the pan from her hands and tossed it to the side. He motioned for her to step away from him, and she snapped out of her stupor, moving quickly, still shocked that she'd actually attacked him.

Looking over at the rest of the group, they all stood with arms trembling, clutching dearly to what they held. Dar worked to make eye contact with each before he started walking forward. They smart-ly moved out of the way, not bothering to attack him any further, just standing ready to defend themselves if he attacked.

At the top of the stairs, Dar found that most of the doors were ajar except for one oversized wooden door with just enough ornate detailing to set it apart from the rest.

The door didn't stay standing for long. The splintered wood crumbled, leaving him a view of three of the Tint family. Dar immediately recognized Mayor Tint and his brother, but he wasn't sure about the other young man.

"Please. We'll pay you," the elder Tint pleaded.

"Fuck that. How dare you come attack us!" Mayor Tint threw up an enchanted branch, and a blast of sharp wind cut across Dar's armor, barely touching his armor or slowing down his stride. It was certainly nothing compared to The White's Staff. "H-how?"

Dar remained silent, just stalking forward towards the corrupted family.

Mayor Tint gave it one more try, launching blade after blade of wind at Dar. Each of the attacks were as ineffective as the last. As Mayor Tint continued, his brother and the young man were taking slow steps back, seeming happy to leave him as a sacrifice and try to sneak out of the room.

Dar shifted, positioning himself in front of the door. It was then that Mayor Tint noticed that the others had been preparing to flee and leave him to his death.

"You bastards!" Mayor Tint shouted, sending the blades of wind flying at his brother. The other two attacked in response, and Dar stood there stunned, watching the family immediately turn on each other. Apparently, there wasn't a lot of love between them.

Blood sprayed from the other two Tint men with each blade of wind, but they pushed forward, trying to get their hands around Mayor Tint's throat. Unfortunately for them, Mayor Tint was victorious. His enchantment tore through both of them before they could reach him.

He looked up from his brother's dead body to once again prepare to attack Dar. Feeling sick to his stomach at what he'd just watched,

Dar decided not to drag it out any further. Moving forward, he removed Mayor Tint's head from his body with a single stroke.

Turning, Dar strode out of the room before he lingered too long and was forced to process everything. For now, he was done. It was up to Prince Gregor to build Bellhaven back up, like it should have always been.

Walking out the door of the Tint's home, he watched as people ran away from him, seeming to not understand that he wasn't out to kill them all, only those that were corrupt. He'd somehow become the villain in the story, his armor now tainted by the moment. But at least their avoidance made it easy as he moved towards his final stop.

Dar knew his hour was up. Mika would be making her way back towards home in the boat, likely livid with him and planning to grab as many people as she could to return. But he'd made a promise to Lou, and he intended to keep it.

Approaching the hanging platform, Dar looked around, working to spot the prison the commander had described. It took him a moment because the structure was partially underground, only the barred windows like gutters hinted to what it was.

Dar walked along them, wishing that he had asked Lou for what her name was so that he could more easily identify her. All he knew was that she was a childhood friend and stubborn. But he decided to take a gamble on her being loyal.

"Who here knows Lou the minotaur? Anybody willing to testify against him will be released from their sentencing."

A clamor of voices came from the barred windows along the street, most more than happy to sell out the minotaur. But there was one voice he'd been hoping to hear that stood out from the rest.

"How dare you! He is ten times the person you will ever be, you racist prick!" her tirade continued.

Walking over to the window where the woman was yelling, Dar was met by fiery green eyes, framed by wild, bright yellow, curly hair. She was petite for a woman that could project so easily.

As he smiled down at her, her eyes turned even more irate, and Dar realized he should probably clear the air quickly.

"I don't mean Lou any harm. I'm a friend. I just needed a way to identify who really was his friend. Seemed like the easy way to weed out the desperate liars."

The woman stopped screaming at him, but her eyes still held distrust.

Grabbing his axe, Dar began slashing through the bars, holding her within her cell. Her eyes became large as she backed up, looking around for a weapon.

"I'm not going to hurt you. Come with me, and I'll get you out of here and to a place where you'll be safe." Holding out his hand, Dar waited. But she didn't take it.

However, she did seem to find her voice. "Look, I'm no brainiac, but when a man covered in armor and blood comes and asks for you to go with them, you gotta question your sanity if you go with them."

Dar laughed, realizing just how intense he must look at the moment. "I get that. But they may also be a really great person to have on your side, especially when the town you're in already wants you dead. I need to keep moving, make your choice. Stay here or take a chance that I'll take you to Lou."

Staring at him a moment longer, she made up her mind and charged forward. He helped hoist her through the small window, her petite frame just fitting.

As he set her on the street, she held out a hand. "I'm Mer."

"Hi, Mer. Most here know me as Black Knight. We'll get into the details once we're out of here. Lou is safe and should be headed up the river with my dao companion. We'll find a safe space to hide out outside the village."

Starting to move towards a nearby gate, Dar made sure to keep Mer near him as he charged forward, the crowd parting for them.

Seeing soldiers starting to line up in front of the gate, Dar sighed. The unnecessary bloodshed was bothering him and Mer wasn't quite as durable as he was.

Sensing a place in the wall that was all granite, Dar turned, changing to that direction. As they approached, Dar created space big enough for both of them to fit through. Pulling Mer in front of him as they passed through, Dar protected her from a stream of arrows that fired, shielding her petite frame with his armor.

Picking her up against his chest, Dar charged forward, running out into the western forest and away from the bloody mess he'd just left behind.

***

Dar was surprised to see the boat still sitting exactly where he had left it. Grumbling to himself, he guided Mer towards the boat.

Mika was standing nearby, scanning the nearby area and spotted him immediately. She ran over, throwing her arms around him. When she finally let him go, he introduced the women.

"Mer, this is my dao companion Mika. Mika, this is Mer, Lou's friend. Speaking of which, where is Lou?" Dar looked around for the minotaur but stopped when Mika's face turned bashful.

"He wanted to leave when it got dark. But I just couldn't repair the enchantment." The small smirk on Mika's face made it clear she hadn't tried very hard. "But now that you're back, we can get going. Why don't you get out of that bloody armor? I feel like you have a story to tell."

Dar removed the helmet, handing it over to Mika. She didn't ask any questions, just walked to the water to wash off the worst of the blood.

They moved to the boat, and Mer ran over to check on Lou. While she was distracted, Dar pulled his armor back into his inner world. He'd deal with it all later.

Dar moved inside the boat, staying out of Mer and Lou's tearful reunion, and fixed the enchantment.

When he had finished, he let out a sigh of relief as he started the boat so they could head back to their village. As he stood at the wheel guiding them home, there was nothing stopping him from thinking. Dar couldn't hold off processing the day any longer.

"I've seen that look before," Mika said, grabbing Dar's face and holding his gaze. "Back when men would come back from a battle between clans."

"I slaughtered so many of them." He looked down, the weight of his guilt firmly on his head.

"For a reason, an important one. I know you, Dar, you wouldn't just kill a bunch of people if it didn't free many more. Now move aside—I'm driving. It seems I need to get you back to Sasha and Cherry as quickly as possible. Having your dao companions around you will help."

CHAPTER 25

Only a sliver of light made its way through the trees as the sun set beyond them, marking the edge of the river. Dar thanked his lucky stars that there hadn't been any major hazards in the river itself.

"Drop the anchor," Mika commanded Lou, who had awoken and had helped spot for any issues along the water. Dar had been lost in his own head.

"Come on." Mika disengaged the boat's enchantment, pulling Dar off the boat. The village had started stirring as they'd been spotted. They were back far later than had been originally planned.

When Sasha spotted Dar, her smile flattened to concern. She grabbed his arm, ignoring those who tried to approach Dar and bringing him away from the villagers. Mika followed.

"What the hell happened out there?" Sasha hissed at Mika.

"Dar will have to fill in a bunch of it, but maybe we go back to the hut first?" Mika suggested.

Sasha nodded, steering them all back over to the hut and motioning for Cherry to follow.

Cherry was quickly on their heels. "What's wrong?" She looked to Dar, and her face immediately grew concerned. She pivoted with eyes of fire to Mika.

Mika just held up her hands in surrender. "We went to check on Bellhaven. Something happened in the city; Dar came back with his armor covered in blood. And we also brought back a demon named Lou and a spirit named Mer. He's been like this since he returned. That's all I know."

"And where were you during all of this?" Sasha started turning on Mika, so Dar stepped in.

"I asked her to wait with the boat and Lou, and make sure they weren't taken if anything went wrong. Lou's friend was going to be killed in the morning, and I promised him I'd help her. I took the opportunity to also purge the city of Mark, Margret, and the Tints, who had taken control of the city. Now the prince stands a chance of saving it."

"And you thought this was your problem to solve?" Sasha's tone wasn't happy.

"It was only bound to get worse, and it has since we left. When I entered the city, there was a spirit's body hanging from the duke's manor like a decoration. Maybe I was rash, but I did what needed to be done." Dar's exhaustion showed in his face, and he sat down on the bed, putting his head in his hands.

The three women curled up on the bed around him, rubbing his back and wrapping themselves around him.

"I'm so sorry, Dar." There was understanding in Sasha's tone.

Cherry spoke first. "There's more though. You wouldn't look like this if that was all of it."

Dar nodded. "There was protection around Mark, Margret, and the Tints. I slaughtered a lot of soldiers in order to get to them and finish it. It wasn't much of a battle; they didn't even stand a chance."

"I'm not saying you're not powerful, Dar, but have you really grown so strong you could take out entire groups of soldiers?" Cherry said it softly, clearly not wanting to upset him.

"I am when I'm the Black Knight," Dar whispered, and instantly Sasha and Cherry understood. "And now the Black Knight is tainted. Too many died at my hand without any type of trial. The prince

promised to hunt the Black Knight now, to show his control of the situation."

"Shit," Cherry cursed and bit her lip. "But I think what you did was right. Killing the prince would have caused more problems, and it wasn't like you implicated Hearthway, yourself, or any of us. And the suit of armor already had a gruesome, if heroic, reputation."

"He can't wear it openly now, though. We don't want it to be tied directly to him or spotted by those in the future who may be from Bellhaven," Mika argued, looking between the group, trying to figure out where she fit in.

"No, Mika. I cannot wear it openly anymore. But then again, I don't want to walk around in that tin can, anyway. All the more reason to focus on making my own body stronger." Dar looked at his women. "I am going to start meditating on the other lesser dao in our family and prepare for the ettercaps."

Cherry nodded slowly. He knew she didn't love the idea of his meditation, but she seemed to understand the need.

"Tonight?" Sasha asked.

Dar looked at the three girls and sighed. "Not tonight. Tonight, I'd like to feel the comfort of the three of you."

"Three of us?" Sasha's eyes gleamed in the moonlight before she looked at Mika. "You know, Blair is going to be so frustrated."

Mika snorted. "Bitch can wait her turn."

It was so sudden that Dar couldn't help but burst out in laughter. Being back with them, in their hut, he felt his gloom start to melt away a bit. He'd do whatever it took to keep his women safe and create a world that would make them happy. If that meant having to destroy threats to them, he'd do it in a heartbeat.

They all undressed and laid down together, and Dar reveled in the feel of each of their flesh pressing against him.

It was only a short time before he drifted to sleep, sandwiched between them.

***

Cherry entered his inner world and kept him company as they fell asleep. He had a sneaking suspicion that she was keeping an eye on him.

That feeling only grew when he woke up to Sasha coaching Mika on what he liked best, and the girls continued to pass him around as they got ready for the morning. There was always one engaging him, keeping him distracted. He bristled a bit at being managed, but he knew their intentions were to help him.

Once they were ready, they headed out to breakfast.

"You look like shit," Blair said, sitting down on a stump near him.

"Uh. Thanks?" He wasn't quite sure how to take that one.

Mika glared daggers at Blair.

"What? He looks like shit, and coddling him isn't going to fix it. No one in the village knows what happened, but he doesn't look injured, just... hollow."

Dar grunted. He was still mentally exhausted from battling inner demons the previous day and didn't feel like dealing with it again.

But Blair didn't take the hint. "He looks like a demon that just went on... oh." Blair's mouth went wide as Sasha and Cherry joined the circle.

"What were you saying?" the dryad asked with an edge.

"Asking if I can get into this game of distracting the newly blooded," Blair answered honestly, taking a bite of food.

Dar scrunched up his brow at that. "Newly blooded? I have killed before."

"Not in cold blood," Blair answered. "I bet you've fought for your life or hunted out of necessity. There's so much that drives that. But killing in cold blood is different, like pushing a boulder up a hill, only for it to roll back on you afterwards."

"Enough," Cherry snapped.

Raising his hand, Dar stopped Cherry. "You sound like you're speaking from experience? How did you work through it?"

"Sex works wonders," Blair answered with a shrug. "You need to distract yourself and come to terms with what you've done. Only then can you process it."

"She's not wrong," Mika chimed in.

Dar remembered that Mika had mentioned similar looks in the eyes of warriors in her tribe. "How did you get past it? All the times a tribe was killed, or your tribe killed another?"

"Purpose," Mika said the word with gravity. "Find a purpose and keep to it. Tell the world that it is better off with you alive than the ones you killed."

Neither Cherry nor Sasha argued with that statement, and they all sat in silence, continuing to eat their food.

Others slowly trickled over. But it was still a relatively quiet breakfast until Russ sat down, nearly bouncing out of his seat, seemingly oblivious to the broader mood of the group. "So, the boat is good to go? We're all ready."

Dar nodded. He knew the chances of putting Russ off another day were slim, and he also knew the village would enjoy the bison if it worked. "Mika, do you think you could give them the rundown and pilot it for them today?"

Mika looked to her other dao companions for a moment before nodding. "Sure."

"Good. Then today I think I should focus on getting more foundations into the ground. And help Bart and his men set frames into the foundations too." After thinking about what Mika had said, he had settled on purpose.

"Great." Sasha did her best to smile.

"Dar!" Neko jumped into his lap, knocking the bowl out of his hands and clinging to him.

He let out a chuckle. "Morning, Neko."

Neko paused, her nose immediately going into the air as her eyes narrowed in on Mika. "Dar, she smells like you." Her words were clipped, but he gave her credit for the full sentence.

"Yes, she does. She's now my dao companion, like Sasha and Cherry."

Blair's head snapped up. "Fuck! I knew something was different today."

Neko nodded. "Fuck."

Mika turned slowly back to Blair. "Dar and I formed a connection before you even met him. Better not fall too far behind." She stuck her tongue out at her friend.

The salt spirit narrowed her eyes at Mika. "Challenge accepted."

Satisfied, Mika turned back to Russ and led the eager demon away, waving a hand high in the air as she left.

"Neko next?" the cat girl asked excitedly.

Blair buried her head in her hands. "Not so fast, Pussy Cat. You're with me today. No way I'm leaving you with mopey or he'll be seven inches deep in you."

Tilting her head in confusion, Neko stared at Blair, then back at Dar to answer what she hadn't understood in the spirit's comment.

Dar held his hands up in defeat. "Not going there."

"Also, seven is low," Cherry commented, causing Blair to splutter into her oatmeal.

"Alright. With that, I'm going to get to work." Dar passed Neko off to the girls and got up, heading into the cave, using his dao to sense where the walls were in the dark cave until he worked his way to the spot in the back. He smiled as he approached the home he'd been carving into the back of the cave, happy to be back in the familiar surroundings.

He took chunks of the granite out, leaving them in spots for future foundations. Glump still had to dig out spots for the foundations.

It wasn't long before Blair came in with Neko in her wake. Dar watched, curious about what she was going to do with Neko. The

salt spirit held a crystal of salt forward that glowed brightly in her hand, illuminating the cave.

"Wait a second, do you have a dao of light?" Dar asked.

Blair shook her head. "Dao of light would be a grand dao. No, this is just the dao of bright. It needs some level of light to work, but then my enchantment can cast a glow from that."

A bit of excitement went through Dar. Bright might help him on the way to flame. But then he paused. He wasn't there yet with Blair, and he shouldn't push it just to get further in his dao journey. But damn, it was tempting.

Realizing he hadn't responded, Dar quickly added, "Fantastic dao. I'm guessing that's not part of salt?"

"Nope, I'm working towards other things as well. Almost have my third greater dao." A smug smile spread across her face.

Dar failed to hide his surprise. "What is the second?"

"Not telling. Not until I'm in your bed, at least." Blair winked.

Dar resisted rolling his eyes.

"Is that the project you've been working on?" She peered around Dar, looking deeper into the cave and the home he had been building into the cliffs.

After setting so many foundations, Dar had removed dozens of tons of granite from the cliff, and the house here had grown considerably. Now he was starting to focus more on the details. But he wasn't ready to show it off yet, and he didn't want anyone to see it before he was finished. Shifting his weight, he blocked off her view.

When she raised an eyebrow, he just shrugged. "I guess I am being a little secretive about it, but I'll show it to everyone when it's ready."

Looking into the dark space, he had an idea. "But would you be willing to make bright enchantments? For this area, and for the village?"

"Sure." She gave a wide grin and pulled Neko along with her as she went to find a spot to pull salt from the cliffs.

Neko looked back beggingly at Dar, but Dar thought it would be good for Neko to spend some time with Blair. He wanted her to have more friends in the village.

Pulling another stone cart from the wall, he wheeled it out of the cave entrance, only to find Bart setting up around one of his foundations with dozens of split logs.

"Are you ready to start building up the frames?" Dar asked.

"Morning. You are getting to work early." Dar didn't miss the way the old blacksmith looked him over carefully. "Want to help us here?"

"Sure. Just setting these into the foundation?"

"Yeah, but careful of that end. There is an enchantment on it. One of Russ' girls has a dao of sticky that's on the bottom of each of the framing pieces. I'll still put nails in the upper sections, but we thought it would help."

Dar looked at the enchantment and then back up at Bart. "We could use something like that for the roofing tiles too."

"Already on it, We're keeping her busier than Russ would like." Bart grinned. "Though I don't think we are going to have enough tiles for more than a few."

"Let me see these for a second." Dar looked at the split logs and pulled his knife from his belt, adding sharp notches, almost like barbs in the wood.

Bart watched him work, curiosity burning in his eyes, but he didn't speak until Dar had finished. "What's the idea there?"

"Think of it like barbs on an arrow, only the frame pieces are the arrow, and the foundation walls are some poor deer. I can fill in these gaps, so hopefully it works as well as wood joinery."

Bart nodded. "I get it. Let's give it a try."

Dar lifted up the first log and leveled it with the short foundation wall before softening the granite and pushing the split log into place. Feeling with his dao, he filled in the notches as he went until the log was set with the foundation bulging around where the log was pushed in.

Bart grabbed the frame and started throwing his weight around, trying to shake it. The piece didn't budge an inch.

"Okay, that's as solid as it is going to get. Let's put in a few more and then my boys can start on the roof. Hopefully, we can get enough lumber for framing all the walls."

It wasn't going to be more than a single-story square box, but furnishing the insides would have to be a winter project.

Bart moved ahead of Dar and started doing his best to notch out the logs ahead of him, leaving Dar to the mindless repetition of pushing each framed piece into place.

While they worked, Dar realized that it might be the best time to talk to him about the dao fruit. Nobody else was around, and they'd gotten into a pattern that didn't need too much focus.

"So, Bart. There's something I've been meaning to talk to you about," Dar started off.

The old blacksmith looked up at him expectantly. "Is this about what happened yesterday or what's changed with my daughter?"

Blinking, Dar realized Bart already knew something was up with Amber. "Have others realized something is different with Amber and Marcie?"

"I don't think others have noticed anything about her or the other girl. But she's my daughter, of course I noticed. But she wouldn't say a word. You gonna tell me?"

Dar paused. He had aimed to talk to the man about the fruit, not have a conversation about how he'd essentially changed his daughter from being a human. He wasn't sure how Bart was going to take it. "So, you know that I may seem human, but I also have dao."

Bart nodded, stopping what he was doing to give Dar his full attention. "I do."

Dar continued, "Well, I helped both of them do something similar. They're now humans who can follow the dao path."

Bart's eyebrows climbed into his hairline. "And that doesn't seem like the sort of thing you should ask somebody's father about before

you do it?" Bart gave Dar a hard look, making him shift uncomfortably before Bart broke out into laughter.

"You should have seen your face!" He continued laughing for a bit before settling down. "I know my daughter. Amber wasn't going to give up a chance like that. We're good." The man turned, going back to his work.

Dar tried to broach the subject again. "So, that was related to what I wanted to talk to you about, but it wasn't quite it."

Bart looked back up, curiosity in his eyes as Dar continued speaking. "I want to offer the same to you and your wife. I'd need to help the two of you, and we'd need to find somewhere private to do it, but I'd like to make you both immortals." Dar paused, hoping he wasn't butchering the speech.

Bart looked shocked. "You can make anybody immortal? It's not limited?"

Dar shook his head. "No, there're limits, but there will be more in the future. For now, I'd like you and your wife to join us."

Bart fumbled for a moment, seeming torn. "I'm fine waiting if you give a couple to the boys cutting lumber. Hell, Frank would be a great choice. My wife and I can wait."

Dar smiled, even more sure that he'd made the right choice in trusting Bart if he'd be willing to step back and give it up for others. "I'm not looking for this to be obvious. At least, not yet. Having Frank suddenly act half his age would be too much."

"Ah. That... makes sense. So you are going in the order of people you trust?" A smile fell into place on his face. "I'm honored."

Dar shrugged. "You bet everything on this trip; you brought all the craftsmen. If I can't trust you, then I think this'll all fall apart."

"Tonight?" Bart asked hopefully.

"Sure. Tonight after dinner I'll send Amber with what you need and have her coach you through it."

Letting out a heavy breath, the blacksmith shook his head. "Crazy times." He turned to go back to work before spinning back. "What sort of dao will I get?"

"The quiet dao," Dar said, feeling a little funny at the one he was offering. "But you can form others on your own after this, and it comes with longevity and a stronger body."

Bart shrugged. "Maybe Tabby won't complain about my hammering in the house if I can be quieter about it. There's a use for everything."

Dar nodded. "You could learn some enchanting and make your house quieter."

The blacksmith's eyes crinkled. "Maybe we should do that to all the young couples' huts." He chuckled at his own joke and Dar joined him while considering that it really wasn't that bad of an idea.

"So, if my daughter is going to live forever, is she going to remain your maid?" Bart asked.

Dar nearly choked. He hadn't given that any thought, but now...

Bart laughed again. "The look on your face. It's fine. I have no doubt you'll treat her right. Heavens, what you've already done for her is enough that I doubt that girl will leave your side, even if you try and pry her off."

Bart snickered. "I've been meaning to thank you. I said I noticed a change, but I mostly meant just how darn happy she's been. And her body had changed a bit, but I figured she was just dressing differently or something."

Dar laughed, realizing he'd assumed so much more. "Oh, of course. I want everyone in my house to have the best I can give them. Even if their stations are a little different."

"Good. Now, if you make Tabby feel years younger with this immortal deal, and we have another girl, you better keep your mitts off her when she turns into a ripe woman."

"Like I'll have time for another woman." Dar let out a sigh. "At this rate, I'm going to be surrounded."

Bart shrugged. "That's a measure of the man you are if they keep coming."

Dar and Bart kept chatting idly as they worked, setting the frames for all of the foundations Dar had made.

CHAPTER 26

Bart's men crawled off the last frame. They had used several days' worth of lumber in a single day of framing, but now the village had rough frames for their homes, and family units were starting to inspect and admire their soon to be living places.

"Good work." Sasha walked up to his side as he watched the village. "Between these homes and the boat, you've brought a lot of excitement to the village."

Dar nodded, somewhat disappointed the work had been completed so quickly. The mindless task had helped him keep some of the thoughts in his head at bay, but it did help to see the villagers so excited as they bounced in and out of the homes.

"It's nice to see them full of hope," Dar said, although he knew his voice betrayed some of his melancholy.

"Yes, and I see we need to keep you distracted again," Sasha replied, giving him a knowing look.

He felt his face warm, not surprised she could read him so easily. Changing the subject, Dar told Sasha, "After dinner, I'm giving Amber two fruits for her parents. I'll let her coach them through the transition."

"Do you think that's safe?" Sasha asked.

"Yes, I think it'll be easier if it passed through people in the community rather than me teaching everyone." Dar realized he'd been

stretching himself thin, and it wasn't something he needed to do himself anymore.

He needed to look forward toward the ettercap issue since the preparations for winter were shaping up. The houses had made a huge leap forward, and in the worst case, people could start making thatch to cover their homes. It wouldn't be great material, and they'd need to replace it come spring, but it would get them through the winter.

Food was being packed away at an incredible rate. Cherry and the farmers were filling two side caves, which were being used for storage now that the housing situation was in a better spot. Dar hadn't realized just how much they were producing every day until he had seen the barrels piling up in the caves.

Sasha watched him from the side. "And which one will be our home?"

"It's almost done." Dar left it vague. It wasn't exactly done, but he was confident that it would be done in time for the winter.

Sasha went to pry a bit more, but she was stopped as Russ came sprinting into the village.

"Dar, good thing I found you. I need your help."

Dar braced at first, ready for a fight, when he realized that the look on Russ' face was closer to a child on Christmas morning. "Sure, let's see what you've got."

Sasha gave him a peck on the cheek and stepped away, back to her own tasks.

"You should see the herd on the other side of the river!" Russ chattered. "Thousands upon thousands of bison."

"Hunting was easy then?" Dar asked.

"Dangerous. When we took the first down, they charged us and circled the injured one."

Dar could see the boat from where they were, and he noticed that more than one large bison was getting pulled off the boat. "How many did you get?"

"Eight! We had to leave two behind. We just had to keep putting them down till they decided it would be safer to run." Russ smiled. "I'm hoping we can get these unloaded quickly and go back for the other two. We did our best to drain and dress them, but they are big fuckers!"

Mika shoved one off the boat onto the ground in front of three of Russ' girls before she looked up and spotted Dar, smiling and waving at him. "Hurry and help them get these back to the village. We need to grab two more."

"You got it. Mind sending the next over the edge? I'll grab it and start carrying what I can back." Dar stepped up to the bottom of the boat as Mika dragged the next one over.

"This guy is big," she warned, before she started to tip it over the edge.

Dar grabbed a leg and did his best to take the whole corpse over his shoulders. His strength helped him carry it, but it was awkwardly large at best. "Maybe we should get one of the carts to help with this, Russ. You grab one and we'll make the first trip back and grab a cart for the rest."

Russ' girls turned to give Russ a small glare before going back to work. Dar suspected that had been the original goal, but Russ had gotten too excited. Either way, they'd get these unloaded quickly.

"We'll get the rest off the boat and head over for the last two quickly," Mika said from the boat.

"Sounds good. I'll see you at dinner." Dar threw the bison over his shoulder and got to work hauling the meat back to camp.

When he and Russ arrived back at camp, there was a big stirring as the women preparing for dinner put down everything. The carcasses were too large for any of their tables, so they started laying out clean cloths and butchering them on the ground.

"How many do we have coming?" Tabby asked, laying down another cloth.

"Eight, and then two more that they have to go back and get."

Tabby blinked at Dar, stunned into silence for a moment. "Ten? What the heck are we going to do with all that meat?"

Dar laughed, knowing it would be a lot of work for the chefs. "We'll pack it in salt and put it in the cool cave. Just need to get it cleaned up." Dar hesitated when he realized she was staring back at him like he was dumb.

"Ten of these. That's going to be... tons of meat. We don't have enough salt for that, and it won't keep long in just the cool cave. If it was winter, we could pack them in snow..."

Dar cut off her panic, understanding her worry. "How about you cut them, and we just apply a surface layer of salt to keep for the night. Then we'll make a run here tomorrow to get more salt?"

Tabby looked at the girls behind her who were listening before turning back to Dar. "We'll do that. And everyone will be eating plenty tonight."

Dar let Russ handle the rest of the bison with the help of a cart, heading off to find Blair to see about getting more salt. He found her sitting down with Neko, the two of them talking in hushed voices.

"I see you two are hitting it off well."

"Fantastic, you might say." Blair didn't miss a beat before turning to him, her eyes meeting his. "You look like you need something?"

Dar sighed. "Salt. Lots of it. Russ came back with ten of those bison."

Blair let out a soft whistle as he hit the number. "There's no way I can pull that much from the cliffs, at least not in a short period of time. Think we can get the boat and go down to the ocean?"

"Yeah, if it isn't too much trouble. I thought you and Mika could maybe go down to get all you can tomorrow."

"All I can?" Her eyes opened wide as a joke before her smile gave it away. "Sure. I'll fill that boat to the brim with salt if that's what you want."

A squeal drew Dar's attention. Neko was sitting, playing with a piece of salt that was giving off bright light.

Dar watched, remembering his other question for Blair. "Think you could bring back plenty of crystals like that to enchant, too?"

"Sure, but be careful. Pussy Cat likes to steal them and play with them. Only way I kept her entertained today."

The cat girl in question turned to Blair with narrowed eyes. "Neko good." The shiny crystal quickly occupied her attention again.

"I feel like we owe you quite a bit for all of this," Dar admitted.

"Oh, I'm taking a chunk of that meat." Her eyes wandered before centering back on Dar. "And a room in your new little fort?"

He should have known she'd go back to inspect what he'd been trying to hide. "Hah, done."

He enjoyed the surprise that flitted across her face, but he knew he wasn't going to get rid of her, and she was becoming a part of the group. She'd have her own bed for the near-term as they figured out where it would go from there.

Her tongue stuck in her cheek, like she was physically stopping herself from saying what was on her mind. He had a good idea of what that might be. She had definitely started meeting him where he was more comfortable.

"Thank you," Dar said, trying to show in his eyes he meant more than just going to get the salt.

She smiled her acknowledgement before stating, "No problem. Just leave it to me and Mika. We've done things like this before."

Dar nodded, not wanting to tell her how to do her job. "Any extra you bring back you should feel free to hold onto. We could trade it when the next river boat passes."

Movement to the side caught his eye, and he noticed Marcie hanging to the side.

"Milord, Amber and I wondered if you couldn't help us with something?"

Dar shrugged. "Sure. Lead the way."

She surprised him by taking him out of the village and to the edge of the northern woods. As they entered the woods, Amber ambushed him, a knife slashing at his back. His red-headed maid was quiet as a

whisper; he wouldn't have seen her coming if it wasn't for her bright hair flashing in the corner of his vision.

Dar jumped back just in time as her knife came up short. His brain worked to catch up with what was happening as he realized that the knife she'd been using was wooden.

"Drat! I thought that would work." Amber looked disappointed.

"Told you." Marcie rolled her eyes.

Dar was still overcoming his surprise. "What are you two doing?"

"Practicing," they said in unison before giggling.

"We tried to learn to fight from Sam's husband, but he just taught us a few simple knife moves and moved on to teaching the others," Amber said.

Nodding, Dar imagined the man didn't think much of two human girls for fighting. "And you've brought me out to see if you could ambush me?"

Marcie shook her head. "No, we wanted help with how to use mana. She just wanted to see if she could surprise you."

"Oh. Well, good job doing that, and thanks for finding us a secluded place." Dar realized why they had taken him out to the forest. "Have both of you filled yourselves up with mana?"

They nodded together. "Yep, I can feel it floating through me. It's very strange, but also amazing."

Dar sat down and started to explain what he'd learned so far, realizing as he did just how far he had managed to come. It was easy to forget it in the need to be so much stronger.

He walked them through what it felt like to flood his channels with mana, feeling his body become much stronger, and pressurizing his mana to use his dao differently.

Both of them stayed quiet, asking a few focused questions and absorbing everything he said.

"Do you want to give it a try?" he suggested once he'd run out of things to share with them.

"Sure." Amber and Marcie got up and paced ten steps away in either direction. Dar thought it was a bit far for a knife fight, but he let them do it how they wanted.

"Go ahead and start us, milord." Marcie's wooden knife creaked as she tightened her grip.

"On three. One, two, three."

Both of them exploded forward with speed that would have made an Olympic athlete jealous. But rather than their blades meeting, they slammed their forearms together and started rapidly slapping away each other's knife hand while trying to control the others' wrist.

When they started switching the knife to the other hand and catching the opponent off guard, it started to get really interesting. Their reactions improved with each move, but Amber changed it up, grabbing Marcie's hair and pulling her head back.

"Ouch!" Marcie yelped before Amber's wooden blade tapped her on the neck. "Not fair! That's cheating"

"I don't think you'd mind, as you'd be dead," Dar said, impressed with what he'd seen. There was a fighter inside each of them. They just needed some training.

It made him realize that he needed to spend some time doing some similar training. He had relied a lot on his dao and enchantments to get him through battles, but he could use some basic combat skills.

Realizing they were both staring at him, Dar added aloud, "That was impressive. Mind if I join, two on one?" He wanted to see for himself how he would stand against them.

"Of course, milord." Amber panted for another second before forcing herself to breathe slowly and stand straight.

Both girls readied their wooden daggers and stepped back, their feet crunching the leaves underfoot as they readied themselves to spring forward.

Dar stretched his arms out and put his hands up. "When you are ready."

"No dao?" Marcie clarified.

"No dao. Just enhancements to your body with mana."

Both women nodded, flexing their hands and getting ready. There was a moment of pause with nothing but the soft patter of falling leaves, while all three of them waited for the other to make the first move.

Amber ended up being the first, lunging forward with her dagger. In response, Dar moved to grab her wrist, but she flipped the dagger to her other hand and stabbed at his arm.

More reaction than anything else, Dar slammed his palm into her chest, sending her flying back, her stab missing his arm.

Marcie filled the spot Amber left in an instant, her dagger going for his throat, moving as silent as a wraith.

Leaning back, her dagger just barely nicked his throat, Dar grabbed her arm, spinning and tossing her, but he wasn't comfortable with how close she'd been to slitting his throat. If this had been a real fight, he'd be feeling a trickle of warm blood on his chest.

Amber had recovered and was running back at him; meanwhile, Marcie flipped over and kicked off a tree. They were coming from both sides. It was smart.

Dar jumped back, putting both of them in front of him again. They moved quickly, throwing themselves at him with a reckless abandon that seemed more akin to assassins than fighters.

The two maids were relentless. He blocked them and threw them off, only for them to be back a second later. Their wooden daggers scratched him if he had the slightest distraction from the other.

Dar had no doubt they would have worn him down if it had been a real fight, and they were still just beginning their practice. He'd had no idea his two maids held such a natural ability towards being great assassins. Where Dar had been relying on brute force and power in fights, they'd started on a different journey, focused on speed and agility.

"Got you."

He felt a wooden dagger press into his back. That moment of distraction had been all they had needed. Dar held his hands up in surrender as the three of them breathed heavily.

"That was great. Both of you." Dar had learned more here than the brute force fighting he'd been doing.

But Amber shook her head. "No, you could have broken our arms or necks with some of those first movements when you grabbed and threw us. You going gentle on us gave us all our chances."

"Not to mention, I'm unsure if we could have pierced you with your dao," Marcie agreed.

"Still, I have to step up my game. You moved so quickly; how did you learn to kick off trees like that?" The agility and the acrobatics both of them had performed during the fight had surprised him.

"Practice and play. We are a lot tougher now and sometimes we just try something. It doesn't matter if we fall, since our bodies can take it now. So we experiment and often end up surprising ourselves at just what we are capable of. It's quite fun." Amber spun the wooden dagger in her hand, looking like she was getting ready for round two.

Dar raised an eyebrow. "Just practice and play, eh? Maybe we need to do this more often."

Both girls looked excited at that prospect. "Yes, please!"

Dar thought about if they should include any others. Their immortal status was a secret, so none of the soldiers would be a good choice. It would be clear very quickly that they held extra abilities.

But then he remembered that Mika came from a tribe that fought for their lives frequently. Even if they were more primal tactics, her experience in fighting other ancients and tribes likely had some form of martial arts she could teach. She'd be a great addition to help them all get better.

"Good. Then I think this is going to become a daily thing before dinner. We'll see if Mika has any lessons for us." Sparring with the beautiful women and improving his fighting abilities sounded like just the right way to spend some of his time.

CHAPTER 27

"You three look ragged." Sasha eyed Dar's clothes, which now had a few new holes in them thanks to Amber and Marcie.

"It was for a good cause, I swear." Dar gave her a quick kiss before taking a seat in their dinner circle.

Sasha looked unamused. "Great. I can't wait to hear it."

The rest of the girls were already there, watching the two of them.

"Marcie, Amber, and I were training in the forest. We focused less on our dao and more on our enhanced bodies." Dar smiled and looked at the rest of them. "I think it should become a family training session every night before dinner."

Shifting his focus, Dar looked at Mika specifically. "I was wondering if you ever had any formal training? From your time in the tribes?"

Mika paused, seeming unsure of her answer. "I've been trained, but it's nothing like what they teach in Kindrake. It's a little more savage, less straight formations and formality."

Shrugging, Dar didn't care what it looked like. It might even be better if they had a unique style that others hadn't trained to fight against. "That's fine. Would you be willing to run us through some of the training routines you used to do tomorrow?"

Blair cleared her throat. "After we get back from the ocean. And am I invited?"

"Of course." Dar paused. "To both of those. We'll do it after you get back, and you are welcome to join us. I trust you to help keep our secrets."

The salt spirit smiled and went back to her meal.

"Excuse us." Amber bowed and stood, pulling Marcie along with her to the central hearth.

"Why are we learning to fight?" Cherry asked.

Dar nodded towards the two girls walking away. "They actually fought very well today. If I didn't have my enchantments, they could have taken me. Given we expect trouble in the future, I realized that we should all hone our skills so that we can best handle any situation. Brute force won't always be what is needed in the situation, and so far, it has been my go-to."

Sasha wrinkled her nose in distaste, but her answer contradicted her face. "That makes sense. I don't want to be anywhere near the ettercaps or a human soldier. Even though I don't want to fight, I don't think I'll have that luxury next to you, Dar. I'll join you in training."

"Neko?" The cat girl pointed to herself.

"Of course. But no claws."

She nodded firmly to herself, flexing her hands with a slightly worried look. Dar did not get the feeling that she was truly confident she wouldn't end up trying to use them in a fight. He decided he should spar with her first, his hard dao ready, in case she slipped up the first few times.

Neko sat there for a moment, extending and retracting her dao of sharp around her fingers, nodding to herself when she'd held it back.

Marcie walked up then, coming back with a bowl of stew and handing it to Dar.

As he went to eat it, Dar realized it really wasn't much of a stew; most of the dish was filled with meat. "They really wanted to use up this bison, didn't they?"

He took a bite; it was gamey but tender. He knew wild kills were hard meat to work with, so he was happy with the surprisingly tasty dish.

Song emerged over by the fire, and Dar looked over to see Russ dancing around the flames with the bison bull's head on his shoulder. He was doing a small jig, swinging around while his women clapped on from the sides to the beat of the music.

Spotting Dar watching him, Russ broke away from his dance and came over to their circle. "Like the meat?" He had a wide grin across his face.

"Very good. Thank you, Russ. The entire village is eating well tonight thanks to your efforts." Dar gave the demon the accolades he wanted.

And the gnoll couldn't have grinned wider at the praise. "Thank you. There's plenty more where that came from!" Then he danced away with the bull head to the next group.

A thought flickered through Dar's mind, and he quickly looked around, trying to find Lou in the crowd. Lou could easily object to Russ dancing around with a bison head, and Dar wanted to cut off any tension quickly. But, when he spotted the minotaur, Lou was sitting with Mer, eating the stew, seemingly happy. They were caught up in some discussion that had Mer giggling and nudging Lou in return.

Relaxing, Dar went back to enjoying his food. "Russ seems happy," Dar commented to the girls.

"He found his place," Sasha pointed out. "I think after everything with the ettercaps, he's figured out where he stands in the pecking order. So now he's focused on doing his role the best he can, including bringing back a bounty of food."

"As long as he's happy. I haven't seen him smile this much before. I'm glad he has a sense of purpose now." A smile touched Dar's lips as he looked around the circle at the lovely ladies that made up his home. They were with him one hundred percent, and he loved them for it.

Glancing around the circle again, Dar's eyes caught on Marcie. She didn't seem quite as pleased as the others; her face was filled with confusion more than anything.

Clearing his throat, Dar asked, "Marcie, mind helping me with something?"

He had noticed there was something on her mind before when they were training, but she'd never spoken up. Maybe one on one, she'd be more willing to open up.

"Sure." She jumped to her feet and handed her bowl off to Amber.

Sasha gave him a questioning look, but he waved to her that he had it under control and walked away with Marcie.

"Milord, where are we going?"

"Just for a walk to talk," Dar answered, and then decided to be direct. "I noticed you had something on your mind earlier and then again tonight at dinner. I wanted to get you alone and see if you wanted to talk about it?"

"Oh." She drew up short. "I—uh. I'm confused."

Dar waited, giving her his attention as they kept walking, letting her set the pace. He couldn't help until she figured out how to put what she felt into words.

"You see, after the other morning, I'm not sure how to feel."

"About when you woke me up?" Dar clarified.

She nodded, some of her hair falling in front of her face. "Amber gushes about how it feels to make you cum with her mouth. She acts like it's the best thing ever."

Dar nodded. Amber had certainly been eager and seemed to enjoy herself, so he wasn't surprised, although it was always nice to hear. "But for you?"

Marcie paused before responding, "It wasn't bad, but it was weird. And, when I went deep, it got a bit uncomfortable. Maybe I'm just no good."

Dar paused, pulling her chin up to face him. "You don't have to feel the same, Marcie. I have no expectations. There are other things we can explore when you are ready."

Her cheeks grew rosy at his comment, and she quickly responded, "I don't mean to say never again. I liked it—I did! It's just... it wasn't as I expected. I think I had just always thought it would taste like... the dao fruit... based on how everybody talks."

Dar laughed. "Well, I wouldn't know, but it seems hard to compete with dao fruit." Turning more serious, he added, "I'm sorry it wasn't what you had imagined. We'll have to play more to find the things you enjoy most. What's it like with you and Amber?"

"Lovely." Marcie blushed and looked towards him.

Dar had seen enough to know the two women were very close. He wasn't surprised that they also enjoyed each other. "What do you like?"

Thinking for a moment, Marcie replied, "Amber sweeps me up and pins me down until I beg her for release. Even then, she just does with me as she wants. It's very... possessive."

Dar nodded, everything becoming clearer for him. "She takes the lead? Pushes you down, aggressively pleasures you, and doesn't take no for an answer till you pop?" That sounded exactly like Amber, and he suddenly realized that Marcie might have been taking tips from a girl who enjoyed the opposite role that she did.

"Yes." She ducked her head.

"And was waking me up with a blowjob her idea?" Dar asked.

Marcie seemed to realize he was onto something. "Yes. That's what she said was so amazing."

He smirked. "Marcie, sex isn't the same for everyone. People like different things. What makes it like a sunrise for the first time for Amber isn't the same for you. Actually, it sounds like it might be just the opposite."

The maid made a silent O with her mouth before coming back to herself. "Then what would make a sunrise for me?"

Dar considered it, coming up with an idea. "How about this: I'll give you a teaser of what I'm thinking, and you can try it with Amber. If you like that, then I think we have a lot of new things to explore."

"Okay." A flicker of excitement danced in her eyes.

Dar continued, "Ask her to tie your hands behind your back. And ask Sasha if she can make you a small silk rope, so it isn't uncomfortable."

Marcie looked confused, but there was an interest as well. "Okay. I... I think I will."

"Just try it. If you like that, I have more ideas."

"Thank you." Marcie blushed, looking away.

Dar turned her to face him once more. "No, thank you for confiding in me. I know this isn't an easy topic to talk about."

"En." She nodded with a small noise of approval.

With that, they turned and walked quietly back to the circle. As soon as they approached, Amber grabbed Marcie's arm, dragging her off. Dar had no doubt Amber wanted debriefing about what they'd talked about. He hoped she'd be open to helping Marcie try it out.

Pivoting his attention to the leader's circle, it looked like they were already kicking off their discussion. Dar went over to join them.

"Evening, folks. I hope you all enjoyed Russ' bison. I found it super satisfying." Dar tried to give Russ the recognition he seemed to crave.

Mindy wasn't far behind him and gave Dar a winsome smile and thumbs up.

Russ puffed his chest out a little more. "If those bison are still here, that means they might be weathering the winter in that field. We'll have easy meat all winter."

"It'll get harder to cross the river, but I'm sure we'll find a solution. It's a big step towards food security for the winter for sure," Dar agreed. "How are the crops, Cherry?"

"We're filling the new containers. Now that we've decided that the smaller cave is for food, we are moving everything into there. We've started plowing out a third field in case we have a few more weeks before the weather turns."

Samantha spoke up. "I don't think we have that long. I can feel winter coming. But I'll be right there with you hoping for it. How about the homes?"

Dar looked to Bart for that update.

"The ladies are making bundles for thatching out of the stalks of the crops. They won't be perfect, and we'll probably need to replace anything we use for walls next summer, but they'll hold for the winter. Wood is coming in, but there's no way we'll be able to make enough planks in time to cover the houses."

"Are we good on the material for the thatch?" Dar asked.

"Reeds and grass would be better, but the girls promise me that the corn husks can work in a pinch. There's apparently a big pile of them they were going to burn, so they were already bundling those for roofing material. We'll have to thatch the walls too, but thankfully, we only have half a wall to thatch." Bart gave Dar a big grin.

Dar noticed that the old blacksmith looked a touch more youthful and gave him a bigger smile. Most people would likely assume it was just that he was more excited and that was causing less stress on his face, but Dar could tell that he'd been successful at working with Amber.

Dar looked around at the rest of the participants before focusing on the task that he was most concerned with. "So. Ettercaps. Rex, anything to report?"

"Nothing from the forest. We are still running double shifts, but the girls are getting worn thin. I was going to ask if we couldn't relax things a bit." The avian demon's expression was impossible for Dar to read, but based on his voice, he had some genuine concern about the girls getting burned out.

Dar wished he could agree, but it was still too risky. "I don't think we can do that. Instead, how about we bring a few more people under you, Rex? Give your girls a break at least."

The entire group nodded at that, and Sam spoke up, "We have enough meat for a week easily. Russ, could you and your girls help give Rex a break?"

The gnoll looked crestfallen that he was about to lose his hunting time, so Dar jumped in.

"Not permanently. Just mix in with Rex's people for a couple days and let his people cycle out for some much needed rest. You'll be back to hunting bison in no time."

Hearing that, Russ nodded. "I suppose we make the most sense, with our skill set being the closest to the guard. But I don't always want to do this."

"Agreed. That brings us to the next point. We need to start focusing on a solution for the ettercaps." Dar looked around the group. "Sam, how's training going with your husband?"

The old lady smiled. "Great. He says the demons are some of the best soldiers he's worked with, and that's not just cotton to stuff between your ears. I can tell by how happy he is that it must be going well."

Dar looked to Rex, who seemed to agree. "Great, I was thinking that, if the ettercaps slow down in the winter, we look at starting to strike into the forest on the first snowfall."

"Get them while they are slow?" Glump clarified.

"Something like that." Dar had a few other plans in his head. It involved mastering the dao of combustion and coaching Amber and Marcie through the same exercise. They'd make up a solid group capable of destroying the webs.

"This is going to be an effort for the full village. Even if we can't kill them all, we have to push them back into the forest. Do we see any during the patrols?"

Rex nodded slowly. "Yes, and it's gotten worse. They have been active in the southern woods the last two days. It isn't like before, where they seemed to come into the woods to attack. They are actively living and hunting in those woods now."

The rest of the group tensed at that news.

"Why is this the first time we are hearing this?" Sam demanded.

Rex held up a hand to forestall her. "One day was an anomaly. Today was the second day, and I'm reporting it. I am also worried, but there was no point in alarming everyone if they were just agitated yesterday and retreated today."

However, Dar was very concerned. Animals moved like that for one reason. "They are hungry, and it sounds like they are running out of food deeper in the forest."

"You're worried that might get them to leave the forest?" Glump asked.

"Best motivator there is for a predator like those ettercaps. If they get hungry enough, I doubt that the edge of the woods is going to be a deterrent."

The group went quiet at that, each of them stewing on their own issue.

"Should we start the palisade again?" Bart offered.

Dar shook his head. "I doubt that will do much to stop these guys. They'd just scale right over it and make some nice webs that completely make a wall useless. They climb into the trees, no problem. Let's continue to monitor and make sure we continue to show a strong force. I want to look like it would be a lot of work to get food from us."

"I could lead a party to harass them?" Russ offered, and Dar suspected he wanted to get out of guard duty for that.

"That might not be a bad idea, but let's get everyone training with a weapon and give Rex's people a rest so they can help you with that. The last thing we need is to lose anyone. Let's not give the ettercaps a taste for humans and ancients."

Russ deflated, still clearly frustrated at being stuck on guard duty, but it was the right thing for the village. If ettercaps were getting more active, it was the most important time for the guard to be alert when they were on watch.

It also meant Dar was running out of time to remove them as a threat.

CHAPTER 28

"Boss!" a kid's high-pitched voice broke into the meeting. Dar looked down to see the miniature version of Glump, the only exception being his bright red hair.

"Kro. This is an adult conversation. Please go back to your mother," Glump said steadily, and Dar could see the little kid deflate.

"I think we were about done, anyway," Dar suggested, not wanting to get too in between a parent and their parenting.

The group nodded, and Bart stood, slapping his knees. "My old bones need some rest. But we are almost ready for winter."

There were murmurs of accent as the leader group broke up, and Kro looked up at Glump hopefully, taking a big step even closer to Dar.

"You can spend time with him as long as you are back in our hut before dark, and you come home if he tells you to," Glump croaked, looking between them. "Really now, you are becoming such a handful."

Kro completely ignored the last part, instead turning to Dar with his first of likely many questions that night. "Is it true that you beat up hundreds of people?"

Dar chuckled. "I don't see everyone walking around with lumps on their heads."

"No! Not here. People say you saved the big guy and his spirit lady-friend from Bellhaven. Beat up all the baddies." Kro jabbed in the air to show what he meant. "You took them all on and were so powerful! And..." Kro was nearly jumping up and down as he recounted all that he'd heard.

Dar herded Kro along with him as they headed back to where Dar's family was sitting.

"Yes, I did beat up some people. But only the bad ones."

"Waaah. So cool." Kro did a few air punches, making noises to compensate for the lack of enemies present. He couldn't help but be cheered by Kro's enthusiasm. Life was so simple in his eyes.

As they approached, the girls looked curiously at the little Kro trailing behind, fists still swinging as he talked and babbled about his imaginary battle.

"So what did you learn today, Kro?" Dar asked.

"Hi, Cherry." Kro froze from seeing Dar's dao companion before remembering the question and answering, although his attention still seemed focused on Cherry. "We learned lots of things, like types of good and bad bugs around the field. Sam taught us about fertilizer and why poop isn't just gross but useful too."

Cherry seemed amused at Kro. "Hello, little troublemaker. Why don't you tell Dar about how you brought mud into the field today?"

Kro blushed bright crimson and muttered something under his breath.

"What was that?"

"I like mud! Mud is great. I thought the plants would like it too." Kro hid his face after he said it.

"Plants like soil and water, but mud is just a bit too wet of soil for them most of the time." Dar reached down, ruffling the kid's hair.

"I know," Kro said defensively, drawing out the word. "Cherry already told me. I won't bring mud into the field again."

The dryad smirked. "You should have seen him, carrying it by the armload into the field and making a mess of himself."

Dar knew that Glump had the dao of mud and that he likely came from some sort of frog. Dar wouldn't be surprised if it was a frog that had his home in the mud, but he found it curious that Kro would also be so drawn to it.

"Do you have a dao?" Dar asked.

Kro looked shocked at the question. "Of course not. But one day, I'll have dao like dad or mom."

There was a gathering of some of the other kids not far from their circle chattering and looking at Kro, who had noticed them by now. They were all motioning for Kro to come join them.

"Thanks, boss. Gotta report back." Before Dar could say anything, Kro was off, running towards the kids and yelling. "He really did beat up hundreds! Even thousands!"

Dar couldn't help rolling his eyes. Kids. Chuckling, he turned back to the circle to see all the women looking at him with big smiles.

"I didn't peg you for someone who'd like kids," Blair blurted out, the others seeming to have variations of agreement.

Dar paused, considering it. He had always figured they would be a part of his life at some point; he just hadn't been at that point yet. "Kids can be fun. I've never had any, but I'm not necessarily against them with the right person at the right time."

Mika licked her lips and looked around at everyone else before speaking. "When is the right time?"

Dar started to speak, but then paused, reconsidering. "I guess it's probably impossible to time it right, but I'd like some stability before bringing a kid into the mix."

Before they could nudge him more on a timeline, Dar pivoted the conversation slightly. "How do kids work with spirits and demons?"

Sasha chuckled and covered her mouth. "Dear Lug, I thought you were already an expert at that."

Rolling his eyes, Dar watched as Sasha smiled, pleased with her joke. "Oh hush. Not that. I meant with dao and interspecies sort of deal," he said.

They looked confused. "Interspecies?"

"Can a spirit have a child with a demon, or a human?"

"Of course," Cherry said, sounding confused that it was even a question. They probably hadn't put all the research into genetics that he was used to and just relied on if it worked or not.

"What about dao? How does that work with kids?" he asked.

That one clearly had a more complicated answer, because the girls chewed on it for a minute before Sasha explained.

"Children among the ancient races are extraordinarily rare. In several hundred years, a pair of dao companions might not even have one child. It seems even worse for those further on the dao path. But, when they do happen, the kids don't instantly have dao. As they grow, they always seem to form a dao close to either of their parents very easily. It's a strange state, where it almost seems like they've started their dao path, but just haven't taken a step yet."

Dar nodded and tried to simplify. "They are pre-dispositioned for dao, but they don't have it yet?"

"That works," Cherry agreed. "They're almost similar to monsters like the hellhounds. They might not have had a true dao, but they are the blood of something that did. A dao runs in their blood so to speak."

"That makes some sense. If we've all used the dao to modify our bodies, then there might be something we can pass along."

The girls all nodded at that, but it prompted more questions for Dar. "Then why isn't there a group of The Whites, or any other celestial demon's children, running around becoming a force to be reckoned with?"

"I've never heard of a celestial demon having a kid," Sasha said sadly.

"Never?" Dar was shocked. They'd been around for thousands of years.

"Cherry said it was rare for those further on the dao path, but that might be an understatement. Most of the children among ancients had parents that only had a lesser dao when they had the child. That Glump is a greater demon with a kid is... special."

"What about a second generation?" Dar was starting to see how humans had taken over if the ancient races struggled so much to propagate.

Cherry shrugged. "I don't know of any."

Dar leaned back and let out a small whistle. "None?" he asked, looking at the rest of the girls.

They all shook their heads. "This seems to shock you," Blair commented, tilting her head in confusion. Dar remembered that she didn't know all about his past.

Sasha started to try to explain it away, but Dar raised his hand to stop her. "It is shocking. Then again, with your longevity, it does make a sort of sense. I just suddenly feel like we took the option of having kids away. I just didn't know."

"We can always try. Trying can be fun." Sasha patted his leg. "You never know."

Dar looked up at the sky, wondering what it meant to be immortal and try with her. Would it help or make it even harder?

"Yes, we can certainly try. If you want kids, I'm open to it." He kissed Sasha, which made her blush and pull back, grabbing his hand.

"Well then, this has been a fun night everybody, but I think I have work for Dar." With that, Sasha got up and dragged Dar away from the campfire quickly.

Cherry and Mika were up in a flash to join them.

"No, we don't get to go with, Pussy Cat." He heard Blair mutter behind him as Neko let out a growl of protest.

***

The next week flew by in a blur of work. Dar busied himself forming larger storerooms in one of the caves. He had needed to remove more stone there and in the house he was building in the back of the large cave.

He used all of the extra stone he had removed to lay a foundation for the palisade. If he kept at it, he'd end up building a stone wall around the palisade, eventually.

When that got tedious, he took a break and started to bring stone out for a foundation around the central hearth. They'd need some better gathering areas as well.

Periodically, Kro would show up at Dar's side, asking all sorts of questions that the kids had come up with, only to run away and report Dar's answers. It appeared he had become the official messenger of the group.

As he walked back into the cave, Dar once again scoped out their food reserves. There had been shock at the camp the night before when they'd announced the final counts for grain. Cherry had been busy and blown away everybody's expectations. He knew it had taken a lot out of her to do so much, but she'd given their town a really great chance at surviving the winter. They also had a lot of bison and fish thanks to Russ, Mika, and Blair's efforts.

Sasha had been busy as well over the week, working with the women preparing thatching. The tradesmen had put down all their other work and were laying it on the houses as fast as it was made. They'd get the roofs and walls filled in for winter.

Dar had hoped they'd be able to have clay tiles, but they were running out of time. It was getting too cold to dry them, and they just didn't have enough. Next spring, they would have to work to replace some of the thatching with the longer lasting clay tiles.

Focusing on his current task, Dar worked on his latest granite project. He was trying to make large containers out of stone, with spouts at the bottom.

"Heya, hunk," Blair said, walking in, pushing one of the village's carts, which was filled with salt.

"I got this one ready. Do me a favor and send the salt up there, so I don't have to carry it?" he asked.

"On it." Blair bent back over the cart, her tight rear outlined in one of Sasha's black dresses. Then she straightened up, and with her came a large mound of salt flowing around her.

She brought it up and over to his new creation. She had to shift up onto her tiptoes to reach the top of the vessel. The salt she had moved flowed over her into the stone tank. When that batch was completed, she leaned back over and repeated the motion.

Dar just watched as all the salt filled the container. Hearthway wasn't going to run out of salt anytime soon at the rate she'd been gathering it. Dar had built this just to store her salt, so they wouldn't keep wasting barrels that were better for storing grain, anyway.

"Like what you see?" Blair asked, arching an eyebrow as she looked over her shoulder with a blush when she was done.

Clearing his throat, Dar coughed away the awkwardness, realizing he'd been staring at her butt while she was leaning over. "So, tell me more about you, Blair."

"Well, what do you want to know?" She watched him, seeming pleased at his interest. "I'm not quite as old as Mika; I'm only about a hundred and fifty years old."

"But you are further along than Mika in your dao?" Dar asked, surprised.

Blair shrugged. "I've spent quite a bit of time on it. Not that Mika hasn't. But I think she spent a lot of time doing other things across the sea."

"She told me about some of those times, lots of war."

"Lots of drinking too," Blair laughed. "When I first met her, she just liked to laze on the beach and drink. I can't imagine it was that different before she came to Kindrake."

"What about you, then? What do you do for pleasure?" As Blair went onto her tiptoes again, Dar shifted the granite under the tank to make a few steps.

Taking them, she gave him a big smile. "Thanks." She moved and deposited another load of salt. "Lots of pushing my dao, plenty of

fun with men. But a good game of cards or dice really gets my blood going."

Dar snorted. "Gambling? Ever play strip poker?" It seemed right up her alley.

"Never heard of it. Tell me about it."

"Oh, well, you play cards, or I guess you could gamble with dice. But you bet articles of clothing you are wearing and lose them accordingly."

Blair's eyes shone and her smile grew a little too wide. "That sounds fabulous. Strip poker," she repeated the name. "I'll remember that one."

Dar had no doubt that she'd find a way to involve him in a future game of strip poker.

"I talked to Mika about the salt you used to sell. She said you had trouble in the past? When we see more riverboats come, do you want us to sell some of your salt?"

"Doesn't matter much to me," Blair said, grabbing another load of salt. "Gathering salt like this is easy. I've never really focused on accumulating a bunch of wealth. Anytime I have in the past, I've lost it gambling, or someone took it from me."

Blair paused, looking Dar in the eyes. "Personal strength is the best source of wealth. Getting my grand dao will be worth more than all the salt I could ever pull from the ocean."

"I'd had no idea." Dar was a bit surprised by the serious tone that she had taken.

"Can't a girl want to be powerful? That, and want the pleasure of a man. The two aren't mutually exclusive." She gave him a wink before going back to her work.

Dar hesitated. He hadn't meant it that way. "I just mean you seemed less serious, more like you'd enjoy a party before you'd train."

Blair snorted at that. "I just like a little D, okay? Well, I like a big one better, if I'm honest. I like the physicality."

"Yet you stayed, even though I wanted something emotional?" Dar pushed her further.

"Mika," was her one-word answer. "She means a lot to me. We have stuck together for a while. If she's in, then so am I."

"Oh, if you are just here for Mika—"

But Blair cut him off. "Oh, stop. If I had zero interest in you, I'd pull Mika away. I'm interested, trust me." A bit of heat blazed in her eyes as they locked onto his. He ended up looking away first. She had such intense violet eyes that it was almost hard to keep her gaze.

Changing the subject, Dar asked, "So how close are you to your third greater dao?"

"Not far at all. I just need one more lesser dao. Something like hard would do just the trick." She looked at him hungrily.

"Funny that. I'm hoping to form a greater dao of flame next. Something like bright would be perfect."

Blair blinked and then broke down into a laugh. "God, it makes both of us sound like absolute idiots. Picking a companion for their dao."

"Yeah, I try not to think of it as a transaction or wanting a companion just for their dao. I feel like that's a slippery slope into treating ancients like tools."

Blair nodded. "I'm sure after what you saw in Bellhaven you would be against that. Mika told me about how you saved her from Henry. Thanks for that; she was in that mess partially because of me." A guilty look flashed across Blair's face.

"About that, she said you two were selling salt in the city before you ran into some hard times?"

He saw her wince, even though her back was turned. "Yeah, I got into a bit of trouble with gambling debts. Then they devalued my salt. It was a hard climb out of it, but they held the ropes the whole way, so I just had to play it as best I could."

Dar had seen a number of those types of situations in the past, where debt was used to keep a person under control. "At least that is done."

"I mean, the debt is still out there. But I don't think they are going to be able to collect on that anymore. At least, not for a while. I'm

hoping that debt gets forgotten." She paused after her latest deposit in the vessel. "All done."

"Great, let me just seal this up." Dar used his dao of granite to seal up the container. It would last better that way.

Blair walked out of the cave with him and got in the cart to drive it away. They were near the southern palisade wall. And, as he inspected it, he noticed something coming out of the forest.

Cursing as he realized his axe was back in his hut, he summoned one of the Black Knight's axes.

"Whoa." Blair looked at the axe. "Wicked."

"Not now," he said, eyes locked on the emerging ettercaps. "Get the guard."

Sensing the urgency, Blair jumped out of the cart, but as she turned, Rex and several of his women were already coming.

"They're out of the forest." Dar pointed. Three ettercaps were milling about outside the forest. They didn't seem to be heading towards the village yet, but their webs were expanding into the bushes outside of the territory they'd kept to.

"It's just a few," Rex offered.

Dar nodded, but it meant that they were going to become a bigger threat, and soon. Jumping, Dar caught the top of the palisade and threw himself over. "But we can't allow them to feel comfortable expanding."

Dar rushed into the first ettercap, swinging his axe to cleave its head off. The first one went down without a fight, but the second two had more time to prepare before he moved for them. They shifted into a fighting stance.

Dar read their body language and dodged to the side before they could manage to tangle him with their webs, like they once had. The training with the girls had helped improve his ability to read his opponent, and it was already paying off.

Rex came down from the sky at that point with a rough spear, slamming it straight into another of the ettercaps, leaving just one.

Dar backhanded the last ettercap, tackling it to the ground and using a knife from his belt to stab into it and kill it quickly.

"You fought well," Rex commented, seeing Dar get up off the ground.

"I feel a little more deadly if I'm honest."

Rex just gave him a predatory smile. "Yes, there wasn't any hesitation."

CHAPTER 29

Dar wasn't quite sure what to think about Rex's comment. Rex had clearly meant it as a compliment, but Dar wasn't sure how comfortable he was with that.

He'd like to rationalize it as a clear choice. The monsters were threatening his village, but Dar also had to admit he still had paused when the village was attacked when he'd first come to the world. Something in him had changed.

That thought lingered as he left to go meet up with the girls for another training session near the northern woods.

"Hey, Dar." Mika waved at him as he stepped around the trees. She already had a sheen of sweat covering her, as did Marcie and Amber. They had started without him.

After saying hi, Mika turned back to Marcie and Amber, continuing where she'd left off. "Here's how you break someone's leg." She thankfully demonstrated it slowly.

So far in their lessons on the training styles Mika had learned on the Mahakhlan islands, Dar had determined that it must have been a brutal place to live. The fighting style was brutal.

There were basic strikes with weapons that seemed pretty standard, but when they got to hand to hand and weapon practice, Mika's martial arts had turned to a more gruesome focus of breaking bones and destroying joints.

Dar felt a shudder threaten to rise up his spine as he recollected one of their earlier training sessions. Mika had wanted to show the moves at full speed and asked that he work to reinforce his body for the hits. He could still feel the ghost of pain in his knees after her attacks.

"Now that you are stronger than even a trained soldier, you can snap the low kick like some of the demons I used to know." Mika pulled a fallen branch from the ground. It was a solid few inches around. She stood it up and raised her knee up parallel to the ground before flexing her ankle and snapping her foot down in such a way that it almost stomped against the branch.

Snap.

"If you hit it like that, you can break their leg just above their ankle."

"Oh." Both the maids nodded, carefully paying attention to every move Mika made. "I can see how that would be useful. It's a pretty quick move. If you can catch them distracted with something high, then..." Amber stepped hard on a twig, snapping it under her foot.

While they were becoming slightly terrifying in their techniques, Dar was also pleased that his women would be able to defend themselves and their family. "Why do I get the feeling that if I leave you three alone too long, you will snap all the branches in the forest?" Dar joked as he walked further into the training area.

Marcie blushed and bowed to him. "Afternoon, milord." Amber was quick to join her.

"Afternoon," Dar replied as Cherry and Sasha walked up to join as well. He turned to speak to all of them. "Perfect, I'm glad you all got here okay. Today is the last day we will practice out here. Ettercaps came out of the woods today; for everyone's safety, I think we need to be a little more careful."

"But—" Amber started to argue and cleared her throat before trying again. "Milord. We practice to become able to protect ourselves. You wouldn't keep us from fighting, would you?"

Dar paused, taking in the hurt on her face. "I am proud of the progress you've made and all you can do, but it doesn't mean that

you couldn't be overwhelmed by their forces. Taking on an army is more than we've practiced."

That seemed to mollify the two of them slightly, so Dar continued, "Plus, after the ettercaps leaving the forest boundary today, we'll most likely have to push them back in the next couple days. Think of it as resting up before we go into that fight."

The hurt on their face turned to a mix of excitement and panic. "You think we are going to go into the southern woods so soon?"

Dar nodded, looking to Cherry. "I think I'm going to miss dinner tonight. Would you mind bringing a message to the other leaders that I plan to try and push back the ettercaps in the southern woods here shortly?"

"Where will you be?" Sasha asked, her eyes narrowed in a look of concern Dar knew all too well.

"I think it's about time I learned the dao of combustion."

He took them by surprise. Up until that point, he'd been putting off meditation, and he hadn't quite told them why. A part of it was that it had wiped him out, and he needed his abilities to prepare the town for winter, but that hadn't been the main reason recently.

After Bellhaven, his head hadn't been in the right space to meditate. It seemed risky to take it on when it could have dangerous consequences, and he knew he wasn't ready. But something with the recent ettercaps he'd killed had helped him at least deal with the slaughter a bit. The ettercaps were a threat, and he'd eliminated that threat to his village. Bellhaven hadn't been so different. It had just been hard to see that in the moment.

"You do look a lot better. Coming to grips with what happened in Bellhaven?" Mika asked.

"Working on it, and I think I'm getting there. I killed two of the three ettercaps that came out of the woods today, and Rex said something about having no hesitation," Dar answered.

Mika nodded, waiting until he continued.

"I really hadn't killed on the offensive before Bellhaven. But just because I didn't wait for them to strike, doesn't mean it was wrong.

I did the best I could with the information I had in the moment. I accept that."

Dar wasn't quite sure it was comparing apples to apples, but he'd take what clarity he could get. "So, I think I'd like to meditate on combustion. And you two" —Dar pointed to the maids—"are going to come with me. We are going to see if you two can meditate on a dao."

"Really?!" Amber jumped up and down.

He checked with the rest of the girls, not seeing any concerns on their faces. "Yes, that's the plan. But after, I suspect we'll be going to battle, so take this seriously."

"Of course, milord." Marcie tried to reign Amber in, but the red-headed maid practically vibrated with energy.

Mika smirked. "If you are so full of energy, then you should spar with me first. Now line up. We are going through strikes again. Cherry, would you make everyone short swords?"

Cherry got to work as her response, and vines began snaking out of the ground in the rough shape of a wooden sword. They each reached forward to the sword near them, picking up their weapons and following Mika through a series of strikes and blocks. She would shout out the name of the move as they completed it.

When the group had each movement down, Mika called their names one at a time. The person called would step forward and complete the sequence, flowing through the attacks while Mika corrected from the side.

Mika had turned into quite the drill sergeant when they were training, and Dar had a feeling she'd done it before. She seemed to be a natural at teaching the moves. It was either that or she'd been through way too many trainings herself and was able to imitate past trainers.

"Overhead block. Thrust. Put your hips into it, Cherry."

Cherry let out a frustrated groan and threw her weapon down. "This is stupid. I've humored you long enough. I don't need to learn how to swing a stick, metal or wood."

Mika glowered at Cherry. "Fine, then. You're first. We start sparring now."

"Hands only," Dar reminded Cherry, who turned and blew him a raspberry.

Mika came at Cherry quickly, but roots erupted all around Cherry and twisted in the shape of a massive fist before punching Mika and smashing her to the ground.

"There. I used my fist. Happy?" Cherry buffed her nails against her shirt with a smirk.

However, Mika was far less than amused as she got up and wiped the dirt off her face. "What happens when you run out of mana? What happens when you fight another grand demon?"

"Uh." Cherry paused. "I just won't run out of mana. And fighting another grand demon isn't exactly the same as fighting in hand-to-hand combat, anyway."

"There are parallels," Mika said, eyeing the large fist of roots that was still hovering above the ground. "Dar, what would you do if you fought that giant fist?"

Dar shrugged. "I guess first see if I could cut through it with strength and enchanted weapons. If I get caught, see if it'll catch fire."

Cherry spoke up, "He's not the first person to threaten me with fire. You'd be surprised how hard it is to burn fresh roots. I just fight with my fists differently."

A small hand of roots rose out of the ground and jabbed at Dar playfully while Cherry smirked. "See?"

Mika gave Cherry a brief glare but continued on with practice. They sparred in pairs without using any dao. Mika insisted that it not even be used defensively; they needed to harden up against pain as part of the training.

Dar sparred with his women, enjoying that they'd gotten skilled enough that he didn't have to hold back if they weren't using dao. And he didn't. The more prepared they were, the less likely he was to lose them.

When he had flipped Sasha over his head and threw her in the dirt, she had scowled, but he could only smile and remind himself that it was the best for the family. Even if he knew, he might pay for it later.

"You are all making me do laundry daily now," Sasha huffed, getting up and dusting off her pants. She had given up wearing dresses to training after the first day. Mika had pulled the dress over Sasha's head and tied it together to prove just how ineffective the choice was in battle.

"Better some extra laundry and a few bruises than losing any of you," Dar muttered mostly to himself, but Sasha's expression immediately softened.

"You're right, it's a trivial thing. But you'll still be punished for that move later." She gave him a simmering look.

Dar smiled, not sure he was sorry about it anymore. "Well, in that case..." Dar moved over and lifted Sasha up onto his shoulders, pretending he was going to throw her and enjoying the squeals she let out in response.

"You will put me down this moment, Dar!" Sasha demanded between her laughter.

"I don't know. I think you are my bounty for such good fighting." Dar crouched like he was getting ready, feeling her brace against him, before he slowly let her back down until her feet touched the floor.

Sasha smacked his butt as Mika cleared her throat, her serious trainer persona back in place as she ordered them back into formation.

Cherry managed to make up for some of her earlier behavior as they continued. Despite her protests, she was actually quite skilled. Dar suspected she had far more experience than even Mika, but no sort of formalized training.

As they finished training, they headed together towards the central hearth. As they neared it, Dar pulled the maids aside. "Are you two ready?"

"Should we eat first?" Marcie asked, her stomach rumbling to punctuate her opinion.

"Sure. But this will take a bit of time, so we should get started. Grab something quick and meet me in the salt cave." Dar wasn't feeling hungry, so he decided to go ahead of them and form a boulder to rest near the entrance, to seal it off while they meditated.

When the girls came hurrying, Dar wiped a bit of food off Amber's cheeks. "Come on."

Leading them inside, he shifted the boulder in place, sealing them in as he lit a torch for them to see. "Okay. I am going to start. I want both of you to watch what I'm doing and feel it with your mana. Here's the character for combustion."

Dar had already set up the cave for meditation. Sasha's book was stashed in the stone floor; he drew it out of the granite and flipped to the correct page. "While I'm meditating on it, I want both of you to try and study it some."

"It's blurry." Marcie frowned. "And it hurts." Her frown deepened.

"I know. Don't push yourselves too hard but do try to get to the point that you can see the character fully if you focus on it."

Both of them nodded, and Dar sat down cross-legged on the cool cave floor. He could feel himself settle into a calm he hadn't felt in a long time. He centered himself with slow, steady breaths.

Peeking out one eye, he checked on Amber and Marcie, who were watching him with rapt attention. He explained what he was doing. "I'm just clearing my mind with a meditation technique in preparation. I'll walk you through it later. Now, I'm going to need that dao character."

They slid the book in front of him.

"I focus on the character and see it clearly, then find the right pattern to cycle those same strokes through the meridians, the channels in my body that carry mana. While I'm doing this, my concentration breaking can cause me physical harm, so please avoid making noise or breaking me from what I'm doing."

After both girls nodded, Dar worked to push them out of his mind as he focused whole heartedly on his meditation technique.

The character for combustion became clear on the page, and Dar let his mana cycle through a few times before trying to form the shape of the dao. As he closed his eyes, he could feel the power of mana circulating through his body. His body hummed with the power.

After a few cycles, he began to work to direct the mana flow. It took a few tries to get the strokes right, but soon mana was flowing into the combustion character.

Remembering last time, he focused hard on the shape, making sure not to let it break as he started to speed it up, chasing the tail end of the cycle to make the character a solid figure in his body and mind's eye.

Pain began to bubble up across his body as it strained to contain the dao character that Dar was trying to imprint upon himself. Spikes of pain began wracking his body; it felt like his very blood was starting to spark and boil under the strain of the technique. But this time, he wasn't worried. He knew his body could weather the storm. He needed to keep his focus and ignore the pain.

He called upon his existing dao of hard and strength to reinforce his body; he continued the meditation, pushing through the pain. As he sank deeper into himself, focusing started to become more difficult. Within his mind's eye, the dao character began to compete with the flashes of faces. Mark, Margret, and the Tints all floated through his vision.

Working to ignore them, Dar doubled down on his meditation, feeling sweat prickle along his skin as sudden doubt blossomed in his mind.

A small voice in his mind wondered if he was worth the power he was trying to achieve. If he could be enough for their town or if he'd destined it for failure. As the small voice lingered, small cracks started to form in the dao character. They split a small bit further, threatening to break the character.

Determination washed through Dar as he crushed the small voice in his head. He'd made the right choice, and he stood by it. He would not let them limit him.

As he felt conviction in that decision, he watched the cracks disappear, as if they had never been there. The little voice was gone, and Dar was left with his dao character, cycling his mana through it.

After a few more cycles, the character for combustion was complete, imprinting into his mind and body. Feeling the sensation wash over him, Dar soaked it in before opening his eyes and taking deep breaths.

The girls startled. "Are you okay, milord?" Amber asked.

"I'll be fine." Dar took inventory of his body. He felt terrible and stiff, but he was nowhere near as weak as last time he had finished cultivating. He smiled at the progress, although his smile was weak. He hadn't been expecting the doubt in his mind to creep up on him like that. He'd need to remember that for the future.

"Maybe you should go grab some food before we start? Maybe clean up your face a little?"

Dar wiped at his face, wincing as he came away with a bloody hand. Dabbing at his face, he realized he had a nosebleed. "Thank you."

"No. Thank you. I had no idea how hard this was," Marcie commented, looking at him with respect.

"What do you mean?" he asked.

"Milord. You whimpered like you were dying, and we've never seen you covered in so much sweat no matter how hard you work in a day," Amber clarified.

Dipping his head, he realized he might have scared them. "It can be hard. But I'll be here to help both of you. Give me a minute, and I'll be right back. You were right, I should eat something."

Dar headed out of the cave and down to the cave with food stores. Grabbing a bowl of oats and a bucket of water, he headed back to the cave.

"You weren't gone very long," Marcie observed.

Dar poured some water into the oats and used his dao of heat to cook the mixture while he splashed a little water on his face to clean off the blood. "I figured I could just make my meal here."

Taking a bite, Dar continued, "Now, you two need to sit down. Cross your legs and focus on the sound of my voice. Clear everything out of your mind. Focus only on my voice."

Dar took a sip of water. "Feel for your heartbeat and focus on that. Feel the depth of each beat across your body. It's your internal clock. Feel that pulse carry life from your chest out to the tips of your fingers."

He became quiet as he watched them settle into relaxed poses, their bodies subtly twitching as they cleared their minds.

Softening his voice, Dar tried not to break their concentration while he coached them. "Good. Now when your mind is clear, open your eyes and look at the page. Find the dao character and begin to trace it in your mind and in your meridians."

Both girls settled back into a trance, meditating on the dao character. Dar quietly started to eat while watching both of them.

He could feel the mana flowing through their bodies as they made the character appropriately. It took Marcie a bit longer, but soon they both were flowing dao through their meridians in the pattern of the combustion dao.

Dar's pride was short-lived as he began to feel the chaos and the storm that brewed alongside the character inside of them. The dao was starting to damage their bodies, and their bodies weren't holding up to the onslaught very well.

Quickly setting his food down quietly, Dar moved himself behind them. Holding out his hands, he placed a palm on both of their backs and worked to infuse them with his own dao of hard and strength.

Kicking himself, Dar continued to try to give them enough to push through the pain. It had been too risky to have them do this so soon.

Amber was the first to cough up a mouthful of blood, but Dar could see the profile of her face as she grit her teeth and pushed through the pain. Marcie cried out, but it turned into a shout of battle as she pushed through as well. Dar braced himself, hoping they wouldn't curse him too badly when they made it out.

The two of them were strong, but his method of walking the dao path was harsh and crude. He would experiment with techniques more before having them try again.

Amber's fingers reached forward, distracting Dar as she sank her nails into her knees, drawing blood. But both she and Marcie pushed through, continuing to cultivate in silence, only broken by a few small whimpers.

Dar stayed there, kneeling behind them, his focus entirely on helping them protect their bodies as they cultivated. He would have stopped it if he wasn't so worried that stopping the process partway would hurt them more than letting them continue.

Hours passed, and Dar started growing more and more concerned, although he could feel them getting close. Exhausted from the use of his dao, Dar needed them to finish soon or he may not be able to continue fortifying their bodies.

A few minutes later, Marcie finished first, gasping for air and falling to her side. "Milord?" she said weakly.

Looking around, Dar realized the light had gone out and Marcie probably couldn't see much. "I'm here but stay quiet. Amber's almost done."

"Sleep," was all she said before he heard her heavy breathing.

Sure enough, Amber finished soon after, crying out in pain and clutching her gut. "How did you get the courage to do that a second time?"

"Need," Dar answered. "Let's get you two some food and water." Dar pulled over the bucket and let Amber drink while he woke Marcie and fed her some of his reheated oats.

"Thank you, milord. We wouldn't have survived without you," Marcie spoke in a barely audible whisper.

Dar still felt guilty for putting them through the process before he'd made it safer, but he was proud of both of them. And they seemed pleased under all the exhaustion. "My pleasure. Let me go get you two more food."

"I can stand," Amber argued, tottering to her feet only to grow unsteady and lean against the wall. "Well, maybe not walk," she corrected herself.

"Lean on me. I'll take you both down to the hearth."

But as Dar rolled aside the rock to help them both exit the cave, one of Glump's dao companions came charging into the cave, breathing heavily.

"Have either of you seen Kro?" she asked. Based on her bright red hair, Dar had often assumed she was Kro's mother, but he wasn't sure.

"No, I haven't seen him since breakfast," Dar answered.

Amber quickly shook her head. "Is everything okay?"

"I don't know. I can't find him. He isn't with Sam, nor has anyone seen him." Taking one last look around the cave, she turned to leave, but Dar stopped her.

"Where have you looked so far? We'll help you."

CHAPTER 30

"I've looked everywhere. He's nowhere to be found. Nobody has seen him." Kro's mother looked like she was fraying at the ends of her sanity.

Dar bolstered himself with what mana he had left and looked to the two maids. "Let's go hunt for him."

Dar knew that Marcie and Amber weren't going to be able to be much help with how weak their bodies were, so he first worked to get them back to the central hearth so they could eat food and work to regain some of their energy. Then he began scanning the area, working to come up with a plan.

Kro's mother hurried off aimlessly, looking everywhere her head could pivot for the mop of red hair. Most of the village seemed to be engaged at that point in the search for little Kro, which made Dar more uneasy. With that many people looking for him, Kro should have turned up already.

"Kro!" a worker shouted by the palisade and turned to him. "You seen Glump's little one?"

"No, sorry." Dar moved on and spotted Shelia patrolling by the wall. "Shelia, you've probably already been asked, but have you seen Kro wander over this way?"

"Huh?" She shook her head. "Sorry, must have zoned out. Getting a little tired here. But I haven't seen the kid."

"You okay?" Dar asked, seeing the bags under her eyes.

"Yes?" It came out as a question before she shook her head. "No, I'm beat, boss. We've had two more visitors creep out of the forest during the night."

"Ettercaps?"

"No, spiders. And something built that during last night's watch." Shelia pointed up to a large web in one of the trees closest to the village.

Dar immediately understood what that meant. "That means something slipped by our watch last night. Can we tear that down?"

"Could, but I don't want to give up my vigil. We're too short staffed to do anything about it," she responded.

Dar nodded. Circling the tree in question himself, Dar didn't see anything up in the tree and decided to do it himself. Swinging up, it was quick work to cut a branch, use it to collect the web, and throw it back down to the ground.

When he finished, he looked back at Sheila, who was swaying on her feet. She looked like she was about to pass out. "Why don't you go rest, Sheila? I'll keep watch while you find a replacement?"

"No, boss. I have a replacement that should be here shortly. I'm at the end of my shift. Normally, I'm more alert, I swear."

Dar gave her a level stare before deciding she could make her own decisions. Shelia knew herself and her limits.

As he walked back, Dar's stomach rumbled. He realized he probably needed to take the same advice that he'd given Amber and Marcie, and swung by the central hearth for some food. He wasn't surprised to find the meal of the day was giant hunks of bison. Russ had flooded their stores with meat.

"Dar." Sasha looked up from her task at a table, the scissors in her hands held perfectly still.

"Please don't let me ruin what you were doing." He ripped off another hunk of the meat.

But Sasha ignored that, putting down the tool and coming around the table to hug him and kiss his cheek. "You're never a bother. I'm

glad you are okay. I saw the girls grab a bowl and head to their hut. They looked pretty worn down. I figured you'd be around soon."

"Of course, I've come to check up on my favorite companion." He squeezed her back. "And to show I'm okay. The meditation went as I had hoped."

"You know, you are going to make me jealous if you fly past me on your dao path so easily."

He breathed in her scent for a moment before letting her go. "Is it really a problem?"

"Yes and no. I love that you are soaring; though, I worry about little ol' me keeping up."

"You don't have to keep up, Sasha. I love you for exactly who you are." He tried to give her the reassurance she needed, but he knew they hadn't had much time together to reinforce it. With winter, things would hopefully settle down and give them more time to spend together.

He changed the topic. "What do you know about little Kro going missing?"

Her mane of black hair fluttered as she shook her head. "They've been looking for over an hour. At this point, Glump is worried sick. I... don't know how to help so I've just been keeping at what I'm doing."

"That's about all we can do sometimes." Dar could see over half a dozen people from where he stood walking about, shouting for Kro to come out. "Hopefully, he's just being a silly kid, and we can laugh about this tonight."

Sasha rolled her eyes. "Kids are so much trouble sometimes."

He noticed Shelia dragging herself through the center of the village, off her shift. She somehow looked even more worn.

"Shelia, get some sleep."

She raised a weary hand at Dar and disappeared into one of the huts. He could have sworn he heard a solid thump of someone falling into bed shortly after.

"We really need to get them some relief," Dar commented. Hearing the guard was worn down was one thing, but they were at their breaking point. And the enemy was starting to get more daring.

"You heard about the two spiders last night?" Sasha worried her lip. "You don't think Kro might have...?" She trailed off, not wanting to give voice to her thoughts.

Dar started to deny it, but he was starting to have the same uneasiness in his gut. If Kro had wandered off outside the town... Dar stopped going down that line of thinking, wanting to stay positive. "I don't think so. We have two people patrolling the palisade. They would have spotted him if he was anywhere near the forest."

Even as he said it, Dar didn't completely believe it. Sheila had been exhausted at her post, and there was already clear proof a spider had gotten past the guard. But he had to believe they would have spotted the rambunctious little boy.

As he even considered it, Dar paused in eating, staring at the palisade. The town was pretty well covered in their search. He might be more useful in extending the borders of the search.

"You're going to go look, aren't you?" Sasha probed.

Dar scratched the back of his head. "Caught me."

"I'll come with you. I feel useless right now." Sasha folded over the cloth she was working on and tucked away the scissors in the spatial pouch under her dress. "Let's go."

Devouring the rest of the hunk of bison, Dar walked with Sasha out toward the southern woods.

Sheila had just left her post, but as Dar scanned the palisade, he didn't see a guard patrolling the south side. Frowning, he wondered if they were both around the other side.

As he went to look, the sound of metal drew his attention immediately. There was a fight in the shadows at the edge of the forest.

"Come on." Dar rushed around the palisade and into the woods. Reaching them quickly, Dar took in the situation.

Two spiders had the guard cornered, and one of his legs was bound in web, preventing him from escaping. The guard looked up to see Dar running and shouted, "Watch out!"

Not hesitating, Dar summoned his axe from his inner world and swung up with all his might. His axe cut made contact with something, and he ducked into a roll as a spider fell from the tree.

"I got this." Sasha sprang forward, using her enchanted wand like a dagger and stabbing into the spider on the left.

Seeing she was handling it, Dar turned back to the guard. In that moment of chaos, the other spider had sprung on the guard, digging its mandibles deep into the demon's back. The guard screamed as the spider thrashed open the wound.

Sasha's ribbons shot out, trying to encase the second spider, but it managed to walk along Sasha's ribbons like a spider would its web. It used her ribbons like a highway straight to her.

The spider moved with its maw wide open, and Dar watched in horror.

But Sasha wasn't as soft as she might have once been. Her palm slapped up at the base of the spider's head and knocked it backwards, a move he'd seen Mika teach her, giving her enough time to ready herself and stab through its abdomen with her wand.

The moment of confusion was the spider's end as the ribbons curled back on it and tangled its legs while Sasha finished it.

Dar was already picking the guard up and removing the webbing. "Are you okay?"

The guard's eyes fogged, losing focus. "Where?"

"We need to get him back," Dar said quickly, hauling the guard back out of the forest and to the village. As he approached, he spotted two men and waved them over.

"Stand watch at the southern edge of the village. If you see anything funny, all you are to do is shout and come get help. No heroics, like this guy."

Their eyes flicked to the guard, whose back was soaked in crimson blood. Both of them nodded rapidly. "Of course."

"What happened?" Tabby was near the hearth when Dar strode in, the crowd parting as he carried the injured man in.

"Looks like he went to check the edge of the forest and got attacked."

Tabby clicked her tongue. "Alright, come set him down. Sasha, can you get some water boiling for me? We'll need to clean out his wounds."

Sasha stepped away and brought back a bucket of cold water. Dar dipped his hands in and got it to a rapid boil in only a few seconds.

"Useful," Tabby muttered as she used a knife to tear the man's shirt off and get a better look at the wound.

Pus was already puffing up around the wound, and there was an oily sheen of poison dripping out. Tabby took the hot water and poured it into one of the wounds. The guard screamed, seeming to come to consciousness just enough to know the pain.

Dar wanted to stop her and help the man, but he knew that she knew what she was doing. He had to trust the process to her.

Curious, he did ask, "Isn't that going to leave burns?"

"A mild burn from this will heal in a few days. That's not his biggest problem. We need to get the poison out of him." She got up to fetch a sewing kit and went to work trying to close the wounds."

Feet pounded on the packed dirt as Rex showed up, looking down at the injured guard. "What happened?"

"Spiders. I think your guard had the same idea as us. Probably went to see if Kro had been anywhere near the southern forest."

Rex's avian face went through a series of emotions and finally settled on anger. "We can't keep going like this, boss. We need to strike back."

Dar clenched his teeth and looked at the guard. They both agreed something needed to be done. Hearthway was in real danger of the ettercaps.

"Get people together. It's time we take the fight to them. At the very least, we need to cause enough trouble to drive them out of the nearby woods."

Rex's eyes flashed with excitement as he hurried off.

Dar had hoped to put it off until winter, but after this attack, there was no way they could increase the guard. And the danger seemed to be mounting with each day. They had to strike back and drive the ettercaps from their home.

"I got this one. Go meet up with my husband and get it done," Tabby huffed and rolled up her sleeves.

"Go, love. I'll join you soon." Sasha smiled before giving Tabby and the guard her full attention.

Dar set off, grabbing men as he went and telling them to meet at the central hearth. It was time they did something about these ettercaps.

"Bart." Dar caught the old blacksmith measuring a piece of lumber. "Get a weapon and meet me at the central hearth. Bring everyone."

His face fell. "What is it?"

"The ettercap problem is getting worse, and now a guard is injured. It's come time. We can't put it off any longer." Dar didn't leave room for argument, nor did Bart argue. Instead, the old blacksmith picked up a sword that had been laid to the side.

"I was thinking we'd be needing this soon." He drew the sword from the sheath to check on it. "Hate that it's come to this."

Dar gave the man a solemn nod. "But we will protect our village; I'm not about to let these devils push us out."

"Aye. I'll be at the hearth in a moment."

Dar saw masses of people with whatever weapons they could find gathering at the hearth. Content that word had gone out and people would assemble, Dar walked slowly towards it, giving people time to assemble, but also trying to figure out what he was going to say to rally them.

Everyone in the village was gathered as Dar stepped up on a bench and scanned the crowd. Rex, Russ, and Samantha all spotted him and came up to stand alongside him.

"We are going to move against the ettercaps. All who agree, say 'aye'."

They looked at each other a moment before all but Samantha agreed. "I don't like this one bit. They aren't bothering us much yet."

"A guard was attacked and nearly killed. And their numbers could overwhelm us if they organize. We can't afford to wait."

"He's right dear." An aged man with a paunch and a sword came up behind her and grabbed her by the shoulder. "Sometimes, for things like this, you need to be the first to strike. You have my sword, lord."

Dar hesitated. "Thank you for it, but I'd ask that you stay behind. We'll have to leave some behind to keep a watch on the children. I can't think of anyone better than you and Sam."

He opened his mouth to argue, but one look from Sam shut the old man up. "Of course."

Dar smiled, knowing the man had likely fought and won countless battles in his youth. But he also needed to accept the limitations his body now put on him. He had trained the young men; they would now pick up their swords and fight for the village.

"Alright, all of you, listen up. If you are able to march through the woods, get a weapon. If you can't leave, or if you have a little one, leave one partner behind. Sam and her husband will be looking after the kids while we are gone."

There were nods in some groups, but more than a few couples started bickering in the crowd.

"Ettercaps attacked us today. We have a guard that's severely wounded. Spiderwebs were placed on the palisade wall this morning. They are getting through our defenses. Right now, it's just a few, but it could be more quickly."

Dar paused, letting it sink in. "We will protect this village, and we will make it a safe place to raise our children. Today, we drive them back and make sure they understand that Hearthway isn't their next stop for a meal."

The villagers pumped their fists. "Yeah. Squash the buggers."

"Everybody needs a weapon and torch. Gather those now. Kiss your loved ones. We head into the southern forest in half an hour. We'll start out from where the palisade wall ends down there."

As he finished, a series of shouts erupted, especially among the young men. They were pumping each other up, preparing for battle. Dar could see some fear across their faces, but they also seemed eager to prove themselves. He hoped the training they'd gotten would be enough to keep them safe.

About to head that way, a commotion at the edge of the crowd caught Dar's attention. At first, he thought it might be related to the fight, but the voices sounded happy and excited.

As the crowd parted, out emerged Kro, covered in mud and dripping from head to toe. He was being dragged into the village by his mother, Glump not far behind.

"You found him?" Dar called from his stump.

"Stuck in the riverbank. Stupid kid worried us sick." Glump stopped, and it looked like he was just now realizing something was up. "Did I miss something?"

Dar smiled. "Glad you got Kro back. We're organizing a group to go attack and push back the ettercaps. It's escalating, and we need to act now."

The old demon sighed. "Well, at least we found Kro first. I was starting to..."

"None of that," Dar cut him off. The last thing he needed was for anyone to lose their spirits before they went out. "Get a weapon and get a torch. We leave here in twenty minutes.

"On it." Glump gave his wife a hug and bent down to talk to Kro.

Dar saw Cherry coming with an armload of torches, and he met up with her, heading to the southern opening in the palisade. When he met her eyes, he let his leader mask slip from his face, showing her the fear he had for the men he was about to take into battle.

Cherry simply nodded, kindness and understanding in her eyes as she leaned up and kissed his cheek. "You were made for this, Dar. And we all stand beside you."

CHAPTER 31

As one, the eighty some villagers left Hearthway into the southern forest. Their torches made great tools for burning through all the webs that they began encountering with their first steps into the forest.

It had changed drastically in the week Dar had been away from it. The webs seemed to cast the whole forest in a gloomy, dying light as they passed by with their torches. Ettercaps and spiders fled from their group as the torch light illuminated their shadowy hiding spots.

Watching the enemy flee seemed to bolster the entire group. Many began raising their weapons and running out a bit further from the group, burning more webs down. He could sympathize with them wanting to reclaim their home, but the last thing he needed was a fire.

"Do not set the forest on fire. Get back in formation," Dar shouted to the column as he saw a pair of men using their torches to burn a web off a dead tree. Its branches started to smolder like little birthday candles.

They grumbled but shifted back, keeping with the column. Dar kept his face blank, but he worried about his ability to command such a random assortment of people. So far, they hadn't encountered trouble, but it was bound to come at some point as they got closer to their keep.

Mika marched next to him, her eyes up constantly scanning the trees. She was entirely a warrior at that moment. The lines on her face were hard and her body moved fluidly as she continuously prepared for attack.

"Devil!" someone shouted, and Dar held up a hand to stop the march, looking around. Sure enough, he could spot small groups of spiders gathering on several trees around them, taking a few steps closer.

"Dar, they are everywhere," Mika whispered.

Dar nodded. They were surrounded. It appeared the spiders were smart enough to organize further out and then press in at the same time. He had hoped they wouldn't be so coordinated.

Projecting as much calm as he could in his voice, Dar shouted, "Everybody, circle up. Take out as many of these bastards as you can and protect your fellow villager. Protect our home."

Rex stepped up, giving his commands like a drill sergeant. "Archers in the middle. Two other layers around them. Tap out when you get tired and shift with the person behind you."

Rex turned, giving Dar a nod. Dar thrust his weapon into the air in return, letting out a billowing shout.

The villagers joined him in his war cry, following Rex's orders. Everyone shifted and tightened the circle, with a number of men going into the center and hovering over the shoulder of another. Dar wasn't an expert, but he had heard of historic battles using multiple lines as a relief was a pretty common depiction of roman soldiers.

Dar stepped up to join those in the outer right. "Afternoon. I'll be between you two." Dar made room for himself.

In his peripheral vision, he saw Sasha, Marcie, and Amber stay back. He was surprised they hadn't joined the front lines until he saw Sasha pulled out her wand and start carving on rocks.

She was going to enchant more rocks to explode. When Marcie and Amber joined her, Dar smiled, a bit excited to see what damage the enchanted rocks could do.

"Neko. Here." The cat girl stepped up next to Dar, shoving the man next to him aside as her tail swooshed behind her. "Fight with Dar."

"And you won't be alone in that," Mika spoke behind him. "I've got your back, and Blair has Neko's, or however it winds up."

Dar shook out his arm and let his axe rest comfortably in his hands. The devils were pooling on the ground, eyeing the villagers like a feast.

"Sasha, now would be a great time to throw the first stone," he called over his shoulder.

In response, a rock lobbed into the gathering spiders, bouncing off one before it exploded, consuming the surrounding spiders in a ball of fire. Two more rocks flew in other directions to the same effect.

The resulting explosions ripped through the mass of spiders, and they screamed. The entire forest filled with their screeches as they surged forward, enraged by the fire.

Dar's focus narrowed to the surrounding few yards as he let himself fall into a trance of battle. He swung his axe, cleaving through spiders and ettercaps with each swing. There was satisfaction in the kills, but like the battles before, the enemy had numbers. More devils crawled over their dead peers as soon as Dar had taken them down.

More than once, Mika thrust a spear over his shoulder while he was recovering from a swing, catching an ettercap that was using its recently dead brethren as a launch pad.

Mana flowed through Dar's body, reinforcing him with hard and strength as he fought what seemed like an endless wave. He nearly spun and attacked when a hand pulled on his shoulder before realizing it was Mika.

Knocking out another spider in front of him, she spoke in his ear, "You're losing focus. Switch."

Dar didn't bother arguing, trusting her combat instincts. He stepped back as she stepped forward with a thrust of her trident, moving fluidly into his spot as she stabbed the spider through the

face. Her movement continuing, she twisted it back out and stabbed the next, taking out another spider.

Sasha pulled Dar deeper into the circle quickly, continuing to lob explosive stones out and over their soldiers into the masses of devils surrounding them. When she stopped pulling him, Dar looked around and realized he was sitting among dozens of spider-gut-covered men, catching their breaths.

"There are so many," Glump croaked, seeing Dar sit down.

"What? Getting tired, old man?" Dar joked.

"I'm not the only one wheezing over here, youngin. I would have thought all those workouts I hear at night would have you in better shape." Glump sparred back, a shadow of a smile crossing his exhausted face.

Dar chuckled, his smile quickly fading as he took a few deep breaths to try to regain his energy. "They just keep coming."

Dar looked over at the men surrounding them, trying to figure out which area needed his help the most as he got back into battle.

Glump grunted and stretched his arm. "Looks like they might be pulling back."

Dar followed his direction, looking out past the ring of soldiers. It did look like the ettercaps were pulling back, but the spiders kept coming, covering the ettercaps' retreat.

Taking his knife, Dar picked up a stone and started to carve combustion into it. Done, he tossed it into the crowd of spiders near what looked like one of their weaker points in villagers, killing at least four spiders with the resulting blast.

Standing back up, Dar prepared to head back into the fray. As he looked over the inner circle, emotion began to sweep over him. The wounded lay packed in a small area. Some of them were too still, either on the edge of death or past it and onto whatever lay past this life.

The emotions threatened to overwhelm Dar, knowing he'd led them into the battle. But he couldn't let himself process those emo-

tions in that moment. There were devils to kill, and townspeople who still needed his protection.

Dar grit his teeth. He'd honor them when they returned to the village. He looked over to Glump. "I'm heading back in. See you next time."

Neko and Blair were on the front line now. Mika had apparently shifted back over their shoulders, protecting them.

The cat girl was a fury. Her hands flew like claws, cutting straight through any spider that got close. Meanwhile, Blair fought with a short sword, but she also had a few crystalline pieces of salt floating in the surrounding air, acting as emergency weapons.

Dar found a man a few down from his original position, who was barely holding his spot. His arm opened with a deep gash. "Get someone to bind the wound. I'll take over here."

"Bless you," the man said, ducking back deeper into the circle.

Dar faced the spiders, once again swinging his axe as he took out row after row.

***

Killing the devils had been grisly work. Now that the field was clear, Dar was amazed at just how many devils they had managed to kill.

But it hadn't come without sacrifice. They had eight dead and three times that who were out of the fight with their wounds. Their initial group of eighty-six was nearly cut in half.

"They fought well," Rex greeted Dar as he stood over the dead. Men were digging graves for them as they spoke.

Dar nodded. He wasn't sure there was such a thing as a good death, but the villagers had died with honor, defending what they had built with their own two hands.

Dar struggled with what to do next. The men around him were haggard from the battle, worn down in the wave upon wave of spiders

they'd encountered. But it was also the best time to press forward, before the enemy could rebuild.

"Come on, sit down." Sasha pulled Dar away from his thoughts. "We have some food, dried berries, and meat. You need to eat."

Dar took what she offered and looked around. His family was still whole. Sasha and the two maids had blood on their clothes, but it wasn't their own. They had helped the injured, on top of creating the exploding enchantments.

Neko was covered in the guts of spiders, wiping at her tail to get some of the guts off. Mika and Blair weren't much better off, spider goo dripping from everywhere. Cherry had been concentrating in the center of the group, bringing the massive stump to bear, crushing large quantities of spiders outside the ring of fighting. From where he sat, Dar could see the displaced roots and the lines of squashed spiders.

"What now?" Dar quietly asked the group as a whole.

"What do you mean?" Mika asked, clearly confused. "We push forward and keep fighting."

But Dar's eyes slid over to the rest of the surrounding soldiers, his voice lowering even softer. "What if I don't think we can push forward?"

"Oh, yeah." Mika's shoulders slumped. "That battle was trying, but we broke them. And we can only hope that it was most of their forces, otherwise..." Her voice trailed off as she swallowed.

"I'm not saying we give up. But what if... what if we pushed forward without the rest? Tried to go straight for the fortress and burn it down? I had joked about it before as a last resort... but I think we are at last resorts."

"Leave this group of armed and trained men, demons, and spirits behind to go do heroics? Sounds like a great way to get yourself killed," Sasha scolded, exhaustion causing her to snap.

Dar held her gaze in return, his voice still quiet but firm. "Look at them, Sasha. That was just one fight, with mostly spiders, and they are already exhausted and worn down. We might have given them a

week's worth of sword practice, but that didn't magically turn them into soldiers."

Even as he spoke, the villagers milled about. They still had spirit and fight in them, but it wasn't the blazing fire they had had when they left the village.

"I don't want to lose any more of them. The seven of us all have the dao of quiet. We could push forward and try to set the massive fortress of webs on fire."

Cherry spoke up, surprising him as she said, "I'm on board with this plan. The less we lose in this effort, the better."

"You agree?" Sasha turned to her other dao companion, and there was a silent conversation between the two of them before she turned back. "Fine. Then I'm on board too. But, for the record, I think this is dangerous."

"Of course it's dangerous. But it's dangerous for us. The rest of the village will be safer. I'm willing to shoulder that risk for them."

"Shit. When you put it like that, how can I say no?" Blair shrugged, scooping a bit more food into her mouth.

Dar met the eyes of the rest of his small family, and each of them nodded in turn.

"Then take an hour. Rest up. After an hour, we head out."

Rex and Glump hadn't loved the idea when Dar had pitched it to them. But all it took was another look at the rest of the villagers for them to agree.

The avian demon wanted to come with, but Dar assured him that they had stealth in the smaller group and that Rex needed to be back to support the second half of their plan to protect the village. If Dar's team failed, Rex would still need to follow through to protect the village.

Settling in after speaking with them, Dar worked to get a quick nap to rest his body. But it wasn't long before the hour was up and it was time for him to head off into the woods with the girls.

***

Dar and the group moved silently through the forest, using their quiet dao to mask any noise they may make. They were in near perfect stealth, well at least as far as noise was concerned.

Webbing connected the entire forest, running up trees and overhead along the canopy. Dar had suspected the ettercaps functioned largely like spiders, so there was a good chance the webs transmitted their prey's motion deeper into the forest. They'd done their best to avoid touching any of the webs as they'd moved.

As close as they were to the fortress with their small team, Dar didn't want to give away their location.

"Careful, I almost didn't see this one," Dar pushed his voice through the other's dao.

"Stupid webs," Cherry muttered. "I should just smash them all."

"Thanks." Sasha looked up from another half-finished dao character of combustion. "I think I almost have enough. You sure these are going to work?"

"It's a lot better than directly confronting them," Blair reiterated. She had been one of the stronger believers in their plan.

"All the spiders can burn, look what they did to the forest!" Cherry had been against the burning of the forest. That was until she'd seen all of the dead trees deeper in the ettercap territory. Now she was out for blood.

Sasha finished and etched the remaining conditionals on the enchanted item. Dar had made them out of granite, and they were shaped sort of like a taser. That way, it fit neatly into their hands. Two tongs rose up and pinched together, with just a bit of space between them.

It was delicate enchanting work that Dar had needed Sasha's help with, but in the end, the small fire starter would try to combust any material placed between the two tongs when activated.

Dar raised his head, once again scoping out the canopy. The trees all around them were gray and brittle looking. By that point, their team was deep enough in ettercap territory that these trees had likely been dead for a long time. It looked like their green leaves had been choked out by spider webs months ago.

"Say, since the spiders are capable of giving a dao in the dao tree, does that mean they are the descendants of some devil that had a dao?" Dar asked. From all the ecology of the ancient races, why the ettercap's spider imparted dao to his dao tree bothered him.

The girls all gave him odd looks. "What would they come from?"

"Never mind. I guess I don't have to make sense of everything," he said, but the idea still lingered with him.

Neko snorted. "Very human. Everything must add up. Why can't spiders just do what they do?" She made conversation as they picked their way through the maze of webs.

"Because we are curious," Dar explained.

Neko moved quickly, covering his mouth. "Curiosity killed cat. Bossy lady tell Neko. Might kill Dar." Neko nodded, as if she was speaking sage advice.

Dar realized she must have heard Sam and taken it literally. Dar tried to suppress a smile.

The girls started snickering, and Neko's ear flattened back against her head. "Neko wrong?"

Dar fought to keep the amusement out of his tone. "It's an idiom, Neko. Like a warning to little children not to be too curious for their own good. Another one is don't poke a sleeping bear."

"Of course," Neko agreed readily, only more confused. "You pounce. Kill lazy bear. Easy food."

Dar couldn't help it at that point. A deep belly laugh ripped out of him at the cat girl's frankness. He had to clamp down on his dao of quiet to keep it from echoing through the woods.

Wiping away tears that had crept up from the laughter, Dar tried explaining again. "It's a lesson in a few words. Like a small lesson. They aren't supposed to be taken literally."

Neko's head tilted, and her ears flopped like a confused kitten. No one had a better explanation, and Neko grumbled, "Stupid words."

"Don't worry, Pussy Cat." Blair rubbed her head. "You'll get it, eventually. Everyone does."

Neko growled. "Neko not stupid."

"Anything but," Dar agreed. "You're learning incredibly quickly."

Smiling wide enough to show off her large incisors, Neko beamed up at Dar before dropping her head again to carefully pick their way through the forest.

The massive spider silk fortress came into view ahead of them, cutting off any playful banter.

"Ready, girls?" Dar asked, taking his own fire starter in his hands.

"Let them burn." Cherry growled.

They moved quickly through the woods, careful to avoid any webs. The spiders remained hanging in their webs, ignorant of their passage as long as they avoided the webs.

A chill passed up Dar's spine as they continued. He hoped they simply would be still until their webs were touched, but it still gave him a foreboding feeling, like a guillotine hanging over his head.

As they continued moving closer to the fortress, the spiders seemed to continue growing larger, and avoiding the webs was becoming harder with every hundred feet. They were having to zig-zag through the area to avoid the webs.

Getting slightly closer, they were out of easy room to move around the webs and about half a mile out from its giant white walls. Dar decided it was time to start using the fire starters. Pushing his into a pile of dried twigs, Dar activated the enchantment, holding his breath at what would happen.

Little bright sparks jumped to life at the edges of a twig, which then combusted again and again as the little tool bore through the stick. It wasn't long till a small fire had started, but Dar left it.

The girls had begun doing the same on objects near them. From leaves to bark on a tree, they were starting small fires and moving clockwise around the fortress.

"Look." Sasha pointed behind them. The orange glow of fire was picking up behind them.

"Good. Let's keep at it. We'll want to circle away when we start this one and burn out another fire between here and Hearthway," Dar repeated the plan.

Smoke was starting to rise into the air, and the spiders were starting to shift, abandoning the areas that had started to burn. Fights broke out among the spiders as they stepped into each other's territory. A rippling effect took place as they started to push further and further away from the spreading fire.

The fire was spreading around the silk fortress, and Dar began to have hope that the plan would work. Emboldened by the success, he started moving faster, setting more fires.

At that point, they had made it almost a quarter of the way around the fortress, but the fire was helping them, spreading across the dry canopy. The dead trees made for great tinder, helping the fire jump across branches.

"Do you think we need to light any more on fire?" Sasha asked, seeing the blaze growing rapidly behind them."

Dar stopped in thought. "Let's circle around the far side and start a fire there. This side should at least drive them away from Hearthway, and the burnt-out forest will make a decent barrier between us and them."

"Wouldn't starting a fire on the other side push them towards Hearthway?" Mika asked.

Dar understood her concern. "It won't if it catches most of them between the two fires. The fires might even put each other out."

The group nodded and rushed to reach the other side of the fortress, repeating the same exercise. By the time they got there and finished setting the flames, their first fire had reached the fortress. The flames licked at the giant web as spiders scrambled to escape.

But the surge of spiders and ettercaps became even more frantic, seeming to even throw themselves into the flames rather than deal with whatever was coming behind. Bracing himself, Dar watched.

Coming out of the entrance was a spider body the size of an elephant. Connected to it at the hips was a gray human-like form. Something about that devil rang alarm bells for Dar.

It almost looked human, but it didn't have the same feel of a demon or spirit. Despite looking slightly human, it felt devoid of any humanity in the way it moved through its minions, easily stepping on and killing any that got in its way.

CHAPTER 32

"What is that?" Dar stared at the half-man, half-spider devil. Fire continued to rage from both sides of the ettercap fortress, filling Dar's nose with the scent of smoke and obscuring his full view of the devil, but the smoke didn't seem to stop it or even really concern it. The devil reminded Dar of a drider from tabletop games, but its human portion was unnatural pale with a face that was too bulbous to be human.

The devil focused his attention at that moment solely at Dar, studying him with dead eyes. Dar saw a spark of intelligence in the devil before it smiled a wicked smile. Clearly, it didn't think it was at the disadvantage.

Dar gripped the shaft of his axe tightly, feeling his skin pull against the smooth grain.

The devil crawled up the top of the silk fortress, letting out a screech as it reached the peak. The screech echoed across the area, causing the spiders to scatter. They were so desperate to escape the wrath of the devil that they went straight into the flames. Cooked ettercap and spider filled the air around them, causing their group to start to gag.

The devil only kept smirking at the destruction around it before once again focusing back on Dar. Right after they locked eyes, the devil vanished in front of them.

"Where'd it go?" Dar's head whipped back and forth. It was nowhere to be found. Dar wondered if it could move that quickly, or if it had some sort of invisibility dao.

"Careful. Don't lose your wits. Stay focused," Mika reminded everyone, turning to position her back to their backs. The others followed suit, quickly forming a circle.

"We have to kill this thing," Dar said. "It seems more intelligent than the others. I have no doubt that, if it is allowed to live, it'll come after us."

"I was sold at giant, creepy man spider. Didn't even need another reason to kill it." Blair's voice dripped with sarcasm.

Feeling uneasy, Dar worked to keep focused like Mika had said and try to solve the problem. If the devil was using dao, it should also need mana as well. Maybe that would help give it away. Relaxing, Dar reached out his senses, trying to see what he could feel.

But as he started to relax to sense for mana, Dar felt a disturbance in the air. Instantly moving, he raised his axe in the overhead block Mika had drilled into him.

Sure enough, the drider was there, its leg smashing down onto Dar's axe with enough force to buckle his knees. Even with his increased strength, it was stronger than he was. Dar started feeling more uneasy.

But, before he could prepare for the next move, Mika was next to him, her trident punching towards the devil's exposed chest.

The devil spun, another one of its spider legs snapping out, catching Mika's weapon and tossing her to the side like she weighed nothing. Dar couldn't help but notice the sharp gouges in the packed dirt that the devil's legs produced as it spun. Each appendage was practically a sword.

Charging, Dar swung up into the devil's mid-section, the girls each starting their own attack at the same time.

The devil jumped back as the butt end of the spider curled under itself before extending back out and spraying Dar down with sticky

webbing. The spray covered the surrounding several meters, making it impossible for him to dodge it.

When Dar quickly tried to rip it off, it stretched and retracted back together with the force of a steel cable snapping into place. It was strong and even his first blast of heat had done little to it.

"Sasha, help me get rid of this silk." Dar had a feeling her dao would be able to mold and strip the webbing off of him in no time.

"On it." Ribbons shot out of her dress, latching onto a tree and whipping her out of the fight over to Dar while the others kept the drider busy.

Mika was bringing her spear around for attack after attack, but the devil was quick, dodging or blocking her attacks while also managing to dodge Blair and Neko's attacks.

Marcie and Amber weren't having much luck penetrating the chitinous armor of the devil, but they continued trying to distract it. They also seemed to be keeping any stray spiders at bay while the three girls focused their efforts on the devil.

Dar looked over, searching for Cherry. He found her sitting down on her own, uprooting a nearby tree to bring it to bear against the powerful devil.

"I'll have you out in a second." Sasha placed her hand on the silk, and it pulled away, curling back into a ball in her fist. "There you go."

"Thanks." He hefted his axe just as the tree slammed itself down on the drider, bringing the fighting to a short pause. "Did she get it?" Dar had to laugh as the image of a newspaper taking out a spider flittered into his mind. This was just a bigger version.

But his glee was short-lived as the tree exploded into slivers of wood. The devil tore the tree apart, screaming incoherently. It was insanely strong, and it seemed much more pissed.

Shifting himself back into the action, Dar swung his axe with all his might, making sure to keep a better eye on its back end.

The drider fought back with its front two legs, the sharp chitinous legs actually managing to turn one of Lilith's enchanted weapons, overpowering him and swinging right back at Dar. They both struck

with such force that small bursts of air buffeted the world around them.

An explosion rocked the drider, and it looked to the side in shock, narrowing in on Sasha as it moved outside of where Dar could attack.

Sasha stood still, surprised at the attention, her arm still extended from the throw. Dar quickly moved himself between the drider and Sasha, making it focus back on him as he completed a rapid flurry of swings.

While it fought Dar, the devil didn't forget Sasha. During part of their attacks, it shot webs straight at Sasha. Dar had a moment of satisfaction when the webs hit her and didn't stick.

Instead, Sasha took control of the webs and turned them around on the drider. As she did, tree limbs snaked out and stabilized her while she held firmly to the spray of web that had frozen midair, still connecting her to the drider.

While Sasha held the drider's secondary attack at bay, the devil continued to exchange blows with Dar, though the chitin on its front legs were scratched and cracked from taking the brunt of Dar's axe.

Not to be left out, Mika and Blair continued attacks along its sides, although they were only partially effective as the devil used its legs to counter the blows.

Another two explosions rocked the drider, as Amber and Marcie took up where Sasha had left off. Neko took the opportunity to leap on the devil's back.

All of that together provided the perfect distraction. In its moment to deal with the multiple attacks and the angry Neko on its back, its legs paused. Dar focused on a particular crack in the chitin, swinging for the fences with his axe and connecting with that crack.

The plating on the drider gave way, and Dar's axe finally bit past armor and into its leg. A sickening crunch sounded as the drider threw its head back in a screech. It sounded like thousands of bugs rubbing their wings together.

All around them, the silk fortress resounded with echoed screams from ettercaps and spiders alike.

Mika didn't even blink, using Dar's shoulder as leverage and jumping over him, driving her trident into the chest of the drider, causing it to slump further to the ground. The other women joined, stabbing into the beast before it could right itself.

Dar went to stab once more, but he paused, realizing the noises of the forest had changed. Listening closer, Dar noticed the sound of scurrying had gone from getting quieter to once again getting louder. Something in that screech had called them back. He turned, scanning around immediately.

Spiders were starting to converge towards them, some still on fire as they passed through the flames, drawn by the call.

"Get back." Dar jumped away and brought up a slab of granite from the ground to shelter him and the girls.

"Um, what is that?" Cherry asked, sliding into the shelter along with the other girls and pointing.

The webbed fortress was moving, or more likely, something big enough to move several tons of webbing was moving. The fortress rippled as the ettercaps and spiders returned to the fortress or whatever was behind those webbed walls.

"Holy shit," Dar breathed the words. He couldn't believe what he was seeing.

A massive spider leg pushed aside the fortress webs. The spider had to be bigger than one of the riverboats, and that was only based on a fraction of it as one of its legs probed outside the fortress, pushing the whole construction of silk aside. The leg slammed down around where the drider lay dying.

Its leg tapped around searching. Not wanting to be identified, Dar wrapped the slab of earth around all of them, molding it to the forest floor.

Stabbing around, the massive spider eventually found the drider's body. Stabbing its leg through the drider's torso mercilessly, it dragged him back towards the fortress. When the body got close, the massive spider's body struck, pushing through the web and devouring the lesser devil in an instant.

With the opening of the wall, part of the mystery became clearer. The back half of the giant spider's body was bound in a web of glowing runes. Only its front two legs seemed to be free of the binding.

The sheer number of dao characters and the style reminded Dar of his body, and he realized this might be one of the seals that Lilith had warned him about. The ones she had put in place to seal off powerful devils.

"Cherry, is that seal something Lilith put in place?" Dar asked, thinking Cherry's past history with Lilith might help her recognize them.

"I have no idea. But I see exactly what you are seeing. Someone had tried to contain this... thing, and it's no longer working."

"Would setting this all on fire even kill it?" Dar asked.

"What on earth—you can't be thinking of fighting that, can you?" Mika gasped.

"How can we leave that here?" Dar shot back. "I wouldn't feel comfortable living on the same continent as this thing."

"Dar. Move." Neko had been paying more attention than the rest of them, and the warning gave them enough time to avoid getting hit as the massive spider's limb crashed down into their hiding spot, jarring Dar and making him clench his teeth.

"What are we supposed to do about this thing?" Dar muttered, pausing to gape at the gathering ettercaps and spiders that were still pouring into the area but going straight to the spider. Instead of preparing for battle, the behemoth of a spider was just devouring them, while they willingly allowed it. It was a disturbing sight.

The giant spider paused and wriggled more of itself free from the bindings.

"Eating them makes it stronger, more able to break the seal?" Dar asked no one in particular.

"If it has been sealed by Lilith, then it stands to reason it at least was weak at one point. But it looks like it's growing stronger by the moment," Sasha observed uneasily.

Dar nodded. He couldn't let that happen. If it was weakest now, this was his best shot at taking it out.

Something deep in his core beckoned him to fight the spider. He could feel the little dao tree pulse, wanting the spider for itself. Like the little dao tree was hungry for the spider. He felt like there wasn't a better option than to see what the little tree could do.

"Then we need to act now." Dar stepped out of the small shelter with his axe in one hand, gathering the dao of combustion in his other. As soon as he hit the web, he pushed, trying to set the fortress and the trees that it was built upon on fire.

The old web burned quickly. Unfortunately, it burned so quickly that it burned itself out each time he pushed another section to combust. He started getting frustrated as flame after flame lit, burnt, and then fizzled out.

"We got this, Dar. Do what you need to." Sasha came up with her fire starter, the others close behind her.

Nodding, Dar pivoted back to the gargantuan spider, watching as it continued to devour more of its brood. A third leg popped out of the binding, working to grab dirt and continue to pull its body further out with the help of the other two free legs.

Moving closer to the ettercaps and spiders marching themselves up for the massive devil's mouth, Dar was pleased when they didn't even seem to notice him. Joining alongside them, Dar moved with them, racing along towards the spider's mouth, but jumping at the last second to land atop its head.

Raising the pitch-black axe and putting all his strength and dao of weight into the swing, he slammed it home into the spider's head. Despite the power he'd put into the swing, the axe wasn't able to break through. The reverberation from the halted momentum rattled up his hands and split his palms.

All eight eyes of the massive spider turned up towards him as it reared up and screamed loud enough to deafen Dar.

Dar latched onto the edge of a chitinous plate that ended at one of the eyes as the devil flailed and Dar rode it like a bucking bull. He

managed it, but only because it was still largely bound and unable to move.

Holding on, Dar worked to come up with a new plan.

Waiting for the devil to stop moving, he raised his axe and aimed for a weaker part of its body, the eyes. Hitting one of them, the spider's eye popped, and mucus sprayed as the creature continued screaming.

Dar smirked, pleased that the plan had worked. Picking up his axe, he started aiming for the second, but he came up short as he watched the eye he had struck grow back.

The eerie black eye stared back at him angrily. Its three legs out of the binding slammed into the ground ahead of it, and the ground around it cracked as the thing heaved itself forward.

A fourth leg popped out of the binding and joined the first three.

Knowing he was running out of time, Dar went to town. Ignoring the disgusting spray of goo, Dar continued playing whack-a-mole with the regenerating eyes. He hoped enough damage might stop it from healing, or at least slow it down.

"If you had a plan, little dao tree, now would be the time," Dar growled, unsure of where to go from here. The situation had been dire and he had put his trust in the feeling he'd gotten from his inner world.

But the spider kept regenerating. Pausing, Dar felt the little dao tree push against his inner world. It was finally making its move.

Deep inside himself, Dar felt a pulse. With it came a wash of clarity, he could sense the complete dao, the underpinnings of the universe focus on this spot. Then another and another, each growing stronger till reality flipped.

His inner world projected itself onto the world around him. All around him was the familiar sight of his inner world. Including the little dao tree hovering right there with Dar. With it came complete control and a brief moment of absolute understanding of everything in his domain.

In that moment of clarity, Dar understood. The massive spider couldn't die. Not if Dar spent the rest of his immortal life hacking away at its eyes.

That was because it was part of the complete dao. So intricately had it woven itself into the fabric of the universe that it was no longer just a massive monster. It was the dark, shadows, and everything that lurked within.

To kill this monster would be to banish all shadows from the world, make it a place where light touched every corner and crevice pushing back everything that used the dark. Catastrophic change that would ripple through the world and undo ecosystems.

While Dar had no love for spiders, or shadows, they had a role in balancing the world. Not to mention all of those aspects of the world that continued to feed into it.

As Dar slowly hacked it apart, it would continue to pull on those aspects to survive. It would take Dar banishing every shadow in the world with light to weaken this thing to the point of death.

But while he realized all of this, he realized there was something else present that was on the same level as the massive spider.

The Little Dao Tree. As weak as it was in this moment, it also was stitched into the fabric of the world, only its pulse was so weak that Dar couldn't see clearly what exactly it was.

As if rising up to that challenge, the Little Dao Tree acted. Its roots rose up and dove into the wounded eye sockets of the spider and they drank up all that it was.

Dar shivered from seeing such a powerful being devoured by the little tree, the spider rapidly turning into a husk before his eyes.

"What in the world," he breathed.

The little dao tree couldn't kill it, so instead, it was taking all that it was and absorbing it. It was stealing the aspect of the world the spider held onto, repurposing it. Into what, he had no idea.

Soon Dar found his feet planted on the forest floor, nothing under him but dust.

"Dar?" The girls ran over, covered in soot and spider guts as a fire raged around them. Their eyes only held wonder and questions at what they'd just seen.

"We need to go," Dar said when he could speak.

All around them, the spiders and ettercaps were idle, like their purpose had been lost.

"Let the fire consume them. We need to go," he repeated, moving through a gap in the flames and rushing out of the fortress that was about to become the center of a massive wildfire.

As he went, Dar let his inner world suck up dead ettercaps and spiders indiscriminately. He didn't have time to take up all the bodies before they burned, but he'd use what he could to produce more dao fruits.

"Dar, what happened?" Cherry panted as they ran. The rest were right behind them, all looking interested in his answer.

"I..." Dar paused. He was at a loss of words on how to explain it. The knowledge and flash of insight he'd felt in the moment had turned foggy, like it was an epiphany just out of his reach. "I can't exactly explain, but that beast was pure dao, and it looks like my body has even more secrets."

There was a shared look of concern among his women at the lack of an actual answer, but Dar didn't know what else he could say. So instead, he just charged forward, aiming to get them out of the forest.

The flames continued to creep closer, quickly getting out of control and filling the air with smoke.

Dar coughed a harsh cough full of smoke, knowing they needed to hurry. The fire was slower to spread downhill, but they still needed to keep moving to stay ahead of it.

Taking the lead, Dar tried to absorb as much of the heat as he could to protect their group.

"Dar, we need to do something so the fire doesn't spread to Hearthway," Cherry reminded him.

"I know." He hoped that Rex and Glump had been able to finish their half of the plan.

Dar and his dao companions rushed out of the worst of the fire and kept on running towards the village, but as they reached the location of the first battle, they found the fighters were still in the area.

Though they weren't idle. No, each of them were hauling cut lumber down. Forty teams of men had been working nonstop since Dar and the girls set out. They were almost done clearing a swath of the forest between two rocky cliffs in hopes of creating a firebreak.

"Did you set the whole forest on fire?" Bart stared over Dar's shoulder, clear concern on his face.

"Pretty sure you told me that was a terrible idea," Russ snorted.

"Enough. We need to burn everything we've cut, anything we can to create a wall right here in the forest. Stack it up on the fire side of the break. We want that side to burn quick and leave no fuel left for the wildfire." Dar didn't wait to see if they understood before moving to take action.

The other men moved quickly. There was no beauty in their movements as they savagely hacked away and hauled away wood, widening the break in the forest as the raging fire crept slowly down the hill.

Cherry went to work toppling small and medium sized trees, while a dozen teams of five brought down trees with reckless abandon that would have made Frank cringe. Just shy of where they were creating a gap, the girls used their fire starters to create a backfire, working to remove anything that might be able to catch and spread the fire down hill.

It was tough work, but the men rallied behind a clear purpose. And when the forest fire pushed them back, it stopped at the line of charred trees created in the backfire.

Slumping to the ground while the flames on the other side of the break raged, Dar panted. They'd done it. Hearthway was safe. He felt a soft form collapse next to him as Sasha's body melted into his. That movement was soon followed by others as Dar's companions surrounded him.

***

When they finally reached the village, they were covered in layers of soot and guts, but their small family was all alive. Dar had led them all back to the village with a smile on his face.

They'd done it. Cheering, he couldn't help but let the joy of the group lift him up.

But that quickly changed as he noticed some somber faces among those cheering. Loved ones had been lost in the process, and many were grieving. Dar felt guilty for his moments of elation, walking over to one of them. Before he could say a word, the woman shook her head, cutting him off.

"Franky knew what he was doing, and he believed in you. I'm glad that he died honorably. You did well for us." She leaned forward, giving Dar a hug before grabbing a few of the other grieving women and moving away from the celebrating group.

Dar watched them go, feeling the weight of leadership along with the elation of victory.

He couldn't ignore that things were changing. Something about that moment with the gigantic spider had felt like he'd taken a giant step towards his destiny. Even now, he could feel something changing inside his inner world.

Part of him wanted to ignore it and just hunker down with his women, but he also couldn't ignore the way his dao tree had called to him earlier. But in this moment, all he needed to do was celebrate their victory.

Dar was filled with equal amounts of hope and dread for what was to come. At the very least, he was looking forward to some downtime with his girls and showing them their winter home. He couldn't think of a better thing to make and celebrate their victory. And he knew the perfect place.

Grabbing his dao companions, Dar started steering them back to the caves, wanting to show them their home.

But, as they made their way, he heard shouting to one side of the village. Dar paused, desperately wanting to ignore it, but in the end, he did his duty and went over.

Jeffrey was pointing his sword and shouting at a richly dressed man and his entourage of men who looked dressed for heavy labor. Dar had never seen any of them before.

"Can I help you?" Dar let his voice carry across the space between them, his axe still ready if need be.

The leader looked up at Dar, his face quickly shifting into one of apprehension, his men behind watching Dar with wide eyes.

Dar tried not to smirk at the man's fear. He knew that, as he was caked in battle gore and ashes, they were likely a gruesome sight. "Devil problem in the woods. Don't worry, we took care of them."

"Oh." The man seemed unable to say much more as his men pressed in closer behind him. A few looked over their shoulders towards the forest, still glowing orange with the fires.

"Where are my manners." The man righted himself, his brain seeming to catch up. "I'm Dane Goodhaul, merchant extraordinaire. Rumors are spreading that there is a village here, so we ventured down, looking for new trade opportunities. But I was surprised to find it empty." He licked his lips nervously. Obviously, other thoughts had occurred to him when he found the village almost empty.

"Not so empty, as you can see. We were taking care of a few things nearby. We protect what's ours." He gave a meaningful look to the man in case empty had made the man think he'd have any stake.

Softening his expression, Dar continued, "But welcome to Hearthway. I'd love to discuss trade, depending on what you have. We are a young village and could use a trading partner."

The merchant bowed slightly. "Then let me be the first to congratulate you. Your little village is officially on the map."

"Hearthway," Dar clarified.

"Hearthway," Goodhaul agreed.

Several of the men looked up, and Dar followed their line of sight to see snowflakes fluttering down above them. "It seems winter is finally here."

Dar nodded, exhausted and ready for a winter slumber. "You are welcome to stay for dinner, but I'm afraid I'm going to need to excuse myself." Dar looked at Dane. "Many of us need to clean up, and then we have a celebration to kick off."

AUTHOR'S NOTE

Book number nine. It feels like I'm a train pulling out of the station and picking up steam at this point. My wife likes to humble me at times, reminding me how excited I was that I made back the cover cost on Legendary Rule. I'm doing fantastic and hope to continue churning out books.

Dao, as you might be able to tell by the ending of Dao Dominion setting the stage to understand a little more about the cogs in the background for what I'm officially calling 'Manaverse'. All my series are intended to be stand alone, with bonus easter eggs between them. But they are in a shared universe.

I hoped you loved the book. If you did, do me a favor and drop a review, you can use the link below for easy access. Also, I wanted to take a moment to talk about how you can keep a series running or even extend a series. It is actually quite easy, talk about the book, make a post, talk to a friend. That is the number 1 best way to get any of mine or another author's series running.

Leave a Review

If you want to follow my progress for future books I do monthly updates on my mailing list and Facebook page.

Mailing List Sign Up

Author Bruce Sentar on Facebook
Patreon

Also if you are a fan of HaremLit there is a wonderful community out there on Facebook where fans and authors chat over the latest and greatest.

https://www.facebook.com/groups/haremlit
https://www.facebook.com/groups/HaremGamelit
And other non-harem specific communities for Cultivation and LitRPG.
https://www.facebook.com/groups/WesternWuxia
https://www.facebook.com/groups/LitRPGsociety
https://www.facebook.com/groups/cultivationnovels

OTHER WORKS

Legendary Rule:
Ajax Demos finds himself lost in society. Graduating shortly after artificial intelligence is allowed to enter the workforce; he can't get his career off the ground. But when one opportunity closes another opens.Ajax gets a chance to play a brand new Immersive Reality game. Things aren't as they seem. Mega Corps hover over what appears to be a simple game. What he does in the game seems to effect his body outside.

But that isn't going to stop Ajax when he finally might have a shot at becoming a professional gamer. Join Ajax and Company as they enter the world of Legendary Rule.

A Mage's Cultivation:
In a world where mages and monster grow from cultivating mana. Isaac joins the class of humans known as mages who absorb mana to grow more powerful. To become a mage he must bind a mana beast to himself to access and control mana. But when his mana beast is far more human than he expected; Isaac struggles with the budding relationship between the two of them as he prepares to enter his first dungeon.Unfortunately for Isaac, he doesn't have time to ponder the

7

372   BRUCE SENTAR

questions of his relationship with Aurora. Because his sleepy town of Locksprings is in for a rude awakening, and he has to decide which side of the war he is going to stand on.

<u>Mana Master</u>

<u>Mana Beast</u>

<u>Mana Immortal</u>

Isaac's story to continue with Immortal Mana Sept 2021.

Dao Divinity: The First Immortal

Darius Yigg was a wanderer, someone who's never quite found his place in the world, but maybe he's not supposed to be here...Ripped from our world, Dar finds himself in his past life's world, where his destiny was cut short. Reignited, the wick of Dar's destiny burns again with the hope of him saving Grandterra. To do that, he'll have to do something no other human of Grandterra has done before, walk the dao path. That path requires mastering and controlling attributes of the world and merging them to greater and greater entities. In theory, if he progressed far enough, he could control all of reality and rival a god. He won't be in this alone. As a beacon of hope for the world, those from the ancient races will rally around Dar to stave off the growing Devil horde.

<u>Dao Divinity</u>

Made in the USA
Monee, IL
12 January 2024

51639087R00207